I0699673

OF GOBLIN KINGS

Complete Collection

EMMA HAMM

*For the little girls who wanted to meet a goblin king...
Or maybe just wish away their baby brother.*

OF GOBLINS AND GOLD

CHAPTER 1

he chime of goblin bells filled the clearing, as they did every first week of the month. Sunlight slashed through the forest beyond in harsh beams of gold that illuminated their strange carts. All manner of fabric and hide covered wooden wheels and rickety beds. Someone had dyed woolen sheep skins bright red and laid them to hide the rotting planks.

Bells were tied all around the edges. Bells that chimed, twinkled, and rang for visitors from all over to see the goblin wares. And there were hundreds of wares. Food from far-off places, jewelry so beautiful it made tears prick a mortal eye, and perfume that would ensure true love.

In short, magic.

Freya tucked the frayed edges of her scarf securely around her neck, over the layers of her dark hair. Usually, she would lift the edge so she could only see the blurry visage of the goblins. It was bad luck to look at them. Such familiarity invited the goblins to join a weary traveler on their journey home. Those people were rarely seen again.

"Freya," her sister, Esther, tugged at her sleeve. "Did you see what they have with them today?"

"You're not supposed to look," she hissed.

"I know," Esther replied. "But today they have—"

"I don't want to know." Freya yanked her scarf out of its neat knot in the bodice of her dress. She tossed it like a blanket over both of their heads. "Goblin wares are not for us, remember?"

Together, they rushed past the goblins who called out in voices sounding like crows. "Pretty ladies! Don't you want to see our necklaces? I've got the perfect one for that swan-like neck of yours!"

Freya held her breath until they had placed a safe distance between themselves and the goblins with their temptations. When she couldn't hear their voices any longer, she whipped the scarf off their heads.

She spun around on her sister, fury heating her face. "What were you thinking? You know the rules as well as I."

Esther's own face turned beat red, but Freya knew that had little to do with her actions and more with anger. "It was a necklace, Freya. A necklace with a moon at the end, just like mother used to wear. I thought you'd like to know."

The words caught her up short. Their mother had worn a half moon necklace, but she knew for a fact it wasn't goblin made. Their mother had hated goblins. She had dedicated her entire life to researching their kind and creating rules for their town of Woolwich to stay safe from their leathery clutches.

The town emerged from the forest like a mirage lifted from their eyes. Though it was a modest town, it had prospered in the days since it had first been built. They were lucky to have the large salt mine in the distance. Though mining was difficult, it had given the town more money than most.

As such, all the buildings were brand new. Their whitewashed exteriors gleamed in the sunlight, accented by warm wooden beams creating criss-crossed patterns like quilts.

Freya stepped onto the dirt path with her sister and ushered them toward the entrance to town. The well was there, and she desperately wanted a drink after their journey through the forest. Then, they would go to the market and buy all the things they needed for the next month.

Again, her sister tugged on her sleeve.

"What?" Freya said. "Esther, we don't have time, if we want to return by nightfall. You know walking past the goblins is dangerous in the dark—"

"Freya!" Esther's shout echoed. Some townsfolk at the gate paused in their stroll, staring at the two sisters like they had gone mad.

Or maybe more mad. Very few of the townspeople liked Freya or her sister. The two girls who lived in a hut outside the village, all by their lonesome now that their dear parents had departed this realm.

She'd heard their whispers of witchcraft. Freya knew how tentative their place was in this village.

Lowering her voice, she stepped closer to Esther and hissed, "Keep your voice down."

"I'm tired of living our life as though we're walking on glass. Mother wore a necklace just like the goblins were selling. Did you hear me?"

"Yes, I heard you."

"And you don't think that's the least bit suspicious?" Esther's eyes were wide with hope. "Maybe she sold it, Freya. Maybe she's still out there and we just haven't been looking in the right places."

Freya's heart cracked in two. Esther had never given up hope their parents would return, emerging from the mist and walking back into their hut like they hadn't disappeared for years. In some small part, that was why Freya continued to live where they did. But she was the more realistic sister.

She didn't stay in that hut because she thought they would return. Freya stayed for the memories that lingered in the walls, like ghosts who haunted her waking dreams.

She reached out and brushed a strand of hair behind Esther's ear. "They're not coming back, Esther."

"All we know is that they went into the forest and they never returned. They could still be out there, Freya. Why do you insist on stopping our search?" Tears filled Esther's eyes, like droplets of pearls clinging to her lashes.

Freya couldn't have this argument again. She took a deep breath, held it, and tried to think of the right words. What would calm her sister down?

A horse and buggy meandered past them. The sweet grass scent of the horse's exhale filled her lungs. Clamoring noises of hammers striking metal, people talking on their morning routine, and the clucks of chickens in the farm beyond all took up space in her head.

She couldn't think with all this noise and sudden sound. Freya's focus had always been off, but with all these distractions, it was even more difficult to provide Esther with the appropriate answer.

"They wouldn't want us to keep looking for them," she settled on. "It's been two years, Esther. They aren't coming back."

What else was she supposed to say? They'd had this argument every week for months now.

Esther's face turned white as snow. She gave one firm nod, then darted through the gate into town. Freya sighed and planted her hands on her hips.

It wasn't like Esther could get very far. Woolwich wasn't that big of a town, and everyone knew everyone. She could ask a single villager where her sister had gotten off to, and they would know exactly where to send her. After all, the witch sisters were hard to miss.

She'd let Esther have some time to herself. The last thing she needed was for Esther to take off into the forest trying to find their parents. Freya had no one left. And a single witch in a hut was easier to burn.

Freya wrapped the scarf around her waist now, creating a makeshift basket for them to place food in. She already knew what she wanted to get. Squash was easy to come by this year, and she could make that go farther. Eggs would be best, since they couldn't keep a chicken to save their life.

Esther said the goblins kept stealing their fowl. Freya thought it was the fox that lived within the thicket beside their home.

"Hello, girlie." The unknown voice was startling for two reasons. First, because she'd never heard it before. Freya knew everyone in Woolwich. And second, because it rumbled like water trapped under ice.

Freya curled her fingers in the scarf and looked up at the horse and buggy that had stopped beside her. The horse was unlike anything she'd ever seen before. A great black charger, perhaps something a warrior might have ridden into battle. Its hooves were painted silver and were so bright, the sun gleamed off their sharpened ends.

The buggy was a patchwork of colorful fabric. She could hardly guess what it was made of, although the ancient wooden wheels gleamed like polished mahogany.

And of course, as she had expected, she could see the bells woven along the edge. Each was perfectly made, reflecting her own pale, startled face back at her a hundred times over.

The wind picked up and all the bells began to chime.

She told herself not to respond. The goblin man couldn't steal her away if she said nothing. That was the rule.

So instead, she turned her face slowly to the side. Forcing her eyes to remain on the town that was only a few steps away. The town he couldn't enter, no matter how hard he tried.

But out of the corner of her eye, she could see him. The bird-like beak where his nose should be. The feathers that winged back from his eyes and accentuated the sharp angles of his cheekbones. He wore a cloak over his head, like that would somehow hide the differences. And she knew, if she looked at him or acknowledged him in any way, he would try to sell her something.

The goblin man reached out a hand into her line of sight. "Are you sure you don't want to buy anything, Freya?"

Her heart stopped at the sound of her name on his tongue. He couldn't read her mind. She knew the goblins weren't capable of magic like that. Her mother had proven it time and time again.

He must have overheard Esther say her name. Nothing more, nothing less.

But that didn't ease the sudden panic in her veins.

Fruit appeared in his palm. The apple gleamed in the sunlight. Its taut skin was so vividly red, she knew she'd seen nothing like it before. Probably never would again. Food grown in the faerie realm was lovely, but it would bind her as their slave forever.

Taking another deep breath, she took a shaky step forward. Away from him. Away from the temptation of the fruit that called out to her because she knew it would be so delicious. So much better than any food she'd ever tried in her life.

All she had to do was reach out and take it. She had money in her pocket. More than enough to buy a single apple from an old man with an old cloak and a horse that eyed her with fire in his gaze.

Shaking herself out of the spell, Freya squeezed her eyes shut and burst into a run. She didn't care if she ran into someone in town. All she had to do was reach the boundary.

Her feet touched the edge of town and all the temptation fell from her shoulders like she'd shaken off chains. She spun around wildly, staring back at the goblin man who remained where he'd been. Seated on the buggy with the reins in his hand and an apple in his lap.

He tilted his head back in the sunlight and laughed. The sound was like that of a thousand voices all screaming over each other.

Freya covered her ears with her hands, but stared him down all the same. She would not be cowed by this goblin who thought he could frighten her. Not now that she was in the safety of Woolwich.

"I will never buy from a goblin!" she shouted.

His laughter died down, and for a moment, she thought his skin was shimmering. The feathers unraveled to reveal grey skin like moonlight beneath. Then his visage returned to the monstrous form.

"Oh," he replied in that stone-like voice. "You are very brave, Freya. But also very foolish. I think you'll buy something from me far sooner than you realize."

She squeezed her eyes shut, blinked, and then he was gone. The horse. The buggy. Even the sound of bells had disappeared like he'd never been there at all. All that remained was the lingering scent of apple in the air. Fresh and crisp, like the last temptation after a day of cooking applesauce on the stove.

With a shaky inhalation, Freya turned around and started into town. She needed to find Esther, and then they needed to get back home.

But she couldn't stop thinking about the goblin man.

Their little hut at the edge of the wood was an odd building, full of subtle mysteries, but it was home. Freya dropped Esther off, then disappeared to wash the grime of the day from her skin.

And perhaps to wash the oil slick feeling from her goblin conversation off as well.

A long time ago, they had sectioned off a room for washing. Their father had been an incredibly intelligent man, and handy to boot. He'd sealed river stones into the wall, covering the wood and preventing the structure from rotting. A single stained glass window let light spread around her. Warped colors made rainbows cascade over the walls. The ceiling he'd left open with a contraption that caught rainwater in a reservoir.

Though sometimes the water was frigid, today it was warm. The sun had the entire day to heat the water in metal pipes her father had weaved across the roof.

Slicking her hair back, Freya tilted her face to the sky and let the water rush over her cheeks. Goblins. She hadn't ever thought she'd get so close she might have touched one.

And who was the man? She knew monsters when she saw them.

They were small, crippled creatures with the faces of animals. Horrible, gnarled things like roots dug out of a garden too late. Rotting. Beyond saving.

At least, that's what her mother had always said. Freya tried hard to never look at them.

But this goblin man was different from the others. Though he'd certainly had the features of an animal, his spine had been straight and rigid. He'd been strong, clearly, and his hands had held the reins with the grip of a powerful man. Even his eyes had stared at her with a shrewdness that denoted intelligence.

Such things went against everything her mother had taught. The goblins weren't strong. They weren't powerful. They were nasty little creatures who could easily be crushed by a careless heel.

Opening her eyes, she reached up and turned off the water. She should leave some for Esther, poor girl. She was still mad about their conversation, and Freya didn't blame her.

Their parents were a sore subject for them both. Neither wanted to admit they were truly gone. No one wanted to say, "Yes, my parents are dead and I've given up searching for their bodies to lay my mind at peace."

But Freya remembered that night when they had left. She remembered the storm that raged through the forest, unnatural in its speed and smelling like the bitter bite of magic. Her mother had been the first to dart out into the night. She'd carried her basket full of herbs and offerings to the faeries.

Of course their father had followed her when she didn't return. He had left with his pistol in hand, and nothing else but the shirt on his back.

Neither had left the forest again.

Freya knew what that meant. The magic had gotten them, whether a witch or fae conjured that storm, it didn't matter. They were gone and wasting any energy on wondering when they might return was foolish. No matter how it eased the pain in their hearts.

She reached out and nudged the amethyst crystal on the windowsill. Her mother had always put crystals in every window, above every doorway, and over their beds. Each had a different meaning, something it protected against.

Freya didn't know how much a rock could really help, but she couldn't bring herself to remove them after their mother disappeared.

She wrapped a towel around herself and grabbed a second to run through her hair. The black locks reached her hips when it wasn't piled atop her head in intricate braids. Brushing it was a burden, but Esther refused to cut it.

And just like that, as she scrunched her hair with the old worn out towel, Freya heard the sound again. Goblin bells.

It wasn't possible for goblins to steal them away from here. Their property was warded, just like the town. Goblins couldn't step foot through the talismans, and that meant they were perfectly safe as long as they were in the bounds of their property.

Well, she supposed if they had made a goblin deal, then perhaps the faerie creatures could. But neither she nor Esther had bought anything from them.

She pressed a hand against her heart, feeling the rapid thump beating beneath her ribcage. Everything was fine. Everything had to be fine.

"Esther?" she called out.

No one responded.

Her sister wasn't so foolish as to walk out and greet the goblins when they were riding back to their realm. Esther had grown up being taught of the dangers these creatures brought with them. She wouldn't have wandered out into the forest without at least telling Freya she was going.

Wouldn't she?

Better check, just in case. Her sister was many things, and reckless was at the top of that list.

Freya knotted the towel between her breasts and stepped out of the shower room. She tried to be positive. Esther had learned alongside Freya what to do if goblins passed by their house. They could watch as long as the wards glowed brightly in the bark of the trees. Maybe that's what her sister was doing.

The sound of bells had come from the front of the house. She was certain of it. The sound had long since died down. She could only hope that meant the goblins had already passed their home, and that Esther was likely buried in a book somewhere and ignoring her calls.

So when Freya strode around the corner, she fully expected to see nothing. Just the trees she remembered with moss growing on their trunks. Perhaps a few pollen motes fluttering in the air and birds chirping.

What she found was a full goblin market set up outside her house.

The market was more beautiful than ever. The jewelry was blinding with gemstones and gold so bright they rivaled the stars and the sun. The fabric was even more vivid than she remembered. Every bit of food smelled divine and threatened that only gods should taste their glorious bounty.

Freya was safe within the wards, she reminded herself. Her eyes flicked to the runes carved into each tree that surrounded their hut. Every ward was still there, glowing because the goblins were far too close.

Movement caught her eye, and she stared, horrified, as she realized Esther was right at the edge of the wards. She was talking to a goblin boy with the face of a rat and a tail that flicked back and forth behind him. Their mouths moved, but she couldn't guess what they were saying.

"Esther!" she screamed.

Freya ran. She threw her body into motion and hoped she could get there in time, but it seemed as though time was against her. Everything moved like she was running in place rather than sprinting across the meadow to her sister. She hauled herself over the tiny fence where they kept their garden and further to the other side. The wards were so close she could have touched them, and yet it seemed like she was miles away.

The rat-faced goblin held out something in his hand. A necklace swung from his fingers. The silver, crescent moon glinted in the sunlight.

"Esther, no!" Freya cried out one last time.

Esther didn't listen, or perhaps she couldn't hear her sister through the spell the goblin had cast. She reached through the wards and grabbed the swinging necklace in the goblin boy's clawed hand.

Freya felt the wards shimmer, shudder, and then shatter as her sister broke them. Each and every one. They popped with little explosions all around the circle of their house. Each one sounded like the cracking of glass on stone.

At the sound, Esther flinched. She jerked away from the goblin boy as though she could retreat to the safety of the wards, but they didn't exist anymore.

Freya grabbed her sister around the waist and pulled Esther into her arms. At least her little sister had the where-with-all to bury her face in Freya's shoulder.

The necklace dug into Freya's ribs, clutched in Esther's hand. The tiny prick of the moon gave her some semblance of bravery, although it would leave a mark in the morning. Either way, Freya had to protect her sister. No matter the cost.

"Begone, goblin folk," she growled. "You'll find no business here."

The rat face boy grinned, then bowed like a prince at a ball. "We weren't looking for business, miss. Just wanted to give a charming thing to the prettiest girl in the village."

As if she would ever believe his poisonous words. Freya knew their kind, and they never gave anything away for free. Hissing out a long breath, she bared her teeth in what she hoped was an intimidating snarl. "Get off my property."

Another voice interrupted them. "What wards will keep us away?"

The sound of burbling deep waters, the grumble of sea, ocean, and lake, could only be one goblin. The one she had met before. He stepped from the mass of feathers, fur, and claws, then let the cloak fall from his shoulders. As the fabric slid away from his face, so did the magic that kept his true form hidden from her gaze.

He really was made of moonlight. Shimmering silver skin, almost like metal but moving like the shadows of a forest in starlight. His pointed ears had tiny tufts of fur at the end, and when he caught her staring, he touched claws to his face. He grinned, revealing sharp canines.

"What?" he asked. "Not what you were expecting?"

His voice was the only thing he couldn't change. Smooth as the sound of a storm rumbling in the distance. He was a tempest, that was for certain. Something to be feared.

Esther pressed her face against Freya's shoulder and shuddered. "I want to go back to the house."

"We will." But she didn't know if that was a lie.

The goblins could come through the wards now. They could walk onto their land with nothing inhibiting them. And no matter how hard she tried to stop them, they could do anything they wanted.

Her mother's words bubbled in her mind. "Goblins can only make deals with the willing."

Her hands clenched on Esther's shoulder. "Did you make a deal?"

"No, of course not."

"Did you buy something from them? Did you buy the necklace?" She pulled Esther away from her shoulder and shook her sister hard. "Did you buy it?"

"No!" Tears ran freely down Esther's face. "I'm not so foolish. He gave it to me, Freya. It is a gift."

She'd never heard of that before, but she also knew the goblin rules. If no deal was struck, and no payment was made, then perhaps her sister was safe.

Drawing herself up strong and straight, Freya glared at the silver goblin. "Get off my property. No deal was made and until then, you are not allowed here."

"Big words for one so small." He looked her up and down. Then those sharp teeth flashed again.

"I am not small. Nor will you make me feel weak. Leave, goblin, or I'll go back into my home and get my shotgun. I know you might be made of magic, but sometimes iron is the only answer to an intruder like yourself."

She met his gaze head on and told herself she wasn't afraid. That her sister shuddering in her arms would not make her break. To her great surprise, the strange goblin relented. He bowed his head, then swept his arm out in a grand bow.

"Lady of this keep, you have banished us. As you wish, we goblins will retreat."

She felt the knot in her chest ease. Maybe they would be all right. Maybe this all would end without losing her sister for a foolish mistake.

She released her hold on Esther, who darted back toward their hut. The tangled vines hanging from the roof would hide her from their gaze, and the solid wood door with the moon carved out of the front would prevent them from entering. She hoped.

Freya waited, clutching her towel to her chest as the goblins packed up their wares. She refused to allow them any time to themselves. Not on her property.

Through all their movement and packing, the silver goblin stared back at her. He crossed his arms over his chest and let his eyes meander over all the skin her towel revealed. She'd never had anyone stare at her this long. Let alone even see her knees.

Freya ground her teeth and let him look. They would remove themselves if she had to stand here all night.

Finally, they packed everything in boxes and crates, and the bells jangled again. Horses emerged from the forest behind them, and the animalistic goblins hooked them up to every cart. The great beasts tossed their heads, jangled the bells, and then the carts moved.

The silver goblin was the last to leave. He uncrossed his arms and gave her a wink. "I'll see you again soon, Freya."

"You're not welcome here," she reiterated.

"Oh, I know. But you see, your sister is mine now."

"She didn't make a deal." Her voice shook in fear because she couldn't lose her little sister. There was no one left, and she'd be damned if this goblin would take away her only family.

He lifted a brow. "What's your definition of a deal?"

The goblin walked away with the rest. They disappeared into the inky shadows of the forest, leaving behind the faint sound of bells and the scent of freshly baked apples.

Freya burst into their home. The door slammed against the wooden interior and dust blew up from the well-worn sheepskin in the living room. Esther stood beside the woodstove. The iron monolith was the largest thing in the hut and was framed by hanging herbs drying in the rafters.

Her sister was wringing her hands in worry. And she should be worried because Freya was going to singe her ears with angry words.

"What were you thinking?" Freya snapped. "You know how dangerous goblins are. You know the wards can be broken so easily. You've left us completely unprotected!"

"I just wanted to get mom's necklace back," Esther whispered. She opened her hand and there it was. The damned necklace that looked eerily similar to what their mother wore when she was still alive.

That's what all this was about? Esther had put them both in significant danger just so she could get back a necklace that looked like mom's?

She was so mad she could have spit fire. Freya didn't even know what to say that wouldn't end in a screaming match. In the end, she grumbled, "You know that's not mom's necklace. Hers wasn't silver, Esther. It was gold."

But that didn't deter her sister at all. Esther closed her fingers around the pointed ends and hugged the jewelry close to her chest. As if it had brought her a little closer to their mother after all.

She couldn't stand the sight.

Freya stalked to the back room. Their bedroom didn't have a door, but there wasn't much privacy here, anyway. Back when they were children, she and Esther had slept in front of the wood stove while their parents slept with a curtain over this doorway. Now, the sisters shared the space.

Esther's side of the room was covered in brightly colored tapestries. She bought a new one each year during the winter festivals, to celebrate the new year. Now, she had exactly sixteen covering the walls.

In contrast, Freya's side was rather bland. She had her small cot, an oak dresser for her clothes, and a small jewelry box on top. It was all she needed, anyway. Esther was more interested in finding things that made her happy. Items. Nik naks. Things that filled their space and let other people know someone lived here. If it were up to Freya, the entire place would be nearly empty.

She pulled out a plain white shift and brown smock to put over it. The goblin's words had gotten into her head, and now she couldn't get them out.

Would he return?

The chill spread down her spine and into her hands, her feet, her very soul. Something inside her said he would absolutely return, and that he would come for her sister.

Swallowing hard, she went back into the center room where Esther waited. At least her sister looked apologetic. Esther likely hadn't wanted to make Freya mad, and the last thing she had planned to do was break the wards. She knew just how dire the circumstances were now that they were unprotected.

Freya only stayed in the forest because of those wards. Her mother had drawn them, and yes, they could recreate the symbols. But that would take time, and night was falling. Wards must be drawn during the day. They drew upon the powers of the sun.

"We have to sew the wards again," she muttered, crossing the room to grab the jug they usually filled with water for tea. She shook it, pleased to find there was enough liquid for her to make a cup.

"Yes, I realize that. I'm so sorry, Freya."

"Don't apologize. Words don't help." She stuffed the wood stove and lit it before adding, "You should get some sleep."

Esther hissed in a long breath. "Look, I know you don't agree with what I did. But I remember mom like it was just yesterday. How am I supposed to forget them? Like you?"

That icy chill traveled down her spine again. Freya straightened and looked her sister in the eyes. "Do you really believe I've forgotten them? Do you think that's even possible?"

"Well, you certainly act like it."

Freya had never been so angry. The rage poured through her veins like her blood had boiled rather than the water on the stove. "Everything I do is in memory of them. I take care of the crystals and the herbs. I grow the plants that keep the goblins at bay. I sew the wards when they break, and I sing the songs to the stream so it flows. What more do you want as proof that I miss them?"

"You could say it once in a while."

Was that what Esther wanted? Freya would not sit here and mourn their parents two years after their disappearance. "Things have to get done around here," she replied, her voice thick. "I can't sit here and wish them back with you. Someone has to take care of us and our home."

She didn't expect that person to be Esther. Her sister was only a child, sixteen and still thinking the world would be kind to two women on their own. Neither of them were likely to get married, not while living within the heart of the forest as they did. Not to mention their dowries had already been spent on food and a new roof. Although, Esther didn't know that yet.

Freya had to step up and take on the responsibilities of both mother and father. She had to do all the things that she might not have wanted to do.

Didn't Esther see that? How could she not understand the difficulty of Freya's position?

Of course Freya had wanted a life different from this. She wanted to live as a normal woman and find a young man who would woo her. She wanted to build her own house in the forest, design it so that many babies could stagger through the halls into the arms of a father who wouldn't disappear into the woods and never return.

Esther shook her head in disbelief. "That's all you have to say? After everything we've lived through together, and all the things that mother and father did for you, all you can say is that you're busy?"

"I don't know what you want from me." Freya made her way to the wood stove and reached behind it. Their father's sawed-off shotgun was in a special iron lined box. No faerie would ever steal it, and no goblin could ever touch the box.

Esther sucked in a low breath. "What are you planning on doing with that?"

"I plan on letting you go to sleep and get your rest. Tomorrow is a long day of ward building. One of us needs to have their wits about them to keep watch for any goblins that might return." She opened the barrel and looked into it, reassured by the sight of two thick bullets. Clicking it back in place, she nodded toward the front door. "I'll keep watch tonight for anyone who might sneak in."

"I told you, I didn't make a deal." Esther stared like Freya had lost her mind.

Maybe she hadn't. But that goblin with the moonlight skin made the hair on her arms stand on end. This wasn't over. She feared what he might plan with magic at his fingertips.

Freya dragged a chair from the dining table into the middle of the room. She sat down hard on the sturdy wood, shotgun held across her chest and eyes on the door. She could see the outside through the moon carving.

"Freya, are you really going to do this?"

She didn't respond. What else could she say that she hadn't already? Yes, she was going to sit here all night and make sure not a single goblin thought they could sneak into their hut.

And yes, this was her sister's fault. Esther knew better. Freya had to fix this situation before they both regretted it for the rest of their lives.

Esther should count herself lucky if Freya ever let her leave the property again. The goblins could take her at any point now if they considered the fine print of a deal as also being given a gift. She had no idea.

Their mother had never taught them what to do in this situation. She'd always said to never get close enough to a deal for goblins to mince words and steal them away. That was the rule.

Esther huffed out a disbelieving breath. "I'll talk to you in the morning then, I guess. I obviously can't have a normal conversation with you right now."

Why she would even try was a mystery to Freya. She didn't look at her sister as she heard clothing hitting the floor and the bed creaking. If Esther got some sleep, even a small amount, that would feel as though she had succeeded.

As much as Esther liked to think Freya was controlling and a horrible sister, she didn't remember their mother's teachings. Esther had always been with their father. He was a kindly man, soft around the edges, and more likely to chat with a goblin than try to keep them at bay.

Their mother had seen the creatures for what they truly were. Faeries liked to kidnap children. They bred mortality into their lines so they weren't so ugly, so disgusting to look upon. They wanted mortal blood and the only way they could get that was by stealing children away.

Sure, the mortal women would cry and beg to be sent back to their homes. They'd want to be in the mortal realm, and maybe they would even wither into a shadow of their former selves. Maybe they would ask to see their loved ones in scrying mirrors or glassy pools.

Time wore away at everything, though. Even love. And eventually, the mortals would forget their lives before goblins, claws, and broods of ugly children.

That was why she stared at the door so fiercely and gripped her gun tightly. She knew what the goblins could do once they sank their claws into children. She knew Esther would eventually forget Freya even existed while she was stuck here in the mortal realm, desperately wishing for her sister to return.

Wishing for her mother.

Her father.

Anyone who would love her because Freya was so scared of losing everything and then being stuck here. Alone. All by herself, without a single person who knew her name.

That future was unacceptable. It made her heart race and her palms slick with sweat. She couldn't survive that fate, and she wouldn't let Esther go because of it.

She tightened her grip on the shotgun. The metal had seen better days. Rust made the handle a little difficult to grip, but that was all right. She knew just how powerful the shotgun was. All she had to do was point it in a direction and fire. Whatever stood in her way wouldn't remain standing for very long.

Goblins were hardy creatures, but she doubted even they would survive a direct shot.

Freya didn't recognize the time passing. All she knew was that she stared for what felt like an eternity. She tried to not even blink, for fear the goblins would appear in front of her as if by magic.

Then she heard it. The chiming of bells that her tired mind thought might be someone tapping a fork against a glass. For a toast, perhaps? Or maybe that was just foolish thoughts because she needed to sleep.

Her eyelids grew heavy. She took a deep breath to force her mind to clear, but all she could smell was the wondrous scent of apples and cinnamon.

No, he couldn't be here. They weren't allowed to come into a house without invitation. At least, that's what her mother had always said. Freya snapped upright again, eyes wide, peering around the room as though he was about to step from the shadows.

When no goblin made himself known, she settled into the chair again. Her hands gripped the wood handle and sweat made them slide dangerously. She needed to get a grip on herself. The sun was coming up, wasn't it?

The cloying scent clawed its way into her nose. It poured into her lungs like someone had tipped whiskey into her mouth and suddenly, she didn't know what time it was. How long had she been sitting in this chair? It felt as though she hadn't been here long, but also as though she'd also been here forever.

She looked out of the little moon carved in their door and felt her hands shake. The sun was rising, but the moon was doing the same. They rose together in the sky until she didn't know whether it was day or night.

"Magic," she muttered. "It's just magic."

And then she heard him. His deep voice whispering in her ear. "Yes, Freya. Of course it's magic."

The sound sent a flutter from her head all the way into her belly. She quivered in the chair, her breath sawing out of her lungs. "What are you doing to me?"

"Nothing at all. I just want you to sleep."

She felt claws on the back of her neck. The cold tips shifted her hair to the side, and then she swore he inhaled the scent of her skin. She could feel the warm heat of his breath brush through her hair.

Freya shook her head, but her eyelids were even heavier. She couldn't keep them open. No matter how hard she tried. "I need to protect my sister," she whispered.

"You need to sleep."

No, just one more breath and she'd be fine. Freya's hands tightened on the shotgun. She would bolt up from her chair, spin around, and shoot him point blank. He wouldn't survive it. He'd never make it out of this cabin alive.

She jolted upright, hands clutching the gun. But as she opened her eyes and spun around, Freya's eyes widened with fear.

The room was filled with sunlight when she had been certain it was still night.

The scent of apples and nutmeg was only a faint trace in the air.

And her sister's bed was empty.

She dropped the gun on the floor and darted into their bedroom. "No, no, no," she muttered, frantically yanking the blankets from her sister's bed. "Esther! Esther, please be here."

But her sister wasn't in the bedroom at all. All that remained was a single, snow white letter on Esther's pillow.

Freya didn't want to touch the cursed page. Goblin magic was all over it. It sparkled like fresh snow when the sun hit its glistening surface, and all she wanted to do was set the entire room on fire.

Esther couldn't be gone. She just couldn't.

Freya's mind refused to believe what was in front of her, but her heart knew the truth. What other choice did she have?

The goblins considered a gift as a debt, and Esther was the only one who could pay that price. They'd cast a spell on Freya and she'd been asleep for the entire ordeal. Had her sister screamed out for help? Had Esther reached for her while they dragged her from the hut, only to realize Freya couldn't help?

Tears in her eyes, she lifted the small note from the pillow and turned it over.

Thank you for your sister,
she'll make a lovely snack.
Please don't try to find her,
we won't give her back.

CHAPTER 4

Freya sat on her sister's bed for hours with the note clutched in her hand. She poured over the wiggly words, clearly written by an inhuman hand. They had to have some kind of hidden meaning in them. Some quest she could partake in to get her sister back.

But the more she read the letter, the more she realized there was no quest. No deal. No way to win back the lost sister in some heroic story. It clearly stated that she wouldn't ever get Esther back.

A swell of emotion was building in her chest. She couldn't think through it. The panic rose into her throat, silencing her voice and bubbling up to her eyes. Tears built, but they refused to spill over.

Freya recognized that she was holding her breath. She needed to inhale or she would pass out, but she couldn't make her lungs work. Not when her sister was gone. Not when she was going to be alone forever and all her fears were finally realized.

The village wouldn't take her in. They'd always liked Esther more than her, because her younger sister knew how to be kinder. Softer. Easier to be around. Freya was all about her work and what she needed to get done. She had little time to pause and talk with villagers who didn't make her own life easier.

They thought she was off-putting. Too difficult, very stubborn, and certainly not the kind of woman who was suitable for a spouse. Let alone friends.

Damn it.

She couldn't survive without her sister. Her family was more important than anything in this world, and the goblins couldn't take her sister from her. Not without a fight.

Freya burst into movement. She thundered through the room, a woman on a mission as she stuffed the panic back into her belly. It rolled there, rumbling through her intestines, but she refused to pause.

Her mother had discovered many things about the goblins, and she had to know more than what she'd told Freya. How had she learned how to make the wards? Who had taught her?

A thought appeared in her mind, one that she would never have dared to think when her mother was still here.

No one knew how to get rid of a goblin better than a goblin.

Long before her parents had disappeared, Freya's father had buried her mother's books in the backyard. He'd said they were cursed. That they drew the goblins to them because such creatures could sniff out magic like dogs.

Freya grabbed a shovel from the shed behind their house and stomped to the garden. Her father had buried it beneath the turnips because no one in their right mind would ever dig up a good bed of turnips.

But Freya wasn't in her right mind.

She stomped hard on the shovel, sinking into the earth she had tilled for years. She heaved dirt over her shoulder, not caring where it landed. Sweat slicked her brow, and the sun rose as she destroyed their garden. The box had to be here. It had to be.

Finally, her shovel struck something hard. She fell to her knees and dug her hands into the soil. Shifting it to the side, she revealed a small wooden chest with golden clasps holding it shut. The wood looked like not a single thing had touched it for years. Perfect. Pristine.

Magical.

The chest where her mother had kept all her books had to be part of that Other realm. Where goblins marched to their bells and faeries flew overhead.

Freya planted her feet on either side of the chest and heaved. Her back strained, aching under the weight and hours of digging, but she didn't stop. Not until the earth released its treasure, and the chest slid out of its tomb.

She pulled it out of the hole in the ground and placed her hands on the golden clasps. Her mother had always said this box wasn't for the faint of heart. Children shouldn't know of the magic that made their realm work.

Freya had never wanted to know what was inside. She'd always been rightfully afraid of the goblins and their work.

Her fingers shook as she flipped the latches up. No locks kept it shut. And within the box, she could hear a faint rustling. As though the wooden frame hid something alive within.

She opened it and threw up an arm, just in case something came flying out. She had no idea what would have survived within the box that long, but magic could do many impossible things.

Nothing flew out at her. No attack, no sound, even the faint rustling stopped.

Freya slowly lowered her arm and peered into the chest.

The contents were rather unremarkable. Four books in the right corner, a small terrarium with plants still growing inside it, a jewelry box, and a stack of loose papers that moved as she watched.

Papers shouldn't move on their own. But they shifted again as she watched.

Was there a mouse or other small creature still alive after years of being buried? She looked back to the hole she'd just dug, and then to the box again. It wasn't possible. There couldn't be a creature living within the chest.

Hesitantly, she reached out and picked one page up. There wasn't anything underneath it, but the page still fluttered in her hand.

"Are you moving?" she whispered.

The page wiggled again.

With a soft sound of fear, she let the page drop from her hand. It wriggled back to the other pages, tunneling under them as though it were frightened of her. But a page of paper couldn't be afraid. It was just an inanimate object someone had written on a long time ago.

Maybe this was why her father had buried the chest. Unnatural things should remain underground.

Shivering, she braced her hands on the sides of the box. "I need to find my sister."

The pages all stopped moving. It almost appeared as though they were waiting for something, or perhaps they were listening. Waiting for her to continue asking them more questions.

Licking her lips, Freya tried to still the shaking of her voice. "The goblins took her. They had a necklace she thought was our mother's, and even though she didn't make a deal, they still gave her the necklace."

That made the pages rustle again. Each loose leaf shifted, jostling with each other to move. They reorganized themselves until a single page was on the top.

Making sure the pages understood her need, Freya added, "I need to go into the goblin realm and find her. I have to get her back."

The top page lifted at the bottom, then slapped back against the others. Almost as though it were trying to say it knew she wanted to find her sister.

Her skin crawled with the magic that made these pages come alive. She couldn't stand the thought that they were listening to her. Or that they could somehow help her, even though they should have just been dormant. They should be still like real paper and not as though they were alive.

Hands shaking, she reached for the top page and lifted it up into the sunlight. The words at first made little sense. Then she realized she was looking at a map.

It was the forest around their hut. Written in her mother's hand because of course she'd been keeping track of the magical things that happened around her own home. She'd been trying to do that for so many years, and here it was. The map of all magical things in the forest surrounding Woolwich.

Freya tilted the map, rotating it in her hands until she was looking in the right direction. There was the town on the bottom left. Their hut was in the bottom right. And then the entirety of the forest spread out like the ever reaching arms of nature.

Her mother had made a few marks. Some of them made sense. A magical pool that must be avoided because kelpies lived within it. A couple spots where she'd seen sprites making away with honey and wine from the village.

But in the very top corner was a marking that didn't make sense. A little square box with lines like the rays of the sun.

"What is this?" she asked.

The pages shifted again.

Without thought, Freya picked up the next page and read what her mother had written.

"While wandering the forest, I found the most fascinating of doors. It stands between two rather impressive old trees. At first, I thought someone was playing a prank on wanderers like myself. But when I opened the door, I realized there was another world beyond it. This is a portal into the Faerie Realm and must be avoided at all costs. I tried to cover it, but no matter how many sticks I placed, when I turned around they were gone. Magic protects the door."

Her mother had drawn a picture of it. The wooden door was unremarkable, but the trees were older than most in the forest. She'd even taken care to draw moss on the bark.

Tears built in Freya's eyes. Her mother had found a portal, marked it on a map, and then buried the knowledge so no one would ever mistakenly go through it.

And Freya was about to do exactly what her mother had taken such precautions to prevent.

It didn't matter. She had to get Esther back because who was she without her sister? A nothing, a nobody. Just the strange girl in the woods who didn't know how to talk to other people because her sister had always done it for her.

Freya could see her future as though she looked into a crystal ball. She would end up alone and the forest would grow in around her. Eventually, she wouldn't be able to keep up with all the things that had to be done. She would disappear into the moss just like the rest of the hut. The villagers would talk about the strange forest woman who they thought was a witch, and that rumor would spread.

The villagers would no longer want a witch on their land. She would be an old woman by the time they decided she had to be taken care of, and the younger people wouldn't see her as a person anymore. She would become a mythical, magical creature who needed to be removed.

None of these fears would come to light if she had her sister, however. Esther would know what to do.

Standing, she raced to their home and grabbed her leather pack off the wall. She shoved as much food as possible into it, a canteen for water, a few pieces of clothing to change into. A second pair of boots. The sides bulged until she was certain that was all she could carry in it. Unfortunately. Now, she just had to start the journey.

Freya threw the pack on, tugged on her thick boots for walking, and threw a plain brown dress on top of her chemise, and raced out the door.

The sun was already halfway across the horizon, and she had a long way to go. The door was at the far corner of the forest, farther than she'd ever traveled with her mother.

Branches slapped at her face, scratching her arms and digging through her clothing to her shoulders. The forest fought back as she advanced through it. Almost as though even the trees didn't want her to find the door.

"What were you searching for in the forest?" she muttered to the spirit of her mother. "I don't understand."

She'd never quite understood why her mother had been so set on finding something in these woods. She'd looked every week for something new. Something magical. And then she'd write it down in her books, or perhaps on the map she found and move onto the next. She had instilled within Freya a deep fear of the magical. So where had this obsession come from?

The sun was setting by the time she made it to the far side of the map. Freya stopped in the dim light, peering down at the pages and looking around at the trees. This was the spot. It should have been, at least.

"Where are you?" she called out as she turned in a circle.

The door could easily hide itself from anyone it didn't want to open for. Magic could do a number of things. All she had to do was find it now.

"Come on," Freya muttered. "Show yourself."

As if those were the words the door was waiting for, it was right behind her on her second turn. Hidden between two trees. The trunks had grown around the solid wood door, pressed against the sides like they were parts of a wall. Leaves crowned the top and spilled over the frame.

A door to the faerie realm, just like her mother had said. All Freya had to do was reach forward and open it, then she would be able to save her sister. Or at least start the journey.

Doubt clouded her mind. Why did she think she could be a hero? How could she save her sister? She was just a mortal who knew nothing about goblins, faeries, or sprites. The only knowledge she held was told to her by her mother, who had hated the dreadful creatures.

"Faerie magic clouds the mind," she said. The words were her mother's, and she knew in this moment, magic was making her think terrible things about herself.

She was strong. She was capable. And nothing was going to stand in her way in saving her sister. This door. Magic. Nothing could ever turn her mind away from what she had to do.

There was no other choice.

Light glowed from underneath the door. Freya reached out her hand and settled it on the golden doorknob that was strangely warm to the touch. She took a deep breath and told herself everything would be fine.

Then she turned the knob and stepped into the faerie realm.

CHAPTER 5

Freya stepped through the door, and the ground shifted beneath her feet. It rolled as though she had somehow stepped onto a wave. She stumbled, then fell onto her hands and knees where the earth tumbled beneath her.

She let out a startled shriek, but the sound didn't stop the magic. Instead, the ground churned up and down until it spit her out. Ejecting her from the tumultuous game it had played, as though she weren't interesting anymore.

Freya pressed her palms into the dirt and tried to get her bearings.

Her head was spinning. A headache bloomed between her eyes and pressed against the front of her skull.

She lifted a dirt smeared hand and pressed it to the ache. The blistering pain didn't stop, but perhaps that was the price of magic. She should have known walking through a magical door wouldn't be easy.

Magic was never easy, according to her mother. Humans couldn't wield it like the faerie kinds could. Goblins used it because they'd already paid its price with their beauty. That's why they looked like animals. Mortals had to continually give bits and pieces of themselves until they were lost forever.

Groaning, she sat down hard on her bottom and held her head until the pounding slowed. She was still very light-headed, standing wouldn't happen for a while without passing out. But at least she could see straight without the world tilting again.

Letting her hands fall down to her sides, she stared at the path she'd been spat out upon.

The ground was covered in beautiful, vibrant leaves of red, gold, and orange. She'd never seen colors that looked so bright. The trees arched over the lane, creating a ceiling of tangled branches and colorful leaves that fell with the passing wind. She could just barely see the sky through the gaps. Bright blue and lovely.

Most concerning, it wasn't fall in the mortal realm. It was the middle of summer, so she wasn't sure why it was autumn here.

Another shower of leaves fell down around her head. She shook them out of her hair with a disgruntled snort. There wasn't anything familiar around her, although it also looked like there wasn't a way off the path. The trees were pressed so tightly against each other, Freya didn't think she could fit past their trunks. Only a small child might be able to fit, and even then...

She stood and dusted off her bottom. If the only way to continue was forward, then she best be putting one foot in front of the other.

At first, Freya kept her eyes on the trees. She wanted to make sure no faeries came charging out at her for daring to step foot in their realm. Not to mention she was concerned there would be a gap she missed if she continued on too quickly.

Then she realized the trees all looked the same. No one was coming out of the forest. And the sun was still in the exact same spot on the horizon that it had been when she first arrived.

Frowning, Freya paused for a moment and looked up at the sparkling light through the leaves. "Curious."

She started forward again. This time, she kept her gaze on the path before her and the faint hint of a shape at the end. A shape that looked suspiciously like another door.

No matter how quickly she moved, the shape stayed in the same spot. A mirage, perhaps.

Freya focused on a tree with a rather distinct curved branch. She watched with rapt attention, forcing herself to stare only at that tree and move forward. But the tree didn't get any closer, no matter how long she ran.

After what felt like hours, she tired herself out. Her legs quivered. Her thighs ached and her stomach twisted into knots. She couldn't take another step forward, but she had gotten nowhere with all the running.

Out of breath, she bent at the waist and braced her hands on her knees. She'd never heard of something like this before. Her mother had mentioned no spell that stuck a person in the same spot while they ran. Was it even possible?

Looking up at the tree again, she twisted her expression into a snarl. Then she looked at that damned hot sun in the sky. In the same spot as it had been hours ago. "Why aren't you moving?"

"I could ask the same of you." The voice came from right beside her, although Freya was certain she had been alone.

She stared down at the creature to her right, and it took awhile to process what was walking beside her. Or who. Actually, she wasn't sure whether to call it a "who" or an "it".

It was a dog.

Or something like a dog.

A black and white dog, with a long snout and soulful brown eyes staring up at her. He walked on his back legs with his front paws held at his sides like a person. A red, crushed velvet suit covered his body as though he were human, but a tail with a white tip stuck out of the back.

At least he wasn't wearing shoes. There was only so much she could handle at the moment.

Clearing her throat, Freya tried to make sense of what was happening. A dog was standing next to her, wearing clothing far finer than any she'd ever touched in her life, and it talked. Because of course that all made sense.

She was losing her mind.

Freya stared straight ahead of them and took a deep breath. "It's not real, Freya. This is all an illusion. Something to make your mind break."

The dog nodded its head. "Possible, I suppose, though unlikely. What illusion would be useful to break your mind? Humans are quick to believe they're mad, and it would be such a waste of magic."

"That's exactly what an illusion would say."

"Or perhaps I'm standing next to you, solid and fully formed. Really, I don't understand why humans are so quick to explain everything away. Perhaps your eyes aren't lying at all."

She stiffened. "Then this is real? You're real?"

He looked down at himself, then back up at her. "Why wouldn't I be real?"

A thousand answers played through her thoughts. Because she'd never heard an animal talk. Because the goblins could easily lock her in this place while she babbled away to a dog who wasn't even real.

A thousand answers, and yet none of them could explain what this little beast was doing.

She reminded herself this was only part of the journey. Esther needed her and abandoning everything at the first talking animal would be ridiculous. She was bound to see a lot stranger things.

"I suppose you're right," she replied. "I can see you're real."

"Solid as they come." He thumped a paw to his chest. "Now, why aren't you moving?"

She didn't have an answer for that. Obviously, if she could be moving, then she would. Freya frowned down at him. "I don't know."

"Ah." He looked around her down the path. "Well, I suppose that's just the path then. I wasn't sure what you were doing."

"I'm trying to find my sister."

"A noble quest." He planted his paws on his hips and the tiny suit stretched across his chest.

She thought perhaps he was some kind of herding breed. In the mortal realm, he would have been working on a farm. Apparently, in the faerie realm, he was a rich dog who could afford red velvet.

The dog snuffled, a sound that was so familiar it made her blink twice before focusing on his words. "If you're on a quest, then you'll have to move faster than you are."

Freya picked her feet up and started walking. Disconcertingly, as she was speeding up her pace, he was standing in the same spot. Not moving, but remaining at her side. Finally, she gave up trying to walk.

Tossing her hands up at her sides, she replied, "See? No movement."

"Yes, I can see that." He tapped his chin with an overly large paw. "What a predicament."

Freya waited again, certain he was going to say something more. A predicament, yes, it was. But he was a magical creature, and surely he'd have an idea that could help her.

She continued staring at him as he tapped his paw.

Finally, the dog heaved a great sigh and shrugged his shoulders. "Well, good luck then." He started off toward the woods without another word.

Furrowing her brow, she watched him leave before shouting, "Wait a second! Aren't you going to help me?"

The dog stopped and looked over his shoulder. "I wasn't planning on it."

She felt her jaw drop open. Leaves rained down on the dog's shoulders, but he didn't seem to care. All he did was huff out another breath that blew one from his shoulder. When she didn't respond immediately, he turned around and pranced away.

"Wait!" she shouted. "Shouldn't you at least try?"

Again, he paused, although this time he looked rather angry. "Why would I help you?"

"Because I need help?" Freya realized that was a flimsy argument at best. "Because I'm asking. I can't be trapped here for all eternity, I have to save my sister."

"Yes, you said that." The dog wandered close to her again. "What do you have to trade?"

She floundered, trying to understand what he was asking for. Her mother had always said faeries were interested in helping humans, but for a price. She didn't want to make a deal with him or she'd end up in the same place as Esther. But this wasn't a deal. He was asking for a trade.

"I won't make a deal with you," she clarified. "If that's what you're asking."

He waved a paw in the air. "Petty magic. Goblins like making deals, yes, but I've risen above my kind."

"So you're a goblin?" She eyed him again, trying to see some semblance of the creatures she knew. He wasn't human enough for him to be a goblin, or at least in her opinion.

The few goblins she'd gotten a good look at always had some kind of human quality to them. Arms. Legs. Skin that wasn't covered in fur. Sure, this creature wore human clothing, but that didn't mean he wasn't a dog in a velvet suit.

He glared up at her. One side of his mouth lifted into a snarl. "Of course I'm a goblin! What else would I be?"

She didn't know, but they were in the faerie realm, so she supposed he could be all manner of things.

Freya pressed her lips together and eyed him. "I just need someone's help. And you look as though you are the kind of person who knows a thing or two about the place we're in."

"Yes, well—" he started as though he were going to argue more, then paused as her words processed. He planted both his paws on his hips then replied, "I do know a lot about where we are."

"And you seem far more benevolent than any other goblin I've met. So I thought it much more likely that you'd be more likely to be a knight in shining armor for a poor woman like myself?"

Freya tried her best to keep the hopeful tones out of her words. Perhaps if she plied him with compliments, then he'd give in. If he could get her out of this forest, then she'd gladly be on her way without him.

He sniffed again. "Yes, I am more giving than the rest. It's what sets me apart."

"I can tell." She pressed a hand to her chest. "My name is Freya of Woolwich. What's yours?"

He touched a paw over his heart. "Arrow the goblin."

"Well then, Arrow the goblin. Would you please help me?"

He seemed to mull over her words. If the goblin relented, that was a better start than where she was at. Surely a goblin would at least know a way out. And maybe he'd know how to find her sister.

"What do you have to trade?" he repeated.

She grumbled out a few expletives before she yanked her pack off her back and tossed it at his feet. "Would anything in there suffice?"

He gave her a rather wolfish grin for such a small dog. "Let's find out, shall we?"

CHAPTER 6

Freya wasn't certain how long they walked. It felt like days, though the sun never moved. She tried to keep up with the goblin dog, but no matter how quickly she walked, she always seemed to tire before him.

At least Arrow wasn't impatient. He paused when she needed to, eyeing her with that dark gaze. Almost as though he were a little disappointed.

Freya didn't know how to prove her worth. She was trying as hard as possible, but she couldn't walk forever. Time passed and her legs quivered. Her back ached. Sweat slicked her skin from head to toe, and still Arrow hadn't given her any guidance on how to get to the end of this path.

Finally, she had to stop. Freya lifted a hand to her sweaty brow, then bent over with her hands on her knees. "I can't," she muttered. "I need to stop for a bit."

"All right, then." Arrow crossed his paws over his chest. "We can stop."

She wanted to grumble he hadn't ever started. The goblin had let her walk and walk and walk while he remained still the entire time. He hadn't lifted a single paw.

With a groan, she allowed herself to sit on the ground. Her butt hit the dirt, and she admitted to herself that she didn't want to be here. She didn't want to sit with a goblin on an impossible path. She certainly didn't want to feel like she was talking to a dog and slowly losing her mind.

But this was the only way to save her sister.

"Damn it, Esther," she muttered. "Why did you take that necklace?"

Arrow settled onto the earth beside her. He laid down just like the animal he looked like, which was disconcerting while he still wore clothing. "Esther? Is that your sister's name?"

She nodded.

He put his head on his paws. "It's a pretty name. I can see why the goblins wanted her. We like pretty names."

"No, they..." She shook her head. "They had a necklace that looked like something our mother used to wear. She disappeared a few years ago, and Esther was certain it was the same necklace."

Arrow narrowed his gaze, then shook his head. "Unlikely. We don't take from the dead. Bad luck, you see."

Such information was new for her to hear about the goblin kind, and she stored it away for the future. Goblins were afraid of the dead. Or perhaps they just honored those who were no longer with them. Similar to humans, really, although she'd seen people dig through graves for anything that was worth a few coins.

She took a deep breath and nodded. "Well, either way. They took her for accepting the gift of the necklace."

"Ah." Arrow grumbled out a sound that was eerily similar to a growl. "The fine print. She really should have read the contract a little closer."

"There's no contract with goblins." Freya's voice snapped through the air like a whip. "They take what they want. Who they want. And this time they took the wrong person. My sister wasn't for barter."

The leaves froze. The wind stopped blowing. It appeared the entire path was holding its breath after her outburst.

Even Arrow hesitated before he quietly replied, "Losing family is very difficult."

"What would you know of that?" She pulled her pack into her lap and rummaged through it. The canteen full of water wouldn't last much longer, but she couldn't stand the thickness of her dry tongue.

Only a few bars of honey and dried fruit were left. She still had a full loaf of bread, but that was only one more day's worth of food. Freya was running out of time and this goblin refused to help her.

Arrow shifted again, standing up and straightening the hem of his velvet coat. "I would know a great deal about that, human child, and I'm offended you think otherwise."

Freya froze. What had she asked him? What he knew of losing family?

Well, now she felt rotten. She set the pack down on the dirt, cheeks burning. "I'm sorry for your loss."

"Not everyone has been blessed in life, as it sounds like you are aware." He looked down at a paw, then back to the path. "My mother's name was Bow. Father was Fletch. Made sense they would name their children Arrow and Notch."

Freya held out one bar of fruit and honey. She didn't think there was anything in it that could hurt him. She never used raisins in her recipe, and that was the only thing she knew dogs were allergic to. At least when it came to dried fruit.

He waved it off, then continued. "They were all like me. Beautiful. Lean. So fast they were in the king's royal hunting party and together they chased down the greatest of prey." He pressed a paw to his chest again, as though the memories ached to think of. "They were all killed in a tragic accident, as the king likes to call it. But I have my doubts. I might never have been in the king's service but I know my family. They tried to save the king but..."

As his words trailed off, Freya reached out a hand for him to take. Delicately, Arrow placed his paw on her palm.

"What a tragic loss," she replied. "My mother and father are gone, although we do not know if they are dead. My sister has been stolen away by goblins for owing them a debt. I am completely alone in this life and I know how difficult it is to feel strong when no one is standing by your side."

He nodded sharply. Arrow blinked a little too fast for her to think him unaffected by her words. "Those of us who are alone must stick together, I suppose."

"That's why I'm asking for your help. I need to get her back, Arrow." Freya stared into his eyes and hoped he saw her sincerity. "Maybe we can help each other so neither of us is so alone."

He huffed out a low grumble, then a growl, and finally took his paw away from her hand. "Fine, fine. What goblin took her and where did they run off to?"

"I don't know." But she did. She must.

Freya tried to consider the options. The rat-faced goblin boy might have been the one. After all, he'd given the necklace to her sister. But that seemed wrong. Unbelievable, if she was being honest.

"There was only one goblin there who might have done it," she murmured. "His skin was like moonlight and he smelled of fresh baked apple pie."

Arrow stiffened. His lips curled back and his teeth glinted in the sunlight. "Apples, you say?"

"And cinnamon. When she disappeared, that scent was very strong in the room even long after they had disappeared."

A low growl erupted from Arrow's jaws. The snarl on his face expanded into a full out sneer. He might be a medium-sized dog, but he could absolutely do damage with those sharp teeth. "I'm afraid to inform you that the Goblin King was the one who stole your sister. If he wanted her, then she's gone forever."

"No." Freya blurted the word out before she could catch it. "I refuse to believe that. She's not gone, and she certainly isn't beyond my reach. No one is that powerful."

"He is." Arrow scuffed a paw in the dirt before looking back to the forest. As though he were pondering whether or not he could slip away from her again. "The Goblin King is the only one we're all afraid of, you see. He's the High King and has been for a long time."

"High King?" She shook her head in confusion. "I thought all faeries were the same."

"Oh, no. We're all split up into different courts and none of us like each other. That much is for certain. But the Goblin King? He's the only one to wrangle all the faerie folk under his iron fist, and none of us would go against him." Arrow started toward the forest with his head ducked low. "Good luck, Freya of Woolwich. I wish you the best."

She'd had him! Freya knew she had convinced the goblin to help her, and now she'd lost him again just by bringing up a man who smelled like apples.

If his own court was so frightened of him, she couldn't imagine how a human woman would stop him. But she had to try.

"Wait!" she called out. "Wait, you said you would help me!"

"I said no such thing."

"You said those of us who were alone had to stick together, and that's a binding verbal contract." She didn't know if it was. Even suggesting such a thing was a stretch, but if the goblins could take her sister over a gift, then perhaps she could convince one to help her over something so silly as the wording of a sentence.

The hackles on Arrow's back rose. She could see the tufts of fur over the collar of his lovely jacket.

He turned with a fearsome snarl on his face. "Semantics, mortal. You're arguing over a dangerous topic. Binding a goblin to you will only end poorly."

"Will it? Or will it force you to help me find my sister?"

He shook his head. Leaves crunched under his paws as he shuffled back and forth. A wind blew between them, ruffling her hair and blowing it in front of her face.

The slight distance from the goblin dog gave him a strange, warped edge to his form. As though magic were what kept him upright and gave him the ability to speak.

Arrow snorted out a breath. "You wish to bind me to help you? Then a deal has to be struck."

"It already has been." She straightened her spine and hoped she was right. "You already said you would help me, and I offered nothing in exchange. Seems to me this is the same situation my sister was in. You offered something freely. I took it. A deal's a deal, goblin."

Perhaps she was right in her assumptions. Arrow's claws dug into the dirt, but he gave her a sharp nod once again. "Fine, then. You want to find your sister, who's in the Goblin King's clutches, you can take that risk. Bind me with a deal, but you're still the one whose head will roll if you mess up."

"I don't care." She did, of course. Her head was rather important in the grand scheme of things, but she wouldn't let this goblin think he had scared her off the battle. "I want my sister back. And you're going to help me get her."

He pointed at her with a paw. "Say it, mortal. If the Goblin King finds us, you're the one who's taking the blame."

"No deal." She swallowed hard, knowing what she was about to say was foolish but refusing again to see reason. "If the Goblin King thinks he can beat me, then he can try his very best. But I will get my sister back and I will break whatever deal she made with him. No Goblin King will stop me."

Arrow's eyes widened in fear just before a crack of thunder split the air. The wind picked up again, catching all the fallen leaves and throwing them into the air. A swirling dervish of colors surrounded them. The sun disappeared behind sudden storm clouds, black as night and ominous.

Her breath fogged as she exhaled, almost as though all the heat had been sucked from the path in the wake of her words.

The dog goblin panted, tiny clouds forming around him and slowly floating up in the air to join the rest of the oncoming storm. "What have you done?" he asked.

Freya didn't know. Why would any of this happen just because she'd said a few words about defying the Goblin King?

She shook her head. "What did I do? I don't know, Arrow!"

"You challenged the Goblin King!" he shouted.

Laughter floated down the path along with a blast of air that blew her hair away from her face. Leaves slapped at her cheeks, scratching the delicate skin and whipping her neck like tiny whips. She threw up an arm but stared at the end of the path. She could see something there... a tall figure who was almost familiar.

Then the figure lurched forward and she could see the moonlight skin clearly. The strange eyes and pointed ears with tufts of fur. She could see the sharp smile in the darkness.

The Goblin King stood there, and he was the one who had taken her sister. Rage burned in her chest.

Without thinking, she leapt toward him. Sprinting with the hope that she could wrap her hands around that pretty long neck and squeeze the truth out of him.

"Freya, no!" Arrow shouted.

This time, she actually moved. Freya struck a wall of magic so hard that it shattered like glass. She plummeted from the path and into darkness so deep it was like she had died.

CHAPTER 7

She tumbled through the air, somersaulting through starlight and past hanging moons until she struck the ground. All the air in her lungs burst from her lips from the sheer force of impact. Freya wheezed, desperately trying to suck in much needed air before her lungs collapsed.

Once she managed, she pushed herself up onto her hands and knees. She stared down at the polished tile floor. Tiny patterns had been hand painted onto each ceramic square. Little stars and moons, lines connecting them to make constellations she'd never seen or heard of before.

She lifted her gaze, looking up to find herself in some kind of... astrological research center? Or something of the sort.

Mobiles of planets and stars rotated above her head. The contraption that controlled them was impressive, if a bit impossible to believe. The stars were represented by five pointed gold creations that looked sharp as knives. A giant planet stood in the center of the room, gilded and patterned with tiny flowers. Rings of gold surrounded it, rotating with the rest of the planets.

Even the ceiling was covered in gold stars, though it was painted a vivid, deep blue.

There were windows, but they looked out into what appeared to be nothing but stars. Impossible. And yet, everything she'd seen thus far in the faerie realm was impossible.

Movement from behind the largest planet caught her eye. Stairs led up to the base of the spinning globe that was easily six feet tall. Silver skin shifted and a man in a black suit stepped from around the corner.

Now, she knew to call him the Goblin King in her mind. He stared down at something in his hand, not even looking at her, although he must be the one who had brought her here.

Freya frantically stood, backing away until her spine hit one of the pointed stars spinning throughout the room.

At her soft gasp of pain, he looked up. Those dark eyes narrowed and the smile on his face could only show his delight at her fear. "Hello, Freya. You've been rather persistent."

She hated him. Never in her life had she felt such a dark emotion, but it flowed through her veins as though raw power had taken the place of her blood. "What have you done to my sister?"

"Who?" He arched a thin brow. "Why do you persist in believing I care where your sister is?"

"Considering you stole her away from our home in the middle of the night, I'd imagine you care very much." She took a large step to her right and avoided the next star spinning toward her head. "You even went through the trouble of casting a spell to make me fall asleep."

"Is that what you believe?" He tilted his head to the side, watching her with a narrowed gaze. "You think I made you fall asleep when you were obviously exhausted? Perhaps you fell asleep on your own."

"I didn't."

That damned arched brow challenged her.

Freya refused to let him get in her head. He wanted her to think that she was the one at fault here. He wanted her to give up because she was the one who had failed her sister.

No. That wasn't the truth. And she wouldn't let him sew lies into her mind.

She balled her skirts in her fists and took another step away from him. "I didn't," she repeated. "You were the one who took her. A gift is not a deal, and I'm here to prove that."

"Oh, we didn't take her because she took the necklace from that boy." The Goblin King took a step toward her, aggressive and seeming to suck all the air from the room. "But you already know that, don't you? Esther has always been fascinated by our kind. Maybe she wanted more than your boring little life."

"No," she whispered. "My sister knows the rules, and she was happy with me."

His hair slid over his shoulder. The long dark locks shimmered in the starlight as they pooled down his chest. "Indeed, she knows the rules as well as you. But what makes you think she follows them?"

Freya would not fall into this trap either. He was getting too close to her with those intense eyes and that creepy smile. She stepped up the nearest stairs and stood beside a planet painted a deep emerald. The star paintings winked above her, glittering and sparkling with magical light.

"My sister respected what our mother taught." Freya held onto one of the gold rings surrounding the planet, as if that would give her the stability and courage she needed. "You cannot convince me otherwise with your lies."

He chuckled. The light glowing from within the planet cast over his features, turning his skin a sickly green. "Esther has alway been fascinated by us. She talks to the fae whenever she walks in the woods. About magic, about goblins, about you and your mother. She's told us a lot of things and none of them required us to stay away."

That sounded like her sister, but talking to imaginary friends wasn't making deals. Esther was never far from Freya's sight, anyway. If she'd been talking to goblins, Freya would have known.

"I don't have to listen to your lies," she whispered.

He rounded the corner near her planet, ducking underneath a passing star. His muscles flexed underneath that skin tight, perfectly pressed suit. He looked like a panther stalking his prey, especially when those silver eyes flashed. "They aren't lies. You remember what your mother taught you. The fae cannot lie, although I will admit we can deceive."

She tried to back away farther, but hit the wall. Apparently even this room had its limits to allow her escape. "My mother was a pious woman who knew exactly what kind of evil rests in your hearts."

This close, his beauty overwhelmed her. The smooth texture of his face was like looking at glass. He still smiled with those sharp teeth, but this time she could see the dimples in his cheeks. The sharp edge of his jaw made him far too handsome, while that sweet scent of his skin filled her nose. Even the faint tufts of hair at the tips of his ears weren't quite so otherworldly.

Gold threads decorated his suit with tiny vines and blooming flowers. His clothing was startling in its luxury. In comparison, she was an ugly weed planted next to a prized rose.

Freya was acutely aware of the poor quality robe she had over her chemise. It wasn't much, just homespun and wool. She also knew she smelled to the high heavens considering how long she'd been running for the past day. Perhaps past two days, she wasn't certain of the passage of time here.

And yet, the Goblin King leaned in and inhaled. "You stink of mortality," he murmured. "And weakness."

"I am not weak."

"Oh, you're not?" He watched her with so much intensity in his gaze that it made her cheeks burn. The silver flecks in his eyes shifted in tight circles, like a whirlpool.

And suddenly, she wondered if he was right. Maybe she was weak.

Hadn't she let her sister get taken? After all the things she'd done to keep her sister alive after their parents disappeared, she hadn't fought to keep Esther by her side. All she'd done was fall asleep in a chair, hugging her shotgun like it was a baby.

She'd done nothing.

She was nothing.

And here she had brought herself to the home of the Goblin King, thinking she could argue for her sister's freedom. Foolish dreams turned people into weaklings who clearly did not know what they'd gotten themselves into.

Freya couldn't yank herself out of the dark place in her mind. She tried to focus on something, anything, in the room that would help her, but the planets kept spinning. The stars kept moving. She was the only thing in the room that was so clearly and thoroughly stuck.

A grey moth fluttered down from the ceiling. It danced through the air, but she could focus on that instead of the constant spinning of the universe. The graceful wings beat at the air until it landed gently on the Goblin King's shoulder.

The dark thoughts parted like the pages of a book. She could see through the magic now. Through him as he had been the one manipulating her mind.

Freya wasn't weak. She had come here when no one else would have dared. She had walked for miles to get to her sister's side, and no Goblin King would change that.

"Huh," he muttered. "Well, that's certainly less fun."

When had he gotten so close to her? If Freya leaned forward at all, she would touch her nose to his. He was peering at her reactions as though she were an experiment he was testing magic upon. And that wouldn't do.

She twisted, ducking underneath his arm and bolting through the planets. She needed space to breathe air that wasn't exhaled from his lips.

Even as she darted away, the sweet scent of him trailed along with her. Not that he wore a masculine scent as she might have thought. Nor even a hint of luxurious perfume, as his clothing would have befit.

"Why do you smell like a bakery?" she snarled as she caught herself on one of the planets. Her lungs heaved for clean air, anything other than the sickly sweet scent.

"A bakery?" He lifted an arm and sniffed the sleeve. "How strange. I don't smell like that to anyone else."

"Impossible."

He shrugged. "I'm the Goblin King. I am designed to charm many people, but temptation comes in many forms. My physicality attracts some. My scent attracts others. Though you might find it hard to believe, some people even enjoy my company for my wit alone."

Freya could hardly believe that. She sneered, the expression twisted and cruel on her face. "Now I know faeries can lie."

He tossed his head back and booming laughter filled the room. "Ah, yes, you are entertaining, madame. I will give you that! I hadn't antici-pated you would be quite so quick-witted yourself."

Was this some kind of test? A meeting to decide whether or not she could have her sister back?

Freya looked around the room filled with galaxies and tried to find some clue. Some detail that would suggest he knew where her sister even was. A map. A drawing. Even just a lock of her sister's hair.

The room was pristine and beautiful, but it was void of anything that suggested a mortal had been here. No footprints, not even a finger print on the golden railing she gripped. Nothing but her own.

She released her hold on the metal and fisted her hands at her sides. "I came here to get my sister back, and you will return her to me."

"And here I was thinking you would be easy to send back to the mortal realm." He tapped a long nail against his chin. "But perhaps this game between us would be suited for more attention than a passing afternoon."

"Game?" Freya spat out the word. "This is my sister's life. Not a game."

"Everything is a game, Freya. Haven't you realized that? Otherwise, life is decidedly boring." He spread his arms wide and descended the stairs toward her. "I'm always willing to make a deal with a pretty woman."

"No." She shook her head. "I won't make any deals with any goblins. I want my sister back, but I will only get her back the right way. I'm not trading my soul for hers."

The Goblin King gave her a censuring look. "The only way to get something from a goblin is to make a deal. So you either take the one I'm offering, or kiss your sister goodbye forever."

Freya shut her mouth with a snap. She supposed he wasn't lying. Her mother had said the same thing about their kind. Goblins never offered anything for free.

The moth on his shoulder fluttered its wings and took off. She watched it fly up to the ceiling and land in the center of a star.

"What do you want?" she asked.

"I want to know that if you fail in this test, you will stay here." He laughed and the sound was mirthless. "Who wouldn't want to stay in the goblin kingdom? And you will fail, Freya. No one has ever beat me before."

"And if I defeat you?" She had to know it was a possibility, not that he was sending her on some impossible trial no one else had survived.

"Then you take your sister home." He closed his mouth, those sharp teeth disappearing underneath his soft plush lips. "Really, Freya, it's a simple choice. Play a game with me. Let's see how entertained we can be before you disappear from this realm forever. That's all I'm asking."

He was asking? She couldn't imagine why he would want the entertainment, but perhaps there was something more happening here that she didn't understand.

Freya didn't have a choice. He would send her home if she didn't take his offer. No matter how many times she fought to return, she would never get her sister back without making a deal.

And the Goblin King knew she had no other choice. Otherwise, he would have waited for her to ask for a deal.

Finally, she grumbled, "What are your terms then, Goblin King?"

The grin returned. Sly and far too knowing, like he had already trapped her, and she didn't know it yet. "Four gifts. Four meaningful items that represent the courts that follow me. Elves, Fairies, Sprites, and Goblins. You need to find the essence of their courts and bring them back to me. It's that simple."

"Why do I expect it's not that simple at all?"

He held out his clawed hands for her to take. "Do we have a deal, Freya?"

She eyed his palms. They were just hands, and yet, she knew they were so much more than that. She was as good as signing her life over to him if she took his deal.

The thought made her skin crawl.

Freya reached forward and placed her hands in his. "You have a deal, Goblin King."

Pain surged through her hands as twin spikes pressed into the centers of her palms. She felt them dig through her skin and into the fine, delicate bones. Twisting and grinding through the muscles.

Gasping, she fell onto her knees before him, her hands still trapped in his.

Her jaw fell open as she tried to think through the pain. She tried to breathe, but the spikes made her fingers twitch uncontrollably.

Then he released her, and the blades slid out of her palms. Freya clutched both her hands to her chest, still shaking with pain.

"Oh, please," he muttered. "It's just a little blood."

The Goblin King lifted his hands and she could see the red slicking his palms. He curled his fingers into fists, waved them in the air, and then she felt the floor disappear.

CHAPTER 8

She landed hard and rocks dug into her knees. Freya dug her fingers into the dirt and growled, "I need to get a better hang of that."

If they were going to continue dumping her on the ground somewhere new, then she had to find a better way to be teleported somewhere. How dare he toss her away like she was boring?

The holes in her palms still ached. Dirt dug into the wounds, stinging like she'd put her hands in fire. But at least it helped get her head on straight.

She had to do this. Find the essence of... wherever the hell she was and then move on to the next. She had to do this so she could find her sister and they could go home. She could do this.

The mantra was almost believable.

Sitting back on her haunches, she looked around her and tried to get her bearings. The sun shone brightly overhead, and she was at the very end of a path. Perhaps the path she'd been traveling for a very long time.

The horizon was filled with cherry blossom trees, each with petals more beautiful than the last. Lavender fields surrounded the woods, although Freya wasn't sure she could even call it a wood when it was clearly an orchard. Pinks and lavenders filled her gaze so much that she started getting starry eyed.

Birds chirped overhead, their songs an eerily familiar tune. Were the birds actually singing here?

"I hate this place." The familiar voice grumbled in her ear, but she already knew it was the goblin dog. Who else would follow her?

"Where did you run off to?" she asked. "I thought you would take the chance to leave."

"I made a deal, remember? You forced me to do so and goblins can't break deals." He stepped in front of her and smoothed a paw down the velvet covering his chest. "But I really do hate this place, so this better be worth my time."

"Where are we?" She pointed at the orchard. "And what is that?"

"We're in the Spring Court, of course." He dropped onto all fours and gave himself a shake. "Nasty lot, but at least they don't bite like goblins."

Freya stood and dusted the dirt and grime from her skirts. "We better go see who we can get to help us then."

She strode away from the path and into the thick, plush grass. Even that was so green it made her eyes water. What exactly was this place? Arrow had called it the Spring Court, and she could easily see why. The entire place reeked of spring. From the colors, to the scent in the air, to the birds who were almost too happy.

Arrow remained on all fours as he trailed along behind her. Every now and then, she could hear him snort out a disgruntled breath.

The sixth time he did it, she spun around with an angry, "What?"

A blue butterfly floated from seemingly nowhere and landed on top of Arrow's black and white head. It opened and closed its wings while he stared at her with big, sad eyes. "That. That is exactly the reason why I hate the Spring Court."

Don't laugh, she told herself. He looked so morose with the pretty blue butterfly on his poor head. How could someone be so sad and so adorable at the same time?

Freya shook herself from such thoughts. He wasn't a dog, even though it was very easy to forget that. Arrow was very much a goblin, and he wasn't to be trusted, no matter how much he looked like a border collie.

She waved a hand over his head and shooed the butterfly away. "Better?" she asked.

"Much. But you can't really fix it until we leave the Spring Court." He loped ahead of her, sauntering through the fields. "You'd think they would clean this place up, but no, of course not. Sprites have to be in a garden otherwise they burn up." He snorted again.

So they were also in a kingdom of Sprites. That was a start.

She followed him all the way to the edge of the cherry trees. Beyond the line of pink was a garden more splendid than she'd ever seen in her life.

Each section of the unending garden was bordered by hedge rows that would come up to her waist. Some of these sections showed the beginning growths of vegetables, but most appeared dedicated to a single flower that were all hovering between just blooming or in perfect buds.

A bubbling river separated the garden from the trees, though its waters were far too sapphire to be real. Stone bridges arched over the rivers, and crystal pillars created handrails that glistened in the sun like glass.

Her eyes took in all the details before she saw the creatures drifting through the greenery. Sprites wandered the hedge rows like ghosts of people. They wore moth-eaten clothing, wisps of fabric, covered in scraps of gossamer so light they looked like they were made of spider webs. Each sprite's face glittered in the sunlight, like their cheeks were covered with something sticky, or perhaps glitter. Their arms did the same, although she could see a fine pattern like veins down their skin.

Far in the distance were countless, ornately carved, white pergolas. Freya couldn't guess their usage, unless that was perhaps where the sprites slept.

A sound of awe slipped off her tongue before she could catch it.

"Oh, no," Arrow grumbled. "That's not the sound you should make, Freya."

"And why not?" She couldn't stop staring at the beautiful sprites in

the distance. "They're stunning! I thought all faeries looked like...
Well..."

He must have caught her looking at him. Arrow's whiskers
twitched. "You thought they looked like me? Like animals or goblins?"

She didn't want to admit that's exactly what she thought. How was
she supposed to tell him that she'd been taught all faeries were ugly
creatures? That they must all be some kind of unholy mixture of man
and beast?

He shook his doggy head, ears slapping against the side of his face.
"Ridiculous. Goblins are the only handsome faeries, you should have
known that. I thought you said your mother studied us?"

She hadn't said that at all, but if he wanted to consider goblins as
the prettiest faeries, then she wouldn't correct him. They were
standing before glorious specimens that she hadn't even known could
exist. How lovely. How strange!

One of the sprites looked over at them. Bouncy curls framed its
perfectly shaped face, but something was off about the features. The
creature's eyes had no whites at all. The startling blue orbs caught
Freya off guard, so she didn't have time to prepare for the sprite
opening its mouth and letting out a loud shriek.

Every single sprite in the garden froze, their hands pressed against
their mouths as they stared at her in shock.

"Oh no," she whispered.

Arrow paused, one foot in the air. Slowly, his tail sank between his
legs. "Oh no is right. This is my least favorite part."

"What's going to happen?"

"You don't want to know," he grumbled.

Yes, she wanted to know. She absolutely wanted to know what to
expect, considering at least ten sprites were now advancing upon them.
She took a step back, then another, until both she and Arrow were in
the middle of the crystal bridge.

The sprites caught them before they could run. The creatures only
came up to about chest height, so they stared up at her with those
unusual eyes.

"Hello," the closest one whispered.

Freya assumed this one was female, considering the rather exaggerated roundness of her breasts. Graceful, thin fingers reached up to touch Freya's arm.

She didn't want them touching her, but if that's what it took to get her sister back... Freya swallowed her pride and her fear. "Hello."

Two of the sprites jumped at the sound of her voice. One of them darted away, only to pause and stare back. As if it had thought she would chase the poor thing.

Freya didn't want to frighten them. They were too lovely, too delicate, and obviously one of the weakest faerie species. She couldn't be cruel to something that was so...

The sprites turned away from her, waving their hands over their shoulders for her to follow them. Freya started forward without hesitation. Arrow remained on the bridge with his hackles still raised.

She glanced back, then waited for him. "Aren't you coming?" she hissed so the sprites wouldn't hear her.

"I hate sprites," he muttered. "They're dangerous and they cannot be trusted."

"They look like they're made of moonbeams and glitter. How dangerous could they possibly be?" Freya glanced over at them one more time. They weren't all that impressive of a faerie species, and she couldn't understand the fear in Arrow's voice.

He shook his head, ears bouncing. "I don't expect you to understand the ways of the fae. First lesson about my kind, Freya of Woolwich, things are never what they seem."

Ominous.

She'd take his warning to heart. If he wanted her to be careful around them, then she would focus her energy on finding what they were trying to hide. Because they had to be hiding something for Arrow to be so afraid. They were far too pretty for her to believe them to be dangerous.

As they trailed along behind the sprites, she tried to consider why Arrow would fear them. Their thin bone structures would make them easy to break. They were short, even Freya could have fought them if she needed to. And sure, those strange glittering textures on their skin were odd, but she didn't think they were poisonous.

The sprite who had spoken to her looked over her shoulder. Those remarkable eyes blinked, and Freya saw a thin membrane slide over the orb of her eye. Like a cat. Or perhaps, like something far more otherworldly.

Once meeting her gaze, the sprite opened her mouth wide and smiled. Freya knew it was meant to be a reassuring expression, but the creature's mouth was filled with razor-sharp teeth. Each one appeared more jagged than the last.

"Oh," she whispered, glancing down at Arrow. "Now I see."

He narrowed his eyes. "Did you really doubt me?"

"I thought maybe you just didn't like sprites."

Arrow plodded along beside her on all fours, the white stripe down the center of his head glowing in the muted sunlight. "I fear very little in this world, but sprites?" A dramatic shudder shook his frame. "I'd be happy to never see them again."

Freya could now assume there was a good reason for that.

They wandered through the gardens, trailing along beside the hedgerows and past sweet-smelling flowers. They approached one of the pergolas, and she saw it was actually a makeshift bedroom. There was a giant mattress in the center, with streamers of lace and chiffon dangling from the ceiling. A sprite laid in the center of the bed, hands folded over her chest, while tiny bubbles floated around her.

Strange. Freya couldn't even guess what she was doing, unless this was just where they rested.

The other sprites continued on without a glance at the other sprite female. Freya followed them, but craned her neck to stare at the sleeping woman.

A thin fingered hand touched the side of her face. The sprite turned Freya's gaze away from the sleeping faerie. Gentle, but there was a strength to her hand that warned Freya she could make her stop looking if she wanted.

The sprite then pressed a finger to her lips, like she was telling Freya to be quiet.

Why?

Did they not want her to wake up the sleeping sprite? And what would happen if she did?

Freya frowned, looked down at Arrow, and hoped the goblin dog could at least tell her what was going on. But he just shrugged his thin shoulders and continued to follow the troop of sprites.

She noted his tail was still tucked between his legs. And that fear traveled through her as well.

Where were the sprites bringing them, anyway? She noted they were approaching a lake now. Its waters glowed in the sunlight, and tiny sparkles danced on the surface like diamonds. Too pretty. Too beautiful. And the more she stared at it, the more she wanted to leave.

"Where are we going?" she asked.

All the sprites spun around and pressed their fingers to their lips. Freya stopped talking. but she couldn't stop the thundering sound of her heart.

They continued on, past flowers and lakes. pergolas and sleeping sprites. She thought they might have traveled for an entire day until they finally paused before another pergola. This one was painted white with gold leafed carvings spilling from the top.

A sprite lay on the bed in the center, although this one was awake. Her eyes were overly large for her head, and the glitter spread over her entire body. She sat up, stretched her arms over her head and yawned.

"What have you brought me?" she asked the other sprites.

They all fell into deep bows, but did not respond.

Freya awkwardly looked at Arrow, who was looking at her. Together, they dipped into bows as well. She didn't know who this sprite was, but obviously the others thought she was important enough to respect.

Freya stayed in her bow until she heard the pitter patter of feet. The sprite had exited her bed and darted over to Freya's side.

"A human?" she asked. "Oh, I haven't seen a human in years! Stand up! Let me look at you."

This sprite was definitely different. Freya straightened and looked at the creature draped in moth eaten lace. The creature was beautiful, with the tiniest frame she'd ever seen, bright green eyes, and long pointed ears. But there was something very wrong with the sprite.

Every time she moved, a blur followed her hands. As though she were moving too fast for Freya's eyes to see, or perhaps like there was a second version of herself moving slower. It made looking at the sprite rather disorienting and, at times, nauseating.

The sprite shifted closer, peering up into Freya's eyes. "I'm the Spring Maiden and I rule the Spring Court. You'll be a wonderful addition to my bed of flowers."

The words sent an electric thrill of fear through her body. Freya swallowed. "Are you going to bury me?" If she wanted to, there was nothing Freya could do to stop her. There were too many sprites for her to fight off, and she'd never been trained for battle.

The Spring Maiden laughed. "Oh no, my dear. I wouldn't do something so dastardly as that. I just want to play with you." She reached up and stroked a finger down Freya's cheek. "Don't you like to play?"

Freya wasn't all that sure she did.

The sprites made quick work of taking Freya where the Spring Maiden wanted her to go. Two of them grabbed her arms, two more wrapped their arms around her waist, and yet another pair gestured for them all to follow. Freya didn't have a choice. She was locked in place.

Craning her neck to look behind them, she saw Arrow was getting a similar treatment. Although, the goblin was light enough that two sprites could simply lift him up off the ground.

He struggled, whining, "Freya! Don't let them—"

He was silenced long before he could warn her of whatever danger was coming. A sprite held his muzzle closed, smiling at her with those shark-like teeth glinting in the sunlight.

"Oh no," she whispered.

And here she was, thinking the Goblin King's tasks would be easier than this. Instead, she was in this strange place, surrounded by hungry faeries who likely wanted to feed her to their Spring Maiden.

She was in so much trouble, and Freya didn't have the faintest idea how to get out.

At least for now, the sprites didn't seem interested in ending her life. Though the Spring Maiden had said she wanted to add Freya to her bed of flowers, they didn't appear to be preparing an early grave.

She was taken to a pergola near the Spring Maiden's, though this bed was empty. The sprites released her arms, and the ones holding her waist urged her to take a seat on the bed.

What other choice did she have? Freya sat.

"What are you doing?" she asked.

"We're going to make you a flower," the nearest sprite said. She had fabric clutched in her hands and a rather maniacal expression on her face. "It's our favorite thing to do, you see. And we haven't been able to do it for a very long time."

"Make me a flower?" Another sprite slapped a hand over her mouth, and Freya couldn't say anything else.

They unraveled her hair from its braid and spread it out over her shoulders. They cooed over the softness and the texture of her hair, but Freya didn't know if such a thing was a compliment. One sprite set about brushing the tangles from her locks while the next pulled her robe over her head.

"Dresses make humans pretty," the sprite whispered.

Freya gulped. But she didn't let the sprite take her chemise off. Not when she didn't know what they were doing. She clutched the sweaty fabric to her chest and shook her head frantically.

"Yes," the sprite said, tugging hard. "Off."

"No," she replied. "This stays on."

Though the sprite frowned, at least she released the fabric.

Two of the others tugged an old wooden chest closer. It had seen better days, with worn edges and what looked like teeth marks on the sides. From a dog long ago? Perhaps from an accident when the chest had been dropped? Freya could only hope that was the truth of it, considering the sprite's teeth were sharp enough to gnaw at wood.

The sprite who had undressed her lifted the lid of the chest. Within were great swaths of fabric. Lace. Velvet. What looked like silk that they shoved aside in a flash. The sprites settled on dragging out a dress made entirely of what looked like very itchy lace.

"Yes," the sprite said again, drawing out the word until it was a long hiss. "This would look so lovely on the new flower."

"I'm not a flower," Freya replied.

The sprite brushing her hair yanked hard. She heard strands snap with the force of the tug.

"Hush," the sprite said. "We said quiet. Flowers don't talk."

She couldn't argue that flowers talked, but this flower did. She wasn't a new plaything for them, but apparently, that's what they thought she was.

The sprites wrestled her into the unusual gown. Lace sleeves fell off her shoulders, and she'd been correct, they were itchy. The bodice was too tight, and the skirt billowed around her as she walked. The scent of moth eaten fabric made her nose burn. She probably looked like some long dead princess who had awoken from her grave.

When the sprites stepped back and looked over their work, they let out sounds of pleasure and delight. "So pretty!" they all said. "How lovely!"

They spread her hair out, brushed too much so the dark locks poofed around her face. Freya didn't need to have a mirror to know what she looked like. Horrific. Tired. Just as she felt.

When they gave her room to breathe, she stepped away and asked, "Now what? Can I please speak with the Spring Maiden?"

Surely the leader of this place would know what the "essence" of spring was. All she needed to get was the information. Then, she had to find Arrow and together, they could figure out how to steal it.

If it was even something she could steal.

Damn it, Freya wished she was more prepared for this world. She'd thought charging into the faerie realm after her sister would be a little easier than this. Not just tossed into the fires of the fae, so to speak.

"Almost done," a sprite said. This one had pretty brown eyes that were as dark as night. She approached Freya with a tiny bottle in her hands. "This is for you."

Freya looked down at the bottle that was clearly meant to be sprayed on her. "Perfume?" she asked.

The sprite nodded and gestured for her to take the glass.

Goodness, if her scent offended them, a bath would be more helpful than a perfume bottle, but she supposed it wouldn't hurt. Freya took the pretty container and used the little balloon to spray a decent amount onto her neck and wrists.

Once finished, she opened her arms wide and said, "Am I sufficient now?"

The sprites watched her with rapt attention. They stared at her face a little too intently. Their eyes were a little too wide. And that was when she realized just how little she knew about the faeries.

Her mother would never have taken something offered like that and just sprayed it on her body. She would have asked what was in the bottle, and then she would have wanted to know why they needed her to spray it on her skin.

There were a million questions she should have asked, and now Freya could only sit and wonder. But, considering their smiles, she didn't think it was good that she'd sprayed the perfume on herself after all.

The most perfect scent finally reached her nose. It was something like her mother's perfume, an aroma she hadn't smelled in so long. A bit of fir, a mixture of basil and rosemary, and underneath it all, the distinct sweetness of lemon.

Her head swam with the memories of her mother. And how much she'd loved to be held in her arms.

The sprites tucked their hands around her waist and lifted her up from the bed. "Come, come with us."

Yes, of course she would come with them. Why wouldn't she? All she could think of now was her mother and the wonderful things she'd done for Freya over the years. How they had rooted in the garden for the perfect carrot for her soups. How her mother had always crushed basil between her fingers and let Freya smell it.

Why wouldn't she go with the sprites? They had given her these memories back. Memories that were long buried underneath years of sadness and pain.

But there was no sadness or pain associated with these memories anymore. Freya took another deep lungful of air and let it settle into her very soul. Relaxation poured through her muscles as they led her through the gardens.

They strode past a smaller lake, a pond really, with a few wooden boats floating on the top. They were shallow edged, with sprites draped over their edges, their fingers trailing in the sparkling waters. So lovely. So perfect.

"Isn't it nice here?" the Spring Maiden asked.

When had she joined Freya? She didn't remember walking all the way to the other pergola, and yet, here they were. In front of the gilded leaves that seemed to sprinkle more gold into the air.

"It is," Freya whispered. "I didn't know it even existed."

"Most don't." The Spring Maiden reached out a hand for Freya to take. "Mortals never remember that sprites exist, but that's quite all right with us. Sometimes we get lucky and someone stumbles into the Spring Court. Like yourself."

A thought bloomed behind her eyes. What did they do to the mortals, and why hadn't she seen any others? A memory was right on the tip of her tongue, something like adding her to a garden.

The thought was dashed away with another lungful of scented air. This time it smelled like the heat of the fire her father always set in the wood stove. The soup her mother would have on the stove, ready for Esther and Freya to eat when they completed their chores.

She loved that soup. But really, the reason the scent meant so much was because she knew it represented spending time with her family. She loved talking with them. Being with them. Speaking to them. Just having those moments when she could feel the peace of knowing they were all well.

Freya had missed that so much.

"Oh," the Spring Maiden said, her voice breaking through the memories as though she had popped a bubble. "So you were a family girl, then? I wouldn't have picked you for that."

"Yes," Freya replied. "I love my family very much."

She blinked, and the memories faded from sight. She was standing in the middle of a garden. Marble tiles were underneath her feet, and flowers grew on the ceiling overhead. Roses were tangled throughout thick leaves, or perhaps they were hedges considering the greenery created the walls of the room.

Was this a garden? Or was this a palace?

No, that word didn't seem right at all. The Spring Maiden lived in a garden. Freya had seen where she lived with all the pergolas and the beautiful flowers. She'd seen the lakes and ponds with faeries floating in their boats.

That was where the Spring Maiden lived.

She blinked again, and everything faded away with the scent of hay and salted meats from the village. Woolwich was always so lovely in the spring. Everyone came together after the winter months to rejoice in the warmth once again. She loved that time of year, especially when Esther and she could stop eating those awful smoked meats.

Esther.

The name blasted through her mind like a stiff wind. Esther was the reason she was here.

Her sister was... gone?

The magical scent fell away until she could see where they were clearly. A garden in a sense, but more like a room. There was a bed in the center that rivaled all the others. It floated above the ground, suspended by vines covered in white lilies.

The Spring Maiden stood beside the bed, all sharp-toothed smile and wide eyes. "You look sleepy, my dear. Perhaps you would like to lie down?"

Freya was prepared for this, now. She was awake and wide eyed as the rest of them. "No," she replied. "I don't think I want to sleep at all."

"You will." The smile on the sprite's face only widened. "Mortals always want to sleep, that's part of your charm."

No, she needed to get her information and leave. That was the only option for her.

Freya took a step forward. Her legs were shaking, although she couldn't imagine why. She hadn't been walking that far, had she?

Getting her bearings, she said, "The Goblin King has sent me on a quest so I can get my sister back. He said I needed to gather the essence of spring from you. I was hoping you might know what that means?"

Those weren't the words she meant to say. All she'd done was tell the Spring Maiden exactly why she was here, and the one thing that would allow her to leave. Wasn't that against everything she should say?

Freya lifted a hand and pressed it to her aching forehead. Everything was going so wrong and she couldn't figure out why. What spell had they cast upon her?

The bed looked comfortable. She couldn't remember the last time she'd had a good night's sleep. A true, restful relaxation where she didn't dream or think about missing family members.

Just one night. That's all she wanted.

She blinked, and the Spring Maiden was right in front of her. The sprite lifted her hands, pressed them to Freya's cheeks, and exhaled directly into her face.

Freya might have thought it disgusting if the sprite's breath hadn't smelled like blueberries freshly picked from the vine. Just like her mother used to gather every year in the fall to bake pies for Esther and Freya.

"Sleep," the Spring Maiden's voice filtered through the memory. "You're such a lovely flower, but so tired. Sleep, little mortal, and when you wake up, you'll bloom all the prettier."

Who was Freya to argue with the sprite when she knew so much? She wanted to sleep. She wanted to fall into the waiting, warm arms of her memories and never wake up again.

Freya was only dimly aware of the Spring Maiden guiding her to the bed in the center of the room. The sway of the mattress shifted as she finally sat down. She felt the sharp prick of the Spring Maiden's nails on the back of her head as the sprite lowered Freya onto the pillows.

She took a deep breath of blueberry scented magic and dreamed.

CHAPTER 10

"You're the prettiest girl I've ever seen," the sprite said.

He brushed his fingers through Freya's hair, and she leaned back into his touch. How long had she been resting in this bed? She didn't know. The sprites came to visit her often, whenever she wasn't resting. They asked her to tell stories about what she had done in the mortal realm.

They were particularly interested in the tiny details. What she ate. How the other mortals talked. If she ever rode a horse or worked in a garden.

The stories were what they mostly wanted from her. But sometimes, like this sprite, they just wanted to sit in bed with her and brush her hair. Their whispered compliments made her blush, but if it made them happy to say the words, then she would allow it.

Freya couldn't really remember her life without them. Of course, she knew what stories to tell them. But the memories felt distant. As though they weren't her memories, just something she'd read about a long time ago.

The sprite wrapped a strand of hair around his finger and lifted it to his lips. "So coarse," he muttered. "Like the tail of an animal. How do you take care of it in the mortal realm?"

She leaned her head against his knee. "I just washed it in the river with a bar of soap."

"A bar of soap?" he chuckled. "And how do you make such a thing?"

"With lye." She remembered the villagers making it. She remembered her mother taking such care, because lye could burn. Or something like that. It all felt so... faded.

"Well, no wonder your hair feels like wheat then." He twisted the strands together in a tiny braid by her temple. "We'll have to help with this. I can make your hair soft as silk. Would you like that?"

"I think so," she whispered.

Freya stared up at the ceiling of twisted leaves, watching as vines threaded through the emerald. The plants were always moving on the ceiling, like a living tapestry that shifted with the Spring Maiden's emotions.

The Spring Maiden....

She was supposed to talk with her about something. Something important, but she couldn't seem to remember what that was. Why couldn't she remember?

The sprite gave a sharp tug on the strand of hair. "Are you listening to me, mortal?"

"Of course," she replied with a wince.

But she hadn't been. She'd been thinking about the Spring Maiden. That gorgeous sprite who seemed to rule all the others with the kindness only an angel could have.

Something twisted deep inside her. A knot that tangled even more because that wasn't right. She didn't know why, but the thought made her nauseous.

The sprite tugged her hair again. "Don't frown like that, you'll give yourself wrinkles. What is the matter, my darling? You can tell me."

He smoothed clawed fingers over her forehead. The pointed ends trailed across her skin, a little too sharp, leaving stinging welts in their wake.

Freya's breathing quickened. She felt as though she was struggling to find something, or perhaps like she was fighting against someone inside her own head. "I think I need to speak with the Spring Maiden," she whispered.

The sprite's movements stilled. He tapped his claws on her forehead and then nodded. "You're more than welcome to visit the Spring Maiden whenever you like, Freya. You know that. She loves your company more than anyone else."

Yes, of course she did. The Spring Maiden was the one who had brought her here, and she loved mortals. She thought Freya was just the sweetest thing. The loveliest flower. That's what she always said whenever Freya walked over to her.

"I'd like to see her," she murmured.

Freya rolled off the bed and onto her feet. Her head spun immediately. She reached out and grabbed onto one of the ropes that suspended the bed, and tried to ease the sudden ache between her eyes. Everything hurt. Her feet, her legs, even her back felt like she'd been laying on rocks.

A whimper vibrated in her throat. Freya could survive this though, because she was going to see the Spring Maiden. She'd make everything better.

Staggering away from the bed and the pergola, she made her way down the steps to the gardens beyond. Her lace dress tangled between her legs. The lace had giant holes in it, and the satin underskirt was yellowed with age. How long had she been here?

Freya kept her arms out at her sides so she didn't fall over. Sounds followed her as she walked. The twinkling call of birds. Bells in the distance, but not the bells she was so used to hearing.

What bells did she remember? She couldn't think of their name.

Someone had once told her to worry about bells. The little spark of fear in her chest warned her of an ill omen. That the sound should make her throat close up and maybe she should run, but she couldn't.

Not yet, at least.

She had to talk to the Spring Maiden first. Then she could run away and do... something that her mind couldn't remember.

The garden path opened up to reveal a makeshift ballroom with marble squares as a floor and roses growing overhead. The petals fell down like a rain shower when Freya walked underneath them. The room was already filled with sprites, although she didn't recognize any of the creatures.

The Spring Maiden walked toward her with her arms outstretched. "My darling girl! Welcome to the ball, I thought you might be joining us."

Ball?

Freya looked around, her brow furrowed again in confusion. The sprite in her bedroom had said she could visit with the Spring Maiden, hadn't he? There had been no mention of a ball. Otherwise, she would have put on different clothing. Not the moth-eaten lace dress that had seen better days.

She looked down at the dress in question, fisting her fingers in the skirts as if that would hide them. But she wasn't wearing the same dress at all. This one was entirely made of pale pink chiffon and floated around her like a cloud.

When had she changed?

Her head ached with the clanging of bells. She looked up and stared into the Spring Maiden's eyes as the sprite pulled her into her arms. "Oh my dear girl, you smell terrible. Would you like more perfume?"

"Yes," she whispered. "I don't think I've put any on today."

"Here." The Spring Maiden pulled out a tiny jar. This was more powerful than the perfume Freya usually wore. Just the scent alone would have overwhelmed her, but she could almost see visions rising off the surface of the solid perfume. "Let me put this on you."

A distant chime said she should worry about that going on her skin. That she should at least try to stop the Spring Maiden from touching her neck. But she desperately wanted to continue smelling fresh baked bread while she remembered her mother singing in the kitchen.

"Freya?"

Though her name should have brought her under the Spring Maiden's spell even deeper, Freya found the sound snapped her out of the trance. Perhaps it was the way the Spring Maiden said it. Just like her sister used to when she wanted something. Or maybe the magic was wearing off.

Whatever it was, the slight break in the spell allowed her to look around the room.

The ballroom wasn't lovely and covered with roses. It was cloying and overwhelming. Sprites wandered the room, but behind them were monstrous creatures. Tall men with bare, broad chests and strong shoulders wearing masks made of vines and thorns. The greenery covered their faces completely. Tiny drops of blood dripped down their necks and chests where thorns were digging into the sides of their heads.

"Who are they?" she asked.

The Spring Maiden followed her gaze to the mask wearing men. "They're our guards, silly. You've seen them before."

No, she hadn't. She would remember seeing such terrifying creatures. There were knives at their hips, clinging onto moth eaten green fabric that made up their pants. Though they weren't much for pants, really. Just basic, plain trousers that did nothing to protect them.

Guards? Why would the Spring Maiden need guards?

The sprite stepped closer and the cloying scent twisted through Freya's lungs. "Come here, silly girl. You still reek of the mortal coil."

But she didn't want to go anywhere. She wanted to take a deep breath of fresh air without feeling as though something were climbing inside her lungs. She needed to feel like herself again, even though she couldn't remember who she was.

"I think I need some air," she muttered. "Yes, I think that's the best choice right now. If you'll excuse me."

The Spring Maiden side stepped, blocking Freya from leaving the room. "Sweetheart, if you'd just let me put this on you before you leave? I don't want you to insult the other sprites, you see."

The grin on the Spring Maiden's face was all sharp teeth and dark intent. But Freya wouldn't be stopped. Not now that she remembered who she was.

"No, thank you," she replied. "I think I'd like to go outside for a bit on my own. I'll stay away from the other sprites. I just need a moment to myself."

The Spring Maiden looked like she would argue. Her expression shifted to one of pure anger and her cheeks turned bright red. But she didn't stop Freya from leaving. Instead, she snapped her fingers and gestured for one of the guards to approach them. "Stay with her," the

Spring Maiden snarled. "You have a few moments, Freya of Woolwich. Then you will be right back here. And you will put on this perfume."

Freya shivered as the sprite's attention diverted from her. She looked at the guard with his eerie mask of vines and thorns. He stared off into the distance, as if he could even see with all that on his face.

"All right," she mumbled. "I guess we're going this way."

Freya didn't look to see if he followed her. She couldn't focus on anything other than putting her feet in front of each other. And when she finally made it out of the ballroom, she darted to the nearest hedgerow and vomited all her nerves into the leaves.

Every heave cleared something inside herself. Some magic was purged in the contents of her stomach. Even as she looked at the puddle of bile, there was something wrong with it. She didn't have any food in her stomach? When had she last eaten? It was all liquid on the ground.

Freya leaned back and wiped her mouth with her hand. Her breath shuddered in and out of her lungs, as if she couldn't quite get enough air no matter how much she gulped. Her lungs actually stung. Like she'd been breathing smoke for too long and now the fresh air hurt to breathe.

"What is happening?" she muttered.

Tunneling her hands into her hair, she stared up at the sky and forced her breathing to slow. In. Out. Three seconds, five seconds, a long break until she was finally inhaling and exhaling at a normal rate. Her stomach still wanted to vomit up more of that liquid, but at least she felt more like herself.

Sweat slicked her brow and made her underarms sticky. She could feel drops sliding between her breasts underneath the many layers of chiffon that made her far too hot. Her hair smelled funny. She lifted an oily lock and sniffed it.

Freya gagged again. She dropped the strand that smelled overwhelmingly like fertilizer and took another step away from the ballroom.

She needed to get out of here. Whatever the sprites were doing to her, it had to stop. She needed to get everything out of her stomach, wash her body for days, and then try her best to figure out why she was even here to begin with.

Then the memory bloomed.

Esther.

She was here to get the essence of spring for the Goblin King and then move on to the next faerie species. She had tasks to complete. Things to do. And she couldn't just stand here being sick.

Her arms were covered in a thick layer of ooze. It smelled like the Spring Maiden's perfume, so she grabbed a fistful of grass and rubbed it against whatever skin she could see. At least that helped the scent dissipate.

"There," she muttered. "That ought to do."

Now, to figure out how to prevent herself from falling back under the spell. Maybe she could grab more of the grass and tuck it into the bodice of her dress. Then she could pull it out and sniff it...

A hand appeared in front of her, holding out a couple seeds on the broad palm.

The guard. How had she forgotten about the guard?

Freya stopped breathing and stiffened. Damn it. She was going to get caught all because she hadn't remembered the thorny creature who lurked behind her.

She let her eyes travel up to the mask. A bead of blood welled on the bottom corner. It dripped onto his neck and traveled down the impressive muscles, to his pectorals, until it seemed to dry on his skin. So many lines of blood.

Her fingers shook as she took the offered seeds.

"What are these?" she asked.

He flattened one hand, then used his thumb to mime crushing the seed with the other. The little orbs looked as though she could pop them if she wanted to. Maybe even her thumb nail could snap through the thin shell.

"Why?"

He tapped a finger against the thorns where his nose might be.

"Will this help block the perfume she's using to control me?" she asked.

The guard nodded sharply, then stepped back to the wall. Almost as though he didn't want anyone to know he'd told her a word. She supposed that made sense.

Freya looked down at the little black seeds, then back at the guard. "Can I ask you a question?"

He didn't move.

She could only assume that was him saying yes. And if he didn't want to talk to her anymore, well, she was going to ask anyway. It felt important as her memories slid back into place.

Freya stepped a little closer, just in case anyone was listening in on their conversation. "Does it hurt?" She paused, then added, "That thing on your face?"

He gave her a sharp nod but remained standing strong and straight.

The seeds burned in her fingers. She could easily run inside, get what she needed, and leave. Freya was certain that the essence of spring was that damned solid perfume the Spring Maiden kept with her. It couldn't be anything else.

But she also didn't feel right without at least trying to help. She couldn't save all the men with these thorns pressed into their skin. This one, though... This one she could save.

Freya didn't care what he'd done to deserve such a punishment. No one deserved to live their lives in constant pain and at the mercy of a sprite like that. Evil spread through time. But kindness spread through actions.

She curled her fingers around the seeds and held her fist up. "I'm going to use these. I need to steal the essence of spring, and I think I know where that is. Once I do that, I'm going out the back door and..." Well she didn't have a plan after that. Freya licked her lips. "I want you to come with me."

He tilted his head to the side.

"I can't leave you here like this." Freya shook her head. "I won't. So be ready. Okay?"

The mask watched her, almost as though he could see her. And then the guard gave a sharp nod.

Freya started back into the ballroom, paused, then reiterated, "You'll be ready?"

At his nod once again, she readied herself for the theft of a lifetime.

CHAPTER 11

She strode into the ballroom with a plan brewing in her mind. All she had to do was get that perfume out of the Spring Maiden's hands. Freya hadn't ever been particularly good with her hands. She was more the brute force in the family while Esther was the one who played piano and had quick enough fingers to steal from pockets.

But maybe she could talk the Spring Maiden into giving it to her. Perhaps if she got the Maiden to put the perfume on her neck, then Freya could snatch it out of her hands and run for it.

Freya walked into the ballroom with false confidence in the set of her shoulders. At least she could look the part, if she were going to pretend to be the hero in this story.

Except it wasn't a ballroom anymore.

Frowning, she looked at the banquet tables that had been set out all across the marble. Giant glowing chandeliers hung from the ceiling, light bouncing off individual strands of glass beads that draped in looping coils. Giant flower arrangements sat on each deep brown table, and drying flowers were strung between the lights. She brushed one of the bouquets away from her face.

Where was the Spring Maiden?

A sprite caught her hand. "Freya! You're just in time for the feast!"

"The feast?" she repeated. "I thought this was a ball?"

The sprite laughed, and the sound made bubbles that danced through the air. "No, silly! Who told you that?"

She wanted to say the Spring Maiden was the person who had told her that, but Freya feared that would show the sprite she wasn't under the spell any longer. Even now, the bubbles that floated through the air popped and settled a fine film upon her exposed arms.

The fog already was building in her mind. She had a hard time focusing on what the sprite was saying, because of course it was a banquet. They were going to have a feast and wasn't that lovely?

Freya squeezed her thumbnail into one of the seeds in her hand. She lifted it to her nose, inhaling the awful ammonia scent, and the fog cleared from her mind again.

The banquet was suspicious, but she suspected the plan had changed simply to throw Freya off balance. What better way to control a person's thoughts and mind than by making them feel as though they were mad?

This wasn't right. None of it was right, but she had to play the game for now.

Freya plastered a fake smile on her face and let the sprite draw her to a table. Many sprites were already seated there, each one more lovely than the last. Glitter dusted their arms and bare shoulders.

Now, she wondered if that glitter was part of the reason why she couldn't think. Maybe that was the essence in the air that made people lose their minds around these creatures.

Their blurry movements returned to the frightening state they had when she'd first looked at them. Their sharp smiles made her uncomfortable again. And the state of their clothing only made her wonder why their items were so mistreated. Just like herself.

"Here," the sprite who had guided her to the table said. She pulled out the chair for Freya and patted the hard cushion. "Sit, Freya of Woolwich. We have so longed for your company."

She sat down and stared at the table in front of her, still grinning. Was that what she was supposed to look like? They all watched her with rapt attention, so she assumed it was the right reaction.

And then, even though she remembered telling them a thousand stories, they all looked away from her. Each sprite tucked into the food on their plate and spoke with each other, muttering as though she wasn't even there.

Freya distinctly remembered them all being enthralled with her stories. That was why she'd been so easily trapped. She couldn't remember the last time someone wanted to listen to her speak. Let alone gave her such undivided attention.

Had she been in a trance the entire time? Was the whole thing made up in her head?

A cold, wet nose touched her knee. Freya glanced around at the sprites to make sure they weren't paying attention to her. But they looked like they'd forgotten she was here at all.

She wiggled her fingers underneath the tablecloth, then lifted it. A black and white face stared back at her.

Arrow.

She'd forgotten about the goblin who'd been helping her. The one who was in a rather binding deal to help her get her sister. Thank goodness he was still here, and the sprites hadn't killed him.

"Keep quiet," he whispered. "Are you back to yourself yet?"

The fog pressed against her conscious mind. Wiggling one of the seeds to her thumb, she broke through it and waved it underneath her nostril. Then nodded. "Yes."

"Good. We have to get out of here."

"I agree with you." She nodded toward the table where the Spring Maiden was sitting. "But first, I need to get that perfume bottle off her."

Arrow didn't immediately respond. She looked down at him only to see his eyes had widened so much, she could see the white rings all the way around his pupils.

"What?" she asked.

"Are you insane? We need to leave now, or they're going to put that spell back over you and I'm going to have to continue pretending to be a dog for the foreseeable future."

She didn't see the problem with him being a dog. He was one. She hated to point that out, however, when he was so enjoying his play, acting at being a goblin like the others.

Freya reached her hand underneath the table and waggled her fingers. "You said you would help me. We made a deal."

"There should be a clause in that deal about risking our necks," he growled.

"Well, there isn't. So." She leaned slightly to the left so he could see her and lifted an eyebrow. "What's it going to be, goblin? Are you going to help me or am I going to make a huge scene and you'll have to run with me and pray the guards don't snatch you?"

This time, she heard the growl. A few sprites stiffened, but at least none of them looked over at her. "What do you want me to do?" the goblin snarled.

"I'll distract her. You steal the bottle of perfume when she isn't looking."

"Are you sure that's the essence of spring?" Arrow touched his cold nose to her leg again.

"Wouldn't you know?" She noted the sprites who stirred at the sound of her voice. Now, they were noticing she wasn't staring off into the distance as she was supposed to.

"No one knows what the essence of any court is," Arrow replied. "It's rumored that no one could ever find all of them."

Right, so yet another thing the Goblin King had lied about. That rat bastard.

She bared her teeth in an angry snarl. "Just go get the bottle. I have to trust my gut."

"You've got it."

Arrow disappeared underneath the tables. The white flag tip of his tail waved as he moved between legs, all the way to the head table.

She had to guess that was the right thing. Freya knew she wouldn't get a second chance at guessing what the essence of this court was. This was her best chance.

Arrow was close to the table now. Thus, the show had to start.

Slapping her hands hard on the table, she stood up. Her chair screamed on the marble floor and every single sprite in the room stopped talking. They all turned as one to stare at the mortal woman who had suddenly woken up.

"Freya?" the Spring Maiden asked. Her voice carried through the room, light as air. "Whatever is the matter, my dear?"

Freya had always been a horrible actress, but she had to try. Arrow was so close now. His tail disappeared underneath the Maiden's table. She'd only get one shot.

She cleared her throat. "You've been keeping me under a spell, Spring Maiden, and I don't appreciate it."

"A spell?" the Maiden laughed. "I've never heard of a spell that would force you to enjoy our company. My dear girl, you are here under your own free will. You've asked to stay, and we have accommodated you in every way possible. Do you not appreciate what we've given you?"

Gaslighting. The sprite was trying to make her feel guilty for complaining about the mistreatment.

Freya snapped a seed and inhaled the acrid scent of sulphur. "You are not treating me well. You've kept me trapped here until I don't know what way is up and what way is down. You're a monster."

The other sprites gasped. A few of them pressed their hands to their hearts, and all turned to stare at the Spring Maiden to see how she would respond.

The Spring Maiden's face turned a bright purple. "A monster, you say?"

Arrow's face appeared over the edge of the table. What was the damned goblin doing? Did he really think this was the best time to steal the perfume bottle? At least get the Spring Maiden to stand up first!

"Yes," she shouted, waving her hands in the air dramatically. "I believe you are a monster. You're a horrible, disgusting creature who likes to think she's beautiful. But surrounding yourself with beautiful things doesn't make you pretty. All it does is highlight the ugliness radiating off you."

Maybe that was a little too far. The Spring Maiden's eyes opened wider with every word, and Freya realized she was very much in trouble. Even if Arrow stole that perfume bottle to the Spring Maiden's right, they needed to run no matter what.

"I think you're tired," the Maiden snapped. "You need to go back to sleep."

"I think I've slept enough."

The Spring Maiden slapped her hand down and caught Arrow on the side of the face. The goblin dog yelped horribly. He flew off to the side with the force of the Spring Maiden's strike.

"No!" Freya shouted.

"Did you think a goblin could steal from me? Me?"

Freya blinked, and suddenly the Spring Maiden was right in front of her. The blurred trail of her sprint remained in the air behind her for a few heartbeats, then disappeared. She held the perfume bottle in her hand, then unscrewed the top and stuck the entire thing underneath Freya's nose.

The scent threaded up through the air, into her nostrils, and raked claws through her lungs. It hurt. Oh, how it sent white hot prongs zinging through her entire body.

But Freya was ready this time. Before the magic could set in, she broke the entire fistful of horrible smelling seeds and lifted them to her nose. Smoke filtered between her fingers, overpowering the perfume with its acrid scent.

The Spring Maiden flinched away with a shout. "What is that?"

"A gift from a friend," she snarled.

Freya threw the seeds at the Spring Maiden with all her might. They bounced off the sprite, but surely left imprints of scent on her skin. A scream erupted from the Spring Maiden's mouth and made Freya's ears bleed.

Maybe faeries thought other people would fight with words, just like their kind. Freya was a human, though, and the Spring Maiden had forgotten that.

She pulled her fist back and let it fly. Her knuckles connected with the Spring Maiden's cheekbone. A sharp crack could be heard, though Freya didn't know if it was from her own suddenly stinging knuckles or the bone of the Spring Maiden's face.

Whatever the thing that made the sound, it made the Maiden drop the perfume bottle.

Freya snatched it off the ground and sprinted toward Arrow. They would expect her to run to the door. Not the goblin dog who still laid in a heap where he'd fallen.

Leaning down, she scooped him up in her arms. "Are you all right?"

He shook his furry head and shouted, "Run!"

That's all she needed to hear. Except there was one more person for her to collect before she finally made her great escape. Freya dodged a sprite's outstretched hands and searched for the guard with a blood splattered pattern she recognized.

There he was. Standing by the door waiting for the two of them.

Perfect, at least he could follow orders.

"Where are you going?" Arrow growled. "Don't you see the guard?"

"Yes, I do," she panted, ducking underneath an outstretched hand. "He's coming with us."

"He's what?" The yelp was so loud her ears rang.

He could argue with her about the decision later. For now, she was going to take the guard with them and regret her choice later. Maybe. Freya sprinted to his side and wrapped a hand around his bicep. "Come on!"

Just like that, the guard ran with them. Together, she sprinted with him out of the ballroom and into the gardens beyond. She hesitated for a brief moment, worried about where she should go next, but the guard seemed to know exactly where to go. She ran after him through the gardens, even as Arrow snarled in her ear.

"He's leading us into a trap!"

"Or he could be helping us. Didn't you see the thing on his face?"

"I saw it," Arrow grunted. "People in pain don't always make the smartest decisions, Freya. Especially the fae."

Well, she had to trust someone in this horrible place. Otherwise, she really was on her own. And how would she ever get out?

The guard stopped in the middle of a hedgerow and gestured with his hand. He waved them over, pointing to a strange hollow in the leaves.

"What's that?" she asked, gasping in air.

Pounding feet followed them. They didn't have time for clarification, but she'd learned her lesson with the perfume.

Arrow answered for the silent guard. "It's a portal. We are not going through that."

She looked at the guard and those horrible thorns. "Will that take us somewhere safe?"

He nodded, firmly.

"Then we're going through it."

She didn't look back at the screaming sprites who were already shouting for her to stop. She didn't look down at Arrow to see if he thought it was the right choice. Freya leapt through the space in the hedges and hoped it would take her to a place a little less dangerous than this one.

Freya clutched the guard's arm as they plummeted through the portal. Yet again, she felt as though they were falling through open air. How did magic always feel like this? She should at least have something to walk on, some sense of knowing where she was.

Instead, she was free falling through the sky until her feet touched something solid.

She stumbled, holding onto the guard and keeping Arrow hugged tightly against her chest. Then, lights blinked on in the distance. As though someone had lit candles just waiting for them to come and rest.

"Arrow?" she asked. "Is that safety or a trap?"

"I think it's fine to go to them."

She'd heard of will-o'-the-wisps before. Weary travelers could easily be lured off the path if they thought there was light and safety at the other end. Then, they would be consumed by the magical creatures who waited for their prey.

"Are you sure?" she asked again, just to be certain they weren't walking to their demise.

He hesitated long enough to make her heart thump hard in her chest. "I think so. The only way to know for certain is to stand in front of them. Since when were you afraid of anything, anyway?"

She was afraid all the time. Every moment she was here.

Freya tugged on the guard's arm and they all made their way to the lights. The closer they got, the more she realized they weren't will-o'-the-wisps. Tiny lanterns, about the size of her hand, hung from the limbs of a giant tree. Each one glowed bright yellow and orange, the flames flickering happily on the end of the white candle wicks.

The tree itself was unlike anything she'd ever seen before. The branches were bent, twisted and warped as though a giant had spent years spinning them around each other. Heavy roots lurched through the ground, appearing through the dirt in a graceful arch only to disappear into the soft moss once again.

Her feet touched the emerald moss that surrounded the tree. It squished underneath her bare feet, but wasn't wet. It was plush and soft as velvet.

"What is this place?" She set Arrow down on the ground.

He gave a quick shake of his entire body, ears flapping against the sides of his head. "An in between place, I'd assume. A resting place for travelers who don't want to deal with any of the faeries in the courts. Or goblins. Or worse."

What was worse than a goblin? Freya didn't think she wanted to find out yet. She'd already had to deal with more than she wanted to today.

Gently, she guided the guard to the roots of the tree and settled him into a comfortable nook. "There we are. Now, let's get a look at this mask."

"Don't touch him," Arrow grumbled. "We don't know who he is or what kind of spell the Spring Maiden put on those guards. If you take his mask off, you might kill him."

"He'll die with it on."

"They were doing just fine before you came in and played hero. Leave him alone, Freya. We got him out of the court, now he can figure this out on his own."

That was cruel, even for a goblin.

Freya shook her head and turned back to the guard. He had tilted his head up for her to look at the mask, as though he already knew she wouldn't listen to the goblin dog. Maybe her thoughts were written all over her face.

"May I touch you?" she asked.

He nodded.

"Okay."

She needed to help him, although she didn't know why. Some voice deep in her bones said he needed to get that mask off his face. She had to see who was underneath the thorns and the vines. What man had suffered through the blood and the pain?

Freya reached forward and ran her fingers along the edge of the mask. Every time she bumped a thorn anchoring it into his skin, she felt an answering twitch in his neck. It must have hurt. No matter what she touched, she was somehow hurting him worse than before.

When her fingers reached his chin, she bit her lip and let her hands fall into her lap. "I don't know how to get it off. It seems like it's attached to your face now. If I try to take it off, it will only rip your skin more."

The guard reached up and placed his hands on the mask. He mimicked pulling it off, then pointed to himself, and shook his head.

"You can't pull it off?"

He nodded.

Freya bit her lip again and frowned. "Can I pull it off?"

He stilled, but then the guard slowly nodded again.

Arrow's cold nose pressed against her elbow, butting into their conversation with all the grace of a bull. "I wouldn't do it."

Freya ground her teeth together and counted to ten. She didn't understand why the little goblin was so adamant that she shouldn't help this guard, but it was getting to the point of ridiculous. "And why not?"

"He's familiar." Arrow sniffed the air near the guard and then took a large step away from him. "Definitely don't take that mask off. I know who he is."

A drop of fresh blood slid down the guard's shoulder, and Freya knew there wasn't another choice for her to make. She didn't care if he was the most terrifying goblin who ever existed. He didn't deserve to be in pain.

She reached forward and grabbed the edges of the mask. "Good, then you can introduce us once I get this mask off him."

Leaning back on her heels, she used her weight to jerk the vines and thorns. They dug into her own hands. Sinking through soft flesh and almost all the way into her bones. Freya refused to let go. The magic could try to fight her all it wanted, but she would free this guard from the sprite's horrible prison.

The guard let out a low groan that made her skin crawl, then the mask slid off his skin with a sickening crunch.

Freya landed on her butt with the mask in her hands. She stared down at the vines and watched in horror as they died. When they withered, they cried out a sound that was eerily similar to a human screaming.

It was awful.

Breathing hard, she looked up at the guard and hoped he wasn't dead. She wanted him to be free, to survive, to leave the clutches of that monster with his head held high.

Freya wasn't certain why she desired that so much, but she did. For once in her life, she wanted to save someone.

But the man leaning against the tree couldn't be real. That moon touched skin was too familiar. The long, hawk-like shape of his nose and the sharp jaw were ones she had seen before. And then he met her stare with those strange, silver eyes.

"You," she coughed out the word like he'd fed her poison. "That's not possible."

The Goblin King cracked his neck to the right, then left, and let out a long sigh. "It's entirely possible. I'm not sure why you insist on disbelieving what's right in front of you."

She didn't believe it was him because he should be ruling from his gilded throne or whatever this insufferable creature did in his spare time. Not gallivanting around, pretending to be a Spring Maiden guard just to... what?

"Were you watching me?" she asked. Though she shouldn't have been surprised, she was stunned he had gone through so much trouble to see what she did after he'd given her this task.

How long had he been there?

The guards were obviously around the entire time she'd been in the Spring Court. She hadn't noticed them while the perfume was altering her impression of the place. He might have been there from the first moment they stepped through the portal.

Was he the one who had made her fall asleep? Was he the guard who laid her into that bed and let her dream away her life?

The Goblin King watched the thoughts play across her face with an expression of rapture on his own. "There it is," he whispered. "You've figured it out, haven't you?"

"Figured what out?"

He leaned forward, planted a hand in the moss, and loomed closer. The fanatic look in his eyes only gleamed all the brighter when she tried to lean away from him. He enjoyed how uncomfortable she was in his presence. How the planes of his chest made her heart beat faster because even now, in this strange place, he was more beautiful than any man she'd ever seen.

He was so close, she could feel his breath on her shoulders. Each inhalation seemed to draw her into the heat of his body.

"You realized I'm invested in this hero's journey of yours. I want to see how you tick, Freya. And so far, it's like a clock that hasn't been wound in a very long time. You find yourself frequently stuck, and when your gut tells you to move, your head tells you to remain where you are."

"That's not true," she whispered, staring into the molten silver of his eyes.

"Yes it is, don't lie to me." He reached between them and caught a lock of her dark hair. He smoothed it between his fingers while saying, "What I want to understand is why your heart tells you to save people along the way. A guard, Freya? Really? What a waste of your precious time."

That wasn't fair of him. Of course she wanted to help someone in pain. What kind of monster wouldn't?

She leaned back on her hands, trying to put some distance between them. "I saw someone who needed help, and I offered it."

"No, that wasn't why, but I can't figure out what your plan was just yet. Did you think to find someone who would protect you throughout the courts?" His eyes darted side to side, watching each of her eyes individually before he shook his head. "No, not that."

"Don't try to pick apart my thoughts," she replied. "I don't appreciate your attempts to climb inside my head."

He lifted a clawed hand and combed through the hair at her temple. "But it's such a pretty little head." He grinned, and those sharp teeth flashed in the lantern light.

His gaze shifted, staring at her lips with a heat that seared through her. He tugged on her hair, not hard, just enough for her to know he could make it hurt if he wanted.

Freya couldn't force herself to move when he tilted his head to the side. Warm breath fanned over her check, spreading a blush wherever it touched. And it burned, god how it burned.

But she still didn't move.

The Goblin King whispered in her ear, lips gently touching the seashell edges, "And I don't think you'd mind all that much if I climbed inside it."

Two paws stamped the ground next to them. "Enough, you two!"

They both turned at the same time to look over at Arrow, who had stood up on his back feet. He crossed his doggy arms over his chest and glared at them. "You're not supposed to be here, Goblin King."

"Yes, well, plans change." The Goblin King leaned away from her and she could breathe again.

Freya gulped in a deep lungful of air. He sucked all the oxygen out of her body, or perhaps the magnetism of his personality conjured her closer. Whatever the reasoning, she needed to put physical space between them or she'd lose her head just like she had with the perfume.

She scrambled to her feet and took a few steps into the darkness before turning back around.

The Goblin King stood next to Arrow, glaring down at the dog as though he wasn't supposed to say anything at all. As if Arrow should have known the Goblin King was there.

"Wait," she said, pointing severely at Arrow. "Didn't you say you recognized his scent?"

"I did." Arrow bared his teeth in a snarl. "I'd know the King's scent anywhere."

"How?" She found it hard to believe the little goblin would know it just from a few passing moments when they met. "You made it sound like you had never met the king before. That only your family who had sadly passed were in his service."

"I—" Arrow looked from her and then back to the Goblin King. "Well, I—"

The Goblin King interrupted them with a wave of his hand. "I'm not going to stand here and wait for you two to finish squabbling. Freya, you've been wasting more time than you have, anyway."

She wanted to argue with them both and force them to explain, no matter how long that took. She needed to understand what was going on here, and if Arrow had been working for the Goblin King. But when he said she was wasting time, she felt the hairs on the back of her neck stand up.

"What do you mean I'm wasting time?"

He grinned. "Well, you only have a finite period for this deal to be completed. And you've already spent nearly two weeks within the Spring Court."

She'd been gone that long? Freya couldn't believe it. Time hadn't passed so quickly without her realizing... had it?

"That wasn't part of the deal," she said, shaking her head in denial. "You said I had to collect items to get my sister back."

"You did, and you do." He twirled a finger in the air as if his hand was the face of a clock. "Did I forget to mention all goblin deals have a time constraint? Oh dear. You've only got a month to gather all those impossible items, and you've spent most of your time in the Spring Court."

Her heart stopped in her chest and she slowly closed her eyes. Dizziness made her head spin. "Do you mean to say I only have two weeks left?"

When he didn't immediately respond, Freya opened her eyes.

The Goblin King stood so close she could see the specks of darkness in his gaze. Specks that looked like black holes, ready to swallow her up. "One month, Freya. That was the deal." He tsked. "I hope you can find her before then."

And then he disappeared.

CHAPTER 13

Forget the Goblin King and his disappearing act. There was someone else who she needed answers from first.

"You're working for him, aren't you?" Freya advanced on Arrow with single-minded intent. She refused to let the Goblin King stop her with an inside man who slowed her process.

Though he was a cute little dog-like creature, her sister was far more important. Arrow had to go. And if she had to chuck him out into the darkness herself, then she would.

He stepped back, balancing on his legs awkwardly as though he had forgotten how to walk. "No! I'm not working with him."

"From my point of view, it looked like you recognized each other. Far more than just your family having worked for him from a distance."

"I recognize him!" He swallowed hard. "I doubt the Goblin King remembers I exist all that often. But yes, of course I know him. He's my king. All goblins know him."

She didn't know if she could believe him. And that frustrated her more than knowing he might have betrayed her. Freya wanted someone to trust, anyone, and now the one person she thought might be worthwhile had betrayed her. The knowledge ripped at her very heart.

Freya needed someone on her side. She needed help, and honestly, perhaps that was why she'd tried to save the guard. Maybe the Goblin King had been right about her, and he'd just seen through the lies she was telling herself.

"If you weren't working with him, then you must have at least known who he was. That he was there the entire time."

Arrow hung his head. "Yes, I did. But I thought you knew! You were the one who made a deal with the Goblin King. I thought everyone understood that came with certain... well. Certain rules that aren't normal for a goblin deal."

"I had no idea." She stepped around him and sat down in the roots of the tree. "And now I'm not sure what I'm supposed to do. Every decision I make is going to be clouded by him, isn't it? He's always going to be there, preventing me from progressing at every turn."

The goblin dog stepped a little closer, then laid down near her feet. "He will do everything in his power to slow you down. Of course he will. The Goblin King has never lost a deal, not to anyone. And you've already gotten through the first step."

"Too late." She touched the perfume in her pocket. "I now have three courts to go through in the same amount of time that it took me to get through one. That's an impossible task."

"It's only impossible if you say it is." Arrow pointed his nose at the glowing lanterns hanging above them. "You're in the faerie realm now, Freya. I don't think you understand just how likely impossible things are to happen. There's no such thing as something that can't be completed. Or a task that cannot be finished."

She stared down at her fingers twisting in her lap. She felt a little better. At least Arrow was here with her. And though he might be a spy for the Goblin King, thus slowing her down, at least she had someone here to talk with.

If she'd been alone while searching for her sister, then she didn't know how long she would last. Though Esther meant the world, it was still difficult for Freya to be in this otherworldly place without support.

"I'm glad you're here," she whispered, hoping her words would ring with the truth she felt in her heart. "Even if you might be spying for the Goblin King."

"There's no friendship between the two of us, if that's what you're implying." Arrow coiled himself like a cat, tucking his tail underneath his chin and staring out into the darkness. "He's the reason I'm alone, you know."

"What do you mean?" Freya leaned back against the trunk of the tree and resolved herself to lose a few moments. What were a few heartbeats to hear a story when she knew how impossible this would be, anyway?

"My mother and father worked for him, like I said. Goblins always work for the king, I suppose, but my family used to sneak through the palace and gather information from the walls. We're small enough to fit, and most aren't." Arrow shook his head. "It all went bad one day and then they were gone. Dead, buried, and he didn't care at all. He did nothing for the people who'd given him everything. Everything."

Her heart cracked open at the last word. Repeated with so much emotion and a bone deep ache.

She knew the feeling. She knew what it was like to miss someone so much it felt like she was bleeding from the inside out.

Reaching forward almost unconsciously, she stroked her hand over his doggy head. She wasn't sure if he would even want to be touched like that. He wasn't an animal, after all. But Arrow lifted his head to her touch and let out a sigh.

Together, they paused for a few minutes in the dim light of the lanterns. Freya lost herself in memories of her family. Her mother and father would forever be a wound in her soul, wondering how they died, or when. Then she turned her thoughts to her sister and felt her resolve harden. She would save Esther or she would die trying.

In some way, she understood Arrow was also thinking of his family. Of his loss, their end, and the journey forward all by his lonesome.

No matter what species he was, what kind of faerie he had been born as, at least they both shared this understanding. He'd experienced a similar life journey. She respected that.

Freya swiped her fingers underneath her eyes—when had they gotten so watery?—and stood up. "Come on, then. We don't have any time to waste if I've only got two weeks to get through the faerie courts."

"I know a way into the Summer Court." Arrow stood as well, shook himself, then lurched up onto his back feet. "I can also get myself some clothes there. Damned sprites are always trying to make me into a dog."

Freya coughed into her hand and tried very hard to keep a straight face. The sprites weren't the only ones who had tried to make him into a dog, but it was hard not to.

"Where is the way into the Summer Court?" she paused, then asked another question. "And what should I be expecting?"

"In what way?" Arrow snuffled into his paw, wiping his runny nose. Then her real question seemed to dawn on him. "Ah. You mean what kind of fae are going to be there?"

"Yes."

Freya needed to know what to expect and how to protect herself around them. The sprites had taught her a very valuable lesson. The fae would stop at nothing to control her, or manipulate the way she thought. She couldn't afford another two weeks pressed beneath their thumb.

"Well, at least this time the Summer Court is filled with elves. They aren't as mean as sprites, but they will try to distract you." He frowned. "I can't say you won't be in danger, but it will be a different kind of danger."

"That's not helpful, Arrow. Be a little more specific." She knew it was against his ways to dance around with minced words and pretty sounds, but she needed the truth.

"Elves are vain. They want to make everything as pretty as they are, and that's the end of it. They're going to look at you and see that you're mortal. Mortals are not pretty nor saveable. To blend in, you must be as noble as them." Arrow stuck out his tongue. It was an expression that would have been funny on a human, but made him look like he was panting. "And they all consider themselves to be nobility."

Freya hadn't heard the term in such a long time. Of course, they were all taught about the nobles when they were little. She remembered learning about their stations and how the teachers had always spoken of them in revered tones. She assumed they were still around, but how would she ever know? Freya wouldn't be the one interacting with them.

"Nobility?" she asked. "How am I supposed to fit in with them?"

"Gesture with your hands a lot." He shrugged, then strode around the other side of the tree. "Honestly, it's not very hard to make yourself seem like you're an important person. All you have to do is never answer a question."

She could do that. She hoped.

Freya followed him around the tree with a frown on her face. "So all I have to do is just... what? Pretend I'm a noble as well?"

"They know nothing about mortals. You could say you were the queen of where you came from and they would assume you were. Keep your chin up a little higher, straighten your shoulders, and lie through your teeth." Arrow stopped on the opposite side of the tree and gave her an unimpressed look. "Humans can lie, after all. The fae can't."

That wasn't the first time she'd heard about the bindings on a fae tongue. But Freya thought they weren't giving themselves enough credit. She absolutely had heard them lie, although they might not have thought of it that way.

Twisting words, telling stories, manipulating the way a person thought... It was all just a different way to lie.

Arrow pointed at the tree with a paw. "That's the way into the Summer Court."

The tree?

Freya frowned and stared at the bark. She'd seen nothing different about the tree at all. It was still just bark. Still the same thing she'd seen from the moment she stepped through the portal. Just a tree. A few lanterns. Nothing all that different from what she might have expected in a forest.

Except... There was something different. All she had to do was look a little closer.

Nestled deep into the bark of the tree was a tiny door. It was about the same size as her hand and surrounded with white mushrooms embedded in the moss. Tiny stairs had been set into the roots, little stones that only a person the size of her thumb could have climbed.

"What is this?" she asked.

"The door into the Summer Court, of course."

Freya could make that connection on her own. Arrow wasn't making the connection of why she would hesitate so thoroughly.

She pointed at the door and then back at herself. "Do you not see the problem?"

"No. It's a door. Doors open and close, people go through them. That's how they work."

The sarcasm that oozed from this dog was ridiculous. Goblin, she corrected herself. She really had to stop thinking of him as an animal or she would make the mistake of calling him one to his face.

Again, she pointed at the door. "There's only one thing standing between us and the Summer Court then."

He looked at the door, then back at her. "Which is?"

"Neither of us is small enough to fit, Arrow. How do you expect me to get through something the size of my hand?" She gestured up and down her body. "I'm not magical. I don't know how to shrink."

The goblin tilted his head back and let out a booming laugh. The barking sound echoed through the darkness, almost as though they weren't out in the wilderness but were kept within a tiny box. "What did I tell you about impossible things?"

"That they're possible here."

"Yes, Freya of Woolwich. So all you have to do is open the door."

Make the impossible, possible. She ironically wondered whether the door would even open for her, a human who hadn't ever considered walking through a door the size of her hand.

But she wouldn't question him. Not when her sister's life was at stake.

So, without too much hesitation, but with plenty of concern, Freya reached forward and opened the door.

CHAPTER 14

Freya wasn't sure how she'd become so comfortable with the faerie realm this fast. Perhaps it was because her mother had talked about it so much during Freya's childhood. She'd known faeries existed. She'd seen drawings of goblins and heard their bells her entire life.

Maybe if someone else was in her shoes who'd known nothing about the fae, they might have struggled with the ideologies. Freya accepted their kind, their stories, and their magic.

There was always the chance that she would wake up from this entire experience and Esther would be in bed beside her. All of this could be some sort of fever dream, or a night after a foul meal of fermented fish.

This world was too real, however. And when she opened the door to the Summer Court, she had the strange sensation of stretching. It was the wrong feeling entirely, considering the door was much smaller than she was. But that was the only way she could describe the sensation that poured over her form and forced her to change.

Freya watched the tree grow larger. Arrow moved along with her, changing his form at the same speed, and the door grew ever larger with the tree. Belatedly, she realized her perspective was backward. The tree wasn't getting any bigger at all.

She was getting smaller.

When the process was complete, she stood at the foot of the stone stairs grown into the massive tree and stared up at the door she had just opened. Light poured from the opening, warm and glowing with the promise of summer. She could almost feel its heat on her skin.

Oh, she missed summer so much. She missed the scent in the air, like the plants were calling out to everyone. Come outside. Lay in the grass and feel the sun on your skin. It was time to grow.

Arrow lifted his nose in the air and inhaled deeply. "Ah, the Summer Court. It's always so lovely this time of year."

"Wouldn't it be lovely all the time? Constant sunshine sounds like the ideal place to live." Freya started up the steps to the door.

"You are correct. It is always summer for the elves." He snorted. "The elves always have it best."

Freya supposed she was about to see why the goblin thought that. Together, they walked all the way up to the doorway and she peered inside.

She stared into a greenhouse with a grey and white marble pool in the center. White and pink lily pads floated on top of the azure blue waters. Rows on either side were filled with every vegetable imaginable and so green the leaves looked fake. The glass walls arched above her head into a lovely point. The entire thing was immaculate and screamed wealth.

Thin hedges framed the end of the greenhouse, each one trimmed carefully into different shapes. One was a dolphin, another a unicorn. She noted a few otters twisting around each other. The topiaries were far more detailed than any she'd ever seen before.

"Wow," she muttered. "Would you look at that?"

"It gets even worse outside of the greenhouse," Arrow muttered as he waltzed in. "This is the safest place to enter the court. Most of the time you end up in the palace, or at the very least in the courtyard."

Well, she was glad they had decided to go this way. At least a greenhouse wasn't so overwhelming as a palace.

Freya strode into the blast of hot air and immediately felt her hair frizz. The humidity stuck to her skin and clung to the delicate spider web fabric on her body. By the time they made it to the greenhouse entrance, her dress was plastered to her skin like a wet rag.

She paused with her hand on the glass doorknob. "Is this going to suit if they're all... noble?"

Arrow looked her up and down, then sighed. "We're going to have to spin a good story for that."

Of course they were. She pushed open the door with a heavy sigh.

The gardens continued past the greenhouse and out into a rich landscape of wild plants. Wide palm trees with branches higher than ten men tall created a canopy over their heads. So much lush greenery filled every corner her eyes could see, other than a thin stone path that led past a small wrought iron seating area, and then disappeared around a bed.

It was so green here. So warm. Birds sang over head and she swore there was a call from a monkey she'd once seen in a passing circus.

Teeth dug into her skirt and yanked her to the side. Freya had her bearings enough to not shout, and dove into the bushes with Arrow as two people strode into view.

They were taller than most mortals, even taller than her father had been. Their lithe bodies moved with grace beneath silken fabric that showed more skin than it hid. Their faces were covered with elaborately painted masks. One was a butterfly. The other a wave.

They spoke in quiet tones that were impossible to decipher, but lovely all the same. She mused that it was like listening to someone sing a song from her childhood, though she couldn't put her finger on what it was.

"What are those?" she whispered in Arrow's ear.

"Elves," he grumbled. "It's always elves."

The red silk fabrics on the one with the butterfly mask were held together by a clasp between her breasts. A large portion of her torso was exposed, and she wore billowing pants that were translucent other than a small triangle at the apex of her thighs. Jewelry covered the rest of her body and hung from her neck, shoulders, and waist. The gold chains danced with even the slightest movement.

The other, a man she assumed although she didn't know why, wore similar clothing. His top was bunched at his shoulder, his pants clung to his skin, and the fabric was bright blue.

He turned toward the female and reached for her mask, stroking her cheek before he pulled it off.

There was nothing underneath it.

Freya pressed her hands to her mouth to still her gasp. She had always heard elves were beautiful. Her mother had told stories about magical beings, revered and honored by both mortals and the fae. They were the most attractive of all the fae creatures. And yet, these beings were completely faceless. There was nothing underneath their mask but a flat surface where features should have been.

"Steady," Arrow muttered. "Elves are beautiful only because they reflect what is around them. With no mortals around, they have nothing to reflect. That's why they always wear the mask."

Heavens above, no wonder everyone thought elves were beautiful. They would change for whatever was attractive to the person they had met, but they were vacant themselves. Completely devoid of anything that would set them apart.

No wonder they wore masks. What a horrific way to live.

Freya kept her fingers pressed against her mouth until the elves moved on. Only then did she drop her hand and let out a croaked sound. "They really look like that?"

"They do." Arrow stood and struggled to get out of the bushes. "And they're quite sensitive about it, so don't bring it up when we meet them."

"We're meeting them?" She furrowed her brows so deeply, she could almost feel them touch. "Why would we ever want to meet them? Can't we just steal the essence of summer and no one would be the wiser?"

"You have to play the game, Freya. That means meeting people."

She freed herself from the snare of thorns and branches, jerking the fabric of her dress until it ripped. "No. I don't want to play the game. I want to get in and out as quickly as possible."

"Unfortunately, we are in the Summer Court and the game must be played or you will be sent back to where you came from." Arrow strode in front of her, his little bottom wiggling as he went. "The elves are more kindly than the sprites though, so you don't have to worry about them trying to make you a pet. At least if you disappoint these fae, they'll just send you back to the mortal realm and forget you ever existed."

That wasn't better.

Arguably, that was even worse. She didn't want to lose the chance to get her sister, and somehow at least staying with the sprites had given her more of a chance than being back home. She didn't even know if she could get back through the same portal.

Sighing, she nodded. "Okay, then. What do I need to do?"

Arrow walked around a corner and suddenly the entire world seemed to open up. No more forest. No more overwhelming greenery. The seaside cliff had a hundred screaming seagulls circling a palace that looked like it was made of seashells. The abalone sheen on the outside gave a pearlescent appearance that she was certain could never be replicated in the mortal realm.

The spires twisted like seashells as well, jutting out of the main part of the castle and into the sky. Beams of rainbows reflected wherever the sun touched.

Elves strode around the palace. Each one wore more lovely clothing than the last, and the masks on their faces differed greatly. Wings, flowers, seashells, images depicting the elements. She noticed that very few wore animal masks. Some of them were wearing insects. Butterflies, moths, even a few dragonfly-like wings.

But none of them were dressed as animals.

She exhaled a low breath and stood at the edge of the gardens with Arrow. "Do we go in?"

"I suspect that's the next step for us. I don't have any idea what the essence of summer might be. Is it safe to assume the Goblin King didn't share that detail with you?"

She shook her head. "He didn't think it was necessary that I know what I was required to gather before I got them."

"Of course not. Otherwise, it would be too easy of a goblin deal." Arrow shook his head, then twisted to cover his chest with his paws. "I feel horribly exposed. We both need to get in outfits that represent our status, otherwise, they'll eat us alive."

A couple of elves approached, although Freya didn't think they had seen the two strangers standing on the edge of their lush greenery. She assumed the two of them were so plain looking, so unremarkable compared to the elves, that one of the creatures would have to quite literally stumble upon them to realize that Arrow and Freya were even there.

She tugged Arrow back toward the undergrowth. "I think we should wait until it's night time then."

"Why in the world would we do that?" He couldn't stop her from moving him, but he did point enthusiastically at the palace. "There's an abundance of clothing inside those walls! We could sneak in, get some clothes, and then they'd think we were a visiting king and queen."

"How are we going to get in without being seen?" She gave one last shove and pushed him underneath an elephant-sized leaf, hiding them from the passing elves.

Just as she suspected, they didn't react. The pair meandered by the two strangers, never the wiser that there were eyes on them at all.

At least the Spring Maiden had guards who didn't let anyone get close to her or her sprites. These people apparently assumed no one would ever attack an elf, and if they even thought of it, surely they wouldn't go through with such an embarrassing plan.

Freya fell onto her knees beside Arrow and shifted a leaf to the side, watching the elves as they walked around the palace.

The goblin remained quiet for a few moments before he muttered, "Well, I look like a dog. I could just walk in and get us items of clothing."

"I'm sure no one would notice a dog leaving with mouthfuls of skirts." She let the leaf fall back in place. "We'll wait until nightfall and then grab what we need. It's easy as that, Arrow. Then no one will see us."

"I don't think they'd notice me," he continued to argue. "But if you're so adamant."

The goblin curled up into a ball and promptly fell asleep. His deep breathing lulled her into a sense of security, but Freya couldn't stop lifting the leaves and observing the elves as they passed by. They really were beautiful, if a little eerie.

And she kept her eyes on the palace. Within those walls was the secret to this court.

All she had to do was find it.

CHAPTER 15

Under the cover of nightfall, they moved through the gardens to the Summer Court palace. Freya tried so hard to stay quiet, even through the gravel on the path. Her foot stepped on a particularly sharp-edged stone, and when she picked it out between her toes, she realized they were walking on crushed seashells.

What a lovely place if it wasn't filled with deadly creatures missing their faces.

She glanced down at the dog beside her. "And to think, I never wanted to meet any fae creature in my life."

Arrow poked his head around the corner of a hedge, peering through the darkness for any sign of elves. "Why would anyone want to go through their life without some kind of fae around?"

"Whatever could you possibly mean?"

He slipped around the corner with a snort. "Life must be terribly boring with no magic in it, is all. And the fae are the only ones with magic."

Freya followed him across the path and into an open area where they would have to move fast. As they darted through the shadows, she realized he was right. She had been so bored back home, but she hadn't realized that was the feeling tearing her up inside.

She had gone through her life as though in a dream. Dazed and numb, she did all the things she was supposed to do. Keep the house clean. Garden. Go to the market and keep her head down when there was conflict.

Maybe someday she would have met a quiet village boy, and still could. They would have started a family of their own and lived in a hut by the forest. Or perhaps he would have convinced her to live closer to town, where her soul would have slowly leaked out of her. A slow bleed, but a wound that could kill all the same.

Seashells crunched under her feet as she raced past a pool filled with glowing fish. One jumped into the air, and the thin membrane of its tail glowed so brightly it cast her shadow in stark relief against the wall of the palace.

Freya hit the abalone wall and pressed her back firmly against it. Lungs heaving, she closed her eyes and tried to still her breath. They needed to be quiet and gasping for air was not that.

The goblin dog snuffled next to her, his nose in the air, before he gave a sharp nod. "This is as far as I can go."

"Excuse me?"

"Here's the thing. Elves hate goblins." He patted his paws on his chest, then swept his hand up and down his body. "I can't go in like this. They'd take one look at me and know what I am, and then who knows what they'd do to someone like me."

"You were the one arguing you should sneak in and get the clothing."

His eyes widened and his nose twitched. "Well, I thought you'd tell me not to go. And you did. You see? It all works out in the end."

She wanted to snarl that he was a slimy little bastard, but there was no time to argue with the ridiculous creature. He wanted her to sneak into the palace by herself? Fine. She would.

Freya wasn't afraid of these elves, or at least, she had survived through worse. She growled, then said, "What do I need to get and how do I find it?"

"Clothing, for both of us. Perhaps a mask." He leaned around the edge of the palace and nodded firmly. "They don't appear to be out and wandering anymore. So you should be able to pick any random room and grab whatever clothing you need."

"And then just walk out?" She already knew panic was written all over her features. Her eyes were too wide. Her hands were shaking. And she could already smell the distinct scent of panic sweat.

Arrow gave her a bright grin. "Don't forget your path through the meandering halls, Freya of Woolwich. You'll make it out just fine."

And then he scampered off with the faint hint of a laugh floating in the wind.

She was going to wring that dog's neck the next time she saw him. Rolling her shoulders back, Freya prepared herself to step once again into danger. She could do this. No one would know she was here. All she had to do was be quiet.

She stalled for as long as she could before darting around the corner. There was an open door right into the palace, which was surprising considering the elves didn't appear to have guards. She supposed there might be some magic that she didn't know about. But nothing stopped her from rushing into the palace and skidding to a stop on the gorgeous stone floors.

Freya barely contained the startled, "Wow," that pressed against her lips.

The room was splendid. Marble floors were lit by a thousand candles leading to a grand stairwell. The railings were covered with all manners of flowers and vines, draping over the edges and dangling to the floor. Candelabras were placed between the plants to cascade their light over every glowing petal.

Freya stared, open mouthed, at the chandeliers hanging from the ceiling and casting shadows with blue flickering flames. The light illuminated a giant mural on the ceiling that was a painting of a thousand elves waltzing in a dance she could almost hear. The entire room hung in suspended silence, as though it were holding its breath.

Why did this feel like a trap?

Freya kept her back turned to the wall and carefully picked her way through the room. She didn't think walking up the stairwell was the right choice, not yet at least. That looked a little too formal, and even as she thought maybe she should try the upper rooms, a warning chimed in her head.

The first rule of magic was to trust her gut. She might not be able to cast spells or knew anything about magic at all. But she knew her body would react to it the right way.

So she headed down a side hallway instead.

It appeared to be the servants' quarters, though there was no one here right now. A long hallway with doors on either side stretched out before her. This floor was dark, like polished obsidian, though the walls still gleamed with unnatural light.

She pressed her ear to the nearest door and listened intently. Faintly, she could hear rustling as someone moved in their bed.

Onto the next.

She continued down the hall, pressing her ear to each vibrantly painted door. This wasn't getting her anywhere, though. Every room had an occupant. And she would not walk into a room when someone could wake up at any moment.

At the end of the hallway, all the hairs on the back of her neck stood up. They only did that when her sister Esther was trying to sneak up on her. Esther had never been successful because Freya always knew when someone was watching her.

She turned around, whipping so quickly her dark hair blew in front of her face. But there wasn't anyone in the hallway. No faceless elf staring at her. No goblin dog pitter-pattering across the marble floors.

All she felt was a strange wind that touched her face with a chilly hand. Magic, she supposed, although she didn't know what it felt like just yet. Letting out a long, low breath, she palmed the door and stepped out into an indoor garden.

The Summer Court sure did like their plants. This room was full of moss with a glass domed ceiling sparkling with stars. A strange structure stood in the center. She might have thought it was meant to be a room, but spiral stairs stretched out of the mossy ground to a small platform at the top. Columns carved with flowers and birds arched over it, creating a space where walls might once have been.

Considering the amount of moss and what looked like algae growing on the pillars, the building likely wasn't traversed often.

The clouds parted and a spear of moonlight illuminated a small chest at the top of the stairs. Freya's gut told her to go. To look within the chest and see if perhaps that would suit. After all, the elves seemed to be a rather strange race. Maybe this was where they kept hidden clothing.

She shouldn't. She should continue on and look within a closet like a normal person.

But her feet moved on their own. The open air around the pillars called to her. Warm breezes darted between the mossy stone and moonlight cast her shadow in a dizzying dance. As though it moved on its own and she was merely watching it traverse the strange pavilion.

Freya reached the peak and touched a hand to a column. She couldn't quite center herself, not yet anyway. The feeling of her stomach falling out of her body made her need to hold on to something. The stairs were far higher than she'd thought.

No walls. No gates. Nothing prevented her from tumbling over the edge, and it was a long way down. She also didn't know how old this platform was or if it would simply give way beneath her weight.

She shifted to the center slowly, feeling out the floor to ensure it wouldn't break.

The chest was quite lovely. Mahogany wood with golden clasps and filigree embellishments that looked like fish darting across the surface.

Surely there was a dress within. She might not find something for Arrow to wear, but the goblin could pretend to be her very loyal dog for all she cared. Let the elves think he was a pet. Maybe that would make him think twice about forcing her to put herself in danger alone again.

She sank onto her knees before the chest and smoothed her hands along the wood. Stealing from the elves felt like a bad idea. What if they knew what she had done? What if they could sense that someone was taking something that wasn't theirs, and they cursed her?

The hairs on the back of her neck lifted again. Someone was watching her. No, not watching. Someone was standing right behind her. So close she could feel their warm breath shifting her hair and shimmying down her neck.

With a sharp gasp, she turned around and pressed her back against the chest. Freya was terrified she'd see a faceless person standing behind her, or worse, a grinning mask that somehow was far more horrifying than a face without features.

Instead, all she saw was shadows, darkness, and smelled the distinct scent of apples.

"You," she whispered. "I know you're here. How is that even possible?"

No Goblin King responded to her, but she would not let him get away with this. Not when she'd discovered him so easily. He had no right to trail her, to startle her, to make her feel so afraid.

Freya stood up and planted her hands firmly on her hips. "Goblin King. I know you're here."

Shadows near the left column beside the stairs peeled away from the marble. He stepped out of the darkness as though he were made of it.

A white poet's shirt billowed around his chest and arms, unbuttoned and showing too much of that smooth, moonlight grey skin. Tight black pants covered his legs, while knee-high boots clipped the ground as he strode toward her.

The Goblin King stopped a breath away from her, his chest nearly touching hers. The heat from him billowed and slicked her skin with a fine layer of sudden dew.

He lifted a hand, those delicate claws almost touching her cheek. "Hello, Freya."

CHAPTER 16

"What are you doing here?" she asked, breathless with surprise.

She didn't sound like herself at all. Freya's voice was watery. Thin, as though he had sucked all the air from the room. Maybe he had. Just standing this close to him was so overwhelming. She could almost taste apple crisp on her tongue. She knew he was grinning at her like the lunatic he was.

That knowledge came with the realization she didn't have to look at him to know exactly what he was thinking. Or, at least, what he looked like.

His dastardly smirk was difficult to forget, no matter how hard she tried. The pointed teeth had been branded into her mind, seeping into her dreams, moving through the fog of her memories until the inky darkness blotted out all other thoughts.

She tried to take a step away from him, but the chest was directly behind her. She caught a heel on the edge and began to fall. The edge of the pavilion was so close, she knew she was about to tumble a hundred feet to her death.

The Goblin King caught her around the waist, tugging her against his chest with a firm arm wrapped around her. His heart thundered against her palms where she had slapped them to steady herself.

This close, she could see how molten his eyes were. The silver within them swirled, constantly moving with unnatural light. His pupils were slitted like a cat's.

He stared down at her and the sharp edge of his jaw bounced. Maybe he was as affected as she was, although Freya thought perhaps she felt this way because she'd never hated someone so much in her life.

Hate and infatuation were sometimes hard to tell apart.

His chest muscles flexed underneath her palms. "Careful, Freya. The game isn't over yet, and I won't have you tumbling to your death when there's still so much left to be done."

"Whatever do you mean?" she whispered. "Wouldn't you love to win that easily?"

"It's not winning if I don't get the best of you." He released her sharply, spinning her into the center of the pavilion and away from the edge. "You're a very worthy opponent, I'm finding. This has already been greatly entertaining."

"Is that so?" She pointed toward the chest. "The goblin you sent to help me thinks I need clothing to speak with the Summer Court. A king, I assume?"

"Now why would you think that?"

"A palace like this would only be built by a man." Although that was a lie. The beauty of this place was haunting and had a familiar feminine touch to the design.

His eyes trailed up and down her body, lingering on the softness of her curves. Slowly, the Goblin King licked his lips.

Freya crossed her arms over her chest, suddenly very aware that the dress she wore was plastered to her like a second skin. She wanted to get out of this tattered lace. Even compared to the Goblin King in his lax outfit, she still felt like a moth who had flown into a garden full of butterflies. Lesser. And not quite as impressive as she should have been.

"Ah, Freya." Her name on his tongue sounded like a sonnet. "You cannot wander elven halls and think they will find you noble simply because of the way you dress."

"I'm mortal, remember? We're quite adept at lying." She didn't know if she was all that good, however.

Esther was better at pretending to be something she wasn't. Even in the village, her sister could fit in with any crowd of people she waltzed up to. Like the elves, Esther had worn many faces and could easily slip into another character. Those she met always thought she was the same as them, shared the same thoughts, even moved the same way.

Freya wasn't good at pretenses. All she could hope was that she could be convincing enough that people didn't notice her presence.

The Goblin King raised an eyebrow, almost as though he knew the thoughts running through her head. "We'll see just how convincing a theatrical show you can put on, then."

"Why are you even here?" she snapped. His words stung. Did he already think she was going to fail? She had come this far!

"I also have to speak with the Summer Lord." He tilted his head toward her, acknowledging that she'd only been partially correct. "My presence has nothing to do with you being here, although I'm surprised you're going in order. Did you think the elves would be easier than the sprites?"

"Arrow said they were less dangerous."

"Oh no, my dear. Pretty things are always dangerous, no matter if they are elegant rather than delicate." He turned around and opened the chest she'd planned to steal from.

He pulled out a gorgeous gown of cerulean fabric. He gave it a hefty snap and suddenly the dress unfurled, then bloomed. Many layers of lapis chiffon were cinched in at the corset and decorated with lovely silver thread. Vines crawled up the corset and ended in chiffon plumes that would fall off the shoulders with lovely grace.

The Goblin King turned around with the dress in his hands. "This will suit you, Freya of Woolwich."

Good lord, he thought that dress would look nice on her? What compliments this Goblin King let fall from his lips.

She took a step forward, reaching for the gown. "I suppose it would. Doesn't matter though, it's only going to be worn to prove a point."

He tugged it away from her reach. "What point is that?"

"That I can blend in with the elves if needed." She tried to snatch it from his hands, but he moved again. Why wasn't he letting her have the dress?

The Goblin King released one shoulder of the dress and gestured with his finger for her to turn around. "Clearly you've never put on a corset before. You can't do it yourself. Turn around, Hero of Woolwich."

"That's not what I am," she whispered, her voice carrying through the moonlight.

"Isn't that what you've made yourself? You're the hero in this story, Freya."

She could feel her heart beating against her ribs with the pounding sound of drums. "Wouldn't that make you the villain?"

The moonlight disappeared and cast his figure into shadows. "I'll be your villain soon enough. But not right now."

She couldn't let him touch her, could she? He asked to help dress her, and she knew for a fact that was too far. He had stolen her sister away. This was the man who prevented Esther from returning home to the only family she'd ever had.

He'd made a deal with a little girl who had little concept of consequences. And sure, maybe the Goblin King hadn't made the deal himself. He had the final say in anything to do with his court. He might not have been the one who had taken Esther, but he was the one to blame.

Freya turned around all the same. She scooped her hair over one shoulder, baring her back to his gaze with a soft, shuddering sigh. "Fine, then."

His claws ghosted over the ragged edges of her lace dress. Rather than unbuttoning the back, he ran the sharp tips beside the buttons, slicing through the thin strands holding the dress onto her body. She felt each pop vibrate through her ribs and belly.

The lace slithered to the marble floor, snagging on her chemise that had seen better days. He didn't move to rush the lace off her body.

Neither did she. They both let it fall on its own accord with a hushed sound against the smooth floor.

Her heart raced. Her throat closed up because she didn't know what to say. How did one acknowledge the villain, as he called himself, helping her into a ball gown?

Gorgeous layers of chiffon landed at her feet. The dress glowed like magic made the colors more vivid. He'd unlaced the corset, she realized. It gaped open, waiting for her to step into the dress and allow him to ease it up her body.

She couldn't do this. She'd faint or fall over or—

"Freya." His voice broke through her worries. "Step into the gown, my dear."

She straightened her spine, stared forward into the darkness, and stepped into the dress. The chiffon was so light against her toes she wasn't certain she'd actually touched it. But he eased it up and over her hips, smoothing his palms along the outside and settling the layers flat.

"Arms," he murmured.

Freya lifted them, and he eased the corset into place. The sleeves fell down over her shoulders, as they were meant to, but her neck suddenly felt very bare. Her collar bone was exposed for anyone to touch. So exposed she could feel his breath on the back of her shoulder.

"You've never worn a corset before, I take it?" he asked, fingers moving behind her as he began the lacing process.

"No, never."

"Why not?"

"No peasant ever sees reason to wear a corset." What should she do with her hands? Did she leave them at her side? "I can't imagine working in the fields with a binding constricting my chest."

"I imagine you'd faint." There was the faintest hint of amusement in his voice. "Peasant. I find it funny the mortals still use the word."

The first tug surprised her. She wheezed with the second and realized very quickly why she would have fainted. Good lord, he was going to break her ribs if he made it that tight. Although, she supposed he would also know the appropriate way to wear a corset.

A voice in the back of her head wondered why she was trusting him to touch her at all. This could be a magical corset that would slowly squeeze her chest until the bones broke.

But another voice whispered that he wouldn't want to win this game like that. Hadn't he said so himself? The Goblin King was entertained by their back and forth. He wouldn't cheat when he could continue to watch her and see what choices she would make.

"Of course, we still use the word," she hissed out a long breath with a particularly sharp sound. "What else would we use?"

"Woolwich, I suspect, would use nothing. Nobles left there centuries ago if I remember right." He remained quiet for a long time before asking her another question. "Is there still a salt mine there?"

"Why do you want to know?"

"No important reason, I suppose." He tugged harder and her ribs creaked in response. "I used to know the people who lived there. Back when mortals understood the fae aren't all bad."

"You were in Woolwich," Freya reminded him. "I saw you in the cart, you know. You were the first goblin I've looked at in years."

"Ah, yes. Your mother had a big voice claiming if mortals looked upon a goblin that we would tempt them into oblivion." He chuckled. "I always thought that was funny, you know. If we could tempt a human just with our looks, you'd think we would be a little prettier."

She placed her hands on the corset and held onto the boning. The shadows shifted around them. She wondered if there were goblins watching them even now. Did they follow him around? Or did he travel alone?

"She was right." Freya didn't know where the words came from. Maybe the corset was squeezing them out of her. "Even if you all wear animal features, you're still so tempting to mortals."

His fingers stilled between her shoulder blades. Heat spread from his fingertips, sinking into her skin like a brand. "Do I tempt you?"

More than he'd ever know.

With every breath she inhaled.

The idea of the Goblin King was enough to make her mind whirl and yes, of course he tempted her.

Freya turned around and met his gaze. "No, Goblin King. You don't."

His eyes squeezed just the slightest bit, narrowing on her as he searched her gaze for the lie. Freya thought she managed quite well to hide her inner thoughts, but then he grinned and those sharp teeth glinted in the moonlight.

"Yes, you are," he growled. "And what a pity that you're tempted by a monster, my dear. Stories like those never end well."

His hands lifted between them and she stared down into a midnight blue mask shaped like twin blooming flowers. Freya took the offered mask and held it loosely in her hands.

"Goblin King," she murmured. She should tell him that she had lied. She didn't know why she'd said such a horrible thing.

But when she looked up, he was gone.

CHAPTER 17

"Pull yourself together, Freya," she whispered, as though the words might snap her out of the dumbfounded stupor.

The Goblin King had dressed her. The gown was far more magnificent than anything that had ever been on her body.

And the Goblin King had dressed her.

Clearing her throat, she noted the sun appearing on the horizon. She hadn't realized so much time had passed, but it appeared she would enter the Summer Court while everyone was waking up.

That was great. What a wonderful thing to happen when she was trying to sneak around and figure out what the essence of summer even was, how she was going to steal it, and how she was going to get it away from the Summer Lord.

At least she knew the elf leader was a Lord. That was the first step closer to whatever she needed to steal.

Twitching her skirts to the side, she placed the mask on her face. Small hooks on either end clung to her ears, and strangely the mask wasn't heavy. It adhered to her skin like it was meant to stick, or like someone had lathered glue on the back. She hoped she'd be able to get it off.

Freya raced down the stairs and back to the mossy floor where she could enter the rest of the palace. Taking a deep breath, she pressed her hand against the surface of the door. She could do this. All she had to do was play pretend.

Shoving the door open, she walked out into the hall filled with elves. This was what she had expected when she'd come into the palace in the middle of the night. A hundred different dresses in every color of the rainbow, a myriad of masks, and so many eyes on her that she could hardly tell who or what she was supposed to be doing.

An elf grabbed her arm. This one wore a mask shaped like a sunflower. "Are you ready?"

She supposed she couldn't ask for clarification on what she should be ready for. Such words would only give away her not belonging, and that she had no idea where she was.

Freya gave a quick nod, and the elf pulled her through the halls. They raced away from the pavilion where the Goblin King had stolen her breath, and out to the stairwell covered in flowers.

Sunlight made it even more grand. She stared up at the mural and tried to square her shoulders more. Lift her chin up to the sky, like Arrow had said. She needed to pretend she was one of them, and no one would give her a second glance. It would be that easy.

The elf holding onto her arm gave her a quick shake. "Are you ready?"

Again that question. Freya frowned beneath the mask but nodded again. This time, they raced up the stairs, down a hallway lined with blue flowers that creeped horizontally along the walls, and then out into a raised courtyard.

The entire courtyard had been set like there was about to be a ball. Sure, there were a few tables here and there, laden with food and drink. But the black-and-white checkered floor couldn't be mistaken for anything other than a dance floor. Vines hung from lines that were strung above their heads, and multi colored petals rained down with every passing wind. Already there were quite a few elves tangled in each other's arms, gracefully swirling to music she couldn't hear.

The sunflower elf released Freya's arm to clap her hands. "My goodness, it's so beautiful! Did you ever think you'd see something so beautiful in your life?"

Freya's stomach churned at the thought this elf might already know she was human. "No," she replied carefully. "I don't think it's possible for anything to be more beautiful. It's existence would burn the eyes of any beholder."

"Quite right!" The elf pointed excitedly to two thrones far away from them. "And the Goblin King is here! Did you know he was coming? I certainly didn't."

Two men occupied the golden thrones, both as handsome as they were opposite. The Goblin King had changed. His dark suit was finely pressed and silver threads sparkled in the sunlight. She couldn't tell what pattern they were from where she stood, but she guessed they were likely tiny flowers.

The Summer Lord was seated beside him in a white suit. Dangerous, considering how much dirt and earth surrounded them. His skin was dark as midnight and had an otherworldly sheen that gave him a pearlescent glow. The crown on his head was made of corals that had been polished, or perhaps metal poured to appear as though it had once been alive.

Freya watched the sunflower elf run from her side and sprint off to the others. They were all standing in lines, preparing themselves to dance. Unfortunately, Freya had no idea what they were dancing to or what the steps were. She couldn't even hear the music.

Another elf strode by her, wearing a mask like the sun. He paused for a moment, then looked over his shoulder and held out his hand for her to take. "Shall we?"

Oh no.

This was the moment they found out she wasn't who she was pretending to be. Their graceful movements were so beyond her knowledge, and worse, if she was too close to an elf, would he be able to smell her? To know she was mortal and therefore deserved to go home?

That's what Arrow said. They could smell a goblin a mile away. They must be able to smell mortality as well.

The elf was waiting. He waved his hand again, as though maybe she hadn't seen him holding it out for her to take. What was she going to do? Her heart rapidly beat faster and faster until she was certain the elf could hear it.

"Summer Lord!" the Goblin King's shout echoed across the dance floor. Everyone paused in their soundless dance, staring at the king who had visited them.

Freya held her breath. She couldn't imagine what he was up to now.

The Summer Lord turned his head to stare, his eyes narrowed. "What is it, Goblin King? You have been invited to my court and now you have all the loveliest of the elven women laid out before you like a banquet. What more could you possibly want?"

Was there a hint of disgust in his tones? Freya assumed there must be. Arrow had made it very clear they didn't like goblins, although she honestly wasn't certain the Goblin King was actually one of their own species.

He looked more... Well. A combination of sprite and elf, more than he looked like a goblin. Perhaps those claws, the tipped ears, and his sharpened teeth came from his goblin lineage, however.

Strange, she never considered he might not be a full-blooded goblin. And the thought felt as though it were very important indeed.

The Goblin King tossed a leg over the arm of his throne and reclined. "Dancing is no longer enjoyable for me. Bad knees, you see. But I do think a stroll through your maze would be quite... entertaining."

"Ah, of course." The Summer Lord sagely nodded his head. "The maze is quite entertaining, and you love to feel something more than just apathy if I remember correctly."

"You do."

They spoke as if they had known each other for a very long time. Perhaps they had. If she peered at their mannerisms hard enough, Freya could even convince herself they might once have been friends. There was a certain comfort to the way they sat with each other.

Although, she also noticed a stiffness in their shoulders. They may have once been friends, but the Summer Lord and the Goblin King no longer enjoyed each other's company.

The Summer Lord opened his arms wide and gestured to all the surrounding elves. "You have your pick, Goblin King. Any of my elves would be honored to be in your presence. Take them to the maze. Discover the secrets at the center, and perhaps you will find someone who captures your fancy."

Freya bristled at the suggestion. Captured his fancy? None of the women could hold a candle to what the Goblin King was. His grey, shimmering skin was like stars in the night sky. His eyes were molten silver and a woman who only mirrored beauty couldn't maintain a relationship with such a king.

Why was she even thinking thoughts like that?

Freya wanted to slap herself. And if she had been alone, she might have. The Goblin King was not an attractive man, nor was he interesting to her in any way, shape, or form.

"I can have my pick?" the Goblin King asked. His voice rang out over the entire ballroom and then some. She swore he almost shouted the words.

A few elves near her bristled. They didn't seem to be interested in being chosen at all. In fact, she would have thought they wanted to get as far away from the Goblin King as they could. Even though they had raced to be here.

Perhaps they hadn't expected their own Lord would offer them up so easily.

The Summer Lord bared his teeth in a mockery of a smile. "Yes, Goblin King. Take your pick of any seashell that catches your eye. They will serve you until you grow tired of them."

Freya frowned beneath her mask. She no longer doubted that the Summer Lord didn't like the Goblin King at all. What she didn't understand was why he'd allowed the King to be in his court at all if they didn't get along.

The Goblin King stood from his throne. He smoothed a hand down the embroidered jacket covering his chest. The tails whipped behind him, trailing almost to his knees as he stepped onto the checkered floor. His knee high boot heels clicked on the floor.

Had he not changed? She narrowed her eyes and Freya realized he hadn't. The Goblin King had just thrown on a jacket over what she'd seen him in before, and somehow he appeared to be ready for such an occasion.

He even stood out from all the elves, no matter how stunning they all were. The Goblin King wandered through them like this was his own court. He smiled. He nodded. Once, he even reached for an elf's hand, twirled her in a circle, and then left her standing alone in the center of the floor.

What was he up to?

Freya tried to piece together his plan, but realized what it was too late. The Goblin King was only a few feet away from her when she knew he was about to choose her. That calculating mind had already caught her in a new web.

She should have guessed he would do this to her. Of course, he placed her in a pretty gown and lulled her into a false sense of security before he made the entire castle crumble to the ground.

He reached for her hand and bent over it. The heat of his breath filtered through her fingers, and then he pressed his heated lips to each of her fingers. The Goblin King took his time worshipping her hand before he looked up at her with mischief dancing in his eyes. "My lady. You are the prettiest seashell here. Dare I say, perhaps more like sea glass than a mere common shell."

An elf nearby gasped. Another pressed a hand to her chest and looked away, as though the words were an insult directed at her.

Freya's mouth went dry. "What are you doing?"

"I'd like to journey through the gardens with you. To meander, as the Summer Lord enjoys calling it. We'll sit in the sun together. Enjoy an elven afternoon. Together."

She swallowed hard. She couldn't say no. Then the Summer Lord and all the other elves would know something was wrong. But she also didn't want to be alone with the Goblin King for any longer than she needed to.

This was a trick.

A well played trick, she'd admit, but it was obviously another distraction.

"You know I don't have time for this," she hissed.

"Precisely," he whispered in return. "Why else would I ask for your time?" The Goblin King spun around and lifted their hands above his head. "I've made my choice, Summer Lord!"

The man in question waved a hand like he didn't care. "Good. Now out of off my ballroom so we can all enjoy the dance."

The Goblin King didn't waste any time. He tugged on her wrist, hard, and they fled the dance floor toward the gardens beyond.

The Goblin King's grip on her arm was firm. He forced her to move, not giving her any chance to shift away from him until she let out a grumbling, "Are you going to let me walk on my own or am I going to be dragged into the maze?"

He released his hold on her, but it felt a little reluctant. "You have a habit of slipping away under surprising circumstances. I'm merely ensuring you don't this time."

"Why would I slip away from you? Where would I go?" She rubbed the wrist he'd been holding, her fingertips white from lack of blood. "Damn, you're stronger than you look."

His eyes dipped down to her hand, then back up to her eyes. A light flickered in his own gaze, and if she hadn't known better, she might have thought that light was sadness.

"My apologies, Freya of Woolwich."

She didn't want his apologies. She wanted her sister back.

Rubbing her wrist, she walked around him to peer at the maze unfurling before them. It was large. The hedges were two men high. Perfectly trimmed and a bright, lovely green. The entrance was framed by two marble statues of women pouring water out of urns.

"Pretty," she muttered. "But then again, isn't everything here pretty?"

The Goblin King strode past her, snagging her mask on his way to stand beside the right statue. He held the flowered creation in his hands and looked down at it, turning the stiff leather. "Sure. Everything is so lovely and pretty and far more impressive to your mortal eyes than it is to mine."

Freya had about enough of this. He didn't get to be melancholy, leaning against the statue with one leg raised. As if he were a poet reciting sonnets to a woman who wanted to hear them.

She was not that woman.

"Why are you doing this?" she blurted. "I don't understand why you're helping me, or not helping me. I don't understand why you would take my sister in the first place for something so simple as the gift of a necklace. I don't understand why you were even at Woolwich to begin with, when there are so many other places for you to prey on mortals."

"I don't expect you to understand any of that."

"Well, you certainly expect something from me." She crossed her arms firmly over her chest and cocked her hip out to the side. "Out with it. Why are you kidnapping people? Why steal children and then send their loved ones on impossible quests to get them back? None of this makes sense."

He dropped her mask onto the ground and lifted his hands in a shrug. Mischief curled the corners of his lips, but the motion didn't reach his eyes. "Eternity is boring."

She didn't care if that was a half-hearted attempt at a joke. Freya let out a choked sound and said with disbelief, "You're doing all this because you're bored?"

"How many years have you lived?" Then heat flashed in his eyes. Not something of interest or even passion, but feverish anger. "A few decades? Twenty years? You couldn't possibly understand the constant turning of the sun and how long eternity really is. I have lived through war and conquest. Through countless kings and queens. They all fight, fuck, and feast. Then they die. Horribly, but in the end, you notice patterns in the way mortals live."

She refused to fall into this trap of pitying the poor immortal Goblin King. Freya shook her head again. "How dare you try to make this about your long life? Should I pity your immortality?"

"Pitying any of the fae is absurd." His hands curled into fists at his sides. "But you should know you're the first human to surprise me in a very long time. Obviously, I want to see where this goes. What you will do next."

An angry retort balanced on the tip of her tongue. Freya didn't care what he wanted. She didn't care that he was interested in seeing where this went, because the end would remain the same whether or not he liked it. She would get her sister. They would return home to their safe life at the edge of the forest. No matter how long that took.

Freya took a deep breath, stilling the anger that burned in her chest. "I'm glad I could be of some entertainment, but I don't have time for this right now."

Let him try to stop her. She turned around and walked back toward the Summer Lord. She didn't know what the essence of summer might be, but someone had to know. Maybe if she found Arrow and got him to sneak through the crowd at a safe distance, he'd overhear someone mentioning it. All she had to do was be patient.

"Freya."

No, she refused to listen to him. She wouldn't turn around, nor would she listen to whatever venom he was about to spout.

"Freya!" he called out again. "How about we strike another deal?"

Was he insane? She wheeled around with a fist lifted into the air. "Are you joking, Goblin King? I sincerely hope so. Another deal? Why would I ever agree to another deal with you?"

The Goblin King opened his hands wide, apparently showing her he had nothing up his sleeves. "No tricks this time, Freya. If you make it to the center of the maze before me, I'll tell you where the essence of Summer is. What it is."

She shouldn't. She should go back and find Arrow, because he could help her where the Goblin King probably couldn't. This was just another trick to waste her time.

But if it wasn't a trick... This would speed up her time here far more than wandering through the crowds, hoping someone was talking about something they shouldn't. Even though Arrow was small and his hearing was much better than hers, it would take time to even convince him to wander through the elves.

She shouldn't, Freya repeated the thought. She knew just how much of a trickster he was.

The temptation called to her, though, and Freya knew this was the only chance she would get. A few moments running through a maze wouldn't waste too much time.

Turning on her heel, she crossed her arms over her chest. "And if I lose?"

"Nothing happens." He held up his hands again, turning them front and back. "No tricks. No rules you aren't aware of."

"Why?" she asked. "Why would you offer me this chance to learn anything about the Summer Court when this could all end now?"

The Goblin King's eyes darkened and twin furrows appeared between his brows. "Perhaps I'm not yet ready for this to end, Freya."

"I don't believe that for a second." A wind brushed past her, stirring her skirts and twisting the light fabric through her legs. "But no matter how hard I argue, you won't give me the truth, will you?"

"The fae cannot lie." He hopped up onto the edge of the statue, seated just below the water pouring from the urn. "Deal or not?"

She didn't have a choice, did she? Was there ever a choice here?

Freya let her arms drop to her sides in defeat. "Fine. You have a deal, Goblin King."

He tilted his head back and let out a sound that was eerily similar to a moan. She almost felt it this time. The deal fell around her neck like a chain of magic that pushed down upon her shoulders. She could feel the power, and that was as horrifying as it was shocking.

She'd thought it would make her skin crawl. Having his magic inside her should have been the worst feeling she'd ever felt. And yet, the magic was soft in her veins. Quiet and calming, like she'd had a glass of wine.

She shook off the strange thoughts. "When do we begin?"

He nodded toward the maze. "Now. Run along, hero. Let's see how quickly you can figure out the famed maze of the Summer Court."

Freya didn't need to be told twice. She took off between the statues, stones crunching underneath her feet. Her father had taught her how to get through mazes when she was very little. Pick a side, left or right, and never let your hand come off the edge.

So that's what she did. She stuck out her right hand and let the leaves play along her fingertips. She didn't care if a few thorns scraped at her palms, they would heal. Besides, the plants she grew at home were tougher. Hell, even cucumbers bit more than these hedges.

The interior of the maze was a dirt path that was almost too dark for her to believe it was still soil. The walls were remarkably the same, with no markers to remember. Unsurprising, considering the entire point of a maze was for it to be difficult. But the farther she entered, the more the hedges grew taller around her head.

They grew until they were three men high. Four men high. So tall she wondered if magic made them appear bigger than they actually were.

Breathing hard, Freya turned a corner only to see him. The Goblin King's dark suit was hard to miss, but how was he in front of her when she'd entered the maze first?

She hadn't taken another turn or doubled back. At least, she didn't think she had. It was impossible for him to have run past her without her knowing. And as far as her mother's studies had proven, goblins couldn't turn themselves invisible to the mortal eye.

"How did you do that?" she muttered under her breath.

Freya darted around another corner and came to a stop before a wall of vines. Frowning, she peered closer to the tendrils that differed greatly from the hedge walls of the maze.

This wasn't right at all. The hedge was very clearly marked. Green leaves, obviously growing and trimmed by gardeners regularly. The vines in front of her were wild and unruly, almost as though they had grown without the touch of a single person.

That made little sense.

Keeping her hand on the wall, she turned and looked back the way she had come. Three forks were behind her. Three paths she could take if she wanted to waste the time investigating where they led.

Or, she could look at this vine wall as an opportunity. The mere idea of cheating had her teeth grinding together.

But would the Goblin King play fair? She was certain he wouldn't at all. Goblins never played fair.

Freya touched her hand to the vines and pushed them aside. She stepped out onto the next path of the maze and saw the Goblin King leaning against one side. "You learn fast," he said.

She wanted to slap the grin off his face. "And what exactly did I learn?"

"Faeries never play fair. And if a maze confuses people, then we'll do our best to make sure they get stuck in the maze forever." He lifted a shoulder in a nonchalant shrug. "Most people won't break the rules, Freya. Apparently, you are not most people."

"I could have told you that myself." She looked side to side, not sure where to go now that she'd removed her hand from the wall.

To the right, there appeared to be a small fountain with water burbling out of a fish's mouth. To the left, the maze opened like the mouth of an animal. Neither appeared to be the right way.

The Goblin King had said the maze was meant to confuse people, so she supposed it didn't matter which way she went. Turning toward the open maw, she left him leaning against the hedge and raced into the clear space in the maze.

Apparently, that wasn't the right choice. The opening was just a circular portion of the maze with ten new passages that revealed themselves. Each one had a unique symbol above the path, but none of them made sense. A fish. A flower. A woman's comb. She didn't know what was at the center and therefore had no idea what she should or should not be looking for.

Frustrated, she spun around, looking at all the clues, before steadying herself.

"A maze meant to confuse," she muttered. "Breaking the rules is the right decision in this case."

What rules were in a maze? Obviously she was supposed to go down one path. The circular space had a hedgerow up to her waist that encircled a small bench at the center. Maybe...

She approached the middle of the maze. The bench was made of twisted silver, pretty metal flowers blooming in the sunlight. But something was off about the ground at the base. Twin lines were scratched where someone had moved the bench before.

"There you are." Freya grabbed the bench and yanked it to the side. The metal screeched on the ground, proving she was correct. This was no ordinary bench, and it didn't lead somewhere normal at all.

The popping sound of magic snapped by her ear. Warm breath touched the back of her neck. "Look at you," the Goblin King murmured. "So few mortals would ever consider that a maze might not be one dimensional."

"Who said mazes only go left and right?" Freya brushed aside dust. A trap door with a metal handle had been hidden underneath the bench, perfectly concealed from sight.

"Who said life isn't the same?" The Goblin King melted away, but his voice remained in her ear. "Hurry up, Freya. Or I'm going to beat you."

She threw the trap door open. Stone steps disappeared into the darkness, but she would not hesitate. She darted into the blackness and threw herself down the stairs. Every step was closer to the center, she just knew it. Every ragged breath brought her that much closer to beating him.

And she realized that was why she wanted to finish this maze. It had nothing to do with her sister anymore. This was entirely about beating the Goblin King at his own game.

With one last push, she burst out into bright sunlight and skidded to a stop. Freya threw an arm over her face so her eyes could adjust, then peered at the splendor with her mouth gaping open.

"Wow," she whispered.

The cliff edge was still far away from her, but it plunged toward a calm sea. Tiny dots of islands decorated the horizon while birds with ten foot long tails floated overhead. Their songs rivaled the most lovely of ballads, and their colors were every hue of the rainbow.

Her breath caught in her throat. The azure sea was so calm it looked like glass. As though some artist had spun an impossible scene and painted it before her, glimmering in the distance. Close enough to marvel at, but never near enough to touch.

Tears built in her eyes because she had the sudden realization that she would never see something so beautiful again. When she returned to the mortal realm, she would also return to the mundane life that had trapped her since she was a child.

This place. This beauty. It was fleeting, and she needed to absorb it through her eyes for as long as she possibly could.

Footsteps approached and the Goblin King paused beside her, hands clasped behind his back. "It is lovely, isn't it?"

"Did I beat you?" she risked a glance behind them. "This is just the end, not the center."

"Really, the center of anything is the perception of the person looking. This may be the center, because there is a world out there neither of us has ever set foot upon." He gestured toward the ocean. "If we were more daring, perhaps we would climb down these cliffs, get into a boat, and sail toward the sun. The maze continues out there, we just haven't seen it yet."

"Philosophy," she muttered. "From the Goblin King himself."

"Everything is a matter of philosophy, Freya of Woolwich." He turned to face her, then sank into a low bow. "I will make good on my word. You beat me to the center."

Freya bit her lip. "Only because you let me."

"Oh no, I would never." But the sparkle in his eyes said otherwise. "The Summer Lord is fond of potions. He always keeps his lucky charm around his neck. I'd highly advise you to consider stealing that from him."

"What?" Freya's own eyes widened in shock as the Goblin King dissolved in front of her. "Why would you tell me that so easily?"

His chuckle floated through the air like bubbles. "Because I don't think you'll be able to get out of the maze."

CHAPTER 19

He was wrong, of course. But Freya thought he might have known that even as he mocked her. The Goblin King might try to get in her head and tell her that she couldn't do certain things, but Freya knew she could get out of the maze.

After all, she remembered every detail required to retrace her steps.

She strode away from the beautiful coastline and back to the bench. She even took care to make sure the metal legs were back in their spots, so whoever tried to go through the maze after her wouldn't find it so easily.

Then, she just had to remember the symbols she had seen before. There was one that was obviously not in her memory, which was the symbol of a sun. That was the path she had to take all the way to the hanging vines, and then it was just swapping hands.

Sure, it took her a while. Longer than she might have hoped. Even running, the sun set long before she had planned on returning to the ballroom. Thankfully, it appeared the elves hadn't noticed. Or if they had, they didn't care.

Many of them were so far into their cups, the dance had turned rather sloppy. As she caught her breath, one elf tripped over their own feet and landed hard at hers.

The elf looked up at Freya and started laughing, pointing to her face. "What kind of mask is that? I've never seen it before!"

Shit.

Freya reached up and pressed her fingers to her face, but the damage was already done. The Goblin King had taken her mask. She was the foolish one who hadn't insisted on carrying it with her through the maze.

She lowered her hand, hoping that the elves were drunk enough that they would continue to think her actual face was just an elaborate mask. "You've never seen one?" she replied, a little breathless. "The mortal masks are going to be all the rage. You should have heard about them by now. What a pity."

The elf's face fell in disappointment, but at least he didn't know what was really going on. The expression meant he believed her lies, and that was a good enough start for Freya to sneak past.

"Excuse me," she muttered and slid through the crowd.

She tried to keep her face down turned so they might not notice she shouldn't be here. Of course, there were a few elves who stopped what they were doing and stared as she snuck by. These were the ones who didn't look like they were drunk. Their eyes narrowed and grew calculating.

All she had to do was get the potion bottle from around the Summer Lord's neck. That was it. Then she could run away, find Arrow, and they could sneak off to the next court with little to no issue.

Sure. Easy.

Freya pressed her back against the stone of the castle, far away from the rest of the elves. She needed to get her bearings in the room. After all, stealing the Summer Lord's potion would be a lot easier if she knew where he was.

Casting her gaze through the crowd of magical beings, she froze when she felt a cold, wet nose press against the back of her leg.

"There you are," she said under her breath, monitoring the elves she hoped wouldn't suddenly smell him.

"You were taking too long," Arrow grumbled from underneath her skirts. "Hopefully there are enough layers to keep my scent away from their unnatural noses. What have you found out?"

"Well," she cleared her throat. "I know it's the Summer Lord's potion we need. He wears it around his neck."

"Get him drunk." She felt the nose touch her leg again and what sounded like a chuckle. "Or more drunk, as it were. The man can hold his drink, but he's really putting the drinks away today."

Freya looked to her right, where the gathering of elves was the thickest. The crowd parted to reveal the Summer Lord in the midst of all those people. And yes, his cheeks were bright red and his laughter a little too loud. He tried to stand, then stumbled.

It was unusual to see any of the fae stumble. They were graceful as a default, so she assumed this was entirely because of the drink.

"How did you know he was drunk?" she asked.

"I can smell him from here." Arrow took a deep inhale, and the exhale blasted against her calves. "Also, I might have been keeping an eye on you. From afar."

Of course he had been. She would have expected nothing less from the sneaky goblin. And though a part of her soul twisted at the knowledge, he'd been watching her, another part was relieved she hadn't been alone after all.

How strange it was to start trusting a goblin. Of all things.

"Thank you," she said. "Are you ready to move?"

"How are you going to get the Summer Lord drunk enough for us to steal the potion?" Arrow shifted with her, staying between her legs with every step. "I can't imagine he's going to enjoy looking at a human without a mask. They don't like your kind any more than they like goblins."

"I'll come up with something." She didn't have much of a choice otherwise.

The elves parted like water before her. They moved out of her way with either laughter or startled expressions. Those who were drunk thought she wore an elaborate mask. Those who were still sober were certain a mortal had walked into their midst. Freya could hear every word they whispered as they speculated who she was.

"The Summer Lord hasn't gone soft, has he? He wouldn't let a mortal into the court."

"No. That's a new mask. No one would dare walk into the faerie realm as a mortal, and they certainly wouldn't test the kindness of the elves."

"If that is a human, she's about to understand why the elves are the most feared of the faerie courts."

Freya swallowed hard, but kept walking. They wouldn't scare her into running. She had to get her sister.

She didn't stop walking until she stood directly before the Summer Lord. He'd spilled a glass of wine down the front of his pristine white suit, but he didn't seem to mind. In fact, he continually pointed out the stain to a few elves near him, while laughing.

"Summer Lord?" Freya asked, but her voice was perhaps a little too quiet.

He ignored her. Gesturing to another elf to refill his cup.

Freya could see the potion bottle hanging around his neck. It contained a single sprig of a plant, perhaps lavender, although she didn't have a clue what that would be for. Her mother always used to use lavender to help them sleep when they were little. A king would likely have a lot of things disturbing his sleep, so perhaps she could use that to her advantage.

Without thinking, Freya snatched the fresh glass of wine out of an elf's hand and passed it to the Summer Lord. "You wanted another drink?"

He saw her then. The Summer Lord narrowed his dark eyes. Furrows appeared on his brow and around his mouth. "Who are you?"

"Freya of Woolwich." She curtseyed low, nearly sitting on Arrow's head. "It's an honor to meet you. I've heard a great many things about your court."

The Summer Lord snorted, then drained the glass of wine in one hefty gulp. "Of course you've heard about us. All mortals find the elves to be interesting. What exactly are you doing here though?"

She leaned away from him as he shifted closer. "I needed to speak with you."

"No, that's not why you're here. You would have run by now if that's the only reason you wanted to see me." He leaned back into his throne, the now empty goblet dangling from his fingers. "So what is it then? A mortal walking into the Summer Court isn't anything I've ever seen before. You obviously have some kind of statement to make. Out with it."

No, this wasn't the way she wanted this conversation to go. Obviously he wasn't drunk enough. He needed to get more wine in him, or perhaps something stronger, and then she could steal that potion around his neck.

"I want to make a deal with you," she said. Her words carried across the dance floor and suddenly, all the sound disappeared. Not a single bird in the sky dared to sing, nor wind dared to brush through the thick fabric of skirts.

A mortal had just tried to make a deal with the Summer Lord. Freya assumed she might be the first one to do so in a very long time.

The Summer Lord's eyes narrowed again, but this time she saw the calculating expression. He was smarter than he looked, she'd give him that. For all he had drunk, he knew a trick when he saw one. Perhaps he saw something of the Goblin King in her.

"What kind of deal?"

"I want that potion around your neck." She pointed at it. "I will not tell you why."

"No one gets this potion."

"A simple deal, if you fear losing to a mortal." Freya smiled her best goblin smile. "Are you afraid, Summer Lord?"

A few elves near her bristled at her tone. They reached into their pockets and she could see the imprints of their knuckles against the fabric as they wrapped their hands around hidden weapons. She knew she was taking a great risk. They could easily kill her, but she had hope.

The Goblin King and the Spring Maiden had shared a similar personality trait. They had to be the best. And to know that someone else had defeated them was the greatest ruin they could face.

But they also wanted to tempt their fate. Their greed and arrogance required them to prove over and over that they were the best out there.

Freya could only hope the Summer Lord was the same as his counterparts.

He watched her too closely, with eyes that saw far too much. But then he smiled, and she knew she had him.

The Summer Lord opened his hands wide, then gestured up and down her body. "What deal were you thinking, Freya of Woolwich? There's very few things a mortal can best me at. Would you like a contest at riddling? Perhaps you'd like for me to read your future or predict your past? What impossible task would you have me defeat you in?"

How adorable. Just like the other faerie leaders, he had underestimated her. Freya knew how to use this to her advantage.

"Oh no," she replied. "I want something far more simple than that. I want to make a deal that if I beat you in a drinking contest, then I get the potion around your neck."

He choked. Rocking forward, he pressed his fist to his mouth while an elf pounded on his back. Once he stopped coughing, the Summer Lord replied, "You realize faerie wine is far stronger than that piss water mortals drink?"

She shrugged her shoulders as if that didn't bother her at all. "I've heard that before."

"And you still want to make this deal?"

"Absolutely."

The Summer Lord pulled the chain over his head and returned to his throne. He set the glass vial on the armrest beside his right hand. Then, the Summer Lord gestured for the surrounding elves to move and they all burst into action. One brought a chair for Freya to sit in. Another brought a table. Soon, they were surrounded by so many bottles of wine, she wasn't sure she could move if she wanted to.

He even poured her glass himself, filling the goblet with wine so red it looked like blood. "I don't even mind that you waited until I was a bit more in my cups than you, Freya. I think this will be entertaining."

Ah yes, the fae loved that word. Entertaining.

She felt a cold nose touch her leg before a hissed whisper, "You can't drink him under the table, you foolish girl! What on earth are you thinking?"

Freya took a deep sip of the faerie wine, but that was all she planned on consuming this evening. Just like the Goblin King had said, there were rules to this game she played with the Summer Lord. But she didn't plan on following any of them.

A deal, apparently, had no requirements that either party remain truthful or honest.

The Summer Lord was already grinning and laughing with his friends. He nudged the elf beside him and muttered, "I'll have this done in two glasses." Then he chugged his wine.

"Would you like another already?" she asked.

"You haven't finished yours."

Freya nodded, then frowned. "Wasn't the Goblin King here? I thought he left, but I swear I just saw him behind you."

Without missing a beat, the Summer Lord exclaimed, "You damned goblin, I told you to get out when you were done!"

It was all the moment she needed to dump the rest of her wine underneath the table. It immediately soaked into the grass and no one would ever be the wiser. Before the Summer Lord turned around, she set the glass against her lips so it appeared she had drank the liquid. When he turned back to her, she was already wiping her mouth.

"There," she said. "Now we're even. Shall I pour you another glass?"

He nodded, but watched her every move with suspicion. Watching as though she were going to pour less into his glass than her own. Unfortunately for him, he was looking in the wrong places.

"Why the masks?" she asked, purposefully slurring her words. "I don't understand why any of you would wear masks when you're supposedly the most beautiful of all the fae."

The Summer Lord removed the cream colored leather covering his face. Underneath was the smooth visage she'd already grown so used to. "Still think we're beautiful?"

Freya tilted her head to the side, squinted her eyes, then nodded. "If I make my eyes go a little blurry, sure. You're still passable. Now, what other masks do you have?"

He turned and gestured for an elf to run off and get more of his masks. While the others watched the elf run, she leaned forward and poured half her own glass back into the Summer Lord's.

And so it continued. They chatted about the Summer Lord's kingdom, because apparently compliments made him look at other elves for reassurance. Every time he looked away, Freya would either dump some of her wine on the ground, never the entire glass, or pour some into his own cup.

Eventually, he was blinking like he was trying to clear something out of his eyes. The Summer Lord lifted his hand and pointed beside her, "When did another mortal get here?"

"When I wanted them to."

He wrinkled his nose, then shook his head. "That's not possible. I would have known if someone came into my kingdom."

This was her chance. He was so well and thoroughly drunk that he wouldn't be able to stop her if he tried. And the other elves could do nothing, because they weren't the ones who had made the deal.

At least, she hoped.

Freya planted her hands on either side of the small table and leaned dangerously close. "You, sir, have been bested. Now I'm real sorry I have to take this from you, and I hope someday to return it. I understand the potion is yours, and I hope you can still sleep without it."

"What?" He tried to grab her hand before she snatched the potion, but his aim was way off. Maybe he thought she was the mortal on the right, not the one directly in front of him.

Either way, she grabbed the potion, turned on a dime, and sprinted through the crowd. No elf tried to touch her, thank goodness, but she heard the growls of anger.

"Goblin!" one of them shouted. "I smell a goblin!"

Arrow darted out of her skirts and raced ahead of her. "This way, Freya! Hurry!"

She lifted her skirts and ran after him so quickly she thought she would trip. A horde of elves chased after them, but they had enough of a head start.

Slamming into the greenhouse door hard, she heaved it open and shoved Arrow through. Together, they raced to the back where the small door waited for them.

"Ready?" she asked, breathless with adrenaline.

"Am I ever!" Arrow nudged the door with his nose and they both disappeared through the portal.

They tumbled out into the warm lights surrounding the old tree. Breathing hard, Freya fell onto her hands and knees in the dirt. Who cared about the dress? She had managed to steal from the Summer Lord!

"Did you get it?" Arrow asked, his own voice warped with stress. "Please tell me you got it."

Freya reached out her hand and let her fingers unfurl like a flower. The potion bottle rested in her palm.

Now that she could inspect it, she was surprised at how plain it was. The cork was old. The lavender sprig within seemed to hover in the air. Sure, there were a bit of magical qualities to it, but she hadn't expected the bottle to look like anything else she might have found in the mortal realm.

"Wow," she muttered. "This isn't what I expected at all."

"No," Arrow replied with his tiny brows furrowed. "It's not what I thought it would look like either."

Freya reached into the pocket of her chemise and pulled out the little perfume tin. While the first was short and squat, the potion bottle was long and flimsy. She placed them both side by side in the roots of the tree, then sat back to stare at them.

A furry butt plonked down next to her. They both turned their heads to the side and watched the two essences of faerie courts in hopes something would happen. Anything. Maybe a magic explosion, or the two items would fuse together. Maybe they would both disappear and leave clues in their wake.

But nothing happened. The perfume tin remained where it was. The potion bottle didn't move or shift. They were just items that she could have found anywhere.

"It's curious," she said.

"Yes, indeed."

"Why do you think these are the particular items I needed to gather for the Goblin King?" She looked over at the furry goblin. "Any idea at all?"

He shrugged his thin shoulders. "I haven't got the faintest idea. They make little sense."

And therein lay the problem. She felt like there was some glaring red flag waving in front of her face and she just couldn't see it. Something along the lines of why the Goblin King was making this easier on her, when he should have been trying to make it even more difficult.

Nothing made sense here. And she didn't know how to process that.

Arrow nudged her arm with his nose. "So what's going on with you and the Goblin King?"

She continued staring at the tin and the bottle. "I'm trying to beat him in this entire charade, and I think he's trying to pull the wool over my eyes."

"No, I mean..." Arrow moved to stand in front of her, then wagged his tail. "You two were in that maze for a very long time is all I'm saying. And when you came out, maskless might I add, you were bright red in the face. What did he say to you?"

"Nothing." She frowned, trying to clear her mind of the current issue and then understand what he was talking about. "Are you insinuating I might have some girlish interest in the Goblin King?"

"I think it's more than girlish." His tongue lolled out of his mouth. "It sure looked to me like you were interested in finding out what he had to say about your dress. The corset is laced quite tight, I might add. Impossible for a woman to do herself. Did an elf dress you? I doubt one did."

She wasn't having this conversation. "Absolutely not, Arrow. Go to bed."

"Oh, we're sleeping now? I thought you wanted to get your sister back as quickly as possible?"

No, he wouldn't goad her that easily. She got up and circled the tree to the opposite side, just underneath one of the bright lanterns. "Good night, Arrow!"

"Seems odd that you want to sleep now that I bring up your infatuation, that's all I'm saying."

"Nothing is going on between myself and the Goblin King," she spat. "I can't stand being near him."

"Is that why you make eyes at him?"

"I'm not making eyes!" She thumped the tree hard, showering leaves down around the both of them to make a point.

The Goblin King was the last person she would ever be interested in. Period. No questions. No ifs, ands, or buts.

Arrow chuckled and replied, "You keep telling yourself that, Freya. You wouldn't be the first person to fall for his charms."

As if he had any charms at all. The goblin dog had sorely mistaken her reactions, and she wouldn't argue this any more. She had nothing to prove. Not even in the slightest.

Freya leaned back against the tree with her arms crossed over her chest. She closed her eyes, but was so angry she couldn't fall asleep. Why would Arrow ever think there was something going on? She hadn't been flirting with the Goblin King. She'd made another deal, sure, but that was just so she could get more information out of him.

And yes, she'd taken his advice and cheated when she made another deal with the Summer Lord.

She was making a lot of deals with the fae, lately. She needed to stop doing that. Her poor mother was likely rolling over in her mossy grave.

Drifting into sleep was easier here than back home. She hardly even noticed, but when she opened her eyes, Freya knew she was dreaming. This place wasn't right. The forest had opened up into a shimmering light that slowly focused until she could see them.

Them.

Esther stood facing Freya, laughing so hard tears were streaming down her face. She had her hands pressed against her belly and was pointing at the young man standing with his back to Freya.

She already knew who the young man was. She'd seen his rat face when he'd given the necklace to Esther. Her blood boiled.

How dare that goblin boy still be around her sister! What new poison was he whispering in Esther's ear? Did he think all those lies would convince Esther to stay with him? Them? The goblins weren't her family. They couldn't have her.

The vision sharpened again. She could see the rat boy clearly now. He had a thick tail that wrapped around his leg, almost as though he were holding it there to keep it still. His ears were wrong as well, big and circular, though they looked soft as velvet.

She shuddered in disgust. The goblins weren't right, that was for certain. They weren't human, and her sister shouldn't be around them when she had other family who loved her.

In other words, she should have chosen Freya over this rat-faced goblin boy.

"I know what you're thinking." The Goblin King's smooth voice interrupted her thoughts and sent a shiver down her spine. "Goblins are ugly, aren't they? Of all the faerie creatures your sister could have chosen, why did she pick a goblin?"

"I don't understand why you're in my dream." She turned her head and met his unnatural gaze. "Let me have this moment with my sister without ruining it, please."

"You think this is a dream?" He materialized out of the shadows, stepping into view. His perfectly pressed suit with metallic silver vines sewn into the edges was immaculate. His hair fell around his face like a dark waterfall, and those silver eyes watched her every reaction. "Or perhaps this is a premonition?"

He would not get into her head that easily. "I don't have a drop of magic in my blood," she snarled. "Premonitions are for witches, and there's never been one in my family."

"But your mother was obsessed with the fae." The Goblin King stepped closer with his hands clasped behind his back. "You never wondered why she was so interested in our kind? Perhaps she was looking for something. Proof, perhaps, of her own magic."

"It's a hilarious thought, but you know as well as I that it's impossible." She tried to gesture at her body, but realized sleep paralyzed her. Freya settled for looking down at her legs, then back at him. "You've seen me. You've worked close enough to know that I'm not magical. Not at all."

He frowned. "Yes, you are quite ordinary, and unfortunately, that only makes everything more complicated."

"Does it?" She told herself not to feel the sting of his words.

Ordinary. As though her not having any magical blood was disappointing. He acted as though he would have liked her more if there was, and perhaps he would. After all, a magical creature must want to surround himself with people of his own likeness.

Mortals must be so boring to him. Less entertaining, and that posed a problem.

Once he was bored with her, would he make this entire deal even more difficult? Would he cast her aside and then she would be forced to flounder in this god forsaken realm?

Before she could open her mouth, he pointed toward her sister. "You're so worried about her well being, but Esther very much enjoys being with our kind."

"She doesn't know what she wants." Freya swallowed the panic his words incited. "She's only sixteen. There's so much of the world she hasn't seen or experienced."

"You're right." He watched her sister and the goblin boy with a soft expression on his face. Almost as though he enjoyed seeing them together. "An entire faerie realm and all she's seen is where I placed her with the goblin boy you so hate. Why are you accepting of Arrow but not of my rat-faced little friend?"

"Because he took my sister." She spat the words out as though they were flames she could burn him with. "He had no right."

"And you have no right to control her. She's her own person, and sixteen is many years."

"Not nearly enough to decide to leave her family forever." Freya refused to believe sixteen was old enough for that. Though she might only be a few years older, she knew that wasn't the right time. Esther would pick a life of adventure and magic.

But then she would regret it for the rest of her life.

The Goblin King shook his head in denial of her words, or disappointment at her stance. "Oh, Freya. I think, someday, you'll learn that your sister is much more intelligent than you give her credit for."

"I give her all the credit in the world. She's the most kind, talented, and giving young woman I've ever met in my life." She struggled against the grips of sleep, wanting to slap the Goblin King so hard he saw stars. "Don't you ever question my love or dedication to my sister."

"I'm not questioning that at all." Again, he pointed to Esther. "All I'm saying is that you're running out of precious time."

Freya looked again and watched as Esther turned around. She walked away with the goblin boy, but something was different about her sister. She'd ripped her skirt in the back so a long tail could poke out of it. A tail with fur as white as snow that waved like a flag behind her.

"No," Freya whispered. Her cheeks grew cold and she could feel her heart thundering in her chest. "It's not possible."

"I'm afraid it is."

Her mother had never mentioned that people could turn into goblins. Goblins were born that way because they were faeries. Mortals couldn't turn into a goblin, and goblins couldn't turn into people. She knew that.

"No," she repeated. "It isn't possible at all. Humans can't become fae."

"I never said she was becoming a goblin." He looked down at his claws, then spread them wide as though inspecting their sharpness. "Magic does strange things to people, especially when you're around it for a long time."

"Then why aren't I changing?"

He looked at her with those molten silver eyes, narrowed with frustration. "That's the question, isn't it? Why aren't you changing, Freya? Or perhaps you're changing more than either of us realize."

She refused to believe it. She wouldn't change here. Freya of Woolwich was a mortal, and she would accept no other option.

She shook her head in denial once again, but the grin on the Goblin King's face made her shiver.

"It's time to wake up," he said. "You don't have much time left."

CHAPTER 21

Freya rolled out of the dream like she was going to war. She planted her palms on the ground with a growl that sounded far more like an animal than any goblin she'd heard thus far.

How dare he?

How dare the Goblin King try to intimidate her with a vision of what was clearly a lie? Her sister couldn't be turning into a goblin. Esther wasn't warped by magic, and she certainly wasn't making friends with the creatures who had kidnapped her.

Esther was smarter than that. She was an intelligent young woman with a heart of gold, but she would not give her life away for another. Especially not a goblin.

Crawling around the tree, she approached Arrow with single-minded intent. She'd gotten enough sleep. He needed to get up as well and take her to the next court. She didn't know how they were going to get there, but surely he did. That was why he was helping her. He knew how to get around the faerie courts, and that was enough to keep him around.

Arrow had curled up in the base of the tree with last year's leaves all around him. He looked rather fox-like with his tail over his nose and ears drooping down in repose. However adorable a picture he made, she refused to let him sleep any longer.

"Arrow," she hissed.

He didn't move.

"Arrow," Freya tried again. She reached out this time and nudged him with her hand.

Still, he didn't move. In fact, she was certain he burrowed deeper into his mountain of leaves that he was using as a makeshift bed.

The little brat. She knew he was awake now, and he was just ignoring her. What he didn't know was that she'd grown up with a little sister who loved to sleep in and parents who expected Freya to help out around the house.

Scooping her hands underneath Arrow, she lifted him up with a great heaving motion and set him on his feet. He wasn't expecting that. He listed to the side, stumbled, and then fell onto his face.

"What the hell?" he snarled. "What did you do that for?"

"We don't have time to be sleeping. We have to get to the next court, and we have to get there now." She nudged him again, forcing the goblin dog to stand. "Up, please. You must know how to get to the Autumn Court."

He plopped down onto his butt and blearily stared up at her. "Why do I have to know how to get there?"

She could feel the anxiety building in her chest. It rose from her stomach and pressed against her throat, threatening to spill out of her body like poisonous bile.

Freya inhaled deeply, but the sound was shuddering and stuttered. "You have to know," she repeated. "You just have to."

Arrow looked her over with a knowing gaze before he sighed. "Fine, then. Come on."

He took off into the darkness as though nothing had happened. Just disappeared into the shadows.

"What?" she whispered, standing still at the tree. "Where are you going?"

His voice floated in the air on a wind that brushed against her shoulders. "You wanted to go to the Autumn Court, didn't you?

Waking me up so early wasn't nice, by the way. Come on, now! Hurry up."

Was he expecting her to walk into the shadows without fear? She expected there to be a portal out there somewhere, but she couldn't see in the dark. She couldn't find the portal or him without light.

Freya looked up at the nearest lantern, but some deep seated worry in her chest made her pause. She looked at the tree, back at the lantern, and then asked, "Do you mind if I take this?"

The tree seemed to lean closer and offer the lantern to her. Almost as though it were alive.

"Thank you." She hesitantly took the light that would allow her to find the wayward goblin. "I'll bring it right back."

She heard the deep groan of a tree shifting back into place, but refused to look at the movement. Her feet crunched through more leaves and then she stepped into the darkness with the light in her hand.

There was a path, she realized. It had been difficult to see because it was covered in autumn leaves. The dirt path had the markings of many feet, and it looked like it was used rather often.

She frowned and continued forward. "Arrow?"

A dark shape darted out of the shadows and sprinted toward her. Freya let out a gasp of horror and fear, then threw the lantern in front of her face. She barely held onto it as it wildly swung. But the metal box was the only weapon she had to protect her against whatever faerie beast was trying to attack her.

The faint sound of a tail thumping against the ground shifted through the leaves.

Letting out a grumble, she lowered the lantern and stared down at the goblin at her feet. "Why would you run at me like that?"

"Because it's fun." He gestured over his shoulder with a paw. "It's not that far. Just need to get out of the tree's magic and then we'll be there."

She wanted to continue forward, but something pressed against her shoulders. A realization that made her so frustrated her feet felt like they'd sprouted roots. "Are you telling me that we've been in the Autumn Court this whole time?"

Arrow shrugged. "Well, yes. That's the only place I knew would be safe for the two of us."

"So we could have gone to the Autumn Court at any point?"

He heaved a sigh. "If we're going to argue about this, we might as well do it while we're walking. I'd very much like to get home, you know. There's a lot for me to do and I've been wandering around the entire world with you."

Freya would have thrown him into the darkness and marched away if she didn't need him around. Seething, she stomped after him while grinding her teeth so hard her jaw ached.

They were in the Autumn Court.

She had slept in the Autumn Court.

Anyone could have come out of the darkness and grabbed them. And he hadn't even warned her. She'd been sleeping on the complete opposite side of the tree!

"Arrow," she snarled. "What kind of fae live in the Autumn Court?"

"Goblins," he replied. The light from the lantern reached him again, and his shadow was ten times larger than him. "Though I suspect you already knew that."

But that meant... "Is my sister here, then?"

Maybe she could beat the Goblin King at his own game. If she could find Esther, steal her away, then they could both run back to the mortal realm and be done with this entire ordeal. And she was certain she could find Esther. All she would have to do was...

"No," Arrow replied. "This isn't where the mortals are brought."

All her sudden inspiration deflated. "Where are they brought then?"

"I don't know." Arrow suddenly disappeared.

Where did he go? She peered around in the darkness but couldn't find him at all. The path just... ended. The light wouldn't break through the shadows no matter how high she lifted it over her head.

Maybe this was the end of the path then.

Freya set the lantern down on the ground. "Thank you again," she said. "If you can take it from here, then I'll leave it. Otherwise, I'll bring it back once I return."

The ground rolled under her feet, and she took that as the tree understood. Then, she stepped off the path and through the thick film of darkness.

Sunlight blasted through the leaves overhead. It was eerily silent here, but so beautiful. Everywhere she looked was filled with bright colors of yellow, orange, and red. The leaves that were still on the trees looked like they were on fire. And the leaves on the ground were so vivid, she wondered if they had just fallen from the branches.

She took a few steps forward, the crunching sound of her steps ringing through the forest. There was no path here. Just trees that were oddly spaced, growing in an orderly fashion that defied logic.

But then again, magic built the forests of the faerie realm. Maybe this was how trees were meant to grow in the Autumn Court.

Arrow stepped out from behind a thick trunk, straightening a new black velvet suit. "There we go," he said while smoothing his paws down the surface. "I feel so much more like myself."

"Where—" Freya shook her head. "Never mind. Who are we going to meet here? What king or queen, duke or duchess rules this place?"

Then she remembered that there was already a Goblin King. She'd met him many times, and he obviously had something for her to steal. But that would be impossible because he was the one who had made the deal with her.

"Damn it," Freya muttered. "This was his plan all along, wasn't it? I can't steal anything from the Goblin King because he knows I'm coming."

Arrow strode up and waved a paw in her face. "You don't have to. The Goblin King is the king of all the courts. Not the Autumn Court."

She blinked. "Care to explain that in a little more detail?"

"The Goblin King is separate from the courts. He's the one who keeps the other leaders in line. His kingdom is..." He shuddered. "Not talking about that. The person we're here to see is the madame Autumn Thief."

Now, that wasn't the name she was expecting to hear. All the other leaders of the courts had some kind of ostentatious name. Even Spring Maiden made it sound as though she were something ephemeral and untouchable. She hadn't expected to hear the Autumn Thief as the leader of this place.

"Really?" she asked. "And she leads even with a name like that?"

"Sort of," Arrow replied with a chuckle. "Her name precedes her, of course. If you were wondering what she does, well, she does exactly what the title says."

So she was expected to steal something from the woman who had titled herself after doing exactly that? Great. Just great. And here Freya had been hoping this one would be a little easier because she had a goblin by her side.

Leaning down, she grabbed handfuls of her overly impressive gown for a forest and then nodded. "Fine. Lead the way, then. Let's steal from the Queen of Thieves. Sounds like an amazing idea."

"Oh, don't be so glum." There was a distinct bounce to Arrow's step as he stepped between the trees and skipped through the leaves. "You might like her, you know. You remind me of her."

"I remind you of a goblin?" The corset around her chest was too tight, that was the only reason she felt something twinge in her chest at the comparison.

It wasn't because the goblin had almost made it seem as though he were fond of her. And it wasn't because she was a little fond of him.

No, she would never let herself stoop so low.

Arrow stepped around a tree, then opened his paws wide. "Here we are, my dear! Freya of Woolwich, feast your eyes upon the Autumn Court." He looked back and winked. "Or perhaps I should say, the goblin court."

CHAPTER 22

Freya couldn't believe her eyes. She knew what goblins looked like. They were monstrous creatures who were deformed, ugly, and they were evil to the core. That was why they looked so horrid. The darkness within them spread throughout their bodies until they were... well. Grotesque.

But these creatures weren't ugly at all.

They were strange. Perhaps even uncomfortable to look at. But most of these creatures were wondrous. They wore black velvet suits, just like Arrow. At least the men did. Their bodies were lean and hard with years of labor behind them. Broad shoulders, thick thighs, biceps that bulged as they moved.

Some of them had rather human faces with pointed ears, but then they would turn around and she'd see a tail waving behind them. Most were animalistic in nature. A gentleman walked past her, his suit a crushed deep purple. She couldn't stop staring at the owl's head that sat atop his shoulders where a normal human face should have been. His head turned completely around, then he met her gaze, bowed, and then continued walking through the forest as though he had some-where to be.

A young woman strode past her. This one wore a velvet gown,

though the front edge ended at her knees and a long train trailed behind her. She was vaguely human in shape, but her ears were long, soft rabbit ears that rested on top of her collarbone.

Freya should have been disgusted by how horrible they looked. But these people moved with an unnatural grace that made her pause and wonder if she'd been wrong all these years.

They weren't human or even slightly mortal in their beauty. They were animalistic and terrifying, with fangs and talons that could rip and tear through her soft flesh.

Fear had sunk its claws into her shoulders for too long, however. Freya felt those shackles slip off her shoulders as Arrow waltzed through the forest and called out to a few goblins by name.

"Lark! Maple!"

Two goblins approached them with wide grins. One was dressed very differently from the others, and Freya eyed the woman's clothing with no small amount of jealousy.

Lark had a beak instead of a mouth and nose, though it was a rather pretty pale beak that she'd painted with tiny flowers. Her blonde hair fell over her shoulders all the way to her waist, accentuating the gold edged corset around her torso. Her skirt was at least black crushed velvet, but it was very short and revealed red and black striped socks.

The other, Maple she could only assume, had leaves threaded through his curly dark hair cropped close to his skull. His suit had the faint hint of a pattern to it, almost like paisley, although the swirls were a little different. When he reached forward to shake her hand, she noted the backs of his hands were covered with a fine dusting of pale fur.

"Arrow," Maple said with a warm grin. "We haven't seen you home in a long time. We wondered when the avenging hero would return."

Avenging hero? Freya stared down at him with a frown. "You didn't tell me anything about being a local hero."

Maple waved his hand for her to shake and only stopped moving when she reluctantly allowed him to hold on to her fingers. "Arrow is a rather shy local hero, if that's what you wish to call him." The goblin bent over her hand and ghosted his lips across her skin. "But when he brings a beauty like you to the Autumn Court, we can forgive him for such flaws."

Freya waited for her skin to crawl. She waited for the discomfort and fear that he would curse her. But it never came. That feeling was something that had guided her for her entire life, and just a couple weeks in the faerie realm had given her more perspective.

The goblins in front of her weren't going to attack. They weren't interested in making deals with her or stealing her away, although they certainly had stolen her sister.

Confused and already starting to panic, she looked back down at Arrow who watched her with a calculating gaze. "Didn't you say we were going to meet the Autumn Thief?"

Lark snorted. "What do you want with her?"

"A great many things," Arrow replied. He placed a paw on the back of Freya's thigh and shoved her between the two goblins he'd called over. "Wouldn't you like to know? Sorry to dash. Important information for the Thief, but only for her ears. You know how it goes."

Freya let herself be thrust through the crowd of staring goblins. She gave Arrow a few minutes to get them far from listening distance before she asked, "What was all that about? You're a hero?"

"Far from it," he grumbled. His ears were flat to his skull. "It's a bit of a running joke. After my parents gave their lives for the Goblin King, people like to say I came from a heroic lineage. So far, I've done nothing to earn the title. That is, of course, until you."

She couldn't take that praise. He wasn't doing anything that would make him a hero with her. She was just getting her sister back and wasn't that going against everything that was goblin?

"Arrow," she whispered as they weaved around a group of cat-like goblins. Their whiskers twitched at the sound of her voice, and their ears swiveled to follow them. "I don't think this is all that heroic, is it? My sister and I are going back to the mortal realm. Shouldn't you be helping stop me if you want to be heroic to these creatures?"

"These creatures are the same as me," he muttered, pushing against her leg with a paw and moving her to the right. "And no. A deal is a deal. Altering it in any way is considered heroic here. It's the game that matters, Freya, not who wins."

None of this ever made any sense. Why would the goblins want to make a deal they might lose? Wasn't that counter productive to what they wanted?

She opened her mouth to ask more questions, only to stop when a creature stepped around a tree. No, not a creature. She had to stop thinking of them as animals when they were far more than that.

Freya didn't think a single person could mistake the Autumn Thief for anyone but the leader of this court. The woman had cloven hooves, her legs ending in delicate deer feet illuminated by a spear of sunlight as she moved. Her legs were clothed in tight leather leggings that led up to a flowing white peasant shirt. A furred, narrow chest was decorated with various lengths golden necklaces. Her face was human, delicate and lovely. Black kohl winged her eyes into sharp points, red curls tangled around her shoulders, and an impressive set of antlers stretched up over her head.

Lovely. Heavens above, this creature was like looking at a goddess who had stepped out of a story book.

Freya immediately dropped into a low bow. For the first time since she'd come to the faerie realm, she didn't know what to do.

The Spring Maiden was an impressive creature, but she had been terrifying. Something about the woman had given Freya shivers of fear and discomfort.

The Summer Lord was strong and powerful, but he had seemed foolish. He was too wrapped up in his own court and revelries to recognize that he was losing at his own game.

This creature? The Autumn Thief stood out from the others. Though this was perhaps a more ugly being, less beautiful and more connected to the earth, Freya could feel power emanating from every inch of the Thief.

"What a polite mortal you've brought to our court," the Autumn Thief said. Her voice was deep and powerful, rumbling like the sound of drums in the distance. "I don't think I've had a mortal bow to me in centuries."

Centuries? Freya hadn't known they could live that long. Why hadn't her mother ever told her that these creatures were immortal?

Arrow bowed as well, sinking onto all four of his feet and placing his head on the ground. "I thought you'd like to see her."

"Why?"

"Because she is looking to save her sister from the Goblin King." Arrow shifted his head back and forth in the leaves. "A dubious deal was struck to take her sister away, and the Goblin King made his own deal with this woman. She seeks representation from each court and then will defeat him at his own game. Thus, winning back her sister."

Hooved feet stepped in front of Freya's vision. She didn't dare look up at the Thief, though she could feel the goblin's eyes staring down at her.

"How interesting," the Autumn Thief breathed. "So you believe you can defeat the Goblin King?"

"I know I can," Freya replied.

"You're an unusual mortal to have made it this far. I'll give you that." The Autumn Thief reached down a hand for Freya to take. "Stand up. What is your name?"

She didn't know if she should take the offered hand, but she did anyway. Freya straightened, then said, "Freya of Woolwich."

"It's a pretty name, Freya." The Autumn Thief's eyes were strange. Big and round in her skull, and shaped just like a deer. Those were eyes anyone could get lost in for days without realizing they'd been staring into an abyss.

"Thank you," she whispered, her voice growing quieter by the minute as she lost herself in the darkness of the orbs staring into her soul. "I need to find my sister."

"And you thought to steal from me?" The sun caught in her antlers. They were covered in a fine dusting of down.

"If that's what it took, yes I would steal from you." Freya didn't know why she was telling the Autumn Thief everything. She should have been keeping this a secret. Why was she still talking? "I will stop at nothing to get Esther back."

The Autumn Thief blinked, and suddenly the spell broke.

Freya stumbled back, taking five enormous steps away from the arresting creature who had trapped her without Freya even realizing what was happening. Yes, this creature was far more powerful than any of the others. She pressed a hand to her chest and tried to control her panting breaths.

The Autumn Thief smiled at Arrow, though the expression was cold. "You did the right thing bringing her here. I was wondering why the Goblin King tried to enter my court without permission. Now, I know why."

"He's a bit obsessed with her at the moment." Arrow stood back up on his hind legs and shrugged. "I think there's something going on between the two of them that neither is willing to admit. But what do I know about affection?"

Though her breathing was still ragged, she gasped, "I am not interested in the Goblin King."

Both goblins looked at her with unimpressed expressions that clearly stated they didn't believe her.

"What?" Freya added. "I hate the man. He stole my sister away from me, and he has been dogging every single step I have taken thus far. He's a horrible creature with monstrous intent. Why would I ever have any interest in such a being?"

They both looked at each other, then back at her.

The Autumn Thief replied, "Because you haven't had a challenge like him in your entire life. You've always lived in a sheltered mortal world, where nothing can touch you but the hardship of merely being alive. The Goblin King answered your deepest desire of becoming the hero in your own story. You wanted adventure and something more than just farming, making babies, and watching the years go by."

"No." Freya took another step back. "No, that's not at all what I want. I want the simple life my mother and father had."

"But your mother and father didn't live simple lives, did they?" The Autumn Thief followed her. Hooves thumped hard against the ground, and the trees seemed to shake with the force of her movement. "They were obsessed with goblins and magic. Perhaps that obsession runs in your blood."

"It doesn't." Her voice shook. Maybe it ran in Esther's blood, but not hers. "I only want my sister back, and then I will leave this place."

The goblin stared her down before replying, "I don't think you will. Regardless, come with me. Let's get you settled with food and drink.

Then we'll talk more about your predicament. I've never been one to pass up the chance to best the Goblin King, and I think you have a rather good chance at succeeding."

The Autumn Thief turned around like they hadn't just shared an intense moment. Freya felt her lungs fill with air once again, before sighing and looking down at Arrow.

He too appeared to be affected by his leader. His tongue lolled out of his mouth and he panted in deep breaths of air. Finally, he looked up at her and met her gaze. "What?"

"I thought only male deer had antlers," she muttered before following the Autumn Thief through the forest.

"Only males, yes." Arrow crunched through the leaves to get to her side, trotting at a steady pace. "But whatever she was born as is no longer what she is."

"Ah." Freya nodded and felt a knot ease in her stomach. At least she'd solved one mystery. "Then where do you think she's bringing us?"

"I haven't the faintest idea."

Why did that sound so ominous?

CHAPTER 23

She followed the goblins to a small glade where the trees had been cleared away. A large table stood in the middle, surrounded by goblins that were far more familiar to her eyes. Little things, tall enough to hit chest height, with furry faces, odd tails, and claw tipped fingers that reached for the mounds of food on the wooden table.

She knew these kinds of goblins, and she knew just how dangerous they were.

Leaning down, she asked Arrow, "Are any of these creatures the ones who took my sister?"

Arrow sighed. "When are you going to stop calling them creatures? Freya! They're just children. Leave them alone."

Children?

Never in her life had she considered that goblins weren't born adult monsters who roamed the mortal realm looking for unsuspecting mortals to trap. She hadn't thought they might have babies, let alone that the ones she had always seen were young. She'd assumed goblins were short and stout monsters.

Now, looking over their antics and comparing them to the adults she had seen in their fancy clothing, she realized it should have been painfully obvious. The goblin children shouted and clamored for attention. They weren't mature. And of course they were curious about the mortal realm. Too curious.

She would have been in their position.

A dog-faced goblin child hopped up onto the table and brandished a spoon at another with feathers on his face. "Say that again about my mother, and I will boil your teeth in my morning tea!"

The feathered child was not going to be bested. He also leapt onto the table with a stick in his hand. "I'll say whatever I want! Try to stop me and I'll wear your toes as a necklace!"

The other children jumped into the fray, everyone shouting and gesturing wildly with sticks, utensils, and some with only their claws. Freya could hardly understand what they were saying, but she could pick out a few random insults.

"I'll eat your hair like spaghetti!"

"I'll suck your nerves right out of your spine!"

"I'll squeeze your kneecaps so hard they pop right out of your leg!"

She glanced down at Arrow with an amused smile on her face. "Is this what goblins consider to be insults?"

"They're threats, Freya." He grinned as well though, the sides of his mouth lifting in mirth. "You're supposed to be terrified of them, remember? You certainly were only a few weeks ago."

"Perhaps," she replied. She watched the Autumn Thief wander into the mass of goblin children and started tossing them apart. "But if they're only children, then that makes them a lot less terrifying."

"Well, children are rarely scary. We never understood why mortals were always so hesitant to speak with them. After all, goblin children go to sell the wares they made themselves."

She frowned, then looked at the little ones with sudden understanding dawning in her mind. "They make the jewelry they sell?"

"Or harvest the vegetables and fruits. Some of them are tinkerers who like to help fix broken things, and mortals have more objects than goblins. We're a lot more gentle on our items." He cleared his throat and shuffled his feet in the leaves. "You can go see them, if you'd like."

"I think I'd rather have the Autumn Thief calm them down first."

"They don't bite, you know."

She looked down into his big, wide eyes, and realized he needed her to do this for him. He needed to see that she wasn't afraid of goblins anymore. Perhaps because he wanted proof that she was no longer afraid of him.

"No more than you do, I assume?" She grinned, then moved to help the Autumn Thief.

Freya squared her shoulders and grabbed a smaller goblin child covered in snakeskin. "That's enough of that, thank you very much."

The child fought initially, then realized who was holding him. His mouth fell open in awe, slitted eyes growing wide, and then he went limp in her grip. Freya deposited him onto a chair with a gentle pat on the head.

She continued pulling all the goblin children away from each other until she met the Autumn Thief in the middle. Freya ducked low underneath the wild swing of the goblin's head. "There we go," she said with a triumphant grin. "I think we settled all the children."

"Good." The Autumn Thief planted her hands on her hips and shook her head. "I'm sure we gave the Goblin King quite a show. You surprised me yet again, Freya of Woolwich. I cannot wait to hear your story."

"The Goblin King?"

At her surprised tone, the Autumn Thief shifted to the side and revealed a strange barrier in the forest. It warped everything beyond a wall of magic, almost like she was looking through glass that hadn't been poured entirely flat. On the other side, she could see the watery image of the Goblin King pacing back and forth.

She gasped, pressing a hand against her mouth for a moment before she let her shaking fingers drop back to her sides. "What is he doing here?"

"He can't come into the court without my permission, if that's what you're asking." The Autumn Thief shook her head, lips curled in disgust. "He gave me too much power long ago, and I'm certain he regrets it now."

He looked like a caged lion. His broad shoulders swayed back and forth with every aggressive movement. Even his face was twisted in a snarl as he watched her with those molten silver eyes.

"He can't come through the barrier?" she confirmed.

"No," the Autumn Thief replied. "Not in the slightest. He gave that ability to me when he gave up being the Autumn Thief himself."

She glanced sharply at the goblin beside her. "He was once... you?"

The other woman laughed, the throaty sound sending birds flying up from the red trees surrounding them. "In a sense, I suppose you could say that. We were very different people then, and we are very different now. He had a higher calling in life, so it seems. Thus, the Autumn Thief became the Goblin King."

He called out to her like some kind of siren from a myth. Freya walked away from the others and toward the barrier that kept the Goblin King away from her. She stopped just in front of the strange magical wall.

Reaching out, she placed her hand on the glass. It was cool to the touch, so perhaps she'd been wrong. This wasn't glass at all.

It was ice.

He watched her with a strange expression on his face. Brows furrowed, teeth bared, but eyes trying to portray some question that she couldn't fathom. He wanted her to say something, perhaps. Or maybe he merely wanted her to walk through the barrier so he could stop her from talking with the Autumn Thief.

His dark hair fell in front of his eyes. He blew out a breath that fogged the glass, then placed his hand opposite hers. She marveled at how much larger it was than her own. His long, lean fingers would have encompassed hers. The claws at the tips left marks in the ice wall between them.

"Wasn't this what you wanted?" she asked. "This was the game you wanted to play. I'm playing it, just better than you thought I could."

The Goblin King watched her mouth with rapt attention, and she felt her lips burn. He never took his gaze off her, even when she stopped talking. And he never said a word in response.

Her hand slid off the glass, and she turned her back to the Goblin King. The others were watching her. Their eyes wide. Some even had their mouths open, as though they couldn't believe she'd taunted the Goblin King.

The Autumn Thief stood with Arrow by her side, both of them watching her with wide eyes filled with horror.

She couldn't imagine why they would be so worried. The Goblin King was behind the wall and they claimed he couldn't enter no matter how hard he tried.

Freya had forgotten all the other goblins stood behind her while she watched their strange king. As though he were some animal in a zoo she could peer at and try to understand.

What was she becoming? Freya knew to be afraid of their kind. She knew better than to even look at them. And here she was, buried neck deep in a deal that would decide the fate of her life and her sister's.

She blew out a long breath, then walked back to the goblins. "Why are you all looking at me?"

Even the children had stopped their crazed banter. Instead, they stared at her with their mouths open and food dropping off the tips of the utensils.

The Autumn Thief took a deep breath, opened her mouth as though she had something to say, then closed it again. She put her hands on the back of a chair and pulled it away from the table. "I think you better have a seat," she breathed. "Why don't you tell me everything that has happened from start to finish and then perhaps we can figure out where to go from here."

"Where to go?" Freya sat in the offered chair. "I need to gather something from this court that is the essence of Autumn, that's all I know."

"And I don't think I can help you without knowing the whole truth of it." The Autumn Thief rounded the table and sat across from her. She braced her elbows on the table and then gestured for Freya to start.

She didn't know how much she should tell the goblin, so she started at the beginning. Freya let the entire story spill from her lips in a deluge of words, sounds, and raw fear that rocked through her body. She even told the Autumn Thief about her strange dream and how she feared her sister was being affected by magic.

Freya hadn't realized how exhausting this all would be to tell someone. She was breathing hard by the end of it, and the words still pushed at her throat. There was more to say. More to make the Autumn Thief understand and yet, she didn't have the right words.

Finally, she stopped talking. Freya took one deep breath, then another, then nodded at the two goblins across the table. "That's it, I suppose. Unless I missed anything, Arrow?"

He shook his head.

She watched as the Autumn Thief and Arrow shared a look between the two of them. What were they thinking? She knew her own thoughts after rattling off the story was that she really was a foolish girl who had gotten in over her head. Esther would be lost forever, and she didn't stand a chance at getting her sister back.

The Autumn Thief frowned, then met her gaze. "So that's why he's fascinated with you."

"Why?" Freya growled. "I've been trying to figure it out since I got here, but you already know? Tell me."

"The Goblin King likes a fight. But no mortal has ever walked into any of the courts and succeeded. I suspect when you first entered the Spring Court, he knew you were going to fall under the Spring Maiden's spell. Every mortal does. You were the first in a very long time to break free of it."

Freya supposed that made sense. She leaned her own elbows on the table to get closer to the Autumn Thief. "You think he's just fascinated because I've done something he didn't think was possible?"

"I think he doesn't understand you. And for someone as old as him, that's downright odd. He's seen a million mortals. He's seen kingdoms fall and kings die. But you surprised him." The Autumn Thief blinked and those eyes seemed to change in color. Darker, then lighter, then red like the leaves above their head. "I don't think you'll find what you seek here, Freya of Woolwich. I can show you the essence of autumn. And you might save your sister. But neither is what you're actually looking for."

That was wrong. All she wanted was to find her sister and get out of this place. Freya refused to even think about the wonders she'd seen.

The magic that ate away at her soul, making her stronger and more herself than she'd ever felt.

"I'd like to see the essence of autumn, please." She swallowed her emotions and turned an icy gaze to the goblins before her. "And then I'd like you to give it to me."

The Autumn Thief watched her closely, then sighed. "As you wish."

CHAPTER 24

Freya followed the Autumn Thief away from the table and down a path she hadn't noticed before. All the leaves were swept to the side and every time one fell onto the dirt path, a wind brushed it away. They reached a wooden bridge with twisted, gnarled roots as railings.

The Autumn Thief gestured for Freya to go first. "Go. I'll join you on the other side, but I'm afraid this is where you must say goodbye to your friend."

Freya wouldn't be saying goodbye to anyone. She looked at Arrow, then back at the Autumn Thief. "No. We have a deal. He comes where I go. He's with me in this until the end."

"And so he shall be. But where I am taking you is for your eyes alone, not his. I appreciate your dedication to one of my very best goblins, Freya. However, I won't allow him into this part of the court. No one but myself can enter." She paused, then nodded. "And now, you as well."

Was that supposed to make her feel better? Freya's entire soul shook at the idea of leaving Arrow behind. She worried about his well being, as he hadn't been treated kindly by his own kind in the past.

"I—"

Arrow waved a paw over his mouth as though he were telling her to be quiet.

Maybe this was another test. Maybe she needed to simply go along with it and he'd join her whether the Autumn Thief wanted him there or not. As he had in the Summer Court.

She gave him a sharp nod, then turned around and walked down the bridge. It swayed with each step, although it was only a few feet above the ground. She couldn't imagine why they even needed a bridge.

Then, the ending of the bridge warped. Shifting so the wooden slats turned into something like golden marble. Freya was so busy staring at the stone steps, she didn't notice until it was too late how the air shimmered at the end. As though what she was looking at wasn't really there.

She stepped off the bridge and into a very long hallway. The golden marble stones on the floor gleamed as though freshly polished. The warm wooden walls were decorated with hundreds of portraits that stretched down the hallway that never seemed to end. She could see so far that eventually the hall disappeared into darkness.

The Autumn Thief stepped into the room with her. "Here we are."

"Where exactly is here?"

"The Hall of Portraits, and it is the only place I would assume the essence of autumn is." The Thief scratched the base of her antlers. "Although I don't know why he'd want you to steal the essence of each court. It's not very helpful or useful."

"That's another question I've been trying to figure out," she murmured.

"The hardest part of any deal is understanding the why of it all." The Autumn Thief pointed down the hall, arm open wide for Freya to follow her. "Shall we?"

Freya moved forward without another thought. She wanted to see what was at the end of this place, although she couldn't imagine what the item from this court might be. After all, the others had been rather small things. She still had them in her pocket.

Reaching into the folds of the once lovely dress, she palmed the two items. The perfume tin was still there, vibrating with magic that wanted to twist her mind. And the potion bottle remained silent, calming, easy to hold in her hand. Almost comforting, in a way, but perhaps that was the magic of summer.

Would autumn be something similar? A little glass figurine perhaps, or hard syrup shaped like a maple leaf? She could only guess at the thousands of possibilities.

The Autumn Thief strode beside her, hands tucked behind her back and eyes on the walls. "Do you have any idea why he might have sent you to collect things from each court? Did he give you any hope of understanding?"

"No," she replied. "We were in this strange room. Like he was tracking the stars, or perhaps the planets. He wanted to make a deal for my sister and I would do anything for her, so I didn't ask questions."

"Classic mortal folly," the Autumn Thief replied, clicking her tongue on the roof of her mouth. "The next time you make a deal, be sure you understand the why of it all. A goblin can't take advantage of you that way."

Something wriggled in the back of Freya's mind. A question that pushed at her senses without rational thought.

All the other leaders of the courts had worked against her. They had wanted nothing to do with the mortal who quested to best the Goblin King. In fact, they had stopped at nothing to keep her in their court or at the very least slow her down.

"Why are you helping me?" she asked. "Arrow, I understand because he's made a deal that he can't get out of. But you? This doesn't make sense that you would walk me down a hall so easily. All I had to do was tell you my story. And then... that's it?"

The Autumn Thief shrugged, but her dark eyes widened just a little. "The Goblin King and I share no pleasant opinions of each other. He was in my place before I was and I had to spend centuries proving to all the other goblins that I was worthy of his position."

"I still don't understand how that's possible."

"The courts are simple." The Autumn Thief pointed to a portrait of a man standing with leaves in his hair, a red suit plastered to his body as he leaned against a pillar with an ornate metal box on top. "Those who rule are given the power of the element. The season, if you will. It doesn't matter who or what you are, the powers still transfer. So when the Goblin King decided he wanted to vacate this throne, I was the one who stepped up to take it."

"Ah." That still made little sense. The Goblin King's position was too confusing.

The courts each had their own ruler already. She could see how dedicated the people of each court were to their own individual ruler, so it made little sense that there would also be this mythical king figure who did... what?

She scratched the back of her neck, sighed, and continued down the hall while shaking her head. "The court system here is so strange. I'm used to a tiered monarchy who leaves the peasants alone and the only people who have any say in the country is those with power."

"That's also accurate here."

"No, it's not." She stopped in front of another portrait and stared up at the man.

This one had a barn owl's head. His hands were warped claws holding onto a crystal clear orb that had a single sprig of lavender floating within it. The blue velvet suit he'd been painted into was quite lovely and yes, the man looked ridiculously handsome even though he was clearly a goblin.

Why did she find them handsome now? It hadn't been that long but...

"The Goblin King said magic can change a person," she whispered. "Is that true?"

Silence rang through the hall. It ate away at Freya's sanity until she felt like there were butterflies in her stomach, fluttering up to her head where they popped behind her eyes.

She didn't want to know if her sister might be one of them now. Although, she supposed that wasn't the right thought in the long run. Her sister wasn't a goblin. She might be a mortal changed by magic, but she would always be Freya's sister.

If only Freya could accept that magic came with a price.

The Autumn Thief nodded. "Yes, of course. Magic changes everything it touches, and I'm certain that your sister has experienced the same thing you have."

"Oh, no, I was asking for my sister. Like in the dream I told you, I saw she had grown a tail." Freya opened her arms wide. "As you can see, I remain unchanged."

The dress had seen better days. Mud stained the lovely azure fabric, and the edges were a little frayed. One panel of the skirt had caught on a branch at some point and she hadn't realized it, so that fabric was ripped and hanging from a thread. Not to mention the goblin children had placed a few sticky handprints on her sides while she had been pulling them off each other.

It was a shame. She had felt so beautiful wearing the gown.

"But you have changed," the Autumn Thief replied. "Haven't you?"

"No." Freya spun in a circle with her arms lifted. "I'm still very much a mortal."

"Not like that. Your sister changed physically because that's what she wanted. Esther has never been all that comfortable with the way she looked. Mortal form isn't for your sister, and that's perfectly all right." Those dark eyes widened, turning a deep green with the Thief's emotions. "But you? You were never happy in your life in the mortal realm, but there were blocks in your mind, like the ice wall that keeps the Goblin King at bay."

"No," she whispered again, taking a step away from the intensity of the Thief's gaze. "You're wrong. I enjoyed my life because that is what I've always wanted. A simple life on the edge of the forest, away from people."

"You wanted so much more than that." The Thief advanced on her, pushing Freya down the hall with nothing more than her burning gaze. "You wanted to see the world. You wanted to experience magic, and all those years of someone else pouring their hatred into you had turned your mind away from us. Hatred for goblins. Fear of power. Anxiety every time you heard the bells, not because you thought we were dangerous but because they called out to you."

Her argument stuck in her throat. Freya still shook her head in denial, but she couldn't say a single word in her own defense.

The Autumn Thief pointed with a fur covered finger. "The portraits in this hall only speak the truth. Look at the centuries of Goblin Kings, Freya, and see what it is you truly seek."

She stared up at the portrait they stood beside and flinched as she saw the Goblin King she recognized. He stared down at her with a wry grin, so realistic he looked as though he could step right out of the painting. She knew that moonlight shimmering skin and those molten, star-like eyes. His gaze was so powerful, even the portrait artist must have spent hours detailing every little perfection in those orbs.

And then she saw something in the painting that didn't seem right. Frowning, she peered closer and realized it was another portrait. There was a painting directly behind him, just like the one she was looking at.

What had the first portrait had in it? A metal box, silver and ornate.

Freya reached into her pocket again and touched the perfume tin that had seen better days, but perhaps wasn't always a small tin.

The second portrait she'd seen had a glass orb with a sprig inside it. She shifted her fingers and touched the potion bottle with its essence of lavender still floating within.

Taking a deep breath, she looked up at the painting before her again. "They're not symbols of the court at all, are they?" she whispered. "They're symbols of the people."

"In a way. They're symbols of who we become as leaders of this place, and perhaps what we desire most." The Autumn Thief leaned against the wall, placing a shoulder against the slatted wood. "Spring always wants to get away from responsibility, so they search for sleep in dust, powder, or perfume. Summer desires nothing more than comfort, thus, you'll see a Summer Lord or Lady with potions. Autumn only wants to know what other people desire. All the gifts came from the Goblin Kings, long ago."

Those dark eyes widened again, inflamed with a passion for knowledge. Freya had the sudden feeling that if she had given the Thief the chance, this creature would have ripped her open just to look through every part of her body for clues.

"So that's why he wants so badly to watch as I go through every step of this deal," she replied. "Natural curiosity comes with leading the Autumn Court, is that it?"

"Yes. And the Goblin King is still part of this court, or at least, some of his soul is. Though I lead it, he came from this place and someday will return. A king has more responsibilities than just a single court, and he has much to do." The Thief pointed back to the painting. "Now, what is it that you want?"

"I don't know what you mean."

"Look at the painting again, Freya of Woolwich. Tell me what you see." Something had shifted in the way the Thief held herself. There was an aggression in her stance. A movement that made Freya gulp and do exactly what she said.

She stared at the portrait and before her eyes, the image shifted. Warping, changing until she frowned deeply.

"What do you see?"

Herself. Standing beside the Goblin King in a gown as blue as the sea. She had a small circlet around her head that looked like a thousand stars had been set into silver metal. But that wasn't what she wanted. She refused to believe it.

"No," she replied. "I need to get my sister."

"What do you see?"

If the portrait was the essence of this court, then so be it. Freya reached up and split it from the frame. The canvas ripped with a horrible sound that echoed down the hall. Each of the paintings suddenly moved. The inhabitants pounded their fists against their frames and screamed in anger that she would dare remove a king from his rightful place on the wall.

Freya bolted back the way they came, rolling the portrait as she went.

The Autumn Thief's voice chased after her. "You can run as far as you want, Freya! But the Goblin King will always find you!"

The portrait had been wrong. The magic wanted her to see a possible future, but it didn't know her truest desires. It couldn't. Because magic couldn't get into her mind and read what she wanted before she had come to the conclusion herself.

Freya burst out onto the wooden bridge and caught herself on the gnarled railings.

Why had she seen herself in the painting? What could it possibly mean other than she wanted to…

No, she refused. That wasn't the train of thought she was going to encourage. She refused to let the goblins get into her head any more than they already were. This was not the life she had chosen, nor was it the life she wanted. They could tell her all manner of wonderful things, and she would still be certain she needed to take her sister back home with her.

The goblins were getting into her head. That was all.

A voice filtered through the wind, one that was so wonderful and peaceful that it made her turn around. The scent of freshly baked apple pie hit her nose, and she knew, *she knew*, she should run.

But she didn't.

The Goblin King stood behind her, framed by that warm, wooden hallway with all the portraits of the kings who had come before him. The kings who appeared to all be goblins and the best of their kind.

"Now you have seen the truth," he said. The silver in his eyes darkened to a deep sterling. His brows were furrowed, almost as though he feared what she would say next. "What do you think?"

"What truth did I see?" She lifted a hand and let it flutter in the air like a dying bird. "That's a hallway of Goblin Kings. I can see that there's something special about everything you told me to get, but I have no idea what you're going to do with any of these. Nothing makes sense. Nothing at all!"

"You haven't put it together yet, and that's all right. I have every faith that you will understand in due time." He took a step closer to her. The velvet of his suit followed the movement of his muscles, highlighting the strength of his body and the unnatural glow to his skin. "You're so much more intelligent than the others, Freya. All you have to do is try a little harder."

"Try harder? I have been fighting for weeks to get my sister back, and all you have to say is do more?" Her face heated with anger and she could feel a heartbeat in her cheeks. "You've sent me on an impossible quest. I want my sister back, Goblin King. And I want her now."

"We had a deal, and I won't give her back before this is done." He took another step closer.

The shimmering swirl in his eyes grew wild and turbulent. It was so lovely, so enthralling that she almost lost herself in that gaze. But not this time. Freya had learned about the faeries' tricks. She knew damn well how to keep her head around them.

"Stop it," she snarled. "I only have one thing left to gather and then I will get my sister from you and we will leave this cursed place."

"Will you?" He tilted his head to the side, a dark swath of hair falling over his shoulder like a waterfall. "No one has told you about the Winter Court, have they?"

She felt an icy chill trail down her spine. "No."

The Goblin King stepped so close their chests nearly touched. He lifted a clawed hand and raked those deadly points through her dark hair. The long lengths tangled on the ends like spiderwebs.

His lips pressed against her ear and he whispered roughly, "Poor Freya. The last part of the game is the hardest."

With a gasp of shock and heat, she wrenched away from him.

He looked down at his fingers. A few dark strands remained in his grasp. "Everyone in the Winter Court is dead, you know. They have been for a long time. Good luck finding someone there to help you."

He melted out of view and she had to wonder if he was ever really there at all. The Autumn Thief had seemed so confident that he couldn't just walk into the Autumn Court whenever he wanted to, and yet, there he was.

Blood boiling, she darted across the bridge and back to the burning forest. Why did every single person she met in this realm want to control her? Everyone had their own opinion of what she should do.

The Spring Maiden wanted her to sleep, while the Summer Lord wanted her to drink.

Arrow wanted her to help him avenge his family, and the Autumn Thief wanted her to accept that she had been looking for this realm her entire life.

The Goblin King wanted her to beat him, or maybe he wanted her to lose. And Esther?

She didn't know what Esther would want from her. That was the largest problem of all. Esther might want to stay here when Freya had gone through all this trouble to get her back. What would she do if she saved her sister and Esther refused to go home?

Her mind was spinning into something that felt eerily similar to panic, and then Arrow stepped into the sunlight with a worried expression on his face. His movements were hesitant.

"Did you find it?" he asked.

"Yes." She brandished the rolled up oil painting. "I think so. Now there's just one left."

"Oh." He rubbed his paws together. "And then you'll be going, I guess?"

"I don't see any reason why I'd stay."

The hurt look on his face made her want to rip the painting in half. She wanted to go home. She was so tired of these new feelings that made little sense in her mind.

Freya had always been the good, dutiful daughter. She listened to her mother's advice and the teachings about the goblins. No one could have convinced her to change her mind, not in a million years. And yet, here she was, looking at this goblin with compassion in her heart rather than hatred or fear.

This wasn't right. She was supposed to listen to what her parents had said. She was supposed to learn from the notes her mother had taken and then move forward from that. But making her own decisions? That wasn't allowed.

Her heart squeezed painfully and her throat closed up. Why couldn't she breathe? Was this another spell?

The ground shifted underneath her feet, tilting to the side. Or maybe that was her head as she reached out to balance herself on a nearby tree. Taking a deep breath through her nose, she felt her lungs expand all the way, but it still wasn't enough air. Almost as though her lungs had shrunk.

Arrow took another step closer and cleared his throat. "Miss Freya, are you all right?"

That was the first time he'd ever called her that name before. Miss Freya. Like she was no longer just a mortal, and he had reason to respect her name.

What was it that he called her all those weeks ago? A woman who wanted to be a hero?

She didn't want the responsibility of being the hero in this story. She couldn't take it anymore because her heart was going to pop in her chest and her head was going to crack open like an egg.

Freya squeezed her hand on the bark of the tree. Time, that's all she needed. Just a few moments to herself where she could get her thoughts back in order. They weren't right. Maybe if she could get back home, then she could paw through her mother's books and see what information lay within those. Maybe her mother had already dealt with something like this.

"Miss Freya?" Arrow asked again. "You don't look so good."

"I don't feel good," she snapped, whirling around. "I know you don't understand it because you've lived here your entire life. But I don't like being in the Autumn Court. I don't like being around goblins. This isn't my place and I want to go back to my own damn home."

"But you have to find your sister." He paused in the middle of the forest and she noted the picture he made.

A dog, standing on his back legs. The fine pressed black suit that fit his form perfectly. The face that was all too human and eyes that saw too much.

He was so intelligent. So kind. If he'd been a human, they might have been the best of friends. She had seen him do more for her than any other mortal. And even though he'd done all those things just because of a deal they'd struck, it had comforted her to pretend he'd helped because she was a friend.

Now, she realized that goblins weren't friends with humans.

They were just like the other faeries she'd met, only better at hiding the horrific side of themselves. They wore their ugliness on their exterior to hide the ugliness in their souls.

She'd fallen for it, so this was partly her own fault. She had really, truly believed that the goblins weren't trying to manipulate her mind. That Arrow was here to help her.

"Thank you for getting me this far," she whispered. "Can you open the portal to the Winter Court?"

"What?" Arrow held his paws up for her to look at. "I can't do magic. We have to find a way into the Winter Court."

She thought maybe he was lying. Now that she'd seen so much, Arrow was surprisingly incapable of magic compared to all the other fae who seemed to live and breathe it. She wasn't all that sure he was just a dog after all.

Panic rose in her throat even more. She tried to breathe in deeply, but all she could manage were gentle pants.

She had to get out of here. And the sick feeling in her stomach was proof enough that Arrow was likely lying. The thoughts repeated in her head until she could hear nothing other than her own voice screaming in her head.

"I will release you from our deal if you open a portal right now." Her muttered words were filled with venom and disappointment. "All you have to do is let me go."

"But... Miss Freya." Arrow took another large step. If he had reached out, he could have touched her with one of his big, speckled paws. "I made a deal with you to help you get your sister. I intend to keep that promise."

"It wasn't a promise, though, was it?" Freya laughed, but the sound was bitter and angry. "I trapped you into helping me, and for that, I'm sorry. But you've been twisting the truth the entire time, and now I don't know who to believe."

No, that wasn't right. She knew she couldn't believe any of them. Trust any of them. And she'd known that from the beginning, but everything had gotten so twisted up in her head because she had been so afraid of being alone.

She only had one more court to go through, and then she'd have her sister back. Then they could return home where they both belonged.

"Open the portal," she said again. "And I will release you from any deal we made now and in the future."

Arrow replied, "Are you sure you really want this? You'll be alone, and you don't know the Winter Court at all."

"I've been alone the whole time, haven't I?" She met his gaze head on, refusing to be upset by the knowledge that she was in the right. He couldn't even look at her. Arrow stared over her shoulder with silence radiating between them.

"You don't have to save the day with me," Freya whispered. "You don't even have to save my sister. All I'm asking for this one last time is to go into the Winter Court by myself."

"You could die." Arrow shuffled his feet in the leaves. "I haven't been entirely truthful about the Winter Court. I knew it would come to this, but I didn't want you to not still believe this was possible. You can still save your sister, even though the faeries in the Winter Court have been frozen for centuries. It's possible."

"The Goblin King didn't think so. But it also made everything so much clearer." She kept her eyes straight ahead. "You've been enjoying this game between us by keeping me in the dark. I needed to know everything, and you fed me the smallest amounts of details, waiting to see when I would fail. Just do it, Arrow. Put us both out of our misery."

"As you wish," he muttered.

Arrow turned around and lifted his paws. The air shifted, shivered, and then split open. Like he'd pulled aside a curtain and suddenly she could see a wintery landscape with a wide open tundra.

"Be careful, Freya." He stepped away from the portal to allow her to walk through. "You're so close to beating him."

"We'll see." She stepped through into the winter storm without looking back.

CHAPTER 26

The silence of the Winter Court was startling after her argument with Arrow. She was prepared for howling winds and a storm that would blow the very skin from her bones. But that wasn't how the Winter Court raged.

Instead, silence louder than any she'd experienced before filled the air. Soft snowflakes drifted from the sky. There was no massive storm. No thunder in the distance, and certainly no creatures attacking her from within the frigid mounds.

This place was quiet as death.

In the distance, she saw a small river winding through the snow. No ice had built upon it, and tendrils of fog rose from the surface. She assumed it was a natural hot spring.

Shivering already, she rubbed her hands up and down her arms. If she got close enough to the river, without getting wet, then she might be able to warm herself for a time. A river had to mean civilization somewhere.

She trudged through the snow. Her toes already were aching with the icy shards, and she worried about frostbite. But she made it numb feet and all.

Lifting her skirts, she stepped into the scalding water. Immediately her toes began to burn, aching and coming back to life where the snow had previously paralyzed them. The entire process was far more painful than she'd expected, but at least it warmed her for the moment. She had a long way to go, and wasn't wearing anywhere near as many layers as she needed to be.

Freya turned left, then right. Neither way gave her any clues at what might be the correct direction. Both were merely snow. A white horizon with snowflakes the size of her thumb falling from the sky in lazy, meandering paths.

The steam from the river clung to her skin. It wet down the fabric of her dress until it was nothing more than a sodden mess. The heat was welcome for the first few moments, but then turned cold and clammy. She couldn't stay by the river or she'd only get more wet. She couldn't leave without freezing.

"What a wasteland," she said. The words fell dull and quiet in the windless evening.

She had to assume it was evening. Freya started her trudging journey to the right and tried to piece together any clues from what the Goblin King and Arrow had said. The Winter Court was dead. All who inhabited it were gone.

No, not gone, she corrected herself. They were dead. Had been for centuries.

And yet the Goblin King had made it very clear that nothing was impossible here. The uncertainty of dead or deathless was a rather complex topic to consider in times like these. Perhaps they weren't really dead, or if they were, then they weren't dead forever. If impossible was possible in the faerie realm, then she had something to work with.

The warmth of the mud sank into her toes, but her shoulders shivered as the steam turned to icy droplets. She needed to find something more than just this dress to wear. Something that wasn't quite so...

Flimsy.

Freya didn't know how long she trudged through the mud and the snow. Sometimes the river disappeared underneath the ground and she would have to forge her way through the mounds of snow that piled up all the way to her thighs. These were the moments she was certain she would lose a limb, or perhaps even worse. Maybe she would just lay down in the snow and no one would find her. Just like the creatures who had lived in this court.

But the river always appeared again, rising out of the earth like a welcoming embrace. Her toes would thaw and Freya leaned down to touch her hands to the warm, life giving water. At least she had this. At least.

Then, out of the snow, a monolith of a castle arose. It was a beautiful building with spires made of glass and ice. It looked like something out of a storybook, one she would have read as a little girl and pretended to be the presiding princess.

Her father had encouraged such thoughts when she was so little. He thought it was grand to have a child who wanted to be the hero in a story. And now that she had her opportunity to do so, Freya wasn't all that certain that she enjoyed the feeling. The responsibilities piled up on her shoulders and now she feared she'd take the wrong step and the glass castle would shatter.

The castle was a chance to get out of the cold, however far it was.

She would have to break away from the river, though. And that posed a problem.

Freya eyed the distance between herself and the doors, then prayed it wasn't so long that she'd freeze to death. The river didn't go anywhere near the castle, and she didn't have any boots.

"Please let me keep my feet," she whispered.

Though it was a price she would pay to get her sister back in her arms, she also knew it was unlikely that she could get Esther back without the important appendages.

Taking a deep breath, she plunged into the mounds of snow and charged toward the castle with single minded intent. If the inhabitants were dead, maybe there was still someone left. A servant. Another type of fae creature that had taken over in the absence of whatever things were meant to be here. Someone had to still live within the castle walls.

Didn't they?

The snow was so cold her feet burned. And then, just before she reached the doors, she couldn't feel them at all. She dragged them through the snow, but she wasn't all that certain she was actually step-ping on them right. She didn't know where her toes were, or even if she was stepping on the flat surface of her feet.

Hissing out a breath, she caught herself on the handle of the front door to the castle. The icy metal stung her hands.

She needed to get inside. And fast.

Freya heaved the door open inch by inch through the snow until she could step through and into the safety beyond. At least it wouldn't be so bitterly cold within. Right?

She was very wrong.

The stillness inside the castle made her hands shake. Snow had blown through the broken windows and covered everything in the greeting room with snow drifts. The furniture looked white now that a fine layer of snow turned them soft around the edges. The chande-liers from the ceiling dripped with sparkling ice. The drifts made it impossible to know where the walls were or perhaps where partitions had been set up to allow courting couples' privacy from their keepers.

A lone chair was in the middle of the room, its back turned completely to ice. But next to the chair was a small chest. White powder covered it in a fine layer of sparkling diamonds. But it was her only hope.

Freya stumbled to the chest and fell onto her knees before it.

"Please," she whispered. "Please have something warm."

She slid her fingers along the lid, but it was hard to find where the clasp was. Ice had wiggled underneath the lip, nearly freezing the entire box shut. But she managed, even with fingers that were slowly turning purple.

Freya opened it with a frustrated grunt and then peered inside.

If she could have thought of anything besides the cold, she might have wondered where the contents came from. A pair of boots, just big enough to slide her feet into. Three pairs of woolen socks, a heavy brocade dress with wool underthings and a cloak. All laid out for her to slip into at the moment she needed them.

But Freya wasn't thinking about who might be helping her or what the fae had in mind. She yanked up her sodden skirts and immediately put all three layers of socks onto her feet. The first pair was hot to the touch, almost as though someone had warmed them already by a fire.

Yanking the boots on, she then tugged her clothing off in one fell swoop. Though shaking, she dressed herself in the woolen underthings before really looking at the heavy over layer.

It had been embroidered with a thousand tiny diamonds. All up and down the hems were patterns of little snowflakes, hardly the size of a thimble. On the larger panels were much bigger snowflakes. All of them were individual, perfectly created, and without a single sign of age.

The cloak had been given a similar treatment, although the inside was lined with a thick layer of pure white sheepskin.

Once all the layers were on her body, Freya felt better. She felt herself warming up, although she still needed to...

She peered into the box and there, at the very bottom, was a bundle of sticks, flint and steel, and a small note. Now, she knew someone was helping her. The Goblin King? Again?

No, she couldn't imagine he would be so bold. She was too close to beating him, and if he was helping her now, then she would assume he was fighting against himself. He didn't want her to win, he'd made that very clear. So this wasn't the king.

Hesitating, she reached into the box and picked up the note.

Whoever finds this crate, I hope it helped you in an hour of need. The fire-place is magical. I'm not certain that will help anyone in the long run, but if you start a fire within it, then it won't go out until you press the button above it. The Winter Court is not without its comforts. Please, make yourself at home. There is light reading provided in the nearby bookshelf, or much darker reading within the side table.

Darker reading?

Freya turned the piece of paper back and forth, as though she thought more words might appear if she rotated it. Who would leave a note like this? It was almost as though they had known they would die and that someone would come into the castle looking for them.

She had no time to ponder.

Grabbing the flint, steel, and tinder, she rushed to the wide fireplace in the back of the room. The edges were carved with elk and bears chasing each other from top to bottom. White marble so lovingly cared for that it was obvious someone had once loved this place.

Steel struck flint, and the tinder burst into blue flames. With that, the entire fireplace came alive and light poured through the room. Heat blasted and melted the snow nearby.

"Darker reading," she whispered.

Though she still shivered and was terrified about what she would have to do in the morning, she also wanted to pass the time until she could rest. Freya opened the drawer in the small end table, the ice thawing at her touch.

The tiny book was bound in black leather with gold caps on each corner. The fine filigree made her pause. Somehow, the strange pattern was familiar. She couldn't hear herself think past the chattering of her teeth, thus the pattern didn't immediately dawn on her.

Sitting as close to the fire as she dared, she thumbed the first page open and read it aloud.

"The history of the Goblin King," she murmured, stroking the edges of the pages. "What Goblin King?"

But she already knew. There was only one man who wore a dark suit with gilded edges. Only one man who could have filled an entire book with his secrets to be recorded for centuries to come.

Only one.

She leaned against the edge of the fireplace and resolved herself to a long evening discovering all the Goblin King's secrets. All she had to do was stay awake.

CHAPTER 27

The story told in the little book was one she couldn't reconcile with the Goblin King she'd met. It was written in his hand, telling of a war between the courts that spilled across the land. Though the tale wasn't kind to the other fae creatures, it showed how much he believed in his own people. The Goblin King didn't want them to fight, but he had fought on their behalf. He'd chosen to support another fae who he thought would end this madness.

And when the fae didn't, the Goblin King had taken matters into his own hands. Such was his life. Such was his legacy.

But the kindness written onto the page, looped with graceful handwriting…. surely that couldn't be the Goblin King she knew. These were the words of a hardened soldier, a man who knew what to do and what it would take.

The Goblin King in her mind wasn't that person. He didn't have a care in the world other than stealing little girls away from their families and then seeing what deal he could get out of it. The bargain of a mortal life for entertainment was the work of a man who had no morals whatsoever.

Except, this book claimed he was so much more than that.

Freya wondered just how much she'd learned about the man who led the courts. She knew the others weren't as simple either. In her journey across the faerie lands, she had only scratched the surface of who they were, what they had done, and the madness that lay within their hearts.

It was the last line of the little book that caught her eye the most. The last line with a flourish that gave her information about the Goblin King.

Freya stroked her finger over the single word and said it out loud. "Eldridge," she whispered. "Is that your name?"

The word filled her with a sense of power. Like she had finally gotten a secret out of the Goblin King that was hers and hers alone. He'd probably never told anyone his real name. No one had referred to him by it that she'd met thus far.

He was a mystery to all who knew him. A mystery to all the people who called him king. Now, she had something to hold above him. Something more important than just a deal or magic that would change the fabric of time.

Leaning back in her chair, she put the little black book back in its drawer and stared into the fire.

Freya had to do something. Sitting in this castle while reading about the Goblin King was getting her nowhere. She had to move forward.

Perhaps there would be details within the castle that might give her a clue about the creatures who had once lived here. Maybe there was a gathering spot. A holy relic. Something that would turn her in the right direction so she could defeat the Goblin King.

Still, her first priority was to get her sister back.

A stiff wind blew through the nearest cracked window and with it, a voice.

"I told you they were all dead," he whispered. His voice was light but filled with disappointment. "Why did you still come?"

"Are they dead forever?" Freya stood up and placed her hands on her hips. She searched the shadows for him, where she knew he was likely hiding. "Or are you just saying that to prevent me from moving any farther? I've almost beaten you, Goblin King."

"You haven't beaten me yet, and I don't think you ever will." His voice was already drifting away from her. "You'd have to be someone else entirely to defeat the Goblin King."

"Oh, I think I'm capable of doing what you least expect." The fire warmed her back and gave her courage. "How far are you willing to go to win this game?"

"As far as it takes."

Was the voice drifting down the hall? That's what it sounded like, although she still couldn't see him. She frowned and followed the sound of his voice.

The halls were very similar to the rest of the castle. Snow drifts made it difficult to tell where the walls and the floors met. It made the entire place look smaller than she had expected a castle to feel. It was, after all, supposed to be home to an entire court.

She watched the chandeliers swing in the wind. Snowflakes drifted down from the ceiling and rested on her shoulders. She could feel their cold touch like little kisses through the thick woolen cloak.

This impossible place had finally convinced her not to question the extraordinary. She would just accept that sometimes, she wouldn't understand what was going on.

And that was all right.

Just like she was following a voice down a hall. A voice that laughed when she peered into rooms, hoping to see the visage of the Goblin King.

"I know your name!" she called out, her words ringing through the ice.

"Is that supposed to frighten me, Freya of Woolwich?" His warm breath brushed the side of her neck. The heat of him lifted the hairs there. "I know your name, too."

She whipped around and stared into the blank space behind her. No one stood close enough to breathe on her, let alone be visible for her to see. But she could still feel him. He was there, and yet not.

Freya shook her head and refused to allow him to intimidate her. This was not how their story would go, and she would rewrite the pages if she had to.

Straightening her back and squaring her shoulders, she ground her teeth and hissed, "You won't stop me. I will get my sister back."

"I have no doubt that is your plan," he replied. Again, from behind her. Like the magic he was using was attached to her back.

Freya heard him at all the times when she least expected it. Maybe he was following her around, holding onto her neck and twisting her head to see the things he wanted her to see. Maybe she had only completed this quest because he wanted her to.

"I will not stop," she repeated, as though the words were more important than anything she'd ever said in her life.

"I'd be disappointed if you did, Freya. But you don't know where to go anymore."

Perhaps she was a little stuck, but that had never prevented her from moving forward before. She might not have Arrow. But she didn't need a guide to find her way through the faerie courts. She had found the castle, hadn't she?

Freya wandered through the halls to the back entrance where she stood staring at a wall of broken windows. A snow filled garden was dotted with stone statues of people and creatures that didn't look real at all. Women in ball gowns that were larger than life. Wings stretched from their backs like giant butterflies, so big she didn't know how they'd carry such appendages.

They were beautiful and carefully carved, so anyone walking through those gardens would have to stop and stare at the masterpieces.

Where to?

Somewhere in this castle was a hidden secret that the Goblin King had hidden. The last piece of this puzzle that would save her sister. Freya could find it, even if she doubted herself.

Taking a deep breath, she closed her eyes and listened. There, on the wind, was the faint sound of goblin bells.

It was all she needed. Freya lifted her booted foot and stepped out of the castle. Her feet crunched through the hard layer of ice on top of the snow with an audible crack. Flakes still fell from the sky, dancing gently as they went.

Though she could feel a slight wind on her face, it stirred nothing in the garden. The statues remained still. The snowflakes fell calmly in meandering paths. And all was silent as death in the garden of the Winter Court.

She stepped closer to the nearest statue and stared up into its face.

With a gasp, Freya realized these weren't statues at all. This was the Winter Court. The man she stared up at had once been alive and handsome as the sun. Frost spread in patterns over his cheeks and dusted his eyelashes with white glitter.

He didn't move. He didn't breathe. The wide wings like a lunar moth spread out behind him with their edges dipped in ice that melted down over his shoulders.

She reached up and placed a hand on his cool cheek. "This is a cruel way to die," she whispered. "I'm sorry it had to be like this for you."

Compassion told her to move. She wandered through the garden, pausing at each of the people who had died where they stood. Not a single one wore an expression of fear or anger. They all looked like they'd fallen asleep. Beautiful and yet eerie.

Who did this to an entire court of faeries? Who would have harmed so many people who were unaware that an attack was coming?

She only knew of one person who was capable of such cruelty, although now she wasn't certain. The Goblin King wasn't what she had expected.

Freya thought about the little book, the one where he had fought a war and still felt guilty for the death he had wrought. How hard he had fought to keep his soul through something that ripped and tore at the goodness in a person's heart.

Eldridge. The Goblin King.

Freya held tight to the name and continued through the garden until she stood in the very center. The frozen creatures here all stood in a circle. They held their hands over their hearts, as though they were praying in the moment they had frozen.

She stepped to the side of one, placing her hand on its back to steady herself. The woman's eyes were closed as well. Her features serene at the end of her time.

At the very heart of the garden, a single glass snowflake rested on top of an altar. She thought the stone statue that held the Winter Court's most precious possession aloft had been granite, although snow and ice had taken away much of the beauty in the stone. The glass snowflake itself was delicate and devoid of any snow or ice. She worried if she touched it, then the entire thing would fall apart in her hands.

And there it was. The end of her journey and the easiest thing to just reach out and take. Freya should have snatched it immediately and crowed to the heavens that she'd beaten the Goblin King at his own game.

She could hear the ticking of time, as though he'd placed a clock against her ear, so she knew just how long she had before her sister was lost to her forever.

Freya had not the faintest idea why she hesitated. She stared at the glass snowflake, the spires that branched off each other, and the delicate way the dim light played on each pronged tip. She stared at the piece that would end all of this.

Instead of rushing to grab it off the ground, to peel it off the altar and steal what was rightfully hers, Freya sank down into the snow beside the nearest figure. She placed her hands over her heart, feeling the rapid beat underneath the many layers keeping her warm.

She sat.

She stared.

And she wondered why she couldn't take it. No matter how hard she tried, she couldn't take that snowflake. Not yet.

Then Freya realized she was waiting for something. Though she didn't know what she was waiting for, she knew it was not yet time to end this game.

CHAPTER 28

S he wasn't sure how long she sat in the snow, staring at the center of the garden with the other faeries. Her mind wandered through all the things that could have happened here. All the horrors these people must have felt as the cold closed in on their bodies and froze their hands in place.

The snowflake was magical. She was certain of that. Light played within the glass even when the dim morning light wasn't hitting it. The colors changed, moving like there was something alive inside the magical object.

The Goblin King's words played in her mind. Everything he said long ago, just now, and then the words in the book which she'd never heard him say but could still hear in her mind. The handsome goblin had made it very clear that his kind was different. That he was different. And she still had a sick feeling in her stomach that she had missed something.

This deal was too easy to beat. Too simple for a mortal like herself, although she was proud of the tiny details she'd noticed. Sure, she had defeated the Spring Maiden, but not on her own.

She had discovered the Summer Lord's secret and bested him, but the Goblin King had given her the details on how to start.

The Autumn Thief was kind to her, but only because she wanted to get back at the Goblin King.

And now?

Who was helping her now, when she had yet to go through a court without a faerie guiding her?

The worry locked her in place until she knew the truth of it all. Until she was certain this court wasn't hiding something from her. Not any longer, at least.

The book had been the first clue. Why would the Goblin King allow a journal of his own to be in a table, lost within the Winter Court, but with a note for someone to find and read it? That made little sense.

Then, of course, his voice in her ear. He had always followed her to see what she would do, but that didn't mean he was so vocal in every place where she'd been. He usually wanted to hide, not guide.

And lastly, the goblin bells. She couldn't see any bells here, and it wasn't right for her to hear that chiming without a goblin to sell his wares. That could only mean the Goblin King was here, or at the very least, that he was trying to hide something from her.

Goblins. Bells. Frozen courts. None of it added up.

Freya was smart enough to know when she was being played, and he was taking advantage of this moment. Perhaps the time had already run out. She didn't know how long she'd been traveling or how quickly time moved in the faerie courts.

Her time might have been up long before she even accepted his deal, and all of this had been some elaborate plan to reveal it at the very end. When she had lost all hope.

She stared at the snowflake and tucked her hands deeper into the cloak. The cold wasn't seeping into her skin. She worried that might be because she had such progressed frostbite that she was incapable of even feeling the cold any longer. Her fingers were still pink, though. Her hands still moved in finite, difficult movements that should have been impossible if she was frozen.

"Eldridge," she called out. Her voice danced across the gardens in a soft hush, like skirts swaying to music she couldn't hear. "I want you to come out, now. I'm finished playing this game."

No one responded to her at first. Maybe he was trying to see just how truthful she was being. Perhaps he thought he could convince her otherwise if only he waited her out.

Freya had all the time in the world. This deal didn't feel right. Her sister wasn't even here, not in the Winter Court at least. And the reality was that Freya didn't know if she could ever get her sister back.

If the Goblin King was being honest, then Esther already had a tail. She already was affected by the magic in this place, and maybe returning to the mortal realm was a foolish thing to ask. What kind of life would her sister have in the mortal realm now?

Esther would have to hide in the forest for the rest of her days. She would never marry. If a husband found out about that tail, then she'd burn on a pyre. The villagers would call her a witch. A servant of the devil who wore his mark rather obviously.

Freya couldn't allow that to happen.

She supposed they could cut the tail off, but what amount of pain would that cause? It was a magical change in her sister's form, and such a curse was dangerous to deal with. The wound might never heal.

"Eldridge," she called out again, this time with a sharp crack to her voice. "I said I'm finished."

Though he didn't materialize in front of her, his voice still moved through the garden. Slithering through the snowflakes like a snake hidden in the grass. "You can't give up now, Freya. Not after everything you've done."

"I'm not giving up." She stared at the altar as though his voice came from within the glass artifact. "I wouldn't ever give up when it comes to my sister's life. But I know this game doesn't make sense. The rules have changed too many times. There is too much for me to under-stand, and I think you have been lying to me."

"Lying?" he murmured in her ear. "It's impossible for a fae to lie."

"No, I don't think it is. I think you can twist words until a person can't tell the truth from story. You told me that the impossible was possible in this place, and yet..." Freya pulled her fingers from her cloak and stared down at the warm digits. "I don't know what's real anymore."

"Everything is real here. All your desires, your dreams, all the things you craved from the mortal realm that could give you nothing." Shadows moved behind one of the frozen faeries. "You have found so much here, Freya. All you have to do is see the magic for what it is."

"And what is it?" She shifted into a crouch, ready to tackle him when he moved around the frozen fae.

"A gift." His voice tickled her right ear. "My gift to you."

"That's a twisted way of looking at it." She watched the shadows slide down the arm of the frozen faerie. The touch was almost sensual.

Except, the more she watched, the more she felt the touch on her own body. His clawed fingers slid down her arm, scraping her skin as it went. But that wasn't possible either. She had on so many layers of clothing. She couldn't feel him touching her.

And yet, she could. More impossible things, proven to be entirely and utterly possible in this unusual place.

"Freya," he whispered. "You are so close to finishing this."

The magic within the snowflake glowed, chipping away at her resolve.

A blast of heat struck her back. She stumbled, reaching out a hand to catch herself. An arm caught her around the waist and tugged her against an invisible, solid chest. "Why are you hesitating? Do you not want to save your sister?"

"You know I want to save her more than anything."

"The last piece of the puzzle is right in front of you. And yet, you refuse to take it. Almost like you want this game between us to continue. If I didn't know you better, I'd be flattered." He released her with a sudden shove that sent her stumbling toward the snowflake. "End it, Freya."

It was right there. So close her breath fogged the glass edges, crystalizing in spidery frost that stretched over the surface. In the reflection, she could see the Goblin King.

He stood in a tight black suit, as always, with his white billowing shirt revealing the solid planes of his colorless chest. His eyes watched her with an intensity that made her blood heat.

He wanted her to take the snowflake. Why? Why did he want to be beaten at his own game?

She watched those strange, swirling eyes turn dark.

"How are you still waiting?" he asked. "Take it. For the faerie realm, damn it, Freya! Take the damn charm and this will all be over!"

Something clicked into place in her mind. Some truth that had been just out of reach the whole time he shouted and tried to convince her that this was the only choice. She lifted her hand, hovering it above the glass surface, watching him for any reaction.

He jolted forward, almost like he was waiting for something to happen. Then he froze in place when he realized she hadn't touched it yet.

"So that's the truth of it, then," she said. Freya turned around and faced him even though she could no longer see the Goblin King. "This isn't the last charm. The snowflake has nothing to do with any of this, does it?"

He remained silent. A wind touched the snow at both of their feet, shifting it around his invisible heels.

She couldn't quite see him, but that didn't matter. Freya knew she had understood what this whole game was about. She pointed at the snowflake and said it again, "That is not the way to get my sister."

Finally, he relented. "And yet again, you have surprised me, Freya of Woolwich."

"Is that what turned all the faeries here to ice?" She looked at the poor souls who were frozen for eternity. Trapped in the same place they were the moment they fell under the Goblin King's spell and touched something that wasn't theirs. Something that should have remained a secret. "Were you going to freeze me like all the others?"

The snow stirred and footprints approached her. Whatever magic had hidden him melted away like he had shaken off a cloak.

The Goblin King stood before her with sadness in his eyes. He lifted a hand and palmed her cheek, his skin so cold to the touch it was like she had pressed her skin to ice. "It's not a bad way to end this story," he murmured. "They have no idea what has happened to them. They live in a world where they see their own happy memories, played over and over again. I promise, they're not in any pain."

"I don't want to relive my memories." She should have pulled away from his touch, but she didn't. Freya soaked in the smooth texture of his palm and the dangerous thrill of his claws touching the side of her neck. "I want to live new experiences. To see new things and to find adventure around every corner."

"And that's something you found here, isn't it? You were just Freya of Woolwich before the faerie realm. A young woman content to live on the edge of the forest with danger so close you could almost touch it. But never did." He stroked his thumb over her cheekbone. "Until now."

"Until you," she agreed. "Now, I want my sister back."

"I can't give her to you." The wind ruffled the dark locks of his hair and the dim light played across the shimmering surface of his skin.

He was otherworldly. So strange it made her heart race, but the way he was looking at her almost made her want to lean forward and press her lips to his. Just to see if a man so dangerous could taste like apples on her tongue.

"You told me to end this," she whispered. "And I want to more than anything else. But I know that snowflake is not the correct essence of the Winter Court."

"Then you have to find it."

"I already did." It was a long shot, but she guessed what was the real essence of Winter. "I think it's you."

His eyes widened. In shock or surprise, she didn't know which.

He still released his hold on her and took a step away. "I told you, the essences of the courts are items."

"No, you never said that." She followed his steps in retreat, forcing him to look at her. "You said to collect them. And I think, considering all the impossible things that you taught me were possible, you're the essence of this court. You were the one who put the snowflake here. You were the one to freeze them and end their lives. Perhaps, in that moment, you became more than just the Goblin King. You became tied to this court for all eternity."

"That is madness." He swallowed hard, eyes darting side to side as he searched for an escape. "No one would ever dare accuse me of being a court's—"

She interrupted him. "You are. And I am claiming you like I claimed all the others. I defeated you, Goblin King. Now, you must return my sister to me."

His wide, horrified eyes watched her approach him. He didn't move when Freya reached out and cupped his face. Just as he had done to her.

The Goblin King sighed, closed his eyes, and tilted his cheek into the warmth of her touch. "Ah, Freya. I didn't deserve you or this challenge. But yes, you have bested me."

"And my sister?"

His hand lifted between them. He covered her eyes with his palm and replied, "It's time to end our story."

CHAPTER 29

The Goblin King lifted his hand from her eyes and she could see only darkness at first. Then, tiny pinpricks of light appeared. Blinking into existence like a thousand stars just waking up.

He stepped away from her and a few more lights bloomed. They cast a silver glow over the room, similar to the first one she'd seen him in. Still filled with stars. Still so thoroughly strange with floating orbs representing planets. These were more like giant glass balls, however. Not at all like the metal ones she'd seen before.

It was beautiful here, but cold, vacant, and vast. She couldn't imagine living here, in this dark place, for longer than a few days. Let alone an eternity.

And she feared the Goblin King had been here for a very long time.

Speaking of the strange man, where had he disappeared to? Turning around in a circle, she tried to see where he had gone. But she couldn't make him out in the darkness.

Then, with a blinking crackle of light, everything fizzled into view. A thousand stars all burning so brightly they lit up the entire room and the man standing in the center.

The Goblin King wore his black suit with gold edges. His hands were held loose at his sides. Even his posture was less straight than normal. It appeared that he was preparing himself for the defeat she was about to give him.

She should have felt triumphant. And yet, she almost felt sorry for him. He was afraid, and for that, guilt ruined the moment.

"My sister?" she asked, clearing her throat.

"Even now, after all the things I've shown you, the only person you're interested in talking to is that little brat of a girl who doesn't care where you are." He held his arms open, not as if waiting for an embrace, but perhaps as though he were questioning Freya's sanity. "I have given you everything you ever desired, and yet you still wish to leave this place."

"What are you talking about?" Her mouth gaped open in surprise. "Given me everything I've ever desired? What?"

"You think I did all this for your sister?" The darkness warped behind him, shifting and changing until she saw herself. Freya could see the Spring Court, Summer, and Autumn. She watched as she struggled and the vision of herself, embarrassing as it was, defeated them time and time again. "You think I would go through all this trouble just to keep a mortal girl?"

"You were the one who kidnapped my sister for a necklace," she snarled.

How dare he try to turn this around on her? As if she was the one in the wrong, or she should be thankful for him providing this adventure. Her sister was turning into a goblin, for heaven's sake!

He tilted his head to the side and watched the emotions playing across her features. She didn't hide them. Let him see how angry she was. How much his words wriggled their way underneath her skin.

And yet, the Goblin King still smiled. He still watched her with those strange eyes, as if he were hoping she would piece together the final bit of their story. "Come on," he said, his voice guttural and deep. "Surely you've put it together by now."

"Goblins kidnap people for making deals," she replied. "That's what you do. Why would I ever consider there was any other reason?"

"Because of what I've done for you!" he snarled.

For the first time, she saw the visage drop from his face. Anger rocketed through him and sparks of magic flew from his hands. Rage changed his entire form, shifting him from Goblin King to a creature of madness and strife.

Freya didn't know how to respond. All that he'd done for her?

The Goblin King had done nothing to help Freya. Sure, he'd guided her throughout the faerie courts, but that didn't mean he was helping. He was self serving and the only reason he was intervening was to tilt her back onto the road he wanted to watch. None of that was for her.

The more she thought about it, the more angry Freya became.

"For me?" she growled in response. "What have you ever done for me?"

He lunged forward, hands outstretched to cup her jaw again. Except this time, he wasn't nearly as gentle. The tips of his claws dug into her neck in tiny pricks of pain.

Freya winced and tried to pull herself from his grip. But he wouldn't release her. Not this time.

The Goblin King's eyes flashed bright silver, like the very moon itself was glaring at her. He bared his teeth in an angry snarl. "How dare you not see everything I have done! When I first saw you in that glade, I thought you were just a meager little cockroach like the rest of humanity. Skittering through the walls of the world to spread disease wherever you went. But then, you challenged me. That fire in your eyes was the first clue you were unhappy in your cottage by the wood, surrounded by people who would never understand you."

"That's not true." She jerked her chin, but his claws scraped deeper.

"Oh, it's very true and you know how honest I am." He forced her to look up into his eyes. Those flashing eyes burned. "I watched you for hours and I knew you wanted more out of your life. You were dying in that pathetic little hovel you call a home. All your potential rotting away as worms ate through to your core. I saw you for who you were and you were begging me to turn your life upside down."

No. He was wrong. She was happy living with Esther in their parent's house. Freya wanted nothing more than to go back to that time and that place, with no goblins to bother them again.

She was.

But why did her stomach twist when she even thought about returning to that mundane life?

He squeezed her jaw one final time, then released her from his grip. "You see?" he asked. "Now you understand the thrill of the hunt and the chase is in your blood. You are like me, Freya. You heard the call of the goblin bells and while you refused us for so long, finally you have answered."

This time, her own anger burned in her chest. Damn him and the beauty of this place. Damn the stars in the sky that he wrapped around him like a cloak, and damn the golden planets spinning wildly around him.

He could pull all the stars from the sky and she would never bend a knee.

Freya lifted a hand and pointed at him with a jab. "You are wrong. And now that I have defeated you, I can say that without question. I have proof. I am here. I bested you. And now I want my sister back. Stop stalling."

He froze in place, and it almost seemed like tears cast a sheen over his eyes.

The Goblin King returned to her, standing so close she could feel the heat of his body. He didn't touch her this time, but he didn't have to. All her attention was captivated by the red stain of his lips, spread across his mouth like he'd kissed someone with blood red lipstick. Pointed teeth worried at a thick bottom lip, and his heart thundered in the pulse at his neck.

The long column of muscle worked in a deep swallow. He stared down at her with misty eyes, as though she'd said something that would forever change the future. As though she had forsaken him.

But she had no ties to the Goblin King. Freya was a mortal woman with mortal desires, and she needed to go home.

Anger still burning in her chest, she closed the gap between them until she could feel his breath on her lips. "Give me back my sister, Goblin King."

"I am offering you the world," he whispered. "You wanted a villain for your story, so I became one. You wanted to fight for your sister, so I made it more difficult for you. And when you stepped off the path, I guided you back to it."

"I want the mortal realm."

"When will you admit that you desire the bright-fire pain of adventure?" He lifted his hand then, curling his fingers around the notch of her hip and tugging her into his arms. "I've seen you ache for a taste of faerie wine, luxurious jewels on your fingers, and the eyes of thousands upon you that glow with jealousy. You never bought from the goblin market, but you stared every day. Esther saw it too. Or did you think she wandered off on her own?"

"Such evil gifts would harm us." The words felt flimsy now that she'd seen the entire realm of the faeries.

He reached up and caught a lock of her hair. He wrapped it once, twice, thrice around his finger. "I know what they say about me and my kind. Beware of goblin men, who march through haunted glen. For the Goblin King has no heart, and heartless things cannot offer what they do not have to give. But I am no monster, Freya of Woolwich. The man standing before you is real and wise. I have lived a thousand years, and now I am the one begging you. Use your common sense. Stay here with me in the goblin realm where impossible is a word that will never leave your lips again."

How was she to say no to that? The Goblin King himself was begging her to stay. The only thing he hadn't done was get onto his knees and press his hands together in prayer.

Freya didn't understand why he was so adamant. She didn't know why he wanted her to stay. And all the problems that might arise when she returned home bubbled back into her mind.

Esther would have to hide.

Freya would have to take care of everything from now on.

The wards still weren't built.

The goblins would still peddle their wares, except now she knew they were children.

Her mind was forever changed by this place, and she feared the boredom of life would soon overtake her again. Would she return to that strange door in the wood? Would she ask for the Goblin King to make her another deal?

She opened her mouth and almost thought she would say yes. But the words she said were, "No. I want my sister back and I want to go home."

The Goblin King flinched away from her, squeezing his eyes shut as though in pain. "I should have made a deal for a lock of your hair, but I underestimated you."

"Yes, you did."

He took a deep, steadying breath, then opened those strange eyes. He leaned so close she could see the stars inside the silver. "I will not make a deal with you again. If I have to lose, then I will enjoy this last moment between us."

The Goblin King tugged on her waist, then pressed his lips to hers. His lips were soft as velvet, brushing against her own in a sensuous slide of lips and tongue. He exhaled into her lungs, sparks of magic that took root in her very soul.

His fingers flexed against her ribs, dangerously clutching her with claws raking at the cloak that cushioned his grip. He tugged her ever closer, devouring all the air in her lungs and yet still demanding more.

She broke the kiss first, desperately inhaling a deep breath.

The Goblin King snarled a short, "I'm not finished with you yet," before he palmed the back of her head and drew her in for a second kiss that seared her flesh from bone.

He kissed her as though his life depended on it, then released her with a sudden shove that sent her careening back.

"I accept defeat," he said. His breathing ragged, his eyes wide and wild. "Get your sister, Freya of Woolwich. Thank you for the memories."

"What?" She felt the magic before it pulled her into a portal.

The last thing she saw of the Goblin King was him turning away from her and holding his head in his hands.

Freya ran through the dark tunnel of the portal like the hounds of hell were on her heels. She didn't want to think about the sadness in the Goblin King's eyes. She didn't want to think about how horrible it made her feel, or how her gut twisted into a knot.

All she wanted was to get her sister and get out of this place. The Goblin King wasn't someone she had to save.

He had stolen her sister.

He had forced her to make a deal that he thought he wouldn't lose.

Whatever he was feeling was his fault. Not hers.

The Goblin King would not get into her head and change her thoughts like that. Goblins were bad, monstrous creatures who lured little girls and boys into the forest where they could turn them into creatures like themselves.

They weren't children who ate like animals at dinner. They certainly weren't the little dog faced creatures who helped her throughout the entire realm and were dear, wonderful friends. They weren't Autumn Thieves with hearts of gold but a darkness hidden underneath their skin, a pain that was soul deep and couldn't be healed no matter how hard they tried.

She slowed as she reached the end of the tunnel. Light split through the darkness of the universe and showed her where Esther was.

Her sister sat in the middle of a meadow with the rat-faced goblin laying at her side. Esther hugged her knees to her chest, tilted her head back, and laughed at something the goblin boy said. He was lying on his stomach, feet in the air, that ugly tail waving as though he had been good. Like a dog.

This was over. She didn't care what Esther had to say. This was all over and they were going home.

She burst out of the portal and stepped onto the emerald green grass that filled the meadow. Breathing hard and already swearing, she charged toward her sister like a woman possessed.

Esther turned around and crab walked into the goblin boy. He threw a protective arm around her shoulders and bared his pointed teeth.

"Who are you?" he snarled.

"I'm her sister." Freya reached for Esther's arm, tugging at her to stand up. The goblin boy rose onto his feet as well, but he didn't try to stop her. "Come on, we're leaving."

She'd thought Esther wouldn't fight. Sure, maybe her sister would argue a bit while they walked away. But that was fine. She had known Esther was a little softer than most, and she'd be unlikely to insult the goblins by leaving immediately.

Instead, Esther ripped her hand out of Freya's and stumbled back into the goblin boy's arms. "What are you doing here, Freya?"

She looked down at her empty hand, then back at her sister. "I thought it was rather obvious what I was doing here. You made a deal you shouldn't have. I came after you."

Esther's eyes widened with every word. She looked at the goblin boy, then at Freya, then back to the goblin again. "I'm so sorry. I didn't know she'd follow me all the way here. If I had—"

He smiled and touched his furry forehead to Esther's. "You have nothing to be sorry for. Talk with your sister, I'm sure this is all some misunderstanding."

Misunderstanding?

Freya's cheeks heated with more anger than she'd felt in years. This rat-faced goblin thought he knew her sister more than her? That they could just talk with Freya as if she was the one who was losing her mind?

Absolutely not. This wasn't a situation they could talk through. Esther was coming with her. Now.

She reached for her sister's hand again, only for Esther to yank it out of her reach once more. Esther glared at her, and for the first time in her sister's short life, Esther put her foot down.

"Freya!" Esther snapped. "I'm not going back with you. I don't know why you would ever think I'd want to return to the woods in that stupid little town we grew up in, but I made this choice. I wanted to go with the goblins, and I did. You will not change my mind."

Any retort she might have had dried up on her tongue. She'd never heard her sister argue before. Esther was the amiable one. The sister who rarely talked back to anyone and would help any person who asked.

Esther arguing with Freya was enough, but to know that Esther was arguing on behalf of a goblin? That gave Freya pause.

She slowly reached forward for Esther's arm one last time and then stopped when her sister flinched away. Again, the goblin boy wrapped his arm around Esther's waist and tucked her into the waiting haven of his arms.

Freya looked between the two of them, frowning. "You want to stay here? With the goblins?"

A long, plush tail curved around her sister's waist and touched her opposite knee. "I don't think I have a choice anymore. Do you?"

And there it was. The permanent changes her sister had experienced and what would keep her out of the mortal realm forever.

All the blood drained from Freya's face. She was light headed, weaving where she stood, staring at the white tail her sister had grown. "No," she whispered. "I guess you can't come home after all."

Esther laid her hand on top of the goblin boy's at her waist. They looked every bit the couple who were wonderfully in love. Who was Freya to break that up?

A part of her had known this might be possible. She should have been aware that such things could have happened in the time she'd been gone.

And she didn't know how long it had been for Esther since they had seen each other. Time seemed to be nothing more than an idea here in the faerie courts. It might have been years for Esther to develop a relationship with this young man.

After all the goblins she'd met along the way, she couldn't think of him as a monster. Or a creature. Or even as anything less than human.

He was a goblin boy, certainly. But he wasn't a monster.

Freya sighed and pinched the bridge of her nose. Sweat trickled between her shoulder blades as the sun warmed her. While she pawed through her thoughts, Freya reached up and unclasped the beautifully beaded cloak. It fell to the ground with a heavy thud, and that was the end of it.

She opened her eyes and sighed. "Okay," she whispered. "I won't make you leave. I just wanted you to come home if you wanted to and I... I defeated the Goblin King for you. I hope that proves how much I love you. And how much I'll miss you."

Both Esther and the goblin boy froze. They looked at each other, then back at her. "You what?"

Considering they both said the words with equal parts horror and fear, she worried that wasn't the right thing to say. Freya crossed her arms over her chest and frowned. "I beat the Goblin King. He made a deal with me that if I could collect an essence from each of the Courts, then I could take you home. I did it."

"But..." Esther looked at the goblin boy as if she was making sure her words were correct. "I didn't make a deal with the goblins. I could have gone home whenever I wanted."

So she could have just asked Esther to come home? At any point?

Freya's blood boiled. That lying, cruel, horrible... "That rat bastard," she swore. She sheepishly glanced at the goblin boy and added, "Sorry."

"No need to apologize, I understand the turn of phrase." His whiskers twitched. "I'm sorry to make you repeat yourself, but did you say you beat the Goblin King in a deal?"

"Yes, is that so surprising?"

"But he can't be beaten." The goblin released her sister and took a worried step forward. "He can't."

"Well, I did." Why was that so hard for everyone to believe? Even a king could be defeated, no matter how much they revered him.

"No, no, he just can't—" The goblin boy didn't have time to finish explaining anything to her.

A sudden rumble shook the ground they stood on. And in the distance, Freya realized there was the faint outline of a castle. Dark and ominous, it hid in the tree line as though it were part of the forest itself. A plume of smoke rose from the walls and another echoing boom rocked the glen they stood in.

The goblin boy reached for Esther's hand and clasped it tight. "We have to run."

"I know," she whispered. Then she looked over at Freya. "The Goblin King can't be beaten. Once he is, he has to give up the throne. That means someone else will take his place, and he'll be locked away for the rest of time."

Freya again felt her entire body list to the side. That couldn't be right. He wouldn't have helped her defeat him if he was going to pay the price. Why would he do that?

She supposed the right question was why the Goblin King ever did anything. He never made a lick of sense, and it had only gotten worse the deeper she dug into his past or who he was.

Her sister and the goblin boy turned as the ground shook underneath their feet. A great rumble rose from the very earth itself and suddenly, everything was falling. All the trees pulled up at the roots. Were they running as well? They were certainly moving as though they were.

Freya darted after her sibling and they all raced away from the castle. She risked a glance behind them and saw a dark cloud was spreading across the land. It reached forward with dark tentacles that slithered through the leaves, searching for whatever it could find.

"Freya!" Esther shouted. "Watch out!"

She faced forward at the last second. A tree was falling onto its side where it had jostled with another. The great trunk wasn't going to stop until it struck the dirt.

With a shriek, she fell onto her hip and slid beneath it. The leaves caught at her hair and beads ripped as she rolled across the ground, but she made it just in time. The sound of the tree striking the earth made her ears ring and for a moment, she was completely disoriented.

Dust and dirt flew up in the air and it took a while to settle. She didn't know which way Esther and the goblin boy had gone, but if she was going to find them, then she needed to get moving. She knew that. But her head hurt so badly.

A hand appeared out of the dust and latched onto her arm.

Esther.

She hauled Freya up, coughing and pulling her out of the wreckage. Together, the sisters raced through the forest to the goblin boy's side.

He held out his hand for Esther to take. "Come on! This way!"

Freya had no idea how long they ran, but they skidded to a stop before a small door in the ground. Like a trap door, really, although she didn't know where it would lead.

The goblin boy wasn't looking at the door. He was staring back at the castle with tears in his eyes. "Oh no."

Freya shouldn't look. This wasn't her fault. The Goblin King had done everything in his power to ensure she won, and of course she was going to. She wouldn't trade Esther's life for the Goblin King's, especially when it was all a lie.

But she did turn around. She looked at the rubble of the castle and the black smoke that surrounded it like an ominous cloud.

"What happened?" she asked. "What happened to the king?"

The goblin boy held both his hands over his heart and shook his head. "The king is gone," he whispered. "Long live the queen."

"The queen?"

He met Freya's horrified gaze with one of his own. "What have you done?"

EPILOGUE

Freya followed her sister and the goblin boy into the trapdoor. It led to a series of dirt tunnels, lit by torches dug into the walls. She had no idea where he was bringing them, but she did trust that he wouldn't hurt them.

But most importantly, she held onto Esther's hand the whole time.

How long had it been since they held hands like this? They must have been children, although she couldn't think of the particular moment. It was like they suddenly just stopped holding hands at one point and never realized they wouldn't do it again. Until now.

She squeezed Esther's fingers. "What does it mean for the fae if the Goblin King is no longer in control?"

Esther shook her head. "I don't know. They waited for him to rule for a very long time. They like him a lot, you know. He's a wonderful king, and he keeps the courts under control far more than anyone else ever has."

Well, that made her feel even worse. Freya knew she shouldn't take this on herself, but somehow, it still felt like it was her fault. If she had realized that Esther couldn't have made a deal, no matter how much the Goblin King said she had, then all of this could have been avoided.

"It wasn't your fault," Esther said, as though she could look into her sister's mind. "If the Goblin King wanted you to beat him, then nothing would have changed his mind. He's a good man, and perhaps a little too manipulative for his own good. You couldn't have known."

No, she supposed not. But that didn't make her feel any better.

She needed a distraction and fast. Freya nodded at the goblin boy. "So what's the story with him?"

Esther tucked a strand of hair behind her ear. "I know I wasn't supposed to talk with them, but I did. Even before the time you saw me. He and I have been friends for a long time, but then we realized we wanted it to be more. He's kind, Freya. So much kinder than any human man I've ever talked with."

The rat-faced boy turned a corner, then peered around it, waiting for them to catch up. She watched his eyes as he looked at her sister. And yes, they were kind. He looked at Esther as though she were all the stars in the sky combined into one person.

Love. She'd only seen the emotion in one man's eyes, and that was her father's. He had doted on their mother just as this goblin boy looked at her sister.

Esther tugged on Freya's hand. She wore a worried expression on her face. "Are you okay with this? I didn't want to tell you, and I probably should have. I just... I knew how much you hated goblins. Maybe you still do, I'm not sure."

"No," Freya replied. She smiled softly and tugged her sister closer so she could wrap an arm around Esther's shoulders. "I don't hate the goblins anymore. I never should have. That was wrong of me."

And how strange it was to admit that. She should have known better than to even be here. Their mother would have shouted until their eardrums bled.

But this was such a lovely place. The people were so strange, and the world was so much bigger than she was used to.

"Damn it," she whispered under her breath. "I suppose the Goblin King was right, after all."

They caught up to the goblin boy, whose ears twisted in her direction. "What was he right about?"

She took a deep breath and let it all pour out of her. "That I was unhappy living in the mortal realm, and I would have done anything to experience at least a little adventure in my life. I would have rotted in that cottage by the wood, and no one could have convinced me there was a better life than that. Not until now."

"We've all been there," the goblin boy replied. He grinned and pointed above them. "We're going up if the two of you are ready."

Freya flicked a clod of dirt off her shoulder. "Am I ever."

The goblin went first, clambering up the wall with his claws sunk deep into the earth. He flipped another trap door up and then tossed down a rope ladder for the two of them to climb up.

Esther climbed up the rope rungs, talking as she went. "What are you going to do now, Freya? Are you going to go home then?"

"I don't think I can." She waited until her sister pulled herself out of the earth before Freya started up the rungs. "I feel a certain responsibility to get the Goblin King back, although I wouldn't have the faintest clue where to start. I don't even know if he's still in the castle."

She caught the trap door and hauled herself out of the tunnel. They were in a warm, earthbound house. A fire crackled in the corner, the stone fireplace billowing heat. A small table with carved animals on the legs stood to her right, and a tiny cot about the size of a child's bed was to her left. A brightly colored quilt was draped at the foot.

"How quaint," she said. "Is this yours?"

Except, when she looked at the goblin boy, there was a new person standing next to him. A small black and white dog with his ears pressed flat to his skull.

Freya was nearly dumbstruck. But she managed to stutter, "Arrow?"

"Hello, Miss Freya." He wrung his paws. "It's nice to see you."

"Oh, it's so good to see you too, my friend." She dropped onto her knees and drew him into her arms for a tight hug. "I'm so sorry for what I said when I left. It was cruel, and you deserve better."

He hesitated before he laid his head on her shoulder. "All is forgiven. Besides, I think I can help you."

"You can?" She drew back and stared into his dark eyes.

"I know where to find the king."

OF SHADOWS AND ELVES

OF GOBLIN KINGS BOOK 2

CHAPTER 1

They plotted rebellion over a cup of earl grey tea.

Three strange figures sat around a small wooden table in the middle of the underground home. A dog in a pressed velvet suit. A young man with the face of a rat and a tail that curled up behind him. And her sister, Esther, with her own fluffy white tail that wagged with frustration whenever one of the men spoke.

Freya stood in the doorway to the single bedroom, leaning against the doorframe, warming her fingers around the chipped, blue teacup in her hand.

It wasn't a particularly good cup of tea, if Freya was being honest. She blew on the top so it at least looked like she was drinking it. Poor Arrow would be insulted if she admitted that his prized talent of making tea wasn't a talent at all.

Her sister and the goblin boy were obviously feeling the same way. They looked at each other, then back to the mismatched porcelain as though the liquid might claw its way into their throats. The tea certainly had a bite to it.

Esther leaned forward, took her sixth cube of sugar, and plopped it into the cup. "So what you're saying is that the Goblin Queen was the least favored candidate for the throne. That's why the King we know took it?"

"Yes," the goblin boy replied.

Lux, Freya reminded herself. He'd informed them that his name was Lux, and he'd appreciate it if Freya would stop referring to him as the rat goblin. Or the goblin boy. Or any of the other nicknames she'd come up with.

Her cheeks still burned at the memory. Old prejudices died hard, and she was trying her best. But sometimes that old hatred of the goblin kind spilled out of her mouth without her realizing just how horrible it sounded.

"If no one wanted her to lead all the faerie courts, then how did she take the throne?" Esther shook her head, clearly struggling with her thoughts. "We all know the Goblin King wanted Freya to defeat him. He practically handed her the victory on a golden platter."

"Excuse you," Freya interrupted. "If I hadn't had his help, I still would have beaten him."

"That's cute." Esther rolled her eyes. "He helped you far more than he should have if he knew he would lose the throne. Why would he be willing to give it up so easily if he had fought his entire life to keep it?"

Arrow stood and padded to the back of the room. He opened up the wall to reveal a pantry so stuffed with food that a couple tins jumped from a shelf and rolled across the floor.

He spoke while tossing random vegetables over his shoulder. "The King has strange ways. Perhaps he already knew the Goblin Queen was plotting against him again. At least losing the throne on his own terms means he has some kind of control."

Freya licked her lips. It didn't sound right, no matter how many times she rolled the theory over in her mind. "I don't think he'd give up that easily. And when I saw him last, it was almost as though he was in pain. Like he knew what was going to happen, and that he didn't want it to happen. But he still let it."

And that was the biggest question in her mind. The Goblin King had made it so very clear that the only thing keeping him happy was that throne. He was proud to be the Goblin King. Everyone she'd spoken to actually liked him as their monarch. Even Arrow, who had lost his family in service to the fickle fae creature.

Pain bloomed behind her eyes, splitting between her brows and scissoring into her nose. The damned headache wouldn't go away, especially when she thought of the Goblin King.

She pinched the bridge of her nose and tried to blink through the pain.

"Cookie?" Arrow asked.

When she could open her eyes again, she peered down to see he had somehow pulled out a tray of tiny sugar cookies in the shape of stars. Maybe some sugar would do her headache good.

"Thank you," Freya muttered before popping one in her mouth and taking another. "Regardless, we need to know what will happen when the Queen is officially on the throne."

Arrow carried the silver tray to the table and set it down. "I think we already know that. The entire kingdom was crumbling around your ears when you ran away from that castle, Freya. She's only going to keep making it worse."

"And do we even know who she is?" That would make all this even more difficult if they didn't have the faintest idea of where to start.

Why did this feel as though she were back to the beginning of the story? Freya had fought through all four courts of the faeries to get her sister back, and she'd succeeded. Esther was sitting right there, within her reach. And yet somehow she was back to the start of yet another quest that would require her to search through places she hadn't the faintest idea how to navigate.

Arrow sat back down and held his snout in his hands.

Painful silence rang throughout the room. Freya looked between all three of them, guilty expressions painted across their faces.

"Well?" She asked again. "Out with it if you all know something I don't."

Lux cleared his throat. "The Goblin Queen is... well, sort of the Goblin King's sister."

He had a family? Freya hadn't ever given it much thought. She knew the other faeries did, of course. She'd seen the goblin children and their messy dinners. Obviously they had families somewhere that she hadn't met.

"Sister?" she asked. "What do you mean, *sort of* his sister?"

Esther frowned as well. "Why would his sister want to hurt him?"

Freya stepped up to the table and placed a hand on Esther's shoulder. They both were aware of what a sister would do to keep her sibling safe and unharmed. Even come all the way to the faerie realm and defeat a king.

"Well, he was born in the Autumn Court. Even became the Autumn Thief for a while there, but then some things happened and..." Lux ran a hand underneath the collar of his shirt. "He decided to go to the Winter Court, where things could cool off. They adopted him. And in the Faerie Wars, he fought by their side. So she wasn't really his sister by blood, but by circumstance. Anyway, after the war he became the Goblin King and sacrificed the entire Winter Court to save everyone else."

Freya remembered that bleak place and all the dead faeries who were forever frozen in time. "I saw them. They were terrifying and beautiful at the same time."

Arrow snuffled. "Sounds like the Winter Court. Regardless, they have a vendetta against the King for freezing them for an eternity. If she's out, that means the Goblin Queen will release all the Winter Court back to their rightful places. And they were known for their cruelty. In fact, I'd argue they were worse than any other court."

"Worse than the Spring Maiden?" Obviously Freya had her own thoughts on the matter. The Spring Maiden's court was by far the most alarming.

"Much worse." Arrow looked troubled by the thought, but he still stated his opinion firmly. "Perhaps we should enlist some of the other courts to help our plan."

"No," Lux replied. "We've been over this. The Goblin King is our problem, and any other courts getting involved would only make this an all out war."

"Maybe that's what everyone needs to see. The Goblin Queen is everyone's problem, not just the Autumn Court's."

"And you want to be one of the warriors in this upcoming war? A small dog with a penchant for suits?" Lux tossed his hands in the air, leaned forward, and the argument was back on.

They had talked about this for days since they arrived in Arrow's small home. Freya had heard every angle of their arguments at least twice.

Arrow didn't want to go into a battle without assistance. He believed the other courts would help them, and that it was smarter to have more allies when dealing with someone as powerful as the Goblin Queen.

Lux wanted to sneak into the castle without anyone knowing. He didn't want the Queen to realize what was happening, and he certainly didn't want the other courts involved. In his opinion, the only court that was worth its salt was the Goblin Court. Everyone else could no longer be trusted.

They would argue until they were blue in the face, but Freya already knew their opinions wouldn't change.

She squeezed Esther's shoulder, then knelt down beside her. "What do you think?"

Esther's eyes widened in surprise. "Well, I don't know. I'm not one to know what to do in a war."

"I don't think it has to be a war." She watched as Arrow stood up on his chair so he was at least the same height as Lux while he yelled. "I think if we get the Goblin King back, then he can take the throne from this woman. Obviously he did it before, and if we give him the tools to do so again..."

"Then he would." Esther nodded. "But how are we going to get him back is the question?"

"I'm afraid my imagination isn't that creative. What do you think?" Freya already knew her sister was smart, but now that Esther had been here for a while, Freya had to assume that her sister knew these people better. "You've lived with the goblins and met more fae than me. Surely you have some opinion?"

Maybe it was the first time she'd asked her sister for something so important. Or perhaps Esther was so used to being the child that she hadn't thought Freya would ask for her help.

Either way, Esther opened her mouth a couple times before she finally spat out words. "Uh, well, I think you should go alone. Or with a single guide. The Goblin Queen must be similar to the other fae we've met. Shiny, new things will keep her entertained while you search for the king. And you were the one who defeated him in the first place and put her on the throne. Why wouldn't you seek out this new queen for her favor? Considering you were the one to put her there."

It was the best plan Freya had heard yet.

Sure, there were a lot of holes in it. She could fail at any point, and most of the concept was making it up as she went along. But it was far better than reaching out to the other courts, and a hell of a lot better than some assassination mission.

Freya wasn't a killer. She didn't even know what she'd do with a sword.

She stood up and pressed her hand to the muscles of her aching back. "Enough, boys."

They continued to argue as though she hadn't said a word.

Anger flashed like lightning in her chest and this time, she shouted. "I said, enough!"

They both fell silent. Lux's cheeks burned bright red, and he sheepishly looked at her sister, then back at Freya. "My apologies, Freya. I got wrapped up in the argument, I suppose."

Arrow, on the other hand, didn't look like he was upset at all. He crossed his paws over his chest and stared at the other goblin with curled lips. "I'm not apologizing. This fool seems to think we're all warriors here. He needs to realize we're nothing more than a dandy dog, two mortal women, and a goblin who is barely more than a baby."

Lux lunged to his feet and pointed at the dog. "I've done more in my life—"

"What did I just say?" Freya snarled. The anger in her tone must have frightened both of them this time. Lux sat back down and Arrow stared at her with wide eyes.

She didn't want to argue with either of them. And she didn't want to scold them like they were children. But they both needed to listen to her without trying to put their own opinions on the table.

"As far as I see it, this downfall of the courts is my fault." Freya lifted her hand for silence when Arrow opened his mouth. "No, listen to me. This is my fault because I was the one who beat him. No one else had ever done so, regardless if he helped. I still was the one to beat him. I was the one to put the Goblin Queen on that throne."

It was hard to admit. The truth sometimes stung, and she needed to figure out how to fix this. If they couldn't ask the other courts, and they couldn't work together, then she would just do it herself.

Freya was used to that, anyway. She almost preferred working on her own.

"So," she continued. "I think I'm going to make a plea to the Goblin Queen."

"Excuse me?" Arrow replied. "You will do no such thing. She's a mad woman!"

"For once, I agree with the dog." Lux leaned back and crossed his arms over his chest. "The Goblin Queen isn't someone you can defeat in a battle of wits. If you thought the Goblin King was difficult, she's ten times worse."

"Then I will figure it out just as I did the Goblin King." Freya shrugged. "This isn't up for debate, gentlemen. I've listened to the two of you argue every single day for the past week, and we've gotten nowhere. I'm the one who gave her the opportunity to take the throne, so she will be more likely to trust me. Don't you think?"

She put her hand on Esther's shoulder and smiled down at her little sister.

Esther nodded in agreement. "I believe this is the best choice for Freya. She'll sneak into the castle. Find the Goblin King. And then we can move on from there. The Queen won't stop her if she thinks that Freya hates the Goblin King just as much as she does."

Arrow curled his lips in a snarl once again. "And just who do you think is going to bring you to the Winter Court?"

"You, actually." Freya turned her grin on the dog. "You know the courts better than anyone else here. So I need you to bring me into the castle, and then you'll be my trusted advisor. An explanation for why I remained when I could have taken Esther and run."

"I think it's an awful plan."

Freya shrugged. "You think every plan is awful, Arrow. Now, why don't we prepare for a new adventure?"

CHAPTER 2

She let the boys continue arguing until they were blue in the face. Arrow and Lux were bound and determined to be the most knowledgeable about their own kind. And while she appreciated the help, most of the time she just wanted a straight answer.

Freya ducked into the single bedroom to gather her things. Not that she had a lot, but she had collected a few items she wanted to keep close to her person.

But in planning to leave, she realized that she would miss this earthen bound home. The dirt walls might have been off-putting to some. She found them cozy, even the little roots hanging from the ceiling. There was a single bunk bed in the corner, too small for either her or Lux to sleep on. So the two of them had laid blankets on the floor. The quilted, patchwork patterns were now dear to her.

These people had become her new family in such a short amount of time. Even the two goblins who she had once hated and feared.

Shaking her head, she tucked as many of her items into a leather bag. First, what little clothing she'd taken from her sister and a few others who had stopped by to visit. Then her boots, because she'd steal

Esther's for walking to the castle. And lastly, the three items that the Goblin King had sent her to get.

She sat on the edge of the bunk where her sister slept and held the three pieces in her hands. A tiny little vial with a sprig of lavender. A little pot of perfume that had made her head spin and her mind forget everything. Lastly, the rolled up portrait of the Goblin King and herself.

How strange it was to think that she'd gathered these items only a few weeks ago when it felt like a lifetime. A battle between herself and the Goblin King should have taken years. They'd packed it into a few months.

Carefully, Freya unrolled the portrait and stared down into the Goblin King's eyes. He watched her with a severe expression befitting a king, but she thought maybe the portrait looked like he was furrowing his brows. In pain?

She leaned closer to look, only for that splitting headache to slice through her skull again. She hissed out a breath and touched her hand to her forehead, letting the portrait roll closed again.

"Freya?" Esther's voice broke through the pain. "Are you all right?"

No, she wasn't all right. This damned headache refused to go away, and it made it so difficult to focus. She could hardly breathe right now, and the pain was only getting more frequent. It seemed like it was coming back daily now.

But she couldn't tell her sister any of that. Not when she was planning to leave again.

Freya shook off the pain, opened her eyes, and smiled through gritted teeth. "Just a headache is all. I think it's from those nitwits yelling in the kitchen since we've gotten here. My ears are constantly ringing."

"The kitchen?" Esther grinned. "I would have called it the dining room."

"Perhaps the living area?"

The sound of her sister's giggle banished any lingering pain. It was so good to hear Esther happy again. Had she laughed since they had lost their parents? Not like that.

Freya reached out her hands for Esther to take and drew her sister to sit beside her. "Thank you for helping in there. I don't think we'd have settled on any plan if the two of us hadn't thought of something."

"Neither of them are thrilled with this plan of ours."

"I didn't think they would be. But I also won't ask for their permission to fix something I broke." The headache bloomed again, and she winced. "I think I need some fresh air, regardless. That's what mother always did for her headaches."

Freya had completely forgotten about their mother's headaches until this moment. She'd always pressed her fingers to the same place, right in the center of her forehead, as though someone had struck her with a hammer.

How odd.

But she didn't have time to ponder what that meant. She had to pack and prepare herself for another journey, when she didn't know how far that journey was going to be. And she had to say goodbye to her dear sister, yet again.

Although, leaving her sister was easier this time. Esther didn't seem like the same little girl she remembered in their cottage. Something in this realm had changed her. Or maybe Freya was just seeing her for the adult she was and likely had been for a while now.

Esther reached for her hands and squeezed them tight. "I want to go with you."

The words hung between them, too dangerous to give proper thought. Esther couldn't come with Freya. Two mortal women wandering through the faerie realm would be foolish. The Goblin Queen would catch them, or some other faerie who wanted to entertain themselves with a human novelty. Not to mention Freya wouldn't be able to focus when she was trying to make sure her baby sister was safe.

"I don't think that's a good idea," she replied.

"Of course it is! We worked well together in the kitchen, and I think we could do that again. The sisters of Woolwich can defeat any faerie who walks before them." Esther squeezed her fingers again. "And I've missed you, even though I also feared what your thick skull would say when you found me."

She should have guessed Esther would say something like that. Sighing, Freya shook her head again. "I don't think the queen will want to see you, Esther. This entire plan is based on the fact that I saved you from the Goblin King, and then I stayed behind. Maybe that's part of the deal with the king, I don't know. I'm going to have to lie through my teeth and you'd be a distraction I can't afford."

Esther frowned, and the expression was one Freya knew well. Her little sister was about to explode with anger, and this little hovel might cave in under the power of her emotion. Esther knew how to shout so loud even the clouds hid from her rage.

But Lux moved into the doorway and cleared his throat. Esther's anger faded as she turned to look at the goblin boy she so clearly loved.

"Arrow has gone out to gather a few things for this new journey," he said. "But I agree with Freya. I think you should stay here with me."

"Why?" Esther asked. "Why should I stay here when there's so much for me to do? I could help her, Lux. You know as well as I that there's so much I could do here in the faerie realms."

"I do know that." He crossed his arms over his chest and his tail snapped with frustration. "I also know there's a lot of people who will need our help here, and I can't manage all on my own. The faerie courts are crumbling as we speak. Faeries from every season need someone to go to, and we're going to be the ones who guide them."

Freya thought that was a rather splendid idea. She met Lux's gaze and watched as he flicked his eyes to Esther, then back to Freya.

Right, she was supposed to help convince her sister.

Leaping into action, she released Esther's hands and got to her feet. "How many people will be affected by this?"

Lux took her cue and ran with it. He stepped into the room and waved his hands above his head. "Countless. Really, every court is going to need someone to guide them through this. The Goblin Queen doesn't care who she hurts as she forces her way onto the throne she's wanted for so long. We need to gather a haven for everyone."

"An army?" Freya couldn't help but poke at the argument he'd just been having.

His brows drew down tight and his jaw jumped. "No," he replied. "Not an army. This will be a refuge camp for those who want nothing to do with the queen. A place for like-minded individuals to find others who want to help."

"Right," Freya replied. She nodded and pursed her lips. "Of course, not an army. However, if I needed you to get involved when I end up in the Goblin Queen's new castle?"

"Freya," he snarled.

Esther stood from the bed with a sigh. "Stop arguing, you two. I can't take everyone being like this. I get what you're both bashing me in the skull with. You don't want me to go with Freya. Neither of you want me to, and apparently my opinion means nothing."

The last thing she wanted was for her sister to feel as though she was unwanted. Freya had just found Esther after tearing the world apart for her, and she craved time with her wayward sibling who always sought adventure.

In a way, Freya supposed that might bother Esther as well. Freya had never been the adventurous one. Esther was more likely to wander into the woods or plunge into a frigid lake to swim. Yet it was Freya who was having all the adventures here. Not the adventurous one.

She stepped close to her sister and cupped Esther's jaw. "If I could take you with me, you know I would. You've proven yourself quite useful, Esther. I couldn't have a more formidable partner if I searched all the corners of the earth."

"Then why aren't you taking me?"

"I need you to be here. With Lux. There are so many people who need help right now, and you two are the only ones who know how to get them to safety." Freya knew the excuse sounded flimsy at best, but it was the truth.

If there were people who needed help, then she would not stand by and let them flounder. Freya was responsible for their losses too. Someday, she hoped, she might be able to make it up to all the faeries who missed their king.

The padding footsteps of a small dog approached them through the earthbound home, and Arrow stuck his face around Lux's leg. "If we're going to the Winter Court, I assumed we would leave right now."

Freya supposed there was no time like the present. They'd already decided on the plan which wasn't much of one. They didn't have to argue about anything now.

Sighing, she reached for the bag she'd left on the bed. "A week off from adventure was rather nice, wouldn't you say?"

Arrow snorted. "You wouldn't know how to live a life without adventure if you tried."

She looked over at Esther, who had covered her mouth to hide her smile. If only the goblins knew just how unadventurous Freya really was. She wished she could play her life back for them in a dream bubble like in the Spring Court. They'd be shocked to see how little she had done in the mortal realm, and how much she had changed in a very short amount of time.

Grinning, she reached for her sister and drew Esther into her arms. "I'm going to miss you so much," she whispered into Esther's hair. "At least this time I get to say goodbye."

"I'm going to miss you too." Esther pressed her face into Freya's shoulder and for a second, it felt like nothing had changed at all.

They were still two sisters who had gone through hell together. They had been raised to be strong and capable, but leaned on each other when they needed to. Even though everything had changed.

Esther wanted to stay here forever. She had a life with this goblin boy who had stolen her heart. And Freya?

Freya still had no one but herself and the hope that she could fix what she'd broken. What would happen after she did that? Where would she go once she'd pieced back together the shards of the faerie realm?

Sighing, she drew back and gave her sister a watery smile. "I'll be back before you know it. Just keep everyone safe while I'm gone."

Arrow's wet nose pressed against the back of her hand. "Excuse me. I don't care who's safe, I just want to make sure my house isn't ruined when I get back. Keep everything clean, Esther. Don't let anyone into the structure who's larger than Lux, for all the faerie realms. They'll tear the whole thing down by the roots and then where will I live?"

Leave it to Arrow to bring them all back to earth.

Freya rolled her eyes, stared up at the roots in the ceiling, then blew out a long, measured breath. "All right, Arrow. How are you getting us into the Winter Court?"

CHAPTER 3

Arrow had created a portal for them in the middle of his garden. Though it had no frame, the colorless surface looked eerily like a mirror. She stared into her reflection that was slightly off, perhaps a little more transparent than she would have expected. Almost as though the portal were made entirely out of ice.

"Ready?" she asked one last time.

"You know, if you keep asking that question, it will not make either of us more prepared." Arrow shuddered. "Just make sure your coat is buttoned all the way up. We're both going to be freezing the moment we step through that portal."

Right. Arrow had insisted she put on multiple layers of clothing, because apparently the last time she'd been in the Winter Court was enough to convince him that she didn't know how to be in snow.

She did. It snowed in Woolwich every year, and she'd always been fine. He still wouldn't listen to the truth that she hadn't exactly had the ability to pack jackets when she was racing to get her sister back before the time ran out.

Huffing out an angry breath, she tugged her hat lower over her ears and fiddled with the mittens covering her hands. "Yes, I realize it's going to be cold."

He looked over at her with a calculating gaze, then nodded. "You look like a ball of yarn someone mangled."

"Thank you?" Though the words were a question. She watched as he stepped through the portal and disappeared.

The dog was a brat. Freya unfortunately didn't have time to scold the little rascal before he'd stepped through the portal. She supposed there was only one way to admonish him now, and that was to follow him into the depths of the Winter Court.

She didn't want to go back there.

Freya stepped through the portal herself and tried very hard not to wince at the feeling of ice shards sliding along her skin. Every portal was different, it seemed. This one was not friendly at all.

The cold pierced her skin in tiny daggers all over her body. It didn't matter that she was wearing warm clothing. The cold sliced through every woolen garment with ease. Icy wind dug into her flesh and poked at her very heart, stealing her breath away.

And stepping out onto the other side of the portal was no better. The very air filled her lungs with more ice shards and the cold stung her cheeks, reaching deep into the bones of her skull. Even her eyes felt like they were freezing in place.

Teeth chattering, she searched for Arrow. He had somehow pulled a hat out of his backpack and tugged it down over his very large ears. A small jacket covered his body from head to toe, but he still shivered uncontrollably.

"Is it colder than the last time I was here?" she asked, rubbing her arms. She thought she'd been able to stand in this barren wasteland in just a ball gown while she followed the hot springs. Now, as she searched for the warm rivers, there wasn't a steaming pool of water in sight. She feared even they might have frozen over.

The entire landscape before them was buried in snow. Drifts of fluffy white ice buried anything that might have once been fences or gates. A few humps in the distance might hide houses, but she wasn't sure anymore. They might have also been giant creatures who had simply fallen where they stood.

Arrow huffed out a little angry breath. "I hate the Winter Court. This is why I didn't want to come with you last time."

The air between them turned even colder, if that was possible. They still hadn't talked about what had happened in the Autumn Court. Of course, she'd apologized, but he didn't wish to speak of the things that were said.

He'd still betrayed her. He'd gone behind her back and worked for his king, when she'd thought he was helping her. And worse, she had made it seem as though they would never be friends again.

Ignoring the conversation they needed to have was turning both of their stomachs. It made times like these with him, when they were both alone and capable of talking about what had happened, turn rapidly tense. The silence between them was filled with the anger of lies and heartbreak.

Was now the time to talk about it? Likely not. But she wanted to heal what had been broken.

Apparently that was a theme in her life these days.

"Arrow," she started, wondering how she was going to say the words that made her heart hurt. "I just wanted to say—"

"We have to keep moving," he interrupted. Arrow trotted through a snow drift, leaping into the air to get farther away from her with every bound. "We'll freeze in place if we don't. There should be a village up ahead where we can rest for the evening."

"Rest?" Freya trudged through the snow after him. "Why would we rest? Shouldn't we find the castle where the Goblin Queen is?"

"She'll find us," he muttered. "Don't you worry about that. No one comes into the Winter Court without her knowing."

Ominous. Freya didn't want to think about what the Goblin Queen would send after them. The Spring Maiden's guards had been terrifying enough, and those were creatures who lived in the season when everything was coming to life. She imagined the Winter Court had frozen ghouls sent after people the Goblin Queen wanted to disappear.

Shivering uncontrollably now, she forced her way through the snow drifts and tucked her hands underneath her armpits. Keeping warm was the only thing she could think about right now, and that took all of her attention. She needed to focus on not shivering so hard that she'd fall onto her knees.

But damn, it was cold. The icy wind stole all sense and reason with every blow. She staggered through the snow and storm, but found it hard to take a step forward sometimes. Freya's mind wandered until she lost sight of Arrow as he bounded through the snow. Only to find him again when he picked up his head.

With the guidance of her trusty goblin dog, they made it to the village. Arrow stood at the top of a snow drift and waited for her to reach his side.

Lungs heaving, she stood beside him and eyed the abandoned place that wasn't yet buried in snow. There were ten houses all together, each with glass paned windows and roofs that were once thatched. Now, snow covered everything and barred the doors from anyone entering.

Or leaving.

Freya lifted her hands to her mouth and blew into them. "Where are all the people?"

"Gone," Arrow replied. "Does it really matter where they went?"

When they could be standing in the middle of a graveyard, yes, it mattered where they went. She wanted to know if these people had left of their own accord, or if some terrifying snow monster had removed them.

"Which house are we going into?" she asked.

"Pick one. I don't think there's anyone here."

She chose a house in the middle of the village. It felt safer to be hidden rather than on the end where any monster could appear out of the snow.

Freya put her mitten covered hands on the metal door knob and pulled hard. It took her ten yanks before the snow finally gave way and allowed enough space for Arrow and her to squeeze through. Once inside, she closed the door with a firm jerk, then locked it.

"You picked a decent one," Arrow said. "Now get a fire going before the two of us freeze solid."

She turned around and took in the interior. It had seen better days, but at least it wasn't dusty or cobweb ridden. Apparently the cold made even bugs disappear.

They stood in what she had to assume was the living area. Four doors on either wall likely led into the kitchen or bedroom. A large area rug covered the floor, woven by careful hands in what might have once been a bright red. Two rocking chairs sat in front of a stone fire-place with patchwork quilts over the backs. Curtains covered the windows in a color that must have once matched the rug.

"Cozy," she said as she approached the fireplace.

There were still logs ready to be lit. Like the first castle in the Winter Court, she had a feeling these were spelled so they would light easily and set off heat. Anyone who lived in a place like this would have to make sure such magic was available.

Bright flames burst into life the moment she touched a match to the wood. Heat spilled into the living area and the light gave every-thing a little more life. She tugged off her mittens and placed her hands before the heat.

"If we're resting for the night, I thought we could at least talk." Freya glanced over her shoulder and sighed.

One of the doors was ajar and there was no talking dog in sight.

"Fine," she whispered. "I guess it's just me for the night, then."

Freya sat down in one of the rocking chairs and set it into motion. She stared into the flames, although she didn't feel all that tired. This adventure was vastly different from the last. She wasn't fighting for her sister's freedom, she was just trying to make up for the mistakes she'd made. And though she certainly was apologetic, part of this still felt like she was being punished for doing what she was supposed to do.

Beat the Goblin King.

That was her task, and she'd done it so well that the entire kingdom had fallen into shambles.

Maybe she should feel a little bad for it, but she didn't. Not really.

That headache bloomed behind her eyes again. This time it was far more painful than normal. It blistered through her skull and would have sent her to her knees if she hadn't been sitting down. The only thing that helped was staring into the fireplace, although that made no sense. Light should have made her headache worse.

She didn't know how long she remained still and quiet, but eventu-ally she became aware that the other chair was moving. A shadow sat in it, or at least the shape of a man, and when she glanced over, her heart leapt in her chest.

The Goblin King sat beside her. He rested his hands on the chair arms, with clawed fingers dangling over the ends. The tufts of his ears were a little bare, and his skin was duller than she remembered. Even his clothing wasn't quite right. The normal crushed velvet black suit was gone, replaced only by a white shirt with an open collar, and black pants that were rather old. His feet were bare, toes curled on the floor as though he was cold. But he was here.

Impossibly.

She blinked a few times to clear her vision, but the Goblin King never disappeared. He really was sitting in the chair beside her, gently rocking and keeping pace with her movements.

"You can't be here," she whispered.

"Freya, haven't I proven to you enough times that impossible things are possible in the faerie realms?"

She gazed into those swirling silver eyes, and she knew it could be no one but him.

The Goblin King had somehow found her.

"I thought you were in a prison or wherever the Goblin Queen puts people she doesn't like." Freya stopped her rocking and noted he did the same. "We had our last conversation, and then the Goblin Queen took over. So you can't really be here."

"And yet, I am." He turned, and she noted how sunken his features were now. Almost as though he hadn't eaten in a very long time. "What are you doing here, Freya? You beat me. You can go home to your little cottage by the forest."

"My sister didn't want to go home. She wanted to stay here with that rat-faced goblin boy." Freya's stomach still twisted at the thought. "She's in love with him, or so she claims."

"Do you think it strange that a human and a goblin could fall in love?" There was a darkness in his eyes she wasn't used to. A serious nature that went against all he was.

Freya leaned forward and met his gaze without hesitation. "Are you all right?"

"Why do you ask?"

"You look..." She gestured up and down his body. "You don't look like yourself."

"Where do you think I am, Freya? In a prison, placed there by the

Goblin Queen. I'm sorry I don't meet your fashion standards." He chuckled though, and the sound softened the bite of his words. "Now you haven't answered my question. Why are you still here?"

She didn't want to answer honestly. He'd take it personally and then run with it. She'd never hear the end of why she was here, and yet, she still had to tell him.

Freya leaned back in her chair and stared into the fire, because she refused to look at him while she said it. "I wronged you, Goblin King. I don't know if I would have changed my choices had I known defeating you meant throwing the faerie courts into a spiral. But I do know I would have figured out a different way. This is me fixing what I broke."

"Oh, Freya." The warmth in his voice had her turning to see a smile on his face. "Does that mean you like me after all?"

"Don't take this personally, Goblin King. I have a sense of honor. This doesn't mean I enjoy your company."

"I think it does." He grinned, but then started coughing.

The hacking sound echoed through the room. It was a horrible, lung deep sound that wasn't healthy. She'd only heard such a noise once, and the person hadn't lived through the night.

Freya leaned forward again, hand outstretched as though she might touch him. But at the last second, she thought better of it.

"Do you want a glass of water?" she asked. "Or is there anything else I can get you?"

"I'm not really here." He shrugged. "I suppose a glass of water wouldn't do anything at all, in the long run. It might make me more comfortable here, but not where I actually am."

"Where are you, then?" If she knew, then this would all be so much easier. She could go directly to where he was and save him.

The Goblin King chuckled. "Freya, you know that's not how any of this works. I can't tell you where I am."

"Can you at least tell me if you're safe?"

The shadows in his eyes darkened. His cheeks seemed to hollow even more, though she couldn't tell if that was the flickering of the light.

"No," he replied.

"No, as in you can't tell me? Or no, as in you aren't safe where you are?" Her heart thundered in her chest.

His answer was so important. He had to know her desire to know he was safe, even if they hadn't gotten along very well in her past adventure.

The Goblin King and her shared a strange bond. They were tied together because he'd freed her soul from a life of boredom and she had... Well, all of this was her fault.

Freya supposed he should hate her for that.

He never responded to her question. Instead, he stared into the fire.

She nodded, resolving not to push him when he was obviously affected by his location. "All right, then. I suppose we can just sit in silence then."

And they did. When she woke the next morning with a nasty crick in her neck, it was as if the Goblin King had never been here at all. Except for the faint smell of apple pie that still lingered in the air.

CHAPTER 4

rrow wiggled his way back into his jacket and sighed. "I don't want to go back out there," he grumbled. "It's too cold."

She also didn't want to dive back into the snow. But the morning came with a bright sun and glistening diamond chips on top of the ground outside the windows. They didn't have time to waste, and obviously the queen wasn't going to find them today.

So they had to continue on. Otherwise, they would get nowhere and the Goblin King would remain in his prison.

"I know," she replied. She shrugged into her own coat with a sad sigh. "I don't want to go out there either. But we don't have a choice, do we?"

"I suppose we don't. Since you dragged me all the way here."

Dragged? That was the game he was going to play? Arrow would pretend that she had forced him to come here, even though he'd volunteered himself for the difficult task.

Lux would have come in a heartbeat. The goblin boy had more in him than most, and he wanted to prove his bravery to any and everyone. Hell, he probably wanted to prove himself to the Goblin King and earn a favor.

She didn't know what Lux's plan was, neither did he, but she knew for a fact that he would have jumped if Freya asked him to come.

What she didn't know was why Arrow wanted to help after all that had happened between them. If he was going to be so awkward through the ordeal, why not just send the younger goblin and be done with it?

If only he would listen to her for a few minutes and let her ask.

Freya put her shoulder to the door, shoved the snow out of the way, and then gestured for Arrow to follow her. "Come on, then. Let's get this over with."

Arrow trotted out into the snow and put his nose up in the air. "There's a strange scent in the cabin this morning. Did you notice it?"

She stepped out into the fresh smell and nodded. "Yes, the Goblin King came to visit last night."

Arrow froze ahead of her. He lifted one back foot up, curling his toes against the cold, and then stammered, "Pardon me?"

"Well, I don't think it was really him," she clarified. Freya crunched through the snow and winced as she broke through the frozen top. "Maybe the right way to say it is that I saw a projection of him. He appeared last night when I was sitting before the fire. He... he didn't look like himself."

"No, I imagine he didn't." Arrow stared off into the distance, then started moving forward again. "The Goblin Queen was not kind to him, even when he lived with her all those years ago. At least, that's what my father always said. I was just a young goblin at the time, but I remember her."

Freya followed him over the ice and snow drifts, hoping that he'd continue the story in as much detail as possible. She found herself curious about the life the Goblin King had led.

"I probably shouldn't call him the Goblin King anymore, should I?" she muttered. "He's not the King. He's not the Autumn Thief either."

"He's just Eldridge now." Arrow kicked snow behind him in an angry gesture. "It seems wrong. He's so much more than that."

"I suppose." The sun beating down on her back at least gave off some semblance of heat. That warmth would make today's journey a little easier. "So what do you think the Goblin Queen's plans are?"

"She'll make an example of him. Eldridge will become a symbol of all the people who rose up against her, and all the people she denied peace or happiness." He frowned, clearly disturbed by the thought. "She was always a twisted creature. She'd rather harm than heal."

Freya followed his winding path, feeling as though she was lucky to actually have a guide this time. At the very least, Arrow pretended like he knew where they were going and that meant the world to her.

But when the silence between them drew too thin, she knew she had to ask more things about the Goblin Queen, or let all the poisonous guilt in her chest fly free. And considering the way his hackles rose whenever she started to speak, Freya thought it likely that Arrow wasn't quite ready to talk yet.

So this time, when she took a deep breath to talk, she asked another question. "What do you mean that the Goblin Queen was always a twisted creature?"

He jumped at the opportunity to explain himself and not talk about the apologies still left unsaid between them. "Even when she wasn't this version of herself, back when they took Eldridge into their family, she liked pain. I remember how the servants said she would kick them if they did something she didn't like. Little things like that. Everyone knew to stay out of her way."

"She sounds like a lovely person," she said sarcastically. "I still don't understand why she'd want to hurt the Goblin King, however."

"Well, he was her brother. And if we were crowning people based on power, she was the logical choice for Goblin Queen. But no one wanted her on the throne. We all knew what would happen if she was given that kind of power." A shiver of dread shook through his body. "No good would come from that. We all knew and none of us wanted to take that risk."

She pushed through a snowdrift that was as tall as her waist and pondered on his words.

The Goblin King had been close to this woman. And she still couldn't even think of the Goblin King by his first name. It seemed like something he should give her, or at least permit her to use. Even in her own thoughts.

She leaned down and picked Arrow up as he struggled to get

through the snow. Holding the goblin underneath her arm, she continued forward as though nothing odd was happening. "The Goblin King and her must never have had a very good relationship then."

"One would think they should feel nothing but disdain," Arrow replied, wiggling his legs to be put down. "But they were rather fond of each other if the rumors are true."

Why did that make her stomach churn in her belly? Even her heart skipped a beat at the thought.

There was no reason for her to be jealous of a cruel woman. The Goblin King wouldn't fall under the spell of a wicked creature like that. For all he was a fickle creature, he had a pure spirit, and he didn't like other people being harmed. Especially his own people.

Shaking her head, she forced the thoughts out of her mind. "And now?" She had to ask the question. She had to know if they were still close.

Arrow still struggled to be free of her arms. "I assume they hate each other now. Put me down, Freya."

She placed the goblin down onto the ground and tried to calm the rolling thoughts in her mind. She needed to focus on the here and now. They were still fighting a very real threat of freezing to death. She couldn't forget the quest at hand just because she'd found out something she didn't want to hear.

Freya put a hand to her head and sighed. "Fine, I don't know why I asked any of this. Where are we going, Arrow?"

"I thought we'd just wander through the snow until one of the Goblin Queen's men found us."

Her heart stopped in her chest. He couldn't be so foolish, could he? They would die out here if they didn't have a plan!

"Arrow," she snarled.

He tossed his head in the air and gave away his jest early before she completely lost her mind in anger. "We're not wandering, Freya. Do you really think I'd lead us in a wild goose chase? You're with me, not Lux."

"Right," she muttered, although she was still angry he'd try to trick her like that. "Then where are we going, if you don't mind me asking?"

"There are some stones nearby that used to be in the Queen's kingdom. She liked to put magic into things that... shouldn't have magic." He stumbled over the words, almost as though someone might be listening to them. "If we find the stones, then we can likely send her a message that we're here."

"I thought you said she'd know when we were in her kingdom?"

Arrow shrugged. He lifted his brows with concern. "She should have. That's always been the Queen's way."

And in the faerie realms, something being different made everyone worried. Freya knew how this went. But why would a quest like this be easy for them? After all, the faeries weren't exactly kind to mortals. They were even less kind to the goblin kingdom.

Taking a deep breath, she plunged through the snow with a little more vigor. They needed to find these stones, that much was certain.

That damned headache came back, but she dismissed the pain. At this point, Freya was learning to live with the discomfort. She still didn't know why she was getting them, but perhaps it was being in the faerie realm that made her head ache. It would explain why her mother had avoided magic so thoroughly.

The day passed slowly. Her thighs ached with the movement of forcing herself through the thick drifts of snow. She took deep breaths to keep her breathing even, but at this point it was impossible to even do that.

They stepped into a gulley between two enormous mountains. The channel had likely been carved by water so many years ago, but now it was covered in ice that was so thick she thought it perhaps stretched all the way to the bottom of what had once been a river.

Leaning her forearm against the stone wall, she heaved in a lungful of air. "Can we take a breath?"

Arrow had his tongue out, he was breathing so hard. Sucking it back into his muzzle, he nodded. "I think a break would be well deserved at this point."

"I thought this was supposed to be easy to find?" she grumbled. "Wouldn't the Queen want people to find her? She's a damned Queen of this Court."

"Well, not anymore." Arrow sat down in the snow. A puzzled expression crossed his face as he stared at her. "No one remains in control of their Court, you see. That's impossible. You can't be the Goblin Queen and the Winter Princess at the same time."

Freya supposed that made sense. There were a lot of responsibilities that went into both positions, and she could only assume there was too much for anyone to focus on both.

She tapped the stone underneath her hand three times. "Maybe that's why she hasn't found us yet. Unrest in her own home would make sense. If she didn't want to give up either throne, then wouldn't someone be fighting her from the Winter Court?"

"Freya—"

"Arrow, this makes sense. Maybe she already has her hands full, and that's why she hasn't found us!" Freya was certain she had figured it out. Now all they had to do was find the person who was opposing the Goblin Queen. Certainly they would help in their quest.

"Freya, stop talking and look at your hand." Arrow's eyes were wide and his tail was tucked between his legs.

Oh no. What was happening now?

Freya looked down at her hand and watched as spirals of blue magic spread throughout the stone. They glowed azure and lovely. Perhaps too bright for her to look at, but she couldn't keep her eyes off the movement. The arcs of light looked like waves she used to draw in the dirt when she was little.

"What is this?" she whispered.

"The Goblin Queen's magic," Arrow replied. "That's ice magic. Only people in the Winter Court have it. I never would have guessed she was powerful enough to fill an entire mountain with her power."

Freya looked behind Arrow at the other side of the gap. "Two mountains." Even those words felt wrong to say. "Two mountains, Arrow."

He followed her gaze, and they both watched as the swirls began on the other mountain as well. They trailed through the stone, seemingly creating a path for them to follow.

"Do you think we should follow it?" she asked.

"I'm not sure. Magic like that isn't always a good thing." Arrow gulped. "The Goblin Queen certainly knows we're here now, though. Maybe you should take your hand off the stone."

Freya pulled her hand off the mountain. A lingering cold bit her fingers as though she'd been holding them against ice too long. Fragile blooms of frost had already coated the bottom of her hand, although they didn't sting as she thought they would.

She closed her hand into a fist. "We're here to see the Goblin Queen, so we might as well follow the path she's laid for us."

"Look out!" Arrow's shout came moments too late.

A burlap bag obscured her vision and the iron band of a meaty arm wrapped around her waist. Though she struggled against the man's grip, she realized quickly there was nothing she could do.

The Goblin Queen's men had found them.

"Arrow!" she shouted. "Arrow, where are you!"

"Fight, Freya!" His next words were garbled, likely shouted through a sack like herself.

She tried to fight, but she wasn't a warrior. Freya kicked her feet and struck back with her elbows. The man who held her made a sound like a soft snort of disapproval, and then something very hard struck the side of her head.

CHAPTER 5

She became aware of her surroundings slowly.

First, she realized there was a new kind of headache pounding through her skull. All the pain seemed to spike from a single point just above her right temple. Confusing, at first, until she remembered the sharp pain of someone striking her in the head.

Though she wasn't certain what he had hit her with, Freya knew it was something hard, round, and likely the butt of a knife. Which meant the people who had snatched them up had weapons. The Goblin Queen's personal guard? No, that made little sense.

She wiggled her wrists and found that someone had bound them behind her back. Rough rope burned the sensitive skin of her wrists, not the silken ties she might have thought a queen like this to use. That was also strange. Faeries were fond of extravagant measures, not burlap and pain.

She opened her eyes but could see nothing. The bag was still over her head. That wasn't helpful. Although, considering the temperature, she was certain she was still in the Winter Court.

The cold stone beneath her wasn't snow, so she supposed that might be a clue. Freya wiggled a bit more, trying to get her wrists out of their bindings.

"I wouldn't do that if I were you." The voice was too soft to be intimidating. Light and airy, like snow falling in an empty field. The man's tones were eerily calming.

Freya should thank him for helping her remain steady. She needed to keep her wits about her and not panic in fear that she'd already been captured and rendered helpless. The Goblin Queen was going to think she was just a foolish mortal who lucked into beating the Goblin King.

Clearing her throat, she tried reasoning with the creature who had tied her up. "I'm here to see the Goblin Queen."

"Yes, I assumed you were trying to find your way through the kingdom when we came upon you." An intense sound followed his words. Was he sharpening a knife? "I understood you and your companion were arguing about the best way to find her. When you activated the magic, you should have known we would find you."

"I didn't know the magic was even there," she argued. "If we gave a grave offense by touching the mountain, I'd like to give my apologies personally to the queen."

Another sharp snicking sound. "I don't think the Queen would care to see you all that much. She's busy these days, you know. Running a kingdom and all that."

Should she tell him she was the mortal who had defeated the Goblin King? Freya didn't know if that would work for her or against her at this point. Maybe telling him that would make all this much worse.

But the threat of having bits of herself sliced off was enough to make her babble like an idiot. "I'd like to know where my companion is before I tell you anything else."

"The dog?" She heard metal being set down on stone, followed by approaching footsteps. "He's somewhere safe. You, however, are not somewhere safe at all."

A blast of familiar pain rocked through her skull. Not the knife this time, but the ache that plagued her for weeks. She winced and hoped the expression was hidden behind the burlap sack.

The scent of apple pie filled her nose. A warm hand landed on her shoulder, then the heat of a breath teased her ear. Impossible, considering he'd have to be inside the sack with her, but she felt him all the same. "Tell him nothing," the Goblin King whispered. "He's going to bring you to the Queen no matter what you say."

She wasn't so certain this creature wouldn't take her fingers off one by one until she told him exactly who she was. Gulping, Freya muttered under her breath, "And what if he starts to chop me up into little pieces?"

"Then you endure." The Goblin King chuckled in her ear, obviously finding her words amusing. "But he will not harm you, Freya. His threats are empty when the Goblin Queen is interested in who you are and why you are in her kingdom."

"How do you know that?" she asked.

The heat of his presence disappeared along with the headache.

She almost swore under her breath and screamed for him to come back. Was that damned headache all his doing? She'd been fighting with it for weeks now! The pain had been unbearable in the beginning and if he was the one causing such horrific pain, she would...

Fingers snapped in front of her face, just beyond the burlap. Light filtered through the holes in the wrinkled fabric, and she could barely make out the shadowy figure of the man crouched out of her reach.

He wasn't a very large man if his outline was anything to go by. In fact, she'd call him downright willowy if she didn't also know he could hurt her.

"Focus," he said, that calming voice soothing the pain in her skull. "I need you to tell me why you're here, little girl. You are a mortal in a faerie realm. I'm sure you know you aren't very welcome."

"I'm not talking to anyone who isn't the Queen." She licked her lips and hoped the Goblin King was right. "I think she'd want to see me, and I think she'd be furious with you if I showed up in multiple pieces."

The shadow reached forward and a chilly edge of metal touched the base of her throat. "You need to talk faster, mortal woman. I'm growing weary of your games."

She was too, if the threat was sawing through the cords of her neck. Freya had never actually been threatened by a faerie before. Sure, the Spring Maiden had wanted to keep her in a drug induced stupor. The Summer Lord had been interested only in beating her with words.

But neither of them had pulled a weapon and threatened to harm her physically.

Who were these feral faeries in the Winter Court?

She had to trust that the Goblin King knew what he was talking about. He'd lived in the Winter Court when he was just a young faerie. Surely he would tell her if there was something to fear.

So she mustered all the courage in her heart, gulped down the fear that shuddered through her chest, and called the faerie's bluff. "I don't think you'll hurt me at all. Not when the Goblin Queen wants to see me. And she does want to see me. I know you don't believe it, but I don't care."

"What makes you think she wants to see the likes of you?"

"You know why. Otherwise you would have left my companion and I to freeze in the snow." At least, she hoped she was right. Perhaps they liked hunting strangers down for sport. "You would have waited until we were nothing more than ice chips, like the faeries I saw the first time I was in the Winter Court."

Another voice interrupted them. This one was much deeper than the first, harsher and more direct. "You've been to the Winter Court before, mortal?"

"Yes." She took a deep breath and broke the rule the Goblin King had told her. The only thing she had to bargain with here was information, and surely this would come out before she met the Queen, anyway. "I was here to gather the essence of this court, sent by the Goblin King. This was the last piece of the puzzle I needed before I defeated him."

They immediately withdrew the blade at her throat. She could hear the faeries step away from her, then their low tones as they whispered together. She couldn't pick out any individual words, but she was certain they were arguing about what to do with her.

Good. Let them be confused about who she was and whether she was a threat to their people. A little fear would serve them right for tying her up like this.

Freya waited for them to approach her again. This time, they reached for the burlap sack around her head and yanked it off so quickly she was blinded by the bright light behind them.

Blinking through tears, she stared at the two figures and waited for them to come into focus.

The smaller one was a very slight man who looked oddly like a birch tree. The patterns were even etched into his skin, the dark streaks looking very much like a tree. His eyes were slanted almost comically, the inner points nearly touching his nose, while the outer edge winged up to his eyebrows. Those eyes were overly large as well, too big to fit his face and oddly raven-like with the dark parts swallowing the white.

The other man was larger than life. He looked like a boulder, with the dark bluish skin to boot. His stomach stretched the shirt that covered him. The buttons were so strained they looked like they might burst at any moment. He stared down at her with black eyes, no whites at all, just black. Were they brothers? Or were all the Winter Court blessed with soulless eyes?

Both of them made a rather intimidating picture that sent her heart racing in her chest.

The big one spoke first. "You are the one who defeated the Goblin King? Speak loudly, girl. This is important."

"Of course it's important," she replied, trying very hard to turn her voice haughty and warrior-like. "Untie me and bring my companion back. Then, perhaps, I'll speak with your Queen about this. But I have no interest in speaking to two lowly guards who were sent to the very outer edges of the Queen's domain."

They looked at each other, then back to her. "How would you know any of that?"

Guessing, really. That was the only way she would know. But they were both ragged looking, and their clothing had frays at the seams. The frozen faeries she'd seen around that icy snowflake had been delicate. Lovely. Their clothing was impeccable and their faces smooth.

These two had pock marked skin and the larger one had spots of peeling flakes where the sun had burned him. If they were living a life that difficult, then they certainly weren't high in the rankings of guards.

She leaned forward dramatically. "I'll speak well of your treatment and how you tricked me. You just have to bring me to the Queen and I'm certain she would let you return from your exile."

"This isn't an exile," the thin one replied with an angry grunt. He reached into his pocket and pulled the knife out again. "I should take your eyes for suggesting such a thing, mortal. You are beneath us."

"Mind, body, and soul far lesser than you," she said. "I'm certain that you think I'm beneath you, but I was the one who defeated the Goblin King. Was I not?"

Freya would have looked at her nails in the silence that followed. At least that body language would have made her appear confident and unafraid. But her shoulders were aching from being tied up for so long, and she'd lost all feeling in her fingers. Her entire body screamed for her to do something, anything that would get her free. And yet, she was at the mercy of these two idiots.

They looked at each other again, and the big one nodded to the back of the cave. They skittered away to whisper in each other's ears. Their hushed tones filled the cave with a sound like trickling water. Freya stared up at the ceiling and prayed for patience.

She'd need more than a little to deal with these two nitwits.

Finally, the smaller one approached her with a frown on his face. "Prove it."

"Prove what?"

"That you were the one to defeat the Goblin King. Everyone knows he's fallen, so you could just be some mortal woman looking to manipulate our queen in the hopes she'll give you enough gold to make you a princess in your land." He scratched his groin, then sniffed his fingers. "We need a little more than just your word."

She tilted her head to the side and smiled, trying to remain pretty and not just angry. "Your entire court gathers their magic from a snowflake that had magic poured into it. It looks like glass, but it's just a snowflake. And your queen has the Goblin King locked up in a prison because she can't let him go. Oh, and all the faeries were frozen in a war. That's why you hate the Goblin King. He did it to you, and the Queen will stop at nothing to punish him for what he did."

She said too much. Far too much. The two guards in front of her weren't involved in the war. If they had fought, they would have died due to some foolish mistake. None of what she said would make any sense to the two of them.

But the big one shrugged and said, "Would she know any of that if she was just a mortal?"

"I don't know."

"Well, I don't either." The big one narrowed his eyes and pointed at her with a meaty hand. "If you're lying, then I'm going to pull all your limbs off your body. One by one."

Freya ground her teeth. "If you did that, then I would die. I'd like very much to stay alive, so I can assure you, none of this is a lie."

"We'll see about that." He stalked toward her, lifted her by a bound arm, and gave her a shake. "Why don't we bring both you and your companion to the queen, eh? She'll know what to do with you."

"I think that's a fabulous idea." Except, now she didn't want to do that at all.

If these two were what the Winter Court faeries were like, then what kind of monster was their queen?

CHAPTER 6

The two faerie thugs dragged her down the crag where she'd first seen winter magic and out into another frozen tundra. They gathered up Arrow who had been tied like a prized hog and then left waiting for them in a snowbank.

He growled when the smaller man reached for his ties. "If you touch me, I will bite your fingers off."

"Arrow," Freya said. "Let them untie you. They're taking us to see the queen."

Arrow's eyes widened in surprise, but he didn't snap at the birch faerie's fingers when he reached for the ties again. The faerie made quick work of the ropes and then lunged away from Arrow as he rolled onto his feet and gave a swift shake.

He quickly trotted to Freya's side. "I don't know why we have these thugs taking us, anyway. They seem decidedly untrustworthy."

"More trustworthy than a goblin," the big one grumbled.

"Debatable," Freya replied with a chuckle. "You tied the two of us up without asking who we are. The goblins gave me a much better greeting than that."

The birch faerie stared at her with those blank, odd eyes. "How did they greet you?"

"With dinner." A soft smile curved over her face as she remembered the food and the madness. "Their children greeted me and I waded into the fray to tame the wild beasts. They gave me food and drink, and memories I could never forget."

She hoped the softness in her voice met Arrow's ears. In a way, it was her apology to him.

The goblins weren't the monsters she'd thought them to be for such a long time. And Freya had a lot of apologizing to do for demonizing them for so many years. All she could hope for was that her words would at least take a small step toward easing the rift between them.

Arrow met her gaze with a soft expression, then blinked his long lashes. "You left a lasting impression on the little ones. They still ask about you, you know. Terrible little beasts, but they want to talk about the pretty mortal lady who picked them up by the scruff of their necks."

The birch faerie snorted. "They won't be asking much longer. They'll have a lot worse things to deal with when the Goblin Queen finally takes over all the kingdoms."

So, that was her plan then. The Queen would take over everything Freya knew and admired, because a Goblin royal had a right to all of the courts. The King or Queen was more powerful than any court leader. That fact had been drilled into Freya's mind.

Blowing out a long breath, she wiggled her fingers behind her back. If she could get out of these bindings, that would be a huge step toward controlling this situation.

"Where are we going?" she asked, trying to distract them from her movements.

"To the Queen, of course." The larger faerie pointed down a cave tunnel that disappeared into the icy tundra before them. "If you don't mind going first, that is. You've been very brave thus far, mortal. Let's test just how brave you are."

Far braver than he gave her credit for, apparently. Freya was ready to get this over with.

She plunged through the snow and into the tunnel that disappeared deep under the mountains. At first, she couldn't see very well. Then light bloomed in the walls.

Thick slabs of ice surrounded them. The Goblin Queen's magic ran through all the frozen walls, turning them a bright, deep blue. The light pulsed brighter, then dimmed, as though it had a heartbeat that she couldn't hear but could see.

This wasn't frightening, even though the faeries had intended it to be scary. It was beautiful, yes, and a wonderful display of the Goblin Queen's power. But not frightening.

Freya held her head high and continued deeper into the heart of the mountain. The floor was slick with ice, but she struggled her way without falling. Freya's heart beat with fear because she knew she wouldn't be able to catch herself if she fell. Her arms were useless tied behind her back.

The birch faerie snickered behind her. "Looks like you've never walked on ice before, mortal."

"I've walked on ice with skates," she snarled. "Or perhaps even with solid boots, but never down a slope made entirely of ice. How are you doing this without falling?"

He grabbed her shoulder and spun her around. She blew out an angry breath, but looked at his foot that he brandished in the air. Four toes, four long claws that dug into the ice wherever he walked.

The faerie bared his teeth in a sinister grin. "I'm made to stroll through these halls, mortal. Are you?"

"Obviously not."

She continued until the slope was so steep that she had to stop. The tunnel extended down into darkness as the light slowly disappeared in the distance. She wondered why it wasn't still glowing down there.

"You have to keep going," the birch faerie said. "We'll leave you here."

"I don't think the Queen would like that." Freya gulped down the spike of fear. If they left her here, she wasn't sure she could climb back out. Her boots would slip and eventually she would fall.

She imagined herself tumbling into the darkness, sliding uncontrollably until she hit a wall. She might live. Or she might bash her head against the ice and die here in the darkness, alone.

The bigger faerie walked by her with a snort. "Not so brave after all, are we?"

He took one step onto the sloping ice and then disappeared. Or rather, he fell onto the ice gracefully for his size and slid down into the darkness without another word. She didn't even hear him as he plummeted into the shadows.

How? How could he do that without having a second thought?

"You next, goblin," the birch faerie snarled.

"Absolutely not." Arrow took a step back while shaking his head. "I'll go when Freya goes."

"Is that the mortal's name?" The birch faerie looked her up and down with that disgusting grin on his face. "Good to know what your name is, my dear. I wonder all the different ways I might be able to use it."

She hoped not to curse her. Her mother had said faeries could do that. All they needed was a name and they could force anyone to do whatever they wanted. Even turn her into something else, like a toad or rat.

Arrow bared his teeth with a snarl and stepped in front of her. "You wouldn't dare."

"I sure would. Especially if she doesn't show up at the bottom with us." The birch faerie reached for Arrow, scooped him up, and then slid into the shadows as well.

Then it was just Freya. She stood with her hands still tied behind her back, staring into what felt like the end of all she knew. How could she do this? She wasn't so brave as to dive into the unknown. What if she landed on shards of ice that impaled her? This could all be some kind of trick from the faeries, and then she was finally out of their hair for good.

"You're afraid of this, but you weren't afraid to make a deal with the Goblin King." His voice soothed the ache in her soul.

This was someone she knew how to deal with. Freya had already defeated the Goblin King. She knew how to manipulate him, or at the very least, she knew what was expected of her.

The Goblin King wanted someone to spar with him. He wanted a verbal joust where she could best him or be beaten. It didn't matter what the result was in the end. He just wanted her to challenge him.

She licked her lips and said, "You were far less terrifying than potentially plummeting to my death."

"But you faced death multiple times while trying to beat me. You might not remember it like that, but you did." He materialized within the ice to her left. Or perhaps not within it, but reflected upon it. Like a mirror. "I find I don't like this version of you that can feel fear."

She snorted. "Sorry to disappoint you, Goblin King."

"Please." He rolled his eyes. "No matter what you do, I highly doubt you could disappoint me, Freya. You were the greatest adversary I've ever battled. And I'm impressed you've come this far. You could have run."

She curled her fingers into tight fists, digging her nails into the palms of her hands until she felt the slightest prick of pain. "Are you really here?" She had to know the truth. "Or are you some figment of my imagination to help me get through all this?"

"Does it matter?" His mouth turned down at the edges and fine lines furrowed between his brows. He was saddened by her words, almost as though he didn't want her to know the truth.

"Of course it matters," she whispered. "I need to know if I'm alone right now or if you're here with me."

"Freya," he scolded. "Would it really make you feel better to know that I was here with you? I'm your enemy, remember? The villain in your story that tried to stop you from getting your sister back. The bad guy shouldn't turn into the one who consoles you in your hour of need."

"I'm asking you to." She took a deep breath and felt her nostrils flair with panic. "I'm asking you to take off your mask of bad guy and villain. Help me, Eldridge."

A shiver traveled through his entire body, rocking his shoulders at the sound of his own name. The darkness in his eyes deepened and those swirling silver stars seemed to glow brighter. "Jump, Freya. I need you to find me."

And then he disappeared again, fading from view like he was never there at all.

She felt something deep inside her stomach twist. Quietly she asked, "Eldridge?"

The word fell in the cold air, disappointing and lacking in life. He was gone. The Goblin King had left her in the cold, all alone, to make this decision on her own.

She shivered in the dark with the strange blue light lighting up the world behind her. "Come back," she whispered. The words choked in her throat as sobs pushed their way to the surface. "Even if you aren't real or just a dream, please come back."

No one answered her. This choice was hers and hers alone, even though the Goblin King had tried to tell her what to do. He wanted her to leap into the darkness without fear. She wasn't a bird who could fly, though, and that fear had been buried deep in her chest since all of this had started.

Now was the time to prove that she was brave.

She straightened her shoulders and tensed the muscles of her back. Awkwardly, she turned around so her back was to the darkness because she refused to slide into the shadows face first. Then she got onto her knees, flopped onto her belly, and let the ice take her away.

Arctic wind blasted through her hair and ice tore at the front of her cloak. The sound of the woolen fabric ripping could barely be heard over her wild tumble. Freya told herself not to scream. Even if this was the end of her life, she would not give these monstrous faeries the satisfaction of hearing her scream.

Then, she hit a flat portion of the ice and rolled to a stop. Her arms felt like they had been torn apart, but at least the feeling in them had returned.

Wincing, she tried to wiggle onto her back without success.

"Well, that was dramatic," the birch faerie said. His hands grasped the ropes around her wrists and he hauled her onto her feet. Settling her with a jerk, he shook her hard. "Are you still alive?"

Though she was peering through the tangled mass of her hair, she still nodded. "I'm alive."

"Pity," he snarled. "I would have liked you better dead. Come on, then. The Queen is in the throne room."

Freya muttered underneath her breath the same thing she'd said to the Goblin King. "Sorry to disappoint."

CHAPTER 7

The two faeries dragged Freya through countless icy halls until they stopped before doors that were three stories high. These white, iced doors were carved with a scene from what looked like a battle. A hundred elves at the bottom level all pointed their sharpened spears up at a monster that looked like a dragon. A single woman stood before the creature with her arms outstretched.

A crown topped her head, and Freya could only assume this woman was meant to be the Goblin Queen herself. But why would she welcome a creature so fearsome as a dragon? Especially when the rest of her people were pointing their weapons at the terrifying beast?

Freya didn't have time to ask questions. The two faeries busted through the doors and shoved her onto her knees. She fell onto her hands and knees, sliding across the ice until she stopped before the stairs.

She would not show fear. Not when the Goblin Queen was likely a very astute woman and would notice any weakness. Freya had to pretend that she was here seeking an audience with the Queen because she wanted recognition for her actions. Not because she was searching for the King.

The cold bit into her fingers and palms. Her breath fogged in front of her face. She stared down at the blue ice of the floor and counted to ten. Only then, when she was certain her expression wouldn't give her away, did she look up.

Freya let her eyes feast upon the sight of the throne room.

Stained glass windows, or perhaps colored ice, turned the walls into a rainbow of overwhelming vibrance. The stairs led up to a throne made entirely of jagged icicles and snow. The arms were carved into twin bears that held the Goblin Queen's throne aloft.

And seated on that throne was the Goblin Queen herself. A pale blue gown floated around her form, carefully laced with individual snowflakes stitched so perfectly, Freya had to wonder if they were actually snow. Her fingers were white, not just pale, but completely white with long pointed nails. The same crown that was carved on the doors sat on her head. Three spikes of ice, like the ones that had dripped from Freya's windows when she was a little girl.

On her face, she wore a mask made of tiny icicles, each creating a beautiful pattern that surrounded her blinding blue eyes.

The Goblin Queen stared down at her with an expression of apathy. "Who is this? Why did you bring a mortal to my throne room?"

The two faeries behind Freya lunged forward, each talking over the other.

"We found her and the dog in the caverns, my queen. They were trespassing on your lands and we thought you'd like to see them," the big one said.

"She said she's the one who beat the Goblin King, and that she wanted to see you. I can't imagine that she did, I mean look at her, but you said you wanted to know who had managed to..." the thin one babbled until the Goblin Queen pointed at him with a sharpened nail.

"You," she snarled. "Say that again."

The birch faerie gulped. "She said she was the one who beat the Goblin King, and that she needed to speak with you immediately."

Freya watched all this happen as if she wasn't even in the room. No one was looking at her or Arrow, who she assumed was somewhere behind them. Freya kept her eyes on the most important person in the room. The Queen.

The Goblin Queen's eyes had narrowed suspiciously, but she still wasn't looking at the mortal on her knees before the throne. Instead, she eyed the faeries as though they were something disgusting she had stepped on.

"Are you certain?" she asked.

The birch faerie looked at the bigger one, then back to the Queen. "Certain of what, my lady?"

"Certain that this measly mortal was the one to defeat the greatest Goblin King this realm has ever seen?"

"Uh," the birch faerie gulped again. His throat worked hard before he whispered, "There's no way to know that for certain, my lady."

"Then it's a shame you thought the risk of wasting my time was more important than the reward you might get." She snapped her fingers. "I don't want to see you in my sight again. You've outlasted your worth."

The birch faerie's eyes widened in horror. He dropped onto his knees, begging, "Please, my lady. I will prove my worth to you! All I'm asking is—"

He didn't have time to say anything else. The frost spread up from the icy floor into his skin. He screamed in pain as the cold froze him solid, but there was nothing he could do to fight against the Goblin Queen's magic. Freya didn't know how long it took for him to solidify. She held her breath the entire time, so it couldn't have taken very long.

The silence that came after shocked her to the very core. His last scream had been one of pain and anguish, but nothing could be done to help him. Not even the big faerie moved, and certainly not his queen.

The Goblin Queen lifted a hand and stared at her nails. "Such a pity your friend wasn't more useful. Perhaps you will find your path to be a little less reliant on hope. Do I make that clear?"

Freya watched the big faerie nod firmly, but his eyes remained on his poor partner. Frozen to the floor with his hands raised forever, pleading with his Queen for mercy.

The Queen stood from her throne and stepped down the stairs. Her skirts swished around her legs, the sound so soft it almost made her forget the horrible thing the Queen had just done.

She strode past Freya without a glance. No, she approached the frozen figure instead.

With a gentle hand, she smoothed her palm over his face. "You were one of my favorites," she told the frozen figure. "This hurts me so much more than it hurts you."

The Goblin Queen planted a hand on the birch faerie's chest and shoved.

He fell almost as though time had slowed. It took a very long time for the icy figure to meet the ground. But the instant the ice hit the floor, it shattered into a thousand bright red pieces. Like rubies someone had tipped out of a jeweler's box.

Freya hissed out a low breath and flinched. She looked away from the horrific sight of a body in so many pieces. That had been a faerie just moments ago. He'd been alive and while he'd been terrifying, he hadn't deserved to die just because he'd done what he was supposed to. Bring the woman who had defeated the Goblin King to the new Queen.

The soft hush of falling snow approached from her left. Freya watched out of the corner of her eye as the Goblin Queen reached out a hand for Freya to take. "Rise, mortal."

Freya should have taken the offered hand. She should have at least tried her best to play along with this morbid game, but she couldn't. She stood on her own and kept her eyes straight ahead.

The Goblin Queen scoffed. "You can act all high and mighty, mortal. But you are not a magical creature. If I wanted to destroy you just as I destroyed him, then I would. Right now, I want to know if you were lying as your kind is so famous for."

"I was not lying," she replied. "I beat the Goblin King at his own game. He kidnapped my sister, and I would have done anything to get her safely home."

"Your sister?" The Goblin Queen stepped around her and stood so Freya was forced to look into her unnatural eyes. "I don't see a sister with you."

"I didn't bring her here."

"Why not?"

The questions were making her head spin. How was she supposed to keep all these lies in order? Freya was going to forget something and then she would ruin the entire plan. All she had to do was... Well, not lie that much. But bend the truth into a little lie she could remember.

For once, Freya was glad she didn't bring Esther with her.

"She wanted to go home," Freya replied. "To the mortal realm with all the rest of our people."

"And you?" The Goblin Queen watched her without blinking. "Why are you still here?"

What would Esther have said? Freya cleared her throat and answered as her sister would have. "I like it here. There is more in the faerie realm for me than in the mortal realm. However, I wanted to come and meet you once I heard that my heroic deeds had freed you and your people. I thought, perhaps, you would be grateful."

That sparked some interest in the queen's eyes. The Goblin Queen blinked, finally, and then reached up to remove her mask.

The queen was a beautiful woman underneath all that ice. Her eyes were not too large for her head, although they were certainly larger than most. Framed with dark, long lashes, they were set into a heart-shaped face that most women would have killed for. Bright, berry red lips stood out in stark contrast to her pale skin. Removing the mask allowed the spiral curls of her white hair to fall around her face as well. Perfect, as Freya would have expected.

A long sigh spilled from the Queen's lips. "If you really were the one who defeated the king, then tell me. What did you do to beat him?"

"He sent me to all the courts to gather the essence of each. I obtained perfume from the Spring Maiden. A sprig of lavender in a spell bottle from the Summer Lord. A portrait from the Autumn Thief." Freya paused for dramatic effect and then added, "And I figured out that the Goblin King was the essence of this court."

The Goblin Queen's eyes widened with each thing Freya said until finally she burst into laughter at the last part. "Ah yes, he is so vain as to not think you would have figured that out. Clever girl. Perhaps you were the one who defeated him after all."

"I am." Freya glanced over at the red ice chips behind the queen and then resolved herself to one last lie. "My name is Esther, my queen.

It was my hopes that you would feel some sort of... gratefulness for my part in freeing you and your people from your prison."

The Queen tucked her hands behind her back and nodded. "So you want something from me, is that it?"

"Just a place in your court for a while. I wish to learn more about this faerie realm, and I do not want to remain in any of the others." Freya swallowed hard and hoped that action looked like mere nerves.

"A place in my court is frequently sought after by more impressive people than you." This time, the Queen's eyes shifted to the side. Almost as though she was the one lying.

But that wasn't possible. Faeries couldn't lie, that was the one thing that had always given her a leg up over the Goblin King.

Unless this one was different.

Freya took a deep breath and plunged into the unknown. "My companion and I hoped we would be welcome here after all the good we've done for you and your people. After all. Without me, you would still be frozen."

The Goblin Queen's expression was calculating. She suspected Freya was lying, although there was no way for Freya to know if the Queen realized that her name was a lie or if she knew there were many layers to this lie.

Finally, the Queen lifted a delicate shoulder. "My darling, of course you are welcome here. You are the only one to ever defeat the Goblin King. I'm impressed a mere mortal could do so, but I'm also happy that you did."

Happy was good. That was a start. She could work with that, even though the expression on the Queen's face made it appear the happiness was tenuous at best.

Not to mention the dead body behind her.

Freya blew out a soft breath. "Thank you, my queen. It's an honor to know that I have pleased you."

The Queen snorted, "Yes, they all say that. But since you were the one to release me, I wish to give you a gift. A token of my appreciation."

All she could hope was that the gift wasn't like the Spring Maiden's gift. Faeries were always spinning things into their own desires, and if this Queen wanted to put Freya into a stupor, then she would realize rather quickly that Freya was not so easy to trick.

Narrowing her gaze, Freya crossed her arms over her chest and nodded. "A gift is always appreciated if it's given with good intent."

The Queen chuckled again. "You have dealt with faeries before, I see. You don't trust me. That's smart. But my gifts rarely have teeth, my dear. You can see I don't hide my displeasure behind falsehoods and ridiculous tactics. This gift is one of thanks, and it will be the only one I give you in return."

"Then I will take the gift."

"Stay in my castle with me." The Queen lifted a brow, surveying Freya's reactions. "Esther, as you call yourself, I think you would make a lovely addition to my court. I'd like you to stay close. I'm curious about your opinions of my court and the people within it. If you could beat the Goblin King so easily, I'm certain you have more use than as only a passing visitor."

That would do. Freya could work with that.

She dropped into an awkward curtsey. "It would be my pleasure, your highness."

"Oh no." The Queen's voice dropped into a low growl. "I assure you, the pleasure is all mine."

The Queen dismissed Freya with a wave of her hand. The gesture summoned a small, pale creature who detached itself from the ice and stepped toward her.

The little monster looked like it was made entirely out of ice. Perhaps as if it were a doll the Goblin Queen used to play with when she was little. Its feet were forever pointed into little high heels that clicked on the floor. Its hair was frost, creating a different color on top of its head, and its eyes were frozen within the water sloshing in its skull. The strange orbs moved through the liquid of its cranium freely, sometimes gathering together, sometimes far apart.

It teetered over to the throne room door, then lifted an icy hand. Waving as if it wanted her to follow it.

Though the beast was strange, she didn't want to stay in the throne room any longer than she had to. The dead body was the only barrier between her and the door. Freya stepped through the red ice and winced as a piece crunched underneath her boot.

The little monster didn't notice at all. Or if it did, it didn't react.

Arrow waited for her with wide eyes and his nose sniffing the air. When she walked by him and touched a hand to his head, he nudged against her warmth. "Well done, mortal."

"Thank you," she whispered. "I thought I blew it a few times there."

"Unlikely. The Queen is curious about you, and that's the best start you could have asked for." He chuffed out a breath of disbelief. "And now we're staying in the castle. Exactly where we need to be."

"Shh," Freya scolded. "We have no idea if the walls have ears here. Unless you want to end up like our friend back there."

Arrow shuddered. "No, I think neither of us wants to meet the same fate. You're right. We'll wait until we can ward our rooms."

Whatever that meant. Freya didn't know the first thing about magic.

They followed the ice creature down through so many halls she was immediately turned around. Freya had no idea how big this castle was, or just how deep into the heart of the mountain it disappeared. It seemed as though they walked forever before the creature turned and pointed to a blank spot in the wall.

Freya cleared her throat. "Am I supposed to walk through the ice?"

The creature rolled its eyes, then waved a hand. A small handle appeared on the ice where it pointed, followed by a screeching sound as the ice cracked in an uneven shape of a door.

Was she supposed to stay there? Freya could just barely see through the warped glass, and the room inside appeared to be filled with snow drifts. "I can't stay here," she said. "I'm mortal. I'll freeze."

It blinked a few times, then made a sound like broken glass. The creature toddled off, and Freya didn't know if she was supposed to follow it or not.

She looked down at Arrow. "Are we going with it again or…"

"It's going to bring you blankets," he replied. "I'm to follow the creature because I have a separate room."

Her stomach turned. "What? No, you will not stay anywhere else. You're staying with me."

He looked up at her with soulful eyes. "I don't think we have a choice, Freya."

Of course there was a choice. There was always a choice, and she didn't want him to go with the ice monster where they had no idea what the creature's plan was for Arrow. She needed him to stay with her because he was the only thing holding her together. Who else would she talk to?

"Arrow," she hissed. "Don't go with it."

The creature stopped at the end of the hallway and made the sound of broken glass again.

Arrow sighed heavily and shook his head. "I don't have a choice, Freya. There are no choices in the Winter Court. We do what the Goblin Queen says, remember? I will be safe."

He reached up and nudged her hand with his nose, and she felt something brittle slide into her hand. A small piece of paper rolled up that he'd been holding in his mouth. When had he gotten this?

Freya closed both her hands into fists and nodded. "Fine, then. But be careful. I can't lose you too."

He gave her an odd look, and she knew it was partly because he didn't believe her. So much between them still needed to be fixed, and she hadn't the faintest idea how to fix it.

Freya stayed in the hallway until the two of them disappeared from sight. Obviously the creature wasn't worried about her wandering around the castle. There were no doors for her to open, not without knowing how to make the door knobs appear. So if she wanted to wander, she was likely free to do so. But Freya would eventually freeze solid and die somewhere in a hallway no one traversed.

She turned and opened the door to her own room rather than tempt that fate.

The interior was rather bland. Just a bed made of ice in the corner, overly large but lacking any blankets. A fireplace carved out of snow, not exactly helpful considering the entire thing would melt. And twin snowdrifts in the back that looked like they might be mounded over chairs.

She glanced around to make sure no one was looking, then unrolled Arrow's note.

"Repeat these words, Freya. It will ward the room from the Goblin Queen's spying. Imagine in your mind a golden bubble forming around this room and this room only."

Was she supposed to perform magic? This was a spell.

She crumpled the paper in her fist again and sighed. He knew she was just a mortal. Freya couldn't do magic. She just couldn't.

A knock on the door startled her. Spinning on her heel, Freya pressed her fist to her heart and watched as the ice creature walked through the door. It held a mound of blankets and sheepskin in its arms. Without a word, it dumped the skins on the floor, then pointed at the fireplace.

Then it made that sound again.

"I can't understand you," she said.

The creature's eyes rolled in the block of its head, then it made another horrible sound and walked back out the door. Through the ice, as though there wasn't a barrier there at all.

Freya turned away with a sigh and stared down at the furs. They were a start to keep her warm, but she wasn't sure how much they would do. Her cheeks already stung in the cold and she desperately wanted to take off all these layers.

No fire. No warmth. She could go to sleep and freeze overnight, passing into the realm of the dead in a peaceful manner, but far too soon.

She had to sleep, though. Especially since her last rest was in a rocking chair. So she stooped down and picked up the spell from the floor. Unrolling it, she cleared her throat.

"I clear this room of all ill intent and spying ears. By the power of the Autumn Court, I banish any energy that might wish to cause me harm. Only those with pure intent may enter these walls." Freya finished and squeezed her eyes shut, thinking of a bright bubble expanding through the room.

Golden light, she thought. Golden light that no one else could get through.

Connecting with the spell was easier than she thought, but she opened one eye and it didn't look like anything was happening. Squeezing them shut again, Freya tried her best.

Finally, she shook her head and tucked the paper into her pocket. "This is ridiculous."

She couldn't do spell work. Trying was just a waste of her time. She set about getting the furs onto the icy block of the floor, trying to cover every bit that her body might touch and then laying the blankets on top.

Already shivering with anticipation of the chilly rest, she rubbed her arms. "This will have to do."

Freya laid down and pulled the blankets high over her shoulders. What she wouldn't have given for a proper fire, not just a cold fireplace carved into the snow. Not the semblance of warmth with none of the reassurance. This place was far colder than she'd thought. And now she was wondering if the Goblin Queen was more of a match than she'd expected.

Sure, the Goblin King had fallen to her wit. But he'd wanted to fall.

She tucked the blanket up to her nose and tried her best to drift off to sleep. And she must have, because when she opened her eyes again there was a fire crackling in the fireplace. The flames merrily danced in the marble carved frame. The snow had melted off the carvings, revealing the real room beneath it.

A dull throb of a headache pounded behind her eyes and then disappeared in the next instant.

The heat distracted her so much that it took awhile for her to notice where the actual heat was coming from.

Stretched out beside her, resting on the ice as though it were a bed, lay the Goblin King. His head was turned toward the flames, the cords of his neck silhouetted by the red light of the fire. His bare chest gleamed, although she didn't know how he could be comfortable while shirtless, sprawled out on ice.

"What—" she started to sit up, only to pause when he looked at her with those dark, soulful eyes.

The Goblin King raised a finger and pressed it against his lips. "Shh, Freya. We don't know who might be listening."

She braced herself on one arm and stared down at him in shock. "You're in my bedroom."

"Don't be so obtuse. Of course I'm in your bedroom, Freya." He shook his head in disappointment, then looked back at the fire.

"No, I just..." Arguing with him would get her nowhere. The Goblin King was a strange man, and if he wanted to be here in her bedroom, then apparently that's where he was going to be. Freya sank back down onto the blanket she'd bundled up as a pillow. "I warded the room. Arrow gave me the spell."

"And you did a good job of it for someone who claims magic doesn't run in her family." The firelight played over the strands of his dark hair, ragged and fallen out of place. "But your mother said the same thing when I first saw her. Magic doesn't always run in bloodlines, Freya. It runs in the heart."

Her own heart thudded frantically at what he had suggested. He'd seen her mother? Did that mean maybe... Maybe her parents were alive?

Licking her lips, she asked, "You knew my mother? You never told me that."

He tilted his head to look at her, then pressed his finger to his lips again. "We cannot talk about it here, Freya. Soon. Soon, I will tell you everything I know."

She was so tired of that answer. He always promised that, and somehow he'd get himself into yet another position where he could tell her nothing. She opened her mouth to argue with him further.

"No arguing," he interrupted. "Your ward was well constructed, but that doesn't mean they're infallible. Soon, Freya. But for now, just pretend that I'm here. And maybe that you don't mind that I'm here."

Freya might have insisted on an argument if she hadn't noticed a strange light in his eyes. Leaning closer, she paused only when his breath fanned across her lips. She wasn't going to kiss him, although he might have thought she would. Instead, she was looking at the reflection in his dark eyes.

She could see herself, but not the room. Behind her own reflection she could see cold stone walls, stalactites hanging from the ceiling, and bars that gleamed red hot. Everything else was iced over and as she stared, a drop of water hit one of the bars and sizzled. Boiling instantly.

"You aren't really here, are you?" she whispered. "Where are you, Goblin King? How can I find you?"

He slowly lifted his hand toward her face, giving her plenty of time to back away.

She didn't.

The Goblin King cupped her jaw and let out a long, relieved sigh. "I can't tell you where I am. But you are correct, I'm not really here. I had hoped tonight we could pretend I was, though. Just for a few moments."

He was in some kind of prison, she knew that. But she didn't know where the Goblin Queen had her prison. She didn't even know if there was one in the Winter Court, or if he was somewhere far out of her reach.

Frustration boiled in her blood. "Why can't you tell me where you are?"

The Goblin King tugged her in his grip, forcing her to come ever closer to his face. His eyes drifted shut. Long lashes dusted his cheeks that were too hollow. "Just for the night, Freya. I want to pretend that I'm not where I am. That you are really here with me and that I am not alone."

Perhaps there would be another time for her to argue with him. Freya gave in and let her forehead fall to press against his. The warmth of his skin burned through hers, almost as though magic spread between them.

A long sigh blasted over her lips. The Goblin King cleared his throat and gruffly said, "I wish you'd call me Eldridge, you know. After all, we've been through, I think you've earned that."

"It feels strange."

"Why?" he whispered.

"If I call you by your name, then it's like we're friends." Freya strangely felt as though she were baring her soul to him. Like she'd ripped open her chest and hoped he liked what she hid underneath. "And we aren't friends. You're still the monster who stole my sister away from her home. The creature who convinced me to come to the faerie realm and lose everything that I love."

"And yet, you're still here. Still trying to save me, even though I'm the villain in your story." He rocked his head from side to side, smoothing his skin against hers. "I have a strange request for you, enemy of mine. I hope you have enough compassion in your heart to pity an evil goblin."

She didn't.

She shouldn't.

Freya knew he was a horrible creature who had done horrible things. She'd read his diary with his history and knew he'd fought in faerie wars that silenced so many, even though he was trying to save them.

She knew a thousand times over that he didn't deserve her pity.

"What do you need, Eldridge?" she murmured. "Only for tonight."

"And then you'll hate me again," he replied with a deep chuckle.

"What other feelings should I have for you? No others. Anything else would surely name me a mad woman." The question was the truth, but tears burned in her eyes after saying them.

His hand shifted from her jaw. Fingers spreading through her hair, he cupped the back of her neck and drew her down into the curve of his body. He settled her head against his shoulder, her torso draped over his. And with another heaving sigh, Eldridge lifted his other hand and clasped her hand to his heart. "Touch me, Freya. Just for the night. You can go back to hating me whenever you want, but I need to feel alive. I need to feel something other than cold."

She stiffened before she realized he meant nothing untoward. He wasn't moving her hand. He wasn't trying to start anything at all.

The Goblin King simply wanted her to rest on his heart and hold him. That was all. He wanted to feel another living person against his heart and listen to the steady rhythm of her breath.

Her resolve shattered like that poor faerie who had died in the throne room. A thousand pieces. All scattered around her like stars in the sky.

Nodding, she tucked herself closer into the crook of his body and eased her full weight down onto him. "You've had a trying time of it. I understand."

A deep rumble echoed in her ear. "A trying time of it. Yes, I suppose you could call it that."

"Only for the night," she repeated.

"Of course. I'd expect nothing less from the conqueror of the

Goblin King." His hand in her hair shifted down her neck and back, resting finally on the curve of her hip.

As they both drifted into sleep, Freya whispered against his shoulder, "I'm going to find you, you know. This isn't forever."

His hand tightened on her waist. "I know, Freya. I have every hope that you will once again succeed."

CHAPTER 9

Freya woke to cold air and icy floors. Her body shivered her out of the dreaming realm and shook her into the present. Sitting up, she rubbed her hands up and down her arms to try to warm up.

She'd been warm last night, hadn't she? There had been a fire in that fireplace that was iced over once again. As if her meeting with Eldridge had been nothing more than a dream.

But that wasn't possible. She remembered him right next to her. He'd been here, and she'd been resting against his warm chest.

Freya flexed her hands, remembering the feeling of his smooth chest rising and falling underneath them. Her cheeks flamed. She'd laid on the Goblin King, even snuggled in close, and that was apparently fine in the moment?

What had she been thinking!

Freya palmed her head and sighed. Why in the world would she have ever allowed him to do that? She should have been screaming at him for even trying to lie beside her, let alone insist that she touch him. Her mother must be rolling over in her grave.

The mother that Eldridge said he had known. That he'd talked to and even hinted that her mother had performed magic.

Yet another reason she had to get the Goblin King out of this prison. Freya had a thousand questions for him to answer, and he would answer them no matter what. If she had to tie him down in a prison of her own making, then so be it. He would give her the answers she so desperately sought.

Then she heard the tip tapping sound of an ice creature walking down the hall. Not a single second would be her own, it seemed. The Goblin Queen's monster walked through the wall without bothering to knock.

She stared, then blinked a few times to clear the grit of sleep from her eyes. "Did you learn how to talk in the time you've been gone?"

"Yes." The creature's voice was still rough and horrible to listen to, but at least it knew her language. "Follow me."

Though she wanted to argue, Freya stumbled to her feet. Her hair was plastered to one side of her head and her clothing was now horribly wrinkled. How long had she been wearing this dress and woolen coat?

Don't think about it, she told herself. She could meet a Goblin Queen in grubby clothing and the woman shouldn't complain. If the Queen wanted her to visit looking like some kind of visiting royalty, then she needed to provide Freya with new clothing.

And it could only be the Queen who wanted her. Why else would this creature be here?

"Where are we going?" she asked, striding toward the door.

"The Queen would like to have breakfast with you."

Ah yes, breakfast. As a normal Queen would want to do.

Freya felt like this was a trap. She needed to prepare for anything. If her previous dealings with faeries were anything to go by, then this was yet another trick to get more information out of her.

As she strode through the blue, icy halls, Freya reminded herself of the lies she'd already told the Queen. She was Esther, not Freya. Her sister had gone back to the mortal realm while Freya had stayed here, because she preferred the faerie realm.

Were there any others? She didn't think so, but this was what she had worried about. Too many lies were difficult to keep track of, and this Queen was intelligent. She'd sense any weakness in Freya and pounce on it like a viper on a mouse.

They didn't go to the throne room this time, although they passed by the horrific doors. Freya swallowed hard when she saw the dragon again. Hopefully those weren't still alive or, if she was lucky, that they hadn't been real at all.

The ice creature's footsteps echoed through the halls, and Freya swore they sounded like the ticking of a clock. A clock that was ticking down to the next time when she would have to face the Goblin Queen. So she steeled herself for the battle that was to come.

They stopped in front of a new doorway that consisted of twisted ice coiling up to the ceiling. Ribbons, she realized. They were ribbons falling down as if some lovely lady had just pulled them off her dress.

What a strange place. The beauty of it was incredible, however, it was also terrifying in its construction. Every detail of this castle had clearly been made with magic that was unfathomable to her mind.

Magic that supposedly she could also use.

Gulping, Freya walked past the ice creature and into what must have once been a dining room. A waterfall of ice covered bright tapestries on the back wall. Long icicles hung from the ceiling and their ends glowed with bright, glistening lights. Snow fell through the air, even though they weren't outside. Tiny, perfect snowflakes danced as they fell.

A silver table had been set up in the back of the room. It was over-laden with food that steamed as she watched, although she was certain the fruit and bowls of porridge would already be cold once she tried to eat them.

The Goblin Queen sat at the center of the table. She'd changed her icy crown for one that was more demure. A small tiara was set in the intricate curls of her hair, dusted with diamonds so bright they looked like the sun. Her gown was so delicately made that Freya wondered if it was frozen droplets of ice on a spiderweb. The long bell sleeves complimented her thin frame, and the wide neck revealed lovely shoulders and a long, swan-like neck.

The Queen lifted one of her manicured fingers and crooked it. She beckoned Freya forward as though she were nothing more than a little girl for her to play with. A toy or a doll, perhaps.

And yet, Freya went as soon as she was beckoned. Who was she to argue with the Queen of this place? She didn't want to end up like the faerie who had shattered on the floor.

Freya was acutely aware of her messy hair, rumpled clothing, and likely sleep lined face. At least there was no one else in the room to see just how horrible she looked, but the Queen seemed like the type who would care about that sort of thing. At least the Goblin King hadn't minded if she was muddy from her adventures. He'd still thought she was equally terrifying because of her wit.

"How did you sleep?" The Goblin Queen asked, gesturing for Freya to take a seat.

"Well," Freya lied through her teeth. "It was perhaps a little cold for my liking, but the room is exquisite."

"I thought you'd think so." With a flourish, the Queen gestured to all the food. How she didn't get her sleeve in the porridge, Freya would never know. "Eat, mortal. It is my understanding your kind needs much of this."

Freya reached for a bowl of porridge and dragged it closer. She tried to put a spoon in it, but the metal clicked against the frozen oats. Licking her lips, she looked to the next item and grabbed a bunch of grapes.

At least if these were frozen, she could still eat them.

"Thank you," she replied. "Why did you want to eat breakfast with me?"

The Queen lifted her hands and clapped them. The thunderous sound rocked through the room, and the icy waterfall cracked open, spilling out twenty women. Each wearing a gossamer gown puffed around their waists. They walked on their toes, like ballerinas, their bare feet silent as they padded over the floor. Ribbons swirled around their wrists and floated in the air as they moved.

Patterns of white snowflakes were stuck to their cheeks. Or perhaps, as Freya leaned closer to peer at the women, they were scarred onto their cheeks.

She realized they were. Scars in all shapes and sizes, but all snowflakes on each dancer's face.

Horrified, she tried not to let that show as the women lifted their arms over their heads and began to dance.

"Do you like the entertainment?" The Queen asked. "I've always found watching them was far more entertaining than music. Don't you think?"

No, she didn't think that at all. Watching these women silently dance, as though they couldn't make any sound at all, was eerie. Strange. It made her heart hurt because she wondered where these women had come from and why they were here, of all places.

But she couldn't say that. Instead, she had to swallow her fear and smile. "They're lovely. Where did you find such perfect specimens?"

"Would it surprise you to know they're from all over my kingdom?" The Queen watched them with rapt attention, as though she couldn't take her eyes off their movements. "Each more lovely than the last. I spent a very long time, when I was young, finding the perfect women for my dancers."

Freya didn't want to think about their families. The lives these women had left behind were just as important as their queen's entertainment.

She reached for a goblet that hopefully still had liquid in it. Tilting it back, she was relieved when coffee hit her tongue. It was icy, and the top had a thick film on it, but this was still coffee. It would at least steel her resolve.

Setting the goblet down, she nodded. "You have impressive tastes."

"Far better than my predecessor." The Goblin Queen lounged in her chair, the position very similar to the Goblin King's limp posture. "Why don't you tell me how you defeated him again? I'd like to hear the story in more detail."

Finally, something Freya could tell without fearing that she'd step into her own lies. She saw no reason she shouldn't tell the Goblin Queen everything that happened. The items were in her possession still, and even then she didn't think they were all that useful. The Goblin King had made up tasks that were inconsequential.

Freya told the story until her voice went hoarse. She spared no detail in the hopes that she would win the Goblin Queen over. After all, that was the plan. Make the Goblin Queen trust her, and then maybe something would slip about Eldridge.

It wasn't a brilliant plan, in hindsight.

When she finished, the Queen smiled at her with too much happiness in her expression. "So you really did defeat him. Well and truly, although you had some help along the way."

"I couldn't have done it without my companion," Freya corrected. "The goblin was exceedingly useful."

"Goblins have a way of seeming more helpful than they actually are." The Queen tapped a finger to her chin. "I'm surprised your people even allowed you to come here. Mortals hate magic, as they should. You're all rather careless with your powers. Like a child beating a drum whenever it wants attention."

Did she know?

Freya felt her stomach drop to her feet at the thought. If the Queen realized that Freya had cast a spell in her room, maybe she would start to suspect her actions weren't genuine. What would happen if the Queen thought Freya was here for other reasons?

Clearing her throat, Freya opened her mouth to plead for forgiveness.

She didn't get the chance.

"No matter, I suppose. You wouldn't be so foolish as to use magic in this castle. I'd know." The Queen gestured to her dancers. "And I enjoy having you around, my dear. I can't wait to hear more stories from your adventures. There is nothing I relish more in this life than hearing about the Goblin King losing."

"I have many more stories to tell," she replied.

"Good. Then I plan on seeing you as often as I can. You'll become one of my new dancers, just with storytelling. How lovely to have met you!" The Goblin Queen giggled. "I think I'll keep you for quite some time. But for now, admire my beautiful snowflakes with me."

Freya was glad for the opportunity to no longer look at the Goblin Queen. She took another deep swallow of coffee and then stared at the young women dancing.

If she could keep the Goblin Queen on her side, then surely the woman would say something. Eventually. She had to know where the Goblin King was being kept, and if Freya became her dear friend, then the Queen would let the truth slip. All Freya had to do was last that long.

Her eyes fell on the dancing women once again. Their hair never moved as they spun across the dance floor. Their skirts swirled in graceful arcs around them, and their arms spun with elegant grace. She'd never seen dancers who moved with such perfection.

Then she looked at the floor.

Blood smeared the ice where their feet scraped the rough ice. Every step stuck their heated toes to the cold floor. To move, they had to rip the skin to take another step. Each movement pulled and broke at the poor dancer's bodies.

And yet, they still danced. They moved with purpose and didn't even flinch when their skin peeled off and revealed the muscle and bone beneath. They kept moving. Whether that was with fear or delusion, she would never know.

Freya's heart raced. She took a deep, shuddering breath and another swift swallow of coffee. She wished it was wine. Or rum.

Something strong enough to get her through this breakfast and whatever the coming months would bring. This place was more than just an ice castle. The entire mountain was a prison, made to horrify and control.

All she could hope was that she didn't end up like these dancers. Broken. Bleeding. Playing to the whims of their dangerous queen.

CHAPTER 10

Freya returned to her room with a heavy heart after watching the dancer's nearly destroy themselves for the Queen. None of them had even complained or winced when they finally stopped. They just smiled at their ruler, dropped into curtsies, and then returned into the waterfall where they disappeared from sight.

Freya couldn't have done that. They must have been sturdy women to not show any reaction or response to tearing their feet up like that.

She stepped into her room after following the ice creature once more. Something else had been bothering her since the moment she realized the dancers were little more than slaves. This creature whom the Queen had made... Was it more alive than she thought?

She turned around as it left and asked, "Is there anything I can call you?"

The creature's eyes rolled in the ice of its head. "Why?"

"Everything has a name."

It pondered the question for a bit before finally replying, "No. I don't have a name."

The little thing toddled off again with its high heels tapping on the ice. She resolved herself to figuring out a name it might like, because she refused to believe it didn't want one. Or maybe because it was made entirely by the Queen's magic. The thought of a name was an idea it couldn't comprehend.

She closed the door and scolded herself. "Freya, you're getting too involved already. Just keep pushing forward, the Queen will eventually give you something to work with."

"Really?" Arrow crawled out from under the ice bed and shook himself. "I don't think she'll admit to a single thing. The Goblin Queen is smarter than we gave her credit for."

"Arrow!" The name burst out of her mouth. Freya lunged forward and scooped the goblin into her arms. "You have no idea how worried I was. Where have you been? Did they make you dance on ice?"

He wriggled in her arms, frantically trying to pull himself from her grip. "I have no idea what you're talking about, you ridiculous woman. Unhand me!"

Freya gave him one last squeeze before dropping him back onto the ground.

He reared up on his back legs and tugged hard on his woolen jacket, forcing it back into place. "You've rumpled my clothes again. Do you know how hard it was to press them without an iron?"

"I can imagine it was rather difficult, I apologize for worrying that the Queen might have killed you." She crossed her arms firmly over her chest. "What are you doing here, anyway?"

"I thought you would have figured something out by now. Obviously I was wrong." He huffed out a breath and walked toward the fireplace. "They didn't even give you a fire?"

"No, I have figured nothing out. Sorry to disappoint." Freya reached out and dusted snow off the top of the mantle. "It was warm in here last night, I swear. I don't know how, but there was a fire and the Goblin King."

"Eldridge visited again?" Arrow grumbled. "He's got to stop doing that. That man will use up all his magic just to keep in touch, when he knows he can't tell us where he is. He's going to hurt himself."

"You think? Or he's going to hurt me." She touched a hand to her head. "I've been getting splitting headaches for a while, ever since he disappeared. I thought it was because of the magic in this realm, but then I realized I've been getting them before he appears."

"So he's wriggling into your head then." Arrow snorted. His ears flopped dramatically on either side of his head. "He knows better than to pry into the mind of a mortal. He could get lost in your head and then we'd all really be in trouble."

"Do I want to know why?" Freya wasn't sure that she did. The more she heard about magic, the more curious she was. And then where would she be?

She was still a mortal. Even the Queen claimed that mortals making magic were clunky at best, and she didn't want to conjure a spell that might go wrong.

Arrow shook his head. "Mortal minds aren't like the fae. We keep everything in nice, neat little compartments in our minds. It's why we sometimes appear emotionless to your kind. But mortal heads? They're labyrinths that are sometimes impossible to get out of. If he's altering the reality you see, that can be even more dangerous. He needs to preserve his strength. Faeries realms, who knows what the Goblin Queen is doing to him."

She had a bit of an idea. Considering how lank and thin Eldridge was looking in her visions of him, she thought it safe to assume the Queen was not treating the previous king to afternoon tea.

Clearing her throat, she turned her attention back to the frozen fireplace. "I've been entirely unsuccessful in finding out anything new. The Queen is keeping me close, but all she wants is to hear how I beat the Goblin King."

"She'll make a mistake soon enough." Arrow's tail wagged, betraying what he was about to say long before he opened his mouth. "But I found something of interest. It's not where the King is, but it's close."

Freya's heart leapt in her chest. He was closer to finding the Goblin King? "Why didn't you say something sooner?"

Arrow shrugged. "Dramatic effect. Come on."

Together they left her room and snuck down the hall. She followed her goblin dog with pure faith that he knew where he was going, because she certainly didn't. Every hallway looked the same. There were no doors. No windows. No differences to keep track of.

Just blue ice tunnels that stretched so far into the distance they disappeared into deep cobalt.

"Where are we going?" she whispered. "Won't someone see us?"

Arrow shook his head, dropping onto all fours to speed up. "Not unless there is a servant wandering around. I don't think there's many people in this castle, Freya."

"Why's that?"

He looked over his shoulder, gaze haunted with memories. "I don't think she's woken most of the Winter Court up yet."

Well, that was even more ominous. Why would the Queen keep her own court asleep when she could wake them? Curiouser and curiouser.

Arrow finally stopped. The wall in front of them was chipped at the bottom, and she could see the faint outline of scratch marks. Deep furrows that looked quite a bit like a dog had been trying to dig underneath the wall.

"How did you know something was there?" she asked.

"I could smell it."

Impressive. She always forgot he could use his nose like a real dog.

Freya leaned down and wiggled her fingers into the gap he'd scratched. The ice was sharper than knives. It didn't take long for her own blood to tinge the icy crystals a bright red. But she managed to get her hands underneath enough to wiggle the door open.

The ice slid forward with a groan, giving enough room for them to slip inside the hidden room. She glanced over her shoulder to make sure no one was watching them and then ducked inside.

Arrow murmured, "Close the door. There's usually guards in front of this, but I made a mess in the kitchen. The servants were screaming when I left. Should take a while for the guards to clean up that whole mess."

"Guards?" she hissed, but went back to work, tugging the door closed. Her fingers screamed with pain. "You said no one was in the halls?"

"And there was no one in the halls when we first got here. None of my words were a lie." He flicked his tail straight up into the air and then started down the long, narrow room. The white tip of his tail waved like a flag. "You'll forgive me once you see what I've found."

Freya huffed out an angry breath and finished tugging the door closed. She hoped they could leave when they were finished here. The door sure seemed stuck. Standing, she dusted her hands off on her now worn jacket and spun.

The room was yet another icy construction. All the walls were a pale color, though. Almost transparent, with small white bubbles of air pockets. There was no furniture, no decorations, nothing that would make this room look like anyone used it at all. The dim light barely even lit up the space for her to see what surrounded them.

"What is this place?" she asked, walking up to Arrow with a frown.

"Step closer to the ice," he replied. His voice was an indistinct murmur of horror. "See for yourself."

She stepped up to the ice and then suddenly the room filled with light. As if someone had spelled it for the moment when another person would step close to the wall. And in front of her was a man who met her gaze with a look of horror in his own. A mortal man, it seemed, although he would never move again.

Freya gasped and retreated from the wall, but the distance only revealed a harsher truth. The soft, golden light illuminated a hundred bodies all hidden within the ice. Frozen in blocks. Still standing at attention as though they could step out of the wall at any time. They were stuck in a single moment with their clothing perfectly preserved and fear still etched on their expressions.

Her hands shook. Freya lifted one to press against her mouth, emotions boiling in her chest. She wanted to rage at the Goblin Queen for taking so many lives. She wanted to scream at the woman who could cause so much hurt and not feel guilt for her choices.

But all Freya could do was shiver in fear. The power it must have taken to suspend all these people's lives... It was unfathomable.

"Who are they?" she asked.

"These are some people from the Winter Court," Arrow replied. "Some of them are merely playthings the Goblin Queen found interesting before she took the throne. They've all been in there for a very long time, I would guess."

Pity made her stomach roll around and her breakfast press against her throat. If she stared for any longer, then she would vomit all over the floor and then someone would know she and Arrow had been here.

A single word played in her mind. *Prison.* They were searching for a prison.

This was obviously a kind of jail, and that meant the Goblin King might be here. Where else would the Goblin Queen have hidden him in this icy castle?

Freya bolted into motion, pressing a single finger against the ice and moving down the line as quickly as she could. "Not him," she whispered over and over until she reached the end of the room. Then, she spun around and did it on the other side.

Arrow let her try to find the Goblin King. He had probably done the same thing when he first found this room, but she had to check. She had to see for herself that they were still going to be in this hellish place because they hadn't found him. Not this easily.

She stopped beside Arrow and pressed both hands to the ice in front of him. This woman was frozen in a beautiful white gown that looked like a wedding dress. She was one of the few who weren't standing. Instead, this lovely dark haired woman was curled up on her side as though she was asleep.

The Goblin Queen had likely trapped this pretty girl in the castle, and then she just never woke up.

Perhaps that would happen to Freya, too.

Her head split open like someone had struck it with a hatchet. Wincing, she pressed her hand to her forehead. The scent of apple pie bloomed in her nose long before she heard the caramel tones of his voice.

"Did you think it would be so easy?" Eldridge asked. "She won't keep me in a place where anyone could find me."

Arrow hissed out a long breath. "My king." The dog bent down until his chin touched the floor. "You're alive."

The Goblin King's reflection stood just beside the sleeping bride. He met Freya's gaze with one of sadness and complete disappointment. "You aren't looking for me hard enough, Freya."

"What would you have me do?" she whispered. "Tear the castle apart with an army of creatures half man, half beast? I could do that. I could get all your old court and force them into another war. Another faerie war that would tear apart the courts and then you could put the pieces back together again."

"Another war?" He shook his head. "No, I don't want that. You know I don't want that."

She remembered the journal, the one he did not know she had read. His diary was nothing more than frantic scribbles and moments of memory from a war that had torn apart his people and his land. But she remembered the emotion in his handwriting. The pain he had felt in knowing that all the creatures were fighting and there was nothing he could do to stop their hatred.

Freya lifted her hand and pressed it against the ice that stood between them. "We're looking for you, Eldridge. I just need something more to work with. If you can't tell me where you are, then tell me something about the Goblin Queen that I can use against her. Something that will convince her to trust me."

He lifted his hand to mirror hers. She could almost feel him through the ice. The warmth of his touch and the magic that came with it. "She hates me, Freya. That's all the clue you need. Fuel that hatred and give her the impression that you hate me as well. Then she will trust you and tell you anything you desire."

She smiled softly. "It shouldn't be too hard to pretend that, now, should it? I do hate you, after all. You're the villain in my story."

"And you're the hero in mine," he whispered. Eldridge flexed his fingers on the ice, as though he desperately wanted to touch her and resented that he couldn't reach through the glass.

His image faded away, and she was left standing alone with Arrow once again.

She took a deep breath. Nodded. Then looked at Arrow with determination. "We're going to find him. We just need to figure out how."

CHAPTER 11

A few days came and went before the little monster showed up at her door again. Freya passed the time by pressing her hands together, breathing into her fingers, and pacing. She knew exactly how many steps it took to get from one end to the other of her room. No amount of pacing helped the anxiety in her chest, however.

They were running out of time. The Goblin King hadn't reached out to her at all since they had stood in that frozen prison with all the Goblin Queen's remaining court. The ones she refused to wake up.

Why?

Why wouldn't the Queen wake up the people who were supposed to be her own? Surely they would be willing and able to help her. They would want to give her more power with this newly acquired throne.

Unless they were the ones who would force her to leave the Winter Court. After all, a Goblin Queen couldn't stay the queen of her own court. Maybe this terrifying woman didn't want to give up her birthright, knew her own people would force her out.

Freya had too many questions, and she knew none of them would get answered without becoming friends with the Queen.

She followed the ice creature through the halls and into an area that split open to the sky. Freya stared up in shock at the sight of the sun. Had they traveled higher in the mountain? She hadn't felt like her legs were working harder. Every hallway seemed entirely flat. But this fissure in the ground had split to the sky. Though the walls were far too high for her to climb.

This wasn't an opportunity for an escape. It was still the same confinement that she'd always been in.

Sighing, she stared straight ahead at what looked like a massive greenhouse. Except, the glass walls were ice that warped her view of what was inside. Other than a single dark figure who stood in the center.

The creature pointed toward the shadow. "The Queen would like to speak with you."

Freya nodded, then looked down at the creature with a small smile on her face. "I think I'm going to call you Frost, if that's all right with you."

Frost blinked up at her and then seemed to frown. "Why would you call me that?"

"Because everyone needs a name." Without thinking, she touched a hand to the creature's head. "Even you, though you seem to think you don't want one. I promise, a name makes you more of a person than just something animated by magic. A name has meaning."

The ice creature touched a hand to its chest as she walked away. Freya heard the smallest whisper as it repeated the name.

"Frost. My name is Frost." The sound of icy high heels clicking over the ground followed the words.

Good. At least now the icy creature might be on her side too.

Freya walked all the way into the greenhouse with its two story high ice walls and gaped at the beauty inside. At least there were no snow drifts here. The floors were a blue marble, not ice, and there were white columns creating a second level. If this had been any other greenhouse, there might have been ivy tangled over the columns and growing in the sun. But even in this room the air was cold. Her breath puffed before her.

There were plants here though, or at least fake ones. Icy roses grew in every corner, and small trees that were carved out of snow. The

Goblin Queen had created the semblance of a greenhouse in this place. But it was still cold and vacant of life.

The Queen stood in the center with her white blonde hair spilling down her back. Her gown today was made of midnight blue, deep and rich in color. It hugged tight to her form, revealing that she was a stunning creature beneath all that fabric. Too beautiful for words.

"Ah, Esther," the Goblin Queen said. "I'm glad you could join me. I was starting to think that you had told my guard that you wouldn't see me."

Esther?

Ah, right. She had lied about her name. Damn it, she was already forgetting her own rules.

Clearing her throat, Freya chuckled and strode up to the Queen's side. "And if I had refused to see you?"

The Queen's gaze shifted, a fire burning in them that was hotter than a regular flame. Blue and white hot. "Then I would have made you, of course. You're in my court for one reason, and one reason alone. My entertainment."

Yes, it seemed like everyone in this court was only here to ensure their Queen was enjoying herself. But that wasn't the way to rule, even Freya knew that.

She took a deep breath and decided to change the subject. This was already going in a direction she didn't want. The Queen needed to be happy, and the Goblin King had said the only way to do that was to talk to her about hating him.

Freya could do that. She could pretend to hate the King. All she had to do was remember how she had felt the first time she had seen him.

Easy.

Walking away from the Queen, she approached the roses and bent down to stare at their delicate construction. "You know, the Goblin King would have hated these. At least, that was my impression of him."

The Queen hesitated for a few moments, then she walked up to Freya's side. "Yes, he would have. Your impression is correct."

"Why do you think he would hate them?" She tilted her head to the side, staring even closer at the roses that were so delicate they almost looked like they were alive. "They're beautiful."

"And delicate. The Goblin King hates anything that's fragile like this. He wants every plant, animal, and person to be strong enough to care for themselves." The Goblin Queen reached out and cupped the nearest rose, then crushed it in her fist. "If something can be ruined so easily, then he thinks it has no place in our world."

Freya now understood why Eldridge was so fascinated with mortals, and perhaps even in Freya herself. It made sense that he would want powerful things to surround him. Stronger than the normal mortal, and certainly a peasant woman would be that. Freya knew how to take care of herself and her sister. But more so, she wasn't a delicate faerie who expected things to be handed to her. She worked for what she had, sometimes struggling for years to get it.

She straightened, trying hard not to stare at the shattered pieces of the rose on the floor. So similar to the pieces of the faerie the Queen had crushed. "And you hate him as much as he hates these roses. Don't you?"

The Queen met her gaze with a small smile that showed her pleasure in the topic. "Oh yes, I hate him more than anything in this realm. And he deserves that hatred. Don't you agree?"

The lie burned on her tongue. "Yes. Most likely. He's a dangerous man who takes what he wants."

"That's why I like you, Esther. I think you understand why I hate him." The Queen reached forward and touched a fingernail underneath Freya's chin. The bitter touch burned. "Tell me why you loathe the monster."

She tried to push all the anger she'd felt at him in that memory into her gaze. Freya forced herself to relive that moment when she had realized the goblins had stolen her sister. "Because he kidnapped my sister for taking a necklace that looked like our mother's. She didn't buy it from the goblin market, she just wanted to see if it was the same one our mother wore. That was all. And then when I realized she had disappeared, I knew I had to beat him and get her back."

The Queen stroked the nail along Freya's jaw, her gaze wide with rapture. "Such passion. You truly think him a beast."

"I told him he was the villain in my story." Freya swallowed hard. "And if I saw him again, I would tell him the same thing. He's still the villain. A demon."

That was the truth, although the anger with the words had dulled. She didn't think he was really a monster anymore. There were layers to his person that she had yet to uncover, and that she was interested to learn.

The Goblin Queen dropped her hand and sighed. Even that movement was pretty and delicate. "You know I used to think of him as my brother?"

"Really?" Freya backed away from the Queen, but then sat on a nearby bench. Hopefully the movement would look like she wanted to rest rather than create space between herself and the horrible queen. "A brother? I thought he was born in the Autumn Court?"

"He was. But his family didn't like him very much, you see. The feeling about Eldridge runs in all the veins of the fae. No one liked him. My family took him in as pity, hoping that he would grow into someone we could love." She lifted her hand and a tiny figure of Eldridge appeared in her palm.

He was young in the swirling snowflakes that created him. His shoulders were held a little straighter and his hip was cocked at a sharper angle. He obviously thought highly of himself. Perhaps that was the posture of a faerie soldier, she didn't know.

Freya's heart leapt into her throat at the sight of him. *Don't react,* she told herself. *Stay angry and don't let her see all the complicated emotions that are swirling in your chest.*

She licked her lips and pointed at the figure. "How strange to think that he would have sought help from the Winter Court. In my experience, none of the faeries of any court like each other."

"We don't. But the Winter Court was more giving in those days." The Queen crushed the figure in her hand as she had the rose. "He used to tell me I was capable of great things and great kindness."

Freya shouldn't have pried even further. She didn't want to know the answer, but some part of her screamed to ask the question. And so she did. "Are you?"

The Goblin Queen's blue eyes lit up with an inner light, glowing with power. "Capable of great things? Yes. Capable of great kindness? No."

Freya's stomach twisted, and she felt nothing but fear once again. None of the other faerie leaders had made her so afraid other than this icy woman who didn't see mercy in the world. The Goblin Queen would stomp upon anyone who stood in her way, and Freya didn't think she would feel bad about it.

This Queen would kill and slaughter and destroy. She desired to see the world at her feet and then to laugh in its face.

Tucking her shaking hands into her skirts, Freya tried to change the conversation yet again. "My Queen, I have a question for you. It's my hope that you have seen worth and value in my presence in your castle."

"Oh, indeed. You are quite entertaining, my dear. I have never been more interested in a mortal, and that's a compliment."

It didn't feel like a compliment. Actually, it felt like a threat.

Freya tried very hard to not let the words bother her. She would survive this, just as she had survived so much more. "If you didn't notice, I'm still in the same clothing I was in when I arrived. My hope is that you may have some great kindness still within you to dress me in something other than an old woolen coat and underthings that have seen quite a few days of travel and freezing."

The Queen looked her up and down, then her eyes seemed to clear. Her mouth curved into a wicked smile. "Oh, my dear. I'm so sorry that I haven't noticed your... predicament. Yes, of course I will clothe you. I have so many things that are leftovers from the old Winter Court, and I think I would very much enjoy seeing what you look like with them on. A mortal, wearing the garb of the Winter Palace."

Was this a good thing? Freya didn't know. This could be a massive mistake to ask the queen to invest even more time in her, but Freya was just starting to hear the story of the Goblin King from this new Queen's lips.

So she would do whatever the woman wanted.

Freya flinched when the Goblin Queen clapped her hands.

"Come, mortal!" she shouted. "Let's see what you look like in clothing made for royalty."

CHAPTER 12

Freya followed the Goblin Queen through a small back door in the greenhouse and then through the winding halls yet again. She was so tired of looking at blue ice. Freya desired to see bright green grass and a splash of pink and red in the sky. Any color. Anything other than damned blue.

The Queen led her all the way into a room that functioned as a sort of closet. The closets appeared to be more tunnels that hid so much fabric it made Freya's head spin. Was this where all the ladies of the court would get dressed? Why wouldn't they have these dresses in their own rooms?

The Goblin Queen lifted her arms. Blue magic spilled in glittering sparkles from her hands and down her arms. It landed on the ground and funneled toward the walls. Deep blue glowed from within the ice, and then ten of the ice creatures stepped out.

They were all slightly different. Their eyes were shaped in round circles or squeezed ovals. Some of them had pointed feet, while others were flat nubs at the end. But they weren't the ice creature she was used to.

"Hello," Freya said.

"You're so polite," the Goblin Queen laughed. "They don't know how to talk. Not like the one I send to go get you. Apparently talking made bringing you to my side easier. It's gotten rather annoying with all those words, though. Would you like a new one?"

That sounded like the Queen would kill the ice creature if Freya was disappointed with it. And she wasn't. She'd just named the poor thing!

"No!" she almost shouted the word. Clearing her throat, she shook her head to emphasize the word. "That one suits me just fine."

"Really, I can make any of them do whatever you want. If that one doesn't look the way you desire, then I can just make another one." The Goblin Queen waved at the ice creatures that approached Freya. "They're much easier than real servants. They don't need food or attention. They just need to know what their job is and they go about it. You see? Already they want to help you out of your clothing. Now, let me pick out the perfect dress for you."

The Goblin Queen turned around and marched toward the closets like she was going to war. And maybe this was her kind of war, Freya didn't know.

Freya thought it was probably not smart to argue with the ice creatures that already had their tiny hands outstretched. If they were going to help her, then so be it.

She lifted her arms and let the monsters go to work. Their icy hands dragged down her body, and she hated every second of their cold strokes. It was like dead things were pulling her clothing off.

A splitting headache preceded Eldridge's voice in her ear. "This is different from the last time a faerie dressed you, now isn't it?"

She couldn't reply to him, damn it. He had to know the Goblin Queen was right in front of her, and obviously she wouldn't be talking to the ice creatures. One of them had stepped on top of another to pull her jacket down over her back and now was working on the laces of her woolen gown.

"What are you doing?" she whispered under her breath.

"Entertaining myself," he replied. The Goblin King stepped in front of her, arms crossed over his chest and head tilted to the side. "Isn't that what Goblin Kings are supposed to do? That's what she was telling you, at least."

Freya gritted her teeth and glared at him. This was too much of a risk. The Goblin Queen could turn around at any point and see him standing there.

"Esther?" the Queen called out. "What color looks good on your skin, my dear?"

She shook her head, breath coming ragged out of her lips. "I don't know."

"You don't know?" The Queen turned around and Freya knew that this was the moment when it all crumbled down. The damned Goblin King had ruined everything once again, sabotaging himself so he'd have to stay here forever in her clutches.

Eldridge remained standing in front of her, watching as the ice creatures undressed her. And the Queen continued to stare at her with a look of impatience.

She couldn't see Eldridge, Freya realized. The Queen couldn't see the Goblin King because, for her, he wasn't really there.

"Esther," the Queen snapped.

"Yes?" Freya whispered the word, too quiet but completely unsure what the question was. Everything in her head was racing, afraid of what the Queen would find out and if she could hide it fast enough.

"You know, if I didn't know better, I would think that wasn't your name at all." The Queen shook her head, then turned back to the clothing. "You never respond as quickly as I want. Get your head out of worrying about what my servants are doing and focus on becoming a more beautiful version of yourself. Pick a color, my dear."

She couldn't pick a color when all this was going on. Freya didn't care what color the Queen picked.

Eldridge watched her with an amused grin. "Yes, Freya. What color do you want to wear? You always look so fetching in blue."

She wasn't playing this game with the two of them watching her like a hawk. "White," she stuttered. "Isn't that the color of your kingdom? White as snow, my Queen. That would be the color I would be most honored to wear."

The Queen clucked, then moved deeper into the closet until she disappeared from sight. "What a color to pick! White. I wouldn't have thought with your pale skin that color would look good on you, but if you insist. It's only going to make you look more pale and drawn, you know."

Then pick a different color, Freya wanted to scream. She didn't care!

The ice creatures finished unlacing her dress. They pushed it over her shoulders until the fabric slumped to the ground. She was left in only her underthings while they gathered up all her old clothes and dragged them away.

Freya wrapped an arm around her chest and used the other hand to hide herself from the Goblin King's gaze. At least no one was looking at her so she could hiss, "Would you turn around?"

"I don't think so," he replied, that stupid grin still on his face. "You're far too lovely, my dear. Would you look at all that pale skin?"

"I'd prefer it if you didn't."

"Oh no, this is a perfect opportunity for me to make you uncomfortable. And I'm enjoying myself." He took a step closer, leaning down to look at her hip. "Where did you get this scar? I must know the story."

She couldn't flinch away fast enough. The Goblin Queen came out of the closet with a massive white gown in her arms. "Will this do? I don't know how warm you have to be."

Freya looked up, panicked. The dress was ugly as sin, but it would do. It didn't matter to her if the dress would make her look like her great aunt. Put it on her and hide her skin. "Yes, that's lovely."

The Queen frowned and threw the dress onto the ground. "That was a test! This dress is ugly, and you'd look awful in it. Really, girl, do you not have any sense of fashion?"

"Wait—" Freya tried to stop the Queen from returning into the closet, but she already disappeared beyond the dresses.

Huffing out an angry breath, she pursed her lips and looked back at the Goblin King. "Eldridge, stop looking at me."

He straightened, eyes glazed and a stupid smile on his face. "Why would I ever do that? You're a beautiful woman, Freya. I didn't know how much more lovely you could get until this moment. I mean really, look at you! You're like a rose ready to be plucked."

"What kind of nonsense is that? Snap out of it, you idiot."

He leaned forward, almost touching his nose to her hair. "Really, I'm not lying. You know I cannot lie. I find you completely irresistible."

"I'm going to slap you." She needed to focus, and he was distracting her worse than normal.

"You wouldn't dare."

She whipped her arm back and struck out like a snake snapping at a mouse. Her hand clapped across his face and the sound echoed far too loudly. Eldridge flinched back with a sound of shock, pressing his hand against his bright red cheek.

"What was that for?" he whined.

"Be better," she snarled.

The Queen came out at the same second, holding another gown that was far more beautiful. The neckline was a modest square, while the skirts flared out only a little at the hips. It would be warm and still give her enough space to move. "Did I hear you strike something?"

Freya struggled to figure out what would make sense. Finally she shrugged and said, "I thought I felt a spider on my leg. I slapped at it, but there was nothing there. Must have just been a phantom feeling."

The Queen strode to her side and held the dress out. "You must tell me if you ever find a spider in my castle, my dear. I hate the dreadful things and have no place for them in the Winter Court. It's why I keep it so cold."

Freya had an idea it was for more reasons than that. Sighing, she took the dress and nodded. "Of course, my Queen."

The ice creatures stacked themselves beside her again, reaching out for the gown with their tiny hands. Freya gave the dress away and let herself be stuffed into the fabric.

The whole time, Eldridge stood behind the Goblin Queen. If looks killed, he would have seared through the Goblin Queen's flesh. Though he wasn't as intimidating as normal. Rubbing his bright red cheek made him look a little... well. Adorable.

Freya held herself still until the ice creatures finished with their work. One of them hopped down, moved to stand by the Queen, and then put its tiny ice hands on its hips. Together, the creature and the Queen looked her up and down until the Queen finally nodded.

"Yes, that will do. Now you look far less like a mortal who stumbled into my castle from the forest. You really were looking like something the Summer Lord would have enjoyed. Too..." The Goblin Queen waggled her fingers in the air. "Earthy."

Eldridge curled his lip in disgust. "You wouldn't know something that looked earthy if it hit you in the face, Lumi. All you see is a beautiful woman who might actually hold a candle to your own beauty."

Was she supposed to respond? Freya furrowed her brows in concentration and forced a smile. "Thank you. I feel more at home here now that I'm wearing something more appropriate."

At least she had sleeves. Now all she had to do was find another jacket that would cover her up, and she'd look more like she belonged here. And the more she looked like she belonged, the more the Queen would like her.

"Yes, before you looked too much like someone, the Goblin King would like. And you know how much we want to avoid that." The Queen reached her hand out for the ice creature to take. "My little servant, would you please go get the fur coat? You know the one."

The creature walked right through Eldridge as though he weren't even there. Or perhaps as though he were a ghost.

She supposed he sort of was in this form.

Freya took a deep breath and tried to think of something else to say. Something that would prove she wasn't distracted. "I'm curious what the Goblin King's type was, then. If he would prefer earthy things, then how did he end up in the Winter Court?"

The Queen's gaze flashed in anger. "Because he enjoys being disappointed, of course. Eldridge never wanted anyone to love him. He wanted to be worshipped, revered, and perhaps even feared. But he never knew what love was, and he wouldn't have recognized it if it had bitten him in the ass."

With a sudden lunging movement, Eldridge put himself in front of the Queen's face and snarled, "You raging bitch. You know damned well that's a lie, and yet those poisonous words can still drip from your tongue?"

Freya wanted to shout at him to stop. She couldn't focus on what the Queen was saying when he was screaming in her face as though he were already standing in the room.

A little whine escaped her lips before she licked them and replied, "That sounds like a horrible way to live. Perhaps you should have pitied him."

"Ah, yes." The Queen smiled and tilted her head back as though rays of sunlight were playing on her face. "Pity for the Goblin King. That sounds like a wonderful idea."

If he could have ripped out the Queen's throat, he likely would have. Rage turned his features into something dangerous and fearsome. Yet, Freya had to keep up this charade that she hated him, when all she wanted to do was save him. To get Eldridge away from this monstrous woman who wanted to harm him and everything he loved.

Blowing out a long, steadying breath, she forced herself to smile and spin in a circle. "Well, my Queen? Are you happy with your work? You've turned this country peasant into a real noble of the Winter Court!"

"Maybe not a noble," the Queen replied, but the smile on her face said otherwise. "But you are certainly easier to look at now, my dear. You could sit at my table and you wouldn't embarrass me."

Freya nearly tumbled forward she moved so quickly. She intercepted the ice creature holding the white fur jacket, snagging it and flipping it over her shoulders with a flourish. She spun in one more circle before winking at the Queen. "Then why don't we go on an adventure, my Queen? Just you and I."

"What adventure would you like?"

"Oh, I don't know." She tried to infuse her voice with excitement, when all she felt was nauseous. "Show me everything. I find myself enchanted by your kingdom, Goblin Queen."

Those were the magic words, apparently.

The Queen straightened, puffing out her chest with pride before holding out her arm for Freya to take. "Then let me show you my world, Esther."

CHAPTER 13

Freya paced back and forth beside her bed. Another week had passed, and she'd gotten nowhere. The Queen had shown her all over the castle and she was no closer to finding Eldridge.

This place was a labyrinth. Larger than the one in front of the Summer Lord's castle. Freya was certain she could spend an entire lifetime trying to figure out this maze, and it would still change before she finished walking through the entirety.

"The Queen makes the hallways realign themselves every few days," she told Arrow. "She changes them so that no one can know how to get from point A to point B without walking through the ice itself."

He stretched on the bed where she had laid out the blankets and furs for him to be more comfortable. "Then we break through the walls."

She shook her head. "They are thick. Too thick, really. It would take me a few hours to break through one, and then she would have already felt the difference in her building. Her magic runs through everything."

"It can't run through everything," he grumbled. "Even the Goblin King wasn't that powerful."

Freya rubbed her eyes, trying to think through the exhaustion.

She'd been trying so hard to entertain the Goblin Queen that she really hadn't had time for herself. Sleeping wasn't an option when the Queen had a new plaything.

"Then she's getting her power from somewhere else," she muttered. "Or something else."

A new voice interrupted them. "Could it be that she's getting her power from someone else?"

She let out a long, frustrated groan. "Of course you show up now. Where have you been?"

The Goblin King sat on the bed beside Arrow, although the goblin dog spared not a single glance for his king. If anything, it appeared Arrow couldn't even see Eldridge.

Arrow lifted his head, perked up his ears, and searched the room for his king. Loyalty ran in his veins, strong and true. He would do anything for his king. No matter how difficult that task might be. "Is the king here?"

"You can't see him?" she asked.

When Arrow shook his head, she narrowed her gaze on Eldridge.

The Goblin King shrugged. "I'm only so powerful, Freya. Sometimes I can't let him see me. Sometimes I have to use you as a guide."

She rolled her eyes to the ceiling, frustrated with life at this point. "Eldridge says he doesn't have enough power for you to see him right now, Arrow. I don't have the faintest idea what that means, or why he would even say it, but here we are. I understand nothing in this realm is as it appears."

Eldridge leaned back on his hands. "Think about what I said first, Freya."

At the same time, Arrow replied, "Ask him what is wrong if he can't use his powers for both of us to see him, then."

She couldn't keep track of everyone in the room talking at the same time. They both needed to slow down because her head hurt so much it felt like it was going to explode.

Maybe Eldridge wasn't the only one getting weaker. The pain in between her eyes was making her shake. Lifting a hand, she pressed it against the side of her head and reminded herself to breathe. "He said that the Queen might be taking some of his power to add to her own. Something along those lines."

"Freya?"

She didn't know which one said her name. Her vision went blurry, and she staggered a few steps to the side. Why couldn't she balance?

Warm hands scooped underneath her arms. "Sit down before you fall down, Freya."

Eldridge lowered her onto his spot on the bed, sinking down onto his knees between her legs. His hands smoothed back and forth on her thighs, easing her through the dizzy spell and bringing the room back into focus.

Taking a deep breath, she inhaled through her nose and out through her mouth. Over and over until the room stopped spinning and she could actually see Eldridge on his knees.

"I'm sorry," she whispered. "I don't know what that was."

"A mixture of exhaustion and me using your mind a little too much." Eldridge reached up and smoothed a strand of her hair behind her ear. "Keep breathing, dear one. You will be fine, but you need to get your balance again. Your body needs to center itself."

"I don't know why it needs to, though." Her heart started racing again, and she couldn't quite catch her breath fast enough. "I just... I don't know what's happening at all anymore. I feel like I'm falling through my own life."

"No, no, Freya, you aren't falling." He shifted his hand to the back of her head and drew her down toward him. Pressing their foreheads together, he took a deep breath with her. "I won't let you fall. I have unlimited power, don't you know that? Magic that would pull the stars from the sky for you if you wished."

"But you're in a prison and I can't find you."

"I won't be there forever." He leaned back and grinned. His thumbs stroked the high planes of her cheekbones. "You're the hero of this story, Freya. You're going to find me. Together, we will defeat the Goblin Queen and restore this world back to what it needs to be. You and I."

She liked the sound of that. At least then she wasn't alone anymore. It wasn't the weight of the entire world on her shoulders, pressing down until she was nothing more than a flattened soul underneath a mountain of responsibility.

Her lungs stopped screaming for breath. Her heart stopped racing. And it even seemed like the ache of the throbbing headache dulled ever so slightly.

She nodded. "All right. It's easier if this is together and not..."

"Apart?" he filled in the word for her.

"Yes."

Eldridge released her and stood back up. "We have never been apart, Freya. Ever since the first moment I saw you, I knew you wouldn't stray far from my soul."

What was she supposed to say to that? She was just a mortal woman, and she'd never even entertained a man at home. Yet this one could string together the most beautiful words she'd ever heard in her life.

A cold wet nose pressed against her arm. "Are you back to yourself yet?"

Of course. Arrow was in the room with them, and she couldn't stare at the Goblin King with moon eyes any longer.

Clearing her throat, she nodded. "Yes, Arrow. I'm so sorry to frighten you. Eldridge, I know it might be difficult, but could you show yourself to Arrow? Take whatever power from me you need. If that's even possible for you to take power from a mortal."

"I don't think you have any more to give," he muttered. "I will try my best."

Freya felt a tug deep in her belly, like he was pulling her spine through her stomach. She pressed a hand to her abdomen and winced, but didn't complain.

Eldridge's form shimmered. Whatever glamour he had put on himself disappeared with the action as well. One moment, he was the ragged looking king. Bruises appeared over his eye and jaw. A cut sliced through the top of his eyebrow and she didn't know if this was due to using the magic, or if he'd just been hiding the wounds from her.

Arrow growled, low and deep. "So she's taken to hurting you, then?"

"Just like old times," Eldridge replied. "There's no stopping her once she starts. You know how she loves to hear people scream."

Freya's heart broke in two. She had known he was in some kind of pain, but this?

"What is she doing to you?" she asked.

"I can't tell you that, Freya. This is just a distraction from what you need to do. You know that." He looked at her with so much hope in his gaze. Hope that she would be the one who finally made a difference. That she could save him even when she knew the likelihood of that was diminishing with every passing day.

She would do what she could. Freya could only move so fast and she hoped she would get to him in time.

Blinking past tears, she nodded. "Fine, then. You have to help us some, Eldridge. I cannot do this without your help. Together, remember?"

Arrow put his paw on her leg. "It's faerie law that no one can help the king, Freya. Not even himself. If he could tell us where he was, or give us any sort of hint, he would have by now."

"Damn the law," she snarled. "I don't care if the faeries say we're supposed to let him get strung up by his toes every night. Laws are meant to be broken."

"Not this one," Eldridge replied. "Faerie law is enforced by magic. I cannot say anything because my tongue won't actually say the words. If I even tried, the only sound that would come out would be a wheeze. You have to do this on your own because you're the only mortal here. You're the only one who can break the rules."

"Eldridge," she groaned. "There has to be something. Tell me something, anything that would get me further into her good graces. I've been doing my best and catering to her every whim, but she still looks at me like some new toy. And no one is going to tell a new plaything anything of importance. Not unless it slips out and then we're merely operating on the hope of good luck."

He tapped his finger against his chin, staring off into the distance as he pondered what he might say. Then Eldridge lifted that finger. "She's not the same person she was when I first froze them."

"How so?"

"The price of resurrection is a soul," he replied. Eldridge started pacing back and forth. "The laws of nature are very clear. You don't get to die and come back. That's basic magic. But because she has, I can only assume that the price has something to do with why she's so different. Maybe that's why she's not bringing the rest of her court back either."

"Like she's leaking," Freya said. "Why else would she need to stay in the Winter Court and take magic from you? She already has the power of the Goblin Queen."

Eldridge snapped his fingers and pointed at her. "Precisely. She's here to take as much power as she can, but no one needs this much. Unless she's planning to use it to create another realm." He paused, then shook his head. "No, she wouldn't know how to do that. I was the only one to discover that spell, and I destroyed it after I read it."

"You know how to create other realms?" she asked, dumbfounded.

What kind of magic had he wielded when he was king?

Eldridge shook his head and waved a hand in the air, dismissing her question. "That doesn't matter. I'll tell you someday. What we need to focus on right now is exposing her weakness. She's hiding something from us, Freya. Something very important to her. Otherwise, she wouldn't be keeping the rest of the court asleep."

Freya tried to remember everything the Queen had told her about her past life. But the Queen was smart. She had revealed nothing personal. Even when they were watching the nightly performance from her dancers, the Queen stayed silent about herself.

Finally, she shrugged in defeat. "I don't know, Eldridge. I don't know what secret she's keeping. Everything is so superficial when we talk."

"Like she suspects that you're trying to uncover something." Eldridge's eyes narrowed.

Arrow snuffled in frustration and sat up. "I think you need to show her you're really working for her. Gain her trust in some big way."

"Like what?" Freya lifted her hands in the air, waving them wildly. "What am I supposed to do now, Arrow? Try to kill the Goblin King in front of her? None of that is going to work because she's still going to see me as a nothing. A no one. A non threat."

They all flinched as a fourth voice interrupted them, echoing like the sound of crushed glass. "That's because you're never going to convince her that you want to help. She's vowed to never trust anyone again. And a faerie vow is binding."

All three of them froze. Freya's eyes widened as she looked over at the tiny ice creature who worked for the Queen. "Frost," she said. "How long have you been there?"

It moved through the wall and stood before them, wringing its hands. "Long enough to know you're searching for a way to beat the Queen."

"Ah." She looked over at Eldridge and knew they both had the same thought.

They needed to destroy the ice creature. As much as it pained her to admit, Frost was now a liability. He would run to the Queen and tell her everything. And then they would fail.

She stood up from the bed, but Frost held up its hands.

"I want to stop her too," it whispered. "I know you don't trust me, but just listen? Please?"

Freya looked back to Eldridge, who gave a slight nod. Then she looked at Arrow, who sighed and hopped off the bed.

He nudged Frost toward the back of the room where the largest snowdrift was. "You better make yourself a seat then, friend," he said. "We're going to need the entire story from you."

CHAPTER 14

Frost sat on a snow chair he had made himself, with his hands wrapped around an ice mug that looked very much like something a potter would have made. His legs were too short for the chair, so they hung dangling off the edge like a child.

Freya was finding it hard not to think the little creature was adorable. She wanted to wrap her arms around the poor thing and tell it everything would be okay, but that was foolish. This creature worked for the Queen.

Even if he wanted to overthrow her.

She sat on the bed with Arrow to her left, and the Goblin King to her right. They all leaned forward and stared at the ice creature the Queen had made.

She still couldn't fathom how this monster had gotten out of the Queen's magical clutches. It seemed to think for itself, which the other servants most certainly did not do. Maybe it was the power of speech? Perhaps that was what had given Frost the ability to think for itself.

"Well," she started. "Why don't you tell us everything from the beginning."

Frost nodded, staring down into his empty mug before taking a deep breath. "The Queen didn't make us as servants, at least not a long time ago. We were supposed to be her friends when she was a little girl. She liked to give life to ice and snow because it made her feel more at home."

Eldridge's knee bounced up and down. "I remember that now. She used to name you all and line you up like little soldiers in front of her bedroom. I always had to ask one of you if the Queen would see me if I wanted to play with her."

A soft smile appeared beneath the ice of Frost's face. "I remember that as well. She was much nicer when she was young. Easier to get along with, at the very least." He cleared his throat and then stared back down into the mug. "Then everything changed when she didn't get to become the Goblin Queen. She hated you for taking that from her."

"Of course," Eldridge replied. "She was always power hungry, even back then. She thought she deserved it more than me."

Thoughts bubbled into her memory. Things the Goblin Queen had said that Freya had dismissed, but now she realized were words of insecurity. Or, in their situation, words of weakness.

She leaned forward and braced her forearms on her knees. "She doesn't think she was given the throne the right way now. It's a hard life to believe you have earned respect, but having no one confirm your thoughts about yourself. It must be driving her mad."

"Indeed." Frost nodded along with what she said. "You see, the Queen spent a long time while you were King plotting against you. She wanted to see you ripped from the throne and on your knees before her. That's when everything started getting... dark."

She didn't want to know how dark. Freya had already seen the dancers with bloody feet and the horrible things the Queen could do. Crushed, bloody ice shards would remain in her memory for the rest of her life.

Lifting a hand, she requested, "Can we move past her transgressions? We all know how evil this Queen is. What I want to know is if you have already found out how to beat her. And if you're willing to share that information with us."

Frost nodded vigorously. He kicked his legs up and down. "Yes! There's only one way for the Goblin King or Queen to lose their throne. You can't just take them off of it, because it doesn't work that way."

She didn't follow. They could be taken off their thrones, otherwise Eldridge would still be sitting in the throne room and they wouldn't have to deal with this Queen at all.

Glancing over at Eldridge, she hoped to find a similar expression of confusion on his face. But it wasn't there at all. Instead, he looked very thoughtful as he pondered the ice creature's words.

"You're right," he said. "The throne can only be abdicated by faerie deal or death. Unfortunately, she is unlikely to make any deals that would unseat her. Not like myself."

Freya touched a hand to his bicep. "You still haven't explained why you did that. You bet your entire world on the hope that I wouldn't beat you and then helped me to do so."

The grin on his face made her want to slap him. "You were so interesting, I couldn't help myself. Besides, I could feel her soul rumbling in the ice. I would not be able to keep any of them trapped for very long. This was inevitable."

"So you wanted this to happen?"

Arrow sank his teeth into her forearm and gave her a gentle shake. "We can have this argument later, children. Focus on the ice cube."

Focus on the ice cube? She couldn't focus on anything other than Eldridge having known this would happen, and he still did it. He still chose to lose his throne, his safety, his sanity for what? To draw the Goblin Queen out and hope that Freya could fix his mess for him?

She opened her mouth again to argue, only for Arrow to sink his teeth even deeper in her arm. "Freya," he said, the words garbled through his grip. "Focus on what we can address now. Be mad later."

Letting out a growl that should have made Arrow proud, she wrenched her gaze from the Goblin King and focused on Frost once again. "Do you think she'll make a deal with me?"

The ice monster shook his head. "No. Your king is correct, she's very unlikely to make the same mistake he did. Mortals are too unpredictable and a deal is something she cannot control."

Freya looked between all the faeries and fae-made creatures in the room. Each one wore a matching expression of sadness, and perhaps even expressions of resignation. Why were they all looking like that? If the Queen didn't want to make a deal, then they were back in the same spot they had been.

Weren't they?

She looked over at Arrow and frowned. "Then we've learned nothing new, right? We're stuck?"

"No," he muttered. "There's another option to remove a Goblin King or Queen, but you aren't going to like it."

"Why am I not going to like it?" she asked. Her stomach heaved and what little she'd eaten that day rose once again. Freya already knew the answer. She just didn't want to hear it.

Frost was the one to answer with his grating, horrible voice. "Kill the Queen."

A cold breeze rushed over her entire body. Goosebumps rose on her arms and scattered down her entire body. Freya knew she'd heard him correctly, but his mere idea made her want to vomit.

Kill the Queen? She wasn't a murderer. She didn't know the first thing about ending someone else's life, nor was she interested in learning more. All she wanted was to get out of the Queen's castle and probably take the throne back for Eldridge. Not kill someone.

She lifted her hands up, palms facing the ice monster. "No. I'm not going to kill anyone. There has to be another way."

"There's no other way to take back the throne," Eldridge muttered.

"We can convince her to give it back to you!" Freya shouted and jumped up from her seat, wildly spinning her arms for balance. "She's not a lost cause! The Goblin Queen might be cruel, but you said yourself that she wasn't always like this. We could at the very least try to convince her to do the right thing."

"I don't have that much time, Freya." Eldridge stared up at her with wide eyes. "I know you don't want to hurt anyone. This is difficult for you, and I don't blame you for that. But we have to make a move on the Goblin Queen, and if taking her life is the only way to wrench my crown from her grips..."

Her jaw dropped. Freya asked with a thick voice, "Is this all about the crown for you then?"

Both Arrow and Frost had wide eyes, staring between the two of them as though their parents were arguing. Eldridge opened his mouth, closed it again, then sputtered, "Obviously not."

"Tell me the truth, Eldridge. You set all this up, so that you had to be saved. You knew I was the only person who could actually save you. So is this all about removing the one person who could have fought you for the throne?" She pointed at him and narrowed her gaze into a frown. "Was this all for your pride and greed?"

His mouth gaped open, closed, and then he simply kept his mouth shut.

She felt her stomach drop to her feet. Of course, this wasn't a mistake. He hadn't suddenly become trapped and needed her to save him. He was just using her again, even though the cost was his own pain.

But what king wouldn't be willing to undergo a little pain as long as he got a throne in the end?

Shaking her head, she felt all the tension drain from her shoulders. "At least now I know the truth," she whispered.

"Freya." He stood, reaching out a hand for her to take.

"I'm going to save you still, Goblin King. Don't worry, I will not let you rot because you deceived me. Yet again." She pressed her fingers to her pounding forehead and sighed. "But after this, I am done with you. You can get yourself out of whatever other problems you dig yourself into. I won't save you again. Not after this."

"Freya," he repeated.

She took a hefty step back from him and shook her head. "No, Goblin King. Go back to wherever you came from while we figure out how to kill a Queen."

"You will need my help," he replied angrily.

"No. We won't. What help can you provide when you're locked up in a prison?" She shook her head one last time, then turned her back on him to stare down at Frost.

She knew when he disappeared because the throb in her skull left with him. Then it was just her, Arrow, and Frost left.

Guilt gnawed in her belly. She should have at least been kinder to him. He was, after all, in a prison cell waiting for someone to save him.

He could have used the kindness, especially since she had just been preaching that they should give the Goblin Queen a chance to change.

But she couldn't do it. Not after everything they had gone through together, and how easily she knew he manipulated the truth.

Arrow hopped off the bed and sat down at her side, staring up at her while wringing his paws. "I don't know if that was smart, Freya. We still might need his help."

"He's been busting his way into my mind this whole time, Arrow. He's caused me pain, forced me to feel so guilty that I would leave my sister again just to help him. And all of that was because he didn't want to see someone challenge him for the throne. Someone he might not be able to beat." She bit her lip, hoping the stinging pain would prevent her from crying.

And she wanted to cry. Very badly. Freya hadn't done so this entire ordeal since she left her small cottage on the edge of the forest, but she'd never wanted to return to her home more than this moment.

She missed the smell of loam and earth. She missed going to the village and getting her food, rather than hoping a faerie would remember she needed to eat. But mostly she missed being around other humans and knowing what to expect when she was talking to them.

Freya needed to pull herself together. There was more to be done and she couldn't fall apart yet.

But she was very ready to have her moment where she could finally let the tears flow. She would greatly love that moment for the release of all this pain and anguish in her chest.

She took a deep, steadying breath, then sat back down onto the bed.

"Frost," she said. "How do we kill the Queen?"

CHAPTER 15

Freya followed Frost through the castle in the middle of the night. She'd never left her room at this wee hour in the morning. And now she was happy that she never had.

All the lights in the castle dimmed as the Queen slept. Some disappeared entirely until they were walking through the halls, relying on radiant light from other areas of the castle.

The darkness made the ice more terrifying. Sometimes she could hear a deep groan echoing through the walls. Her mind spun nightmares of some ancient creature trapped underneath the castle, and its pain traveled through the ice.

At least they were moving quietly. She'd put on her old clothing, the brown coloring made her easier to overlook. Besides, these clothes were much warmer than what the Goblin Queen had provided her. And the boots were more comfortable than soft, rabbit lined slippers.

"Are you sure we're going the right way?" she whispered.

"Yes," Frost replied. They had covered his feet with some of Freya's old clothing so the ice wouldn't tap as they walked. "It's just this way."

A small part of her worried that the ice creature was bringing her back to the Queen. He was, after all, made by the Goblin Queen's magic. Surely it would be impossible for him to go against her wishes.

Frost had explained that magic always had a price. Sometimes, like giving him a voice, it meant that her control would break. He was a free thinking creation now, and he didn't like what the Queen was doing.

The explanation seemed a bit of a stretch to her. But she didn't know all that much about magic and knew better than to question those who did.

They stopped in front of an icy door and he pointed at it. "This is the door. Go straight through the snow and you'll find a bog. Don't talk to any of the faeries within it. Touch nothing other than the compass at the center. That will bring you to the weapon you seek."

Weapon. It still sent shivers down her spine. Was she entertaining killing someone because she couldn't imprison them?

Killing the Queen wouldn't be easy. The Goblin Queen knew how to say the right words that wiggled into Freya's mind. All she could hope was that in the moment when she needed to take action, that she would. Freya feared she would freeze.

With a sharp nod, she pulled the hood of her cloak up and over her head, then buttoned it tight around her neck. "How cold is it going to be out there?"

Frost gave her an unimpressed stare. "Freezing."

Of course, it would be. Why had she even asked the question?

Freya yanked the door open and plunged out into the waist deep snow. The mountain loomed over her head, dark and ominous now that she knew what it hid within it. But the sheer cliff of the mountain stopped here, and the ground was a great tundra of snow and nothing else. A blizzard raged over her head, but none of the snow touched her. Almost as though the blizzard wasn't actually there at all.

Frowning, she tugged her hood down and tried to step in a straight line. She often had to turn around and stare behind her, double checking that her footprints were orderly. It was hard to tell, but she assumed they were.

The blizzard made everything white. The sky, the ground, everything her eyes could see. Eventually, even the mountain disappeared from view.

"Keep going straight," she whispered to herself. The raging blizzard overhead stole her words and tossed them over her shoulder. The wind was bitter and ruthless, never giving her a second to breathe. Or at least, that's what it felt like.

Freya had no idea how long she struggled through the blizzard and the ice. It could have been mere moments, hours, or even days. But when the wind stopped howling, she knew she had reached her destination.

Another mountain, though much smaller, appeared in the distance. The monolithic structure was surrounded by what looked like hot springs. Tiny dots in the distance broke through the snow and the ice at her feet. The blizzard didn't touch that place, it seemed. Snow still blasted all around her, whipping her hair in all directions, but it stopped in a wall of white. Raging in one area, but if she stepped through the storm, it would be silent on the other side.

The moment she stepped out of the blizzard, all the raging sounds of the storm stopped. Disappearing as though it had never existed at all. The howling winds dropped away and then... nothing.

The silence was terrifying.

Swallowing hard, she trudged through the snow until she reached the very edge of the hot springs. She knew this was the place Frost had spoken of, yet it still felt as though she were intruding upon something that no mortal was supposed to see.

Frost had claimed this was a swamp. The hot springs were more like pits with bubbling water that had a thin layer of goo on the top. Each bubble took a while to build, then even longer to pop. A fine layer of algae grew on the top, but the green coloring was too minty for it to be familiar. Pale and thin, the thick scum on the water shouldn't have grown there at all.

She stepped over a few stones, picking her way through the bog. Her feet sank into the thick mossy ground. She lifted her foot and felt the ground suctioning her boot.

"Careful, Freya," she reminded herself. "If you fall into this water, you'll freeze solid."

Moving through the bog was a little easier than she'd expected, although she had to backtrack many times. The paths through the hot springs sometimes ended. Pools would collide with each other, and she'd have to choose another way.

Freya didn't know what she was looking for. A compass, is what Frost said, but he hadn't given her any idea how to find the darn thing. He'd made it seem like it would be obvious where it was. Obviously, he did not know how difficult it would end up being to find.

A cough echoed over the bubbling water. Freya froze where she was, one leg lifted to take a step. Her brown skirts swayed around her and slowly, she turned to look to her left.

Three faeries were huddled inside one of the pools. Their skin was covered in a fine layer of pale green mud, cracking where they hadn't dunked their bodies underneath the warm water in a while. The one in the middle had her arms around the other two who looked like they were male.

Their ears were incredibly long, almost longer than their entire head. They wore no clothing at all, just the layer of mud.

She wanted to take her cloak off and give it to one of them. Or all three.

Freya opened her mouth to tell them to get out of the water. That was step one. If they could get dry, then they could find something to put on and then huddle near the warm water, but not within it.

Then she remembered Frost had told her not to talk to anyone. She couldn't speak with any of the faeries in this place, although he hadn't given her a reason why.

Perhaps they were dangerous. Or maybe this was a curse that would pass on to her if she tried to converse with any of them. Freya didn't know, but she knew the faerie realm was a very dangerous place. What looked like it was impossible was very possible, as the Goblin King would say.

The thought of him made her shiver and step around the pool with the three faeries in it. Even though she was still angry at him for setting this all in motion, she also realized why he'd done it. This was the only way to bring the Goblin Queen out of her hiding. He had few choices, didn't he?

Stomping through the muck, she came upon two more pools with faeries. One held a single occupant who shivered uncontrollably, holding his arms around his head. A faint whining sound could be heard, although she wasn't sure if he was trying to speak or if he was crying. The third pool was full of faeries. Ten, eleven, she couldn't count because they were all massed together.

Who were these creatures?

Freya noticed there was a small podium in the distance, but she couldn't figure out how to get there. That had to be where the compass was held. It was surrounded by many pools filled with the mud covered faeries with only a single path to get to it.

Goal in mind, she squared her shoulders and figured out the maze to get to where she needed to go.

It took a little while to retrace her steps. She paused a few times with her finger in her air, tracing the lines of the path that she could see. But finally, she made it to the path that would take her to the podium.

A small compass rested on top of the stone structure. She was so happy to see that it wasn't made out of ice, she planned to kiss the stone when she reached it.

Lifting a foot, she went to set it down, only to freeze at the last second when one of the faeries lunged forward. It slapped a muddy hand onto the moss before her and glared at Freya with hatred in its eyes.

"None may pass," it rasped.

She had to pass. This faerie wasn't going to stop her.

If she wasn't supposed to talk to them, then she wouldn't entertain this threat. However, Freya assumed she also wasn't supposed to touch them. Why couldn't this have been a little easier?

There wasn't another way over the path. She reached into her pockets and tried to find something she could give the faerie that might convince it. There were just a few bits of bread and dried fruit that she'd grabbed to keep her stomach full on the journey. Nothing else was useful.

She pulled out a handful of raisins and let them drop from her fingers into the outstretched hand.

The faerie blinked its enormous eyes and twitched its ears. It looked down at the raisins, then retreated into the waters. The dried fruit was held in its hands like she'd given the faerie gold coins.

Maybe that was the secret. These creatures obviously hadn't eaten in a very long time. They were all emaciated and shivering in the water. Surely that would be her way to get them to leave her alone?

She took one step onto the moss and then stopped again when another faerie's hand darted in front of her. Over and over, she handed them bits of food, making sure not to touch them or utter a single sound.

The food ran out before the faeries. There were still three more, each watching her with hungry eyes. Her heart broke for them.

Don't apologize, she told herself. Say nothing until you're in front of that damn podium.

Freya gathered her skirts in her hands, took a running start, and leapt over the faerie's outstretched hands. They shrieked in anger, but at the very least she had gotten to the podium.

The ground was more sturdy here. As though the moss had grown over stone instead of dirt. She stomped her foot to make sure it wasn't ice, and that she wasn't about to fall into a trap, but nothing happened.

The compass sat on top of the podium, unsuspecting with no guards or visible wards. It looked like a normal metal compass. The same kind she'd seen a hundred times in her life.

Hesitantly, she reached out, then snatched it off the podium. She waited for something to happen. Some big, booming sound that would echo all around her. Or perhaps the hot springs would overflow and she'd have to run from the boiling water and the faeries who were released.

But nothing happened at all.

She stared down at the compass and the pin that swirled in her hand. It wasn't pointing north, that was for certain. Instead, it seemed to be wildly moving and waiting for something.

Magic. She'd never get used to it.

Leaning close to the metal, she whispered, "I need to find the weapon that will kill the Goblin Queen."

The pin stopped spinning. It pointed behind the podium at a wall of pale green ivy that had seen better days. Narrowing her eyes suspiciously, she stepped closer to the ivy. It moved with a wind that she didn't feel, so she could only assume...

Freya reached out and brushed some of the tangled plants aside. Thorns bit into the mittens on her hands, sticking to the wool. She didn't care. Because there was a cave hidden behind the plants. A cold, damp cave that was full of darkness.

She frowned into the shadows. No one would walk into that without some kind of light or a torch. She needed something.

But when she looked around, she realized there was nothing to give her light. No sticks. No fire. Nothing.

And this was the only chance they had at stopping this horrible Queen and saving the Goblin King. So even though she was terrified, Freya plunged into the darkness. She only hoped there wasn't something waiting for her.

CHAPTER 16

Once her eyes adjusted to the darkness, she could see vague shadows and shapes around herself, although she had no idea what they were. They could be stones. They could have been armored fae watching her every move.

The compass had a small light within it. The needle glowed on its own and never wavered from the same direction it always seemed to point. So she used that as a guide to get through the tunnels of the cave until she burst out into an enormous cavern.

Sunlight speared from a slight crack at the top of the cave and illuminated the stones. Small mossy patches shone emerald green and were brighter than the sun itself. Or perhaps she was so starved for color, that anything looked vibrant.

Golden sun slashes caught on a stone giant embedded into the rock walls. Only his outstretched hand and bowed head poked through the mountain. The rest was hidden within the stone. Bald, with a polished skull, he stared down at the ground as though defeated in battle long ago.

She wondered what the giant's story was. If the carving was created by an artist, then the emotion was so painful and pure it made her heart ache. But she had a feeling a person hadn't created this masterpiece. This was the faerie realm, after all, and this giant was most likely an actual person who had once been alive.

Freya thought it possible that the Goblin Queen had turned this man into stone. Maybe it was the Goblin Queen's parents, although a giant such as this would have been depicted in the tapestries.

He didn't look like the kind of person who attacked villages or castles. The soft expression of sadness on his face was one she had only seen in the kindest of souls. He held out his hand as though waiting for something. Or someone.

She stepped down into the cave, remaining as quiet as possible because she wasn't sure if she was supposed to talk yet. Could she speak to this creature? Or was that breaking the rules yet again?

She reached out and held onto his thumb that was as tall as Freya. Hauling herself up onto his palm, she walked forward and saw there was a small inscription in the center of his hand. Someone had carved into his stone flesh, "Warm the giant, and he shall provide all you seek."

At least she knew she could talk to him.

Freya looked around for something that might heat this great being. There was a compact bundle of sticks where someone had once built a fire, not in the hand, but at least close enough. She hopped down and gathered it all up in her arms.

A flint laid nestled between stones, with a small leather thong attached to it. She tried very hard not to think about the people who had come here before her.

She stepped back up onto the hand and set her wood into a pattern that she knew would catch ablaze. Putting her hands on her hips, she surveyed her work and then nodded. "That will do."

Carefully stepping back down onto the floor, she returned to the flint and leaned down to pick it up. She lifted it, and a rattling sound startled her. Freya stared in horror at the skeletal hand still clutching the flint in its grasp.

With a shriek, she dropped the flint and shook her hands to rid herself of the shock. She hadn't noticed the bones poking out of the ground where the flint had laid, but apparently someone else had already tried this way to wake up the giant.

They had failed. But she still had to try.

Shaking the skeletal fingers off the flint, she settled her nerves once more. "Stop it, Freya. At least you'll get warm even if this won't wake the giant."

She'd think about this later. And she knew in that moment, she would grow ill knowing she had touched a dead body. Perhaps she would even vomit. But for now, she would start a fire and hope this time, a fire was all the giant wanted.

Using the giant's hand as a lever, she heaved herself back up onto the great palm and set to work building a large campfire. Once the roaring flames crackled, she sat down near the warmth and tried to get some feeling back in her numb fingers.

It was hard to get comfortable in this place. She couldn't even heat her own body up, let alone a giant like this. How was she supposed to thaw the ice that had dripped from his nose and frosted his brows?

She'd need a fire big enough to fill the entire cavern. And then she'd choke herself with smoke after the attempt. It would take her months to gather that much wood, anyway.

"There has to be another way to warm you," she muttered. "Now, what is it?"

Warming a person might not be physical. Freya was always warm in her very soul when she talked about the things she loved. Maybe that was what the giant was waiting for. He wanted a story that would warm him from the inside out.

It was worth a try. And a better plan than she'd come up with thus far.

Freya wrapped her arms around her legs and hugged them close to her chest. What story did she tell first? There were a lot of stories that made her heart squeeze in her chest, but none of them would interest a giant. She wasn't someone who had created a life story worth listening to.

"When I was little, my mother used to take me into the forest," she started. "She didn't like being in the shadows of the trees, but she always brought me there to teach me how to live on my own. Just in case I ever found myself lost in the woods.

"One day, when I had wandered too far from my mother's side, I heard her calling for me in the bushes. I knew nothing about faeries at that point. So I wandered away without worrying what might wait for me. I didn't notice the slight differences in the words, and how the voice didn't sound exactly like my mother.

"I remember her crashing through the brush, screaming my name. And instead of getting mad when she found me, likely just before some faerie had kidnapped me, she pulled me into her arms. I will never forget the love in her voice when she told me I was the most important thing in her life. And that losing me would feel like losing her own heart."

Instead, her mother had forced her children to lose her instead.

Freya frowned. That memory had always heated her to the very soul, and yet, it wasn't doing that at all. She was sad when she remembered it now. She feared what had happened to her mother, and all she could think about was living with her sister on their own. Her mother had spent so many years worrying about losing her children, only to make them suffer the very fate she had tried to avoid.

No, that memory wouldn't do. The giant would only pity her for a childhood ill spent.

Clearing her throat, she tried a different memory. One that always made her laugh.

"My sister lived with me my entire life. She's always been my shadow, right there with me, even when I didn't want her to be. When she was just a child, she used to put frogs in my pockets because she liked to hear me scream."

Freya grinned, this time remembering how much she loved being with her little sister. "She'd fill my drawers with snakes every chance she had. Sometimes, in the middle of the night, I'd catch her in the window talking to the spiders outside. She's always been more interested in things that made other people uncomfortable. Or even afraid."

Like goblins who kidnapped little girls and stole them away to a faerie realm. A magical place full of dangers and monsters. Or, if the little girls were lucky, full of Goblin Kings and fairytale quests.

Yet again, she discovered this place had tainted another memory. She couldn't feel warm about the thought of her sister in the mortal realm when she knew just how much Esther had hated living in that place. Now that Esther wanted to remain here, thinking of her in their home felt... wrong.

She imagined her sister back home, where Esther had felt like she wasn't free, and her stomach turned. Freya couldn't bear to put Esther in a cage again. Not after everything her sister had accomplished.

Frustrated, she tucked a strand of hair behind her ear and tried to think of another story. Anything that was from her old life that might have made her feel better, and thus inspired the giant to come alive.

She couldn't think of a single thing.

The strand of hair fell back in front of her face, pulled out of place by a warm hand.

"I was wondering when you would show back up," she muttered, putting the hair back behind her ear so it wouldn't distract her any more.

"I always show up when you need me," the Goblin King said. His breath played along the back of her neck, hot and warm and all too distracting. "After all, you're out here telling a giant stories of the mortal realm. You already know what stories you should tell him to heat his soul."

"I don't know what you're talking about." But the words were a lie. She knew what the Goblin King wanted her to say. There were only a few memories that left her breathless, and he knew all of them.

After all, he'd been there for each one of them.

His claws dragged over the fabric of her cloak and down her shoulders. "Why don't you try telling him about me, Freya?"

"He's not interested in learning about the Goblin King. I don't think a giant would care very much about your story."

"He doesn't care about me. Or my story. What he cares about is feeling some warmth in that icy soul of yours." He leaned closer and whispered his next words in her ear. "Or have you been in the Winter Court so long that you've forgotten what passion feels like?"

"Stop it," she breathed. "Thoughts of you don't make me feel passion."

"We both know that's a lie."

The Goblin King disappeared back to whatever prison he was in, but his presence still lingered. The scent of him. The feeling of his fingers on her body.

Rolling her eyes, she let the story of the Goblin King tumble from between her lips. She told the giant everything, holding nothing back. How she was confused by the attention of an immortal faerie, but also how it made her heart sing that he would give her any attention at all.

She was nothing and no one. He saw something in her that had captured his attention, and she really didn't understand why.

But his kisses were amazing.

And she hadn't stopped thinking about his lips since he had kissed her. That was problematic. She hadn't ever entertained a man before and adding that stress to this quest only made everything that much more difficult. She didn't want to think about a man when she had a job to do. Freya was better at focusing on what had to be done, rather than what could be done.

The fingers surrounding her twitched, shifted, then curled in toward her. Gently, the giant lifted his arm from the rocks and raised her closer to his face. "You're only feeling conflicted about this because you've never felt this way before. It's perfectly natural to be confused when you have no idea what is happening. You need to give yourself a break."

She stared up into the eyes that were larger than her torso and gulped. A giant was talking to her. A very kind, albeit extremely large, giant who was frozen in the side of a mountain just a few moments ago.

Yet, her story was the one that had woken this fantastical creature. And it wasn't her warmed soul or passion for the Goblin King that had convinced the giant to wake up.

It was that she needed someone to talk to about her relationship with the Goblin King. She needed advice.

Apparently, that advice would come from the lips of a giant.

CHAPTER 17

Freya stared up into the eyes of the giant and tried to close her jaw. Goodness, he was big. Bigger than a house and even larger than some of the castles she had seen in this faerie realm. He held her so carefully, like he knew how easily he could crush her, but didn't want to scare her.

She appreciated that.

Clearing her throat, she stuck out her hand as though he might shake it. "Freya of Woolwich."

"Nice to meet you, Freya. Now why don't you tell me more about this Goblin King that you're falling in love with?" He grinned, revealing chipped teeth that looked as stoney as the rest of his visage.

She frowned. "I'm not falling in love with the Goblin King."

"You most certainly are. I'm afraid that's just how it goes when you're around someone as much as you two have been. It sounds like there's a rather extensive amount of sparks, as well. Have you thought about talking to him about your feelings?" The ground rumbled, and he pulled his other hand out of the earth.

The giant cavern it revealed beneath him made her head spin. If she took one step in the wrong direction, then she would tumble into that dark hole. What would happen then? Would she plunge to her death, breaking every bone in her body before she settled in a mess of broken bones and scrambled flesh?

He must have noticed her staring. The giant shifted her away from the hole, then propped his head on the other hand. Leaning against his fist, he tilted his head to the side and then shook his hand.

She stumbled, apparently moving as he wanted.

The giant asked, "Well? Are you going to admit it or not?"

"Admit what?" she reached out and held onto his thumb for balance. "That I'm falling in love with the Goblin King? I'm not."

"Then why did it disappoint you so much to hear he'd put himself in danger? If you didn't care for him, you would have recognized it as the smartest decision he could make to flush out the Goblin Queen. You would have seen the logic in his choice." The giant lifted a brow.

She disagreed. But a sickly feeling made her stomach turn, because what if he was right? "Are you suggesting if I were falling in love with him, that he isn't feeling the same? And that's why he could put me in danger to save his throne?"

The giant rolled its eyes. "My dear, is there any reason for you to think he doesn't view you as in high regard? He has moved space and time for you. He trusts you to be the only person who could save him from the Goblin Queen. So much so that he actually went through with this insane plan."

Right. And she had just as good as admitted the giant was correct and that she was falling wildly in love with this Goblin King.

Sighing, she flopped down into his palm and cradled her head in her hands. "What am I going to do? I can't be considering this. He's a faerie. I'm a human. We don't mix."

"Historically you mix very well." The giant's cheek squished as his palm shoved it up. "You see, most goblins marry mortal women. Their animal bloodline gets a little too strong if they don't, and faerie blood always overrides mortal blood. It's as easy as that."

She dropped her hands from her face and stared up at the giant again. "How much do you know about goblins? Or the courts?"

"Everything." The giant looked pointedly around them. "This is the Chamber of Memories, my dear. I watch everything that happens in the realm. Nothing is said, done, or thought about without me knowing of it. That's why you're here. I'm the only living person who knows where the knife was hidden."

Freya waved her hand in the air, dismissing the knife entirely. They'd get to that. But first, she wanted to find out everything she could about the Goblin King and the very new Queen.

"The Queen said Eldridge used to live with them in the castle. But there's something that I just don't understand. Her hatred for him runs deep. So deep I have a hard time believing it's because he took the goblin throne from her."

"You haven't pieced that together yet?" he asked. His eyes squeezed shut and his lips turned down at the corners. "Eldridge always saw her as his adopted sister. And though they were of similar age, he considered himself to be part of the Winter Court when they took him. It was as simple as that in his mind, and he never considered another future."

Though the thought had occurred to her, Freya hadn't given it any merit until this moment. "But the Goblin Queen... She didn't view him as a sibling, did she?"

The giant shook his head. "No. In her mind, he was always the Autumn Thief. A very handsome, very strange young man who had appeared from another court. And he catered to her every whim, as he thought a good brother should do. They went riding together. He taught her how to prank her parents, and he marveled at the ice magic she could control when she was but a child. They were inseparable."

She shouldn't feel pity for the Goblin Queen, but she did. A strange mixture of emotions pulsed in her chest.

Jealousy because she didn't want anyone else to have claim to the Goblin King. She didn't enjoy hearing about another woman who had been such an important part of his life. But she also realized just how tempting he could be. How the thought of his arms around her had consumed her mind so easily.

The Goblin Queen had only hoped for something more from the young man who had come into her court. Instead, she had been given a brother who would remain a brother no matter how hard she tried to convince him that she wasn't his blood relative.

Such unrequited love could destroy a person. Or, in the Goblin Queen's case, make them hell bent for revenge.

Freya sighed, all her emotions filtering out with the breath. "So she loved him, then."

"In whatever way the Goblin Queen could love anyone. Her heart is cruel, Freya. I wish I could say she was once a good person, but she always leaned toward darkness and pain." The giant moved his hand, wiggling his fingers until she stepped off of him and back onto the ground. "You should not feel guilty for what you are about to do. The last remaining good part of her wants this as well."

"I find that hard to believe." She stared around them at the cave and the moss that dripped from the rocks. This place couldn't really be so cruel as to let a woman die because she'd loved the wrong person? "I don't think she wants to die. I think she wants revenge."

"And then what?" The giant waved his hand in the air. "She won't stop there. Revenge is an empty plan. Once she gets it, then where will she go? What will she focus on? The next person who harmed her? You need to see what she was like during the faerie wars. Perhaps then you will understand why I say she needs to rest. Forever."

Freya remembered what Eldridge had written in his journal. The faerie wars were brutal, yes, but the nobility of the Winter Court had remained in their castle. He had done what he could to protect them on the battlefield. But none of them were out there with him.

She opened her mouth to argue, but the giant interrupted her with an all knowing stare.

"Freya," he muttered. "Do you believe everything you found in a journal? Of course the Goblin Queen fought. This was her court and people were trying to take her from the throne. They wanted to murder her and her family. The fight was exactly what she wanted. She fought with her soldiers, side by side, and she never stopped fighting. She loved the bloodshed."

"I..." What was she supposed to do with this knowledge?

Freya didn't know why it was even important for her to believe the Goblin Queen was a bad person. After all, there was no other way out of this. Eldridge, Arrow, Frost, they all had said the Queen had to die.

And Freya was the only one who could kill her, apparently, even though she had never killed anyone in her life.

Frustrated, she wrapped her arms around herself and muttered, "I don't know why it's so important for me to believe this. Does it matter if I think she's an evil person or not?"

"It does," the giant replied. "Because you cannot hesitate. And if you don't truly believe that this is the only way, you will. She has lived hundreds of years. All that time gave her experience that you could never dream of. If you want to beat her, Freya, then you must not question your resolve."

Freya was already questioning it. She questioned everything the fae told her because none of it sounded like the truth. Even though she knew some of it had to be. Or at least the vague shadow of truth when they were always trying to hide something.

Hesitation was part of how she had survived this world.

"Freya," the giant groaned. "Perhaps it would be best if you simply saw what she has done. I fear everything rests on your shoulders now, and that you don't realize just how important this is."

"Of course I do." Freya wanted to argue that she had listened. Everyone kept telling her what to do and how to do it, but she was certain this wasn't right. There was more she could do. More that they could at least attempt to convince the Goblin Queen to listen.

Why were they all giving up on this woman who had wanted to be loved?

But she didn't get the chance to argue. The giant shifted and pulled himself out of the mountain. The ground grumbled in anger, shaking beneath her feet and rocking her dangerously close to the edge of the abyss from which the giant emerged.

He lifted a hand and slammed it down on the other edge of the cave. The wall shifted, then broke as if someone had punched a hole through the stone itself. Light speared through the space, revealing an enormous field on the other side filled with fog and drifting clouds.

A field that was barren of snow, though still dusted with pale greys and whites.

"What is this place?" she asked.

"It is the final battleground of the faerie wars," the giant said.

"Many faeries died here. And sometimes when a faerie dies in a grue-some manner, they don't leave the spot where they met their demise. No matter how many people try to convince them to leave, they will remain exactly where they died. You need to speak with these remnants of a time long past."

She didn't want to talk to ghosts. Freya had already talked with faeries, and that was more than enough for her lifetime.

"Spirits?" She said the word as though it were a curse.

"In a manner of speaking. They are quiet souls who have no desire to harm you, Freya. They merely want to talk." The giant pointed toward the opening in the cave. "Go. There is no other way out."

She didn't want to. But apparently, like everything she'd experi-enced in the faerie realms since coming here, Freya didn't have a choice. She had to go through this hole in the wall. Speak with the ghosts like that was something she did every day.

"I don't know why I need to be convinced," she grumbled. "I just need the knife."

"And they are the only ones who will tell you where it is, now. I certainly won't." The giant quirked a brow. "They will bring you to it if they deem you worthy."

"Another test." Freya picked her way over the stones and out onto the fog covered fields. "It's always another test in this place."

CHAPTER 18

Freya stepped onto the ashen fields and heard the stones knitting themselves back together behind her. She didn't turn to look. There was no need anymore, magic was simply what it was. She didn't worry about it anymore, even though it still felt a little strange to see sometimes.

Compared to the cave, this place was eerily quiet. She hadn't realized just how loud the sound of dripping water and the giant's breath had been.

This place had no sound at all.

No wind.

No breath.

Nothing but the faint hush of ash shifting in a breeze that was sluggish and low. The grey clumps on the ground looked almost like snow. It was so thick a blanket that the ash covered whatever was lying beneath the surface.

Although Freya knew what the ash hid. She wasn't so naïve that she couldn't guess what remained on this battlefield.

She stepped over what looked like a ribcage. Bodies laid everywhere. Some of them were completely bare, leaving just the hint of bones and what might have once been a person. Others didn't have a body left at all, but their armor remained where they had once lain.

Swallowing hard, she bent down and picked up a shoulder plate. The silver had been polished once, but now was dingy with age. Fine filigree decorated the edges, standing out against the flat metal. Tiny dots and swirls might have meant something once to this person who had worn it. A family crest, perhaps.

The person had died wearing this armor that was supposed to protect them. They had given up everything for this war and their court, only to fall here and then be forgotten.

Footsteps behind her proceeded the scent of apple pie. Eldridge stepped to her side, and she realized he didn't leave any footprints in the ash. He bent down as well, sinking onto his haunches, and reached out his hand to touch a small pile of ash.

Peering closer, she could make out the shape of a skull beneath his hand. The teeth still stood out in stark relief, even though the ash looked like a white blanket had been laid over the head.

"This was where it all happened," he said. His voice was full of haunted memories. "The last stand as all the courts battled with each other because we all refused to admit there was only one person worthy of being the Goblin King."

"Why?" she asked. "Why wouldn't they all fall in line under a single person?"

"Because every court wanted someone from their own to take the throne. It was the first year in recorded history that it might be possible. The Autumn Court had always given up their Thief to become the King or Queen. But that year it could have been anyone from any season." He stared down at the skull as though it could look up at him. "And it was partly my fault. I didn't want to take the throne, and I made that very clear. I gave them false hope."

He turned his head, and she gasped in horror. The side of his face that had been turned away from her was horrifically burned. The ragged edges of blistered skin stretched all the way into his hairline. It was the worst around his eye, where someone had clearly tried to take out the orb.

"What happened?" she whispered, reaching out a hand to touch him.

"The same thing that has been happening since she first captured me, Freya. Nothing new." He leaned away from her touch. "Did you not hear me? All this life lost is my fault. I was the one who encouraged them to battle and I am the one to hold the weight of this guilt."

She looked around the battlefield and saw all the carnage that had once been here. "Perhaps you do," she replied. "But do you not dishonor all the souls who were once here by not taking the throne again? You were a good king, Eldridge. Everyone I've spoken with agrees. They love you as their monarch, and they want you back."

"I suppose that's what every king wants, isn't it? To prove we're worthy of their adoration." He stood up slowly, as if the movement pained him. "I didn't want you to see these memories. The giant knew that."

"You don't always get what you want." Freya stood as well. "The giant said I needed to see it for myself. So I don't make some mistake that we're incapable of reversing, I guess."

"Like not killing the Goblin Queen when you have the chance?" There was something in his gaze that she couldn't name. Some emotion that was almost like hope, but poisoned with regret.

"Why are you so sad?" she asked, taking a step forward. Eldridge retreated from her. She took another step closer to him and chased him through the ashen fields. "I don't think I've ever seen you like this. Do you not want her to die?"

Something twisted in her chest. Maybe he had buried all that emotion in his heart for so long and was just now realizing that he was in love with the Goblin Queen. That he had denied her his attention for such a long time, but that he hadn't wanted to deny her at all.

What if this was his revelation and now Freya was just standing in the way?

She could return to the mortal world. Without her sister, of course, because Esther had already started making a life for herself here.

Why did that hurt so much? The mere idea of leaving with no one to come home to stung, but it wasn't that emotion that churned in her belly. It was the jealousy and the heartbreak that maybe she was too late.

The anger that he had put himself in danger and used her as an escape. That emotion had made her too late to tell him how she really felt. She couldn't do anything other than accept whatever his choice was. Because she couldn't control him.

Swallowing hard, Freya stopped where she was. "If you don't want me to kill her, then we can find another way. Perhaps you two can share the throne. Perhaps—"

"No." He stepped forward and caught her around the waist.

Eldridge tucked her into the curve of his body. Those starry eyes swirled, hypnotic and oh so very enthralling. Freya couldn't breathe when he looked at her like that.

"I know you two were close when you were children," she whispered. "The giant told me a lot of things. And I think you need to reconcile that history with her before you make any decisions. Maybe she doesn't have to die."

"You are willing to give up so much to save someone who means nothing to you." He lifted a hand between them and tunneled his hand into her hair. "That heart is part of the reason I am so fascinated with you, Freya. You choose to forgive and to allow people to live their lives even though it may make yours harder."

"It's not always about me," she replied with a shrug. "I can give up some of my comfort as long as it helps someone else in the long run."

"And that is very unfaerie-like of you." He sighed, the breath fanning across her lips. "I know you're mad at me, Freya. You have every right to be. But if there could have been another way for me to do this, you must know that I would have chosen that path. I would have done anything to spare you this pain."

She didn't know that, not really. Even now, a part of Freya didn't believe that he would have changed anything. He knew how to manipulate and warp the truth into something that suited him. That included changing reality.

But she knew she was already tired of being angry with him. She was so exhausted and the safety his arms provided was so tempting. Even though she knew it was only temporary.

Freya rested her head on his shoulder, taking the comfort he offered. "I know you aren't really here right now, but I wish you were."

She felt the press of his lips against her hair. Those lips curved into a smile that spread heat from the top of her head to the bottom of her toes.

Eldridge chuckled. "Don't tell me you're growing fond of my presence, my hero."

"I wouldn't go so far as to say that." Of course she was. She shouldn't have allowed herself to think like that at all, but... She was.

Every time he was with her, she felt stronger. Like she could do more than the average mortal.

And then she remembered her jealousy when she had thought he might want the Goblin Queen more than her. Even though it was all in her head, she felt like she might have lost him only a few moments ago. And this was her chance.

If she didn't want to lose him, then she had to say something. She had to admit her feelings or it was entirely possible that he would decide it wasn't worth it to chase her through the faerie courts again.

Even if it made her pride sting to be the first one to admit it.

Freya sighed into his shoulder and shook her head. "Actually, I think I might like having you around."

"Excuse me?" He reared back in surprise. "Are you admitting that you're fond of me?"

"I'm admitting that looking at you doesn't make me sick to my stomach." No, that wasn't the right way to say it. She wasn't a child. Freya cleared her throat. "And that, maybe things are better when you're around."

He leaned closer, his eyes locked on her lips. "Is that so? I'll admit, I've been waiting to hear those words for some time now."

"We don't have time for this." She stared at the berry red color of his mouth and wished there was more time.

She wanted to taste him again, to feel his hands on her body and see what a faerie king could do with those long fingers. After all, she wasn't a child anymore. When she might have been afraid of a Goblin King in her younger years, now she wanted to know what he desired.

His lips barely brushed hers in a featherlight touch, like a butterfly resting against her for a mere moment. "If only there was more time. I would convince you that you should never leave this place. But we have company, and I'm afraid ignoring the dead is a poor decision."

The dead?

Her mind was so foggy she couldn't imagine what he was talking about. She wanted him to kiss her again. A real kiss this time, not just some feather touch that left her wanting more.

Then the word pierced through the fog of her mind and she remembered they were standing in the middle of a battlefield. Particularly one that was known to be very, very haunted.

Gasping, she lurched out of his arms and spun around. Eldridge had been staring over her shoulder. She could only imagine what was behind her.

The spectral figure was ethereal and delicate. The silver edges of its form moved in the wind, though she couldn't make out who or what the creature was. It wore a cloak covering its head and face. The spirit rode the ancient ghost of a reindeer that was slowly rotting. Freya tried hard not to stare at the skull of the steed that lacked any flesh.

The cloak draped over the body of the reindeer, and the spirit reached forward to use the beast's horns as reins to direct the beast toward Freya and Eldridge.

The strange rider stopped a mere ten feet from the only two living people on a battlefield of the dead.

"Why have you come?" it asked. The rumbling tones were deep and rode the wind like the howl of a wolf.

"I need to know how to kill the Goblin Queen," she replied. She stepped out of Eldridge's arms and closer to the ghost. "I was sent here to relive her memories so that I could see why she needs to be removed from the throne."

Although, it seemed like everyone feared Freya wouldn't do what needed to be done.

The spirit inclined its head, the hood shifting just enough for her to see the white skull beneath it. "So be it. If you wish to have the weapon, then you must know what happened to us. You must see for yourself the torment."

She swallowed hard and looked to Eldridge for one last reassurance.

Except Eldridge wasn't there anymore. He had disappeared, returning to wherever his torture was enacted.

Freya was alone in this, again. Only this time she was certain she would succeed.

Straightening her back and squaring her shoulders, she returned her attention to the ghost before her. "I accept that I need to experience to understand. Please, lead the way and I will follow."

CHAPTER 19

The spirit reached out its hand for her to take. "Come with me, Freya of Woolwich. Hero of the Autumn Court and beloved by the Goblin King."

Beloved? She felt the blood drain from her face.

"Oh, no," she corrected. "He doesn't..."

"Stop talking," the ghost scolded. "You said you wanted to experience it. And experience you shall. But there will be no more arguing or trying to explain your beliefs. I am dead. Trust in the knowledge of the spirit realm and allow us to show you what the real history of this place is."

She clamped her jaw shut and stared at the bones of his hand. There were a few grisly pieces of flesh still hanging from him, and she could only assume that his body was around here somewhere. If she wasn't careful, she might even step on it.

Swallowing all her fear, she nodded and took the boney hand. "Show me everything."

Freya had expected to travel again. She had thought the ghost would bring her to yet another place. Instead, touching him allowed her to see into the spirit realm. Thus she was forced to watch as a thousand faerie souls all burst into view.

They fought with wild abandon. Their swords gleaming in sunlight she couldn't feel. The sound of axes striking shields was so overwhelming she could hardly even hear her own thoughts.

A great beast, perhaps an orc or troll, swung a hammer over her head. She ducked down low, but the hammer never touched her. Instead, it collided with the skull of a beautiful pixie behind her. She watched in horror as the other warrior's head exploded.

Flinching away, she closed her eyes and tried her best to breathe through the sudden nausea. "Why are you making me watch this?" she gasped through gritted teeth. Her stomach heaved again.

"This is not the only thing you need to see, but you must understand the pain of battle," the spirit replied. "Follow me, Freya. We need to find the Goblin Queen. Although, at this time, we all knew her as the Winter Princess."

It was a new name for the same face. Freya didn't care what they had called the woman. All she cared about was the way to defeat her.

Freya allowed the spirit to drag her across the battlefield. Her senses shifted, the living realm colliding with the world of the dead. She could see the people as they were when they battled, but also feel their bones crunching beneath her feet.

Her stomach clenched again, but she refused to allow the gorge to spew out of her mouth. She couldn't throw up. She was stronger than this.

So she walked through the battlefield with her head held high. Even though she was terrified of all the things she saw along the way.

A goblin with the head of an owl wielded a sword nearly as long as it was tall. That sword took out so many fae who couldn't get anywhere near the owl headed woman. Until an archer without a face caught her in the throat with a gold fletched arrow.

Scenes like that played out before her in the hundreds as so many people lost their lives. Until they got to the very heart of the battle where a small tent stood.

"What is this place?" she asked.

"The spirit realm exists in the now, the then, and the time in between," the cloaked ghost said. "While these spirits battle, this was what happened the night before. Here you will discover all that you need to know."

She approached the tent and reached her arm toward the swaying curtain. But at the last second, she looked back at the ghost. "This is the moment that will convince me to kill her?"

The hood shifted to the side, and she saw for a second what the ghost had been. A handsome goblin man, with the face of a brown tabby cat, and the paws to match. He'd once been very handsome, and yet, now he was nothing more than a spirit.

He moved again, and the visage of what he had once been disappeared. "No, Freya. You need no more justification to take a life. There is never a good reason to do so. What you are about to witness will show you the truth. She didn't become evil. She wasn't always bad. But she still made choices that would give her power. Now you will know where that came from, and such knowledge should be used wisely."

A gust of wind blew him out of existence, leaving her with a thousand unanswered questions. Frowning, she turned back to the ghostly tent. This would explain it all? She didn't know what she might find the Winter Princess doing, but she supposed the only way to find out was to pull back the curtain and step into the past.

Freya stepped into the tent and eyed the three figures around a large table in the center. They weren't ghosts like the others. The interior of the tent was bright with color and vibrant with life. This was a memory, not just the remains of the faeries who were left here.

The Goblin Queen looked different back then. She wore silver armor that appeared more pretty than functional. Freya had thought the Winter Princess would be more likely to wear something aggressive. Instead, her blue skirts were heavier than normal. Her hair was left unbound and wild around her face. In youth, the Winter Princess had been a lovely, delicate thing. Not the hard edged woman who was apt to kill her servants.

Two men stood beside her. One tall and white haired, too similar in appearance to be anyone other than the King of the Winter Court. He wore a crown atop his silver head and a finely made blue suit with silver embroidered edges. The other man was entirely clad in armor, including a silver helm that hid his face.

The Winter Princess pointed to a map on the table. "We should attack them here."

Her father shook his head. "No, daughter. That would leave Eldridge alone with his force. And then we will lose them all. I taught you better than that."

"Precisely. You did teach me better." The Winter Princess looked to the man in armor and then blinked. Her father froze in place, as though time had stopped. Then she said, "Did you get everything in place?"

"Yes. Eldridge will assume we made a grave error in choosing to attack this section of the battlefield. The Summer Lord has agreed to capture him on one condition." The guard widened his stance, as though he were afraid to tell her what the Summer Lord wanted. "He wishes for the promise of your hand if he succeeds."

The Winter Princess snorted. "I will have no husband, but if this succeeds then I will be able to destroy the Summer Lord once and for all. With the Goblin throne, the powers of the Winter Court, and Eldridge at my side, I will have so much power that no one will ever question me again."

"How exactly are you going to take his power from him?" The guard tilted his head to the side, then moved to the other side of the table. He watched the Winter Princess intensely.

Freya thought maybe he was in love with her. The Winter Princess brought that sort of attention to herself. Her story was one of many unrequited loves, her own and others.

The woman who would become the Goblin Queen tilted her head back and laughed. "My dear. Magic is easy to syphon off of anyone that I desire. A little pain can go a very long way."

"You would harm him? I thought you wanted him for yourself."

The Winter Princess stared back down at the battlefield map, and her lips curved into a dangerously dark smile. "I did. I do. But he will come to me of his own accord, because he wishes to be with me. If that is only to end his torture, then so be it. He will desire me. No matter how long that takes for me to convince him."

Freya's stomach rolled again. So that was the plan this whole time? The Goblin Queen was stealing his magic, as they had thought, but she also wanted to torment him until he finally caved? That wasn't finding a lover.

It was creating a slave.

She didn't need to watch any more of this madness. Stumbling out of the tent, she fell onto her hands and knees in the ash. A pang of pain rocked through her entire being. As though someone had shoved a knife in between her ribs.

Sucking in a deep breath, she pressed her hand to what she was certain would be a mortal wound. Except, there was nothing there when she pulled her fingers back.

Another blast of pain echoed through her head. Crying out, she cupped her skull in her hands and rocked back and forth until the ache disappeared.

What had just happened? She'd felt pain before from Eldridge trying to reach out, but never like that.

Gasping in air, she forced herself to stand again. She had to get moving. She had to get the knife and then... then what? She had no idea.

The hooded ghost materialized before her. He'd pushed his hood back this time, letting her see the strange skull beneath it. Fanged teeth clacked as he spoke. "The Queen is taking what she needs from Eldridge. But that doesn't mean she cannot be beaten."

"Her servant said there was a knife that could take her life," Freya replied.

Her head still felt like it was splitting open. The pain made her vision skew to the side. Why was this happening now? What could cause pain like this?

She had to know. And this figure before her was the only one who might be able to explain.

"My head," she started, pointing to her temples. "It's throbbing in a way I've never felt before. It's only hurt like this when Eldridge has been trying to contact me, but I don't see him. Why is my head hurting?"

The ghost looked through her for a moment, his attention diverting somewhere she couldn't follow. Finally, the skull tilted back and paid attention to the mortal standing before him. "The Queen knows you're up to something. She's realized you're not there, and that means something horrible could happen after all. You need to hurry, Freya. The King needs you."

She was trying to hurry. But no one else seemed to be in the same rush. "I need to find the knife before I go anywhere. I've come all this way just to find it, and if I return empty handed, then all of this will be for nothing."

The ghost lurched forward, reached for her, and grabbed her by the collar of her jacket. It dragged her closer until she was staring into the bottomless pits of its eyes. "Will you kill her? I need to know if you can actually do it."

She gasped and held onto the skeletal wrists. "Yes!" Freya struggled to free herself from the grip, but couldn't wiggle herself free. "Yes, I can do it if I have to."

"And you will have to, Freya of Woolwich." The ghost released her and retreated.

He reached into the folds of his cloak and pulled out an ice blue knife. It was made in the old ways. A metal handle with leather wrapped around it for a grip. The blade itself was made by chipping away the edges of the ice so it was sharpened by brute force alone.

This was not a weapon to hold with finesse. This was meant to kill.

The ghost held it out for her to take. "Wield this wisely. Save our king and stop all the horrors that this Queen desires to commit."

Freya took the blade and hissed as a bitter chill seeped through the thick wool of her mittens. The cold was white hot, enough to freeze her fingers off if she wasn't careful. She wrapped it in the edge of her jacket, up and around, until she could tuck the entire thing into the jacket's pocket. That side of her body would be colder, but at least she wouldn't get frostbite from the enchanted blade.

"Thank you," she said. "I will make sure that she doesn't do what you all fear. I will stop her."

"I hope you will." The ghost turned away from her and lifted its hood. "The king believes in you, and he doesn't give that regard lightly. Now, he needs you more than ever, Freya. Save him and defeat the Queen."

"How am I going to get back fast enough?" She stumbled after the ghost. "I don't even know where he is."

The spirit lifted a thin hand and pointed to the rotting reindeer. "Take your steed, Hero."

She supposed she'd done stranger things in her life than ride the spirit of a reindeer. Freya hurried to the beast, reached up, and used the horns to haul herself onto its back. "The beast knows where to go?"

The edges of the spirit were already wispy as it disappeared into the fog. "Yes. Trust in the magic. It will take you where you are needed most."

CHAPTER 20

Freya held onto the reindeer's antlers for dear life. They practically flew away from that haunted battlefield with the thousands of ghosts who remained behind. The beast's sides heaved as they thundered across the land and ran headlong into the blizzard that surrounded the Goblin Queen's palace.

The reindeer never faltered, even when they struck the side of the storm with all the force of a battering ram. Icy shards of snow blasted Freya's face, tearing at her sensitive skin in tiny daggers. Bits of the reindeer fell off with the sheer force of the wind.

Still, they went forward.

Sides heaving, the reindeer moved faster when a blast of icy air tried to force them back. It tucked its head, forcing Freya to press herself lengthwise against its back. They rode with a ferocity that she hadn't known a beast like this still had in it. She would have assumed the great beast had fought its final battle long ago.

But then again, this was the steed of a goblin warrior. Of course, the creature knew how to continue forward when something was driving it back.

She tried to reach out to the Goblin King in her mind, but he did not respond. She whispered endearments in the hopes he would answer. "Eldridge," she called out. "You have to wake up. You have to talk to me."

No one responded.

Freya realized with horror that she was more clear-headed than she had been since Eldridge started reaching out through her mind. She just hadn't realized how foggy her reality had become. She'd gotten used to dealing with the ache behind her eyes. The strange feeling of floating had just been because she was in the faerie realms. Not that he was dipping into her perception and altering the reality that she saw.

Now, she wondered how long the Goblin King had been meddling with her head.

The snow made it impossible to see what direction the reindeer was running. She didn't know if they were heading back toward the castle, or if they were going somewhere else. Freya could only pray this faerie ghost was taking her where she needed to go. And that was away from the Goblin Queen's castle.

If Eldridge had been in the castle, she would have found him by now. Wouldn't she have?

After all, she had pawed through more of those rooms than she could count. And no matter how hard she tried to snoop through the Goblin Queen's home, one thing had been very clear. No one other than the Goblin Queen was awake.

Other than those two strange faeries who had brought her to the castle. The faeries who had been sent to the very outer reaches of this land to watch for intruders.

Or at least, that's what Freya assumed they had been sent out there for.

Maybe she knew nothing in this story. Maybe there was so much more yet to be revealed.

The reindeer tossed its head and the thundering hoofbeats slowed. Though the storm still blasted overhead, she could almost feel the reindeer's intent to stop. It wasn't going to continue for much longer, which meant they had to be near something important. Didn't they?

With the thought came a frigid blast of wind. And then, appearing out of thin air, an ominous prison emerged from the fog.

It was tall and dark, as though the ice that made up the sharp edges was so deep and thick that it had turned black. No light could penetrate the tall, jagged structure that rose into the air like daggers being thrust at the sky. They created a strange pattern around the open archway that led into the prison. Perhaps like a snowflake, if they could look that ominous and threatening.

Swallowing hard, she gripped the reindeer's last remaining fur as it trotted up to the archway and then stopped.

"This is the place she's keeping the Goblin King?" she asked. Her voice wavered with dread.

The reindeer tossed its head, almost as though it were saying yes, this is the place.

Suddenly, Freya second guessed coming here on her own. And though she still had the magical dagger clutched in her fist, she worried that it would do nothing to stop whatever beast lurked in those darkened doors.

What if the Goblin Queen had some kind of guard in the prison? What if she was supposed to battle off some great wyrm like the carving on the throne room doors?

The reindeer didn't give her an option to fear any longer. It reared up, tossing her from its back without a second thought. Freya tumbled through the air, then struck the ice and snow hard. Breath wheezed from her lungs while the ghostly beast disappeared. Fading from view as though it had never been there at all.

"Thank you for the help," she said. The wind caught her voice and dashed it away. She could only hope it somehow found the spirits who had helped her find the Goblin King.

Getting back onto her feet, Freya swept the snow from her skirts and the long edge of her jacket. She patted the knife where it was still in her pocket, releasing her grip on the hilt that was the only comforting thing in this realm thus far. She should have known this wouldn't be easy.

And yet, the sight of this prison was enough to make the hairs on her arms stand up. It loomed above her, eerily silent even though she knew there should have been some kind of sound.

Where were the guards?

Where was the beast that would prevent people from walking in without permission?

Freya had more questions than that, but those two were the ones that stuck in her mind. The Goblin Queen was no fool. Surely she would put Eldridge in a cage guarded by a hundred men. All armed to the teeth and ready to battle at a moment's notice.

Unless...

No, it couldn't be true. But the facts were laid out before her as she stepped into the mouth of the cavern that was the Goblin Queen's prison.

There were no guards here. Because the Goblin Queen had believed no one could find this place.

Because no one else was awake.

Yet again, a faerie had underestimated Freya. She walked into the prison without a single person telling her to stop. Her footsteps echoed inside the main cavern, the only sound in the entire building.

There obviously should have been guards. Armor still hung on the walls, and it looked as though someone had painted scenes of battle behind them. Although the ice distorted the paintings now, warping the warriors even more than their faerie bodies already were.

Doors led off in all different directions, though there were no iron bars on them, so Freya had no idea which way each door led. The long line of doors continued down through the hall until it disappeared into the darkness at the end.

Benches lined the walls, likely for guards to take a rest while they were guarding those the Winter Palace wanted to lock away.

There should have been people here. A lot of people. And yet, this ancient cavern was filled only with the ghosts of prisoners who had lost their lives in this place.

Gulping, Freya pushed open the first door on her left. There was no one within the prison cell. The icy magic of the Goblin Queen filled it to the brim. The walls were made of ice, white and blue light slashing through in intervals that made her immediately nauseous. Over and over, the light pulsed. The strange pattern was disorienting and horrible.

Maybe that was the point.

She pushed open another door and saw this one was completely black. The ice was so thick that she wondered if it was even ice anymore. It looked like stone.

The third room was filled with a thin layer of ice and water in between the walls. This one also made her feel ill, but mostly because of the strange fish that stared at her when she entered. They hovered inside the walls, their mouths full of sharp teeth and a bright light hung from their heads. Obviously, these creatures were starving, and they wanted a piece of her flesh to feast upon.

Freya closed that door with a solid thump and continued her way down the hall.

She might have kept going forever if one of the doors hadn't hidden an occupant behind it. She paused and stared at a faerie who looked very familiar. It was the big faerie who had first found her when they entered the Winter Court. The faerie who now sat on the floor, tears dripping down his cheeks, with a pile of ruby red ice stacked next to him.

Was that the birch faerie?

She could only imagine it was. The pieces of that faerie's body were hard to forget. The sharp edges had faded a bit, likely from the big faerie touching them so much. A stacked pile of ice stood before him, little pieces of what had once been his friend carefully stuck to each other in the hopes that he might put the other faerie back together.

Freya stepped into the room. Her heart squeezed for this poor man who had only wanted to help his friend. The one who had wanted to impress his Queen, only to fail in the worst way imaginable.

She cleared her throat. "Excuse me? Do you think putting him back together will bring him back?"

The big faerie looked over his shoulder, large brown eyes filled with tears. "The Queen said I had to do this, mortal. I don't know if this will bring him back, or if it's just another of her punishments. I hope it does. You see..." He reached forward and touched a hand to what had once been the other faerie's knee. "He was my dearest friend. My oldest friend. We were born at the exact same time, and our mother's always said that meant we were supposed to look after each other."

Carefully stepping around the pieces of the birch faerie's body, she crouched down beside the living one. Freya stared at the work he had completed thus far. It was an impressive amount of pieces, and the big faerie had put quite a few of them together in a manner that made sense. The frozen creature was looking more like himself.

"I need to find the Goblin King," she muttered. "You know that, but now I think you know why as well."

"You want to defeat the Goblin Queen." He nodded, then picked up another ruby red piece. "I don't think you'll succeed. You've seen what she can do. Why would you even try?"

She pondered the question, because it was a hard one. Freya could give him the normal, heroic speech that anyone else might have provided. She could tell him that she was trying to right her own wrongs, save her own soul, bring back order to the courts and become a legend to the faeries.

Instead, she decided to tell him the truth. "Because it's the right thing to do," she replied. "Someone has to try."

Ever so carefully, she reached out and touched the very edge of the frozen faerie. Even though he had terrified her in life, he still deserved to live. All faeries terrified her. That didn't mean they should die.

The big faerie nodded again, his eyes watching her hands with rapt attention. As if he thought she might hurt his friend.

When she did no such thing, he heaved a great sigh. "Your Goblin King is in the very last cell, if that's what you're looking for. But I don't think he's going to be much help."

"Why's that?"

"I think he might be dead."

The words zinged through her as though she'd been struck by lightning. Dead? No. The Goblin King couldn't die. He was far too stubborn for that, and he was the type to wait for her just so he could laugh that she had worried about him.

He couldn't be dead.

Her heart beating out of her chest, she stood and raced to the door. "I hope you get your friend back together!" she shouted over her shoulder as she raced away.

The hall turned dark and ominous. She put her hand on the wall to guide herself as she continued running. It didn't matter if something on the floor tripped her. She'd get back up so she could find the Goblin King faster.

Genuine fear made her breath catch in her throat and her hands shake. What if he really was dead? What if she was too late?

Freya struck the wall at the end of the tunnel hard. Her forehead bounced off the ice, leaving her dazed as pain scattered her thoughts. Though the pain was familiar, considering how often her head ached these days.

She'd give her left arm for that headache back if it meant that Eldridge was still alive.

Shifting to her right, she opened the first door and prayed it was his cell. It wasn't. This one was empty just like the others, black and devoid of life. Spinning on her heel, she reached for the other cell and threw it open with a resounding crack as it struck the wall.

This cell differed from the others.

The walls, ceiling, and floor were composed entirely of crystals. Jagged edged and sharp, they glowed with a dull purple light. Freya had only seen such crystals once in her life, and they had been in her mother's study. Amethyst pillars were supposed to help calm a person's mind.

Obviously, that was not the intent of these. The sharp edges were like daggers. The points were clearly meant to be spears, thrown into the skin of any person who dared to step into those awful, horrible rooms.

At the very back of the cell was a lean, dark form. Crumpled against the floor where streaks of blood turned the crystal pillars red.

The Goblin King had been forced to lie upon the floor at some point. Harsh wounds on his sides turned his white shirt blood red. Strips of his skin laid against his sides, only made worse by a sudden shiver that rocked through his body.

All the tension blasted from her lungs and her shoulders slumped forward. He was alive.

Thank all the gods and the faerie worshipped beings that the Goblin King was alive.

Freya was suddenly very glad for her sturdy boots. The sharp edges of the crystals dug through the thick soles of her shoes, though they never quite reached her feet. They tried their best, though. A dark magic filled these rocks with a lust for pain and anguish. It seemed that they almost whispered with the screams of all those they had harmed in the past.

The Goblin King's shivers only drove the crystals deeper into his skin. The bright blossoms of color on his shirt were spreading too fast. Every time he shifted, she could see the crystals dig deeper into him, like roots tangling through the earth. He was wedging himself into the painful spikes and she didn't think he even realized it.

And she could see a thousand cuts all over his skin. Some were shallow, like on his hand that appeared over his shoulder, his fingers curling as though he were trying to hug himself. Some were very deep, like the ones she could now see on his thighs. Each a perfect puncture wound in the shape of a crystal.

Soon, she would get him out of here. He just had to make it a few more minutes and then they would be free.

Finally.

She crouched beside him and reached out a hand. "Eldridge?" she whispered. "It's me."

He rolled at the sound of her voice. She could hear the wet suction of crystals coming out of his skin, then sliding back into wounds they had already created in his back. His eyes searched for her, but those dark, lovely, silver eyes were fogged over with a thick layer of film. One was so bruised around the socket, she could only imagine someone had tried to take the orb out.

"Freya?" he muttered, his voice weak and thready. "I know you can't really be there. I'm too weak to reach you. What spell is the Goblin Queen sending to torment me now?"

Tears built in her eyes and spilled down her cheeks. The warm droplets fell onto his face, sizzling where they struck because his skin was so cold. "It's me, Eldridge. I'm really here. Didn't I tell you that I would find you? All you had to do was wait for me."

He lifted a hand, though the movement was obviously painful. He touched the tips of his claws to her cheekbone, his hands shaking. The soft, sad smile on his face made her heart bleed.

His voice was still strong, though. "Oh, my darling hero. You aren't here at all, because the Queen has had her way with you. We failed, don't you know? Perhaps she sent your spirit to me."

"I'm no more a ghost than the giant in that cave. I haven't joined the creatures on that battlefield and neither will you." Freya leaned down, peering at the crystals still lodged in his back. "We have to get you out of here. But I don't know if I can lift you."

He apparently wasn't listening to her at all. Eldridge stared up into the ceiling and let out a half hearted, sad, chuckle. "You know, no one's ever beaten me before. I think that was why I was so fascinated with you. Obsessed, really."

She tried to wiggle her fingers underneath him, but the crystals created a wall of sharp edges. She would have to haul him up, yanking the crystals out of his back in the process. And though that sounded painful, there was no other option. "Yes, well you helped me defeat you, you know."

"Not really." He moved one of his shoulders, wincing. Although his reaction was more one of discomfort rather than absolute agony. "You would have done it without my help, it just would have taken you a little longer. That's why I was helping. Just to see if I could get you to do it faster with a little help."

"I still would have failed in the Spring Maiden's court. I would still be asleep if you hadn't gotten me out of there." She picked up his hands and gripped them tight. "Eldridge, I'm going to pull you up very quickly. It's going to hurt, I imagine. I need you to stay quiet, because we don't know if someone will hear."

He frowned, then tugged her closer to him. He used her hands as leverage, yanking her to his face that she almost fell down onto the crystals herself. "I need you to understand this, Freya. I was interested in you. Not because you beat me, but because you are one of the most fascinating women I have ever met. And if I could have kissed you a thousand times in your lifetime, I would have. I should have."

"We don't have time for this, Eldridge."

"There is always time for romance." He smiled and some of the fog cleared from his eyes. Just a bit, as he ran his claws through the dark locks of her hair. "There will always be time for us, no matter how many armies stand in my way."

She took a deep breath and decided to rip at the wound. She needed him to focus on the now, and not whatever drivel he was spitting.

Even if it did make her heart flutter.

"There is no us, Eldridge. There is only what is happening currently and what has to happen later. And right now, I need you to get up so we can get you out of this room."

He frowned again, those delicious little lines appearing between his eyes. "I'm trying to tell you that I'm falling in love with you, you ridiculous woman. And yet, you refuse to listen to what I have to say?"

"Yes, I will listen to whatever you want when we get out of this horrible palace and this disgusting Queen's clutches, but I won't listen to another thing for a moment further." Even though she lost all the air in her lungs at the word love.

He couldn't love her.

They hadn't known each other very long, and in that amount of time they had fought against each other, and then he'd been stuck in a prison. He was merely saying the words because he could very well die alone in this cold, painful place.

That was the only reason. Definitely not because he had these feelings for her that he just couldn't shake. She refused to believe it.

If she did, then she would have to admit her own obsessive thoughts were the same thing. That she was falling in love with the Goblin King and that meant everything had to change. Everything.

So instead, she shook her head and drew away from him. "Eldridge, we have to go now. I need you to stand up."

He was still ignoring her. Willfully staying in that floating place where he didn't have to feel this pain or realize that he was about to get out of his prison.

Freya stood up and braced her legs on either side of his prone body. She would have to do this with one harsh tug, but it shouldn't be as difficult as she had originally thought. He'd lost a lot of weight since the last time she'd seen him, and he was always on the thinner side.

In contrast, she'd likely gained weight. All this walking and running and doing gods know what in this place had packed on the muscle. She looked more like the Viking women her mother used to idealize than a noble.

Good. She'd rather be terrifying than beautiful.

Freya grasped his hands again and tried to warn him one last time. "This is really going to hurt Eldridge. Don't scream. Neither of us know if she decided guards weren't necessary or if they just happen to not be here right now, all right?"

He stared up at her with a bright smile on his face. "You are beautiful. I'm glad you'll be the last thing I see."

"Idiot," she muttered.

They might as well get this over with. He was going to scream and if she had to haul him out of the prison herself, then this would take more time than they had. So they couldn't afford to wait any longer.

With a great heave, she used her legs as leverage and yanked him out of the crystals. The wet sound that echoed through the room made her stomach lurch. She couldn't throw up. Not now, but damned if she didn't feel the acidic vomit pressing against the back of her throat.

Eldridge too made a horrible sound. A cross between a moan and a groan, he collapsed into her arms with a ragged wheeze.

Freya struggled to hold on to him, blood slicking her palms and making it incredibly difficult to hang onto him. Why was he so skinny? Damn it, she needed something to hold on to that wasn't just wound covered bones, but that was all his form was at this point.

"Eldridge," she grunted. "Wake up. I need you to stand on your own, I don't think I can carry you out of here."

"Trying," he weakly muttered in her ear. "I can't... I can't feel my legs. Am I doing it?"

Not even close. He was still limp, hanging off her like she was lifting a corpse.

This would get easier, she reminded herself. He would be able to stand up on his own, just not right now. And maybe it was the room. Maybe this cave was part of how the Goblin Queen stole his magic.

If Freya got him out of this prison cell, then he might be stronger, gain his own power back. Or, at the very least, she could set him down on one of those benches and then they could figure out their next steps.

Freya wished the reindeer hadn't taken off. She could really use that beast at the moment.

But she could do this. She could lift him up and prove herself to be stronger than any of the faeries' had thought she was. Freya leaned down, hooked her arm between his legs, and draped him across her back.

Step by agonizing step, she made her way across the crystals. They sank into her boots, digging through the leather and reaching for her feet. By the time she made it halfway to the doors, they succeeded in what their dark magic desperately wanted. Every step dug deeper into her heels, blistering pain rocking through the bones of her feet and into her very soul. She left thick, bloody footsteps in her wake.

The magic threaded through her mind, and then she understood why the Goblin King had thought she wasn't real. The magic in the crystals was a kind of poison that dug not only into the flesh but also into the mind.

"Freya!" Her sister lunged into view with her arms outstretched. "You can't take him out of the cell. He will die!"

She gritted her teeth and took another step. "No, he won't. He'll die if he stays in this cell."

"You have to listen to me. You're about to make a very grievous mistake. We can't afford to lose all this time. If you don't leave him in this cell, then he will die and everything will be for nothing."

"No," she snarled. "And you aren't my sister. Go away."

The image of Esther faded from view, only for the birch faerie to appear in front of the door. His entire body was cracked, as if the big faerie had finished, but he hadn't healed. Instead, his form had become a mosaic of flesh and bone. "You aren't going anywhere, little girl."

"Yes, I am." Freya took two more steps, then paused to catch her breath. "And you're going to move."

"I'm going to use your name against you. I'm going to whisper it into a curse that makes you take this visage on." He waved a hand up and down his body. "You're going to become me."

"Well, that's a cute threat, but it's not going to happen." She blew a breath at the hair that had fallen in front of her face. "You can keep trying to threaten me, but nothing is going to change. I'm taking him out of this cavern, no matter how many of you try to stop me. You're just figments of my imagination."

The Goblin Queen waved a hand through the birch faerie and he disappeared. But the Queen stood there with a grin on her face. "Am I, Freya? Or did you just walk into the trap I laid out for you?"

Freya froze. Was she really here? Or was this just another part of the poison that wanted to drag both her and Goblin King back into the crystal spikes?

No one knew Freya was here. The big faerie wouldn't have told the Queen... Would he?

In her brief hesitation, she could hear the cackling laughter from within the crystals. They had stopped her. And whether the Queen was real or not, she was going to stay in this cell because she didn't want to fight against the Goblin Queen.

The vision of the Queen put her hand on the door to the cell. "You're going to stay in here with him, if you want him so badly. But nothing that you do, little girl, is going to slow what I have planned. I will become the greatest Goblin Queen to ever live, and a mere mortal has no chance of defeating me. Even with the Goblin King at her side."

She refused to believe that was true. Because even if she got out of here, even if the Goblin Queen wasn't real, then she was still going to fight this woman. She still had the crystal dagger in her pocket.

If now was the time for her to kill the Goblin Queen, then why was she wasting any more breaths?

Freya took another step forward. Then another. "You are not going to stop me. No one is going to stop me, no matter how hard you try. He's not staying in here a moment longer."

She stood directly in front of the Queen and glared up at her. Freya still didn't know if this woman was a mirage or if she was really there. But the Queen would step aside, regardless.

The Queen looked her up and down, then sneered. "I'm going to lock you up in here for the rest of time, little mortal."

"No," she replied. "You aren't."

Freya stepped through the vision and into the hallway beyond the crystal cell. Immediately, all the weight that had been tugging her backward, the magic that wanted to do her harm, fell away. Eldridge even felt lighter on her shoulders, as if much of the weight pressing down upon her had actually been from the magic. Not him.

Now she could breathe. Now, she could release all the tension that had been riding on her shoulders and she could take a deep breath.

Gently, Freya shifted the Goblin King down onto one of the nearby benches. He flopped a little, but shook himself when she got him seated. Eldridge put out a hand and braced himself on the stone.

He blinked rapidly, and with each fluttering movement, the fog over his eyes cleared.

"Freya?" he asked, reaching for her. He caught a lock of her hair between his fingers, gently moving it back and forth as though he couldn't believe the texture. "You were really in that horrible cell with me?"

"Yes, I was." She slapped his hand. "Stop doing that. Of course I was in the room with you. I said I would get you out, didn't I?"

He let his hand fall back to his side. "You did. I'm afraid I wasn't all that optimistic at the end there."

"Oh, you know better than that," she said with a laugh. "How many times have I surprised you, Goblin King?"

He reached for her again, drawing her down onto the bench with him. "I thought I told you to stop calling me that? You know my name, Freya. Use it."

The heat from his mouth tempted her greatly. She wanted to press her lips to his. To feel that heat that always spread through her body the moment he kissed her. The warmth that only Eldridge could seem to bring.

"Eldridge," she whispered, knowing he could feel her breath. "You had to know I was coming for you. You had to know that after all this time, I wouldn't let you suffer alone."

"I did," he replied. "I made an error in forgetting that you are the hero of this story, Freya of Woolwich. However, could I make that up to you?"

"I can think of a few ways."

She leaned forward and pressed her lips to his. The soft, plush comfort of his mouth hadn't changed in all the time that he'd been stuck in his cell. He was still passion incarnate, tasting of apple pie and sweet treats.

Eldridge slid his hand to the back of her neck, drawing her closer. He dipped into her mouth with tongue and lips, devouring her whole as though she was the only water and he was a dying man in a desert.

Perhaps he was. Perhaps he found some nirvana in her kiss because he didn't act as though he'd been wounded, or even as though he had been in a cell at all.

Eldridge took. He feasted. And when he finally pulled back for air, Freya gasped in a breath of shock. Her stomach clenched in desire and her heart raced in her chest, pounding against her ribs as though the organ itself wanted to be touched by him.

The Goblin King dragged the back of his hand across his lips, the fire in his eyes so bright it burned her very soul. "I've been waiting to do that again for a very long time."

She sucked in a long, shuddering breath. "Was now really the right time for it?"

"There's no right time for romance," he repeated with a wink. "Or had you already forgotten that so quickly?"

"Right." She took a step away from him, clearing her throat. "You did say that, didn't you?"

He nodded. The grin on his face was a little too prideful for her taste. "You said you had the dagger."

"I do." Back to business as usual, apparently, as though nothing had happened between them. She didn't know if she should be relieved, or if it should sting a little. "I still don't know what to do with it, but I have the dagger."

"It's the first step. The second is getting me out of these bloody clothes and back into something a little more... intimidating." He smoothed a hand down his chest, wincing when his fingers bumped over wounds. "And perhaps a bath."

Another voice interrupted them. The big faerie boomed down the hall, "I can get you back into the castle, if that would help."

Eldridge lifted a brow, then called back, "It would, friend!"

Freya met Eldridge's questioning stare with a shrug. "I don't know, he seems like he hates the Queen as much as we do by now. I think we can probably trust him."

"Then let's get back into the castle." Eldridge started toward the voice. Each step was an exaggerated limp, but at least he was walking on his own.

Freya rushed to his side and tucked herself under his arm. At the very least, Eldridge had someone to help him now. And that was a start.

CHAPTER 22

They snuck through the castle halls, a little slower than Freya would have liked, but at least no one knew they were there. The big faerie left them at the hidden entrance with a nod and a sharp-edged smile. "Kill the bitch for me, would you?"

Freya didn't know if that meant he was supporting them, or something worse. He could ruin this all for them if he decided to get involved. But she didn't want to kill anyone and still had a small amount of hope that she wouldn't have to. Unfortunately, her reality was setting in.

As she helped Eldridge limp down the hall toward her private quarters, she had to come to terms with the reality that she was going to have to kill the Queen. The dagger burned a hole in her pocket, poking at her with its sharp edges and reminding her that she was, without a doubt, the hero of this story. Which meant she was also going to hold all the guilt herself.

They made it to her room without anyone seeing them. She shoved it open and helped push Eldridge through, then slammed it shut behind them before any ice creature realized they were back.

She wanted a few minutes with the Goblin King to herself. Then, all of his subjects could come rushing in and ask him whatever questions they might have. And she understood their desire to see him. He was their king. And the only good one they'd had in a while. Arrow, at the very least, had every right to see that Eldridge was healthy and whole.

But for a few moments, just a few, she wanted to pretend that it was just the two of them.

They hadn't gotten such a respite before, and Freya wanted to know what would happen if they did. If she was alone with him for more than a few moments, with no rush to save someone else, what would happen?

Her heart raced as she turned around and pressed her back to the door. Eldridge was standing near the frozen fireplace, staring down at it with a frown.

He was a picture of strength, even bloody and broken as he was. A king returning to a castle where he found only disappointment and changes. Perhaps, in other circumstances, he might have been glad to return to this castle where he'd spent some of his formative years. Instead, he looked saddened by everything he saw.

Eldridge cleared his throat. "You know, this used to be the most beautiful palace in all the courts. Winter was known as the place for artists to gather when they wanted to be inspired. I met so many people here who had more talent, more heart, than any people I've met since. The art this place influenced would have made even the most hardened of hearts weep."

She could imagine it was so. The few pieces she'd seen here were immaculate. "What was it like when you lived here?"

He chuckled. "It was more than this. More than some icy, snowy room where so few people could ever survive. It was warm and wonderful and so filled with hope. Before the wars. Before... Well. Before I did what I had to do."

"Do you really believe that?" She took a step closer, holding herself in check so she didn't launch herself at his back. "It doesn't sound like you believe you did what you had to do."

"You can't deny my part in all this. I have spent a large portion of my life trying to make amends for all the pain I wrought here, but nothing I do seems to matter." He turned away from the fireplace, staring into her eyes as though she held the answer to something. Like she could heal him. "I don't think you understand, Freya. I froze them all into mere sculptures of themselves. They were incapable of movement. Of dreaming. Of doing anything other than remain exactly where I put them because that was the only way I knew how to stop her."

"And you were right to stop her," she replied. Freya took a step closer, lifted her hands, and pressed them to his heart. "If you hadn't done what you needed to do, then she would have done all this sooner. She hasn't even woken up the Winter Court. Just those two faeries who she sent out into the middle of nowhere to watch for someone who might end up in the kingdom. She doesn't care about the Winter Court. She just cares about herself."

"Yet, I haven't stopped her again." His hands moved as if by their own accord. Eldridge slid his fingers into the soft dips above her hips, drawing her closer into his arms with a long sigh. "This place was beautiful before her. I miss it. Just as you must miss your home."

She did, but not as much as he might think.

Freya tilted her head back and stared into his eyes. "I miss my home because of the warmth that it brought my soul, but I don't miss the place. I miss the feelings that came with it."

Some of the tension in Eldridge's thin shoulders eased. "Yes, I suppose you're right. There wasn't much here for me in the long run. Just a family who had always wanted a son, and a sister who thought I would give her the world on a silver platter. I failed them all, in the end. And maybe that's why I feel so guilty being here."

Freya didn't know how to tell him that the Goblin Queen was actually in love with him. That was a bridge they would need to cross. But how did one say that his sister was in love with him? The words felt twisted on her tongue. So wrong that it was impossible to believe they were true.

And yet, they didn't share blood. Could she blame the Goblin Queen, when she herself was falling for the same man?

"Eldridge..." She licked her lips and figured it was better to tell him now rather than later. "I think you need to know something. The Goblin Queen, she's not doing all this just because she wants power."

"I know." He nodded, the fog returning to his eyes for a moment before clearing. "Do you think I didn't know all those years ago? Even when we were children, she wanted us to be something more. She wanted a life that couldn't happen. And though she tried to force that life to take form, it wouldn't. To live like that, in constant frustration and disappointment, turns a person into something twisted and ugly."

Freya flinched back from the words. She didn't know what she would do if he had called her ugly. And not physically. She knew the Goblin King meant the Winter Princess had always been an ugly person deep in her very being.

The words were cruel.

But they were truthful.

Freya cleared her throat and nodded. "Well, then. As long as you are aware of that."

"I need to clean this blood off me. And I'm afraid I must ask you to uphold a promise you said to me a while ago."

"Which is?" She didn't remember all the things she'd said, but a promise? Freya wasn't certain she had ever offered such a thing. Although, he would remember better than she supposed.

He drew her even closer, tucking her underneath his chin and pressing his lips to the top of her head. "You offered some of your own energy. That I could take some of it to use magic again. Is that still something you'd feel comfortable with?"

Freya didn't have the faintest idea what that would entail. He would take some of her own life and then transfer that into magic? Would that mean she would be weaker, or would it feel like she was ill?

Anything was a risk she was willing to take. The Goblin King was a much stronger person than she was, and far more useful in their fight against the Queen. He knew the Goblin Queen better than anyone else, and he needed to be prepared for anything she threw their way.

So she nodded. "All right. If it would help you, then yes. Please take whatever you need and we'll see what happens."

"You won't feel a thing," he whispered into her ear. "I promise. You know I would never hurt you."

Of course he wouldn't, at least not on purpose. Freya let him take a little more of her weight and then sighed. "Tell me a story about when you were younger, then. Just to keep me distracted."

He chuckled. "You make it sound as though you'll need me to. There will be no pain, Freya. You won't even feel it."

"You don't know that," she argued. "Neither do I."

"I know you won't. I've done this before." He tightened his arms around her waist, and she felt the slightest tug in her belly.

It was a faint feeling, like a butterfly was playing through her torso. Not quite anxiety, but certainly not comfortable either. Blowing out a long, relaxing breath, she tried very hard not to focus on the sensation of her own magic leaking out of her body.

Magic. As if mortals even had any.

"When I first came here, there was a single person who entertained me more than anyone else. It was a little boy by the name of Hugo. He was a very small child, more pixie like than one of the fae in the Winter Court. I never really thought much of him other than the slip of a boy was cute. He used to play pranks on anyone he could get his hands on." Eldridge tightened his grip around her waist. "You reminded me of him when I first saw you."

Freya scoffed. "As if. I was never a prankster, and I certainly wouldn't have been interested at that age. I was much too serious."

"So was he. Until he wasn't anymore and then suddenly, it was like all the chains had come off him. He wanted to live more than he wanted to see life pass him by." He combed his fingers through her hair, tugging on the strands and playing with the ends as he always did. "I saw you and I wondered what would be the thing that makes you realize you needed to live."

"What was it that made this little boy want to live?" She shifted her hands around his waist, holding onto him even though it must have caused him great pain.

His wounds were underneath her hands. The ragged edges of flesh pressed against her fingertips and she wanted to go back in time so that he would never have to endure this. If she had known this was his plan, she would have stopped the damned man long before he ever thought about bringing himself here.

Eldridge's breath stirred her hair. "He lost his sister. She wandered off into the snow and no one knew what had happened to her, or how to find her. It took them seven weeks to find the little sprite again."

"And then? Was the little girl alive?" She stiffened, hoping that the child hadn't been found frozen to the ground.

"She was fine." He chuckled in her ear. "She'd just wanted some adventure and a change of pace. So she'd gone into the forest where the trees talked and the wind whispered secrets in her ears. She was a faerie child, after all, and everything out there called to her."

Freya lifted her head from his shoulder to glare at him. "Did you steal my sister because you thought you could replicate this story?"

He shrugged. "Maybe a little. Your sister did want to come to the faerie realm, though. She practically begged us to kidnap her in the hopes you wouldn't come thundering after her like some great beast assured that we were damaging her honor."

"Well, you did." Freya thought back to her sister's fluffy white tail and sighed. "No one would ever marry her in the mortal realm now. She couldn't even become a spinster with me, heaven's forbid. That tail would have people putting her on a bonfire faster than they could say witch."

Eldridge tugged her back into the haven of his arms and his laughter rumbled through his chest. "I think she would be honored to be called a witch. Esther seems more interested in that lifestyle than you."

"You're right, she probably would have practiced magic if I had let her."

Freya could just see it now. Her sister would have taken strengthening the wards into creating her own. Then she would have tried to spell a few things in their house to move on their own, and suddenly they would have been two witches living in a hut together. The villagers would have hated it, but Esther might have actually been happy.

Ridiculous, but her sister had always been the adventurous one.

Underneath her fingers, the open wounds moved. The skin shifted and shuddered as though there were snakes underneath her hands. Freya gasped and then realized the skin was knitting back together. All his wounds were closing, progressing with each inhalation that the Goblin King drew.

He was healing himself.

How?

Those wounds had nearly been fatal. She had seen them herself, had felt the blood on her fingers.

Drawing away from his embrace, she lifted her hands and stared down at the blood that still coated them. The liquid was still sticky and warm. But the wounds she had been touching were no longer there.

"How?" she whispered.

Freya moved forward and caught the edge of his ragged shirt in her hands. She lifted it up and over his head, revealing lean planes of muscles and ribs that were too harsh. But not a single wound remained open on his blood slicked chest.

She pressed her fingers to where she had known there was a weeping hole. "How is this possible?" she whispered.

"Anything is possible here, remember?"

The expression on his face tugged at her heartstrings. He looked at her as though she were made of magic. Maybe she was. After all, it was her life force that had healed him.

She released a ragged groan, then threw herself into his arms. Freya kissed him as she'd desired for so long. Open mouthed, rough, and raw. She poured all her worries and fears into the kiss.

Gnashing teeth bit at lips and she didn't care if it hurt him. He could handle a little more pain as punishment for all that he'd put her through.

"How dare you put yourself in danger like that," she hissed against his tongue. "You chose to do this to yourself."

"I did, but never again." He vowed. His fingers flexed against her sides, dragging her closer.

As if she could get any closer to him. Freya was pressed to his body from thighs to shoulders. She wanted to crawl inside him, or perhaps for him to crawl inside her. It didn't matter. She needed to be tighter against him. To get to a point where she didn't feel like they were two people, but one.

She clawed at his chest with her hands. Her palms couldn't get enough of the heat that now poured off him in waves. The muscles bunched underneath her fingers, beckoning her to touch more. To drag at his flesh and press her lips where her fingers had just claimed.

Freya had never felt like this. She'd never been so consumed by desire that she didn't know which way was up or down. It didn't matter. Direction, sense, self, all of it fell in the wake of her passion.

Eldridge flexed his hands at her waist again and then gripped with a punishing strength. He lifted her up, scooping his arms underneath her thighs and forcing her to wrap her legs around his waist. She balanced herself on his shoulders, drinking in his kisses like fine wine.

She knew wherever he touched would be bruised, or perhaps he'd only leave red marks. But the thought gave her a thrill that rocked through her entire body. She was slick and overheated, needing him to touch everything and nothing at once.

If he touched more, she feared she'd lose herself to his passion. But if he didn't touch more of her, then Freya was certain she would die. Either was a horrific and entirely unsatisfying end to something so thoroughly wonderful.

Eldridge groaned into her lips and pulled himself free from her kisses. She let out a tiny sound of disapproval before silencing herself. He had only moved away to put his lips to her neck.

Dragging his teeth and tongue down the long column, he hissed out a breath. "You hold yourself with such swan-like grace. You will surely be my undoing, you beautiful woman."

She shouldn't have been so proud that she had distracted him, and yet, the words sent a zing of passion straight into her belly. "Good," she replied. "I want to be your undoing, Goblin King. I want to unmake you so that you are something new. Something whole. And mine."

He drew back then, releasing his hold on her neck to stare deeply into her eyes. "Haven't you already seen? You have made me into a new man already, Freya. I hardly recognize myself in the mirror, but I think I like this version better than what I was before."

All the stars in the skies reflected in his eyes. She could see a thousand galaxies, a thousand possibilities all waiting for her there.

She opened her mouth, likely to let her emotions spill from her tongue.

Someone cleared their throat in the doorway. The sound of Arrow's padding footsteps entered the room, and everything came crashing down around her ears.

The Goblin Queen.

The throne.

A life that she would have to take.

And they were kissing in private, like they were two teenagers trying to sneak away from their parents.

Cheeks burning red hot, she untangled her legs from around the Goblin King's waist and cleared her throat. "Arrow. It's good to see you. I apologize."

The Goblin King also cleared his throat, the tops of his silver cheeks darker than the rest. "Give me a moment, would you? I need to put myself back together, apparently. This is..."

He didn't finish the sentence. The Goblin King walked straight through the wall and disappeared.

CHAPTER 23

Freya crossed her arms over her chest and decided not to look at the smug expression on Arrow's face. And she knew it would be there. She didn't even have to look at the dog to know that he was grinning from ear to ear.

"Stop," she muttered.

"Stop what?"

"Stop looking at me like that." She had never hit a dog in her life, but Freya thought it entirely likely that she could if he didn't turn around and leave the room.

"I'm not doing anything. You were the one just kissing the Goblin King like he was hiding something behind his tongue. Did you find anything, by the way? I know a lot of ladies are very curious whether or not he's got a secret back there or if he's just a boring kisser."

Actually, Arrow wasn't even a dog. He was a goblin who looked like a dog, and she thought that meant it was fine for her to kick him. Maybe a few times before she threw him out of the room and then buried her head in the snow.

How was she supposed to look at the Goblin King again after that? He had completely crawled his way underneath her skin and more. He looked at her like... like...

Well, as though he enjoyed her company. As though he enjoyed kissing her, and that was a problem. They couldn't kiss each other when there was a Goblin Queen to kill, a throne to save, and her sister back in the Autumn Court who was apparently falling head over heels for a goblin too.

No. Freya stopped that thought process. She was not falling in love with a goblin, just like her sister. She couldn't. Goblins and humans didn't mix, and she was leaving it at that.

"Arrow," she snarled. "You will keep this to yourself. Do you hear me?"

He pressed a paw to his muzzle, miming that he was going to keep his mouth shut. But somehow, she doubted that he was going to do that at all. There was too much mischief in his eyes, mixed with a very healthy dose of pleasure that he had finally caught them.

Where was Eldridge anyway?

He said he had to go put himself together, which she could only hope meant he was as affected by their kiss as she had been. Or was that even a kiss at this point?

She wandered over to the ice block of a bed and sat down on the edge. Pressing her fingertips to her lips, she stared at the empty fireplace and tried very hard to not think about what had just happened. She needed to force her thoughts back to what they were about to do.

She needed to think about anything other than his taste that still lingered on her tongue. Or the way he had gripped her hips like she was his only lifeline. Or the sounds he made in her ear when he had shifted away from her mouth and down her neck...

Arrow cleared his throat again. He sat directly in front of her, though she didn't know when he had gotten there. How had he moved without her realizing it?

"What?" she asked.

He looked pointedly at her neck and then back to her gaze. "I think you'll want to cover that up before we see the Goblin Queen."

"Cover what up?"

"The giant red mark that Eldridge left." His tongue lolled out of the side of his mouth and his eyes danced with laughter. "I think trying to convince the Queen that you mean her no harm will be a little difficult when you let the love of the Queen's life put a hickey on your neck."

"He did not!" Freya lunged back to her feet, trying to find a piece of ice that was at least a little reflective. "Did he?"

Of course, there wasn't any reflective ice in the damn room. She needed to know now if the Goblin King had marked her.

Arrow trotted to the bed and hopped up onto the icy block. "I thought the King would be a lot worse for wear than what it appeared he was. How strange. I guess I overestimated the Queen's hatred. She didn't really hurt him all that much. And here I was assuming we'd get him back in pieces."

Freya stopped her frustrated searching and shook her head. "No, she did hurt him. He was stuck to crystals in the floor like they were daggers. I helped to heal him."

"You did?" Arrow's jaw dropped open. He sank back onto his haunches and then lifted a paw to tap his muzzle in thought. "How is it possible that a mortal healed a faerie? And a king at that?"

"He took some of my magic," she replied. "Or something like that. I'm not sure. Remember when I said he could take some of my life force if he needed to? Well, he did. Again."

That damned jaw remained open. Arrow stared at her as though she'd grown a third head.

She frowned, looked around her, and then asked, "What?"

"You healed him?"

"Apparently. I think it's more accurate to say he healed himself and used what little magic he could take from me." But he was still looking at her strangely, and she could only assume that meant something was very, very wrong. "Arrow, why are you making that face?"

"Well... I..." His tail thumped once, twice on the bed behind him. "Humans can't do that."

"I don't think you're right, because I most certainly did. He took whatever he wanted. I could feel him doing it. Just the faintest tug, like he was pulling something out of me." She shuddered. "I don't want to feel that again."

"Miss Freya, what I'm trying to say is... Well. Mortals don't have magic. If you were entirely human yourself, then you wouldn't have been able to give him any magic at all. Pulling a life force to make his projection easier to see, that's one thing. But healing him physically?" He looked her up and down, almost suspiciously. "I suppose that tells us why you were able to hold your own against the Goblin King all this time."

Her mind refused to believe what he was saying.

She was just a human. Both she and her sister were mortal. They came from the realm where magic was a struggle and only performed by those with questionable morals. That was the truth, plain and simple.

"That's not possible," she said. "I know my history. I know my family. There is no magic in my line, Arrow. I'm just mortal."

He grinned. "I guess you were wrong."

Freya didn't want to argue with him, but she could prove that there was no magic in her blood whatsoever. Opening her mouth to begin, she was stopped by a door on the interior of her room slamming open. She hadn't even known there was another door in this room.

Flinching, she leapt away from the fireplace and back into a safe corner of the room. The Goblin King strode through the new doorway, straightening the fine lines of his crushed velvet suit that he so dearly loved.

And that she very much appreciated him wearing.

Though he was still too thin, and that would take time to fix, the suit hugged his muscles in a very satisfying and distracting way. His shoulders bunched as he reached up and tugged the wrist of his shirt into place. "This is so much better, don't you think?"

Arrow practically wiggled in his place on the bed. He stood up onto his back legs and bowed deeply. "My King. You look the same as the first day I met you. Impressive. Delightfully powerful. I am surprised you managed after all the Queen had intended to do."

He looked at the goblin dog and grinned, sharp teeth glinting in the dim light. "Arrow. My old friend, I should have known you would be the one to guide the hero of this story. And I thought you wouldn't step foot in the Winter Court ever again."

"Only once in a blue moon," Arrow replied.

"And it will be a blue moon when we are done, my friend. Mark my words, we are going to change the very fabric of time." His eyes flashed bright and filled with malice. "Lumi won't know what hit her, poor dear. But I should have done this a long time ago."

Freya was still stuck on their previous conversation. She wasn't mortal? That couldn't be possible. Her mother wouldn't have hated faeries as she had throughout their life. One couldn't hate a person for being faerie, but then love her daughters who were of the same blood. Such complicated emotions weren't... well. She supposed they were entirely possible after all.

Had her mother experienced something tragic? Was her father not even her real blood sire? After all, Freya had always thought she looked more like her father than her mother, because the similarities were obviously there.

And her mother wasn't a faerie. She was certain of that. Her father couldn't have been. He was too simple of a man and had never been interested in magic like her mother. He was more interested in farming than wards or spells.

Freya's mother was obsessed with the faerie realm. She was obsessed with magic and all the things that came with it. But only to prevent anything from happening to her family.

Right?

Wasn't that the way of it?

"Freya," the Goblin King's voice broke through her thoughts. "Are you ready?"

Ready for what? Freya wasn't ready for anything. She wanted to reach through the veil of death and strangle her mother for leaving nothing but questions in her wake. It wasn't fair that Freya was left here with Esther and no one else to answer the questions of their lineage.

"Hmm?" she settled on asking. She looked up into his frowning face and wondered what he saw behind her eyes.

"We have to focus." His tone was almost scolding, and he had every right to do so.

Freya knew what they had to do would be very difficult. They both needed to focus on everything that was about to come to pass. They had to be ready for whatever the Goblin Queen might throw at them.

And instead, she was standing here with her head in the clouds, completely incapable of listening to anything. "I'm sorry. I was caught up in my own thoughts for a bit. What were you saying?"

"I was telling you my plan," he replied, frowning. "Did you hear any of it?"

"No." Freya at least could answer honestly, considering this was a very important plan that she needed to be ready for. "Tell me again, Eldridge. I have a lot on my mind."

His expression softened, and he reached to touch a finger to her chin. "Yes, you do. You play a very important part in this, my dear, and I'm sorry for it. We're going to her banquet, together. She likely has no idea I've escaped her prison, or there would be a thousand of her self made guards running around this palace. We'll catch her by surprise and force her to see us as actual threats."

It was as good a plan as they were going to get. She realized just how much of a stretch this was. The Goblin Queen might be surprised for a few moments, but that was all they had. The woman thought on her feet with the best of warriors, ready to plan her battle at a moment's notice.

"Understood," she replied. "And while we're at the banquet, how am I supposed to get close enough to kill her?"

"While we dance, of course. Lumi was always the one who wanted to see everything go as planned. She loves anything that requires her to be the most beautiful woman in the room. I will force her to wake up more of the Winter Court. Bring them all to the dance floor, and then we will show her what true beauty is. We'll frustrate her. Anger her. Put her in a position where she feels like she has to prove herself." Eldridge reached for her waist, tucking her against his side once more. "She will hate you. And that is when we will strike."

Right, like that was going to work. Freya wasn't more beautiful than the Winter Princess who was now the Goblin Queen. A woman with that much magic at her fingertips would make a mortal look plain and boring.

She pointed to the white dress crumpled in the back of the room.

The fur coat sat next to it, now slightly yellowed with age. "That's all I have to wear, unless you want me to show her up in a plain brown traveling gown."

Freya wiggled out of his arms and lifted her hands over her head. She gave him a little spin, showing just how plain she was.

His plan required a beauty. A woman who could outshine even the brightest of stars. And what he had was a vaguely polished rock, but still a stone from a riverbed.

Eldridge smiled, and the expression lit up the room. His hands glowed with power and he lifted them to gesture up and down her body. "You are more lovely than you know, Freya. But you will not walk into her ballroom as one of the Winter Court as she would so like to claim you. You are mine, and thus you will be dressed in the regalia of my true court."

She felt the magic before he even started. It tickled her feet, tingling around her legs and sweeping up her frame. The fabric of her dress unlaced itself, changing structure and form, weaving into something new and entirely different.

Dark amethyst spread from the bottom of her new gown. Tiny sparkles of silver stars dusted the hem near her feet, then cinched her waist in tight with more tiny stars. Moons and planets spread up the bodice that hugged her small waist and drew her chest up higher. A thin cloak of midnight blue clasped around her neck, decorated with diamonds that sparkled as she moved. Freya felt her hair slithering up the back of her neck, becoming an intricate coil of braids and loose tendrils of curls.

Suddenly, she was no longer the same woman. She was beautiful and remarkable, a faerie princess rather than a human who happened to find herself in this miraculous place.

Freya smoothed a hand down her bodice, the boning nearly uncomfortably tight, then looked back up to Eldridge's pleased expression. "Well, do I look like a woman who could distract the Goblin Queen?"

He held out his hand for her to take. "Yes, Freya. But you were always that woman, regardless of the clothing. Did you not see the jealousy in the Goblin Queen's eyes when you were changing? She wanted to make you ugly. She did not succeed."

His words seemed like a stretch, but she would take the compliment. Freya slipped her arm through his. "Are you ready to kill a queen, my king?"

He grinned. "Oh, I've been ready for a very long time."

CHAPTER 24

They walked through the halls of the palace toward the room where this had all started. Or at least, the first time Freya had actually talked with the Queen rather than shivered with fear. The hall where ballerinas had danced until their feet bled. The place where frozen food had proven this quest to be more difficult than she had thought it would be.

Teeth chattering, Freya looked up at Eldridge who was quickly looking to be more himself. His cheeks were rounding back to their normal chiseled form. And when he turned his head to meet her gaze, he didn't appear nervous at all. Instead, his eyes were lit with excitement.

"Everything is going to work out as planned," he said. "You shouldn't be so worried, Freya."

She wasn't a fool. Things could easily fall by the wayside if they underestimated the Queen. After all, hadn't he made the same mistake with Freya herself?

"I think we should prepare for anything," she replied. "What is the plan if this doesn't work?"

"It will work."

"And if it doesn't?" she insisted.

He paused them in front of the banquet hall door, his hand braced on the icy surface. "We're going to keep her off guard. That's the plan. If it fails, then we fail. So we will keep ourselves ready for anything and everything that she might throw at us. Because she will throw everything she knows. Thankfully, I happen to understand her thoughts. I grew up with her. I know what she's going to do."

And Freya had grown up with Esther. She'd never guessed her sister would take something from goblins, let alone be happy to live among them.

"Trust me," he reiterated.

She would try her best. But Freya feared he was making a grave mistake. One they couldn't so easily come back from.

Eldridge closed his eyes, and she saw his hands start to glow. The warmth of his magic spread through the door, melting the icy structures and turning it back into warm mahogany wood.

Freya gasped in surprise as the magic spread. Ice fell in great, slushy waves that soaked the cold floor, warming the ground and heating it back to the original white marble. His magic spread even further, pulsing down the hall and no doubt into the room where the Goblin Queen waited for them.

Only once the hallway was unrecognizable did he stop. And though he was still weak, he held himself with pride in the set of his shoulders, then smiled at Freya. "Now we're ready."

He shoved the doors open and held out his arm for her to take. Freya slipped her hand onto his forearm and allowed him to guide her into a completely different ballroom.

The walls were painted bright yellow with tiny daisies falling from the ceiling that was made of stained glass. Silver metal ivy crawled over each individual panel. All the seats had melted from their icy structures, back into the warm, caramel wood. The Queen waited at a banquet table where there was a mountain of food and steaming liquids.

Freya's gaze flicked to the back wall where the dancers had emerged from the frozen waterfall. Now, it was a bubbling fountain, impressively large, with brightly colored goldfish swimming within it.

The Goblin Queen's chair screeched as she shoved it back. "What is the manner of this magic?"

She wore a pale blue gown made of ice. The bodice stretched up toward her neck in tendrils frozen to her skin. The fabric hugged her beautiful form, and her white hair was piled atop her head with long pillars of white ice as a crown. She was as lovely as ever, and suddenly, Freya felt plain again.

Eldridge swept into a low bow, tugging Freya with him. "I thought the castle should return to its former glory. All this frozen nonsense would make the Queen ill. You know how she hated the cold."

The words were a challenge. The Goblin Queen braced her hands on the table in front of her and snarled, "You're looking at the Queen, Eldridge. And you know I always loved the cold. No matter how much my dearly departed mother wanted to wipe it from existence."

"You would have been happier if you listened to her tastes. She was always more interesting than you, however. She was ready to take the world by storm. And you?" He tilted his head to the side, looking her over as if he was disappointed. "You turned into the spitting image of the woman your parents never wanted you to be."

"Such a shame." The Goblin Queen rounded the table, her hands glowing bright blue at her sides. "And yet, I'm more myself than I've ever been. Perhaps they were flawed parents who never saw the use in a daughter so powerful. How did you get out of your prison, Eldridge? I hope you enjoyed your adventure, because I'm afraid you need to go back now."

"I won't be doing that." He tugged Freya closer to his side. "You suspected nothing when we were right under your nose. I'm disappointed, Lumi. I thought you would be better at sniffing out a rat."

Freya bristled at the term. They were talking like she wasn't even there, and this wasn't the plan. Wasn't she supposed to be the one distracting the Queen?

But this conversation felt personal. These were two siblings who were fighting about everything they could. Each word was a barb meant to wriggle under the other's skin, and for what?

They would not change each other's minds. And throwing insults like this would not make anyone feel better.

The Goblin Queen tilted her head back and laughed. "Eldridge! This adorable rebellion is cute, it really is. But nothing is going to stop me. Not you. Not your little human pet. Did you think I didn't know you were talking to her?"

"You didn't," Freya interjected. "You let me wander about the castle unsupervised."

"He wasn't in the castle, darling. The longer you spent searching these halls, the more time I could take his magic. And now he has none at all." The Goblin Queen's smile was sharp and cold. "That was the last of it, wasn't it? One more trick. A show that would make me think you still had power. I know you, Eldridge. And I know when you are weak."

He stiffened. "Perhaps," Eldridge replied. "But you don't know everything, Lumi."

The blue light of her magic spread from her fingertips. It touched the table first, turning all the food back into frozen chunks of ice. The tendrils of cold spread across the floor, reaching the fountain where it shifted the water back into its original rigid structure.

Eldridge did nothing to stop the magic from spreading. Maybe the Goblin Queen was right. He had used the last bit of magic that he'd stolen from Freya to turn this room into something warm and more inviting.

He watched the magic spread with a bored expression. "Lumi. Are we going to fight by turning the room from cold to warm? I came here to offer a truce. Why don't we dance like we did in the old days? Wake the court up. Bring at least a few of them back so we can enjoy each other's company. I'm bored staying in the prison cell."

The magic paused at his offer. "Is that why you're here?" The Goblin Queen asked with a laugh. "Eldridge. You know I'm not going to let you out. And I'm not going to have a dance."

"I think you will," he replied. "For old time's sake."

The Queen drew in a deep breath. She looked Eldridge up and down as though thoroughly disappointed. "Is this your plan? To make me wake up the court and then convince them to rebel against me? You're too weak, Eldridge. And you forgot that I am no fool."

"But you are a fool who loves me," he replied. He released his hold on Freya and took a step closer to the Goblin Queen. "I'm asking for one little thing. A favor, if you will."

"You think this will distract me," the Goblin Queen said. She shook her head in disbelief. "You think a dance will be the end of this all. What is your plan? To try to kill me once we all spin wildly across the floor?"

"Wouldn't it be a fitting end to our story?"

"There is no fitting end to our story. You want me to die so you can take the throne back. I'm not going to give you that satisfaction." She leaned around him, staring at Freya with death in her eyes. "Once I put you back in your prison, I'm going to take your pet apart piece by piece. We'll see just how brave she can be. I've always wondered what was inside a mortal, you see. We don't get them around here so often."

Eldridge lunged forward and caught Lumi's face in both hands. He forced her to look at him, his hands shaking with some unnamed emotion. "Lumi," he whispered. The word was guttural with emotion. "I'm begging you."

Freya's heart fell into the pit of her stomach. She'd heard those tones before, but they were always when he was trying to seduce her. Watching him do that to another woman was like breaking apart pieces of her soul and tossing them into a river. The Goblin Queen didn't have to rip her apart, after all.

She hurt. Physically, even though she hadn't realized that was possible. Her entire body ached as though she'd been in a fight, or a battle, or perhaps only realized that a Goblin King had many layers to him and some of them were at her own expense.

Lumi melted at his touch. She moved closer to the king as though her body couldn't stay away from him. "You want a ball so desperately, but my dearest, my love. You won't defeat me while we're dancing. I will make you regret ever trying to beat me."

"That's a bet I'm willing to take," he replied. Eldridge released her and stepped away, tucking his hands behind his back and clearing his throat. "If you think you can prevent us from stopping you, then please. By all means. Lumi, I want to see if you can do it."

"A test then?" The Goblin Queen tucked her own hands behind her back and turned. She sat down at the banquet table and touched a finger to her chin. "You believe you can stop me. I believe you can't. Whoever remains alive by the end of the ball will win. How does that sound?"

Awful. Freya wanted to step in and tell them both that they were being foolish. No one could win a bet like that. No one could possibly make that bet thinking that either of them would triumph. They would just lock horns for the entire ball and then... what?

Eldridge nodded. "Of course, that sounds like a deal to me. And if no one wins by the end? If we're both alive?"

Exactly, that's what Freya would have asked. Obviously they needed to come to some kind of understanding. The likely end was that neither of them would kill the other.

The Goblin Queen tapped a long-nailed finger against her chin. "Then I win. You return to your cell like a good little goblin, and I get to do whatever I want with your human pet."

Absolutely not. They could not agree to a deal with her like that, because then they would always lose no matter what. Freya knew for a fact she wouldn't be able to put a dagger through this woman's heart in that amount of time. It was just impossible.

The Goblin King wouldn't be so foolish. Eldridge was a risk taker, yes, and he enjoyed a battle of wits. But a ball wasn't enough time to get everything aligned that needed to be aligned.

Freya looked to him for a scoff, or an angry snort that the Queen would try to pull the wool over their eyes like that.

But her heart stilled when she saw his expression. That calculating look was him considering it. And worse?

He nodded.

The Goblin King agreed to the deal. "We'll accept your deal. If we don't kill you by the end of this, then you win."

"And what do I win?" The Goblin Queen asked. She leaned forward, nearly crawling onto the table as she awaited his answer. "I want to hear you say the words, Eldridge. I want to know that this deal is exactly what you have always feared."

He cleared his throat and avoided Freya's questioning gaze. She would have stepped in front of him if it wouldn't have ruined their plan.

But she had to try something. "No," Freya interrupted them. "This is a losing deal. We won't take this one, nor any other with the likes of you."

The Goblin Queen looked at her with a bored glance. "Dear, he's already accepted. We can't go back on that now. What we have to decide is what the other person wins."

Well, that couldn't be Eldridge. He wasn't going back to the prison, or she'd failed in everything she'd attempted. Freya created a shield of her own body, shoved in front of Eldridge, and squared her shoulders. "Then you win me."

The Queen laughed so hard the sound turned into unladylike snorts. "Do you think I want you more than him? That's adorable. Really, Eldridge, I understand your interest in the little thing now. She is a cute little adventurer, isn't she?"

Freya bristled at the tone. She was more than just adorable or cute. She was the mortal who had defeated the Goblin King, and she could do it with this witch as well.

Eldridge put his hand on her shoulder and moved her back beside him. "No, Freya. You aren't going to offer yourself up for this deal. Obviously the Goblin Queen only has one desire, and I'm more than happy to put it on the line." He straightened his shoulders, inclined his head, and replied, "You will win me, Lumi. We all know that's what you want."

Every fiber of Freya's being screamed with rage. Why would he do that? Why would he offer the one thing they couldn't give?

Grinding her teeth, Freya clutched the fabric of her skirts in her fists and tried to stay quiet. She'd yell at him later, if she got the chance. But he had to stop making these decisions without her.

Otherwise, they'd keep getting into situations like this.

Lumi grinned, then lifted her hands and clapped them loudly. "So be it, Eldridge. You have yourself a deal. Now, the Winter Court is waking and we shall throw a ball unlike any this court has ever seen before."

CHAPTER 25

Freya flinched away from the doors as they slammed open again. She feared they had both been unaware as the Goblin Queen's icy creatures snuck up behind them. The Goblin Queen didn't care about honor, she could easily have been distracting them while her magic built giant beings to throw them both into prison.

But it wasn't an army that entered the banquet hall.

Faeries flooded into the room. They were the same faeries she remembered from when she had first come to this terrifying court. Each one was beautiful with delicate butterfly-like wings. Some large. Some small. Frost patterns decorated their cheeks and any skin that was bare from their clothing.

Their dresses were made of gossamer. Their suits of fine linen and silk. Pale blues. Beautiful, deep midnights. Every color was a shade of blue and so incredibly appealing. Snowflakes and ice made a prominent feature in all the clothing that the faeries wore.

But they all had a similar expression of confusion on their face. None of them seemed to understand where they were, or how they had come to the ballroom.

The Goblin Queen stood, clapped her hands for attention, then smiled at the members of her court. "Welcome home," she said. "You've all been asleep for quite some time. But you're back now. So you might as well make a show of it. The previous Goblin King has asked for a ball. We will remember him fondly now that he passes the crown to me. The rightful goblin heir."

The winter couple nearest to Freya bristled. They looked at each other with horror in their eyes, before turning back to stare at the Goblin Queen. They wisely kept their mouths shut, but Freya knew what they were thinking.

What had happened while they slept?

Why had all their nightmares become reality?

Music danced through the air. At some point, a few faeries of the Winter Court had walked to the back hall and brought out instruments. Violins, cellos, even harps were dragged from some hidden room and set up away from the others. All strings, Freya noted. The musicians lifted their instruments, saluted the Queen, then filled the air with the haunting tones of the Winter Court.

Snowflakes fell from the ceiling. And though it was strange, they never touched the ground. Freya reached up and caught one on her fingertip.

It was as lovely as it was delicate. The snowflake hovered for a second on her finger before melting into a small teardrop. She couldn't help but fear the tiny thing was a metaphor for Freya herself. A mortal in a faerie court. Caught between two nobles who wanted to destroy each other.

How was she supposed to survive this?

The Winter Court drifted into their places as though the entire dance was choreographed. They raised their arms as one, took their dance partners into their embraces, and then whirled into an intricate dance. They moved so quickly that Freya had a hard time guessing what the steps even were.

This was different than the ballerinas who had twirled like tops spinning out of control. Every couple was perfect. Their steps were measured, and they weren't just dancing because the Goblin Queen bid them to. They were dancing in happiness at finally being awake.

They had each other again. Their arms full of someone they loved. Even if their new Queen was a monster.

The winter faeries wrapped each other up with warmth and affection. They whispered endearments in each other's ears and how much they had missed each other. That dreams couldn't hold a candle to the reality of holding a loved one in their arms.

The Goblin King stepped up to her, reached out his arms, and waited until Freya looked at him. He fit in here among these faeries. She hadn't realized how much until she saw them all together.

The Autumn Court was one thing. Those creatures with mixed animal features had wiggled their way into her heart. They were the misfits, the unfortunate, and the odd. But that wasn't who the Goblin King was.

Each faerie in the Winter Court was a masterpiece of perfection. And so was the Goblin King. His cold features, the silver skin, even the tufts of hair on his ears were meant for this place.

Perfection could not stand flaws. Freya had many.

"I don't think I can do this," she whispered. She stared at him with fear shaking every limb. "I think we're going to lose, Eldridge. And I don't want all of this to be for nothing."

"We aren't going to lose." He winked. "Didn't I tell you to trust me?"

"I do trust you." Or at least, she should. But this moment felt like he had no control, and neither did she.

Eldridge lifted a brow, impatience radiating in his expression and the set of his shoulders. So, she allowed him to pull her into his arms and thrust her into the dance.

She couldn't say she doubted him. Of course she trusted the Goblin King. Eldridge was a mastermind at using other people's emotions to get them to do what he wanted. He'd played her easier than the musicians were playing their instruments. He knew every thought in Freya's head, and he certainly knew how to play the Goblin Queen, too.

But she didn't think this was the right way to go about it. She didn't think they would win this wild game. And she believed they would regret these decisions. Every single horrible choice would put them right back to square one.

Eldridge tugged her closer, pressing her against his pounding heart. "You are worried," he murmured in her ear. "I can still feel it. So can the Goblin Queen. You need to control yourself and know that I would never let anything happen to you."

"I'm not worried about myself," she corrected. His hands flexed at her waist, then he lifted her up as all the other faeries did with their partners.

Freya watched the fabric of their gowns spin. For a moment, she could pretend they weren't even in the Winter Court. All this magical movement was like a dream. Like she had been transported into a fairytale story that her mother would tell her as a child. Of gowns and princesses falling in love with princes at a ball.

When her feet hit the ground again, she wrapped her arms around Eldridge's neck and inhaled his familiar scent. "I'm worried about you."

"There's no need. We're going to win." His eyes strayed toward the Goblin Queen where she was surveying the dancers. Likely to pick out who her partner would be. "The Goblin Queen's faults are the same as mine were. She thinks too highly of herself and that will be her downfall."

"Isn't it dangerous to assume it won't be yours? You still have that flaw, Eldridge."

He shook his head in clear denial. "She will do everything that I want her to do. I would fall for this trap, and so shall she."

And there it was. He already illustrated that he understood why she was so nervous. He said the words she had feared he would say, but he didn't understand that he was falling right into the same web he thought he'd spun for her.

"Eldridge, listen to me."

But he was already lost. The Goblin Queen beckoned him to her side, and he went like a moth to the flame. The partners in the dance changed. She was thrust into the arms of a man with blue hair and eyes black as coal.

He leaned closer to her and whispered, "You've already lost him. Why don't you entertain yourself with me for a little while?"

She smiled at the man when he leaned away. This was a game she knew how to play. A faerie tried to distract her, and Freya was getting rather good at telling them off.

This man was just as impressive as the others. His suit was finely pressed, with miniscule white snowflakes on his shoulders that grew larger until they met the hem at the bottom of his jacket. His blue hair was perfectly quaffed. Handsome, yes, but those black eyes lacked the emotion of the other faeries.

She didn't trust him. Freya kept the false smile on her lips and replied, "While I'm certain you would be a wonderful choice, I'm afraid I can't give up on him just yet."

The faerie looked surprised that she would deny him. "Why would you care what a fallen king does? He's already walking to his own ruin, little human. At least you'd be safe with me."

"Would I?" She didn't think she would be safe with anyone.

Eldridge swung the Goblin Queen into a wild dance. He spun her closer and closer to Freya, and she knew this was the moment. She was supposed to reach into her pocket and pull out the knife. Then, when he got close enough, she would simply hold it out. Together, they would slice through the Goblin Queen and spill her blood on the floor like rubies.

But the faerie who was holding onto her suddenly tightened his grip. He clutched her against his chest, the grip punishing. Bruising. The bones of her arms creaked in the tight squeeze. She lost all the breath in her lungs.

Eyes wide, she met that black gaze with realization dawning.

He grinned down at her with sharp, shark-like teeth. "None of this is real, Freya. Did you think she would risk losing control for even a second?"

"Eldridge," she croaked. "It's a trap."

And of course it would be. The Goblin Queen was no fool.

All she saw before everything exploded was the wide-eyed stare Eldridge gave her. He looked like he was shocked that the Queen had beaten him. But that always had been his downfall, hadn't it?

He underestimated the people who wanted to overthrow him. He underestimated Freya and now he underestimated the Winter Princess who was far more capable than Freya could ever be.

Time slowed, then stopped. All the faeries froze in place once again. Solid structures wearing expressions of horror. Their time in the living world had been short, but now they were thrust back into the dreaming realm where they would likely remain for the rest of their lives.

The Goblin Queen didn't freeze Freya. But that was expected. She wanted the mortal to see what happened when someone tried to beat a Goblin Queen.

Eldridge coughed. The ragged, rough sound preceded a bright blossom of blood that stained his berry red lips. The floor warped and ice surrounded his feet. Holding him in place.

He swung a clawed hand that froze solid just before the Queen's neck. He would have killed her if the wicked tips of his fingers had touched her throat. But of course, they didn't. Nothing sharp would ever touch a woman that powerful. Not unless she wanted it to.

His beloved face turned bright blue, just like all the other frozen faeries. The ice consumed him until the Goblin King wasn't even a prisoner anymore.

He was a decoration piece.

Freya's breath fogged in the air. The room turned even more frigid as the Goblin Queen stared at the man she had finally ruined. After all this time, perhaps centuries planning her revenge, she had turned the Goblin King into nothing more than her own personal plaything.

"Don't you think he looks better this way?" The Goblin Queen asked. "I think he looks more like someone we could both handle. Don't you, my dear?"

Freya didn't know how to respond. The tears in her eyes blurred her surroundings. She could make out the strange, frozen shapes of the faeries who had returned to their previous forms. But it seemed like there were more shadows walking among them. Shadows that looked like the spirits of those who had lost their lives once again.

She swallowed hard, biting the insides of her cheeks so the tears didn't fall. "I prefer him warm and moving."

"Of course you do." The Goblin Queen rolled her eyes and turned back to Freya. "You would have wanted him to beat me. You wanted to help this story become something others would talk about for ages, didn't you? All at my expense."

"Yes." What reason did she have to lie? Freya told the truth. She was trapped. The frozen faerie's arms were still wrapped tightly around her, and there was nothing she could do to get out of them. She wasn't strong enough to break the man's arms. And she wouldn't want to, even if she could.

The Goblin Queen meandered to her side, hands pressed against the bodice of her icy gown. "So what was the plan, Freya?"

"We were going to kill you," she replied. "The ball was supposed to be a ruse so that you would let your guard down. Then we would have an opening to remove you from the throne."

"I'm sure that was a good plan at the time. But you had forgotten the most dangerous thing that Eldridge taught me." She leaned in close and pressed her icy lips against Freya's ear. "I trust no one."

And if Eldridge had listened to Freya, then they wouldn't have been in this mess. They might have succeeded. But no. Of course not. They were in his old home and he was the one who knew best.

She wished she could go back in time and slap some sense into the idiot. At least then she wouldn't have to face down this terrifying woman all on her own. And the reality was that there were no more moves in this chess game.

No one could stop the Goblin Queen, now.

Arrow was safely in their room, waiting for Eldridge and Freya to return. He wouldn't come looking for them for a while. Plenty of time for the Goblin Queen to rip Freya into pieces. Just as she had told Eldridge that she would.

Freya was well and truly alone.

Biting her lip, she decided to take control over her own fate. "What do you want?"

The Goblin Queen blinked her long, white lashes. "Excuse me?"

"You wouldn't keep me alive unless you wanted something from me. You're talking, asking me to tell you our plan, for what reason? You're stalling. Or you want something from me and you're trying to figure out the best way to ask it. So go ahead." She hoped she was right. Freya was making the biggest mistake of her life if she wasn't. "What do you want from me, Goblin Queen?"

And there it was. The light that burned in Lumi's eyes when she thought she had trapped someone. The Goblin Queen drew herself up straighter. Her hands left her waist and floated at her sides as though she were preparing to cast some spell. But she didn't.

Instead, the Goblin Queen grinned that pointy smile and said, "You can still save him, Freya. And I want to know if you're willing to give up everything to see the Goblin King breathe again."

Freya's eyes widened. "Save him? You're the one who cast the spell to freeze him. You're the only one who can save him now, not me."

"Oh, you see, this is all his doing. The Winter Court is still under the curse he laid on us all those years ago. We are frozen, and though I can lift the curse for some time, it's difficult to battle for more than just myself." The Goblin Queen sighed, then pressed her hands to her heart. "It takes a toll on me. Or had you forgotten how easily you discovered I'm using three sources of magic to keep myself awake?"

Was that the truth of it, then? Had they missed something so simple, so easy to discover, and yet there it was?

Eldridge's magic was powerful. He had complete control over all the magic given to the Goblin heir, but also the magic that was innately his. So of course the curse he had cast upon this place would be more powerful than the average spell.

The Goblin Queen was trying to stay awake.

Freya let out a low breath of shock. "Of course," she muttered. "That's why you're always using magic. You're still fighting against his curse."

"And you could break it." The Goblin Queen lunged forward again, brushed her claws down either side of Freya's face. "You beat him once, Freya. All you have to do is break the curse. Take my place, and then he will breathe again. I'll let him go. He'll live again and you will be the one who saved him. I promise, I won't let him forget that."

Something was missing from this explanation. Something horrible and evil because that was who the Goblin Queen was in her core.

"You said I would be able to see him breathing," Freya quietly said. "That's how you started this whole deal. Was that the truth?"

The Goblin Queen's gaze shifted into darkness. "No, my dear. You won't see him alive again. This story will end in tragedy, I'm afraid. But you will know that you gave up your life so that he could live. And if anyone could beat me, it would be him. So wouldn't it be smarter for you to make sure Eldridge has that chance?"

But Freya could beat her. She had beaten Eldridge at his own game, so couldn't she do the same for this woman?

Those claws scraped down her cheeks. Tiny pinpricks of cold trailed from her eyes as though she were crying frozen tears.

The Goblin Queen hissed. "No, don't think like that, Freya. You're only going to disappoint yourself. You cannot beat me, and you wouldn't ever have the chance again. If you don't agree to this deal, then I will simply take matters into my own hands. You will join the goblin man you think you have fallen in love with, and everything will end now."

Well, she didn't have an option then, did she?

Freya took a deep breath and then let it out with all the tension in her body. "I will take his place then, Goblin Queen."

CHAPTER 26

The moment she agreed, the frozen faerie's arms moved. He released her with a creaking sound, like an iron gate opening. Freya stepped out of the frigid grip and shook herself.

A fine coating of snow already laid on top of her starry cloak. The fabric was ripped at the edges, too light now to give her any amount of heat. The ice had taken its toll on Eldridge's magic. As it would for all time, she supposed.

"Follow me," the Goblin Queen said. She lifted a hand over her head and then strode away as though she didn't worry that Freya would come along behind her. Freya was merely a pawn in this game.

And that was the root of the problem, wasn't it?

The madness of the ball, the sudden and swift change that happened in the matter of seconds had shocked them all. Eldridge had been so prepared to destroy the Goblin Queen with one nimble blow. But they hadn't worked together on this at all. He had run the entire battle without telling his soldier where to go.

Meanwhile, the Goblin Queen simply controlled all her pieces on the board with finesse and grace. She had created a mindless army that did her bidding without question. That plan still had its flaws, though. Freya knew those weaknesses were equally dangerous.

Soldiers who could think and feel were the only ones to see situations from another angle. The Goblin Queen was relying on herself and herself alone.

That was an opportunity.

She just had to figure out how that was an opportunity before the Queen froze her solid.

Taking the Queen's place in Eldridge's curse was a risk she was willing to take. Freya could only stall for so long, but she needed time right now. Time to think. To plan. To live, if that's what it came down to.

Freya reached into her pocket and touched a hand to the knife that was still wrapped up in fabric. The sharp edges were wearing away at their covering, and she knew it was a sign. She had to use the knife. She had to at least try to finish this game, even if that meant fighting to the bitter end.

Otherwise, she would die. She didn't trust that the Goblin Queen would let Eldridge go, either. Right now was the moment Eldridge had spoken of.

The Goblin Queen thought she had won. All of that confidence was running through her veins, telling her that no one could beat her now. She could let her guard down. The ball simply hadn't been the right moment to strike.

Freya followed the Queen through the blue ice halls. Head held high and jaw set as though she knew she was going to her grave. It was easy to pretend, because she very well could be seeing her last visions of the place.

As they strode through the halls, swiftly moving over the ice, Freya only had one regret.

She wished she had apologized to Arrow better. She wished they had talked about the awkwardness between them, and that she had the time to mend their relationship before she had to take this risk. After all, the goblin had become a very dear friend to her.

Even if he was a goblin. Perhaps that was the strangest change in her life. Not the Goblin King. Not losing her sister. But becoming friends with one of the creatures she had once hated. Close friends that she could only hope would get a chance to know each other better.

The Goblin Queen opened a door at the very end of the castle and gestured for Freya to step out into the storm. "Walk, mortal. This is your last chance to see the beauty in the world. So I suggest you look your fill."

At the end of her words, the storm stopped. Snowflakes fell gently through the air, settling in a fine layer of untouched diamond dust. A light wind blew through the flakes, ruffling the snow mounds and revealing a frozen lake of the purest blue. The sky overhead mimicked the color until the whole world was painted white and azure. The air was filled with a heady silence. Like it was waiting to be filled with song.

This was hidden behind the storm? All this natural beauty that filled the heart with a longing for something unnamed.

Freya knew she was staring. That her eyes were ridiculously wide and that maybe her jaw had fallen open. But she hadn't realized the castle was surrounded by so much elegance. So much possibility for it to be a lovely place that artists flocked to for inspiration. Why would she want to hide all this with a storm?

The Goblin Queen paused beside her. A faint wind stirred her curls that had fallen out of their tight braid. "Lovely. Isn't it?"

"Yes." Freya furrowed her brows and clenched her hand in the fabric of her dress. "Why are you letting me see this now?"

"I'm not a heartless wretch," the Goblin Queen replied. "I know he wanted you to think that my heart is frozen, but I know the sacrifice you're going to make. I understand that you must feel afraid of death, even though I will never experience that myself. No one should go through that fear by herself."

A moment of kindness from a woman she had been led to believe didn't know how to feel that emotion at all. Freya wished she could convince the Goblin Queen to change. To give them all a chance to figure this out together. But she knew as well as the other woman that there was no stopping what either of them had to do.

The battle of wits had only just begun.

They walked across the ice together. Quietly admiring the sunlight dancing on the mirror-like surface and the frozen bubbles rising beneath their feet. The ice was crystal clear and perfectly flat. Though no fish swam in the depths, Freya had a feeling they would come alive if only a little heat were allowed to enter this place.

Finally, they reached the end of the lake where a great, twisting sculpture of ice created large gates. They stood open, waiting for anyone who wanted to enter with open arms.

"What is this place?" she asked.

"It's the royal burial grounds." The Goblin Queen stepped through the gates, her gown swishing around her legs. "This is where I laid my mother and father to rest. It's where most of the Winter Court waits for the curse to be broken. And it will be where you remain for all time."

Buried. She was going to be buried alive?

Freya's stomach twisted in fear. She walked hesitantly after the Goblin Queen, now understanding just how grave any misstep would be.

The burial grounds were exquisite, just like the rest of the Winter Court. Her fears dimmed as she saw the many altars instead of graves. The winter faeries didn't put their bodies in the solid ground, apparently, although that made sense considering how difficult it would be to dig up the frozen earth.

Instead, each person was encased in an ice coffin. Like tiny little greenhouses placed all around the grounds. Each coffin was unique in its own way. Some of the patchwork patterns of silver framing resembled snowflakes. Others had created a warm biome inside the ice, flowers growing through their finger and vines wrapping around their wrists in loving embraces.

Freya would rather be warm in death, she supposed. Though it wasn't really death, was it? She was expected to take on a curse. Alive, but not awake. An eternity like that would seem as if she would live in a dreaming world. Would she even be able to hear someone talking to her?

"Here we are," the Goblin Queen said. Her words sliced through Freya's nightmarish thoughts.

In the very center of the burial grounds was a large stone altar. A large ice cover protected the woman within, although this one was made of pristine, clear ice. Freya was horrified to realize someone was already laid to rest upon the altar.

The woman was unnaturally beautiful, with long dark locks that reached her waist in fluffy curls. Her blue gown spilled around her hips and draped over the grey stone. Whoever had buried her, had folded her hands gracefully on her chest. Long dark lashes fanned out over her curved cheeks.

"Who was she?" Freya asked.

She stepped up to the altar and looked down at the hands delicately folded over the woman's heart. Tiny half moons of blue decorated her nails.

"Someone who everyone thought was so lovely that the sun wouldn't set on her face." The Goblin Queen snorted. "Obviously the sun sets on anything and everyone. And though she is still pretty in death, I highly doubt anyone wants her now."

The Goblin Queen planted her hands on the ice top and gave it a quick shove. The arced ice slid too easily, slipping off the altar and hitting the ground. It shattered like too thin glass. Shards spilled over the ground beyond the altar, skittering every which way.

Freya almost expected the woman to open her eyes in fear. The sound was loud enough to wake the dead, and yet, the woman remained still and silent.

The Goblin Queen then put her hands on the corpse and shoved. The body slid from the altar onto the ground with a wet thump that had Freya turning her face away from the desecration. Sweat slicked her palms, and she squeezed her eyes shut in hopes that this would all go away.

Who was so cruel that they would remove the dead from their final resting place?

"So much better." The Goblin Queen dusted her hands off on her dress and grinned. "I think this place would be more fitting for you than that little witch."

"Obviously you did not like the woman," Freya observed. She took a deep breath to still her nerves, then forced herself to look back at the Queen.

"No. But I do like you, Freya. I want to put you in a place of honor so that when the time comes, we can all look at the woman who broke Eldridge's curse. We'll make sure to put flowers on your coffin, I promise you that." The Goblin Queen lifted her hands and blue magic spilled from her fingertips in a sparkling rain shower. "I'll make yours the most splendid one in my garden."

Garden? Was this what the Goblin Queen called her garden?

Freya reminded herself that she still had to play the game. She couldn't sit around waiting for the Goblin Queen to make a misstep. She had to take control over this situation or everything would fall apart. Just like she was afraid it would.

So she played the game.

Freya clambered up onto the altar and sat down with a hard thump. The stone was ice cold. The backs of her legs ached, and she wished for more layers in her skirts. Compared to the woman who had laid here before, Freya felt small and insignificant. Her feet weren't even close to the end.

Patting the stone around her, she arranged her legs as the previous woman had them. "Now what?" she asked.

"Now you are going to take the curse from me." The Goblin Queen frowned. "I thought you knew that? Lay down, Freya. I'll transfer it to you and then everything will simply go dark for you. It will be painless, my dear."

Why did all the faeries keep saying that to her? None of this was painless. For any of them.

She tried to hide her shaking hands in the folds of her dress as she laid down on the cold stone. She could feel the pinpricks of ice digging into her back. The sky spread out above her, not a cloud in sight. And yes, it was a beautiful day to die.

But she had no intent on dying.

Blue tendrils of magic spread from the ground. They slithered over her body, stretching over her arms and hands, holding her down onto the altar. Like thick icicles, they forced her to remain still as the Goblin Queen began her chant.

Freya could feel the curse. Strangely, it was familiar. Eldridge's magic had been around her for such a long time, it would be hard not to recognize the feeling. It moved through her body, solidifying her legs first. And what a horrible thing to attack. It meant she couldn't run if she wanted to. That claustrophobic feeling might drive a person mad long before the curse put them to sleep.

And though she wanted to put her plan into action now, she waited. Because she wasn't the kind of person to rush headlong into battle. She would take her time. She would wait until the moment was right.

The ice stretched up to her hips, then her chest. Her heart stuttered in the cold grip of magic. It wanted to keep beating, but the ice wanted it to stop.

As the magic reached her neck, Freya croaked out a simple, "Wait."

She hoped the Goblin Queen suffered from the same flaw as every faerie she had met thus far. The flaw that meant they all were so easily controlled, even though they didn't realize that was what happened.

Curiosity.

The Goblin Queen fell into her trap with almost no complaint. The magic stuttered, hesitated, and then held her frozen in place.

Lumi, the Winter Princess, and now Goblin Queen, leaned over Freya's prone body. Her beautiful face was silhouetted by the vivid blue sky. "What is it? Last words are an honorable thing, I suppose. But if you could hurry up, that would make this all easier."

Freya purposefully kept her voice too quiet to hear. She whispered nonsense that no one would have been able to understand. Because the words didn't matter, she just needed Lumi to get closer.

"What?" The Goblin Queen leaned down until her ear almost pressed to Freya's lips.

It was all the opportunity Freya needed. She had remembered what her mother always claimed, and the teaching that would actually save her daughter.

Magic came down to one thing. Belief.

And in that moment, she let Arrow's words fly through her soul. She let his belief consume her and fill her heart.

She had magic. She was more than just a mortal and she could break this Goblin Queen's power if she wanted to. And so she did.

Her arm shifted, wiggled beneath the grip of ice and cold. Freya wrapped her fingers around the hilt of the icy blade and gripped it tight.

"Your greatest flaw has always been your pride," she whispered into the Goblin Queen's ear.

And then she lifted the blade between them and plunged it deep into Lumi's heart.

A sound echoed through the graveyard like a great boom of an ancient beast screaming. The Goblin Queen arched away from her, a gasp echoing through her lips that turned into a painful wheeze. Cold blood dripped down the hilt of the knife. Freya's hands turned slick with it.

The Goblin Queen pressed her hands against her chest where the hilt of the blade had stuck. She braced herself with one arm over Freya. This time, it was Lumi's eyes that were held wide with shock.

The strength of the Goblin Queen's magic faded. Freya's body warmed, though it was still too chilly for comfort. And there were more important things here than her own comfort.

She shifted, holding onto Lumi and helping her ease down onto the altar. The once Goblin Queen gasped in a few breaths, though they were stuttering and slow. Each pant seemed to come at a great price as dark blood spread from her back.

Freya stared down at the woman who was so certain she had won. Her heart filled with pity.

She couldn't leave this woman to die alone.

So she sat beside her and held Lumi's hand. With soft touches, she stroked the palm that had once controlled so much magic.

Freya sighed. "Unlike you, I am actually kind. You were right, you know. No one should have to face the fear of death alone. I think you would have left me alone, and you would have liked knowing I was afraid. I won't do that to you."

Lumi's hand flexed. Her fingers clawed at Freya's, desperately trying to hold on to the mortal woman. "I don't want to die."

"No one does." Tears slipped down Freya's cheeks, warm and likely undeserved for this woman who had done so much harm. "But you won't face it alone. I promise."

Freya stayed. She didn't know how long it took for this evil woman to slip away. But even in the darkest moments of Lumi's life, she was still that heartbroken little girl. Weakened by magic and pain.

She waited with her enemy until the last rattling breath filled the burial grounds.

The Winter Princess lost her grip on the mortal hero's hand. The delicate fingers slipped down onto the altar where they would remain for all eternity. Limp. Powerless. And finally at rest.

Freya leaned forward, held her head in her hands, and sobbed.

CHAPTER 27

Freya had no idea how long she sat in those burial grounds. It might have been a few moments, it might have been hours.

She had killed a person. Even though the Goblin Queen had been evil and horrible, she still had a right to live. Or at least, that's what it felt like now that Freya had murdered the woman.

Eventually, her tears dried up, and she knew she had to go. People needed her. She couldn't remain here feeling sorry for herself. Even though killing someone for the first time did feel appropriate to languish in agony.

The blood had dried on her hands, but it still soaked her dress. The Goblin Queen's magic had changed the fabric of her gown where her life force lingered. It was a pale bluish lavender now. Completely lacking in the vibrant colors the Goblin King had given her.

The hem was soaked in blood. Her hands were covered in it, and a splatter had stained the side of her dress. She was quite literally marked as a killer. Anyone who saw her would know what she had done.

Would she ever get better at this? The wound she had inflicted on the Goblin Queen seemed to spread through her own body until she couldn't quite tell whether she had harmed herself or not.

Perhaps the smartest thing to do would be to get out of this place where dead people rested.

She stood, stumbling off the altar and making her way to the entrance. The frozen lake spread out before her and the storm hadn't started up again. Was that all the Goblin Queen? The blizzard might have been a symbol of the Queen's internal struggle. Or... Something. A cry for help? A wish she'd made as a child gone wrong?

Freya's mind wasn't working right. Belatedly, she realized that was an issue she would have to figure out. Her heart wasn't in it anymore. She wanted to go home. She wanted to break down and cry, or maybe just fall over and let all of this end here. After all she'd done, she was so damned tired.

Freya shambled over the ice like one of the dead had risen out of the cemetery. Each step was a shuffle of sorts. Picking up her feet was harder than it had been before she had this massive amount of guilt on her shoulders. She could feel that guilt weighing her down, dragging behind her with every movement.

"Freya?" Eldridge's voice called out over the ice.

The frozen lake groaned beneath her, almost as though it didn't want the Goblin King to find the woman who had killed Lumi. Or maybe she was the one who had groaned.

She knew what she must look like. Blood stained gown billowing in the slight breeze. A knife clutched in her hand, but one she didn't remember removing from the Goblin Queen's heart. When had she pulled that out? Or had she ever really let it go?

She stared down at the blue blade and could remember the popping feeling of flesh. It had slid in between the Goblin Queen's ribs so easily. Like she had been born to kill someone. As if it was easy, when it should have been very difficult.

"Freya," Eldridge called out to her again.

She wanted to turn away from him and run. He shouldn't see her like this.

No one should see someone after they had so easily taken a life.

Eldridge slammed into her like she'd hit a wall. He tugged her hard against his chest, catching the hand that held the blade and holding it away from the two of them. They must have looked like they were dancing.

"My hero," he whispered into her hair. "You're covered in blood, Freya. Where are you hurt?"

"I'm not." She pressed the words numbly into his shoulder. Her lips stiff with cold. "I'm not hurt at all."

"Who's blood is this, then?" He sank onto his knees, drawing her down into his lap on the cold ice. "Freya, you're frightening me. Please, tell me what happened. Let go of the knife, darling."

She tried. She really did. Freya wiggled her fingers, but the cold knife was stuck to her fingers. Fused, as if it didn't want to let go of her.

Eldridge leaned back and helped pry it free from her grip. Painstakingly, he opened each and every one of her fingers, drawing them open and shaking the knife off of her skin.

The blade hit the ice with a solid thunk. Then, the lake split like the mouth of a fish opening up. Bubbles from deep beneath them caused the fissure, traveling through the ice until they reached the knife. They devoured the magical object, drawing it deep into the darkness until she couldn't see it anymore.

At least the Winter Court had taken back the only weapon that could destroy the person who would lead it. Freya didn't want the responsibility anymore.

Eldridge cupped her face, forcing her gaze to return to his. "Are you hurt?"

"No." Not physically. She wasn't sure yet what was going on in her head. She had a sick feeling in her stomach that this memory would come up again for a very long time.

Lumi's eyes hadn't been that magical blue when she died. They had faded into an almost silver. Metallic, dull, and lacking of any emotion.

Had she been afraid when she died?

His thumbs smoothed over her cheekbones, eyes searching hers to see if she was telling him the truth. "What happened?"

"It's over." She couldn't tell him everything that she'd done. She couldn't. Freya stared at her bloody hand resting on his shoulder. "The Goblin Queen is gone."

"Yes, I knew that. I woke up and I can feel all my powers are back, as well as the responsibility of my throne." He squeezed her jaw ever so slightly, forcing her to focus on him. "You don't seem like yourself, dear one. Not at all."

She didn't feel like herself.

Wiggling free from his grip, Freya tucked herself underneath Eldridge's chin and tried very hard not to start crying again. "I didn't want to do it," she whispered. "She didn't deserve to die, but I didn't... There wasn't another way."

"I know." Eldridge tightened his arms around her. "I know you did all you could to convince her otherwise. She wouldn't have changed for anyone, Freya."

"But she did." Her voice was thick with emotion. Memories from just an hour before burned behind her closed eyes. "She wanted me to see the sky before I died. The storm disappeared long before we reached the burial grounds. Lumi still wanted me to see something beautiful before I saw nothing at all. Surely that meant she was still capable of some kindness."

"No, Freya. It means she saw the value of beauty, that's all." He splayed his hands across her back, rubbing gently. Easing the torment of her soul. "I will remind you a thousand times over if you need me to, but you did the right thing. My dear. My wonderful hero of this story and every tale that you are drawn into. You saved us all."

But why did it feel like she had saved no one? Or she supposed that she had saved everyone at the cost of someone who maybe hadn't deserved what she got?

She shook in his arms. No matter how embarrassed she was about her reaction, she couldn't stop shivering. And she wasn't cold. She didn't feel the frigid air or the ice beneath them.

Eldridge's arms flexed, and a blast of warm air surrounded them. "I think I am the one who needs to help you, now."

"How so?"

"You're missing pieces of yourself. It happens when you..." He drew back and cupped her face again. He threaded his fingers through her hair, gently scraping his nails over her scalp. "We won't talk about it for a while. But when you're ready, I'll help you. I promise."

Though it didn't make her feel a world of difference, at least she knew he would be there for her. And when she found the pieces she had lost... Freya hoped that he would give her the smallest bit of kindness and handle them with care.

Footsteps echoed over the ice. First, the sound of heels, then clicking claws, then a thunderous sound like a hundred feet all approaching at once. An army?

Freya lifted her head from Eldridge's shoulder and watched with shock as what appeared to be the entire Winter Court walked over the frozen lake. Many of them she recognized from the dance. But some were new faces she'd never seen.

Arrow and Frost led them toward the couple who were curled into each other. Both her new companions' faces were filled with shock and hope that this was all over. That after every moment of fighting and scheming, that their true King had returned.

She didn't want them to see her like this. Pressing her face back to his warm neck, she blew out a long sigh. "I'm covered in blood. They're going to think me mad."

"No, they're going to think you've saved them all." He tilted his head and kissed the side of her face. His lips burned, and she wondered just how cold she was. "But if you'd prefer not to show any signs of your battle, then I suppose I can help with that."

Magic warmed her from the toes up. All the blood washed off her body like she had taken a shower and she felt her dress rip at the hem. It dissolved at her feet, the gown now knee length and still as lovely as ever.

The magic made her feel fresh and clean. Not like she had just killed a woman, but that she was taken care of.

The transformation did remind her, however, that she wasn't the same person as she had been walking into that graveyard with the faerie she'd left behind.

She was a new woman now. Not a faerie, not a mortal, but something in between.

Eldridge helped her stand up and face the crowd of people. He held her hand in his, connected and united. No matter what the Winter Court thought of them after they had killed the Princess.

"My King!" Arrow called. The grin on his face was infectious. Even Frost looked like he was smiling underneath that strange icy cage of a head. "We're glad to see the rightful king take back his throne."

"Not quite yet, my friend. I still have to return to the Goblin castle and piece it back together." Eldridge squeezed her fingers. "There's still a lot of work to be done."

She couldn't help but feel like he was talking about her, as well. And there was a lot of work for her to do. Yet again, she felt like she was floating and there was no one there to catch her when she fell off the edge of the waterfall in her mind. Sure, she was holding onto Eldridge like he was the only lifeline she had. But what if he didn't want to be that person for her?

Her breathing was too ragged. She was going to lose it in front of all of these people. They wouldn't understand what was happening to her. How could they?

Faeries killed each other all the time. They waged wars, and they dealt with the emotions that came from them. If they even felt guilt at all. But she had never killed anyone before today, and that weight pressed against her shoulders. It held her down into the ice like the Goblin Queen herself was still holding onto her shoulders. Whispering that she had become a monster while trying to be a hero.

Arrow padded closer, his brows drawn down in a frown. Wringing his tiny paws, he stared at her with hope in his eyes. "Freya? Might I be of assistance?"

She released her hold on Eldridge's hand and dropped to her knees. Dragging the goblin dog into her arms felt like she was finally hugging a friend. Someone who could see her fall apart without judgement, because he was and always would be there for her.

"Arrow," she whispered into his furry neck. "I'm so sorry for everything that happened. I didn't know how to... I still don't..."

He rested his head on her shoulder and let out a long, happy sigh. "I forgive you, Miss Freya. I will always forgive you. No matter what."

At least some weight lifted from her shoulders.

Someone cleared their throat and stepped out of the crowd of icy faeries. He was taller than the others, with broad shoulders that tapered into a trim waist. He held his hands at his sides, open and inviting. "My King. Please allow me to be the very first to welcome you back."

Eldridge looked the man over with a light in his eyes that she knew was a little too calculating. "So you'll be the one who takes over for her, is that it?"

This man would be the new Winter Prince?

Freya looked him over and tried to see through the thin veil of his power. She wanted to know if he would be a good man. Or in the very least, if he would take care of the court she and Eldridge were leaving behind.

Shockingly, she could suddenly see his future. Glimpses of what he would be, or could be, if he let himself.

He wouldn't be the kindest of leaders. He would fall in with the other court rulers very well, though. His heart wasn't pure, and his intentions weren't just, but he would lead the kingdom well. They would understand his desires. They would agree to do what he ordered.

Order was a good word for him. He liked things neat. Tidy. Exactly where he placed them.

When Freya looked up at Eldridge, he had stiffened in shock. His hands flexed at his side, but he wasn't looking at the other faerie. He was looking at her.

"What?" she asked.

He swallowed, Adam's apple bobbing up and down. "What do you think of him, Freya?"

"I think he'll suit the court just fine." She tightened her grip on Arrow for a brief moment before releasing him. "And I think for once, I'd like to not worry about the Winter Court for a little while. Don't you agree?"

Eldridge was still too stiff. He nodded curtly and then replied to the faerie man, "You'll do. Take the throne and do your people proud. Be a better leader than the one who fell, would you?"

The faerie bowed, low and deep. His dark hair nearly touched the ice, melding in with the color. Freya lost control of her balance. She couldn't tell where the ice was and where the faerie man's hair started. When she looked at the other faeries to try and distract herself, all their dresses seemed to meld into the frigid surface as well. There was no longer an up or a down. Just a constantly moving ice that threatened to swallow her whole.

She might have laid down to still her stomach, but someone else interrupted her thoughts.

Pale hands streaked with dark smudges snapped their fingers in front of her face.

Jerking back, she stared up in shock at eyes that were very familiar. Black eyes that had caused more trouble than they were worth.

"You?" she whispered.

The birch faerie grinned down at her. And sure, he wasn't exactly put together right. In fact, she would argue that the cracks along his face made him look like a mosaic. Just as she had feared.

But he was alive. Well. And apparently healthy, considering he hopped away at Eldridge's angry growl.

"I wanted to say thank you," the birch faerie said. "You helped my friend put me back together, and I know I wouldn't be where I am today without your intervention. That means a lot, Miss Freya. And I don't usually say such pleasant words."

No, she suspected that he didn't.

Releasing her tight grip on Arrow, she shakily stood. "Well, it's the least I could do for taking your Queen."

The faerie's cheeks turned bright red. He looked over his shoulder at the big faerie who had remained in the crowd. "We never much liked her anyway, miss. She always made things a little too... difficult. We had to focus on staying alive. Play to her whims. When really we just wanted to focus on each other."

Oh.

And there was one of those pieces she had been missing, like Eldridge said. It fit right into her soul where she remembered how important it was to save people like this. People who had forgotten how to love, but could now do so freely.

Tears in her eyes, she pressed her side against Eldridge's. "Can we go home now?" she asked.

"The mortal realm won't look kindly on you or your sister," he replied. "Are you sure you want to take that risk?"

She hadn't even realized she'd said the wrong word. Or perhaps the wrong term for what she thought of as home now.

Freya looked up into his starry night eyes, and said, "I want to go home with you, Eldridge. I want to see my sister and help put the kingdom to rights. I don't want to go back to my cabin in the woods."

His eyes widened. "Oh."

"Yes. Oh." She smiled, though the expression felt fragile now.

Eldridge wrapped an arm around her waist and pulled her beneath his arm. "Yes, Freya. We can go home now."

Though strange, returning to the Goblin Court did very much feel like returning home. Freya hadn't realized how close Eldridge lived to the other courts. It felt as though that starry kingdom was so far removed from the others, that he could never have seen them.

And yet, his castle was right around the corner from the Autumn Court. But then again, when she thought about it, that made a lot of sense.

He would want to be close to his home. Why wouldn't he? Though he'd left the Autumn Court for a while, they were still where his roots had grown.

Arrow stopped with them just before the castle, then bowed low. His suit was looking a little ragged, but he still somehow appeared quite noble as he bowed. "My King, as always, it is an honor to save the kingdom with you."

"And you, my friend." Eldridge looked on, amused, as Arrow stepped up to Freya's side.

"Miss Freya." He wrung his paws, looking first at the ground, then up at her. "I hope you will come and visit a lonely old goblin in his meager home someday."

She tapped a finger against her chin, taking her time to ponder the question. "Will you have tea?" she asked.

"I suppose if you want tea, then yes I could have some ready for you."

"Arrow, I don't know how to tell you this, but your tea is quite horrid." She tried very hard to suppress the smile on her lips, but couldn't quite contain it. "I'd prefer it greatly if you didn't serve me tea any longer. Then I'd be happy to come to your home. Quite happy indeed."

And just like that, it was as if she had never said those things all those months ago. It didn't matter that she had been careless. Nor did it matter that she had tried to end their friendship when it had just begun.

Freya and Arrow's relationship was fine again. And for that, she was very grateful.

Arrow dropped back onto all fours and left. He was likely returning to his home, hoping that her sister and Lux hadn't destroyed the place. She could only hope that they hadn't, although Esther wasn't particularly neat.

She had a feeling they would all know if Esther hadn't treated the goblin dog's home with respect.

With a soft smile on her face, she returned her attention to the Goblin King. He stood in the center of a small field, his castle silhouetted behind him. The spires twisted with stairs on their exterior, beautiful and unreal. Stars could just barely be seen glittering in the sky around the castle, although the sun was still on the horizon. She didn't know how it looked like a galaxy flared to life behind the building, but it certainly did.

He reached out his hand. "You said you wanted to come home."

She did. More than anything. Freya took his hand without hesitation and let him draw her toward the very sky where he had made his kingdom. "Where do you think my sister and Lux are?"

"If I know the friends of the Goblin King, then I think your sister and Lux will be waiting for us in the castle." He wrapped his arm around her shoulders and drew her close. "Now, the story I'm going to tell everyone will be quite tragic. I want them to pity me, you see. It's been a long time since I've been in such trouble that someone has had to save me."

"Ah." Freya nodded. "Of course. You will want their sympathy, that makes sense. How can I assist in this elaborate lie?"

"It's not a lie." He pressed a hand against his chest dramatically. "I would never lie to anyone. I'm a faerie. This is merely the same story that we just lived. Elaborated, perhaps, but only for dramatic effect."

"Isn't that a lie?"

"Of course not." He winked. "It's the gift of a storyteller and every bit my right as the person who suffered so greatly to defeat the Goblin Queen."

They strode through the front gates of his castle, and she shook her head. "Absolutely not. I was the one who defeated the Goblin Queen. You can't take that title away from me. I am now the only person to defeat not one, but two people who hold your very station."

He stuck out his tongue. "I suppose you're right. It is unbefitting of a gentleman to steal a lady's title without asking."

"Truer words have never been said."

Eldridge remained silent for a few moments. He waltzed them all the way to the front door before clearing his throat and asking, "Then I suppose it does no harm to ask if I might steal your title. Just for dramatic effect."

Freya laughed, looking up at him with all the mirth she could muster contained in her chest. "Thank you very much for asking, Goblin King. But no. I would like the title for as long as I might keep it."

He sighed, then draped himself over her shoulder. She stumbled with the sudden weight that was hanging off her. Like he was some war battered man who needed her to help keep him upright. "Then you will tell them I was gravely injured, which I was mind you, and that I needed to be carried back to my throne. Then, when I sit on it, we will reveal that I have been healed by the power of the Goblin King, and everyone will be left in awe."

The laughter that burst out of her was filled with a sense of relief. He was back to his normal self, finally. Ridiculous and quite possibly the strangest man she had ever met. But he was back to being her

Goblin King. "I will do no such thing. But I can help you into the castle if you need a woman to drag you."

"Would that make me look weak?"

She stared into those swirling silver eyes and shook her head. "I don't think you could ever look weak, Goblin King. You took the throne back, even if you had the help of a mortal woman."

His joking expression softened. Eldridge tucked a strand of her hair behind her ear and quietly said, "Or perhaps not so much of a mortal as we thought. You used magic on the ice, Freya. I think that shouldn't just be swept under the carpet so quickly."

"Perhaps not. But let's get settled into this new life first, shall we?"

Together, they opened the doors and strode into the room where she had first met the Goblin King. The golden planets weaved overhead, although they weren't so dangerously close as to hit them now.

Three figures stood in the very center of the room. Two with tails, and one with horns that just missed clipping a passing planet.

"Freya!" Esther shouted, running to her sister and throwing herself into Freya's arms. "You made it! I can't believe it, but you actually did it!"

Lux grinned behind Esther and added, "Again. You did it again."

"Did you ever doubt me?" Freya peeled herself out of Esther's arms and tried very hard to look at least a little disappointed. "I beat the Goblin Queen, yes. But it wasn't easy."

"Beating the leader of a court is rarely easy." The deep, smooth voice was one that Freya had hoped to hear again in her lifetime.

The Autumn Thief strode toward them with her hands tucked behind her back. There was the slightest bit of fur on her antlers, and Freya feared that meant they would shed soon. She quite liked the antlers on the redhead. This time, the Thief wore a lovely corseted dress in a deep, vibrant green. The bodice was tight to her flat chest, and the corset created a lovely hourglass figure tucked in tight at her hips.

"Autumn Thief," Freya said with a grin. "It's good to see you again so soon."

"With information you'll be pleased to hear this time." The

Autumn Thief extended her arm. "Would you follow me, please? I've been waiting quite a long time to speak with you."

Freya frowned. She looked at Eldridge, hoping he would have some kind of reaction. But he appeared just as confused as she was.

They had only walked in the doors a moment ago. What else could she need to hear that was so important?

Esther nudged her toward the Thief. "Go on, Freya. I'll fill in the Goblin King. But I think you need to hear this from the Autumn Thief yourself."

Did her sister know what the Autumn Thief was going to say? That made everything even more suspicious. Freya didn't have the emotional capacity to handle returning to the court, let alone whatever else had gone wrong.

But she would go forward and do whatever the Autumn Thief wanted. Because of all the court leaders, this was the only one she thought had Freya's best interests at heart.

She followed the Autumn Thief past a few of the planets to an alcove she hadn't seen before. The space was filled with tiny silver stars hanging from the ceiling and softly dancing in a breeze she couldn't feel. A metal bench had been poured to look like it was the tail of a comet that burst out of one side, glowing with a faint white light.

Freya sat down, pinned her shaking hands to her lap, and cleared her throat. "All right, then. What is it now?"

"Not just yet. I want to make sure you're all right, first." The Autumn Thief sat down next to her and gathered Freya's hands in her own. "You just went through a great struggle. I can feel that much. I don't want you to fall apart at the seams, Freya. Your place here is still very uncertain, but I believe you to be capable of far greater things than you've even accomplished thus far."

Freya nearly broke down again. She wanted to let the words tumble from her tongue that she wasn't all right. Maybe she never would be again. She was still haunted by the image of the Winter Princess dying. The knowledge that she had taken a life, and that she hadn't really fought all that hard to not take it.

But she couldn't blame anyone other than herself. The knife had been in her hand. She had made the decision to plunge it into the Winter Princess's breast and it had been far, far too easy.

The Autumn Thief squeezed Freya's fingers, bringing her back into the present. "Dealing with death is never easy. I'm afraid I cannot help you with that. But perhaps I might address an underlying issue that is causing your inability to focus on anything but what you had to do in that frozen place?"

Nothing else was bothering Freya. She couldn't focus on anything other than what she'd done.

Frowning, she stared into the Autumn Thief's eyes that slowly changed from a deep brown to a vivid green. "I don't know what you're talking about. I can't think of anything else but her."

"You won't let yourself think of anything else. Because if you had a few moments of rest in your mind, you would realize you fear that you no longer have a purpose. There is no more evil villain for you to defeat. No more reason for you to be a hero." The Thief tilted her head to the side. "Look inside yourself, Freya. Do you really fear the memory of death? Or the sudden existence of a threat you cannot fight?"

She swallowed hard. "I will make a place for myself here, in this court."

"No, you won't. You're so certain that no one could ever need you here, that you will continue to apply yourself to this one, singular memory." The Thief smiled softly. She released her grip on Freya and smoothed a hand down her corset. "But I am here to give you a new purpose. Ever since you were in my court, I knew there was something different about you. About your sister. There were too many questions left unanswered. So I did some digging."

Freya pressed a hand to her aching temples. This time, not from Eldridge's magic, but from the pounding of too much pressure. "I don't think I can take another person musing that I'm not human. I've already heard it from enough people today."

"That's not what the Autumn Thief is trying to tell you," Eldridge said.

She startled at the sound of his voice. Freya pressed her hand to her thundering heart and wheezed out a long breath. "Don't sneak up on me like that, Eldridge."

"Sorry." He put both his hands on her shoulders, squeezing tightly like he was here to give her support. "Go ahead and tell her, Thief."

Oh no.

What were they going to say?

Worry spearing through her chest, she waited for someone else to hit her over the head. What could be worse than the Autumn Thief knowing what kind of faerie she was? Or had come from?

The Thief cleared her throat. "I know where your mother is, Freya. She's alive and I believe she's currently being held in the Spring Court."

A scream built in Freya's chest, but she refused to let it out. Instead, she whispered, "My mother?"

"Yes, my dear. She's here in the faerie realms."

Eldridge held tight to her shoulders as she started to shake. Freya didn't know what to do with this information. Her mother was dead. She had been dead for many years. Missing, of course. But eventually a person had to give up looking and realize that the loved one who had run away was no longer alive.

Except she'd been wrong.

Eldridge sat down beside her on the bench, pulled her against his side, and pressed his lips to her head. "We'll find her, Freya. I promise you."

So many promises.

She put her head to his heart and for the first time in her life, prayed to the old gods and the new. Her prayer was a simple one.

Please, let the Goblin King keep his promise.

OF PIXIES AND SPELLS

CHAPTER 1

What does a hero do when there's no one left to save?

Freya found it was a lot of sitting around and talking. To anyone who would listen to her, although most of her visitors wanted to hear yet another part of her story.

The faeries already knew all the stories she'd told. They still wanted to hear them a thousand times over. If they could have played the stories on repeat, they would have. Mostly it was goblins who made their way to the Goblin King's castle. They slipped in through the cracks in the walls and then hunted her down for their daily fix.

But today, Freya didn't want to talk to any of the furry little creatures. She wanted a little time to herself.

If she was being honest with herself, time to herself was all she got these days.

Esther was very busy with Lux. While they were gone in the Winter Court, the two of them had stepped up in a big way to make sure the courts ran smoothly. They'd become a sort of go between for a lot of the faerie creatures. Esther was kind enough to understand their individual points of view from each court, and Lux could translate their words into something the other faeries understood.

Obviously, her sister and Lux didn't have time to visit Freya.

She could visit Arrow. He loved it when she came to his little home, even making her tea, though she hated every drop.

But he had gotten into the Goblin King's library and the faithful dog had disappeared. Now, whenever she tried to talk to him, all he wanted to speak of was the newest fact he'd discovered in between the pages of an old tome.

She found that information interesting most of the time. But there was only so much old history a woman could take.

And Eldridge? Well. Eldridge was busy being king. He didn't have time to entertain her, nor did it feel right to drag him away from it all.

Nearly every court needed his help to put their kingdoms back together after the Goblin Queen had destroyed many of them. The crumbling she'd seen in the Goblin Court had spread in their absence. Everyone had broken houses. Fractured court systems. Things that needed fixing and only the king could force them to work together.

She admired him for his patience. But she missed him a bit.

Freya left the castle in the stars and strode into the gardens. Eldridge kept many wild plants here that grew nowhere else. And it was one of the few peaceful places in the castle. She sat on a stone bench carved with twin lions and tilted her face back to the sun.

Her life here wasn't all that bad. She should have been happy to have a few relaxing months to herself. After all, it had been a very long time of fighting with the faeries.

She'd had to save her sister. Then had to get the king back after her actions had nearly destroyed all the courts in one fell swoop. She was a busy woman.

But it still felt like she was missing something. At home, at least, she had things to do. Freya was never still for very long in that cabin in the woods. The wards needed tending. The garden needed weeding. Most of the time she had to crawl on her hands and knees into the basement of the house just to get some wild creature away from their cold storage. She was busy all the time, and there was never a shortage of things to do.

Here, she touched nothing. All the items in the faerie courts were magical. Eldridge had made that very clear. If she wanted to blow herself up, then she could go about and poke whatever she wanted. But if she desired her fingers to remain attached to her hands, then she wouldn't touch unfamiliar objects.

So she'd stayed in her room. Like a good little human pet, waiting for when Eldridge would tell her she could leave. Except that moment never came.

She mused that she was now a princess locked away in a castle. Incapable of doing anything other than waiting for her prince to come and save her. Or, in her case, a king.

Freya opened a single eye at the sound of scuttling footsteps and stared down the small stone path that led back to the castle. A little goblin child stood in the middle with wide eyes, staring at her as if she might bite.

"Hello," she breathed. "What are you doing here?"

"Well." The boy was part cat, part human child. He had long whiskers on his face that bounced when he talked. Lifting a paw, he licked it and then rubbed behind his enormous ears. "My friend said that the woman who defeated the Goblin Queen lived here. He said you would be in the gardens but... You don't look like the lady who could do all that."

"I don't?" She lifted a brow. "And just what must this paragon look like?"

He lifted his paws into the air and flexed his claws. Sharp claws flashed in the sunlight. "She'd have claws like these."

"Oh." Freya nodded sagely. "Of course she would. And what else?"

"Um..." The little boy looked up, then back down. Finally, he used his paws to push back his lips and showed his long canines. "She'd have fangs like this!"

Or at least, that's what Freya thought he said. The garbled words were a little difficult to understand.

She supposed if someone was going to believe that the Goblin Queen was a monster, then it must take another monster to beat her. Freya wished she knew how to change her shape so that she could impress the child. But he wasn't the first to be a little disappointed when he met her.

Smiling, she shrugged. "I don't know what to tell you then. I'm the one who killed the Goblin Queen, and I don't have claws, fangs, horns, or other animal appendages, I'm afraid."

"You?" His eyes opened so wide they nearly fell out of his head. "You're the Queen Killer?"

Freya winced. She hated that nickname. The faeries had been trying it out for size, and she didn't know how to ask them to stop. It was a name that brought with it sad memories and guilt.

She didn't want to be known as the Queen Killer. Just Freya was fine. Or maybe the Goblin King's... friend?

No, that was a horrible path to go down. The last thing she needed was to be wondering what she was to the Goblin King when he had made it clear he didn't know the answer to that question either.

Sighing, she patted the bench beside her. "Why don't you come sit down? I'll tell you anything you want to hear."

"Really?"

"Really."

The goblin boy bounded to her side, plopped himself down on the bench with purpose, then hauled his tail out from under him to hold. "Did you want to kill the Queen?"

Freya blinked at the child. That was the first time anyone had asked her that question before. "Um..." She narrowed her eyes and furrowed her brow. "Why do you want to know that?"

"Well..." He looked side to side, then whispered, "I think killing a person must be hard, is all. And if you wanted to kill her, that would make you a lot scarier."

Oh, her heart was breaking for this soft hearted child. He deserved to be showered with praise for the massive heart he hid in his cat-like chest. Leaning close, she whispered, "Do you promise not to tell anyone?"

His eyes widened even more, if that were possible. Nodding frantically, he stared into her eyes with slitted, dilated pupils.

Freya hoped she wouldn't disappoint him by telling the truth. "No. I didn't want to kill her. But sometimes there's no other option for bad people."

He nodded, although there was a question in his eyes he obviously didn't feel comfortable asking. "Did it feel weird?"

"Did what feel weird?"

"Killing someone." He looked down at his hands, then back up at her. "It's just... Well. My father died a while ago, and someone said that was because an elf had killed him. They said he deserved it, but..."

She didn't think her heart could hurt anymore, but there it went. Hurting even worse for this little boy who had lost a loved one. And his father, of all people? A boy needed his father.

How did she go about this without causing the child even more pain? Clearing her throat, she tried her best. "I think that would be a different situation, don't you? The Winter Princess was a horrible monster. She would have hurt all the faeries in every court if we didn't kill her. I don't think your father could have been that bad."

"He wasn't." The goblin boy tugged on the fabric of his pants. "I liked him."

"Then I don't think it's the same. Your father isn't like the Winter Princess." Freya wrapped her arm around his shoulders and leaned back against the bench with him. "How about we stay quiet for a little while? You can count all the birds that fly by."

"I do like birds!"

They waited in silence for all of ten heartbeats before the boy started rambling again. But at least this time he wasn't talking about how his father had been killed. He named every bird that flew by them. Some of them were nonsense, others were merely the species, but some he took the time to give proper names.

And when she was about ready to go mad from the imagination, this child held within him, the boy sighed. "I should go home. My mother probably misses me."

"Did you tell her you were going to sneak into the castle?" Freya knew the answer before he said it.

"No, of course not. She would have told me not to come, and then I never would have met the Queen Killer." He hopped off the bench and started down the path like he didn't need to even say goodbye. Like he was confident he would eventually see her again.

Leaning back on the bench, she let the sun play across her face. Though the boy's story had been sad, at least he could return to his mother. She'd likely be angry when he made his way back to their little home. But if she was anything like Freya's mother had been, then she would still hug the child tight with happiness that he'd made it home. Even if he'd lied about where he was going all day.

Her heart twisted in her chest at the thought of her mother.

Her mother, who was alive. Somewhere.

Freya couldn't find her though. She had to rely on other people to find information on the woman who had birthed her. The Autumn Thief understood the need for finding out information quickly. But it would never be quick enough.

Who knew what the Spring Maiden had done to her mother? Was that why she was so interested in Freya to begin with?

She ran her fingers through her hair in frustration. Whatever good feelings the goblin boy had brought disappeared in the wake of her mother's predicament. All Freya wanted to do was run out into the wilds and fight everyone who knew nothing about her mother's whereabouts.

But that wouldn't change her situation.

All she could do was sit. And wait. And hope that the faeries were doing whatever they could to find her mother. Even though she knew the likelihood of that was slim.

"Time for another walk, I guess," she snarled. Freya stood up. The anger shaking through her frame couldn't be contained, and the only way she knew how to ease the feeling was to walk.

So she did what she had been doing for too long. What she'd been doing every day since she returned to the Goblin King's court.

She walked.

CHAPTER 2

Freya realized she could no longer spend time indoors. She worried too much about what cursed object she would touch. So the Goblin King gave her freedom to travel throughout his kingdom, and it was easy to find places to sit and think.

Lately, she had taken to wandering all the way to the very edge of his kingdom where a small stream had split through his wards. The water wasn't magical. It wasn't sent by another person to attack the king, or even a risk to be near at all. The stream was shallow, simple, and the tiny eddies that swirled through it were lovely and relaxing.

Leaves from the Autumn Court danced on top of the water. They were little boats meandering their way down the stream to wherever it exited. She wasn't sure where it went. Freya had never followed it, but that was part of the appeal.

Not knowing where the water went gave her some semblance of normalcy. She wasn't the hero of this story anymore. She was just Freya. And as a normal woman in these parts, she probably shouldn't know what was going to happen or where everything went.

Sighing, she leaned back on her hands and watched the leaves twirl on their wild ride down the water. Someday, she would like to ride on a ship through the sea. Maybe she would even visit some strange faerie land like she had seen off the shores of the Summer Court.

The adventurous thoughts stalled when she remembered the major problem standing in her way.

Her mother.

The memory always darkened whatever dreams ran through Freya's head. Her beloved mother was missing and there was nothing she could do about it.

She had to sit here, with her hands tied, hoping someone would do what was right. And it was downright frustrating. If she didn't get some kind of information or relief from this torment, then she was certain she would go mad.

A leaf fell from above her head. Bright crimson and so vibrant she wondered if it were on fire. It floated through the air like a snowflake. Not that she'd ever be able to look at snowflakes the same again. Not after her time in the Winter Court.

A hand appeared out of nowhere, snatching the leaf midair and holding the lovely foliage in front of her eyes. "Were you staring at this so intently because you wanted it? I could make it last forever if it's leaves that you want."

Eldridge stepped in front of her. He wore his customary black suit with golden embroidery on the shoulders. The sun turned his black hair into an oil slick color of blues, purples, and hidden reds.

He'd gained weight since they returned to the Goblin Court. Finally. After months of torture at the hands of the Goblin Queen, it had taken a while for him to return to his normal handsome nature.

Now, it was hard to even look at him. He was too attractive. Too otherworldly. Suddenly a Goblin King once again, and not just someone she had to save.

Taking a deep breath, Freya reached for the leaf and held it by the stem. Twirling it in her hand, she tried to appreciate the gift for what it was. An olive branch. Eldridge and her hadn't been themselves lately.

She supposed it was to be expected after what they'd gone through.

"It's lovely," she replied. "And surprising to see anything from Autumn in your court."

"Did you think it would be all darkness and gloom?" He flipped the tails of his coat up and sat down on the ground beside her.

She hadn't expected him to risk getting the suit dirty and noticed how he hid a wince. Eldridge had important news, that much was apparent. Otherwise, he never would have sat on the dirty ground.

Or something else had gone wrong, and he needed to be on the same level with her so she didn't tackle him to the ground.

Immediately suspicious, Freya turned toward him and asked, "What happened?"

His eyes widened in surprise. "Nothing happened! Why would you even suggest that? Nothing at all has happened. I just wanted to visit with you. It's been a while since we had time to ourselves and... well." He struggled to find his next words, only to throw up his hands and shrug.

That wasn't good either.

The Goblin King was never at a loss for words. And though she didn't want anything to be wrong, she was ashamed to admit her heart picked up its pace. If something was wrong, that meant they needed her. That she was still someone to go to when the faeries needed help.

Even though she'd never been that person in the first place.

She sighed and tried to think of something to say to him. Something that would pull out the words he wanted to tell her, even though he didn't know how to say them.

Freya settled on gesturing all around them. "The sun is shining, Goblin King. The stream is burbling and the leaves are falling like rain around us. This is a beautiful setting to say something difficult, so you might as well spit it out. I don't think you'll get a better chance than this."

Though he obviously was still struggling, Eldridge relented. "You don't seem like yourself, Freya. That's all. You wander around my kingdom with a lost expression on your face, and I don't know how to help you. I want to, you know."

"But you're busy being king." She broke away from the hope in his gaze and stared down at her fingers she'd twisted in her lap. "You have more important things to focus on than a human woman you picked up on your travels."

At her words, Eldridge lunged forward. He shifted until he was on his knees before her, then reached out for her hands. He squeezed them tight between his own. "Freya, that is not how I feel about you. Surely you know that you are so much more than some stray I picked up in my wanderings around the kingdom."

Did she?

Logically, yes. They had a connection between them now. Their travels would have attached most people, though. She felt a connection with Arrow as well and wondered if the romantic feelings were only lacking because he was a dog.

Her thoughts were all messed up in her head. Jumbled like she had thrown them all into a bucket and shook them around too hard.

But leaving him on his knees, though highly appealing, felt wrong too. Eldridge needed to know what was going on in her head, especially if she was distracting him from being king.

"I know," she replied, shaking her head and squeezing his fingers in return. "I just can't focus on anything when I know my mother is out there. She's waiting for me to find her, or maybe she's stuck in that horrible nightmare realm. There's a thousand possibilities of what is going on. How am I supposed to do anything? Think of anything but her suffering?"

He released his hold on her hands and moved a lock of hair behind her ear. His fingers lingered, warm and smooth and comforting. "You are a hero at heart, Freya of Woolwich. I should have known your wandering soul wouldn't want to linger here for long."

She supposed that was a way to look at it, although it didn't feel right either. Freya wasn't just some wandering soul. She was a daughter who feared for her mother. Simple as that.

But could a faerie ever understand that suffering? She'd never seen them show any familial ties at all. Even when it came to killing their adoptive sister.

That dark memory haunted her, too.

It seemed like she couldn't get away from her sins. All the memories of what she'd done, where she'd been, how she'd beaten two very powerful faeries. They all lingered until she didn't know which way was up and which way was down.

And the guilt, as well. A wonderful, talented, strange man knelt before her, begging for her attention and for Freya to return to normal. This was her chance to see what a life with the Goblin King would really be like.

She'd ruin all this if she didn't dig herself out of this hole.

Freya opened her mouth to apologize, but no words came out. She just stared at him with her eyes wide, hoping that he would understand what she was trying to convey.

She needed time.

To find her mother.

To feel like the hero in her own life again. Faeries be damned. She needed something to happen that would return her power.

He slid his hand from behind her head, down her neck, and stopped over the pounding beat of her heart. "I came here to tell you that I will never let you linger in the dark for long. Not alone. You must know that."

"I do." After all they'd been through, Freya trusted that he had her best interest at heart. He really wanted her to be happy here.

Namely because he assumed she still wanted to run back to the human realm. She didn't know how many times he'd asked her if she missed her little cabin. Freya even had to clarify with him if he was asking so much because he wanted her to leave.

He didn't. She had to remember that.

"Good," he replied with a soft smile on his face. "Then I want you to take what I have to say next as hope. Do you understand me?"

She shifted forward with excitement brewing in her chest. So he did have something to tell her. Something very important if he was certain she would take it wrong. "What is it?"

"We received a letter from someone I'm sure you will remember." He leaned away from her to pull a small piece of paper out of his pocket. "Apparently an old friend of ours knows where your mother is."

Heart racing in her chest, she reached for the letter he held in his grasp. An old friend? She didn't have many friends here, and she knew Arrow wouldn't have written a letter to them. The goblin dog would have stomped to the castle, radiating with anger.

"From who?" she asked, opening the envelope and pulling out a small card.

The smell hit her first. Like someone had thrown a bouquet of roses into her face. Then she saw the glitter on the edges of the card and she knew who had sent them the note.

Freya frowned and looked back at Eldridge. "The Spring Maiden?"

He nodded. Small, worried wrinkles appeared between his eyes. "Just read it, Freya."

The note had crumpled edges, likely from Eldridge's fists when he first read what the Spring Maiden had to say. Neither of them had fond memories of the leader of the Spring Court.

My dear Eldridge,

I know much time has passed since we last saw each other. I hope you've been well.

It's my understanding that you have in your charge a very unique mortal woman. I have also met this fine creature and only realized recently that I know where a certain motherly figure to this woman resides.

Just thought you'd like to know.

If you find yourself curious, come and visit for a while, would you? It's been too long since the Spring Court has seen the Goblin King.

Yours,

Spring Maiden.

Freya frowned at the signature. "Why would the Spring Maiden reach out after all this time? She never mentioned my mother while I was there. Did she mention her to you?"

Eldridge shook his head and stood up. He held out his hand for her to take while replying, "No. Even when I was hiding myself as one of her guards, I never heard her say a single thing about another mortal woman."

A letter like this made little sense, then. Freya took his hand belatedly and let him pull her up to his side. She stared at the letter, trying to piece together this mystery even though she didn't have enough information to do so.

"I just don't understand," she muttered. "Why now?"

With a muttered curse, Eldridge plucked the paper from her grip.

Freya let out a snarl of frustration and reached for it again. They held it between them, tugging back and forth until she finally let go before it tore. "Eldridge, what are you doing? I need to figure out why she sent the letter."

"And we will." He wrapped an arm around her waist and tugged her against his chest. "This is more fire in you than I've seen since we beat the Winter Princess. Let me enjoy the battle between us for a moment."

All the wind blew out of her sails. Yes, she supposed she had been rather boring while she was trying to forget all the bad things that had happened.

Freya placed her hands on his shoulders. She smoothed her fingers over the muscles beneath his jacket, feeling them shift and twitch at her touch. "I've been rather boring, haven't I?"

"You don't know how to sit still." He lowered his head, lips so close to hers she could feel their heat. "But I missed this side of you, my hero."

"Don't call me that when no one needs saving." Freya leaned closer, flirting with touching him but never quite letting their lips finally do what they both wanted.

And she did still want to kiss him. Every fiber of her being wanted to lean in, press their lips together, and let him warm her from the outside in.

Maybe she could. Just this once. Even though she still didn't feel like herself, maybe kissing him would make her feel a little more like the hero he kept calling her. She could be that person again, if only she gave herself the chance.

She leaned forward, eyes drifting shut.

Eldridge slid a hand between them and pressed a finger to her lips, stopping them from ever touching his.

Freya's eyes popped open again, flying wide in shock.

Mischief danced in his gaze. "There will be time for that, my dear."

"There's time for it now."

"Perhaps, but isn't the wait that much more delicious?" He released her with that wicked smile on his face. "We have to go see the Spring Maiden, you know. There's a lot of planning to do. And packing! My goodness, we have to pack half the castle if I'm to come with you."

"Why would you come with me?" She shook her head to clear the fog of desire from her mind. "We're trying to find my mother, not yours."

"I would certainly hope she isn't my mother. That would make all this attraction between us very awkward." He danced out of her reach, nearly falling into the stream behind him in his excitement. "Come on, Freya! Back to the castle we go. Adventure waits for no hero."

She followed him with a smile on her face for the first time in what felt like forever. He was a ridiculous man. A foolish man, even.

But she hoped someday she could call him hers.

CHAPTER 3

She stood in the courtyard of the Goblin King's castle, a place she hadn't realized existed, and blew at the hair that fell in front of her face. "We're traveling in that?"

A carriage stood before her. A normal, entirely mortal carriage. Or at least, similar enough that she knew what it was without having to clarify. The wooden sides were black, not painted, but actual black wood. But the wheels were normal. The horses were normal as well. They stamped their hooves in impatience at the goblin man at the front of the carriage. He held onto the reins and stared straight ahead, rabbit ears twitching at her question.

Eldridge stopped beside her and adjusted the sleeves of his midnight blue suit. "Yes, of course. Did you think we were going to walk to the Spring Court? That would take all day."

All day?

She twitched the pale blue skirt of her traveling gown. "I've always traveled through portals to get from one court to the next."

"Yes, I remember. Arrow loves his portals because he's deathly afraid of horses. And the two of you were in a rather large hurry to get between each of them, were you not?" He nodded at the horses again. "I don't mind a few hours of travel, and I assumed bringing all our belongings would be a little easier this way than having to travel through the portal eight times. I brought a lot of clothing, Freya."

She knew he had packed more outfits than she could count, but... "How close is the Spring Court to yours?"

With a sigh of impatience, Eldridge shaded his eyes with his hand and stared off to their right. "About a few hours by carriage ride that way. You can't see it from here because the trees block that dreadful garden the Spring Maiden loves so much."

"I..." She blinked, then swallowed hard. "I didn't realize all the courts were so close to each other."

"They're close to my kingdom, if that's what you mean. The Goblin King has to be between all of them, so they all touch the land that is officially mine, even though no one lives here other than me." Eldridge winked. "I'm glad there are still things in my kingdom that can surprise you, Freya."

"It's never boring in the faerie realms," she agreed. She took his offered arm and let him lead her down the steps to the side of the carriage, although she was still a little surprised.

All the courts touched this land? They were really all that close to each other?

The goblin at the front nodded to her. The bubbles of his cheeks moved up and down, like a rabbit sniffing at something. She could only assume that was a smile as Eldridge opened the door and tucked her inside.

This was really a lovely carriage. The interior had been painted with a thousand stars and a bright galaxy above her head. The dark cushions were comfortable and the plush back cupped her spine. Magic. She would never get over how useful it was to have in her everyday life.

The carriage shifted as Eldridge entered. He settled himself and then tapped the ceiling.

Off they went. Too easily and far too simplistic for her liking.

Freya stared out the small window, then looked back at the Goblin King. "We're the only ones going?"

"Yes."

She chewed her lip. "Won't we need some of the others to help us? The Spring Maiden is very untrustworthy. We both know that."

Was he trying to hide a smile?

He took a few moments to reply to her, staring out the window with his hand pressed against his mouth. Finally he said, "This is a political meeting. She's a court leader who has officially invited her king to come see her. I don't think we need to show up with an army at her doorstep."

"What if this is a trick, though?" Freya didn't trust any faerie leader other than him. And mostly she didn't trust the Goblin King either. "She could be trying to take the throne, just like the Winter Princess."

"Dahlia is not so powerful that she could ever take the throne. If she managed to kill me, it would go to the Summer Lord now that the Winter Princess is dead." He leaned back in his seat.

"That doesn't mean she wouldn't try to kill both of you then. I think we should at least bring Arrow, or let him know where we're going." Her heart raced. Was this another situation when he underestimated his opponent? What if the Spring Maiden had cooked up this plan to take out all the court leaders in one fell swoop?

Was it hot in the carriage? She was hot.

Eldridge nudged her foot with his own. "Freya. Not everyone is out to kill me. I know the Winter Princess might have made you think that, but there has been no struggle between the courts since I became King. You don't have to worry so much."

But she did. Because he wasn't worrying at all, and someone had to think of these things or... or...

He tapped her toes hard. Nearly stomping on her foot to make his point. "Freya, I realize I've given you no reason to think faeries aren't warring creatures lacking hearts. I know your experience with us thus far has been trickery and strife. But we are very similar to the nobles in your realm. Not everything is about battle and winning wars."

How did she tell him that she didn't trust his judgement? After their experience in the Winter Court, and her own experience with him, it didn't seem likely that her opinion of them was wrong. Sure, his experiences differed from hers.

Eldridge forgot Freya was mortal. The Spring Maiden didn't like her kind. She was more likely to have Freya's mother locked away in a dreaming world to watch her memories than actually know where her mother was.

This was a trick. She was certain of it.

If the Goblin King didn't want to believe that, then she would just have to be that more on her guard. Ready for anything, no matter what that cost her.

"Freya," he repeated. "The worst we can expect is that she'll want something in return for information about your mother. This is the same kind of deal the Autumn Thief has been helping us make across the kingdom. We haven't come up with anything real. If anyone would know about a mortal in their court, it would be the person who leads it. Don't you think?"

Her thoughts must have played across her features like an open book. Eldridge rolled his eyes with a grin and stared out the window for the remainder of their ride. And that was fine. Freya didn't want to talk when she had to plan how to keep them both alive.

The landscape was a little distracting, though. Even she had to admit it.

Autumn was the theme of the Goblin Kingdom, although it was a little darker than the Autumn Court itself. She watched the sky move from twilight into the bright morning of the Spring Court. The moment they entered the Spring Maiden's kingdom was painfully obvious.

The ground shifted into emerald green like someone had unrolled an impressive carpet. Flowers dotted through the grass, bright and almost too vivid to be real. Fluffy white clouds danced through the sky. Birds started singing. Their chirping warbles reminded her of her time in this place, and how easy it had been for the Spring Maiden to capture her mind.

Freya shivered.

"Remembering your last visit?" Eldridge asked.

"Yes." She pointed to some of the pavilions just out of sight. "I remember those a little too well. They had me laid out like I was nothing more than convenient entertainment."

Eldridge frowned, his own memories turning his expression dark.

"I've always hated the way the Spring Maiden sees your kind. She thinks mortals are weak minded, but idolizes your lives. The two don't fit, but she would never explain her thinking to me."

"I don't think she wants to be one of us. I think she's just fascinated with the way other people live." At least the Spring Maiden had been kinder than the Winter Princess. The Spring Court was more about satisfying their strange leader's needs. And less about causing other people pain.

"Don't give her so much credit." He touched a finger to the side of his face where thorns had broken through his skin. "There's a lot I need to talk with her about, and one of those things will be her treatment of the guards."

The words were refreshing. At least someone was going to hold the court leaders accountable for the pain they had caused.

Leaning forward, she placed her hand on his knee and squeezed. "I had completely forgotten you immersed yourself in this court to watch over me. More than anyone, you would know of the pain here."

"Every court likes to cause pain. Such desires are part of who we are as faeries." His eyes darkened. He stared at her like he wanted to take a bite out of her, but Freya didn't think he would.

He'd always been so gentle with her. So calm when he could have been forceful and rough. Surely he wasn't one of the faeries who liked pain...

Was he?

Considering the light in his eyes, she feared she might be wrong. Perhaps that was the reason he'd put some space between them.

Leaning back in her seat, she shoved her spine hard against the back of the carriage. If he wanted pain, then she didn't know if she could go through with this. Freya knew nothing about the acts of love. Let alone causing another person pain.

It was a lot to think about. Maybe too much, when she rolled it over in her mind.

Eldridge wrapped his knuckles against the ceiling, hard. She jumped at the sound, thinking he was mad at her or warning her of what was to come. But he was just letting the goblin man know that they were stopping.

Suddenly, she found herself a little fearful of the Goblin King all over again. And that wasn't fair to him. Not after everything they'd gone through.

Freya would look deeper into that reaction later. But for now, she needed to be on guard in the Spring Court. "Stopping so soon?"

"The Spring Maiden doesn't let anyone enter her court much farther than this. Even the Goblin King." He threw the door to the carriage open and stepped out. "Come along, Freya. Someone will find us soon enough, and then the game is on."

She could only imagine that game would be difficult to play.

She exited the carriage and waved goodbye to the goblin man as he steered it back the way they had come. He gave her another odd smile that was more a bouncing of cheeks than anything else.

At least the goblins liked her now. Freya considered that to be a success.

The Goblin King straightened his coat one last time. She had seen him do the action so many times, but now she wondered if it was a nervous tick. He always seemed to check and make sure he was presentable before he took on another adventure.

If he was nervous, then at least she knew he wouldn't do anything foolish.

Freya stepped up to his side and put her hand on his arm. "You said someone would find us?"

He jumped at her touch. "Ah. Yes. The Spring Maiden has wards at her borders that tell her servants when someone arrives. They're the ones who greeted you the last time, if you remember."

"I do." She squeezed his bicep. "I didn't know you were watching even then."

The anxiety in his gaze eased. He reached up and placed his hand over hers. "I was watching you the entire time, Freya. Even in the moments when you felt like you were alone."

God, if that didn't heat her to the very core. She wanted to kiss him badly. She wanted to jump into his arms and say they didn't need to find the Spring Maiden yet. If only they could have a few moments when she could prove to him that even though she had been distracted, she still wanted him.

Someone cleared their throat, interrupting her thoughts. "Goblin King. It's been a very long time since you entered the court."

They both turned to see a pixie behind them. The strange creature pulsed its wings slowly, the dragonfly texture casting rainbow beams onto the surrounding flowers.

She'd forgotten how beautiful the spring faeries were. This one had golden curls tangling down to her bottom, with a heart-shaped pale face that reflected the sun. She wore a lovely, short dress made of spiderwebs.

They were so fragile in appearance. Freya always wanted to ask if they needed help walking, but she supposed that was part of their dangerous magic. Pixies didn't need help. Their mouths were full of razor-sharp teeth and they moved with unnatural speed.

If anyone needed help in the Spring Court, it would be Freya.

Eldridge squeezed her hand one last time. "It has been a long time. However, the Spring Maiden summoned us. We're here for a visit."

The pixie looked Freya up and down, then bared her sharp teeth in a smile. "I remember you. Your memories were so sweet to watch."

Freya gulped. "Thank you?"

Apparently there was nothing else the pixie had to say to the mortal. She turned around and waved a hand for them to follow her. "The Spring Maiden has been expecting you. I'm to show you all the changes in the kingdom, Goblin King. Then she will meet us at the end of your... tour."

They followed the pixie, and Eldridge leaned down to whisper in her ear, "Stalling? Maybe you were right, Freya. Something strange is happening here."

An icy shiver trailed down her spine. What could be happening in the Spring Court?

CHAPTER 4

The pixie led them through waist high flower fields. Freya's nose filled with the scent of lavender and rose. Once, she would have marveled at how lovely it all smelled. But now she remembered the Spring Maiden's cursed perfume and how it had made her do whatever the Spring Maiden wanted.

She hated the thought that someone had controlled her so easily. The spell had been intense and impossible to break.

If Eldridge hadn't saved her, she still would have been in these fields entertaining the faeries with her memories.

She didn't want to think about what would have happened then. These faeries hadn't necessarily been cruel to her. They just hadn't seen her as anything other than a new toy to play with. They thought mortals weren't alive, and that was part of the problem.

She couldn't help herself. The pixie who guided them through the gardens had claimed to remember her, but Freya couldn't conjure up the face in her memories.

There was no other option. She had to ask. "I'm sorry, I don't remember you. How do we know each other?"

The pixie grinned again, sharp teeth glinting in the sun. "My brother used to brush your hair. And when he was finished, and you fell back to sleep, I would braid it into a thousand tiny braids all over your head. You looked so lovely sleeping like that, you know. Much better than now."

Freya touched a hand to her loose hair. Sure, it was pin straight and falling around her shoulders. Maybe a few strands were frizzy, but she hadn't had time to think about her hair lately. She bathed. It was clean, and that was enough.

"My hair?" she asked. "I don't remember you braiding my hair."

"Like I said, mortal, you were asleep. So few of our flowers remember anything once they enter the dreaming realm." The pixie held out her arm for them to go ahead of her. "These are the new dreaming chambers. After you left, the Spring Maiden realized there were a few flaws in the original design. We've completely remade them."

Freya didn't want to know what they had created. These pavilions were always so dangerous to begin with, but she didn't remember any flaws. She hadn't escaped from them at all, so surely they had functioned appropriately?

Apparently she was wrong.

What had once been an open area was now closed off. The dreaming person was held down onto the bed by a hundred vines that shifted and moved while they slept. The thick tendrils looked like garden snakes writhing over the prone form of the poor man who had laid down to sleep.

A leaf touched his cheek tenderly, then moved again as it continued in the strange, wrapping coil.

At least the man was asleep. Freya thought if he had awoken and seen what was happening to him, he might have screamed in fear.

"Why did you change it?" Curiosity got the better of her. And she felt more brave with the Goblin King standing beside her. "At least before I could wake up a few times and breathe fresh air."

"The Spring Maiden realized that was the flaw. You were only able to escape because she let you wake up and play with us." The pixie touched a finger underneath her eye, wiping away an imaginary tear. "Now we don't get to play with them anymore. But at least we can still watch their dreams."

Freya shared a horrified glance with Eldridge.

He looked deeply disturbed by what they had found. And something in his gaze said he would speak with the Spring Maiden about this terrifying development as well.

Small consolation, but at least someone wanted to help these poor people.

Clearing her throat, Freya tried to get as much information as she could out of the pixie. "How many dreamers do you have? I remember there were quite a few of us."

The pixie grinned and shook her head. "You don't remember any such thing, Freya. You were sleeping. And when you weren't, the Spring Maiden's perfume kept you in a silly little stupor. Don't think it will be that easy to trick any of us. We're the ones who are masters at trickery, not you, mortal."

"Easy," the Goblin King snarled. "She is the hero of these courts. The one who saved us all from the icy grasp of the Winter Princess. You will offer her respect and nothing else, pixie, or I will rip your wings from your back."

Another person interrupted Eldridge, and the sound of her voice sent shivers down Freya's spine.

"Please don't threaten my pixies, Eldridge. Of all people, you should know how protective I am of my dear, darling creatures." The Spring Maiden rounded the corner of the pavilion. "You're just as protective as I am, my king."

Why did Freya feel like she had to curtsey? This woman had done nothing but haunt Freya's dreams for countless nights, and still she felt like she needed to offer respect.

The Spring Maiden was just as lovely as she remembered. The ethereal quality of her nature was the same, although perhaps her pale features were a little more drawn. Her white hair fell lank around her face, rather than shining with oil. And her clothing had more moth-eaten holes than Freya remembered.

In short, the Spring Maiden looked rather ragged. That in itself was a warning.

But just because the Spring Maiden was tired, didn't mean her teeth were gone. She moved in that blurry way that always made Freya ill. One moment, she was standing beside the sleeping man, and in the next, she was directly in front of Freya.

"Hello, my dear," the Spring Maiden rasped. "I don't think you know just how much I missed you and your lovely memories. They were a joy in the darkest of times."

Freya tried her very best to not flinch as the Spring Maiden dragged her claws down Freya's face. This was too close to what it had been like in her trap. And Freya hadn't realized how traumatic the experience had been until she returned.

Now, she remembered the feeling of drowning. How she had been stuck here with no one to save her, no hope at all. So of course she had fallen under the perfumed smell. She wanted to escape from this nightmare so badly that she would have done or taken anything that offered her some kind of relief.

Eldridge's hand snapped out from her left. He grabbed onto the Spring Maiden's wrist and forced her away from Freya's face. "I'm glad her memories were so satisfying then, Dahlia. But as I reminded your pixie, this is no longer a mortal woman who stumbled into your court. She saved us all, and you would do well to remember that."

Though his grip must have been punishing, the Spring Maiden merely smiled. Her teeth were sharper than their guide's. It was like looking into the mouth of a shark. "Yes, I understand what she did to Lumi. But I wanted to ask just how much input you had in those decisions? Weren't you and the Winter Princess close? How strange to hear she died just after capturing you."

He stiffened. "You know I had no hand in what happened."

"I think you did. After all this time ruling with you, Goblin King, I know the signs of your hand. You killed another court leader, and that alone is enough to suspect your intentions in being here." Those teeth gnashed with every word. The Spring Maiden was only barely holding herself back from biting Eldridge. "Wouldn't that be a concern for all of us if you were trying to pick off the court leaders, one by one?"

"You know I'm not doing that," he snarled.

"I think you have a lot of plans, Goblin King. And I don't think any of those plans include us. So I wouldn't know what is going on in that head of yours." She stilled, the blurry motions that always radiated around her disappearing. "Perhaps if I could take a peek into that head of yours, I could tell the other leaders that you aren't plotting against us. I'm a more powerful ally than I am an enemy, Eldridge."

Oh no. If Eldridge got on one of those beds, then Freya knew damned well he would never wake up. She had just gotten him back. She refused to risk losing him again so soon.

She whipped out her own hand, grabbing onto the Spring Maiden's other wrist. She squeezed hard until the Spring Maiden's wrist turned bright red. "He's not letting you watch him dream. And you aren't going to peek into his head. He is the king of all the courts. Your king. You will give him the respect he deserves."

Perhaps the Spring Maiden hadn't thought a mortal could be so strong. Or perhaps Freya had come across even more aggressive than she'd planned. But whatever she'd done, she had surprised the Spring Maiden.

Those big blue eyes, with no whites at all, stared at her in shock. Blinked. And then the fine lines of movement rippled around the Spring Maiden once again. "You defend him with such passion when you hated him only a few months ago. What changed?"

"That's not for you to know," Freya snarled. "You're the one who called us here. Not for the courts. Not for Eldridge to undergo a firing squad of your own questions. You claimed to know something of my mother, and I will hear what you have to say. Anything else, I'm afraid you'll have to send another request for Eldridge to visit your court at a separate time."

"A mortal speaks for the king?" The Spring Maiden tilted her head back and laughed. One might think the two of them didn't have complete control over the Spring Maiden.

Eldridge shifted his grip, forcing the Spring Maiden's attention back to him. "Yes, she speaks for me. When one finds the other half of their soul, one keeps it."

He shouldn't have said that. Freya didn't even know where their relationship was going, or what would happen between the two of them. Why would he declare his feelings to a court leader? That should have stayed between the two of them until they could have talked about it a little more privately.

She was going to kill him. It was the only way to get out of this embarrassing situation and not feel her cheeks burn any longer.

The pixie behind them coughed into her hand. They had an audience of more than just their guide now. Pixies from all over the Spring Court had surrounded them without Freya noticing the veritable army the Spring Maiden had summoned.

And they had all heard what the Goblin King had said.

Freya was going to drag him into the first dark corner she could find. And she wasn't sure if she was going to hit him, kiss him, or do both in that order because he'd just declared them a couple. Without asking her permission. But her heart still fluttered in that odd little thump.

The Spring Maiden wriggled in their grip. "Well, if that's the way of it, let me go. No more games, Goblin King. I understand that you intend to find this woman's mother and stake your claim. Unhand me."

Oh no. He would not stake his claim when they found her mother. Freya didn't want anyone staking any claim over her. She was her own person.

Eldridge interjected before she could say anything that might insult the other woman. "We just want to find her mother first, Dahlia. Then we'll see about whatever I might have to say to the woman. You claimed to know where she is."

He released his hold on the Spring Maiden, so Freya reluctantly followed suit. She still wanted to squeeze the woman's arm for a little while longer, or at least until she could make the Spring Maiden feel the same way she had.

The pixie leader took a step back and shook out her hands. "Like the rest of the people you've asked, I've only heard rumors. But I won't tell you anything without a deal, you know that."

Eldridge nodded. "I understand. What do you want in return for information?"

The Spring Maiden licked her lips. She looked left and right, then gestured for the other pixies to leave. Not another word was said until they were alone, giving Freya enough time to realize two things.

First, the Spring Maiden looked worse for wear because she was exhausted. The deep bags under her eyes cast horrible shadows in the sunlight. And second, the Spring Maiden was afraid.

Very, very afraid.

When they were alone, the Spring Maiden leaned forward and rasped, "I need your help. I have to show you something, Goblin King. I don't think you will like it."

CHAPTER 5

The Spring Maiden led them away from the field of dreamers and down a smaller path lit by will-o'-the-wisps. Freya remembered these bridges with their tangled white roses covering them. It was just as beautiful as she remembered, although she couldn't decide if that was a good thing or not.

She felt like she should hate this place. Every inch of it was created to lure mortals into a lifetime of doom, and yet, she couldn't feel anything but awe.

The pixies here were terrifying, sure, but they were still faeries. Still part of the same whole that had created her dearest friend and now, the man that apparently everyone knew she was infatuated with.

"I can't believe you said that with everyone standing there," she hissed. "Now they all think we're... We're..."

"A couple?" He wrapped an arm around her shoulder and jostled her. "I know we haven't talked about it, but frankly I can't have you falling head over heels for yet another poor sap with a thorn mask."

"That's why you said it?" She was going to slap him. Where was that dark corner when she needed it? "Eldridge, I don't go around falling head over heels in general. Let alone for another guard."

"You tried to save me last time without even knowing who I was.

I'm just making sure everyone knows you aren't available." He grinned, and the expression was far too satisfying on his face. "Besides, I like it when you argue with me. Your cheeks get all flushed and it's such a pretty color."

A childish part of her wanted to clap her hands to said cheeks so he wouldn't get any satisfaction from his argument. If he liked her pretty red cheeks, then he should only see them when he'd earned the right to do so.

For now, she was intent on making sure his ears blistered by the time she finished yelling at him.

"Lovebirds, this is highly entertaining and I would cherish listening further, but I need you to focus on me." The Spring Maiden had stopped at the end of the bridge and was waiting for them. "People tend to get lost in this part of my court, and Eldridge, I'm not all that confident you remember how to get to the castle."

"I remember," he grumbled, forcing his attention away from Freya and back to the woman waiting for them. "I'm not that dense."

"Well, we will have to agree to disagree. I remember you getting lost the last time you tried to find it, and I had to send all the pixies out to find you." She shook her head. "You'd think someone as powerful as the Goblin King would remember a few simple directions."

Eldridge released his hold on Freya and stomped toward the other faerie. "They weren't simple directions, Dahlia. You purposefully made them confusing so you could laugh at me."

"So you admit you couldn't find the castle on your own then?"

"I'm admitting nothing! I'm simply stating the facts. Unlike you, who seems very intent on making sure that I'm embarrassed in front of this woman." He pointed to Freya. "She knows me well enough to see right through your exaggerations. Freya, tell her."

She wasn't all that sure the Spring Maiden was wrong.

Looking between the two of them, Freya chose the safest option. "I think I'd very much like to see the castle of the Spring Court, and that standing here arguing is only delaying the inevitable. It doesn't matter which one of you is right."

His nostrils flared.

The Spring Maiden grinned and rolled her eyes. "I always liked you, Freya. Your memories were refreshing and I'm glad to see reality is the same. Come on, you two."

She raised her arms and whispered a few words. The hedges in front of them parted in a wave of movement, undulating under the Spring Maiden's power. The greenery revealed a land beyond that was unlike anything Freya would have guessed in this kingdom of spring.

A giant castle stood with twin stairways that arced away from the white marble structure. More gardens grew about this part of the Spring Court, but these weren't manicured like the others. All the plants here grew wild and free, without a single hand to cut them or change their natural shape.

Somehow, this made the land even more beautiful.

The castle itself was more like the ones she'd seen in the mortal realms. The shape was boxier, without the long parapets and twisting spires like the Goblin King's castle. This one was sturdy, meant to last through anything that befell it. And while that was unexpected for the beautiful Spring Maiden's court, it somehow fit the impressively strong woman she knew the Spring Maiden to be.

A few of her guards wandered past them, their faces covered by those strange masks. Eldridge's expression tightened.

If Freya didn't speak up, they were going to argue again and who knew how long it would last this time.

"Spring Maiden," she asked, her voice slightly panicked. "You said you knew where my mother was."

Of course, Freya had already figured out that wasn't what the Spring Maiden had meant in her letter. She'd already admitted she had no idea where her mother was, but that she had the means to find a lost mortal in her court.

The Spring Maiden glanced behind her, then replied, "I don't know exactly where she is. But I do know she's in my court. Surprisingly, we lost track of her for a while."

"How did she end up in the Spring Court?" Freya tried to piece together the story, but it just made little sense.

The portal behind her childhood home hadn't led to the Spring Court. It had placed Freya in an in-between place, waiting for another faerie to bring her somewhere else. That was how she had left it, at least. Arrow had helped guide her through the magic and to the Spring Court itself.

But her mother wouldn't have had such a guide. She wouldn't have had any way to get to the Spring Court, not without help, at least.

The Spring Maiden gestured to one of her guards, and he sprinted ahead of them toward the doors of the castle. Once he had opened them, the Spring Maiden replied, "She was looking for something. I don't know what, the pixie who brought her here didn't know what she wanted. But your mother did say that she was certain she could only find it in the Spring Court."

That, at least, made sense. Her mother was a collector of strange objects. It made sense that her curiosity and passion for magical items might bring her here. "Why do you think she's still here, then?"

The Spring Maiden turned around. Her strange eyes seemed to widen, but it wasn't with happiness or glee as Freya expected. No. The Spring Maiden's eyes were welling with tears. "My dear, I know when anyone enters or exits this court. There is not a single place in the entire Spring Kingdom that isn't warded. My borders are air tight and no one has ever broken them. I knew when your mother entered Spring, and I have no question that she never left this place."

The eerie words filled her with a sense of dread. If her mother had never left, then what was she supposed to do? How was she going to find a woman who had disappeared in Spring and never left?

"Come with me," the Spring Maiden said. She strode into the shadows of the castle's interior, leaving them with only one option.

Follow her.

Freya tried very hard to keep her mouth closed as they walked past countless magical paintings with inhabitants that moved. The floors were a carpet of thick moss and the walls were covered with a hundred flowers, all dripping nectar on the floor. The colors were so bright here, in contrast to the Winter Court, which was filled with only shades of blue. The Spring Court was a rainbow of color, sight, and sound.

"Lovely, isn't it?" Eldridge murmured. "Most faeries spend their childhood here."

"I had no idea there was even a castle," Freya replied. "It seemed like there was nothing but gardens when I was last here."

He nodded, then pointed to a painting above them. This one appeared to be a map depicting a large country with various towns and a capital in the center. "That is the Spring Court. I know it seems like most of the courts are a small portion of an entire kingdom, but most of them are extremely large. Spring is by far the largest. It acquired more and more land as the younger faeries wanted to spend their youth in Spring."

"Wow," she whispered. The word echoed through the hallway. "It's beautiful, but I didn't know so many people lived here. I thought..."

At her hesitation, he filled in what she was going to say. "You thought you saw all of this court when you were here."

"Yes, I suppose I did."

"There's so many more surprises for you to see," he replied with a chuckle. "I think you're going to love seeing just how beautiful the Spring Court can be."

Or she would hate it. This place wasn't exactly in her fondest of memories.

The Spring Maiden stopped in an archway created by bluebells dripping from a trellis. "Shall we? I don't think I can explain what's going on better than I can show you, I'm afraid."

Eldridge lifted a brow. "Then by all means. I must admit, I'm curious what has you all worked up, Dahlia."

"The worst thing that's happened to this kingdom." The shadows under her eyes deepened to a dark purple. "I've spent every waking hour trying to fix this, and yet... This is out of my league. I'm glad you came, because I didn't think you would. And then the Spring Court would be alone in this matter."

Frowning, Freya trailed Eldridge as he rushed into the room beyond.

Green ivy climbed up the walls to the ceiling. Bright light speared through their leaves, suggesting there was no covering above their head except plants. Moss covered in morning dew cushioned her feet. They approached a large wooden crate in the center of the room.

"It's in there," the Spring Maiden said. "At least, the proof of what I'm going to tell you is in there."

Eldridge cleared his throat. "Well, this is all rather ominous. Do I want to look in the crate or not?"

"It is ominous." The Spring Maiden walked over to the crate and threw the lid open. "Someone is hunting pixies in this kingdom, and I don't know who. They're growing more and more angry with me for not controlling this threat, but I can't even guess what would do this to a faerie capable of protecting themselves."

Freya tried to believe that she had a strong stomach. She wanted to be the powerful, brave woman who could look at what was in that crate with a calculating eye that searched for clues.

Instead, all she managed was a faint gag when she peered inside the crate.

The pair of wings were still bloodied at the ends where someone had ripped them off a pixie. The nubs were still shimmery with magic, but without the powerful beat of a pixie attached.

Heavens above, what could do that to a pixie?

Freya spun around, putting her back to the sight and squeezing her eyes shut.

"Horrible, isn't it?" the Spring Maiden murmured. "I keep getting pieces shipped to me from all over the kingdom. Not from the killer, mind you. Just other pixies sending me whatever is left of their loved ones in the hopes I might be able to find the rest of them."

Freya heard the crate lid being shut, and only then did she turn back around.

Eldridge couldn't seem to tear his eyes away from the crate. His breathing was ragged, shoulders moving with the emotion that poured through him. "How long has this been happening?"

"A few months now." The Spring Maiden's lip curled as she too looked down at the crate. "The remains are entirely useless. My magic is bound to the living. I can't use pieces of dead things to find any clues, and I'm afraid my hands are tied. I've been struggling to find the murderer, and we are running out of time."

"How many?" Freya asked. "How many have already fallen to whatever monster plagues you?"

"Fifty two."

The horrific number rolled through her mind. Freya pressed a hand to her mouth. "So many."

"And there will be even more if we don't stop this monster soon." The Spring Maiden watched Eldridge with hope in her eyes. "Goblin King, we need you. And I understand we may have a mutual need for each other. If you help me find this killer, then I will help you find Freya's mother. You have my word. The first thing I do afterward will be to locate the human in this realm. Do we have a deal?"

Eldridge looked at Freya first. There wasn't another option. She couldn't trade all those pixie lives to rush finding her mother.

She nodded.

"You have a deal, Spring Maiden." He crossed his arms over his chest. "We'll find your killer."

The Spring Maiden gave them their own room. She watched them with a sly smile on her face and a quirked lip as she brought them through the halls of her castle.

"You two will be very comfortable here," she said. "And now that I know the Goblin King has a consort, I will make sure to provide as much privacy as the two of you require. I know how difficult it is to find alone time when you are with the king."

Freya didn't want to even guess what the woman was hinting. If she had previously been a consort, for Eldridge or for another Goblin King, that could stay in the past. The last thing she needed was to feel uncomfortable comparing herself to a faerie woman who looked like she was made of silk.

The door closed behind the Spring Maiden, and Freya tried to take in the gilded beauty of the room.

All the greenery on the walls and ceiling was made of poured gold. The leaves that tangled up the posts of the bed, the flowers on the ceiling, even the floor, were metal. And Eldridge walked over it all like it was nothing special. As if he'd seen a room like this a thousand times before in his life.

Maybe he had. But Freya hadn't.

She was afraid to touch the small vanity in the corner with its mirror that reflected her own horrified expression back. She didn't want to even think about the fingerprints she'd leave on the giant chest in the back of the room that she was certain they had to put their clothing in.

What could she touch? Anything at all?

Even the bed looked like she would ruin it if she dared place her grubby fingers on the posts. Or the headboard. Or the footboard, for that matter.

"Why do you look like you swallowed something awful?" Eldridge asked with a chuckle.

"This room... It's... It's..." She struggled for the right word. Exquisite wasn't enough. Magnificent was too plain. There wasn't really a word to describe how this room made her feel, or the tangled knot in her stomach that she was going to break something worth more than everything she owned.

Eldridge walked up to her and cupped her face in his hands. "It's just like any other room in this castle. She didn't give us anything special, and no, you won't break anything. You aren't so strong that you could bend gold, Freya."

"But what if I scratch it, then? I could do some damage, and the Spring Maiden is terrifying." Those sharp teeth could pull out Freya's throat, and then where would she be?

Probably back in the dreaming realm with no control over her life. And that would mean her mother would remain wherever she was, lost for good. Esther would at least have Lux, but that wasn't going anywhere fast. Her sister and the goblin boy were fighting when she'd left, and Freya hadn't taken that as seriously as she should have. If she had known the Spring Maiden was going to kidnap her again, she would have tried to help mend her sister's relationship.

"Freya." His soft voice broke through her panic. "You're spiraling, and I need you to focus. We have to find a killer, remember?"

Some of the panicked fog in her mind disappeared. A killer. Yes, they were supposed to find a murderer who was sending bits and pieces of his victims back to the Spring Maiden. In crates.

She shook her head and squeezed her eyes shut. "I don't know the first thing about tracking down a murderer. I can win in a battle of wits, sometimes. But a murderer? What am I supposed to do to help, Eldridge?"

"I suppose we'll just have to think like the killer. Why would anyone want to kill pixies?"

She had a few opinions on that. Because they were terrifying little things full of vibrating magic that liked to put people to sleep so they could watch their memories? It was all a horrible practice. Any manner of person might have disagreed and wanted to stop them.

All of that and more, really. She opened her eyes again and was yet again overwhelmed by the value of everything surrounding them. A single leaf from the bedpost would have fed so many people in her village. And here? The faeries thought this was normal decoration.

How far had she come in her life? It was hard to say. Freya still wasn't used to this place or these people, and nothing in this room was hers. Yet she still felt as though she had stepped into a life far better than her last.

Eldridge moved in front of her line of sight again. "I don't think we'll be able to think much in this room. Why don't we get some rest? What do you think?"

"Yes, I guess I'm tired." But she wasn't. Not really. Freya was so afraid to fall asleep again in this place. She didn't know if she'd ever wake up again.

They got ready for bed, and Eldridge yanked some of the pillows off the bed to sleep on the floor. Though he had claimed they were a couple to this entire court, they still weren't that close. Not yet, at least. But she had hopes that someday they would be.

Maybe.

Freya willed herself to sleep, but couldn't manage a single moment of it. Every time she drifted off, her mind would snap back awake with the fear that she had returned to the dreaming realm and would never wake back up again.

She spent most of their "night" staring at the ceiling, waiting for Eldridge to wake. He didn't snore, at least. That was a small blessing.

The hours passed while she relived all her memories in this dark place. How she had felt so weak and afraid here. How the Spring

Maiden had enjoyed her weakness, even controlled it by forcing Freya to go to parties like a doll she controlled. Freya had seen an illusion. The pixies saw reality and laughed at the weak mortal.

And yet, after all that had happened, she had returned. Now she was here helping the very people who had made her life so difficult. Who had caused her so much suffering.

She supposed that was only right, though. She should help these people because they needed it. Even if they were evil to their very core.

Eldridge eventually stretched his arms over his head and winced, moving his head from side to side. "I haven't slept on the floor since I was a child. I forgot how uncomfortable it was."

"We could always ask them to bring us a second bed," she said. Her tone was a little too hopeful, and she feared Eldridge would hear the exaggeration in her words. She wanted to get out of this place, and the night by herself overthinking everything hadn't helped.

He narrowed his eyes, then sighed. "You can't think when you're in this room, can you?"

If she spoke, she would cry. Freya simply nodded her head while holding her eyes a little too wide.

He rolled onto his feet and held out his hand for her to take. "Get out of bed, then. No one should be awake just yet. We can get some air and clear our heads. How does that sound?"

It sounded like he was taking care of her, and Freya didn't know what to do with that. He was the trickster. The manipulative Goblin King who got her into the most ridiculous of situations, but always found his way out with wit and charm.

He wasn't supposed to be the kind hearted man who wanted to make her more comfortable.

But maybe she liked this version of him. He seemed like someone she could get along with. And less like someone that required her guard to be up at all times.

Hesitantly, Freya reached out and put her hand in his. "I could use some fresh air. Maybe that will clear my mind."

"She taught you that was necessary in this place, didn't she? Fresh air was the only safety." The shadows in his eyes were a little too familiar. Freya had known it would be hard for him to be here too, but she had never learned what happened to him in the Spring Court.

He had dove head first into his disguise, and perhaps he regretted that choice. She knew better than to pick at old wounds, however, when he wanted to take her away from all this.

Freya allowed Eldridge to draw her through the gilded halls with their white marble floors. Plants dripped from the ceiling, coiled through the windows, entirely unkept and wild in their growth.

It was as if the Spring Maiden wanted everyone to see the groomed gardens and think she was well put together. But her home revealed the madness within.

They exited the castle out a small servant's door and burst into a wild tangle of lavender tails and blood-red poppies. Eldridge threw his head back and filled his lungs with clean, crisp air.

"Ah," he said on an exhale. "Now that does feel better, doesn't it?"

It did. She could think easier out here, whether that was a spell in the air within the castle, or just her own memories tainting her lungs. Either way, she was grateful to no longer be in that golden room. "This is much better."

He held out his arm like a gentleman in a fairytale. Or at least one of the stories her mother used to tell her when she was just a babe. "Walk with me?"

There wasn't a reason in the world she would ever say no.

She linked their arms and together they moved through the lavender field. She imagined the Spring Maiden would have had a fit seeing them trudge through her gardens like this. They didn't stick to the path. They walked wherever their hearts decided they wanted to.

This sort of freedom was what she had needed in this place. Freya glanced around, still expecting some pixie to wander into view. But no one disturbed their stroll or even rustled the hedges.

"Why aren't there any pixies here right now?" she asked.

"They all sleep. There is no night surrounding the Spring Maiden's castle, so it always seems like its day here. But they sleep just like mortals." His bicep clenched. "The guards watch over them. In all the two weeks I was here, I never saw a guard sleep."

"Surely they must sleep, though," Freya replied. "It would be impossible for them to not."

"Perhaps they sleep standing up," he muttered. Eldridge's spine stiffened at the thought. "I know I used to lean against a wall to get some form of rest. Whatever they do, they aren't treated like they're alive here. To the Spring Maiden, her guards are statues animated only for her purposes. No thoughts. No dreams."

The thought was deeply unsettling. Freya licked her lips and had to ask, "Are they pixies or mortals?"

He shook his head and helped her over a particularly muddy spot filled with lavender bulbs. "I don't know. They never take off their masks, but they also don't have wings. Mortal, perhaps, or other faeries from the courts. There's no way to know who or what they were, and that's been bothering me since we returned."

She frowned and let the topic drop. The guards were another detail they needed to fix in this court, but there were more pressing matters at hand.

Her mother needed to be found.

They had to unmask a murderer.

Why couldn't anything in the faerie courts be easy? Of course, she had been sitting in the Goblin King's home waiting for an adventure. She just hadn't bargained for the one that would be quite so... well... urgent.

Blowing out a breath at a wayward strand of hair, she pointed at a pavilion on the horizon. "What about there? I wouldn't mind stopping for a bit and getting out of the sun."

"Why would you want to get out of the sun?" He tilted his head to the side. "It feels good, doesn't it?"

"Yes, but if I stay in it for too long, then I will get even more freckles." She gestured to her face and then to her arms.

"I think your freckles are lovely." Eldridge wrapped his arm around her waist and tugged her closer. The warmth from his body was searing, and the strength in his arm was like an iron band. "I wouldn't mind spending the afternoon counting them. How many do you think there are?"

"Quite a few," she planted her hands on his chest and gave a little shove. "We're supposed to be finding a killer, Eldridge."

"Indeed." He leaned down and dragged his nose up the length of her neck. He stopped right at her ear, gently biting the lobe. "But I think we have a few moments to ourselves. After all, the Spring Maiden did say she wanted to give us some privacy. And I haven't seen this side of you in a very long time. I'm intrigued, hero of mine."

All the breath in her lungs stuttered. She couldn't quite inhale all the way, and the tiny panting sounds she was making were embarrassing. "Intrigued by what?"

"You." He scooped her up in his arms and raced toward the pavilion.

Her stomach bounced against his shoulder, but she couldn't stop laughing long enough to tell him it was uncomfortable. Freya slapped her palms to his back, giggles bubbling from her lips and filling the clearing with the sound of joy. He didn't slow down for a minute until he placed her on her feet in the pergola.

Thankfully, there were no dreamers in this one. There was a smaller bed in the corner with silk sheets and white roses above it. Petals fell like rain from above their head.

Freya was breathless. A few more giggles escaped her mouth, and she pressed a hand to her lips to contain them.

"Oh, don't do that," Eldridge murmured. He took her wrist and pulled it away from her face. "I love the sound of your laugh."

Her heart skipped a beat. He hadn't said he loved her, and she doubted he ever would. That was a ridiculous fantasy of a young woman who had grown up hearing about faeries. But the words were so close. They were so close to saying that he loved her, or making some other wonderful declaration, and her heart thudded against her ribs.

"Eldridge," she whispered.

He stroked his thumb over the high peaks of her cheekbones. His eyes watched his hands as they moved, as though he couldn't get enough of looking at her. As though he thought she was beautiful.

And in that moment, she felt like she was.

Freya let her eyes drift shut as he held her. Even if he never said he loved her, at least she could enjoy his touch. She languished in the addicting allure of the Goblin King's attention that he gave to no one else but her.

For now.

She waited for the kiss, but he didn't lean any closer. Freya didn't feel the fan of his breath or the warmth of his lips close to hers. She grew tired of his teasing.

Patience worn thin, she snapped her eyes open, ready for another battle of wits. Except Eldridge wasn't teasing her. He wasn't even moving. His entire body was frozen exactly where he had been, eyes not moving, chest still as if there were no breath left inside him.

It was as if time had stopped.

"Eldridge?" she whispered.

Freya wiggled out of his grasp, then shoved his shoulder hard. "Why aren't you moving?" she asked. "What magic is this?"

A faint growl erupted from the bush beyond the pavilion. The sound was deep and haunting, too rough to be a pixie and not like anything she'd ever heard in the faerie realm. But she'd heard the sound back home before.

The memory was buried deep in her subconscious, but the sound made it come roaring back. She had been a little girl. Her mother was waiting for their father to return from the market, where he had been intent on buying a new hammer and tools to patch their leaky roof. The growl had been a wolf, her mother claimed. A lone wolf in the forest looking for something to eat.

They had remained locked in their cabin, shivering in the shadows, until her father returned. Her mother had shouted out the window that there was a wolf, and he'd thundered into their home with wild eyes. Her father had taken his shotgun outside for hours, searching for the beast, but he never found it.

Now, she had to wonder if the monster had been a faerie creature.

Heart pounding, she stepped around Eldridge's frozen figure and walked to the edge of the pavilion. There, just beyond the hedges nearest to her, the leaves rustled. Movement of some beast that was large enough to shake the entire hedge.

And as she watched, twin red eyes appeared through the green. They met her gaze from the shadows.

CHAPTER 7

Any rational person would have stayed with Eldridge. She should have cowered beside the Goblin King and hoped the wolf couldn't come into the pavilion because this space was protected by the Spring Maiden's magic.

Freya found herself to be less and less rational the longer she was in the faerie realm.

The wolf took off through the hedges and Freya's stomach twisted in worry. She'd never heard of a creature like this in the faerie realms. She would have heard the fae talking about the beasts. Wolves were dangerous, and they were always meddling with sheep or chickens. At least, they did in her village.

The faeries had to eat. They must have farms and livestock that they used to put food on their tables. The wolves around here must have hunted those beasts, but no one talked about them.

Or...

She shuddered to think this beast had come in from her realm and was now running rampant through the faerie realm. What if this was the pixie killer? A wolf was just a wolf. Freya had seen the men from her village hunt down packs before when they were too unruly and were getting too brave. If a wolf was what plagued the Spring Court, then that was something she could work with.

Eldridge was a warrior. He should be able to hunt down a single wolf and ensure it killed no more pixies. This would be easy if a wolf was their problem.

Except, she didn't know how time had stopped. She could easily dismiss such a thing as the magic of the court affecting Eldridge. But why wouldn't it also freeze Freya where she stood? It should have been the other way around.

If the beast was magical and that was how it hunted its prey, then she would need proof. Freya didn't care that the wolf might have hurt someone, or even that it was always a threat regardless of that death. She wouldn't kill an innocent animal without proof.

Quickly, she walked over to Eldridge's frozen form and tapped his face. "Are you going to wake up? If you don't, I'm going to do something very foolish on my own."

He didn't move.

"I'm going to take that as relenting that I should absolutely follow that wolf and report back when I figure out what's going on." She patted his face one last time and then headed out. "Good talk, Eldridge. I'll let you know what I find out."

She was quite certain that if he was awake, he would yell at her to stop what she was doing and get back here.

But he wasn't. She hiked up her skirts, hopped over the hedge, and took off in the direction the wolf had gone. The traveling gown was rather uncomfortable to run in, and she'd need to talk with Eldridge about that. If they were going to be running off into the wilds, then she needed to be wearing pants. Like him.

As it was, the brambles tugged at her clothing. She pulled her skirt from their grip with a rough tug, and the fabric ripped at the edges.

The wolf had gone into a section of the Spring Court she'd never seen before. Although, she supposed she really hadn't seen much of the Spring Court at all. The gardens gave way to the wild and unknown.

All the plants turned into recognizable bushes. Thorns, brambles, fallen branches of trees that had seen better days. This wasn't the kind of greenery she was used to from the Spring Maiden.

And it was all so close to the gardens. That was the most confusing part.

Freya reached up and knocked a branch out of her way. The branch was covered in moss, but had been snapped by a careless hand. Or a beast that had passed here before her.

She slowed her wild rush to catch up with the animal and searched the ground for signs it had been here before her. And there, in the mud at her feet, was a large padded footprint. Except... Well, it didn't look right.

Freya crouched down to get a closer look. Holding her hand next to it in the mud, she blew out a long breath at the size. "You're a big beast, aren't you?"

The sight of a wolf's footprint that was larger than her hand unsettled her. The thought that this was a wolf who had escaped into the faerie realm slowly dissolved. She wasn't dealing with a wolf from the mortal realm.

This was something different.

She swallowed hard, realizing she'd put herself in a rather precarious position. If the wolf's feet were this large, then she didn't stand a chance if it found her first. Likely she could climb a tree, but would she be fast enough to get away?

Right. She needed to think things through before she ran off into a faerie forest. Maybe she'd gotten a little too excited.

But she was in it, now. And if this fae beast was going back to its home or hovel, then she stood a chance at figuring out if this was the faerie killer. Freya couldn't stop now, even if she was much more afraid than before.

Picking her way carefully this time, she walked through the forest while following the giant footsteps. The beast had slowed. The prints were much closer together and easier to find.

She had to dodge between hedges and branches, but eventually she found herself on something like a path. An animal path, certainly, but she had walked on these in the forest where she lived before. Usually deer made them. Not this path, however, considering the amount of paw prints that padded through the mud and tamped down the earth.

Light appeared at the end of this strange tunnel made of thorns and arched branches. She slowed down, hesitating to enter the clearing beyond. What if the beast was waiting for her to step out? Wolves had incredible noses. The beast might have smelled her already, and she had no weapon.

Leaning down, she tugged at a large root near her foot. The blunt stick wouldn't do much, but it made her feel better to hold some kind of club in her hand. Just in case.

Getting onto her hands and knees, she crawled through the mud to the very edge of the path. There, she peered through the grass at the clearing beyond and sent up a silent prayer that she wouldn't meet that horrifying red gaze again.

But the beast wasn't in the clearing beyond.

The grass was classically emerald green, almost painfully vivid. Why would it be so lush when the rest of the forest hadn't been? Tiny white flowers dotted through the field, and from the back corner a lovely pixie woman emerged.

She wore a pale white dress, her wings fluttering behind her as she landed in the field. She held a woven basket in her hands, clearly intending on gathering something that grew in the field.

Perhaps that was why the Spring Maiden's magic grew in this field.

Curious, Freya lifted up onto her elbows. That was when the scent hit her. It was too much like the perfume the Spring Maiden had used to keep Freya under her spell. Though, there was no magic tainted with the scent this time.

Was this where the Spring Maiden grew the ingredients to keep the dreamers in their deep sleep? It would make sense, in a strange way. But Freya hadn't ever thought to see this place for herself.

It was hidden. Completely and utterly hidden from any eyes that might have accidentally found it.

So this was where it all started. The pixie leaned down and started plucking the white flowers, then placing them in the basket she held. She hummed under her breath and Freya watched the shadows for the wolf.

She should get out of this path and tell the pixie it wasn't safe. The wolf might not be the one who was hunting them down, but the beast was still dangerous.

Freya didn't get the chance to warn the other woman.

The dark furred form charged out of the forest directly at the pixie. And Freya wanted to shout a warning. She wanted to scream for the pixie to fly, but nothing came out of her mouth other than a faint squeak as she flattened herself to the ground once again.

The wolf's jaws flashed in the morning light. Gleaming white fangs caught one of the pixie's wings and ripped it off before she could even think about flying. The woman let out a cry of pain and anguish, reaching for the wound that flashed bright red.

Then the wolf disappeared.

It was gone as quickly as it came. The pixie stumbled, falling onto one knee as her eyes widened with shock.

The faerie wasn't so weak, however. She bared her teeth and lifted her hands, ready for another strike. Freya tried to get up again to help, only to drop again when she heard the angry snarl.

The wolf appeared from the opposite side of the field. It was so fast that the beast moved in a blur. One moment it was in the back corner of the clearing, and then suddenly it was upon the pixie again.

Those teeth flashed, sharp and too terrible for her to look at. The last wing ripped off the faerie's back with powerful jaws clamped down on the dragonfly pattern. But this time, the pixie was ready.

She whipped around with a scream of rage and raked her nails down on the wolf's back. It let out a howl that chilled Freya to the bone.

This time, the beast didn't run away. It didn't use the shadows to get the upper hand. Instead, it stayed right where the pixie was. It circled her with gnashing teeth and Freya had to look away.

She knew what was going to happen. Anyone watching would have known, but there was nothing she could do to help.

Freya had no weapons. No magic. Nothing that could save this pixie from her fate.

She didn't even have the stomach to watch.

A scream echoed through the clearing, cut off by a crunching sound that Freya would never forget. That horrible sound made her stomach roll. She squeezed her eyes shut and tried to still the beat of her heart. She had to keep her own scream locked up tight in her chest or the wolf would know she was there. Then, she would be the next victim it claimed.

When it had been quiet for too long, she opened her eyes to see what the wolf was doing.

The beast was hunched over the pixie, jaws working hard. But the moment her eyes landed on the creature, it was like it knew she was watching.

It stopped feasting and looked over its shoulder, staring into the shadows where she hid. The red eyes seemed to glow with magic and power. Freya knew this was no wolf from the mortal realms that had discovered how to plague the pixies here. No, this was a monster who had been born in this realm. A monster created to terrorize and instill fear in any who saw it.

Hands shaking, she tried to move back on the path.

But then the beast moved. It planted its paws firmly on the ground and then stood.

Shaking its shoulders back, this wolf-like monster stood as a mortal man did. Its hunched shoulders proved to be broad and commanding. The beast's hips and legs were awkward, but this wasn't like looking at Arrow stand.

This was a monster. Half man, half beast.

"A werewolf," she whispered.

Her face crumpled in fear. Her mother had told her about these legendary creatures, but even she hadn't believed they were real. A man who was bitten by such an animal would forever be enslaved by the horrifying curse that beckoned good souls to kill and devour.

The beast shook again. It straightened its spine even further, puffing out its heaving chest as it returned its attention back to the dead pixie at its feet.

It leaned down and picked up the body. Holding the limp, bloody, and broken faerie in its arms, the werewolf met her gaze.

She should run. Freya should disappear down the path and seek out Eldridge immediately. But she was frozen in place, staring at the monster as it stared back at her.

The werewolf opened its mouth wide, baring its teeth in a snarl. And then a ragged sound came from between those awful lips.

"Freya," it snarled.

Her body suddenly moved again. Freya scrambled onto her feet and bolted back down the path with fear nipping at her heels.

CHAPTER 8

She slapped branches out of her way in her wild escape from the monster in the clearing. Heart racing in her chest, lungs heaving for breath, she ran all the way back to the pavilion.

"Please be awake," she muttered as she raced to Eldridge's side. "Come on, you have to wake up. We need to go."

Freya threw herself at the Goblin King. Hands scrambling to grab whatever she could, she tugged at his form hard.

"I will not leave you," she growled. "The beast is coming and we have to go. Now! Wake up, you damned faerie man. Come on!"

Whatever spell the werewolf had cast wore off. Eldridge blinked, then lowered his hands with a frown. He stared down at his fingers, not allowing her to move him even though she was clearly distraught. "What happened?" he asked, his face furrowed in a frown. "How did you move away from me so quickly?"

"God damn it, Eldridge. I will explain later. We have to go," she shouted.

He grabbed onto her shoulders, holding her still for a moment when she would have bolted back to the castle. They needed to put more distance between themselves and that creature in the clearing. Freya had no idea if it was following her.

Stalking her.

What if she led it back to the castle?

Obviously it had a taste for pixie flesh, so that wouldn't do. She couldn't put everyone in the Spring Maiden's court at risk. Not without warning them about what was coming.

Eldridge shook her hard. "Freya, what is going on? You're shaking like a leaf!"

She hadn't realized how badly she was shaking. But there wasn't time to worry about her. They had to warn the Spring Court. They had to tell the Spring Maiden that a terrifying werewolf who stood ten feet tall was hunting down the pixies.

Out of breath and still running on adrenaline, she stammered, "We have to warn the Spring Maiden. She needs guards. An army. All the guards possible to stand watch. Because we can't stay here. We have to go back to the castle because he's coming, but I also don't want him to catch them off guard. What if we lead him to them, Eldridge?"

He shook her again. "You're not making any sense. You didn't go anywhere, Freya. What you saw must have been some kind of premonition, or... What did you see?"

She stared over his shoulder with wide, terrified eyes. Were the hedges moving? Had the werewolf shook them while it hunted her down? "I did leave, Eldridge. You were frozen in place, like someone had stopped time. And I followed the wolf, who was in the hedges. I saw him kill a pixie. He ripped her wings off like it was nothing, and then I realized it's a werewolf."

How did one explain that a mythical creature was real? How did she tell Eldridge that a creature from her own realm, the kind of monster they told stories about at night, was now plaguing the Spring Court?

Were werewolves something the fae had even heard of?

He released his hold on her shoulders and took a step back. Eldridge shook his head at her words. "No. That's not possible. You saw a wolf, Freya. Nothing more."

"He stood up," she whispered. She pressed her shaking fingers to her mouth. "He stood up after he killed her. And then he looked me in the eye and he said my name, Eldridge."

His eyes widened in shock. Stumbling back, Eldridge sat down hard on the edge of the bed behind them. "There hasn't been a werewolf in the faerie realm for over two hundred years. No one would ever believe you."

"He could be following me. We need to go."

"He wouldn't." Brows furrowed, Eldridge clutched the edge of the mattress. "They don't go so far. The fact that he's even coming this close to the Spring Court must mean that he's starving or... I don't know. It's unusual for a werewolf to be this close to any other faerie creatures. They hate us after we hunted them down."

"I'm telling you, he looked right at me and said my name." Why had he done that? She couldn't imagine how the creature would even know who she was.

"Perhaps he worked with the Winter Princess," Eldridge murmured. "Perhaps he's hunting you, not the pixies."

Freya sank to her knees in front of Eldridge. The marble beneath her was warmed by the sun. "He didn't try to hurt me. He just said my name, holding her body like we were going to have a conversation over the corpse."

The shock wore off and Eldridge lunged forward. He wrapped both his arms around her shoulders, yanking her against his heart and holding her too close.

He pressed a kiss to the top of her head and breathed some words that she didn't understand. His hands slid down her arms, then back up. He sank his fingers into her hair, muttering more words that made little sense.

What language was he speaking?

Freya pressed her hands to his shoulders. "Eldridge, what are you doing?"

"Shh," he scolded. Then continued with his strange ritual.

Over and over he touched her shoulders, head, arms. Freya felt a faint tingle on her skin. A prickle of electricity as magic weaved over her body and through the fine threading of her clothing.

"Eldridge, are you casting a spell on me?" Her skin crawled at the thought.

He finally stopped and heaved a ragged sigh. "I have to do something. It's not much, because I don't have everything I would need for a true protection spell. But you have to have something, Freya. A werewolf is no creature to toy with. He could tear your head from your shoulders with no thought or struggle."

"I'm aware," she snarled, pulling herself from his arms. "How dare you cast a spell on me without my permission?"

He allowed her freedom from his grip, but anger turned his cheeks a dark silver. "What would you have me do? You said a werewolf was hunting you down because you so selfishly took off without any warning. I have to protect you, Freya."

"At least ask. You know I'm not comfortable with magic. You know I wouldn't want..." She rubbed at the tingling feeling still vibrating down her arms. "I don't like it. You can't cast spells on me whenever you want."

He stood up so quickly the bed screeched backward. "You are so fragile, Freya! You have no idea just how vulnerable a human is in this realm. Would you have me watch as you run around without armor or any protection at all? I cannot have you without some form of... Of..."

"Magic?" she asked. "You know that's not how I grew up. If I have to get metal armor, then I will. But I don't want to wear magic as a second skin. It's not who I am."

"Isn't it though?" Eldridge shouted the words and threw up his hands. Black shadows poured from behind him, sinking through the leaves of the plants that shriveled at the touch of his unbridled anger. "You performed magic. We both know that. I saw you do it in the Winter Palace, and I'm certain you did it while you were searching for your sister. You have as much magic as I do, and that says something."

Anger boiled underneath her skin. He knew damned well that she didn't want to talk about the strange power that ran in her veins. She didn't want to think about the implications when there was nothing she could do to figure out where she had come from or how she had gotten these powers.

"What does it say, then?" she asked, crossing her arms over her chest. "By all means, let us argue while a werewolf stalks us. Even now he's probably watching us with a grin, getting a show before his meal."

"They hunt one prey at a time," Eldridge snarled. The sound rivaled that made by the werewolf himself. "I would not put you in danger so carelessly."

"And isn't that the problem? You've taken on this role of protector when I never asked you to be one!" She threw her hands up in the air. "You claim I have magic, but that I am weak. You say I need someone to look after me, but you're the one who keeps falling under spells. I was the one awake. I took the opportunity presented, and I found the Spring Maiden's killer."

"At what cost?" Eldridge clenched his hands into fists and a blast of magic rocked through the ground. The marble beneath their feet split, cracking open to reveal ugly, tangled roots. "You could have died. If there wasn't a pixie to distract this monstrous creature, you would have been in his jaws. Not her."

Freya swallowed hard. Maybe he was right. Maybe she would have been the creature's prey instead of the pixie, but someone had to do something. She refused to believe the only option was to wait.

She was tired of waiting for everyone else to do something.

Squaring her shoulders, she clenched her jaw and met his angry gaze head on. It didn't matter that his magic was killing all the plants around them. It didn't matter that he was arguably the most powerful faerie in all the realms.

He could not talk to her like that.

"If you want to claim we are together, Eldridge, then we have to be in a partnership. You don't get to pick and choose when we are equals. Just because this moment didn't satisfy you, doesn't mean I didn't do the right thing." She planted her fists on her hips. "I will have to take risks to help you find this killer. Those risks won't always mean I will put myself in danger. But many of them will. If you want a partner, then you have to let me be one."

His eyes watched her with so much sorrow in those big, wide eyes. He hated the words coming out of her mouth. And she understood it, in a way.

Eldridge took a step closer, and the shadows merged back into him. They gathered behind him in a dark mass, standing tall and proud. He reached out a hand and tunneled it into the hair at the back of her neck. "I'm afraid, Freya," he whispered. "Afraid of losing you. Afraid of the horrible death this monster would have given you. The day I lose you will be the day I hold you in my arms until you can say goodbye in comfort. I will not see your end by clawed hands and strong jaws."

Tears built in her eyes. Her lower lip wobbled, because those gruesome words were the kindest anyone had ever said to her. "I'm not asking you to watch me die a horrible death. I'm asking you to trust me."

With a rough groan, he pulled her against his chest again. His hands glided down her back, and he pressed his lips to her hair. "I do trust you, Freya. But when you told me you had left without me... It was like someone had ripped my heart out of my chest. I am unaccustomed to fear."

"Well, you're going to get used to it." She turned her head, pressing her cheek to his chest and feeling the thundering of his heart. "I know you don't want to put me in danger. But sometimes, I'm going to have to be."

"I know that," he muttered. "I just don't like it."

She scoffed. "No one likes being in danger. Even you."

"I do, actually. I quite like the thrill of the chase. If I had seen that werewolf, I would have called out for it and run in the opposite direction." He squeezed her tighter in his arms. "But the thought of you facing down a creature like that alone? It makes my knees weak."

Freya leaned back in his arms with a grin. "I make your knees weak, Goblin King?"

He touched a finger to her chin, tilting her head back and staring down at her with a serious expression. "Every day, Freya of Woolwich. Every day."

Heart skipping a beat, she cleared her throat and replied, "We need to go warn the Spring Maiden."

"Indeed." He released her and stepped back, straightening his suit sleeves. "Shall we tell her we're hunting a werewolf?"

CHAPTER 9

They summoned the Spring Maiden immediately. Freya and Eldridge met her in that hidden room with the wooden crate no one had moved yet. The box was a reminder that they still hadn't succeeded in stopping this horrible creature.

The Spring Maiden swept into the room wearing a white gown decorated with flowers that spilled from her hips. "What is it? You've already found something?"

Freya licked her lips and looked at Eldridge.

He was staring at her.

Was she supposed to tell the Spring Maiden what had happened? Damn it. She was really hoping he would take this one.

Clenching her teeth, she tried to manage a supportive grin but only bared her teeth in a grimace. "It's a werewolf."

The Spring Maiden's eyes widened even more than their normal state. "Pardon me? I don't think I heard you right, girl. Did you claim that a werewolf is hunting pixies?"

"Yes." Freya clenched her hands in her dirty skirts. "A werewolf. I saw him myself."

The Spring Maiden's tongue punched the side of her cheek. "I see."

The silence that followed was filled with shock. Freya looked over at Eldridge, who shrugged. Apparently he hadn't thought she would take the news so well, but Freya saw it as something else. This reaction suggested the Spring Maiden had known it was a werewolf.

But that couldn't be possible. No one would have allowed a monster like that to wander around their court. And Eldridge had said the faeries had killed off most of the werewolves, if not all of them.

"Were you hiding werewolves here?" Freya asked.

"No," the Spring Maiden replied. The calculating look had returned to her gaze though, and that made it hard for Freya to believe a word the woman was saying. "Why do you ask?"

"Because you don't seem all that surprised to hear it was a were-wolf." Freya crossed her arms over her chest. "I saw what that creature did to the pixie in that field of flowers you use to create the perfume that controls the dreamers. It's hard for me to believe that you are unaware of what's going on. If you know whenever someone walks through your borders, surely you knew he was here?"

Eldridge watched her speak with a grin on his face and pride in his expression. It looked like the Goblin King was impressed with her.

Freya was rather impressed with herself, if she was being honest.

"Astute," the Spring Maiden said. "But you aren't correct about everything, my dear. I have not been housing the werewolves in the Spring Court since we started a killing spree, although I thought perhaps there was someone here I wasn't aware of. You see, the borders are infallible. I am not."

The Spring Maiden lifted her hands and clapped them loudly. The doors to the room opened and a small pixie was pushed between them.

He was particularly small for their kind, and pixies were already so short. His hair was cropped close to his head and his ears were larger than most. Big, black eyes stared at them with fear in his gaze. He was shivering out of his boots. The poor thing.

Eldridge took a step closer to the terrified pixie, admonishing the Spring Maiden. "Go easy on the poor thing, Dahlia. He doesn't know what's going on by the looks of it."

"I do, Your Highness." The pixie cleared his throat. "I've just never been before so much royalty before."

This was something Freya could help with. She plastered a smile on her face and walked to the pixie's side. Offering her arm, she kept the grin on her face and hoped it looked soft and kind. "I have also never been around this much royalty. Between the two of us, I think we might be able to manage them."

His eyes got even wider, if that was possible. "But you're the Queen Killer, ma'am."

Damn it. Apparently her reputation had preceded her.

With a frown, she let her arm drop to the floor and shrugged. "Well, you can't say I didn't try. Spring Maiden, why in the world did you bring this pixie to the room? Unless he's seen the werewolf or knows where it lives, I don't think we need more proof that your people are dying."

"Oh, he has proof." The Spring Maiden sauntered over to the crate and sat down on the lid. Crossing her legs delicately, she waved at the pixie man. "Go on. Tell them what you told me."

He opened his mouth, then clamped it shut as the Maiden interrupted him with a sharp snarl.

"From the beginning, pixie. I don't want you skipping any details like you tried to do before. Show them the truth first, and then I'll let you go."

Freya still didn't know how the Spring Maiden could be so cruel to her own people. The pixies were as mishandled as the guards, now that she was seeing it all. And suddenly, she wasn't the person the Spring Maiden's hatred was directed toward. What an odd turn of events.

The pixie man shuffled his feet, before clearing his throat and beginning his tale. "All the pixies who work in the fields have heard of this beast. He takes many forms, some of them claim. A werewolf. A magician. A kindly old man with a crooked cane and a long white beard. But all of them kill pixies, because he hates the lot of us."

Eldridge frowned. "A lot of people hate pixies. There's not much to go on there."

"Well, sir, most of us know that he's hunting pixies and not any other faerie. If you cover up our wings, then he'll leave us alone." The pixie shuffled his feet. "So we figured out a way to hide our wings and thought maybe he would leave us to work. It's the only thing we could think of to save ourselves."

The Spring Maiden circled her hand in the air. "Yes, yes. We all understand that you had to do something to keep him away from you. Now turn around and show them what you've all been doing."

Freya watched the pixie wince with a strange mixture of pity and mirth. After all, most of these creatures had tormented her while she was here. They'd made it very clear that she was nothing more than a toy to them, and while she pitied the fear they felt while being hunted, she also thought they were getting what they deserved.

He reached for the hem of his shirt and pulled it up and over his head. Then he turned around and showed them the strange contraption on his back.

A small zipper ran down his spine. And Freya was certain it was a zipper. It even had a little tab at the top, just between his bright, shimmering wings.

"What does that do?" she asked, curiosity spiking at the sight.

"It keeps us hidden from the wolf, miss." The pixie reached over his shoulders and tugged the zipper down.

With a flex of his back muscles, he curled his wings in toward the zipper. Carefully, he tucked them into the hidden pocket that he'd created with magic, then he reached and zipped it back up.

The expression on his face was pinched, almost as though holding his wings like that hurt. And she could imagine it did. His skin bulged where the extra flesh had been packed in beneath it. But the wings were gone. Contained as though they had never been there in the first place.

Eldridge stepped up to the pixie man's side. "May I?" he asked.

"That's why I'm here, Your Highness. As proof that the pixies are doing whatever we can to prevent this creature from knowing what we are." The pixie squared his shoulders. "If you must touch them, then you may."

Eldridge reached for the zipper and gently pulled it down. The wings unfurled again, though they were a little crinkled in comparison to the first time the pixie had walked in the door.

Freya couldn't keep her mouth shut. She had to ask. "Does that hurt?"

"Quite a bit, miss." A muscle in the pixie's jaw jumped. "But it's better than being dead."

She supposed that was the better way to look at it. Hiding their wings like that had to cause them immense pain, however. And no one was trying to stop that pain for them. Instead, they were suffering with the hopes that someone would eventually put an end to these dark times.

It didn't settle well with her.

"So you hide your wings, that's a good first step. We're trying to hunt it down though." She hoped the words weren't too harsh, but knowing that the pixies were hiding themselves didn't help their cause. They needed more concrete evidence. "Do you have any idea where the creature hides? It has to sleep. Somewhere it has to have a den."

The pixie stepped away from Eldridge and pulled his shirt back over his head. "The only thing I've heard is that he is seen more around the mines. That's where the zipper comes from. The faeries in that area were the ones to figure it out, you see."

Mines?

Freya hadn't realized the Spring Court was so large. Eldridge had told her that it was, but there were mines in the Spring Court? Why would they need those?

Frowning, she looked to the Goblin King for whatever information he could give her. He was staring off into the distance, contemplating the words the pixie had said. "So he probably has a cave where he lives, then. If I remember correctly, the mines are full of abandoned shafts."

"You're correct, Your Highness. There are plenty of caves and cave systems that we don't go into anymore." The pixie shivered in fear. "There's a reason we don't go in them anymore, though. I wouldn't advise to search without knowing where he is."

"Would someone there know more than you?" Eldridge took an excited step forward, a little too quickly.

The pixie flinched back as though the Goblin King was going to hit him. He held up his hands, "Yes! Yes, I'm sure they would know something. But I don't, Your Highness. I'm sorry. I'm so sorry to disappoint."

Why was the pixie reacting like that? Did the Spring Maiden hit them?

The more she discovered about this court, the less she liked the place.

The pixie man started to slink toward the door. He clearly didn't want to be here any longer than he had to, but he froze when the Spring Maiden cleared her throat.

She still sat on the crate, staring at him with aggression and anger in her eyes. "Now tell them the last part. If you don't tell them that, then I look like a liar. And you don't want me to look like a liar, do you?"

"No, mistress." He swallowed hard, the knot in his throat bobbing up and down. "The werewolf is said to have been seen with a mortal woman. Once, a long time ago, he was hunting a pixie, and she stopped him. Ever since then, he's been obsessed with finding her again."

"A mortal woman?" Freya's heart leapt into her throat. "Do you know what she looked like?"

He nodded. "Like you, miss. Dark hair, dark eyes. She was pretty, the last time people saw her."

"Who was the last person to see her?" Was her luck changing? If someone in the Spring Court had actually seen her mother, then she could start there. They might be able to find her mother after all.

She couldn't breathe through the excitement. This was her chance. Her first real clue when they had been searching for so long.

"The last person to see her lives near the mines, miss. They said they saw her confront the werewolf. She saved a pixie life all those years ago, and no one saw the werewolf for years after that. Because... well... Because..." He tugged on the collar of his shirt. "The werewolf took her, miss. He cast some spell on her and she fell asleep. He dragged her off into one of the tunnels and no one ever saw her again."

Before Freya could ask another question, the Spring Maiden interrupted them. "That'll do. Off you go."

The pixie didn't pause to see if they had more questions. He darted out of the room like they'd set him on fire.

Freya put her hand on Eldridge's arm to battle the dizzy spell that threatened to drive her to the floor. Her mother was alive. The werewolf had taken her, but her mother had to be alive. People had seen her.

"I—" She shook her head. "I can't believe it."

The Spring Maiden stood and strode up to her. She tucked a finger under Freya's chin and tilted her head back. "I keep my promises, Freya. I told you if you helped me find this monster, that I would find your mother. This is only the start."

She met that dark gaze without hesitation. "It's a damn good start. Now what do we do?"

The Spring Maiden grinned her shark-like smile. "Now we hunt."

CHAPTER 10

It took them days to figure out their next steps. The Spring Maiden wanted to send them with the appropriate amount of guards. She said it was important that they arrived in the mining town with the forces of the Spring Maiden. Otherwise, the miners might not want them anywhere near them.

Eldridge half agreed with her. He wanted the guards, but he wanted them to remain hidden at all times. That way, they could speak with the miners as if they were friends. He said he would dress as one of them. Walk through their ranks and lure the werewolf to hunt him rather than the pixies who were obviously incapable of protecting themselves.

They woke up every morning to go meet with the Spring Maiden and argue. But every day they landed on the same realization. Neither of them agreed on anything.

Freya was reminded of Lux and Arrow arguing before she went to the Winter Court. Everyone had their opinions on what should be done, but no one was willing to listen to anyone else. Was this a faerie trait? Did they all have this foolish trait of digging their heels in even when they might be wrong?

She grew tired of it on the third day and stopped Eldridge after they had met with the Spring Maiden. "I don't think we're going to settle on anything, Eldridge."

"She'll come around. I know her very well, and I understand her argument. But I think that the Spring Maiden doesn't realize her people are afraid of her." He reached for her hand and placed it on his forearm. "I know you're worried about all this. She wasn't always this ridiculous woman who wanted to cause harm. I still see her original personality in there. We have a chance with this one, unlike the Winter Princess."

"That's not..." Freya sighed as he dragged her down the hall toward the exit they always used. "Where are you taking me?"

"I thought we could go for another walk. There's so much you haven't seen in this court yet, and I'm taking this as an opportunity to prove how lovely my home is." He grinned. "Every court is mine, really. I think you would want to see it all."

"They aren't yours," she argued. "And I think we need to talk about this more. You two can argue until you're blue in the face, but nothing is going to happen. Has anyone even gone to get that pixie I saw die?"

"I'm sure someone has." He held the door open for her and gestured for her to walk in front of him. "They wouldn't let their own stay there to rot in the sun."

"Are you sure?"

"I'm positive, Freya. Things like this take time. The pixie was right. We can't just thunder into the mines intending to hunt this terrifying beast. We'd get lost in the dark, and then the werewolf would find us. Or something worse." He gestured again for her to go, again. "Go on. I have a surprise for you."

She'd learned a long time ago that she didn't like faerie surprises.

But his eyes gleamed with happiness, and she could at least give him a chance. Eldridge was so excited. Neither of them had worn that expression on their face in a very long time. So whatever had gotten him all riled up, it had to be good.

Freya left the Spring Castle and stepped out into the gardens beyond. "Where are we going then?"

"To the right."

If he wanted her to lead, then she would. Freya walked around the corner of the castle still muttering about faeries who thought everything would work out just fine and who didn't realize that not everything could be fine if they ignored it.

"I can hear you, you know," Eldridge called out to her.

"I know you can! I was hoping you'd take something to heart."

"Maybe someday. But for now, I think it's important that you relax a bit. This wasn't meant to be all work and no play, after all."

What did he mean by that? They were here to find her mother. Of course it was work. They had to step into the role of hero and king again. Did he think they had come to the Spring Court to... what? Galavant around?

If he really believed that was why they were here, then she would turn back around and get to work on her own. She could find her own mother, now. Freya had plenty of information to get started, and the miners were more likely to talk to her than the man they knew as king.

"Eldridge," she growled.

"Just look in front of you, Freya. Faerie realms, not everything has to be so serious." He waltzed ahead of her with his hands in his pockets. The wry grin on his face challenged her to disagree with him.

But she did. Maybe she wouldn't have a little while ago, but now she had seen multiple people die. She had been the downfall of a kingdom and a queen. Though she had saved one of those, the guilt of the other would ride on her shoulders forever.

Killing someone changed a person.

Losing one's mother changed them too.

"Eldridge, look, I know you think that life can be all fun and games but—" The words stuck in her throat.

A giant glass structure stood behind him. The building appeared to be some kind of conservatory melded with a greenhouse. Steel rungs allowed the glass to bubble out on the sides, and a thousand different flowers bloomed inside the glass. Heat waves radiated off the edges of the building like the movement of a pixie.

"What is this place?" she asked.

He held out his arm, pointing at the strange building in the distance. "That's for us to find out. Your surprise is inside, by the way. But if you don't want to know what it is..."

"No, I do," she quickly corrected him. "I was just saying we have little time for these kinds of fun and games."

"Of course," he replied with a wide grin. "No more fun and games than necessary, Freya."

She highly doubted he was agreeing to that. Curiosity still got the better of her. She picked her way over all the plants and vines standing in their way, then reached the front door of the conservatory. Opening it blasted her with a wave of hot air that immediately made her hair frizzy from humidity. But it felt so good to feel warm.

Tilting her head back, she let the heat and sun play over her features. A smile graced her features, and she felt all the tension drain from her shoulders. "This is beautiful, Eldridge. I never would have guessed the Spring Maiden would keep a place like this in her kingdom."

"Like I said, there are a lot of secrets you don't know about." He put a hand on her hip and shoved her forward. "Keep going. There's more."

Fascinated now, she stepped into the observatory and made her way past flowers the size of her head. Everything was larger here, like it had been infused with magic to make it more impressive. She would have stood and stared at each lovely specimen, but there was something in the middle of all this extra large greenery.

A small blue blanket with two white sheepskins laid out on it. There was a bottle of wine waiting for her, with two tall glasses next to a basket full of bread, cheese, and what looked like a bottle of honey.

He'd planned a picnic. And here they were, ready to enjoy the afternoon with each other.

She had to work, though. Freya sighed and readied herself to argue with him. But he slipped his arms around her waist and tugged her back to his chest.

"I know the faerie realm is vast and there is so much you have yet to explore. We could get lost in a lifetime of adventure." He pressed his lips to the side of her neck. "But I am certain the greatest adventure is getting lost in you."

She melted back against him. Prettier words had never been said, and no matter how hard her mind struggled, her heart said to stay. So she did.

Freya stopped arguing. She stopped fighting for him to see that they had work to do and let herself enjoy an afternoon with an immortal creature who courted her. Freya of Woolwich. The little girl who had grown up on the edge of the forest with a mother who hated his kind.

They spent the afternoon eating and drinking in the middle of that wonderful oasis. Freya shed the outer layers of her clothing that were meant to keep her warm. He took off his jacket. If anyone had wandered into the observatory, they would have thought the two of them mad.

But they were laughing. Telling stories about their childhood and enjoying each other's company without feeling forced.

Freya laid her head in his lap, laughing so hard she could barely breathe. "So, wait! You're telling me that your greatest accomplishment growing up was stealing the whiskers of a visiting noble?"

He coughed into his wine glass, his own gusting laughter choking him. "Yes, that's exactly what I'm saying. I snuck into his room in the middle of the night, used scissors to snip them all off his face, and then ran as fast as I could. I still have them somewhere."

"That's disgusting!" she said, trying to stop giggling but incapable of doing so. "I have no idea why you would keep those. They're whiskers!"

"They're trophies of war."

She gave him a censoring glance, although her eyes still crinkled with mirth. "He told you not to climb the curtains while he and your father were having a business meeting."

"And he should have known that a goblin boy would not stand for such a ridiculous request." Eldridge drank deeply from his wine glass, then snorted into it again. "You can't tell me you weren't a wild child, as well. You must have played pranks on your family or friends."

She shook her head. "No, not really. I was a very serious child. Esther was the one to run wild and terrorize my parents. She was the funny one. I was supposed to be the big sister and take care of her. No matter what."

"That's a shame." He brushed his fingers through her hair, smoothing each strand behind her ear and lingering once he got them settled. "But if a serious childhood is what brought you to me, then I suppose I cannot be so angry at your parents."

Her cheeks burned. "Eldridge."

"What? Am I not allowed to admire your beauty? Your strength?" He lifted a brow. "You know that I'm interested in you, Freya. More than I could ever say. I haven't felt like this before."

She shouldn't encourage him, but she wanted to know. "Like what? What are you feeling?"

He took a deep breath, expression serious and grave. With a gentle touch, Eldridge traced the barest tips of his fingers along her arm. He wrapped his long fingers around her wrist and lifted it up. Gently, ever so gently, he curled her fingers in his and pressed their hands to his heart. "I couldn't put a name to it if I tried. All I know is that this feeling is vast and deep. It is ancient and powerful, and I can hardly contain it in my fragile body. When I see you, I am both light as air and heavy as stone."

Oh, and what words those were.

I'm falling in love with you, she thought.

Freya couldn't say the words, yet. Instead, she pressed her lips together and held them in. Hoping her flesh could contain the feeling that fluttered in her chest.

Eldridge followed the line of her brow to her temple and then trailed his pointed nails into her hair. "I have no expectations, Freya. I'm merely telling you what is in my soul."

"I know," she whispered. "I'm glad we got this time with each other. Alone."

He grinned, leaned down, and pressed his lips to hers. "As am I, my hero. As am I."

CHAPTER 11

Another week flew by and yet again, nothing changed. Freya grew tired of inaction and arguments.

Yes, she understood that there was a large amount of tension in the air. The pixies were a secretive sort, and the Spring Maiden was the worst of them. Some part of that unnatural woman didn't want them in her mines.

The longer she thought about it, the more Freya was certain she had figured it out. The Spring Maiden put up a front at the entrance to her kingdom. She wanted people to believe this place was beautiful, manicured, so no one could ever question how lovely it was. The inhabitants of the Spring Court were meant to reflect that.

But the reality of this place was much darker. Though there was of course beauty, there was also a lot of darkness.

Perhaps the Spring Maiden disliked that truth because the kingdom was a bitter reflection of her own soul.

Whatever the reason, Eldridge wouldn't convince this terrifying woman that they needed to go to the mines without guards. And the Spring Maiden wouldn't convince Eldridge that he needed more information before he charged into a werewolf den. Yet again, two faerie leaders had locked horns and neither would let go.

After a week of that nonsense, she was quite done. Freya enlisted the help of a few pixies, who were a little hesitant to help until she told them her plan. After that, they were quite pleased to go about and gather all the things she needed.

Freya would not run into the darkness head first. She wasn't trying to get around either of the leaders in secret. She merely wanted to know what they were up against, how to beat the creature, and then maybe she could move forward with confidence. With or without the faerie rulers.

The pixies were pleased with her plan. One of them even smiled at her and whispered, "This is how she killed the Queen. It must be!"

And though the words made her flinch, at least it meant they had some faith in her.

Half of another week passed before everything was finally ready. Freya stepped into the courtyard where a large cart rolled into view. It was stacked high with mounds of books that apparently would give her the appropriate information on werewolves in the faerie realms.

Freya knew the very first way to solve a problem was to search for a solution within the pages of a book.

"Is this everything?" she called out, approaching the cart with her hands behind her back. Her pale pink skirts swished around her legs, the bodice hugging tight to her curves. And though her arms were bare, the sun warmed her skin to a lovely shade of peaches and cream.

"It is, miss." The pixie at the front pulled the horses to a stop, then hopped off his twisted metal seat. "Every book we could find that was related to werewolves. It'll take you a while to get through all of them."

Freya could hear a faint rustling within the books. One of the stacks toppled over, and a small snout appeared over the lip of a navy colored book. That snout belonged to a rather handsome black and white dog who stepped down off the cart while standing on his back legs. He wore a fine red, pressed velvet suit with a white collar popped around his jaw. Dashing, really, if it had been on anyone but a dog.

Arrow used his paw to shift the page of the book he held in his grip, eyes still on the pages. "Yes, I'm certain it would take her a rather long time. These books are drier than the desert. But thankfully, she'll have a little help."

The grin on her face almost hurt.

He was here. Finally, her dearest friend who knew how to help her through every adventure was here.

The pixie beside her stared at the goblin with his mouth dropped open. "How long have you been in the cart?"

"Long enough to hear you sing that horrible song. I thought pixies could sing?" Arrow finally looked up from his book to glare at the faerie beside her. "You have a horrible voice. There are people who can help with that, you know."

The pixie pressed a hand to his chest, and Freya burst into laughter.

"Oh, my friend." She snagged the book out of Arrow's paws and dropped to her knees to give him a hug. "I missed you so much."

He patted her shoulder with a small paw, struggling to get out of her grip already. "Yes, well. Good. You should miss me as I'm more helpful than these oafs. I've already looked through most of these books while we were careening through the forest. Not much help here, if I'm being honest."

She released him with one last squeeze. "Is that so? I was certain someone would have a story that would give us something to work with. How are we supposed to fight a werewolf if no one knows how? I thought the faeries had killed them off before."

"They did." He bared his teeth in a snarl. "But those battles were hard won, and we lost a lot of good faerie warriors in the process. No one knew how to stop the wolves, so we just... fought until they eventually died."

"That doesn't seem effective." Freya stood and dusted off her skirts. "Are we back to square one, then?"

Arrow reached into the pocket of his vest and brandished a very small book about the size of her palm. "Of course we're not. Square one would suggest we have no books that might help us. This one will. No one in the kingdom would have such knowledge. Other than me. Of course."

Her eyes widened and her heart stuttered. "What do you have there, Arrow?"

"My father was a collector, of sorts. He liked to know what the other creatures were doing, and thoughts about their existence. Before all the werewolves died out, he found one that was dying. Promised he wouldn't sell the secrets, however..." Arrow waved the book. "This will give you more information on how to communicate with the beast and perhaps how to kill it. If we have to."

She pressed her hands dramatically to her chest. "My hero. What would I do without you? You are a fantastic, incredible, wonderful partner, you know that?"

"I do." He rolled his eyes, holding the book out for her to take. "And you'd be on that never ending path without me. Still. Might I remind you."

"Indeed, I would be. I owe you my life." Freya couldn't get the grin off her face. It was just so good to see him after days filled with pixies and Eldridge. Finally she was around another forward thinking indi-vidual who wasn't quite so perfect.

The doors behind her opened and a wave of warmth struck her back long before she heard his voice. It hadn't taken the Goblin King very long to realize one of his own court was in the Spring Court.

"What is Arrow doing here?" he called out. Anger made his voice a little more gruff than usual.

Right, so they were going to argue.

Freya squared her shoulders and got ready for what he was going to say to her. He wouldn't like having Arrow arrive in the Spring Court, considering Eldridge had said he didn't want to bring anyone with them. But they needed the help! And who better to help them than the goblin who had started this journey with them?

She ground her teeth and turned around. "I had a pixie inform him that we need his help."

"We don't need his help." Eldridge stopped right in front of her, teeth grinding and eyes narrowed. "We've got this handled with no one else getting involved. He has a life to live, Freya. Arrow is not your servant."

"Nor would I want him to be. He'd make a terrible servant." She reached out her hand and laid it on Arrow's shoulder. "He's here as a friend because he wants to be. And he's brought us all the information we need to understand this creature, and where to go next."

"The Spring Maiden won't let us enter the mines without her

consent," he snarled. "Have you not been listening at all to our conversations? You're in the room with us, Freya!"

How dare he suggest she wasn't taking this seriously? Of course she was. They were looking for her mother, for heaven's sakes!

Freya pinched her nose and tried to calm down. Arguing had gotten them nowhere so far, and it wouldn't get them any farther. She needed to calmly and rationally explain to him her reasoning. Not shout.

Thankfully, Arrow stepped between them before she could even think of the words to convince him.

"My king," Arrow said. He bowed low for Eldridge's attention. "Freya was right to call for me. I am, after all, the same kind of species as a werewolf if you think about it. I know how to find another dog. Besides, I already brought you information that you'd need."

"Such as?" Eldridge snarled.

Freya held up the book. "A recounting of a dying werewolf, written in Arrow's father's hand."

"And..." Arrow turned around and walked back to the cart. "If you two would follow me, I think you'll find this rather interesting. I found it in your library, Eldridge. Before I left, I wanted to see if the Goblin Kingdom would have more information. It did, of course."

The confidence in this goblin dog never ceased to amaze her. Freya had to bite her lips, so she didn't grin. Arrow always knew how to convince the king to do something, even though their own relationship had started on rocky footing.

She trailed along behind the two of them and realized her heart was full again. Not because she was on an adventure, but because her family was together. Parts of it, at least. But it was so damned good to see these two working by her side.

Arrow hopped up onto the cart and sat down between a stack of crimson books and a mountain of scrolls. "This is a map of the Spring Court. Not the map that the Spring Maiden would give you, I'll make that distinction now. This is the real map."

And just like that, the curious lines between Eldridge's eyes appeared again. She recognized that expression. He was excited by the possibility of what might happen next.

Eldridge reached for a folded up parchment beside Arrow's right foot. It was the same size as a book until Eldridge unrolled it. And then it was a man's arm span wide.

"Would you look at that," Eldridge said with glee. "She would be furious to know this exists."

Arrow nodded. "I'm sure she would. But that's why it was in your castle and not in the Summer Lord's clutches. Hidden away for safe-keeping, just in case something happened that a Goblin King would need to step in to take care of. I assume a werewolf hunting down pixies suits?"

"It most certainly does." Eldridge snapped the map down and met Freya's stare. "Do you know what this means?"

That they could finally get on with finding the werewolf? That they could leave these wild gardens and actually find her mother?

Freya shrugged. "Oh, I don't know. What does it mean, Eldridge?"

He growled at her, and the sound echoed through her entire being. It wasn't a sound of anger, but one of passion and desire. She'd explore that sound later if he would let her, but for now, they had an audience and a place to go.

Eldridge folded the map back up and set it on the cart where Arrow was staring at them with a rather smug expression.

Licking his lips, the Goblin King planted his hands on his hips and stared at the two of them. "We still have to convince the Spring Maiden that we're allowed into the mines. Just by ourselves, now that we finally have a map, we can follow without the threat of getting lost."

"Why do you need her permission?" Freya asked. "I think it would be more logical that the Goblin King could go anywhere in the courts. I'll inform her that we have to return home to see my sister. She's falling in love with a goblin, you see, and that's a rather difficult thing for a mortal woman. She needs her sister by her side."

The frown on Eldridge's face was almost comical. "You know, it's rather easy to forget you can lie."

"Why's that?"

"I don't think of you as a mortal anymore," he murmured. "How strange."

Arrow snorted and rolled his eyes. "Strange indeed. I didn't miss your moon eyes. Both of you are sincerely uncomfortable to be around. Just get on with it already, would you? I already picked where we need to go."

His words snapped Freya out of the strange trance. The Goblin King's eyes were just so captivating when he stared at her like that. As if he wanted to devour her mind, body, and soul. And she'd let him if he wanted to try.

Clearing her throat, she looked back at Arrow and shook herself. "Where do you think we need to go?"

He flipped the map open again and pointed to a small symbol in the center. It was right next to a sign for the mines that stretched over half the kingdom. "The town's name is Mudgate. Everyone there has been mining for a very long time. From what I've heard, no one leaves it."

"You think they'll know about our werewolf?" she asked, leaning over the map.

"I do."

Eldridge placed his hand on her back and peered at the symbol with her. "It's a good start. If they've been mining for a long time, then they'd at least have heard the stories. We can talk with a few of the older pixies. Get a head start on the werewolf returning to his den."

"It's a better plan than we had before." Freya looked up at Arrow and asked, "What's next?"

He snuffled, then stood up on his back legs and walked to another book. "I have more research to do. You have to go lie to the Spring Maiden. And Eldridge? Try not to mess any of this up."

CHAPTER 12

Their carriage rattled down the old road filled with potholes and deep ruts. Freya was bundled up next to Eldridge while Arrow sprawled on the opposite bench. Though he was the smallest one here, apparently he took up most of the room.

She should have known better than to allow Arrow to ride in the carriage with them.

A wheel hit a particularly large bump, then she heard the tell-tale crack of a wooden wheel. The carriage rolled precariously, then slowly dropped onto its side. She barely held onto the wall but prevented her head from cracking against the side.

They were nowhere near the town. Or at least, she didn't think they were.

She bit her lip to keep an "I told you so," in and then looked over at Eldridge. "A portal wouldn't have gotten us there any faster, huh?"

"I thought we'd want some time to catch up. It's been a while since we have talked with Arrow. Just the three of us." Eldridge gripped the lip of the window and looked for all the world as though he was entirely relaxed. Like nothing had happened.

"Eldridge. The wheel just broke," she snarled.

"Yes, it does appear that it has broken. The driver may take a while to fix it." He looked at the door behind her, the one that was currently staring almost straight up at the sky. "Perhaps we should get out of the carriage and walk the rest of the way."

"That might be the plan." She reached for Arrow and tucked him into her arms.

Very carefully, she opened up the door facing the sky and clambered out. At least she wasn't wearing one of those dreadful travel gowns, or Eldridge would have been looking right up her skirts. Instead, she'd stolen from his wardrobe and put on a pair of dark leather pants, and a white billowing shirt that looked better on her than him.

Freya placed Arrow on top of the carriage and then sat with her legs dangling into the carriage. "Are you sure you want to get out?" she asked. "It looks to me like you're enjoying yourself down there."

Eldridge reclined with half of his body still on the cushions of the seat, and the other half bracing himself. "I'm perfectly fine. But if you're in a rush, hero of mine, then perhaps you should move your legs and I'll join you in the fresh air."

"Ah, the sarcasm," she replied with a grin. "I did miss the bite."

"The bite?" He reached up and pressed a clawed hand to her calf. Squeezing tight, he stood in the broken carriage, his lips close to her ankle. "I wouldn't say my sarcasm has a bite, but there are a few things that do."

Arrow made a gagging sound behind them. "Stop. Stop it, that's more than enough. The two of you need to realize we're hunting down a killer and we don't have time for whatever it is you think you're doing. Besides, we're right next to the town."

They were?

Freya stopped looking at Eldridge and glanced around them. Shockingly, there was a town just down the road from them. Although it wasn't what she had expected from the Spring Court.

In fact, it looked downright similar to the mortal town she had come from. The buildings were rundown and old, patches on the sides creating a patchwork pattern. There were three levels of the buildings, it looked like. Railings were on some of the other levels, but most were broken and didn't appear like they would stop anyone from falling.

The road led right to the town where it stopped and split off in a spider web like pattern. The map had warned them that Mudgate would be difficult to navigate. Freya just hadn't realized how challenging it would be.

Eldridge poked his head out of the carriage, a bright grin on his face. "Ah, we are closer than I thought we were. How fortunate."

She moved aside to let him emerge into the sun. Their pixie driver was standing beside the carriage with her hands on her hips. At the sight of them leaving the carriage, she shrugged and unfurled her wings. "If you're all walking to the village, I'll head back to the court if you don't mind."

Eldridge waved her off.

If only they could fly to the town. Freya wasn't excited to walk all that way and then attempt to figure out where they were staying.

Apparently, her two companions weren't of the same mindset. Arrow shook himself, then stood on his back legs and started toward Mudgate. Eldridge whistled as he followed the goblin dog. The damn fool.

"You two look far too happy to be doing this," she muttered, trailing after them.

"I like Mudgate," Eldridge said.

"You've been before?"

"No." He straightened the sleeves of his borrowed jacket that was a little more worn than most he would wear. "But it does look like an adventure and a half. Doesn't it? There could be robbers."

Freya furrowed her brow. "And that sounds exciting to you?"

"Immensely."

If he kept whistling, she was going to hit him. Robbers were not an exciting surprise to add to their journey. The last thing they needed was to deal with vagabonds on top of trying to stop a killer werewolf and find her mother.

Was she the only responsible person in her party?

Freya trailed after the two men and marveled at their differences. The tall, lean, Goblin King walked with a swagger that suggested his confidence had no end. Arrow, on the other hand, sometimes hopped a bit in his walk as though he were trying extremely hard to appear human, even though he never would look like one of them.

They were both so near and dear to her heart, though.

The mining village became crystal clear as they walked toward it. Upon first observation, she had thought it was empty. That was not the case. People were walking around to get wherever they needed to go. They were just sticking to the shadows, hiding from anyone who might see them.

Strange. She had thought they would at least feel safe in their own town.

She stepped closer to the two men and muttered, "Why does it feel like we're being watched?"

"Because we are," Eldridge replied. "I think it's safe to say they rarely receive strangers here."

He was most likely correct. The few pixies she could see were staring at them with wide eyes. Dirt streaked their cheeks and their brown clothing had seen better days. Everything here was in tatters. The people. The buildings. Freya could only hope the mines had seen an easier fate than the people who moved around them.

"What do we do now?" she asked under her breath.

It didn't appear that anyone was going to give them a room. The moment they stepped toward one of the pixies, the creature disappeared through a back alley that they hadn't noticed.

No one wanted to speak with the unknown, apparently. Although she couldn't blame them if their entire life had been living in this poverty.

Arrow pressed his cold nose against the back of her hand. "I don't think it's smart for us to stay here, Miss Freya. We should look for another town nearby and then return tomorrow."

She glanced over at Eldridge, but he was looking at her to make the decision. "I don't always know what is the right choice," he said with a bemused smile. "This place is likely dangerous. I'm sure there are plenty of reasons to leave, and plenty of reasons to stay. But Arrow and I will be fine. You're the mortal."

Sure, leave it up to the human to decide their destiny. Freya blew out a frustrated breath and looked around them one last time. It really was run down. The pixies didn't want them here. Even the sky was clouded over and fog descended from the heavens as though even the sun was ashamed to look upon this place.

But they were closer than ever to finding her mother. Closer to finding out the truth.

She couldn't give that up so easily. Not when it was all within her grasp.

Freya shook her head and gestured around. "There has to be an inn somewhere, doesn't there?"

Arrow grumbled out an angry sound. "Sure, an inn. That will definitely keep us safe from the robbers and vagabonds filling the streets here. I'm sure they aren't interested in kidnapping a mortal woman and trading her for something meaningless like... Oh, I don't know. Food."

His words wouldn't get under her skin. She had known this wouldn't be easy, and of course she was aware there were dangers in this realm that were unlike anything she had dealt with before. But Freya would take the risk if it meant her mother was saved.

Eldridge stepped close to her side and placed a hand on her back. "You know I wouldn't let anyone touch you."

"I do." She smiled up at him and felt warmth bloom in her chest. For the first time, she really did believe that he would protect her with every breath in his body.

Even if he had made more mistakes than she could count, at least she knew that Eldridge was a good man to his core. He didn't want to see her injured or harmed. He'd throw his own people into the mouth of the mine itself if they tried to harm her.

Arrow chuffed another angry breath. He walked away from them, tail straight up in the air. "Nice words, Goblin King. But I don't think even you could stop a mob if these pixies decide they don't want any strangers in their mix."

They wouldn't create a mob... would they?

Freya tugged her jacket tight to her sides and stayed close as they wandered through the streets. The deeper into the mining village they went, the more she was shocked at the conditions these people lived in.

The air was filled with the acrid bite of metal and loam. Each house tilted dangerously to the side, so much so that she had to assume magic was the only thing keeping them from crumbling. Every street they walked on grew narrower until she could have reached out and touched both buildings on either side of her. Freya felt her throat closing up as claustrophobia set in. Everything was too close now. If someone wanted to attack them, then there was nowhere for any of them to go.

"Eldridge?" she whispered. "Do you think we're close to the inn yet?"

"Indeed we are." He stopped underneath a sign with a carved falcon on the front. "I do believe we've made it, Freya. Now, let's see if they have any rooms available."

Part of her hoped they didn't. Then they wouldn't have to stay in this inn that looked like it hadn't seen patrons in years. But the other part of her wanted to get this over and done with. She eyed the dirt smudged windows that were so grimy she couldn't see inside. "All right, then. If you think it's safe."

"Nothing here is safe." His expression darkened. "Arrow was right about that."

Great. Just great.

They walked into the inn and she fully expected it to be filled with smugglers and other unsavory sorts. But the interior was... well. Sad.

The bar in the back appeared abandoned. There were only a few glasses of whiskey left, but they were covered in a fine layer of dust. Three tables stood near a fireplace, but two of them were missing legs and were only standing up by luck itself. And then there was the floor, which was also fully coated with filth, dirt, and apparently some sort of slick oil because Freya had to hold her arms out at her sides so she didn't slip across the length of the floor.

Perhaps the most strange and eerie detail was that there was no one in the inn. No one at all.

Eldridge cleared his throat and called out, "Excuse me? We're looking for a room for the night!"

A bang echoed from behind the bar. Or actually, from beneath it.

The few remaining bottles rattled, and a pixie appeared from underneath the bar itself. He looked worse for wear. A thin hat on top of his head had been crushed against the side of his dark brown curls. He wore an old, dark brown suit that had seen better days. A rip over the chest might have been where a pocket once was, although one could never really know with pixies. His eyes were ringed with red and his nose was overly large, also bright red.

Why had he been under the bar? Perhaps that was where the creature had been taking a nap. However, considering the man clutched an empty bottle in his hand still, Freya thought it more likely that he had drunk himself into a stupor.

"A guest?" The pixie muttered. He rubbed his eyes with his empty fist, as if by doing so that they would suddenly disappear. When they didn't, he cleared his throat and noisily dropped the bottle. "By all the faerie realms, you're really here."

"We are." Eldridge frowned. "Is this establishment no longer open?"

"Oh, no. It's open. We just haven't had any guests since... since..." The pixie scratched his head. "Well, I can't honestly remember. It's not like a lot of people want to visit a mining village. You know?"

She could imagine that was the truth of it. Though why a mining village would even have an inn was her next question.

The young pixie was shaking as he stared at Eldridge, so she thought perhaps it would be better if she intervened. Stepping into the dim light, she smiled softly. "I assume you're the caretaker of this place. My name is Freya, what's yours?"

Hastily, the pixie man yanked his hat off his head and ducked into a low bow. "Claude, madame. Welcome to the Shrieking Falcon."

Well, at least they had a name for where they were. She'd have to pull out that map again and write down the name of the tavern so they could find it again in the winding streets. "It doesn't have to be a fancy room, Claude. We're hoping to only be here for a few nights."

Claude's bright expression diminished. His bottom lip stuck out in disappointment and he heaved a massive sigh before nodding his head in defeat. "I understand. Only a few nights. Let's see what rooms are available, shall we?"

Freya frowned in confusion. Hadn't he just said that no one had stayed in the inn for a very long time? Surely that meant all the rooms were available.

The pixie reached underneath the bar and pulled out a scroll. With an elaborate flick of his wrist, he unfurled the paper all the way to the floor. He reached into his pocket, pulled out a pair of round glasses, and popped them on his nose. "Yes, I do think there might be a few rooms ready for you. If you'd follow me this way, I'll get you all set up."

They had to trust the strange pixie, even though she wasn't sure if he owned the place or not. Freya met Eldridge's confused expression and shrugged. "I'm quite tired. Might as well see if we can rest our head here, shall we?"

He nodded, and all three of them followed the strange faerie man. Except, she realized there were no wings on Claude's back. Strange, she decided to ask him about that. It might have something to do with the werewolf they were hunting.

He shifted slightly and his suit moved. At the base of his neck was a small brass pull tab. He was hiding his wings like the other pixie had shown them. Tucked into his back even while he was hidden underneath the bar.

Freya's heart twisted in her chest. She had to help these people, just as much as she had to find her mother. Their safety, and their lives, were equally important.

"Here we are!" Claude said jauntily. He tripped and fell against the door, then pulled himself together at the last second. Tugging on the bottom of his suit jacket, he met their gaze with a grin. "I hope you'll find everything up to your standards. If you need anything, I will be in the common living area."

Freya eyed his staggering walk and sighed. "He's drunk."

"Very," Eldridge replied. He pushed open the door to their room and gestured for her to step inside ahead of him. "But at least we have a room."

"At least we have that."

She should have held her tongue. Freya's gut twisted the moment she walked through the door.

The floor was at least cleaner than downstairs, but not by much. A four poster bed in the corner was missing a post. The blankets were still crumpled at the foot of the bed where someone else had clearly slept. A fireplace in the corner was likely meant to keep them warm, but she could see even from here that soot filled the chimney so thoroughly that she wouldn't dare light a fire in fear they would set the entire place ablaze.

She looked over her shoulder at Eldridge, who chewed on his lip. "Well, this is less than satisfying."

"That's a word for it," Arrow grumbled.

Freya didn't want to leave. She was so tired, and this place was so... so...

"Awful," she said.

"But not impossible to stay in for a single night." Eldridge wrapped his arm around her shoulder and spread his fingers wide in front of them. "The hearth might be cold, but that's just a reason for all of us to snuggle a little closer together. The bed might have bugs, but we don't need a bed to be comfortable."

She lifted a brow. "Don't we need at least that?"

"Oh, mortal of little faith." He released his hold on her and winked. With his classic Goblin King flourish, he whipped off his jacket and laid it down in front of the fire. "Come, Freya. We'll all keep each other warm."

"On the floor."

"Perhaps, but it will be the best night's sleep you've had in a while." He was trying. So hard.

Freya sighed and relented. "All right. Tomorrow we'll start asking around for anyone who knows something about the wolf."

"At first light." Eldridge waited until she laid down, then arranged himself around her. Tugging her against his heart while Arrow curled up in the hollow her body made.

And though she was still tired, Freya was warm. Tomorrow they would find out all the things they needed. Tomorrow, she would take on the pixies and prove to them she was trustworthy.

But tonight, she would enjoy being safe in the arms of her Goblin King.

CHAPTER 13

Maybe she thought she was comfortable a little too soon. Freya woke long before the two goblin men. She was shivering uncontrollably and the two of them were snuggled up together like the human woman with them didn't exist.

Arrow had apparently gotten up in the middle of the night and shifted sides. Perhaps he had tucked himself against the Goblin King's back, but then Eldridge had rolled over. Now, the Goblin King was the big spoon with his arm wrapped around the goblin dog.

It was an adorable sight, and she might have taken the time to enjoy it if she wasn't shivering so hard. As it was, she was mad that they were comfortable while she was not.

Blowing into her hands, she tried to bring some life back into her fingers before standing. It had been warmer in the room below with the pixie man.

She couldn't imagine it would be dangerous to speak with him on her own. After all, no one else had been in the inn. She could talk to a faerie without having Eldridge right behind her. Couldn't she?

Freya tiptoed to the door, biting her lip and wincing with every step. The floor creaked. One of them was going to wake up and yell at her for even thinking of leaving on her own. But they didn't. She made it to the door without issue and opened the squeaking wood.

Seriously, couldn't Claude have at least oiled the damn thing?

She closed it behind her, then listened for any movement in the room beyond. When she heard nothing, Freya assumed she was in the clear. The two of them needed to sleep, anyway. They were going to be more useful in making decisions than Freya. At least they knew something about this realm. Freya was just walking around hoping these faeries took pity on her and gave her a nugget of knowledge.

Making her way down the stairs, she walked into the front lobby of the inn. Claude was nowhere to be seen.

She had a feeling she knew where he was. And that wasn't the best of places, considering she had hoped he would take guests as a reason to be more awake.

Quietly, Freya made her way to the bar and leaned over the edge. Just as she suspected, a pixie laid on the floor with one of the last bottles of whiskey in his hand. At least this one wasn't empty like last time.

"Claude," she said.

He snorted in his sleep, curling into himself and clutching the bottle a little tighter to his chest.

"Claude," Freya said again, this time with a little more passion.

Nothing again.

She looked at the bar and stared at a glass next to her right hand. This was an inn. He must have plenty of glasses that he could fill, so it wouldn't be all that bad if she just...

Freya nudged the cup from the top of the bar. It hit the ground with a solid thunk right beside Claude's head. Surprisingly, the glass didn't break. She was impressed at the craftsmanship, at the very least.

Claude let out a tiny sound of fear, skittered backward with the bottle held against his heart, and stared up at her with wide haunted eyes. "Please, no! There's nothing here, I tell you. Nothing at all!"

She held out her hands. "No, no. I'm not going to hurt you. See? It's just me. Freya. I'm one of your guests that you let into the room earlier?"

He blinked his eyes, and eventually the panic cleared from his eyes.

"Miss Freya. Madame. I am so sorry. I have bad dreams, is all. What can I do to help you?"

That kind of reaction didn't come from bad dreams. That came from a man who had suffered greatly in his life and was expecting everyone to swing at him. Freya was certain this town was rough to live in, but she hadn't expected it to be quite so brutal.

How did she make it clear that she didn't want to hurt him? She wanted a little more information on how to find the werewolf. Of course, that might be a sore subject as well, and he was unlikely to speak about it if he was afraid of her.

Freya eyed the bottle in his hand and tried on a whim, "I couldn't sleep. I remember seeing you had alcohol and wondered if you would be willing to share."

He looked down at the bottle as well, then back at her. "People don't really drink in these parts."

"That's surprising. Considering this is a mining town, and it looks a little... down on its luck." She chose the most gentle way to say this place looked like it hadn't seen a coin in centuries. "I'd imagine most people would seek help at the bottom of a bottle."

"Most people here are miners." The tension in his shoulders relaxed. "Mining while drunk could kill you, and everyone else in the shaft with you."

"Ah." She nodded. "I understand. But I'm not a miner."

The pixie opened his mouth, a question in his eyes. Then it dawned on him what she was trying to say.

Miners might not drink, that was certain. And understandably so. But since Freya wasn't one of those folks, she could drink with him without putting anyone in danger. Or at least, not as much as most.

He narrowed his eyes on her and cleared his throat. "You'll have to be very plain with your reasoning, Miss Freya."

"I find it's not nearly as entertaining to drink alone as it is to drink with friends." She braced her elbow on the table and popped her chin in her hand. "My companion has plenty of money for it, if that's what you're worried about. I'm certain he wouldn't mind paying for a drink or two."

That lit a fire in Claude's eyes. He was obviously a man motivated by two singular things. Drink and money.

The knowledge of those traits made it very easy for Freya to plan out how she was going to ask him about the werewolf. He lived in the mining town. This strange faerie must know about the werewolf. Or at least the existence of someone else who did know more than just fear and superstition.

Claude reached for a new bottle of whiskey and slammed it down on the bar in front of her. "I'm afraid there's only one kind of poison here, my dear."

"That's quite all right with me. You'll find I'm not very picky about my... poison." She pointed to the tables behind them. "Shall we sit?"

"None of those chairs would hold either of our weight, I'm afraid." A glint in his eyes suggested this was a challenge. As if he didn't think someone like her would be comfortable drinking at the bar, rather than at a table.

There weren't any stools for her to sit on. Freya had never been one to shy away from a challenge, however. She heaved herself up onto the edge of the table and sat with her legs crossed. Prim and proper, but still shockingly wrong for a lady of her status.

At least, that's what she assumed he was thinking.

She gestured for a glass. "Well? Tell me about yourself, Claude. I like to hear a story when I'm drinking."

It was the right thing to say. He poured her a hefty glass and then told her his entire life story with rather impressive drama.

He had been a young pixie when he first came to this town seeking fame and fortune. The metal that made magic mirrors could be sold for as much as an entire pixie home, he claimed. But eventually the mining got to him. His lungs betrayed him, but he didn't have enough money to get back home.

That's how he ended up in the inn. He worked here for the previous owner, cleaning rooms back when the mining town had been booming. Now that there were a lot of magic mirrors, and very few people would risk breaking something that powerful, the town had died.

As did the original owner.

He spewed the story with all the flair of an actor. Freya found herself more and more captivated by the tale. Perhaps it was the drink that rushed straight to her head, but she teared up when he claimed he missed his family, but there was no way to get in touch with them.

She pressed her palm against her heart. "I would do anything for my family."

"I could tell that when you walked in the door." He hiccuped and then winced. "You're a kind hearted woman, Miss Freya. I knew that with the first look I got of you."

Those blasted tears returned again. They filled up her eyes, and she held them open frantically so she didn't start crying. "That's an awful nice thing to say."

"Well, it's the truth." Claude lifted the bottle to his lips and took a large swig.

When had they started drinking straight out of the bottle? She'd thought they were drinking out of glasses.

But when she looked down at her own hand, she wasn't holding the glass. She was also holding a bottle that was about half full of whiskey. Good lord, had she drank that much? She'd been sipping while Claude was telling his story and then... then...

Sighing, Freya put the bottle down on the bar and slid it away from herself. She needed her wits about her for this.

"Claude?" she asked. "I came here for my family, you know."

"Here?" He narrowed his eyes, trying to focus on her but looking over her shoulder. "Why would any of your family be here? This isn't a place for anyone like yourself, or even those men upstairs."

"My mother came here." Freya couldn't look him in the eye when she told this story. She needed to focus on the words, not his reaction. And for some reason, that was very difficult with so much alcohol in her system. "I don't know why, but I plan on asking her when I find her."

"For love?" Claude leaned against the bar but somehow still weaved side to side. "I know a lot of people who came here for love and then fell out of it. She could be anywhere by now. Or in another, better, part of the Spring Court."

"No, you see... The last person who saw her said she was unconscious after trying to fight a werewolf." She looked up then to meet his wide-eyed stare. "I know she's not dead. And he has her somewhere."

Claude's throat bobbed in a heavy swallow. The fear in his gaze was proof he was well aware of the beast she spoke of. He'd heard of this werewolf, and he feared it with every bone in his body.

She needed him to tell her what he knew. That determination banished some of the fog from the whiskey, enough so that she could lean forward and put her hand over his. "I think you know what I'm talking about, don't you?"

He nodded and pressed his lips together. "We all know about the werewolf, miss. That's who I thought you were when you woke me up. I was certain the shadow looming over me was the wolf come to claim my wings."

"Why your wings?"

"So we can't fly away while he's killing us, miss. Every pixie knows to be afraid of the wolf." He moved away from her and wiped the back of his hand over his mouth. "You don't want to find that creature, miss. If she went with him, then she's gone for good. You might as well give up."

Freya shook her head fiercely. "No. I will never give up on finding her."

"You have a death wish, then." He set his own bottle down and backed away from her. "Maybe you should go back to sleep. I don't think the werewolf is going to walk through those doors any time soon."

She looked over her shoulder at the solid wooden frame. The frosted windows revealed nothing that was happening on the street beyond, but she knew the danger that still lurked in the shadows. And that knowledge filled her with a sense of purpose and adventure. Unlike the pixies who lived in a constant state of fear.

"He is out there, though," she murmured. "Isn't he?"

"Not on the streets." Claude cleared his throat. "At least, I hope not. The last time he came into the town, he left a trail of carnage in his wake. Twenty five pixies all dead in their beds. No one heard him enter, and no one heard them scream. It was over in a moment of blood and pain."

The clinking of glasses caught her attention. Freya looked back to the pixie who was arranging things behind the bar. For the first time in a very long time, it looked like.

"Claude," she mumbled. "You know how you feel about seeing your family again? How you said you would do anything to get out of here and hold them in your arms?"

"It's a pipe dream. I can't see them again because I'm never getting out of here. Don't compare that to your story, Miss Freya."

She shifted closer, swinging her legs to the other side of the bar. "It's the same thing, though. I know she's out there. I know, if I tried hard enough, that I would be able to hold her in my arms. I don't care if it's a death wish to take on the werewolf. I need to find my mother. And I need your help to do that."

Claude turned away from her. He braced his hands on the edge of the shelf where most of his remaining whiskey was held. His shoulders curved in on himself and she could see his shirt moving where his wings were trying to flutter underneath the skin. "I can't help you rush to your death. That guilt would stay with me for the rest of time."

"I'm not going to die." She hopped off the bar and placed her hand on the wings slithering beneath his skin. "The man with me is the Goblin King. And the goblin dog is his faithful companion. If anyone could rid you and your people of this nightmarish monster, it is us."

Perhaps it was the alcohol loosening her lips. She was certain Eldridge wouldn't have wanted to tell the pixie who he was. At least, not yet.

But she spewed the words in the hopes they would get one step closer to her mother.

And it worked.

Claude heaved a sigh. "You need to speak to the Magician then. He's the only one who knows anything about that creature."

"How do I find him?" She tried to control the excitement in her words.

"I'll draw you a map."

CHAPTER 14

"Freya."

The words split through a headache that made her entire world spin. This was worse than when Eldridge had been forcing her mind to live through his magic. Worse than any pain she'd ever felt in her entire life.

Groaning, she put her hands to her temples and whimpered.

"Freya," again the word came. Although, this time it was at least said a little more quietly. "We were terrified when we woke up without you. What were you thinking?"

Thinking? She wasn't thinking at all through the pain in her skull. Who was talking to her, and why were they doing it so loudly?

She blinked open her eyes that felt like someone had thrown sand in them. She was face down on a wooden slab which was strange enough. But as she forced her head to raise, she realized she was also staring at an empty bottle of whiskey.

Oh.

Maybe that was why her head was hurting.

Groaning again, she eased upright and rubbed her hand on her cheek. "I don't remember."

"What do you mean, you don't remember?" Eldridge tucked his hand underneath her chin and forced her to look at him. "Did that pixie hurt you? What spell did he cast?"

Another voice interrupted them, yet again far too loud for comfort. "That 'pixie' did nothing to her. I take offense that you'd assume I would harm a patron. She just can't hold her alcohol. The girl said she wanted to drink, and faerie realms she did. But apparently a bottle of whiskey was a little too much for her."

Yes, that was right. She had come down in the middle of the night because the Goblin King had been spooning his goblin dog. And she had wanted to talk with Claude on her own. He'd offered her whiskey and then...

Nope. Nothing. She remembered absolutely nothing from the night before.

Maybe if she could focus on something other than how the ground was moving beneath her. Was there an earthquake? It felt more like she was standing on the bow of a ship instead of the shuddering of the earth. But she was in the faerie realm. She didn't know what an earthquake would feel like here.

Eldridge sighed. "You're hungover."

"Very." She felt her stomach roll, then pressed her fist to her mouth, so she didn't spew liquid all over the Goblin King.

"Arrow and I planned to find food. I see you are in no shape to join us." He patted her head, while clearly angling his body away from her just in case she threw up. "Why don't you go back up to the room and get some rest? I'll wake you when we return."

That sounded lovely. Even if she could find a little water to splash on her face, that would be ten times better than what she was feeling right now. Freya nodded and slid off the bar. "I think I probably need that."

"Then it's a plan." He smoothed his fingers over the tousled locks of her hair. "You're a never ending surprise, Freya."

She didn't have the mental capacity to guess what that meant.

Freya staggered back to their room and stumbled to the corner where someone had placed a bowl of water. If Eldridge had already used that to clean himself this morning, then she didn't care. She needed some water on her face, immediately. Otherwise she was going to keep this grimy feeling on her body forever, and she just couldn't stand that.

She splashed the cold water on her face and let it settle the strange rolling. Her head cleared enough for her to at least think. She patted the stand the bowl sat on and realized there was no towel.

Dripping, now cold, she sighed and grabbed the end of her jacket. At least she could wipe her face with that.

Her hand hit the edges of a piece of paper tucked into her pocket.

That was strange. She didn't remember putting anything in there, but she remembered little from last night.

Blinking away the water droplets and the last remaining fog from her eyes, she tugged the piece of paper out of her pocket. It was a map of the winding streets of Mudgate. And a tiny spot marked on it which was penned, "Magician."

Strange. "Magician?" she whispered.

The sound of the word blasted her with all the memories from last night. Suddenly, she recalled the conversation with Claude and how he had been certain this Magician would know how to get her to the werewolf.

And Eldridge was out with Arrow somewhere. Damn it.

Racing from the room, she leapt down the stairs and back into the main entrance of the inn. Breathless, she slammed into the bar once again. "Claude. How long did the Goblin King and his companion say they were going to be gone?"

He looked up from his position on the floor. "They didn't say."

"Do you think it will take them a while to find food?"

He lifted the bottle to his lips, then smacked them. "Considering I didn't tell them where to find anyone who would give them the time of day? Probably until nightfall."

Damn it. That wouldn't do. She needed to find this Magician, now. Freya had never been one for patience, especially when she was holding the answer to all their questions in her hand. All she had to do was follow the line on the map. How hard could that be?

After all, she had traveled through the faerie courts on her own before. The Spring Court couldn't be that different from the others.

Pressing the map to her chest, she backed away from the bar. "I'm going out, then. Do tell the Goblin King that I'll be... busy. If he asks, just let him know I'll return. Does that sound like a plan?"

Claude lifted a hand in a salute. She could just see the tips of his fingers over the edge of the bar. "You can trust me, Miss Freya!"

Somehow, she doubted he would even remember they'd had this conversation. Eldridge would be angry with her, but... this was their chance. And she didn't want to wait.

She opened the door and charged out onto the street. Ready to take on any pixies that might step into her way or try to stop her. She was the fearless Queen Killer, and no one was going to stop her.

Freya walked into a broad chest, slamming her nose into a sharp collarbone.

"Ouch," she muttered.

Fear didn't have the opportunity to speak. She knew that chest, the apple pie scent, and the soft clothing that had only barely cushioned her nose. The Goblin King had not gone with Arrow to go get food.

"I thought you couldn't lie," she snarled, rubbing her face.

"I didn't lie." He watched her with an all knowing gaze. "I had a feeling when I left with Arrow that you weren't in your right state of mind. I decided at the last second not to go. And that I would wait outside the door just to make sure you didn't do anything stupid. Like this."

"I'm not doing anything stupid." She brandished the map at him as though that would make this situation better. "I'm going to find someone who can help us with our werewolf problem."

"And where did you get that?" He snatched it out of her hand. "This is a dangerous part of Mudgate. You aren't going there on your own."

"Well, I planned on it." If it was dangerous, however, she was grateful he was here. Even if that meant that he had to sort of lie to protect her.

Freya was still angry he was lurking at the front door like some kind of bodyguard.

She reached for the map again, only to have him pull it out of her reach. "Eldridge. I would have been perfectly fine."

"You most certainly would not have been." He snorted. "You aren't even controlling your magic. Even though you shouldn't have any to begin with. We really need to dive into that, by the way. How do you know how to cast spells?"

"I don't," she growled. "What would you have done if I snuck out the back instead of the front door?"

"I assume you would have been deterred by the pixies who are sleeping in the back alley." He shrugged. "But if you were foolish enough to try climbing over them, I suppose I would have known where you were by the sound of your screams."

She hated that he was right. She hated that he was anywhere near close to guessing what her plans had been, and that she would have still tried to get over those pixies.

Freya jabbed her finger at him. "You don't know me so well, Goblin King. Don't get any of this twisted in your head. Just because we're..." She gestured wildly between them. "Whatever we're doing. It doesn't mean that you know me, yet. We haven't even talked about each other all that much."

He backed her against the door to the inn with an arm braced over her head. "I do know you, Freya. I know you're brave and you're thoughtful. I know you're foolish too, and that you'll stop at nothing to get your family back. Even follow a Goblin King into the faerie realms and somehow think you might beat me."

"I know I can beat you," she whispered.

Why was he so close to her? She couldn't think about anything other than the heat of his lips and the pulse at the base of his throat. She wanted to press her mouth to the strong column of his neck, to taste him again because it felt like forever since the last time she had. It had been too long.

She cleared her throat and said, "I think we should get going if we're going to find this Magician."

"What's the hurry?"

"My mother is the hurry." She refused to believe he didn't understand that. "Claude made it very clear what kind of monster we're hunting. It's his opinion that my mother couldn't have survived this long in the werewolf's clutches."

"And yet, the Spring Maiden seems to believe she could have. She wouldn't have made a deal with us, otherwise."

Freya wasn't so certain. All the leaders of the courts did what they felt was necessary to get what they wanted. Including throwing other people into dangerous situations. Maybe the Spring Maiden didn't know if Freya's mother was alive and only assumed she was. They still might find her mother and then realize with horror that she'd been dead for a very long time.

What would that be like? She didn't think she'd survive that disappointment.

"We have to go," she repeated. "My mother might only have a few more days to live. There's no way for us to know either way, Eldridge. If this Magician can get us closer to her, then we need to take the risk now. Waiting might only make it more difficult."

He sighed and released her from the door. "Yes, fine. But I don't understand why we couldn't have waited until after breakfast."

"Because Claude didn't tell either of you where to go to get that food," she replied. "He made it very clear that you wouldn't find it without a map. Arrow won't be back until tonight."

"Excuse me?" the Goblin King exclaimed.

"You'll have to walk on an empty stomach," she said with a grin. Freya tapped her hand against Eldridge's chest and took off to follow the markings on the map. "You've done that before, haven't you?"

The streets were closer together here, and wound in a strange network of avenues placed where they needed to be. Not that it made sense to the average person. The grey stone streets, drab walls, and black soot made it seem like all the color had disappeared from the world.

Eldridge grumbled something under his breath and raced after her. "Freya!"

"What?" She glanced over her shoulder and grinned. "I know you probably haven't worked on an empty stomach before, but I think most people here have. Maybe it'll help you connect with them. What do you say?"

"I say I'd like to pick up some food along the way if we see it." He was frowning so hard his brows nearly touched.

She supposed they could do that, but doubted they would find anything suitable to the Goblin King's taste. Honestly, she could forget her grumbling stomach if they found the Magician.

Freya could only hope it would be easy to find him.

CHAPTER 15

"Freya, we have to turn right." Eldridge pointed down a dark side alley that certainly didn't look correct.

She held the map up and peered at the three streets in front of her. Something was wrong. The map said there were four offshoots here, not that there were three. The main road didn't count, it clearly said so. And turning right would only send them down the third street, not the fourth.

Frowning, she tilted the map to look at it from another direction. "I don't think we do."

"I know it might seem strange, but these streets change all the time. The map says to take a right. It doesn't matter that one of the streets is missing," he responded. Eldridge had been getting grumpier the longer they walked without getting him food.

She stored the information away for another time. Adorably, the Goblin King got angry when he didn't eat first thing in the morning. She would have to tease him about that later.

"I really think that's not the direction," she replied. "Look at this with me, would you?"

Stomping over to her side, Eldridge pointed to the map. "Even if we were missing a street, this one would still be the correct one to go down."

But that didn't seem right. The Magician's store should be beside them. It was in the first building on the street, and it wasn't the way he wanted to go.

"This is a magician's store, Eldridge. Don't you think he might try to hide it from people?"

"Not from potential customers." He strode over to the wall where the street should have been. "What do you think I need to do? Cast some spell over here so the Magician will let us in? There's nothing here!"

Nothing but a wall with a few posters on it. She eyed the paper, mostly sketches of people who were missing. So many families hoping to find each other and praying no one was lost to the werewolf.

"I guess not," she replied. "I just thought it would be here. That's all."

"Nothing but the reminder that we are running out of time." He turned with a solemn expression. "Look at all these people. So many pixies are looking for so many lost souls."

She walked up beside him, holding the map against her heart. "Do you think they all fell at the claws of the werewolf?"

Though his eyes darkened and his jaw worked, Eldridge never replied.

Freya's heart twisted in her chest, beating hard against her ribs because her very soul knew that they had a larger purpose here. Sure, it was easy to forget when she was also trying to find her mother. But look at them all.

So many faces of so many people. Each one was sketched by loving hands, although some were more talented than others. Their eyes stared out through the pages, begging her to help them. To find them. Or, at the very least, kill the creature who tormented all the pixies in the Spring Court.

"Wait a minute," Eldridge narrowed his eyes and shifted one of the missing posters aside. "Would you look at that?"

A small mark was painted on the wall in front of them. It was the vague shape of an eye, though the iris was a spiral of color rather than an actual eyeball.

"What is it?" she asked.

"The mark of a magician," he replied with a grin. "You were right after all, Freya. There is another street. We weren't looking in the right place."

Eldridge placed his thumb in the middle of the spiral. The wall groaned, then shifted. Dirt and dust rained down on top of their heads, but the wall moved to reveal its secrets. Another street, shrouded in darkness, with small street lights lit by three candles in each.

This place wasn't so dusty or soot covered. It looked as though it had just rained on these cobblestone streets. They were slick and reflected the glimmering, warm light. There also appeared to be only one shop.

Glass windows poked out into the narrow street, warm light spilling out of them. A single sign hung above the windows with a potion bottle inscribed on it.

"Ah." Freya muttered. "A magician would hide their shop from prying eyes, I suppose."

"There are many who would like to steal the secrets of a magician. Of that I'm certain." Eldridge still wore a frown, however. "I hope he hasn't laid any traps."

"How would he sell anything if people couldn't walk down the street?" The question seemed logical, but Freya had learned a very long time ago that logic had no place in the faerie realms.

Eldridge bit his lower lip. "I'm not sure he wants to sell things, Freya. I think the only people who go to this man are the desperate and the depraved."

How quaint. And now they were here.

She wondered which category they fell into.

She wouldn't wait any longer. Taking a deep breath, she strode down the street toward the shop and hoped nothing was about to attack her. Every step echoed, as if another person were walking right beside her. Except, Eldridge didn't make any sounds at all when he walked. So that second person couldn't be him.

"What are we going to ask when we find him?" she whispered as though someone was listening to their every word.

"I would suggest we be as truthful as possible. Magicians are... difficult." Eldridge struggled to find the right descriptor. "They have a lot of magic at their fingertips, but they rarely use their magic for any reason other than satisfying their own desires. We have to make him want to help us."

Right, because that would be so easy. Can you help me find my mother, sounded like something the Magician had probably heard a thousand times before. What set Freya apart from the hundreds of pixies who had begged for the same thing?

She'd have to come up with something, and fast.

Freya paused in front of the door and licked her lips. "What are the chances of him wanting to help us out of the kindness of his own heart?"

"I would say the chances of that are zero at best."

Pressing her hand against the door, she repeated, "At best?"

"Negative chances, honestly. I wouldn't expect the Magician to be a good man at all." The warm light illuminated only one side of Eldridge's face. The other was cast in a terrifying shadow that made it seem as though he had two faces.

As if he were two people in this moment, not just one.

Shivering, she pushed the door open and entered the Magician's shop. The bell rang over her head, and she was immediately greeted with a wall of objects on shelves. Skulls, mummified creatures, gemstones that seemed to swirl with smoke. A thousand objects, all brimming with dark magic. They were terrifying and fascinating.

An orb sat on the middle shelf within eyesight. Smoke swirled within the glass, writhing and moving with some inner power that called out to Freya.

Touch me, the smoke seemed to whisper. And see what the future holds.

She couldn't do that. Nothing in here should be touched by a mortal, and yet everything was so infinitely tempting. Perhaps that was the power of the Magician. He made people give themselves up by touching some cursed object, and then he never had to deal with them at all.

Eldridge's hand came down on her wrist.

Freya snapped out of her thoughts and was horrified to see her fingers were a mere inch from touching the orb. It would have been so easy to move a little more, and then she would have answered the magical object's call.

"Don't touch that," Eldridge snapped.

"I wasn't trying to." Freya shook him off her and rubbed her wrist. "I didn't even know I was reaching for it."

"Freya..." He took a step closer to her, dropping the volume of his words until she could barely hear them. "We need to talk about your ability to use magic. A place like this is more dangerous for you if you don't know what kind of power runs through your veins."

"I do know," she replied, stepping away from the shelves. "None."

Freya walked around the wall of shelves to the interior of the shop. A cauldron bubbled in the corner, freestanding and floating in mid air. Glass vials lined the walls, filled with every type of object. Some earth. Some water. And even a few that seemed to be filled with tiny bones. She hoped the Magician had gotten those from a bird or a rat, rather than some fae creature she hadn't met yet.

And seated at a desk on the far wall was a very elderly gentleman. He had a long white beard that nearly touched his hips. Round spectacles sat on his nose and magnified his eyes, making them extra large. He wore a robe the color of the sea, and she half expected to see a pointed hat on his head.

The man was rather exactly what she had expected a magician to look like. Freya didn't trust him already.

"Ah," he said. His voice shook as he spoke. "I have been expecting you two today. Took you long enough to find the street."

"I'm afraid it wasn't very easy to find," Freya replied. "You were expecting us?"

"I don't get customers every day. But my dear Arabella let me know you would be here soon. She's never wrong, you know." He stood and rounded the desk.

The Magician used a curved cane to move around his shop.

Although she wasn't certain if she could call it a shop when there didn't appear to be anything available to buy. His spine was bent in on itself, like the oldest of people she'd seen before.

In fact, he looked very much like every mortal she'd met.

Frowning, Freya looked at Eldridge with his silver skin and tufted ears, then back to the Magician. "Are you a mortal?"

The grin on the old man's face let her know that she was at least in the right line of guessing. "Mortal is a rather limiting word, don't you think? The right question, my dear, is if I'm human."

More riddles. Yet another person who wanted to talk around the truth rather than just say it.

"Well, if you're human, then you've been in the faerie realm for too long. You're already speaking in riddles, old man." Freya shouldn't have grumbled at him, but she was so tired of being treated like this. "From one human to another, I thought you'd be more helpful."

Eldridge choked behind her.

But the Magician laughed. "Such spirit! I wouldn't have expected anything else from a woman who tied herself to a Goblin King."

Maybe Eldridge didn't understand the game here. She had walked in expecting a powerful faerie creature who would tear her apart with just one look. But this man? He was a human, like her. And he probably hadn't seen one of his own kind in a very long time.

She didn't have to convince him of anything. All she had to do was give him a little taste of the world he had been missing.

Freya looked over her shoulder at Eldridge, then snorted. "And I would have expected more from a fabled Magician. You're old, sir. And yet, I'm supposed to be afraid you'll cast me down with a curse?"

Yet again, another choked sound from Eldridge erupted before he leapt in front of her. "Please don't take her up on that. We both know you're very capable of cursing us into toads. I prefer her in the form she's in. If you don't mind."

The Magician watched the Goblin King's antics with a bemused smile on his face. "Yes, I imagine you are rather fond of this form. She's a beautiful young woman. And more intelligent than you."

Freya didn't want to torment poor Eldridge much longer. She'd taken a risk in teasing the old man, but she was certain the Magician would want to be treated like he was back home. Ribbed a bit for his age. Teased by someone who was much younger, while he still held all the power in this conversation. Obviously, she wouldn't be here unless she needed something from him.

She walked around Eldridge and grinned at the Magician. "I imagine it's been a long time since you've seen another human."

"And a talented one at that." The Magician struck the floor with the end of his cane. "What is your name, miss?"

"Freya."

"Ah, what a lovely name. Your mother must have had wonderful taste." He pressed a hand to his chest. "My name is Soren. And Arabella is over there, if you have a care to meet her."

She followed the line of his finger to the Madame Arabella who had foretold their arrival.

A human head sat on a small podium in the back corner. Her mouth was affixed open, her eyes as well. She had once been a lovely blonde with pouty lips and big blue eyes. Now, she was a frozen head who apparently spoke to the Magician whenever he wanted her to.

The reality of their situation crashed down on her head. Eldridge was right. She hadn't walked into some famed magician's workshop and wooed him because she was a mortal just like him. He was a dangerous man with more power at his fingertips than she could ever imagine.

She should treat him as such.

Gulping, she kept the smile on her face and returned her attention to the Magician. "I was hoping you could help us," she said. "We seek the wolf."

The Magician grimaced, but nodded. "Yes, I knew you were looking for that cursed beast. I thought maybe I'd get away from talking about him today. Come on, then. Have a seat and I'll get you some tea. You have questions that will take a long time to answer."

Freya didn't want to stay in this room any longer than necessary. Looking over her shoulder, she met Eldridge's wide-eyed gaze. Apparently, he was also in a rush to leave.

Unfortunately, neither of them could.

She kept the fake smile plastered on her face and said, "Tea sounds lovely."

CHAPTER 16

They sat at a table far from Arabella. Thankfully, Eldridge took the seat where the severed head remained within eyesight. Freya wasn't sure she would have been able to peel her eyes away from the macabre figure.

"He's not going to poison us, is he?" she whispered.

"I don't think so, but you were exceedingly rude to him so one can never know." Eldridge crossed his arms over his chest and glared at her. "Why can't you ever trust me? I said to woo him. Not to call him an old man incapable of magic."

"I didn't say he was incapable of magic." She didn't think. Freya could admit she'd gotten a little carried away in their banter.

It had seemed like the Magician was enjoying himself, though! How was she to know that he might get insulted? That's how he would have been treated in the mortal world. A little ribbing. Some fun jesting from a much younger woman. He had appeared to enjoy the comical moment.

Now, she wondered if it was all a big show so he could go behind the curtain near his desk and get poison to put in their tea. He was a magician, after all. No one would know where the Goblin King and herself had gone. It wasn't like Claude would remember and tell Arrow.

They were on their own here.

Cheeks burning, she wiggled lower in her seat. "I guess we just hope it's not poison, then?"

"If we're lucky," Eldridge snarled.

The curtain flipped open and Soren came back out with a pot of tea in one hand and three teacups floating in front of him. "I'm not going to poison either of you. You're both so dramatic."

Freya rushed to help him with the cups, her chair screeching on the floor in her hurry. She snatched all three out of the air and gently set them down on the table. "You could have asked for help, you know."

The Magician smiled at her, but there was an edge in his smile that made her a little frightened. "Trust me, Miss Freya. If I needed help, I would have asked for it."

She supposed he wasn't the type of person who needed help from anyone. "Well, you have survived this long on your own in the faerie realms. I don't think I'm the one to question you on whether or not you need help."

"And don't you forget it."

Soren set the teapot on the table and took a seat with them. There was one chair left empty, and Freya had a sickly feeling that it might be for Arabella. The Magician didn't bring his head over to the table with them, but there was still a presence in that chair that she could feel.

He took a long time pouring the tea. He made sure there were enough tea leaves in each cup and set a small mesh net down afterward. It was a rather clever contraption that would save them all the bitter taste of fresh tea leaves. Once he had poured the hot water, Soren clasped his hands and sighed. "Now we can talk. I find there's less to say without a cup of tea in my hands. Don't you agree?"

She wasn't sure. Freya had never had issues talking after she'd come into this realm.

But if the Magician wanted her to drink something, then she would drink. Freya lifted the cup to her lips and blew on the hot liquid. "I suppose you're right. You know why we're here, it seems."

"Werewolves. It's all anyone talks about in Mudgate." Soren shook his head in disapproval. "I never know why. They aren't all that interesting as far as magical creatures go. Easy to track. Easy to kill."

That was reassuring to hear. Especially from this magician who was unlikely to hide details. If they were going about finding a werewolf, then he would be honest in how difficult it was.

Or at least, she hoped he wouldn't hide any important facts.

Freya sipped the scalding tea. "I'm glad he'll be easy to kill. I was expecting you to tell us that it will be much more challenging."

"In a way, it will be. You can find the wolf. You can kill the creature. It's navigating the mines that you should be the most concerned about." Soren leaned back in his chair and eyed her with a look that suggested he knew something she didn't. "And perhaps what you might find about yourself as you walk through the magic mirrors. You are a curious one, my dear."

Eldridge nodded and took his own teacup in hand. "I've told her the same thing. Walking through a magical realm without control over her own powers is dangerous."

"Indeed it is. But, considering the look on the young madame's face, I don't think we're going to have this conversation for a while yet." Soren grinned. "Am I right, Freya?"

She was about to throw her teacup at both of them. Already Freya imagined sending the scalding liquid into Eldridge's lap and knocking the old man over the head with the porcelain cup. Maybe then they would take her a little more seriously.

Her magic wasn't what they were here to talk about. And yes, she understood that there was something strange going on with her.

She'd cast a few spells in the Winter Court, and she didn't know how she'd done them. It was almost a natural response to something she wanted, which no human should be able to say. And yet, here she was.

More confused than ever.

But she would answer those questions soon. Not here when they should use this time to find out more about the werewolf, her mother, and the terrors the pixies lived with every single day.

Instead of arguing or hitting the two of them over the head as she wanted, she lifted her teacup again and took a steadying breath of peppermint. "We're not talking about that right now. We're talking about how to find the werewolf and my mother."

"Your mother?" Soren sat up straighter, his eyes wide and his shoulders suddenly broad. "Your mother's name wasn't Astrid, was it?"

Her blood ran cold through her veins. "That was my mother's name, yes. The Spring Maiden sent us here because she thought we might be able to find her. She was last seen here. The werewolf dragged her away after she tried to save a pixie from him."

Soren's chair screeched as he stood. He tapped his fingers on his head, drumming them like he was playing the piano on his temples. "No, no, no. This isn't right. You shouldn't be here, that's what he said."

"Who said?" Freya stood as well, trailing the old man through his workshop. "Did my mother talk with you?"

He shook his head and backed away from her. Soren's shoulder clipped one of the shelves, and all the jars that contained shimmering dust rattled where they were kept. "I won't say a word. Not to you, not to anyone."

But that wasn't right! She was here to find her mother, and he knew where she was! Or he'd spoken with her. Something had obviously come to pass. Some reason why he didn't feel like he could tell Freya about her own mother.

It wasn't fair.

It wasn't right.

She hadn't come all this way to be so disappointed because an old man wouldn't tell her what he knew!

Anger blasted out of her in a shattering echo that thundered through the workshop. Energy seared through the air, making the jars rattle even more and blowing Arabella's hair behind her. Even the severed head opened her eyes even wider, as though she was shocked that a mortal had powerful magic.

Freya pressed her shaking hands against her belly and tried to look like she was strong. But really, she was horrified at what she'd done.

Nothing like that had ever happened. Nothing had ever proven so forcefully that both Eldridge and Soren were right. She had magic, and she had no idea how to control it.

"That," Soren said, lifting a gnarled finger and pointing at her. "That is why your mother didn't want you to know where she was."

But that was cruel. And wrong. If her mother knew something about Freya's past that would explain all this, then Freya had a right to know. She had the right to understand why her mother had hidden so much from her daughters.

Her hands were shaking even more now. That anger and disappointment bubbling in her chest.

Soren twisted his hand in the air, and she felt something come down over her shoulders. As though he'd drawn a wet blanket over her that was heavy and lined with... something. Something that wouldn't let her even attempt to use magic.

"No more in my shop," he growled. "I don't care that no one taught you how to control it, little girl. There are too many priceless objects in here for you to break them with carelessness."

Eldridge stood and joined them by the shelves. He put his arm over her shoulders and drew her back to the table. "Sit, Freya. I imagine you are tired after such a show."

She wasn't, that was the strange thing. She'd also thought to be tired by what had happened, but she felt more awake and invigorated than before.

Soren reluctantly met the Goblin King's gaze. "I won't help anymore, if that's what your plan is. I think I've made it very clear where I stand. Sending your untamed witch on me won't change my mind."

"I wouldn't dream of it," Eldridge replied. He held his hands tucked behind his back, ever the gentleman and the politician. "I've been around longer than her, you know that. I'm here to make a trade for information. Not about her mother, but about the wolf. We still need to find it."

Soren narrowed his eyes. "What's the trick, fae?"

"No trick. I want to get out of this damned mining town sooner rather than later. And if that means a trade, then that's what we'll do."

A calculating light bloomed behind the Magician's eyes. "What are you willing to give?"

Freya was the one who answered. "Anything."

Sure, Eldridge could glare at her all he wanted after that declaration, but she meant it. If he asked for her soul in trade for finding out where her mother was, then she would willingly give it.

Perhaps that was her greatest flaw. She would do anything for her family. Even give herself up.

Eldridge sighed and pinched his nose. "We will not give you anything. Ignore my companion's ridiculous statement. But I will let you take a bit of her magic to research it, or add to your own collection. That's up to you, Magician."

Soren vibrated with glee. He burst into movement that was surprisingly swift for a man his age. He charged through the room, grabbing bottles off shelves and holding them in his arms. Though he did pause for a second to whisper something in Arabella's ear. The head closed her mouth and then smiled with a wicked grin.

If that wasn't unsettling, then Freya didn't know what was. She shivered with disgust as the Magician approached her, a vial outstretched.

"You will not fight me on this," he warned. "It'll only hurt even worse."

She supposed she didn't have a choice.

Freya braced her hands on the arms of the chair and stared straight ahead. The sensation was very similar to when Eldridge had taken power from her back in the Winter Court. It felt like someone was pulling at her soul, yanking off a piece that might have been important, but she wasn't all that certain why.

Her stomach flexed, and Freya felt something coming out of her mouth. Gagging, she opened her lips and a pale mist erupted from her throat. It spiraled through the air toward the small vial the Magician held out.

"Yes," he muttered. "That's it."

Finally, the Magician corked the vial and everything stopped. Freya slammed her back against the chair and heaved in a breath. How strange. How awful.

Soren lifted the vial and watched the mist swirling inside it. "This is impressive. I wonder what I'll find when I really look through it. What do you think it is, Freya?"

Brows furrowed in confusion and fear, she shook her head. "I don't know."

"We'll find out, eventually." He pocketed the mist and then held out a small, circular jar.

There was a tiny light inside it. Freya took the bottle and realized the light was the smallest person she'd ever seen. A tiny woman with glowing skin and bright wings that she gently beat inside the bottle.

Soren tapped the side, and the woman fell onto the bottom of the glass. "A will-o'-the-wisp. Dangerous creatures if not contained, but she'll be able to lead you to the werewolf."

"How?" Eldridge scoffed. "She's a faerie who's likely been in that bottle for many years. You can't expect us to believe she will lead us through the mines."

"She used to work in them. This was one of the faeries who guided miners to their doom. She liked to watch the werewolf tear their wings off." Soren bared his teeth in a dark grin. "When a dwarf captured her in a jar, I paid a pretty price to have her on my shelf. If anyone knows where to go, it's this one."

Freya's stomach churned. Having someone guide them who wanted to see people get killed, felt a little like asking a butcher to watch her pig for a few hours. "How do we know she won't lead us to the slaughter?"

"You don't." Soren waved a hand, and suddenly her chair careened toward the door. "Now get out of my shop."

CHAPTER 17

It took them a while to get back to the inn, but they still beat Arrow. And though their companion had found them some food, Freya didn't feel like she could keep anything down. Not yet, at least.

Her mother had really been here. Now it wasn't just the Spring Maiden claiming that Astrid was in this court.

Suddenly, this all felt too real. She hadn't realized how it would feel to know that she had been lied to. Or perhaps more accurately, that she'd wasted so much time because she'd been certain no one could survive that long in the wild.

Did this mean her father was alive too? Had they both been waiting for her to find them, help them, save them, only to realize that they were alone?

It turned her stomach for days.

Both Arrow and Eldridge agreed they had to wait a little while to go into the mines. They needed the proper tools, and then they needed a guide who could actually get them through without causing a cave in.

Few miners were likely to help them. Arrow had decided he would be the one to talk with the pixies, namely because neither Freya nor

Eldridge looked trustworthy. At least Arrow fit in here with his grubby, dirt smudged nose and constant scowl.

Freya and Eldridge stood out too much. So, they were both stuck in the inn. Together. When all she wanted was to move, and all he wanted was for her to slow down.

It was frustrating, to say the least.

A week later, she wandered to the inn's bar in the hopes that she might find Claude. At least he had pleasant conversation and a bottle of whiskey to spare. She wasn't sure where he was getting all the alcohol, considering it always appeared that he had very few bottles left, but she never failed to find him underneath the bar where he had drank himself the night before.

Unfortunately, it did not appear that Claude was there today. In fact, she couldn't find him at all.

Freya braced herself on the bar and peered underneath it. Nothing. No pixie man and no scent of alcohol either.

"Strange," she muttered. "I thought he would be here."

If he wasn't here, then where in the world was Claude? She wasn't all that confident the pixie man even stayed in one of the rooms. She thought it more likely that he was always close to the bar and the front door.

Whether that was because of his fear for the werewolf, or his fear that someone might steal his alcohol, she'd never know.

Freya straightened and blinked her eyes in shock. The room had changed into something else entirely. Or... well. Somewhere else.

Candles decorated every surface. Wax had splashed around their bases, dripping off the tables and leaking onto the floor in delicate puddles of cream. The warm light danced in a slight breeze that she didn't quite remember feeling before. Tiny faerie lights hung in loose arches from the ceiling like a network of tiny stars.

"What is this?" she murmured, walking around the corner of the bar and out into the main area of the inn.

By the door, a trail of rose petals littered the floor. They led back to the stairs she had walked down just moments ago. More pale candles melted onto the railing of the stairs, delicately creating a lace-like pattern of wax. The rose petals spilled over the stairs as well, leading all the way up the warm wood.

She followed the path to the top of the stairs. A faint tickle trailed from her toes all the way up to her head. Freya lifted her arms and marveled as the Goblin King's magic rewove the fabric of her pants and shirt. He turned the entirety of her clothing into a graceful, silken night dress. Simple but elegant.

What was he up to?

Heat bloomed in her chest. He'd gone through a lot of trouble to make this moment special, and she could only guess at what he wanted.

Freya put her palm on the door and pushed it open. The Goblin King stood in the center of their room, wearing his own matching set of pale silk sleep pants and an unbuttoned shirt. The floor was covered in red rose petals and a fire danced in the hearth, turning the dismal sadness of their room into a warm and inviting place. He held a bouquet of white roses in his hand that he held out for her to take.

"I thought you might want an evening to ourselves," he said, watching his fingers on the thorns. "A lot has happened since we came here, my hero. And for all that we've done, I know you have been overwhelmed."

She took the offered roses and buried her nose in their petals. They smelled like spring, when metal and soot had filled her nose for weeks now. Sighing, she held the roses against her heart. "I suppose it has been a little overwhelming."

"A little?" He raised his brow. "I went through all this work for nothing, then?"

Freya snorted. "You used magic to do all this and we both know it."

"Maybe." Eldridge held out his arm for her to take and guided her toward the fireplace. "But I asked both Arrow and Claude to give us some private time together. They're both out at another establishment, probably getting into horrible trouble if I know my companion."

He was probably right. Arrow loved to enjoy himself when he was given leave.

Setting her fingers on his arm, Freya followed him to the blast of heat that rolled off the fireplace. Together, they sat down on the rose petals that filled the air with their lovely scent. She set the bouquet beside them and sank her fingers into a sheepskin that he'd placed beneath the petals. "You put a lot of effort into this, I'll admit that."

"Thank you." He hesitated, swallowed hard, then asked, "Do you like it?"

For such a powerful man, he could be rather bashful about this. Freya wondered how many times he'd gone out of his way to make a day special for another person. Or even to woo another faerie woman that might have haunted his dreams once.

The flare of jealousy in her chest was a warning to stay away from such thoughts. This was about him and her, not whatever image of perfection her mind conjured up.

Impulsively, she reached out and cupped his face with her hand. "It's perfect, Eldridge. Thank you for thinking about me."

He grinned and tilted his head into her palm. "This isn't all, you know. I wouldn't be so careless as to set this all up without something for us to eat and drink."

With a flourish of his hand, a plate appeared in front of them. It was laden with cheese, meat, and grapes. Another flick of his wrist brought about a glass pitcher full of red wine, and two gold goblets.

"Impressive," she said with a quirk of her brow. "Where did you get all this from?"

"My own court," he replied defensively. "I'm not stealing from anyone, if that's what you're insinuating."

"Just checking." Freya reached for a grape and popped it into her mouth. Flavor exploded on her tongue, far more than she remembered with fruit from the mortal realm. "Is this going to doom me to the faerie realm for good? My mother used to say a person couldn't eat faerie food unless they wanted to be trapped forever."

He reached past her and took a few grapes of his own, setting them on his tongue one by one. "If you're stuck here, then I suppose I am too. I don't think that rumor is true, though. I've seen mortals eat our food and return to their home when their faerie captor grew bored with them."

"Have you? How many mortals have you seen in the faerie realms?" Freya was morbidly curious if there were more people like her. People who had come hoping to save someone, and who had eventually failed.

"Hundreds." Eldridge grinned. "Would you like to hear the stories?"

"Absolutely."

And so they passed the evening with him telling her countless tales about the humans who had tried to win their siblings back. She listened with rapt attention, laughing at the right points and solemnly nodding at their failures.

In a way, all the stories were the same. They either wished away their sibling, or the foolish child had made the same mistake as Esther. Their sibling had traveled all the way to the faerie realm and been given a few tasks by the Goblin King. Some were very difficult, most were rather simple in nature.

No one had bested him until her.

"It's rather sad, don't you think?" She had laid her head in his lap over an hour ago. "They are willing to go through so much trouble to get their family member back, but you always knew they would fail."

"I suppose." Eldridge ran his nails through her hair, gently raking her scalp. "But now I wonder if they were all practice for the moment I would meet you."

What a fanciful thing for him to say. Freya didn't think he was preparing for her. He hadn't even known she was alive! And yet, the questioning expression on his face made her wonder if he was really considering such an insane thought.

"Eldridge," she said, sitting up to look him in the eye. "You don't really think you were preparing for me this whole time, do you? That's a ridiculous thing to say. I wasn't even born when many of these people were in the faerie realm."

"No, you weren't." He cupped her face in his hand, stroking his thumb over the peak of her cheekbone. "But that's how it goes with faeries, you know. We only find someone who completes our souls once in a lifetime. Every step of our existence is preparing us for meeting that person. If we lose them, then it is a fate worse than death. A parting of a soul that has torn into a thousand pieces, never to be healed again."

Her tongue stuck to the roof of her mouth. Was he saying she was his soulmate? Wasn't that as good a declaration of love as she would ever get?

Maybe it was the wine talking, or maybe it was that she'd wanted this for so long, but Freya was finished with talking. He'd made certain that her evening was special and that no matter what, she felt like they were together. Even while hunting a serial killer and tracking down her long lost mother.

She cupped his neck ever so gently. Freya scraped her nails down the back of his head and neck, lingering on the cords of muscles that worked in a swallow. No more words were necessary between them. Not tonight, at least.

Tugging him toward her, she kissed him as if she were trying to brand a promise against his lips. That she would always appreciate his attempts at romance. And no matter how far life drew them away from each other, she would always let her heart sing for him.

He slid his tongue along the seam of her mouth, reaching forward to hold on to her jaw. Freya let him. She flexed her fingers on the back of his neck, then climbed into his lap. One leg on either side of his hips, she finally felt like she was where she belonged.

Eldridge wrapped his arm around her waist, holding her jaw with the other, and slowly rocked himself against her.

Though he was stiff and hard, Freya didn't find herself frightened of what would come next. She'd never been with a man before, had only heard rumors from other girls in the village when they spoke of their secret lovers. She had thought this moment would terrify her.

Instead, all she could think about was the flavor of sugar on his tongue. His hands gripped her waist, not bruising or punishing. Eldridge learned the shape of her body with every gentle press of his fingers.

Wrenching away from her lips, Eldridge pressed his face into the crook of her neck. He inhaled deeply, then set his teeth to the place where her neck met shoulder.

Freya gasped as something happened in her body. A clenching sensation along with a flood that forced her hips to glide against his. Rocking back and forth as she had never done before.

He breathed out a long sigh in her ear. "You are mine, Freya of Woolwich. Mine and mine alone."

"Not yet," she replied. Freya teased the seashell of his ear with her tongue, biting down on the lobe hard before adding, "Not until you make me yours, at least."

His hands flexed on her back and a low growl reverberated through his being. "Don't challenge me, Freya."

Oh, it wasn't a challenge, it was much more than that. Freya wanted him to devour her mind, body, and soul. She wanted to forget that they were in a freezing cold inn and that she didn't know where her mother was. She wanted to forget everything but them for a night.

Licking her lips, she leaned back even as she continued rocking on his lap. "I want to make a deal with you, Goblin King."

His eyes flashed bright silver. "I thought you were done with deals?"

"I guess I'm not after all." Her next words would take more bravery than she felt, but magic pulsed through her veins. Freya swallowed and said, "Make me enjoy this, Goblin King. And I will give you the entire night."

The tufts of hair on his ears moved as though the pointed tips twitched on their own. "Oh, I'll need much more than a single night, Freya."

And with that, the time for talking ended. The fire flared bright behind her back as the Goblin King slid his hands up her thighs. He drew the fabric sensually over her skin. Taking his time so he knew she was feeling every slide of silk. Freya tilted her head back and closed her eyes.

His hands slid higher, drawing the nightgown to her hips and revealing her glistening center to his gaze. She gasped. Eldridge slid a single finger through her folds as his other hand continued to push the silk higher.

Lips and teeth took hold of her nipple as he stroked her core. Freya heard a moan follow a long sigh. She was tense in his arms, waiting for something. Anything. Some peak or tension that she hadn't realized a man could bring her to.

The swirl of magic pressed against her back. She relaxed into the sensation of another set of hands, knowing without a doubt that it was the Goblin King. He drew the nightgown up over her head and then pressed both his palms to her inner thighs, spreading her even farther.

Hours might have passed where he teased her with lips, tongue, and fingers. Or it might have been seconds. She didn't know. All she could focus on was the sensation rising in her body, waiting and hoping that he would listen to her every gasp.

Eldridge rolled her on top of him, then eased his hands down her arms and drew her hands to his shoulders where he pressed them firmly. He stroked his hands down her sides, settling over her hips where he gently lifted her.

She felt the tip of him press against her entrance, but again, no fear. This was what she wanted. No, what she needed.

He didn't move her again. Instead, she felt his hands relax on her hips even as his shoulders shook beneath her hands. He wasn't going to force anything, instead, he was letting her take the lead.

Freya opened her eyes and stared down into that moonlit gaze. She shifted her fingers, tensed her thighs around his hips, and lowered herself onto him. Inch by mind numbing inch.

He shuddered, eyes rolling back in his head. The deep, guttural moan that erupted from his chest sent a zing of electricity to her very core.

When she was fully seated upon him, it felt natural to keep moving. She rose and fell, riding the waves of sensations until she just barely reached a peak. Only to have it fall out of reach. Over and over again.

Finally, he groaned again and took hold of her hip firmly. He held onto her, settling her into a different rhythm, their movements more powerful. Eldridge kept one hand on her hip and eased the other between them, pressing between her legs on some part of her body that made her back arch.

There it was. That was what she had been looking for.

Sweat glistened on both of their skin, and in that moment of rising she thought they both looked like they were covered in diamond dust.

His magic pressed her down harder. His fingers turned bruising as he gripped her, making her move faster while he stroked that impossible place she hadn't realized existed.

She rose higher.

Higher.

Then the stars opened up, and she saw oblivion.

Freya cried out in his grip, holding onto him as he arched into her, plunging deeper a few more times before stilling with his lips pressed against her neck.

It was done, and yet it still felt as though she had been filled with some kind of impossible magic. He was still inside her, stretching her almost to discomfort, and yet... she didn't want to let him go. She didn't want to move from his chest while he held her limp body against his own.

Freya could hear his heart beating against her ear. She tasted the salt of his skin, no longer sweet, but mortal and fae mixed into one.

And she didn't regret what they had done.

Pressing a kiss to his shoulder, she tucked her head into the crook of his neck. "I think you won our deal, Goblin King."

He chuckled, still breathing hard. "Well, at least I beat you once."

Freya didn't even try to stop the smile on her lips. He made her happy, and she couldn't remember the last time she'd felt like this. Or if she had ever been this happy before him.

The Goblin King made her feel real. Like she was more than just a mortal. More than a woman who lived in the forest. She was Freya to him, and he worshipped the very ground she walked on. He'd proven that with every kiss he pressed into her skin.

Eldridge shifted, pulling himself from her and leaving her empty. With a soft moan, she tried not to let him go.

He chuckled, "My dear, I'm just moving us to the bed rather than the floor."

"Why would we do that? The bed is covered with bugs."

He stood, then scooped her up into his arms. "It is not, because I cleaned it. And I believe the deal said I get you all night, now." He grinned down into her shocked expression. "A deal is a deal, Freya."

CHAPTER 18

Freya woke the next morning and reality hit her over the head like a tree had fallen on top of her. She'd slept with the Goblin King. And not just slept, really. They had spent the entire night exploring each other's bodies, learning the sighs and moans that came from each other's lips, and...

Oh god.

She would never get the image of him out of her head. Freya would look at him and every time would remember the tension in his features as he leaned over her. She'd see the cords of his neck as he threw his head back while he was deep inside of her.

Sure, she'd known this was where they were going. Of course they were approaching that singular moment when they would finally taste the forbidden.

Freya just hadn't realized how embarrassed it would make her feel. After all, she was still draped over the Goblin King's chest, completely naked, and he was fast asleep. Likely Eldridge wouldn't feel awkward at all, but how many times had he done this?

She had never felt another person's touch like that. Never been that close to a living being, and... well. It was a little overwhelming. Like everything else in her life.

Freya peeled herself off him, taking care not to wake the sleeping Goblin King. Tip toeing across the room, she gathered her clothing and pulled them on. The nightgown had turned back into her shirt and pants. The flowers and candles had disappeared. The room had returned to the dismal, disappointing atmosphere it had been when they first arrived.

This was where her first time had been. In a mining town's inn. On a bug ridden bed in the middle of nowhere.

Her first time was supposed to be something to remember. Something honorable and wonderful and... and...

Freya shook the thoughts out of her head. Those were romantic things to think about, but real life wasn't a fairytale, nor a romance. If she had wanted to be wooed like that, then she should have approached him when they were both in the Goblin Kingdom. Then she would have had the experience to tell others about.

Shaking her head, she gently opened the door inch by painstaking inch, waiting for the squeaking hinges to wake him. When he remained asleep, she squeezed herself through the small gap and padded down the stairs.

Hopefully Arrow had returned and found something. Then she could get her mind off what they had done. She could focus on the future and put all her mind power into planning their next steps.

As luck would have it, Arrow was waiting for her by the bar. He and Claude were bent over, whispering to each other as if someone might overhear their plotting.

Freya snuck up behind them, then cleared her throat. "What are you two up to?"

Claude straightened so quickly she heard his back crack. He let out a startled squeal, then relaxed when he saw who was standing in front of them. "Miss Freya! You are impressively quiet for a human. I didn't even hear you come downstairs."

The goblin dog sniffed and wagged his tail. "Neither did I, which is impressive on its own. And we weren't up to anything, I'll have you know."

"I found you two huddled together in the shadows, whispering."

Freya lifted a brow. "I'd think that the body language of two faeries up to something."

His eyes canted to the side, and Arrow finally heaved a sigh. "Fine. We were just talking about who was going to wake you two. We need to get going."

She kept her brow lifted and stared him down. That wasn't everything. She wasn't a fool. And he would have to tell her the rest if he wanted her to move. Now, all she had to do was see which one of the faerie men broke first.

Arrow was far too stubborn to give in to her disapproval. He stared right back at her with his own brows furrowed in a glare, teeth slightly bared in an impressive snarl.

But Claude caved like a stack of cards. "We were musing about what we'd find when we interrupted you and the Goblin King. That's all. Arrow thought you two were caught in a lovers' embrace. I thought it more likely you were both exhausted after dealing with the Magician. He's quite terrifying, as you know."

She did know how terrifying the Magician was. Freya wouldn't forget that experience soon, but she was also disappointed that the two faeries were gossiping. How terribly beneath them to speak of her own private life. And time.

Squaring her shoulders, she used her best motherly disappointed face and glared at them. "The Goblin King and my private time is none of your business. Either of you. I think there are more useful things for the both of you to be doing than gossiping about what was happening upstairs."

Eldridge's voice echoed down from the stairs. "Oh, go easy on them, Queen Killer. Curiosity is the natural state of a faerie."

She tensed at the sound of his footsteps approaching them. What was she supposed to say after doing that with him all night? Good job? Should she pat him on the back and congratulate him for spending the entire evening on her body, just as he had said he would?

Awkwardness spread through her until she didn't know what to do with her hands. She crossed them over her chest, then thought that might seem like she was pushing her breasts up for him to look at. So she shifted onto one foot, then felt like he might consider that a rather tantalizing pose.

Arrow watched her every movement, frowned, then looked between the two of them as Eldridge finally joined them. "Good heavens and faerie realms, I was right, wasn't I?"

"Right about what?" she snarled.

"You two—" He waved a paw between them and then pressed it against his mouth. Arrow gagged a little, then added, "You were together."

Panic raced through her veins. She looked at Eldridge, then back at the goblin dog. "Stop it, Arrow."

Eldridge tossed an arm over her shoulders and tugged her against his side. "What's the matter? I don't care if he knows. Let them talk. We're the only two that know what actually happened last night."

If he continued talking, she was going to burst into flames. Her cheeks already burned so hot she was afraid they would sear. "All of you stop it. I don't want to talk about this in front of an audience."

The grin on Eldridge's face was far too proud. She hadn't even said he had done a good job, yet he was acting like she had called him a god. This wasn't fair. She didn't want to publicize her private life!

She shook his arm off her and stepped away from them all. "I'll say it one last time, I'm not talking about this with all of you."

Every face in the room fell. As if they all suddenly realized that she was very uncomfortable and they were the ones who had made her feel that way. Good, let them be guilty. They'd all stepped out of line and she wanted them to feel bad about it.

Crossing her arms over her chest, Freya hugged herself tight. "Arrow, did you find someone who can bring us to the mines?"

He was staring at her with those sorrowful eyes. Obviously he knew he'd done something wrong, but he didn't know what that wrong thing was. Finally, he cleared his throat and nodded. "Yes, I think I did. I still think it'll be equally dangerous, but at the very least, we won't get lost."

Good, at least she could focus on that rather than the knowledge that everyone now knew she lost her virginity. Idiots.

Freya knew they had meant nothing by it. They were all merely happy that their loved ones had taken a step toward being more of a couple and less of two people trying to figure out where the other person was. She understood that. But publicly talking about it all?

She had to draw the line somewhere.

Wincing, she took a step back and leaned against the bar. "Who is it?"

He shook his head, ears flopping against the side of his cheeks before replying. "Well, there aren't a lot of savory sorts around here, so I will say I'm not sure that we can entirely trust him. But he works in the mines, and said he goes to the areas most won't because that's where the good mirror ore is."

Eldridge turned his gaze from her and frowned at the goblin dog. "Why does he go where others won't? That seems suspicious."

"I thought the same," Arrow replied. "But he wants to get out of here, so he's willing to take risks others won't. He said he needs to get back to his family sooner rather than never. The more ore he gathers, the better it is. He'd rather get the money and run, even if it costs the tunnel collapsing on his head."

Freya wasn't entirely opposed to following a risk taker like that. It sounded as though the pixie knew how to get around the mines, and that's what they needed. The tunnels were where the werewolf hid. And potentially where her own mother waited for them to save her.

"All right," she said, bracing her fists on her hips. "So he thinks he can take us through the mines, and perhaps to the werewolf?"

"Maybe." Arrow looked up at Claude, then back to them. "I've yet to find a pixie who will really talk about the beast. They're all terrified of him."

Claude snorted and headed to the back of the bar where he kept his spirits. "And for good reason. A lot of the older pixies refuse to talk about the beast because they're certain even mentioning his name will summon him to your house. I'd keep your voice down if you're saying the word in the mines. They're more likely to kill you for speaking the wolf's name than guide you through the tunnels."

"So we need to keep it quiet that we're hunting the beast." Freya tapped a finger to her chin, still angling her body away from the others.

"How are we going to convince this pixie to take us where we need to go, then?"

Arrow coughed into his paw, then sat down on all fours. "That's the problem, unfortunately. We're not going to convince any miners to take us where the werewolf is hiding. For two reasons. The first being that none of them know where he is. The second is that... well. This was the only miner I could find who would guide us at all, and he'll only take us to where they build the mirrors. Anything else, any other exploring, he made it very clear that we're on our own."

Right. Of course. Because why would it be so easy as to have a guide that would take them directly to the creature they were hunting.

She lifted her hands and cracked her knuckles. "Then how in the world are we going to find the wolf?"

"Easy." Eldridge reached into his pocket and drew out the tiny faerie trapped in the jar. She was bright blue today with her hands pressed on the glass walls that kept her away from the fresh air. "I do believe that's why the Magician gave her to us, after all. She's going to lead us directly to the werewolf. Aren't you, my dear?"

The will-o'-the-wisp stuck out her tongue at the Goblin King, then sat down hard on her bottom. She ignored all of them staring at her, and Freya worried that meant she wasn't planning on helping at all.

That little faerie creature was their last hope of finding the werewolf before the monster found them.

Sighing, she turned her gaze up to the ceiling and sent a silent prayer to the heavens. "I guess there's no time like the present, then. Shall we go find our pixie guide?"

They left Claude at the inn with a hefty purse full of gold and a few hugs goodbye. He'd teared up a little when they left, saying how he wished they would find Freya's mother and thanking them for giving him the chance to leave this horrible place.

Freya could only hope it was enough money to get him home. Of all the people she'd met here thus far, Claude had made a special impact on her. The kindly alcoholic deserved a little happiness in his life. At whatever cost.

Arrow led them through the winding streets, past multiple stores and a hundred faeries with haunted eyes. The deeper they got into Mudgate, the worse poverty she saw.

If only they could help all of them. More than taking care of the murderous werewolf plaguing their home.

Finally, Arrow paused in front of a door that was cut crooked so it fit into the wall that was nearly falling over. "He lives here. Said to meet him early if we wanted to have a guide." Arrow's nose twitched. "He didn't say what early was, though. Hopefully, we're not too late."

The door slammed open at the end of his words. "You are late, dog. But I had a feeling you were coming and free gold is free gold."

The pixie who stepped out to lock the door was entirely unexpected. Freya was used to their kind looking delicate and beautiful. Like the petal of a flower plucked from the stem.

She couldn't guess what flower this man had come from, but maybe it was something thorny.

He was huge. His shoulders spanned the entire doorway and then some, so large that he'd had to tilt his body to get out of his house. And rather than the zipper she was used to seeing the pixies wearing ragged silver scars were visible through his threadbare shirt. His dark skin glistened around the marks, as though magic was trying to heal him and to grow back the wings that had once been there.

Had he ripped them off himself? Or had someone else surgically taken them off?

Freya tried to wipe the disgust from her face, but she feared she wasn't very successful. She couldn't understand how someone willingly gave up a part of themselves that was so beautiful. So rare.

He turned around and yellow eyes stared her down. "Well? You said you wanted to go into the mines, didn't you?"

Why was he looking at her?

Freya looked to her companions, then back to the pixie. "I do want to search the mines. My mother is said to still be in there, and I plan on finding her."

The pixie never looked away from her gaze. Those piercing yellow eyes saw through her words and into the quaking of her very soul. "If your mother was lost in the mines, you aren't going to find her."

"I think I will." She straightened her shoulders and refused to let him intimidate her. She would find her mother if that was the very last thing she ever did. Just because he was a miner, didn't mean he knew everything about the place.

Apparently, he thought differently. The miner snorted, then shrugged. "Sure. If you want to get lost in the mines with her, be my guest. Follow me to the mirrors and that's where we part ways. I'm not looking for a woman foolish enough to get her head turned around by the mirror ore."

And with that, he walked away from them. He didn't even look over his shoulder to see if they were following him.

Freya looked at Eldridge, who shrugged. He started after the miner with a quick statement tossed over his shoulder. "I guess we better follow him."

She supposed that was one way to look at it, but if this man was so certain they were paying him for nothing, shouldn't he actually play the part of a guide? At least he could tell them something about the mines.

Hurrying to catch up with the man, she strode beside him and reached out a hand for him to shake. "My name is Freya. What shall we call you?"

"Whatever you want to call me, human." He didn't even look at her. "We won't know each other for long enough to care what the other's name is."

"Why would you think that?" she asked, frowning. He could at least pretend that he was interested in their plight.

Surely it wasn't often that a human and two goblins ended up in the Spring Court asking someone to take them into the mines. He must have been at least a little curious about... well. Anything.

The miner shook his head. "I'm going to make it out of the mines tonight with more coins than usual. I'll eat my dinner, then rest my head on my pillow and forget I ever met you."

Disgruntled by how rude this man was, Freya clenched her teeth and snarled, "And you think I will remember you?"

"No." The miner turned down a side street sharply. "I don't think you'll leave the mine at all. You'll be in that cold, barren place, wondering if you should have listened to me in the first place. People like you don't belong in the mines, human. You'll be lucky to see the sun again."

Eyes wide, she tripped over her own feet. The miner stomped away and turned another sharp corner. Disappearing for a few moments before she could catch up with him again.

Eldridge put his hand on her shoulder and forced her to step back. "I don't think he wants to talk with you, my dear."

She couldn't imagine why. She was an unusual creature in this world, and he was about to bring them into a mine where he thought they would die. The least he could do was give them decent conversation. This man was so rude that it made her blood boil.

Frowning, she followed the miner quietly and tried not to take this personally. After all, they had a long way to go, and the miner seemed like he knew where he was taking them. At the very least, they would get to their destination in one piece.

The streets opened up to a wide area that looked as though a giant had taken a huge chunk out of the earth. She stared, wide eyed, watching as pixies zipped out of the cavernous maw with silver chunks of metal in their hands. The one nearest to her brought his large piece to a giant melting pot to their right. He dropped it in, made eye contact with another pixie who nodded, and then he flew back into the cavernous maw of the earth. Apparently to search for more.

The sun overhead wasn't quite as bright as it should be, though. The steam that came off the melting pot filled the air with a cloudy, thick substance.

Their miner grunted. "Don't breathe it in."

"Breathe what in?" Freya asked.

He pointed to the clouds. "That. Mirror magic is dangerous for faeries to inhale. I haven't got the faintest idea what it would do to you if you breathed it in."

Tip understood. She wouldn't take the risk.

Freya trailed along behind him, watching the miners with wide eyes. She was stunned that they could move so quickly. Some of the miners weren't using their wings. Most, actually. Even their miner got into a cart system that brought the others into the darkness of the earth.

The system was strange. She'd seen tracks like this before, but they were always for wealthy people to move around the kingdom. These rungs were rickety at best, and the cart was held together by steel bars. At least that looked sturdy enough. The seats were plain boards, uncomfortable and designed to be useful rather than aesthetically pleasing.

He gestured for them to sit in it with him. "Come on, then, There's no other way into the mines for the likes of us."

Freya waited for her companions to get in before settling against Eldridge's side. Her curiosity burned too hot to not ask, "Why don't you use your wings like some of the other faeries? It seems like it would be faster for you to gather ore and bring it back."

The miner glared at her, then reached forward for the center pull. "I don't owe you any answers, human. Remember that."

With a quick tug, the cart careened on the tracks down into the shadows.

Wind whistled in her hair and Freya's stomach rose into her throat. She let out a long scream that was stolen by the air blasting past them. She could see nothing but darkness. Shadows that moved in the distance, perhaps that were miners or... she didn't know. All she could think about was the speed that they were rolling on these tracks and how difficult it would be to stop this ridiculous cart from hitting the bottom.

Lights appeared on all sides. She caught glimpses of miners with their pickaxes, hacking away at the earth in the hopes that they would find some magical ore that would give them the ability to get back to their family. Just a nugget. Anything that could be put into that giant melting pot.

The cart slowed, and the lights illuminated their miner, who had leaned forward to grasp the brake system. Freya's stomach dropped back where it belonged, and she could breathe again.

Now that her back wasn't pressed against the cart, she could look around.

One of the pixies lifted his lantern high, illuminated the small piece of ore in his hand. It was silver and beautiful, but steam rose off it like it was hot. Considering he held it with a bare hand, she assumed it wasn't heat that was rolling off the metal. Instead, it had to be magic.

The miner gave another quick tug, and the cart rolled into a large chamber in the center of the mine. Metal squealed as they slowed again, but they stopped smoothly and with no jolt at the end.

"Here we are," he growled, hopping out of the cart and heading over to a large bucket that held a bunch of pickaxes and leather bags. "Good luck finding your mother, human. You'll need it."

She was still angry that he wasn't at least helping them any further. Was he incapable of feeling pity?

Stomping over to his side, she watched as he picked up an axe and held it up to the light. His skin gleamed like he was made of ore as well. Perhaps the mirror magic had rubbed off on this pixie who took his time inspecting his weapon of choice.

"Well?" she asked, fists on her hips. "Don't you have any words of advice for us as we wander through this labyrinth?"

"Not really." He dropped the axe down onto his shoulder and met her gaze. "Don't wander off like your mother. They aren't forgiving, and no one is going to save you. If you scream, no one will hear you. No one but the wolf, that is. And if you want to find him, well, then you're just asking to be killed. Aren't you, little sparrow?"

With a jaunty whistle, he headed off for an empty mine shaft and left her standing there with her mouth open.

Eldridge joined her, chuckling though he was at least trying not to be too loud. "Miners aren't exactly the pixies you're used to, are they?"

She tried to close her mouth, but couldn't quite get over how rude that miner had been. "I don't understand. Why does everyone around here think that I'm going to get killed?"

He wrapped his arm around her shoulder and tucked her into his side. "Because they don't know the Queen Killer, my hero. No one has heard your story, and they're underestimating you."

Freya let him draw her away from the mines and back toward the center chamber, but something twisted in her stomach. Something that made her feel a twinge of fear for the first time since they'd been hunting this monster.

What if the miner was right?

"I think the smartest way to proceed is to ensure we have some direction to go," Arrow said. He drew them away from the cart system and padded through the tunnels with his nose in the air like he was actually a dog.

The wind had blown his fur up in comical directions. He looked very much like he'd been struck by lightning. Of course, he didn't care what he looked like when they were about to go into the tunnels to hunt a beast, but Freya still thought it was funny.

"Where are we going?" she asked.

"The miners said this tunnel would lead us to where the mirrors are created. If anyone knows the older tunnels, it's the dwarves." Arrow's ears perked up, standing straight on his head as he listened for any sound ahead of them. "The wonderful thing is that I adore dwarves. I'm very much looking forward to seeing some again."

Eldridge grabbed onto her arm and forced her to slow down. They lingered in the tunnel far away from Arrow, but still let him lead.

"What is it?" Freya turned toward those starry eyes and tried to keep them moving forward at a quicker pace. "I'm not talking about last night if that's what you're about to insist."

"No, I don't want to talk about last night," he hissed. "I'm trying to warn you about the dwarves."

"Arrow likes them. How bad could they be?" She remembered the stories her mother used to tell her about the creatures. They were wonderful beings with talents in metal and jewelry. Their only rivals were the goblins themselves.

Everyone knew goblin jewelry was cursed, though. That's why no self-respecting human would buy or take anything goblin made. Wearing such a gift would curse the wearer, and who knows what kind of curse that would end up being?

The dwarves were good, talented creatures who had moved into the faerie realms only because there were so few magical creatures left in the mortal realm. At least, that's what her mother always said.

"Arrow doesn't always have perfect taste," Eldridge hissed. "Dwarves are territorial at best. Just... keep quiet when we meet them, would you? They don't like humans, and Arrow has clearly forgotten that."

She thought he was overreacting. The Goblin King worried about her more than she worried about herself.

Rolling her eyes, Freya hurried to catch up to Arrow. "Sure. I'll be careful, as always."

If she wasn't mistaken, he muttered, "You're never careful," before catching up with her.

The tunnel opened up to the most incredible cavern. Large white marble pillars filled the space and connecting planks created walkways where hundreds of dwarves moved quickly. Hung on giant wires in between these columns was almost a hundred mirrors as well.

They were in every shape and size. Some circular, some large and rectangular. Some of them were even the size of her palm with ornate frames and tin handles.

The dwarves were rather unusual in shape and speed. They all had beards, even the women with their prominent breasts. Their legs were shorter than human legs, but she was surprised that they were still quite tall. In fact, they would have come up to her shoulder. Most of them, at least.

One of the dwarves raced by them, shouting to get out of the way because he was handling hot metal.

She jumped to the side and narrowly missed the steaming cloud of mirror magic that followed the dwarf.

"How can they breathe that in?" she asked.

Eldridge shrugged and held out his arm for her to go ahead of him. "Dwarves aren't like the rest of us. I hesitate to even call them fae. The rules don't apply to their kind. They can lie, cheat, steal. Their tongues aren't locked by the same magic as my kind and for that, it's hard to trust them."

She tilted her head to the side and raised a brow. "Do you not trust me? I can lie."

"I'm certain you can." He rubbed a hand over the back of his neck. "But I like to think you wouldn't lie to me. If given the chance."

Freya's face split with a blinding smile. "You're right. I wouldn't lie to you."

"Good." Together, they braved one of the strange wooden walkways and followed Arrow as his voice rang through the cavern.

"I love dwarves!" the goblin dog shouted. "Look at these mirrors. Are they not the most magical things you've ever seen?"

Freya couldn't take her eyes off them. Some of the mirrors seemed to have something, or someone, inside them. Shadows moved behind the glass. They twisted like a person was watching them traverse through the cavern.

She didn't know if she should be frightened or not. These weren't just magic mirrors. They were living things.

The dwarves weren't using their magic to create mirrors like in the stories. Mirrors that could tell the future or predict who a princess would marry. These mirrors had a mind of their own, and she could feel their power every time they walked by one.

It was unnerving.

Unnatural.

And yet, she still wanted to wake one up and see what it had to say to her. What if the mirror knew where her mother was?

"Freya." Eldridge put his hand on her shoulder and drew her away from the large standing mirror. "They're very mesmerizing to look at, but their magic is dangerous. You need to keep your wits about you in this place. Do you hear me?"

She did, but it was so hard not to look in the mirror. There was a shadow behind the glass in the shape of a woman. Was the mirror trying to tell her where her mother was? What if the mirror was already reaching out? Trying to get her to see where her mother had been hidden?

This was her moment. She just had to ask the mirror what she wanted and then... and then...

Two hands slapped both sides of her cheeks. Freya lunged away from the painful ache, blinking her eyes and holding her face in her hands. "What?" she snarled.

And there, standing in front of her, was a dwarf.

This must be a female dwarf because her breasts were rather impressive. Her beard was shorter than the others, trimmed neatly to her face and gelled swirls on her cheeks. Her dark hair was nearly black as night, and her searing blue eyes burned with anger. "What do you think you're doing, looking into a mirror like that?"

She had a thick accent with lilting tilts at the ends. Freya might have even enjoyed listening to the woman speak if she hadn't been scolding.

Still rubbing her cheeks, Freya frowned down at the other woman. "What do you mean? It's rather hard not to look into them. Don't you think?"

Eldridge pressed a hand to his mouth, snickering behind the dwarf. Why hadn't he helped Freya? After all they had done last night, she expected him to be a little more protective. He should have jumped to her defense and tossed the dwarf into the darkness below them.

But no. Of course not. The Goblin King was snickering into his hand like a child because Freya had been slapped twice at the same time.

She'd get him back later.

The dwarf planted her hands firmly on her hips and shook her head in disapproval. "This is why mortals aren't allowed in the mines. You get too wrapped up in the magic, and then what are we supposed to do? Make sure you don't wake up an evil mirror? It's not my job."

"Then what is your job?" Freya asked. She finally dropped her hands from her cheeks, even though they still stung horribly.

"I make the mirrors," the dwarf snarled. "And apparently now I'm supposed to watch you and make sure you don't break anything."

Freya had less intent on breaking any magic mirrors than she did dying in these mines. She knew how much bad luck she'd get from breaking a normal mirror, let alone one that had a mind of its own. "I'm not going to break anything."

"Accidents happen, and then you find yourself trapped in a dimension you didn't know existed." The dwarf walked away from them, shaking her head. "Follow me, would you? And stop trying to touch things."

She looked back to Eldridge, who shrugged, then followed the dwarven woman. Apparently they now had a new guide, and they hadn't even had to ask for one.

Speaking of... She frowned and called out, "You wouldn't have seen a black and white dog around, would you? I apparently lost my companion."

"Oh, he's waiting for us." The dwarf shouted back. "He's the one who found me and said you were getting yourself in trouble."

Freya sighed. Of course Arrow had said she'd gotten herself in trouble. He was worse than the Goblin King.

They picked their way across the ramparts and through the columns. Freya made sure she wasn't looking at any of the mirrors this time, lest they capture her attention so thoroughly that she couldn't break free. Besides, she didn't want to get slapped by that dwarf again.

The woman was stronger than she looked.

"Are we going to a tunnel?" she asked, leaning to look around Eldridge to the smaller dwarf ahead of him.

"We're going to the place where we keep all the finished mirrors. The ones we've put to bed." The dwarf rolled her eyes and picked up her pace. "My name is Rose, by the way. I make all the handheld mirrors here. The ones that are particularly dangerous for your kind."

"Ah." Freya smiled. "My name is Freya. This is Eldridge. He's—"

"A goblin friend," the Goblin King interrupted her. "I found her in the woods."

"The woods?" Freya mouthed when he looked back at her.

She could understand that he might not want the dwarves to know who he was. That was fine. The Goblin King in the mirror mines might make a few people feel a little uncomfortable. Especially if they hated having a human here this much.

But the woods?

Rose the dwarf chuckled, and the sound was the happiest she had made thus far. "That sounds like a mortal. She wandered into the Autumn Court then, hm?"

Eldridge laughed with her, likely at the thought of Freya being foolish enough to do that. "Something along those lines. It's a story we'll gladly tell you in return for a few directions."

"Yes, your goblin dog has already told us all of your plight. It's a horrible thing what happened to her mother." Rose's expression fell into one of great sadness. "I think we might be able to help you, but I fear you may already be too late. The werewolf likes to eat quickly, you see. His hunger is impossible to sate."

The words shivered down Freya's spine. She hurried to follow the dwarf into another cavern that opened up before them. This one ended with stairs leading to the floor, where countless mirrors stood with blankets over their reflective surfaces. Effectively hiding them from anyone who might seek to use their magic.

Freya thought it was rather adorable. The dwarves had actually put the mirrors to bed.

Rose stood in front of the largest mirror and planted her hands on her hips. She watched them with an angry expression, then blew out a breath. "Arrow, I believe you are hiding behind a mirror somewhere. You'll have to come out to listen rather than sneaking about like you've been doing."

The soft, padding sound of dog feet could be heard. A small black and white dog looked around a mirror to their right, his expression one of sincere apology. "I know that, Rose. I was just looking around. How often does one get an opportunity to be around this many magic mirrors?"

"Never, unless you're a dwarf. The three of you won't speak a word of this to anyone else either, do you understand?" The glare on the dwarf's face made it hard to think of doing anything other than agreeing with her.

Arrow joined them, and they all nodded their heads forcefully.

"Good," Rose snarled. "Then I will help you. And only because this werewolf is a threat to all magic mirrors. If he continues destroying the pixie population, then we will never get the ore we need. Dwarves are not miners. We are artists. I'm going to make that very clear right now in case any magical law enforcement gets their hands on your memories. I am doing this to help the dwarves and everyone else who might ever want to use a magical mirror."

Apparently whatever Rose planned on helping them with was breaking every dwarven rule in the book. Freya knew she should be solemn in this moment, and thankful that anyone would be willing to take this risk. But really, she was excited. Fueled by the energy in the room.

Rose pointed at Freya. "You. Come here and stand in front of this mirror."

"You said it was dangerous for a human to do that," she replied, trying very hard to not be too snarky.

"How adorable. The human remembers things." Rose rounded the mirror's edge and grabbed onto the sheet. "You'll be with me the entire time. I made this mirror when I was first apprenticing and learning how my magic can give life to metal. He won't dare harm you if I'm here."

It was a small reassurance, but Freya also realized it was the only one she was going to get.

Stepping up to the mirror, she took a deep breath and watched as the sheet fell away. This standing mirror had to be at least eight feet high. It towered over her with a silver ornate frame that was decorated with thousands of lilies. They might have been beautiful if Freya also didn't know how poisonous those flowers were.

This mirror was meant to be beautiful and deadly.

It heaved in a shuddering sigh and then a man stepped into view. He stood behind her reflection, and Freya belatedly realized that her two companions weren't in the mirror. It was only herself and the magic mirror right now.

He wasn't anyone she might have thought to be so powerful. The man had mousy brown hair and a soft, trustworthy smile. He wore a white peasant's shirt and brown pants. His features were unremarkable. If she had seen him in a crowd and someone asked her to point him out again, Freya didn't think she'd be able to. Maybe that was the magic.

"Hello," she said. "My name is Freya."

"And I'm your magic mirror," he replied. "What is it you seek?"

This all felt rather easy. She'd thought it would be difficult to convince the mirror to help her, or Rose. But they were all working together to get her to the werewolf... why? Because he was a plague upon the pixies?

She supposed that would make sense. Freya was so unused to faeries being helpful. But Eldridge had claimed the dwarves weren't fae at all, so maybe that was why this one was kinder.

"I'm looking for my mother," she said. Not the werewolf at all, but they were intertwined. No matter what she did, the werewolf always led back to her mother.

"Ah," the mirror said. "That's not what I was expecting you to say at all. Rose claimed you were looking for the wolf."

"I was." Freya felt like she was talking through water. Her voice wasn't loud enough, no matter how much she shouted. "I am. I want to stop the wolf, but I also want to find my mother."

"It's an interesting question, you see. Your mother's fate and that of the wolf are... the same. In a way." He frowned, shaking his head. "Even my magic cannot break through the guise of enchantment that wraps around your mother. She is hidden, covered in fur and flowers. It seems."

"Flowers?" The fur she could understand. After all, the werewolf had kidnapped her. Of course she would end up in some place that was full of the beast's shed. But flowers?

"Yes. In a meadow of sorts, I suppose that means she's in the Spring Court."

"In a way," Freya corrected. "She's here in the mines."

He frowned, and the background changed. He was suddenly in a tunnel, not like the one she stood in, but dark and dank. Stalactites hung from the ceiling and water dripped down on his shoulder. "This is the place that will bring you to her, but I cannot go any farther."

"This is one of many tunnels," she sighed. "I cannot find her if you don't give me more direction than that."

"My magic is strong. But whatever hides your mother from my gaze is far stronger."

Rose stepped into view behind Freya. "Can you show us more of the tunnel? I might know which one it is."

The mirror man nodded. "I can."

He moved to the side and Freya noticed a few adjoining tunnels split into this one. In a particular tunnel there was a minecart still full of ore, and a large cave in behind it. At the top of the ore pile was a single gemstone, glowing bright blue.

"There we go," Rose murmured. "I know exactly what tunnel this is."

CHAPTER 21

Rose brought them to an ancient tunnel in the cave system. Warning signs hung from every sturdy rock they could.

"Don't go this way."

"Danger ahead."

"Falling rocks and cave-ins."

This was the last place Freya wanted to be. It seemed of all places in the mine, this was the one that was the most dangerous. The pixies had over mined this area. Shafts overlapped and caused cave-ins. Every step was a cautionary one, and no matter how far ahead she moved, there was always the risk the next step would be her last.

Swallowing hard, she stayed very close to her companions and their guide. "How much farther?" she asked.

"Not much longer until we reach the place the mirror showed us," Rose replied. "But there's a lot farther for you to go after that, I imagine."

Eldridge touched a hand to the pocket where he kept the jarred faerie. "I think we'll be all right. We still have a few tricks up our sleeves to find the wolf."

The look the dwarf gave Eldridge was unimpressed. She knew he had more tricks, and she wasn't happy about it. "Just don't cause another cave in, you hear me? There are a lot worse things than the werewolf in this mine, and I understand if you have to run. But a cave in here might cause another one farther down. There are still people working nearby. They don't deserve death because all of you couldn't be careful like I warned you."

Maybe this was what the miner had warned them about. They were going into the mines, ones that had certainly caved in already, and that threat was the nightmare of novices like them.

Now, she could only hope that they all stepped carefully.

The darkness threatened to devour their torches. Every shadow shifted and moved on its own. Freya didn't know if that was because hidden ore still remained in the walls of this cave, or if her mind was playing tricks on her.

The walls weren't filled with anything. They were just stone. She had to keep telling herself that.

"Watch your head," Rose called back to them.

Arrow didn't have to, but Freya and Eldridge both put their hands over their heads to touch the ceiling. It got lower and lower until she was walking bent over. That's when Rose stopped guiding them and moved to the other side of the tunnel.

"This is the place," she said.

There was a tunnel that was caved in, but Freya didn't see the cart. "This can't be the place. We're missing the cart filled with ore."

Rose pointed to the collapsed tunnel. "It's behind those rocks."

"Then how are we supposed to get there?"

The dwarf set her pack down and pulled out a few lanterns. "Take these and look in the other tunnels. You want to find the cart, that's the first start. And then you can continue down the tunnel the mirror showed you behind the cart."

"No." Freya shook her head in disbelief. "You were supposed to bring us to the same tunnel. You said you knew where we needed to go."

"I did." Rose finished up placing all the objects on the ground, lit one lantern, and then dusted off her hands. "And I've gotten you as close as I know how. All the other tunnels are too dangerous. If you want to risk your life, then by all means. Do so. I won't go a step further."

She didn't give any of them a chance to argue. The dwarf disappeared back down the tunnel as if the jaws of the werewolf were gnashing at her feet. And then they were alone in the dark, yet again.

Freya couldn't have been more shocked if the dwarf had smacked her cheeks again before leaving. They had a guide for all of a few heartbeats before they were back on their own in the mines.

"You'd think she would have left us with a map at least," Freya snarled.

"There are no maps of this place," Eldridge corrected. "There are no maps of any mines. Those who work here, know the way. And those that don't? They get lost and someone eventually finds their body when they reopen the tunnels."

Well, that was ominous.

Freya stared into the darkness at the networks of shafts that splintered off all over the place. She couldn't guess which one would lead around the cave in and back down the tunnel they needed to walk into.

"Which way should we go?" she asked.

Both Arrow and Eldridge looked at each other, then settled down on the ground beside the lanterns. Why were they sitting? They still had a long journey ahead and stopping now would only be a waste of time. What if her mother needed them and they got there too late?

"Freya," Eldridge coaxed. "We can't go any farther until we get some rest. All of us need sleep."

"I'm not tired." She leaned down and reached for a lantern. "Resting now isn't an option. We have to keep moving."

He put his hand over hers, stopping her from lifting the metal light. "We will. Once we all rest our minds so we can manage this labyrinth appropriately. If we go into this blind, tired, and full of fear, we will get lost."

Her hand shook in his grip. "What if the werewolf finds us in the middle of this tunnel?"

"And I thought it impossible for you to let fear decide your actions." Eldridge tugged her down onto the stone floor beside him.

"Rest your head, Freya. We have to do this or we will make a grave mistake."

She didn't agree. Not at all.

But she also realized there was no argument here. She could try to navigate the tunnels alone, and she would most likely find herself lost within moments. She could take the jarred faerie. Wander through the tunnels following the bright light and hope the will-o'-the-wisp wouldn't lead her to certain death. But what would she do if the tunnel caved in? There would be no one to help her. No one to know.

Freya sat down with them and kept her mouth shut. She didn't argue, even though she disagreed with this choice. She kept her head down and decided it was smarter to listen to the faeries.

Both Eldridge and Arrow fell asleep quickly. She listened to the steady sound of their breathing and reminded herself that they were all safe. This place hadn't bested them yet, even though it had tried many times.

The dwarf had to be a cruel hearted woman to bring them all the way here and then dump them. She'd asked Rose for help! The mirror had seemed like it wanted to assist them as well, but Freya realized that very few people in the Spring Court were interested in helping those they did not know.

She settled on the ground beside her companions and let her mind wander away from this terrifying tunnel with all its threats of death. Her thoughts drifted back to an evening with the Goblin King, where he had only been interested in attending to her every whim and desire.

Freya didn't know how much time passed in that dreaming world. She remembered every detail of their secret night where they had finally explored every inch of each other's body. The sounds of his voice rang in her ears as she rolled over and opened her eyes.

Arrow was curled up in the crook of her body. His head laid on one of her arms and his breathing remained deep and quiet. He was a lovely little animal, even if he wasn't really a dog, her heart still twisted at the sight of his adorable sleeping face.

She rolled a bit more, trying not to disturb the goblin dog while also searching for Eldridge. She wouldn't put it past the blasted man to go off on his own while the two of them were asleep.

He had moved while she dreamed, rolling so his back was facing her. His ribs lifted and fell in the comfort of deep sleep. Thank all the faerie realms that he hadn't done the same thing she would have done. Sneaking away would only cause them all to waste even more time.

As she watched, Freya noted a slight difference in the shadows beyond Eldridge. Had he cast an illusion over them before they fell asleep? It would make sense for them to be protected.

Then the shadows parted and red glowing eyes appeared.

Freya opened her mouth to shout at Eldridge that the werewolf was here. But she couldn't move. She couldn't speak. She couldn't do anything but watch as the beast stepped out of the darkness and loomed over the man she was falling in love with.

The werewolf was just as terrifying as she remembered. His broad chest was covered in hair, his legs bent at an awkward angle, and his wolf head was too large. Too real.

The beast's lips quivered, then parted to reveal shiny teeth that gleamed with drool. A long strand of spittle dripped from his mouth as he leaned over Eldridge. The Goblin King was still asleep.

The man she loved barely reacted as the werewolf leaned over him. A monster's snarl echoed through the shaft. Freya shivered in fear and realized she still couldn't move. She was frozen in place. Completely at the mercy of this monster who wanted to kill her and everyone she loved.

She couldn't breathe.

Eldridge, she wanted to call out. Wake up!

Those teeth gnashed above Eldridge's face, lingering over his neck as though the monster wanted to tear into the Goblin King. He wanted to cause pain and see blood pool on the floor. Freya could sense that.

But the beast stopped at the last second. He froze, then looked over at her with red, terrifying eyes.

An emotion flickered in the depths of those wild orbs. Freya almost thought the monster recognized her. As if it knew she was the same mortal it had seen in the meadow, the same one whose name he knew.

Deep, guttural tones shook the beast's throat. And yet again, just like last time, the werewolf growled, "Freya."

With a gasp, Freya sat straight up. Arrow tumbled off her lap with a grumble of complaint before he rolled back over onto his side. She sucked in air and wildly turned to look at Eldridge. But he wasn't asleep on his back. He was facing her on his side with his arm outstretched, as if even in his sleep he was trying to hold her hand. There was no beast leaning over him. No werewolf in the darkness.

She'd been dreaming.

Slapping a hand to her forehead, Freya eased back down onto the ground. She'd had a nightmare, and of course she would in this place. Her mind was in turmoil, even in sleep. All she needed to do was calm down a bit.

Her heart continued to race in her chest. She was terrified that Eldridge had almost died, even though she knew very well that wasn't how it worked. Dreams weren't premonitions. Dreams were her mind sorting through all the things she'd thought or learned the day before. Easy as that.

Blowing out a long breath, she rolled Arrow over until he was closer to their heads. Then she gently crawled over Eldridge so she was the big spoon. She put her own back to the darkness because she didn't think the werewolf would hurt her.

The thought was crazy. The werewolf was a monster, and he would hunt down anything that stood before him. Everyone they'd met had said so.

But the recognition in his eyes, at least the first time she'd seen him, made her hesitate. It was more than knowing her. Those eyes were familiar, kind, and full of love. She'd seen them before, she just couldn't remember where.

Shaking her head, she turned so her back was pressed against Eldridge's and met the darkness head on. She stared into the darkness, unafraid. Let them try to intimidate her. Freya had seen more terrifying things than her own nightmares, and she was not the same weak little girl who flinched from shadows.

This time the shadows remained still and quiet. No red eyes stared back at her, and she knew for certain this time that the werewolf had not visited them.

"It was just a dream," she whispered. "Nothing more than that, Freya. Go back to sleep."

She closed her eyes and nudged a little closer to Eldridge. Like him, she stretched out her arm and laid her head on her bicep as a pillow.

Just as she was drifting off to sleep, she realized her hand rested upon a small tuft of coarse fur.

CHAPTER 22

They all woke at almost the same time. As if someone had rung a bell through the tunnel, all three of them sat straight up, gasping for air and reaching for each other.

Freya didn't ask what the other two had dreamt. She knew. Of course, she knew. They'd all had the same nightmare of teeth, claws, and fear.

Nightmares had no place to be voiced here, however. She refused to even think of the werewolf haunting their dreams, because he had no right to be in their minds. Simple as that. She wouldn't give the creature any more power than it already had.

Standing up, she reached for the oil lantern and turned it brighter. "More light would probably do us all some good, don't you think?"

Eldridge nodded, still sitting on the ground and hugging his knees tight to his chest. On the other side of the lantern, Arrow also nodded. Even he wasn't getting up just yet. They both stared into the lantern with haunted expressions.

"Come on," she muttered. "The sooner we get this over with, the sooner we're out of this cursed place."

"I didn't know it would be like this," Eldridge whispered. "If I had known, I never would have brought you both here."

"Well, you wouldn't have gotten far without me. I would have followed you to the ends of the earth if you were going to save my mother." Freya reached out her hand for him to take and wiggled her fingers for his attention. "Stand up, Eldridge. We have a long way to go."

He looked up at her, eyes wide and brimming with tears. "I can't tell what's real and what's not, Freya."

"I'm real," she whispered. "As real as I was when I saved you from the Winter Court. I pulled you out of that prison and I will do it again if you need me to. But you have to stand first."

He stood, allowing her to draw him into her arms for a few moments. The hug cleared the dream from his thoughts, apparently. He pulled away from her and wiped an arm over his eyes. "Right. We have a long travel day ahead of us. Arrow, can you walk?"

The goblin dog stared straight ahead of himself, ears drooped down and tail tucked tight to his body. "I know that dream wasn't real. I know he wasn't really here, but those teeth..."

She met Eldridge's pointed look and nodded. Freya plucked the goblin from the ground and heaved him into her arms. "That's all right, Arrow. I'll carry you."

She had never guessed it would be this difficult just to walk through the mines. Something was in the air here, and all she could hope was that it wasn't the ore turning their minds insane. They still had to keep their wits about them if they were going to make it out alive.

Eldridge reached into his pocket and pulled out the tiny, glowing faerie. "It's time for you to go to work, my dear. I'd like to make a deal with you."

The power of the words laced through the air. And with all this strange magic swirling around them, she could almost see the power of his words. It swirled around him in a galaxy of color, blooming from his lips and wrapping around the jar. A few tendrils drifted off from the others, reaching for Freya before they returned to their master.

The will-o'-the-wisp pressed her hands against the glass jar. She nodded vigorously, listening to every word Eldridge said.

"Good." Eldridge held her jar up high to the light. "The Magician said you were bringing people to the werewolf's cavern. Is this true?"

She nodded again, pounding her fists on the glass.

"All right, then the deal is very simple if you follow the rules. I will let you out of this jar if you promise to take us to the werewolf's lair." He leaned close to the glass and glared at the tiny creature. "If you try to trick us, or if you don't bring us directly to the lair and try to lose us in this cursed place, then my magic will drag you right back to the jar wherever I leave it last. You will rot just like us in this cavern. Do we have a deal?"

Freya could see the tiny creature gulp. The fate would be worse than what would happen to them if the werewolf devoured their bodies. At least Freya and the others would be dead. This faerie would be trapped for all eternity.

Finally, the tiny faerie gave a sharp nod.

"Good enough for me," Eldridge snarled. "You made a deal with the Goblin King, wisp. Remember that."

Freya hoped the threat was enough to scare the faerie into actually guiding them correctly. Eldridge twisted the top of the jar and released the will-o'-the-wisp into the world.

She spun as she left her prison, stretching her arms over her head and coiling through the air like a ballerina. Every movement was grace-ful, and Freya could easily see why so many people would follow one of her kind into the darkness. The glittering brightness of her body and wings, the sheer joy in her expression, made Freya want to trust anything this creature said. Even though she knew how dangerous this little beast was.

The wisp turned around and gestured for them to follow her. And though they tried their best, it was difficult to follow something zipping so quickly. The faerie took a while to get her bearings, too. Though she'd been with them traveling, she had been stuck in Eldridge's pocket.

Every time the wisp darted down a tunnel, Freya's heart would jump in her chest. No one knew where they were going. This wisp was the only way to get them to the werewolf, and now she feared they would never get out again. The wisp wouldn't help them again, at least not without leading them to their death.

But she was shocked to see the wisp was actually showing them the right direction. They turned down a particularly narrow tunnel, and there was the cart they'd been looking for. Filled with mirror ore and a single gemstone seated on top the size of Freya's fist.

She glanced over at Eldridge and smiled. "I think we're getting somewhere."

"Ever closer." But his expression remained grim.

Freya didn't know if he was worried about what would happen when they found the wolf, or if he was concerned about the same thing as she was. How were they going to get out of this labyrinth?

They followed the wisp for what felt like hours before Freya noticed the veins in the walls. The silver mirror ore was stunning to look at, but it pulsed with magic like the power was blood flowing through the ore. Like the earth was alive, and these were actual veins the miners were ripping out.

She leaned a little closer to a particularly large chunk, watching as it pulsed again. Not with light. That only came from the lanterns both she and Eldridge held. The pulsing was the actual movement of the ore. Like it was liquid and not solid. It undulated within the walls.

"Eldridge?" she asked. "Are you seeing this?"

Freya straightened and realized her companions had wandered farther from her. Arrow had sat down in the middle of the tunnel nearest to her, and Eldridge leaned down to stare at another vein, much farther away from them.

But they were both frozen. Stuck in place like they didn't know how to move anymore.

Frowning, she called out again, "Eldridge?"

He didn't respond.

She left the ore she'd found and stumbled across the floor. Why couldn't she move her legs correctly? That was odd.

Staggering down the tunnel, she reached out her hand and braced her hand on the wall near Arrow. "What's going on, Arrow? I don't think I feel very good and I don't know why."

Her voice warbled, the same way it had when she had addressed the magic mirror. That should have meant something. A voice screamed in her head that the way she sounded was incredibly important, but she couldn't remember why. Or she couldn't focus on why. The thought danced out of reach like the glittering light of a wisp who was supposed to lead them through this madness.

She waved a hand through the shadows, slapping at the strange light bobbing in front of her eyes. She needed Arrow. He'd know what was going on.

Freya took one step, then fell onto her knees beside her faithful goblin companion. Squinting, she tried to touch his head, but it looked like he had four of them now. Which one was actually his head? It took her a few tries while her mind tried to focus on the sharp stones biting into her knees.

Finally, she set her hand on his skull and felt the soft fur of his ears underneath her fingers. "There you are," she whispered.

A blast of cold air trailed between her shoulder blades. She felt that thing inside her, the magic or power or whatever Eldridge had called it, unravel its wings. Suddenly, she saw herself and Eldridge further down the tunnel. They were walking away with their arms around each other, but Arrow's leg was stuck underneath a rock.

"Wait," he called out, his voice a hoarse croak. "Please! I'm right here. Don't you see me? I'm hurt!"

The image of herself and Eldridge did not stop. They looked at each other with glowing white eyes, kissed, and then walked on.

"No," Freya whispered. "No, my dear friend. We would never leave you."

But Arrow couldn't hear her. He was stuck in the vision of this nightmare and no matter how many times she called out to him, he never heard her.

Eldridge would know what to do. He could snap the goblin dog out of this horrible spell. All Freya had to do was get to him. Arrow might not be able to hear her, but Eldridge and her had a powerful connection. This wasn't the first time they'd conquered dark magic together.

She slapped her hands to the stone floor and pushed to stand. The long, grueling walk to his side was a staggering embarrassment. She fell onto her knees multiple times, crawling toward him with her hand outstretched. This was ridiculous. She knew how to walk, damn it.

Finally, she reached his side. And though she had to squirm on her belly to get there, Freya still reached out and wrapped a hand around his ankle. "Eldridge," she rasped. "We have to help Arrow."

But he didn't move. He stared into that ore and she already knew that something was horribly wrong. He was going to show her his own nightmare, and this time she didn't know if she would survive it. What was a Goblin King terrified of?

Mist poured off the ore he stared into. And then she saw a vision of herself down the hallway. Arrow wasn't in Eldridge's nightmare. A small blessing, she supposed.

Her image reached for Eldridge to take. "Come on!" she said, her voice strange and thin. "We're almost there! Just a few more steps and we'll finally save my mother."

How was this his nightmare? Did he not want her to find her mother?

Freya had worried about this. Eldridge had to know she would not leave him once she found her mother. Freya's life was here now, and even the woman who had birthed her wouldn't change that decision. Esther was here. Eldridge was here. All her new family and friends had made her life infinitely better in this place.

Then she saw those glowing red eyes again. They loomed out of the darkness behind her. Eldridge's image peeled out of his body, lunging for Freya in his vision.

He was too late.

The werewolf wrapped his jaws around her throat and shook his head once, twice, and the third time was enough. In a wild spray of blood, her head was removed from her shoulders. The werewolf kept the head in his mouth while her body dropped onto its knees, hands limp at her sides.

The sound that came out of Eldridge would haunt her for all eternity. A wild, keening cry of an animal in so much pain, she was certain he wouldn't survive it. He dropped onto his knees as well, that aching moan echoing over and over again.

With a gasp, she released her hold on his ankle. She couldn't watch that any longer without feeling her soul rip from her chest. She couldn't lose him like that, and he apparently couldn't lose her either. What a match.

She needed to get away from this ore or she'd be locked in this horrible dream state as well. What Freya didn't know was where to go. The ore seemed like it was everywhere.

Every tunnel she crawled past was filled with the silver stuff. She forced herself onto her knees, but that was no faster. She would drag her limp body and confused mind through this entire place until she finally grew too tired. And she was tired. So damned tired. All she had to do was lie down.

Perhaps she would die here alone, but wasn't that always going to be the case? Freya wouldn't have gotten out alive. She might have found the wolf, but her mother wasn't here anymore. And if she was, all she would have found were the bones that remained after the wolf had devoured her mother's corpse.

Freya had led her dearest friends into a trap. They would experience their worst nightmare over and over, and she would slowly rot away. Alone. Unloved. Forgotten by the world above.

Cold stone pressed against her cheek. When had she lied down? A stone pressed against her eye, a little too jagged and uncomfortable, but she couldn't move it. She couldn't move anything at all.

This was what she deserved. She should stay quiet, lay here, and wait for the inevitable.

Bright light flashed in front of her eyes. Bright, blue light that sparked a small nugget of hope in her chest.

The wisp. She was still here, somehow, and fluttering in front of Freya's face. Even as she struggled to open her eyes, the wisp was patting Freya's cheeks. Not quite as forceful as the dwarf, but enough to get her attention.

"I can't," Freya whispered.

The wisp flew back an arm's length, then launched herself at Freya's face. Her entire body slapped Freya's cheek, and that was enough to get her up. Freya lunged forward, sitting straight up and gasping in air.

This was just like the Spring Maiden's perfume. She knew how to get out of a situation like this. Hold her breath, stay cognizant of the world where she was. Though she didn't have those small buds to break open, she wasn't completely without tricks in this cavern.

She reached for the sharp stone that had dug into her cheek. With that in her palm, she stood. The overwhelming magic of the ore pressed down on her shoulders, but this time she dug the stone into the meaty flesh of her palm. The pain shocked her out of the trance.

"That'll do." She nodded at the wisp. "Lead on. Let's get out of here, and I'll come back for my friends."

And though it broke her heart to do it, Freya knew she couldn't snap them out of the daze they were in. The magic here was too powerful. All she could do was continue on.

She left a bloody trail in her wake, crimson droplets falling from her fist. If one of them woke before she returned to save them, perhaps they could still find her in this labyrinth.

CHAPTER 23

It took a long time to drag herself out of that tunnel. The wisp continued to come back and flutter in front of her face every time Freya started getting lost to the ore again. The bright, waving light was just enough to remind her that she needed to dig the rock into her hand again. Thus, Freya would.

And every time that pain zinged up her arm, she would force herself to take a couple more steps forward. Onward. Always onward until she burst out of the tunnel and fell onto her hands and knees.

Clean, fresh air filled her lungs. She could finally breathe without feeling like someone was holding her down. The magic released its hold on her reluctantly, but it had no choice.

Lifting her head, she stared at the strange place where the tunnels had spat her out. It was a field. She was kneeling in a field full of daisies of every color. Pinks, yellows, blues, whites, all dancing in a slight breeze that cooled the sweat slicking her skin. Green grass filled in the spaces between flowers, emerald in color and so lush it felt like her fingers were sinking into moss. And above all that color was a bright blue sky dotted with fluffy white clouds.

She had never thought that the mines would connect to a place like this.

Slowly, she stood. The flowers reached up to her knees, dancing as she stumbled forward. Freya tried her best to walk, but... why had the wisp brought her here?

The little faerie was nowhere to be found, either, so this must have been the right place. Unless the faerie had brought her to safety and the Goblin King's magic had sucked her back into the caves.

Freya doubted that was the case.

She walked into the center of the field and tilted her head back. The sun's rays played across her cheeks and the last remaining tension of magical control drifted away from her shoulders. She was free.

Dropping her head, she froze in shock. The werewolf stood at the edge of the field. His hands were held loose at his sides that heaved with great, powerful breaths. She thought he would run at her, teeth bared and slathering jaws open wide. She was in his meadow. This was the place where the wisp had brought people to die.

The werewolf didn't move.

He stared at her. She stared back at him, and Freya realized he wasn't going to move at all. The wolf was waiting for her to take the first step, and that was an intelligent response she hadn't expected.

Taking a step closer, she called out, "Hello!"

Any normal beast would have flinched at the sound of her voice. The wolves back home would have run the moment they heard a human shouting, and they wouldn't have stuck around to see what she wanted.

The wolf didn't react in any negative way. His ears flicked forward, and he tilted his head, but he stood there the same as before. Like he wanted her to keep talking.

She lifted her hands to show that she wasn't a threat, then took another step forward. "I've been looking for you. Did you know?"

He moved his head in the slightest of nods.

"Good." She took a few more steps closer this time, testing to see how close he would let her get. "A pixie told me that you took my mother. She fought with you in the caves and when you beat her, you dragged her into the tunnels. No one has ever seen her again."

His ears twitched again. He nodded again, and Freya knew she was getting somewhere. This beast was not an animal. He knew what she was talking about. Who she was talking about. And this was the closest she'd ever gotten to finding her mother.

"Please don't run from me," she whispered. "I don't know who you are, or why you took my mother. But I need to find her."

The wolf turned away from her and headed off through the meadow. She felt her heart fall in her chest. She'd wasted her chance. Now the creature was running from her.

But the beast stopped and looked over its shoulder.

Did he want her to follow him?

Freya looked back at the dark mouth of the tunnel she'd left. Her companions were back there, caught in a nightmare and waiting for her to save them. It was the hardest choice she'd ever made. But she left them to follow the beast in the hopes she would return to this tunnel sooner rather than later.

She trailed the werewolf through the meadow, marveling as he fell onto all fours. It was easier for him to move like that, she thought. His back was hunched awkwardly, but he moved faster. Much faster.

Soon, she had to run to keep up with him. And what a strange feeling to be running through a meadow with a wolf at her side. They raced through the fields toward something she had missed until they were on top of it.

A mound of earth had been piled here. The flowers grew much thicker, creating a carpet of colors that led up to a small glass coffin. Inside, a very familiar woman laid with a bouquet of daisies clutched in her still hands.

The woman had cornflower curls laid out artfully around her head. She wore a blue overdress, the brass buttons that closed it at her shoulders still gleaming. Her white undergown hadn't aged a single day since her mother had left. It was the same outfit Freya remembered the last time she'd seen her mother. And she was the spitting image of Esther, just with a few years added to her life.

Freya gasped and felt her eyes fill with tears. "Mother," she whispered.

Some part of her had wondered if the wolf was her mother. She didn't know if the beast was male or female, she had simply assumed because of his broad chest. But now she could see with her own eyes. The beast was not her mother.

She stepped up to the coffin, nerves churning in her belly. She was irrationally afraid that her mother would open her eyes. And that was what Freya wanted more than anything. Proof that her mother wasn't lying in that coffin, dead.

But what would her mother say when she saw Freya had followed her into the faerie realm? Freya was terrified of her mother's disapproval. But Freya also knew her mother wouldn't open her eyes. After all, a coffin was only used to remember those who had passed.

Carefully, she set her fingers on the glass. Though she smudged it, the mark at least made her feel like this all was more real.

"My mother was an amazing woman and I love her very much," she said through thick tears. "Thank you for preserving her."

A blast of heat hit her back. The wolf had stepped too close, towering over her. She tensed, afraid he was about to put her in the coffin with her mother.

Instead, he tapped the glass over her mother's chest with his claw.

Her mother was still breathing.

Freya lunged forward again, pressing her hands to the glass and staring down at her mother with new eyes. "She's still breathing," she whispered as though she couldn't believe it. "She's alive."

The wolf nodded and moved. He stood on the other side of the coffin, awkward in nature but still clearly invested in whether or not her mother died.

He opened his muzzle and struggled through his words. "She... Sleep."

Freya frowned. Asleep? But that was magic only the Spring Maiden seemed to have.

She shook her head in disbelief. "I was placed under a similar spell before. The Spring Maiden was the one who made me fall asleep, and I couldn't wake up unless she let me."

Again, the wolf nodded. "Found in... mines. Curse hard... to break."

If he was suggesting what she thought, then that changed everything. It meant the Spring Maiden had not only lied to them, but she had willfully led them astray. She'd sent Freya, Eldridge, and Arrow after this wolf in the hopes that they would fix her problem while knowing she had caused Freya's greatest strife.

Where had all the air gone? Freya couldn't breathe.

She stepped away from the coffin and waved her hands in the air, counting all the reasons this didn't make sense. "So you're claiming all of this is the Spring Maiden's doing?"

The wolf nodded vigorously. He didn't move from where he was, but watched her with those all knowing red eyes. Those eyes that were so familiar because she had wanted them to be her mother's so desperately. Now, she realized this animal was just what the Spring Maiden said.

She pointed at him. "You're still a murderer. You've been hunting down pixies for how long? Killing them horribly. They find pieces of your victims and send them to the Spring Maiden in the hopes she can cast some spell that would find you."

The werewolf looked at her mother, then back to Freya.

"I know she was put under a spell. What does she have to do with pixies?" Freya shouted the words. But then it dawned on her.

Of course he had been hunting pixies. They were the only way to get a message back to the Spring Maiden that what she had done was wrong. The werewolf wasn't a serial killer at all. He'd been trying to save her mother.

Frowning, she took a step closer to the wolf. "Did you want to kill the pixies?"

His eyes flashed bright red, and he bared his teeth in a snarl.

"Tell me," she insisted. "I need to know if you wanted to kill them, or if it was a message that you were sending to the Spring Maiden. Your answer changes everything, wolf."

He looked her dead in the eye and lifted both of his clawed hands. He gestured with the left, then the right, and finally brought his hands together, interlacing his fingers.

Freya sighed, disappointed at his answer. "They're one and the same, is that what you're saying? You wanted to send a message, and you wanted to kill them."

His snarling grin sent shivers of terror down her spine. Of course he had wanted to kill them. He was, after all, a wolf.

A memory bloomed in her mind's eye. Her father sitting beside her in front of their fireplace, cleaning his gun. He'd claimed all wolves were bad at their core. Some of them could wear sheepskin that would confuse people. They appeared good at first glance, but then they showed their true colors, eventually.

This wolf might be interested in her mother, perhaps because she was the first mortal he'd seen, but that didn't make him good. He was still a serial killer. Still the villain of this tale, even if she didn't want to believe that.

But there was the matter of what he'd done. He'd saved her mother's life. He had taken care of her body even while she slept under a dreaming curse for all these years. And Freya couldn't forget that debt.

"She's my mother, and she means more to me than life itself." She looked at her mother's sleeping face and sighed. "For that, I am forever grateful. I don't think it's right to not give you something in return. What do you want?"

The wolf lifted his claws and pressed them against his heart. He then lifted them to the sky, then back to his chest once more.

"You want to live," she whispered. "Is that it?"

He nodded and took a step away from her. Away from the coffin as well. His eye darted to the vast landscape of the meadow, and Freya understood that bone deep desire that echoed through him.

The werewolf only wanted to be free. He didn't want anyone to hunt him as he let go of this strange, unusual job of watching over her mother's body. After all, a werewolf was a wild animal, and right now, he wasn't fulfilling that nature.

"Go," she said. "I won't know where you went. It will be hard to find you, but I suggest that you don't stay in the Spring Court. They're all watching you."

He pointed to her mother, a question in his eyes.

"I will look after her now. I give you my word that I will break this sleeping curse." Freya was surprised at the fervor in her own voice. "I vow it."

And with that, the wolf gave her a sharp nod, dropped onto all fours, and disappeared over the horizon.

Freya made her way through the meadow back to the tunnel. Thankfully, she still remembered how to get back to that hidden place. It was a beautiful walk, enough to calm her mind and settle her back into the role she was most comfortable in.

Hero.

Freya knew what to do now that she was moving forward. She had a goal. Wake her mother and break the curse. She had a villain to defeat. The lying Spring Maiden, although she wasn't sure how the venomous woman had convinced them all she wasn't involved. These were tangible goals she could attack with reckless abandon.

But first, she had to get both Eldridge and Arrow out of the mines. Then they could work their magic and get all of them out of this meadow. Back to the Spring Maiden's castle, where she planned to wrap her hands around that skinny little neck and squeeze until the Spring Maiden's face turned purple.

Freya paused at the mouth of the cave. Already she could see the wisps of mirror ore magic reaching for her. This mine wasn't just dangerous. It should be sealed on both ends so no one would ever make the same mistake she and her companions had.

Someday she would return and make sure that happened.

"Wisp?" she asked, her voice echoing through the cavern. "Are you still there?"

It was a shot in the dark, really. She didn't expect the wisp to still be there. The tiny creature had done everything that she'd promised, and then some. She was the only thing that had gotten Freya through that nightmare.

No one responded.

She didn't blame the poor thing. The wisp had been in a jar for so many years, she likely wanted to go home. Or, at the very least, find whatever remaining family she had left in those mines.

That left Freya on her own, yet again. And she didn't have the faintest idea how to proceed this time. Was she supposed to plunge into the darkness? Her hand still ached from digging into the fleshy part of her palm with that rock. And she didn't have another sharpened object, so wouldn't she fall under the same curse?

She had no more tricks up her sleeve. All she could do was stare into the shadows and hear the Magician's words in her head.

"The question you should ask is if I'm human, not mortal."

That horrible old man had performed magic. And she'd done it before in the Winter Court, without thinking about it. That had to count for something. Freya had magic inside her. All she had to do now was figure out how to use it.

Taking a deep breath, she tried to remember what she'd felt in the Winter Court. The unknown man had approached them, the one who was now the Winter Prince. He'd walked up to them with confidence, and it wasn't that she had been afraid or nervous. She had just been tired. Freya hadn't wanted to deal with yet another faerie man who wanted to spit strange words and riddles at her. She'd wanted it all to be over.

Maybe that was the trick. She didn't have to bend the magic or know how to create some complicated spell. She had to give the control over to something else. Something she knew would take her away from this meadow and this madness.

Her next exhale flowed with power. The clean, crisp air from the meadow surrounded her. The breeze hugged her tightly, like a person was behind her. Even though she knew it wasn't a real person. It was magic. Magic that wanted her to know it was here with her and when she was ready, they could walk through the tunnel without fear.

She took a step into the darkness and waited for that horrible sensation of pressure on her shoulders. Instead, the wind she'd summoned from the meadow squeezed her shoulders gently and pushed her forward.

So she continued.

It was easy to walk this time. And when it grew too dark for her to see through the shadows, the wind brought her tiny daisies. They floated through the air. Some whole, some only petals. And they glowed with the most beautiful and delicate of light.

They illuminated the tunnel that had seemed so vast and unending when she first walked through it. But this place wasn't magic. Her mind had been under the influence of powers greater than her own. This was only a tunnel in the earth with gleaming silver ore embedded in the walls. That was all.

There was nothing to be afraid of in a place like this. The earth was magic, yes, but that magic could be manipulated into revealing what she wanted. Freya blinked and suddenly she could see lines in the floors. No, not lines, she realized.

Footsteps.

Singular imprints where she had walked before. They were close together, then staggering, then simply the dragging motion of her knees on the ground. But they were her footsteps and that meant she could follow them back to her companions.

"Thank you," she whispered.

The breeze swirled around her shoulders and filled her lungs with the sweet scent of spring. She remembered this scent from when her family had gathered sap every year. The air smelled like maple syrup and hope.

She took a deep breath and plunged through the darkness with more confidence than she'd felt in a long time. Eldridge wasn't that far, really. He was still frozen, staring at the wall with his eyes wide in horror.

How long had he been made to watch her die? And how many times had he relived that horror?

"Help him," she said as she put her hand on his shoulder. "No one deserves this."

The wind flowed down her arm and through their path in the tunnel. It wrapped around his shoulders, billowing fresh clean air into his lungs. Freya hoped it was enough to wake him. She desperately wanted to see those eyes open and watch as he recognized that she was standing right here in front of him, not wherever the image of her was.

"Eldridge," she said, calling out to him. "Eldridge, I'm okay. I'm right here."

His head tilted to the side, though his eyes remained trained on the ore.

She tried one more time, adding a little more lyrical quality to her voice. Cajoling him out of the nightmare. "You know I wouldn't be so foolish as to die in front of you. Goblin King. Come back to me."

Eldridge lifted his gaze from the ore and looked at her. She saw the hold of the ore's magic lift from his shoulders as if he was suddenly twenty pounds lighter. He heaved a sigh and then his eyes filled with tears.

He lunged for her, wrapping her in his arms so tightly she couldn't breathe. Repeatedly, he pressed his lips to her hair and whispered things that made little sense. "I'm so sorry. This was all my fault. I should have known what would happen. I'm sorry, Freya. No apology is good enough. My hero, my darling. My love."

The last word rocked through her entire being. She wrapped her arms tightly around his waist and held him close to her heart. Tangled in his arms, she remembered what it was like to be so afraid that she would lose him. She remembered seeing him in that horrible prison in the Winter Court and in her nightmare when the werewolf had killed him. How could she not?

Freya was as afraid to lose him as he was to lose her.

Pressing her lips to his jaw, she drew back to kiss him. She lingered on the corners of his lips. The salt from his tears slid onto her tongue and she knew they were filled with love as well. So much love that they hadn't had the time to talk about yet. But they would. They had all the time in the world now.

"I need to get Arrow," she whispered, her throat closing with her own tears. "And you need to go back to the meadow. Follow my footsteps on the ground."

He didn't release her, but peered over her shoulder. "What footsteps?"

Had they already faded? That was annoying. Freya spread her fingers wide, feeling the tug of magic pulled from her navel. She didn't have to look behind her to know that the footsteps were glowing again. "The wind from the meadow is keeping the ore from tangling in your mind again. You won't fall under its spell as long as you follow in my footsteps."

"I won't leave you." He squeezed her tighter. "We stay together, Freya. That wolf is still out there."

She stared up into his horrified gaze and watched understanding dawn in his eyes. "He's not there, Eldridge. I already took care of it."

"You what?"

"Not everything is as it seems. You were the one to teach me that." She released her hold on his waist and forced him to let go of her shoulders. "I'll tell you when you get to the meadow, but I have to get Arrow out of this. You didn't see his nightmare. He... He..."

Eldridge shuddered and she could physically see the mantle of Goblin King descend. Though he wanted to remain with her, to wrap her in his arms, he understood the game of being the hero. The one who had to save everyone.

He took a step away from her, toward the footsteps, and nodded. "I know his greatest fear. He was abandoned as a child by his family, though they died tragically, it was still only him left. He fears that happening again."

"He does." Tears pricked in her eyes. "I can't let him suffer any longer, and I can't watch you at the same time."

He nodded again. Eldridge hesitated for a few more moments, his eyes sweeping her from head to toe as though he was checking one last time that she was alive and well. Then, the Goblin King turned and ran down the tunnel toward safety.

One down.

One to go.

Freya took a breath and continued. Arrow should only be a little distance away, but she was getting tired. Slogging through the ore's power felt like she was constantly moving through thigh deep snow drifts. She didn't know how much longer she could pull the wind with her.

There he was. A tiny black and white dog, curled up in a ball so tightly he looked a quarter of his size.

She lifted her hand and whispered, "Go."

The wind spread from her fingertips, gently wrapping around Arrow and weaving into his lungs. Freya picked him up in her arms. He didn't move. His body was so cold, she feared the worst, but whatever his horrible outcome, she knew she would never let him stay here in this tunnel.

He was hers, just as much as she was his. Their lives were intertwined now with so much love. He was her dearest friend, and she would do anything for him.

Step by painful step, she left the tunnel. Arrow stirred in her arms, his nose snuffling at her neck, before he lifted his head. "Freya?"

"Who else would it be?" she asked, turning around a corner and seeing light at the end of the tunnel.

"You came back for me." His voice was thick and tight with emotion. "I didn't know if you would."

"I never left you, Arrow. It was the magic, that's all. I had to go to the meadow to find the werewolf and put an end to all this." She smiled down at him and brought them both into the light. "It's already over. Now we only have a few loose ends to snip before this part of our story is complete. But know that we will end it together, as always."

The goblin dog wiggled in her arms and she put him down in the daisies. He lifted his nose into the air. His tail wagged happily, then he stood up on his back legs. "The sun is much better. The air here is..."

"Much better," she finished the sentence for him with a soft smile. "Now where is that Goblin King?"

She already knew where she would find him. It wouldn't take long for Eldridge to get his feet back under him, and the very first thing he would have done is explore this meadow. He'd want to make sure there was no danger to them. Namely in the shape of a werewolf.

Freya wandered through the daisies toward the coffin where her mother was laid to rest. And as it appeared on the horizon, the vision of a dark silhouette appeared, standing beside the glass where her mother lay.

"Is that..." Arrow cleared his throat. "That's not who I think it is, is it?"

"Yes, it's her." She tried very hard to not allow her voice to sound reverent, but... wasn't this a fairytale?

She'd listened to her mother tell her this story before. A woman who was waiting for true love's kiss, laid out in a field of daisies while resting in a glass coffin. This was the thing that stories were made of.

Stepping up to Eldridge's side, she put her hand back on the smudge she'd left before.

He was staring down at her mother with a frown on his face. "She's beautiful, Freya. You look very much like her."

Not really. Esther looked more like their mother, but she supposed there were a few similarities. She shared her mother's nose. There was that at least. They both had the angular features that her family shared. But that was where the similarities ended.

"I wish I looked more like her," she mumbled. "Esther favors our mother, though. If you had seen my father, you would have said I looked just like him. We were both lean and dark, while Esther and Mother always favored the light."

He put his hand on top of hers. His fingers were so much larger, stronger. "Where is the werewolf, Freya?"

"I let him go." She stared down into her mother's serene expression and wondered what Astrid would have done.

She probably would have killed the beast, regardless. Her mother wasn't one to let a faerie go just because it had saved someone else. All those lives of the pixies meant more than the single life of a mortal.

And yet... She couldn't kill the beast. Freya had to give him a chance.

"You let him go?" Eldridge repeated, stunned. "Why would you do that?"

"He was keeping her safe. She went into the mines. But I don't think he was killing pixies back then. She fell under this spell while they were meeting and he tried to protect her. He recognized the spell that was laid on her and he put her here." She turned her hand around and laced their fingers together. "He kept her alive in the hopes that someone would come to collect her someday. I had to let him go."

Tiny lines appeared between Eldridge's eyes. "A sleeping spell, you say?"

"Just like what the Spring Maiden did to me." Finally, she met his gaze without flinching. "I don't know why she lied to us, but this is all her doing. She put my mother to sleep, just like she did me. And then she sent us to kill the beast who was trying to force her to recognize her own mistakes."

He let out a low growl. "Then I think we need answers from the Spring Maiden."

Arrow stepped up and placed his paw on top of their hands. "She's the only one who can wake your mother. The sleeping spell she uses is one she thought up on her own. The flowers you saw, Freya. Those might be the key."

Freya looked at her companions and realized how lucky she was to have them. Together, they could overcome any obstacle.

She straightened her spine and squared her shoulders. "I suppose it's time for us to take down yet another faerie noble, gentlemen."

CHAPTER 25

It was easier to say they were going to take down the Spring Maiden, than actually doing it. Their plans took over an entire afternoon and then spread into the next night. A day turned into much longer as they paced through the meadow.

Eldridge summoned food and water for them. They could have portaled into the Spring Court, but that would get them nowhere. The Spring Maiden had planned all of this in detail, thus she likely would know they had found her out.

She was sacrificing her own people to a monster. But why? It made little sense. Nothing about this added up and Freya wanted to understand before they went on the attack.

Her two companions were more than happy to rip apart every step of their journey. They hashed out every detail that the other might not have been a part of. They told their story a hundred times over, pouring details into each other's head. But no matter how many times they rehashed what had happened, everyone landed on the same thing.

This didn't add up.

The Spring Maiden had never cursed someone where she couldn't look into their heads. She had certainly never let one of her dreamers escape from the Spring Court. So why was Freya's mother different?

Freya had taken to sitting next to her mother's coffin. Eldridge had summoned a small stool out of thin air, so Freya sat and braided little flower crowns like her mother had taught her so long ago. The repetition of moving her hands helped ease her mind.

"Why were you here?" she asked every day. "You hated the faerie realms. You hated these people and yet you were here. The Spring Court is the worst of them all, so why, Mother?"

If only she would wake. Then Freya could ask her a thousand questions. Her mother had always helped her to see the world in a different light.

"Did you want to find more books?" she asked. She had found the chest in their garden. That was how Freya had gotten into the faerie realm to begin with.

But again, she hadn't entered the magical realms in the Spring Court. Freya had been spit out into that in-between place. That world between the realms, not here. So how had her mother traveled so far?

And then there was Eldridge. He'd said he loved her, or as good as said it. She didn't know how many times he'd been hinting at it, but whatever the hints, she now felt a little strange being around him. Not uncomfortable per say, but like her heart was going to burst if she didn't say it back.

She wasn't ready to say it. But he'd said that he loved her, so shouldn't she say something back? At least to reassure him that his affections were reciprocated. But she didn't know how to say she was in love with a creature her mother had trained her to hate.

The flower in her hand fell apart in her tight grip. Damn it. Now she was going to have to find another flower to replace this one, and she didn't want to leave her mother's side while she was feeling so... so...

A wet nose pressed against her wrist with the perfect flower held between his teeth. "Miss Freya, you can use this one."

Though the words were garbled, the meaning was still behind them. Of all people, Arrow would always be the one to take care of her.

"Thank you," she said. The flower stem was the perfect length to weave into the last piece of this flower crown made of entirely white daisies. A rarity in this field. "I think this one is going to be my best yet."

"Well, you have a whole stack of them to choose from." Arrow looked at the dozens of crowns strewn around her mother's coffin. "Are you all right, Freya? You don't seem like yourself."

"I don't think I've been myself since I came here." She sighed and set the crown down in her lap. "When I struggled with my first quest, it was a time when I had to defy everything I had learned. I had to suspend disbelief and realize magic was real. Then I had to go to the Winter Court and save Eldridge, finding out that I have magic too. And here... Here I have become something different. Someone different. I hardly recognize myself and I don't know where to go from here."

He set his head on her knee and sighed. Arrow stared at her mother with those big, sorrowful eyes. "I don't think there's an answer to what you want, Freya. We're all changing. And no mortal comes to the faerie realm without being affected by the magic. Look at your sister!"

But she didn't think it was the magic that had changed her. Nothing about the way she had manipulated the wind made her feel like she had changed in this place. She'd pulled on something deep inside her very soul to do it. And that power felt like it had been there for a very long time, waiting for her to use it to communicate with this realm.

She shook her head. "I don't know. I don't know why all of this is happening now when my mother would have stopped at nothing to make sure it never developed."

In the reflection of her mother's coffin, she saw Eldridge step toward them. He was every inch the Goblin King. His perfectly pressed suit. His handsome features, silver skin glowing in the light. The wind ruffled the tufts of fur on the tips of his ears.

"Your mother may have been protecting you," he said. "Magic in the mortal realm will get you killed. That is the danger of being like us."

"Like us?" she repeated. Freya stared up at him with wide eyes. "I'm not fae, Eldridge. You know that. I'm just a mortal woman, like my sister and my parents. Nothing about me is different except this... this..."

"Magic." He said.

The Goblin King sank down beside Arrow. All three of them turned their attention to her mother's coffin. Perhaps it was easier for them to look at the sleeping woman rather than each other.

Freya struggled to talk about this. She wasn't different, and yet she was. Every fiber of her being wanted to shout that she hadn't changed because she was so afraid that her mother would wake up and not like what she saw.

Freya had always been the good, dutiful daughter. She was the image her mother had wanted to create. A capable woman who never touched magic. No matter the cost.

Now, if her mother woke and saw her daughter using magic... What would she do? Would she lose her family all over again when she had only just found her?

A groan escaped her lips. Freya folded over her legs, pressed her arms to her knees, and held her head in her hands. What was she supposed to do?

Eldridge touched the back of her head and pressed his lips to her hair. "My darling, we will handle this together. I know there is so much you fear, but we cannot do anything until we wake your mother."

"I know," she whispered. "This would all be so much easier if I wasn't so frightened of what she will say when she sees me."

"Perhaps you should be more frightened of what the Spring Maiden will say." He drew her back up to sitting, a smile on his face. "Focus on the first obstacle, and then we will continue our story from there."

The first obstacle. She could do that.

Freya steadied herself and tried to remember this was what she had wanted. An opportunity to put her family back together. And Eldridge was right. They could do nothing about how her mother would feel about Freya's choices until she was actually awake.

The Spring Maiden would have to do that. And the rage Freya had originally felt that the horrible faerie noble had taken advantage of her family needed to fuel her.

She closed her eyes and let that anger flow through her entire body.

Heat blasted through her veins, warming her to the very core because she knew now was the time for her to rise to the occasion. The Spring Maiden was in the dark, and that was because, like all the other faerie court leaders, the Maiden had underestimated Freya.

"I don't think she even thought we'd make it this far," Freya said. She squeezed her eyes tighter. "She sent us here because she thought the werewolf would kill us. Two birds with one stone and all that."

"Perhaps." Eldridge took her hands and squeezed them tight. "Or perhaps she thought that she could get us out of the way until she completed whatever this was supposed to do for her. Perhaps it has something to do with your family line."

Her family was no more special than the average mortals. But it didn't make sense that the Spring Maiden would target her mother. It didn't...

"Gah." She abruptly opened her eyes and stood. "I need to speak with the Spring Maiden or all these possibilities are going to drive me mad. How do we get there?"

"We don't without a plan." Eldridge stood as well. "Do you have a plan, Queen Killer?"

He knew how much she hated that name. Glaring, she shook her head. "No. I don't have a plan. And I don't think we need one."

Her two companions shared a look, then Arrow asked, "Come again?"

"The Spring Maiden likely thinks we're dead already. Isn't that how this should have worked out? We find the werewolf. He kills us. We never know about my mother at all." She pointed off in the direction the werewolf had run. "She didn't anticipate the werewolf still having his wits about him. I don't know why he gave me the chance to talk with him, but he wanted to explain himself. There was humility in his eyes, Eldridge. He was not a monster. She needs to answer not only for my mother, but for him. Right now, we have the surprise advantage."

He tapped his chin with a long finger. "Or she might be expecting us to rush back, and this was all some elaborate ruse. She may know we'll run back to her court and that's where the real trap lies."

"No." Freya refused to believe that. "She's not that crafty. She always thinks she has the upper hand."

And in this case, she didn't. Freya would catch her off guard and then they would question the Maiden. Now, they had to find a way to get into the Spring Court without anyone seeing them.

She narrowed her eyes on Eldridge. "Did you leave anything in our private room so we could teleport back to it easily?"

His eyes widened in shock. "How did you know that's how I teleport?"

Well, that was an awkward question. She hadn't really known at all. At least, he'd never told her such a thing. Had she been using magic to get that answer? Freya didn't know.

Instead of wondering if she'd somehow crossed yet another line, she shrugged. "Does it matter? I need to know if we can teleport into the castle with my mother. I want to hide her. Leaving her here is leaving our best bargaining tool behind. Besides, I don't trust the Spring Maiden not to try to move her again."

At least he didn't try to argue with her. Eldridge gave a sharp nod and reached out his hand to place it on the coffin. "Do you want the entire thing moved, or just her body?"

The awful question was the first of many, she was sure. Bringing an entire coffin was bound to get tricky. So she leaned down and pushed off the lid. The same as the Winter Princess had done all those months ago.

The glass hit the ground but didn't shatter. A loud thunk was all it made before it settled in the daisies.

Her mother was within reach. Freya shouldn't feel like she was looking at a dead body, but she did. With a shaking hand, she touched her fingers to her mother's warm cheek. "We're going to wake you up, Mother. I promise."

Eldridge winced and placed his own hand on her mother's shoulder. "Everyone touch me. Teleporting isn't easy and I want us all there in one piece."

Freya reached out, grabbed onto him, and squeezed her eyes shut. It was time to confront a faerie noble.

Yet again.

They landed within their room in the castle, a little harder than Freya would have liked. She stumbled to the side. Frantically, she searched for her companions and was relieved to find Eldridge holding her mother in his arms.

"Is she all right?" she asked.

"She's still asleep if that's what you want to hear." Eldridge carefully laid her mother in the gilded bed. Flowers had grown in the canopy in their absence. White roses rained petals down on her mother's head. They lingered in her hair, tangling through the golden curls.

"She looks like a princess," Freya murmured.

"There have been many princesses in the same predicament." Eldridge rounded the bed to pull her into his arms. "And they all woke up, I'm happy to say."

Arrow grunted. "All the ones you know about. I'm sure there's still some in those beds."

"Arrow!" Both Freya and Eldridge scolded at the same time.

"What?" He trotted toward the door. "I was just saying what everyone was thinking."

Freya rolled her eyes as Arrow pressed his ear to the wood. Sure, he meant well. But she didn't want to hear about how there were many others still trapped by the Spring Maiden's magic. She would wake her mother up. No matter what the cost.

Stepping out of Eldridge's arms, she looked between the two of them. "Arrow, would you mind staying here with my mother? Just to make sure no one comes in and tries to steal her."

He pulled away from the door and rolled his eyes. "I know you're trying to keep me out of trouble. What am I going to do if a pixie walks in to get your mother? Hmm?"

He'd seen right through her plan.

Freya cleared her throat and asked, "Bite them?"

"Right. Because they'd be so afraid of a dog bite." But he still hopped up onto the bed and curled up next to her mother's feet. "Fine. That's fine. Leave the goblin dog because he doesn't have any magic. I see how it is."

"That isn't the only reason and you know it." She knelt and hugged him tightly around the neck. "I'm sorry, but I need you to stay. I don't know what the Spring Maiden might throw at us, and I can't keep track of both of you. At least I know she won't be inclined to attack the Goblin King. But you? If she had her way, I'm certain she would try to harm you because you mean so much to me."

He grumbled but at least seemed appeased.

And she now knew someone was watching over her mother, which was a small blessing. If the Spring Maiden tried to move her mother's body, then she'd have to move Arrow, too. And Freya knew she could find Arrow no matter what.

She reached for Eldridge and took his hand. "Time to find the Spring Maiden?"

"It's time." He dragged her out the door.

Together they raced through the halls until they found the servant's exit that he'd taken her out last time. Eldridge slowed down in front of the door, squeezing her fingers tight and watching her with wide eyes. "Are you sure you're ready for this?"

"I defeated the Winter Princess, didn't I?" Somehow, that felt a lot harder than what she was about to do. Sure, the Spring Maiden was terrifying. But she wasn't nearly as powerful as the witch who had become the Goblin Queen.

This was easy compared to the creatures she'd beaten before. Even if the Spring Maiden didn't believe it.

Freya put her hand on the door as if she could feel the powerful creature beyond it. "I don't intend on fighting her, Eldridge. We're not going to waltz in there and throw spells or brandish swords. I want to reason with the Spring Maiden first. Like I wanted to with the Winter Princess."

He nodded, albeit slowly. "We'll play this one by your rules then, Freya. I trust your judgement."

Now, she just hoped she was right.

Freya pushed the door open and walked into the gardens beyond. There were countless pixies all pruning the flowers. Some were up trees, trimming the blossoms that fell to the ground and filled the air with a sweet, apple blossom scent.

She counted twenty pixies within eyesight, and that meant the Spring Maiden had more back up than Freya wanted her to have. The pixies all had sharp teeth and wings. They could easily overcome both her and Eldridge.

She had to be certain the Spring Maiden was caught off guard and didn't order her many pixies to attack.

Leaning over to Eldridge, she muttered, "Can you freeze these pixies when I tell you to give us some privacy?"

He glanced around at them, seemingly counting each and every opponent. "There's not that many of them. I should be able to do it, but if anyone walks into the fray, then they won't be frozen."

"That's fine. I don't think I'll need that long to convince her." Freya found the Spring Maiden in the middle of all the pruning.

The lovely lady of this court sat at a delicately made table and chairs. The twisted metal was painted bright white, and a tea set sat on top. Beautiful porcelain gleamed as white as the table, with tiny yellow flowers painted all over it. The Spring Maiden sipped from the smallest teacup Freya had ever seen.

And she was alone.

Perfect.

"Give us a little privacy, Eldridge." She narrowed her eyes on her prey. "I think the Spring Maiden and I should have a talk."

Freya relied on surprise being her only weapon. She had nothing but her own wits about her, but that should be enough. Where the Winter Princess loved battle and showing her teeth, the Spring Maiden only wanted to be regarded as powerful.

She didn't actually have the ability to be powerful herself. Not really.

Every pixie in the garden froze at the same time. Eldridge's magic didn't touch the Spring Maiden, and it took the noble faerie a few moments to realize her subjects weren't moving.

The Spring Maiden frowned as Freya took a seat opposite her on the table. "Hello," Freya said. "It's been a while since you and I talked. Hasn't it?"

The teacup fell from the Maiden's hand and shattered on the table. A soft whimper escaped her lips, and she looked down at the mess she'd made. "My goodness, that's hot tea. You should stay away from that mess, my darling. Your delicate hands would get scalded."

"Would they?" Freya reached forward and caught the Spring Maiden's hand. "I think you're stalling. You didn't expect me to be back so soon, did you?"

"Or at all," the Maiden grumbled.

Freya bristled. This woman wasn't even trying to hide the fact that she hadn't wanted Freya or her companions to return. And though she knew the fae couldn't lie, Freya had hoped that the Maiden would at least pretend to be a little remorseful.

Instead, what she got was a woman who cared very little that Freya was here and struggling. The Maiden didn't even feel guilty for what she had done and all the people she had harmed along the way.

Freya clutched the side of the table until her palms ached. She could not let herself fly into a rage, nor could she launch over this table and grab the Spring Maiden around the neck. That was what she had told Eldridge that she didn't want to do. Fighting would only get them so far, and that progression would be nothing compared to what diplomacy would do.

She couldn't repeat what happened in the Winter Court. Freya wasn't sure she would survive it.

The death of the Winter Princess weighed on her mind even now.

Which was why she was so settled on giving this faerie a chance. "You knew my mother was under your own spell. I want to know why."

"So you found her, then?" The Spring Maiden reached for Freya's teacup and shakily brought it to her lips. "How odd. I didn't think you would find her at all."

"Yes, I did. And I found the wolf as well, who was quite adamant that he wasn't the monster you painted him to be." Freya leaned forward and narrowed her eyes. "You knew he was sending you dead pixies as a way to ask for help, didn't you?"

The Spring Maiden's hand was shaking so badly, she had to put down the teacup. It clattered against the metal table and she immediately waved for one of her servants to come over.

Freya had already suspected this would be the Maiden's plan. Freya knew she would try to get out of this conversation, disappearing into the morning mist. The woman was less confrontational than any faerie she'd met in her travels.

When no servant appeared, the Maiden licked her lips. "Of course. You have Eldridge helping you."

"I don't need anyone's help to stop you. I want that to be very clear." Freya bared her teeth in a snarl. "Or have you forgotten my new name? Your people call me the Queen Killer for a reason."

"The Winter Princess let you kill her. Or you had help from Eldridge the same way you did when you beat him." The Maiden's face turned bright red. These words weren't lies. They were what she wanted to believe. "You are still just a mortal woman and one such as you could never defeat the Spring Maiden. Not for good."

Freya tilted her head and watched the Maiden's expression slowly shift into one of fear. "You know that's not true. Otherwise you never would have gone to such lengths to hide the truth from me. So what is it really, Maiden? I'm giving you a chance to not end up in the same place as the Winter Princess. I don't want to kill you. Despite all the flaws I saw in that horrible mining town, I believe you love this Court. And that, given the right tools, you could fix all the wrongs here."

She honestly wasn't sure that the Spring Maiden could. And she was surprised to realize that she wanted to give the woman a chance.

After all the Maiden had done, Freya still believed the Spring Maiden could be better than the other fae.

Dahlia was more fierce than the others. And though she loved luxury, her own castle was the truest to her season. Beautiful on the outside, but deadly on the inside. The Spring Maiden wanted to let that side of herself emerge. That darkness wanted to be free and to rule as she should, rather than how other people expected her to.

And that was the chance Freya grasped.

The Spring Maiden looked at Freya, then glanced around them. Clearly searching for Eldridge. "I don't know what you're talking about, my dear. The werewolf has hunted us for generations. Your mother was in the wrong place, at the wrong time. That's why I told you she was here. There's no hidden meaning behind my words. I'm not hiding anything from you."

The lies must have burned. And Freya watched with pleasure as the Maiden's face turned green. The faerie pressed a hand to her stomach and the other to her mouth as she held in the vomit from the lie.

"You want to purge yourself of those words, don't you?" Freya asked.

The Maiden glared.

"I know your kind can't lie, and this is the price you must pay for trying to do so." Freya leaned back in her chair and looked at the dirt underneath her nails. Anger simmered just underneath the surface of her skin, and she felt that age old confidence rise inside her. The magic that had been passed down through her blood. "I can make you tell me, you know."

"Well, that would be a trick to have a mortal forcing a fae to do anything."

Freya lifted her hand and squeezed her fingers in the air. Like she was choking the Maiden as she so desperately wanted to do. Eyes wide, the Maiden reached up and touched her throat.

The air twisted between Freya's fingers. Almost like it gave her the semblance of what the Maiden's neck would feel like. She squeezed a little tighter.

"It's not a trick," Freya hissed. "But I think you know that. Why else would you keep my mother locked away? You know something I don't. Last chance, Maiden. I have no interest in playing around. I'm sure there are more people in this realm that know what you know. So spit it out, or I will move on to the next person to question."

Eyes wide, the Maiden slapped at her throat until Freya released her. Long wheezes echoed from the Maiden's lungs as she gasped in air.

Freya patiently waited until the Maiden could breathe again. Then she raised her brows.

"I always suspected," the Maiden rasped. "I never thought it could be true. Your mother was meddling with things no mortal had any right to look at. She was obsessed with magic while remaining entirely human. When she came into this realm, I thought it better to put her to sleep rather than allow her to find more faerie secrets."

"That's it?" Freya shook her head in denial. "That's not the entire story."

The Maiden bared her sharpened teeth. "Your whole family was cursed. The more I looked into it, the more I feared what your story truly was. Your father, your sister, even you. Everyone was touched by magic and you never should have been. Mortals living in the mortal realm with magic? No. That's never allowed."

"So you put my mother to sleep?" Freya furrowed her brow. Pieces were missing from this story. "What about my father?"

"I never met the man."

"But you must know where he is. If you had my mother, then he wouldn't be far behind." Freya said the words hesitantly, however, because she wasn't so sure.

No one had been in that meadow with her mother. And Father would never have let her mother remain in that state. She would have been less surprised to find him dead, draped over her mother's coffin. But not there at all? That was suspicious.

The Spring Maiden swallowed hard. "I have told you everything I know. Your father was not with your mother when she arrived in the Spring Court."

Freya wanted to deny it. But there was always more to a story, no matter how much she wanted this to be the end. "You'll wake her now."

"No," the Maiden said, then frowned. "I will not wake her until we find out why she was here. Why she was cursed. You were supposed to help with the werewolf, and obviously you were sidetracked."

"I took care of your werewolf problem. That was the deal, and I upheld my end of the bargain." Freya stood and leaned over the table, her nose nearly touching the Maiden's. "Now we're making another deal, and you're going to take it. You wake up my mother and I will let you live. If you refuse one more time, then you will join your sister in her icy grave."

The Maiden's eyes widened.

"Yes. I don't plan to bury you here when I'm done with you." Freya cupped the Maiden's cheek and tried to smile in the same feral way as the other always did. "I'm not so kind as to let you stay in your home, even after death. It's your choice, Maiden. But I don't think you question whether or not I can actually do this. I think you know if I wanted to end your life, then I could. With just the snap of my fingers."

The Maiden swallowed hard, then slowly nodded. "I'll wake your mother when we're finished here."

"Now."

"I can't..." The Maiden's eyes darted left and right, then she relented. Her shoulders curved in on herself and she looked very small. "Now. As you request."

"Good." Freya straightened and patted the other woman's shoulder. "And in thanks, once I find my mother alive and well where I have left her body, I will ensure the Goblin King sends you more assistance. Your people need you. And despite all this, I still believe you are the one who can help this court."

Freya left the Maiden sitting where she was and joined her Goblin King on the other side of the castle.

Heart pounding in her chest, Freya met Eldridge's questioning gaze and said, "It's done. Let's see if my mother's awake."

CHAPTER 27

Her stomach churned with every step up the stairs. Freya had thought if she ever got the chance to reunite with her mother, that she would be intensely excited. She'd expected to run up the stairs and throw the door open with love and hope in her heart.

But all she felt was fear. What if her mother didn't recognize her? It had been years.

And what if her mother was disappointed? There was no getting around the fact that Freya was in the faerie realms, as her mother had always told her not to do. And she certainly couldn't explain away the Goblin King. Or the goblin dog, who was likely sitting on the bed with her mother right now.

She scratched the back of her neck and stared up at the ceiling, stopping at the top of the stairs. "Hang on," she muttered. "I need a few minutes."

Eldridge paused as well. He put a hand on her back and rubbed the tension between her shoulder blades. "What is it? I thought you'd want to see your mother as swiftly as possible?"

"I thought so, too." But she couldn't breathe. Every muscle in her body locked up tight and her thighs quaked with fear.

Her mother was going to be so disappointed that Freya had done everything in her power to go against what she'd been taught. She was not only in the faerie realms, but she'd fallen in love with the enemy. One of the dreaded creatures who... who...

She looked up into Eldridge's eyes and realized she couldn't even think such dark thoughts any more. Oh, she loved him more than anything in the world. She'd even give up her family for him, if he asked her to. It wouldn't be easy. And it would feel like ripping her own heart out of her chest. But she would do it.

Eldridge was more important than anyone else now.

Tears burned her eyes. Freya launched herself at his chest and wrapped her arms around him. "I'm not going anywhere," she whispered against his shirt. "No matter what she says. I don't want to go anywhere. I want to be with you wherever you are."

"Oh, Freya," he replied with a chuckle. Eldridge held her tightly against his heart. "I never worried about that. You're a grown woman and you've proven yourself more than capable in my world. Who else could have saved your mother from the clutches of a sleeping spell? She would have been there for all eternity if you hadn't done something about it."

"None of that will change her opinion on you or your kind." Maybe that's what she was worried about. Freya wanted him to be happy and to fit in with her family. Like the man she'd always thought she would end up with. But the problem was that Eldridge wasn't that man.

He was a goblin. A terrifying, monstrous creature who her parents would have hated.

Would hate.

It was hard to start thinking about her mother in the present tense. The woman was waiting for her disappointing daughter, Arrow probably talking her ear off, and Freya didn't even think she could walk inside.

Pulling back, she sniffed loudly while trying to keep the tears from falling. "Do you think we should get Esther first?"

"And leave your mother in the Spring Court for even longer?" He rolled his eyes. "Freya, I think you're stalling. Your mother can't be all that bad."

She thought back to the countless times Astrid had struck Freya over the knuckles for even daring to question her teachings. How many times her mother had scolded her for daring to think that the fae could maybe be a little more complicated than just bad.

And she remembered how her mother had warded their property like a mad woman, insisting that no faerie ever step foot on their property because they were horrible creatures with nightmarish features.

"No," Freya replied, her voice soft and brows furrowed. "She can't be that bad, I suppose."

Releasing her hold on the only person who felt like a lifeline, Freya turned back to the hallway that would lead her to her mother. Had it gotten longer since they left? It sure seemed like it took a thousand steps before she stood in front of the door she had to open.

Freya froze. She didn't want to open the door. She didn't want to see her mother when she knew what the other woman would say.

That Freya had disappointed her.

She'd fallen into the same pit as Esther, and in doing so, had become a shame to their family name.

Her fear was valid and true. It shook through her very core and trembled down to her bones. Freya put her palm on the door and listened quietly.

Screaming was to be expected. Her mother would shout at Arrow, then likely try to attack him. The goblin dog would not bite her mother, so she wondered if maybe he was harmed in the battle.

But when she pressed her ear to the door, she didn't hear any of that. All she heard was the quiet murmuring of a soft conversation on the other side. A conversation that sounded nothing like what she would have expected from her mother.

Eldridge put his hand on her back once again. "Freya. I promise you that nothing is going to go wrong. But if we want to understand what is happening, then we have to talk with your mother. Don't you think?"

She did, but that didn't make it any easier.

Sighing, she replied with nothing more than a firm nod. Flexing her fingers on the wood, she nudged it open.

The hinges swung open to reveal her mother sitting up on the bed.

White rose petals still tangled in her blonde hair, although now her eyes were open. She stared at Arrow, who sat at the foot of the bed like a normal dog would. Perhaps to keep her at ease. He was talking though, and that would be the first indication that he wasn't entirely an animal.

Her mother was cross legged, hands resting on her knees, and for all purposes looked rather calm. When the door opened, she looked at them with kind, intelligent eyes that didn't immediately flare with rage when she saw Eldridge behind her daughter.

Freya didn't know what to do. Did she walk into the room? She felt a bit like an intruder who had interrupted an important conversation that she had no right to interrupt.

In contrast, her mother immediately stood and rounded the edge of the bed. Astrid paused ten feet from her daughter, watching every movement with wide eyes that brimmed with tears.

"My girl," her mother choked. "I never thought I'd see you again. Look how much you've grown."

"Well, it's almost been ten years." Freya suddenly realized how angry she was. So angry she was shaking.

She needed an explanation.

Freya and Esther had been alone for too long. They had struggled through life because their parents had disappeared without a single word of warning, and now she found out that they were alive? How many years of her life had she given up to become her mother, when the woman was still here?

Freya ground her teeth and tried so hard not to let the venomous words slip off her tongue. She glared at the woman who dared to be happy to see her.

Astrid took a step back and shook out her hands at her sides. "I suppose I have a lot of explaining to do."

"More than that," Freya snarled. "You were here? You told us to never go to the faerie realms, no matter what happened. I came here to get Esther back and now I find you've been here the whole time? Why? Where is Father? What were you doing in the Spring Court of all places?"

A thousand questions spilled from her lips and she knew that her mother wouldn't answer them all. But she wanted to advance on the older woman, spitting angry words and bitter heartbreak that she'd suffered since her mother had left.

A daughter deserved her mother's attention, time, and love. Freya had suffered without it for too long and that space where her love had once been, now filled with anger.

"I'm sorry," her mother replied. "I know it's not enough."

"No, it's not." Freya turned toward the fireplace. It was the only spot in the room where she wouldn't have to look at her mother.

The clicking of dog paws hitting the ground didn't make anything better. Arrow trotted over in front of her and sat down hard on the floor. He glared up at her as only her dearest of friends could do. "Your mother has a lot to tell you."

"I'm sure she does. But now that she's awake, I'm not so sure I really care to hear it." Freya looked beyond him, back toward the fireplace. "She can speak with Esther if she needs additional help. Considering she was here, I assume she was looking for something in the faerie realms."

"Freya." Her mother touched her shoulder. "This is something you need to hear as well, my darling. You have every right to be mad at me. There just isn't enough time for us to have this argument."

That anger boiled in her chest. She should control it. Contain it. Be the daughter her mother wanted her to be.

Snarling, she whipped around and threw her mother's hand off her shoulder. "We don't have time? Do you know how much time I had sitting in that cottage, waiting for you to come home? I was fourteen!" Freya dashed at the tears in her eyes. They weren't helping. "I didn't know how to take care of a child, let alone myself. I wanted my mother to come home. My father to protect us. Instead, I had to grow up. I had to be the one to everything for Esther and myself!"

"I know!" her mother shouted. "Do you think I'm unaware of what I put my daughters through? There wasn't any other option for your father or I."

"No other option?" Freya screamed the words back.

How dare her mother even suggest that? There was always another choice when children were involved. Hands shaking, she lifted them in the air and pretended she didn't see the way the furniture in the room rattled against the floor.

Every angry retort and frustrated argument rose from deep within her soul. She hadn't realized just how much hatred and anger had built in the absence of her mother, but here it all was. All rising to the surface at the same time.

She had been abandoned by the one person who should have stayed.

Power rippling through her voice, Freya growled, "You could have brought us with you. Every other choice would have been better than what we suffered through. I made sure Esther lived, and I did everything you said. I sacrificed everything because you couldn't be a good mother and stay with your children."

She had thought the bitter, angry words would make her mother argue all the more. She'd been that kind of woman when Freya knew her. Even the thought of her daughter's rebelling had made Astrid punish them.

And here she was. Silently watching her daughter rage, clearly using magic when that should have made her mother even more angry.

Instead, Astrid stood in the center of the room and let her daughter expel all that awful energy. Her face was calm as the glass of a magic mirror.

When Freya finished yelling, Astrid took a step forward and cupped her daughter's face in her hands. "Your father is the werewolf, Freya. The same one you hunted. Arrow informed me of the quest given to you by the Spring Maiden. We were both hunting the same quarry, but for different reasons."

The words echoed through her head.

Her father was the werewolf.

She'd been hunting the only man who had been her support structure. Her kind-hearted father with soulful eyes and a skill for music.

He was a werewolf.

Freya realized Eldridge had caught her by the elbows and was lowering her into one of the chairs by the fireplace. But she couldn't focus on the surrounding world when her mother had ripped the floor out from under her feet.

Her father couldn't be a werewolf. There were no werewolves in the mortal realm, not anymore. Hardly any werewolves even lived here, in the faerie realms.

"How?" she muttered. "How is that possible?"

Astrid sank to her knees before her daughter, placing her palms on Freya's legs. "He wasn't always like this. The incident happened after you and Esther were born, you see. He had come from the faerie realm. Not a fae, but a changeling child. It's... complicated. But, he went back to see his family and when he returned, there was a wound on his shoulder. We had hoped the curse wouldn't pass to a mortal, but... well. Obviously we were wrong."

She couldn't understand a word her mother was saying. So much of it was wrong compared to the story she knew.

Her father wasn't a changeling child. He was the son of a farmer from a different town who had met her mother in the market. The story had always made her heart warm in her chest because what were the odds of meeting your soulmate in a busy area of town?

"What?" she asked again. Her voice thin and reedy. "Father can't be a changeling. They're not mortal."

Eldridge responded first. "He was the mortal babe the fae stole to replace their child. So to us, yes. He's a changeling." He frowned and started pacing behind her mother. "I don't know what happens to those mortals. The magic here is strong and affects adults, but a child growing up here? He might as well have been fae."

No. None of this made sense. It wasn't right with what she had thought had happened and... And...

She couldn't breathe.

Finally, Freya shook her head and asked, "Why were you here, though? In the faerie realms at all?"

"Your father turned that night. He changed into the beast you saw when you found me, I suspect." Her mother leaned away from her, looking to Arrow, who gave her a little nod of encouragement. "He went through the portal in our woods. I followed him because I didn't want him to be here alone. I didn't know where he was going or why he would even try to find the faerie realms."

"And that's when you met the Spring Maiden," she whispered.

"She didn't want me to find him. As you know, time is... different, while traveling here. For your father, it was months before I got out of the portal and to the Spring Court. He'd already lost his mind and started killing." Astrid shook her head. "It was only a few pixies, but it was enough to set off the bloodlust. I went after him to see if he would listen to me, but the Maiden didn't want me to."

Freya could believe this part of the story. And though it wasn't the one she'd made up in her head, she also recognized that this was very much the truth. Her mother had come here intending to save her father. She'd failed, and thus, Freya had stepped into her shoes.

Frowning, Freya held her head in her hands. "Why did you think you could get him back? This is the faerie realm. It's nothing like our home, and finding him in an unknown land would have been impossible."

Her mother stared at her with wide eyes, as though she didn't recognize her own daughter. "Because I love him. I would have done anything to keep him alive, and I still will. I have no doubt that I will find your father and I will bring him home."

Freya recognized the fierce love in her mother. The kind of love that ended worlds and toppled kings from thrones.

Maybe that's where Freya had gotten it from.

Letting go of all the tension in her shoulders, she released her anger. At least for a little while. "All right, then. We'll find him together. But first, I think you need to see Esther."

"I wouldn't expect it any other way. Arrow told me that your father ran after you took me from my coffin." Her mother stood and her features hardened. She returned to the imposing, terrifying woman Freya knew her as. "Let's go to this Goblin King's court and find my husband together."

CHAPTER 28

As fierce as her mother was, a sleeping spell was much stronger. And so Astrid slept a lot on their trip back to the Goblin Kingdom.

Eldridge thought it was smarter to not travel through a portal. Too much magic in a mortal body was bound to hurt, he reasoned. Considering how long her mother had been affected by this spell, Freya wasn't going to argue.

They traveled in a small carriage all the way back to Eldridge's domain. And yes, it was as awkward as Freya feared it would be.

She hadn't expected talking to her mother to feel so... uncomfortable. They had a lot of mending to do in their relationship. Freya needed to work on her abandonment issues, and her mother needed to remember what it was like to be alive and not asleep.

Astrid kept her head against the carriage window and drifted in and out of the waking realm. Freya worried the spell wasn't entirely broken, but Eldridge insisted this was normal. Spells like that took a long time to wear off. And though most people would have thought the poor victim would be wide awake, often they wanted to return to sleep.

Apparently, a sleeping spell wasn't all that restful.

Freya watched the Goblin Castle appear on the horizon. The strange galaxy of stars appeared behind it, even though the sun was still out. The dark silhouette of the imposing building made the tension in her chest ease.

She was home. Even though her mother was a stranger and they had yet another person to save. At the very least, she was home.

The wheels rattled on the cobblestone and woke Astrid. Sitting up straighter, her mother rubbed her eyes and yawned. "Are we here?"

"We are." Freya watched the front gates open and saw two figures waiting for them in front of the door. One with a rat tail that waved behind him, and one with a fluffy white tail that wagged in excitement.

What would her mother think now that her baby girl wasn't human anymore? Freya would protect Esther from any words that would insult her looks. Esther was just as beautiful as she was before. No one would ever tell her otherwise.

The carriage stopped and Lux opened the door.

Her mother flinched away from the rat-faced boy who held out his hand as though nothing had happened. "Madame. Welcome to the Goblin Court."

To her mother's credit, she took Lux's hand. "Thank you. It's not at all like I expected."

"I imagine not." He helped her to the ground and then bowed low over her fingers. "Know that we are not a threat to you or your daughters. The two of them have made quite an impression in a very short amount of time."

Freya pressed her palm against her mouth to hide her smile. If Lux was trying to get on her mother's good side so she wouldn't mind her daughter being in love with a goblin, then he was doing a good job of it. He looked every inch a nobleman who was about to ask to court her daughter.

Good. Let him sway her mother first. He was much more terrifying to look at than Eldridge.

"Mother?" The shout echoed through the courtyard. Esther shot across the cobblestone and slammed into their mother with all the force of an avalanche, locking her arms around Astrid's waist and sobbing into her neck.

Maybe that's how it should have gone between Freya and Astrid. But she just couldn't do that.

Freya wished their reunion had been one full of tears and love. She would have loved to fall into her mother's arms and purge all the emotions the past few years had brought her. That had never been their relationship, though, had it?

Her mother had poured all her teachings into Freya's head. Not a single day went by when she wasn't trying to train Freya in some kind of lesson that made little sense but was important. Esther was the one who got the love. The hugs. The adoration and the bedtime stories.

Freya was supposed to take care of her sister. And Esther was the one to be taken care of.

Sighing, she turned to look at Eldridge and tried to muster a watery smile. "She's home now. Esther will be so happy to have her back."

He tucked a strand of hair behind her ear, brows furrowed and worry twisting his expression. "And you?"

"If I had known she was alive, I would have been searching for her just as I did Esther." Although, that would have proven much more difficult considering she had only been a child when her mother had disappeared. Traveling to the faerie realm might have been more dangerous when she was that young.

"Freya!" Esther shouted. "You did it!"

She waved a hand over her head awkwardly. "I did!"

Esther bounded to her side and grabbed her hands. "Now that we have Mother back, everything can return to normal. We'll be like a family again."

Why was she the one who always had to break her sister's heart? Astrid was here. She could tell Esther all about the horrible things that had happened to their father, and that their lives weren't going to slow down any time soon.

No, she wouldn't be this person anymore. She didn't want to see the light die from Esther's eyes. Not when her sister was looking at her like a hero, yet again. As though Freya could defeat any monster that was thrown at her.

She liked it when Esther looked at her like that. It reminded her of all the times she had chased away nightmares.

Softly smiling, she ran her fingers through Esther's hair, settling all her flyaways back into place. "Mother has a lot to talk to you about, but I'll let you two get settled before we tell you anymore. Get her rested and well, while we clean up. Will you?"

"Of course." Esther's grin didn't waver. "It's so good to have her back. I never stopped believing she was alive, you know. I'm glad I was right."

Her sister ran off to grab her mother by the arm. Esther would drag the poor woman all over the castle before she finally let her sleep again. But this was what her mother had missed for all these years. Hopefully she would indulge her youngest daughter in listening to what Esther had to say.

After all, Esther had earned this time for the heartache and loss she had suffered.

Eldridge pressed his hand to the small of her back and nudged her toward the side of the castle. "Come with me. We'll let your sister handle your mother for the time being."

"Oh?" Her stomach flip-flopped. What did he want to talk with her about? Was this going to be a conversation about indulging in each other in that mining town?

Freya hadn't even had the chance to think about that. She had a bit, but really, now was the time for her to sit down and measure the repercussions. She'd slept with the Goblin King. Not many people did that. Or at least, not many mortals.

Now that she thought about it, though, maybe a lot of people did. Maybe it meant nothing to him and she was over here worried that he was going to... to...

"Freya," Eldridge said with a chuckle. "I can see your mind racing. Would you follow me and see what I have to show you? Stop over-thinking everything and just be for a few minutes."

Just be.

She could do that.

Freya trailed along behind him through a set of wrought-iron gates covered in ivy. She wondered how similar the layout of this castle was compared to all the others. Were the leaders together when they built their homes? Or did each castle have its own labyrinth-like quality that differed vastly from the others?

He led her into a small garden. This wasn't at all like the Spring Maiden's flowers. Instead of bright pinks and pastels like Freya was used to, this garden was filled to the brim with deep emerald colors and black petals. A garden of midnight blooms.

"How beautiful," she said.

And it was. She could feel the tension leaking out of her by the minute. No longer were her eyes overwhelmed by the sight of so much color and brightness. Instead, he'd given her the opportunity to ease into the shadows and be forgotten by the world. At least for a little while.

Eldridge drew her to a bench carved out of dark stone and set her gently on the surface. He knelt before her, staring up into her eyes, and holding her hands in his. "I know you're overwhelmed. So much has happened in such little time. I would be surprised if you knew how to handle this all without bursting at the seams."

Don't cry, she told herself. Don't cry because he's being nice to you.

She feared if she spoke, then all the tears would pour out of her. So Freya nodded sharply and stared down at their hands.

"I need you to know that I am here," he murmured. "Not as the Goblin King. Not as your rival or your companion in a quest to find your mother. I am here as the man who loves you."

His hands clenched on her fingers, forcing her to stay still when she might have ripped her hands out of his and retreated.

"No," Eldridge chuckled. "You aren't getting away so easily. I need to tell you this, Freya. And you need to hear it."

"What if I'm afraid?" she whispered.

"Of what?" Eldridge leaned back with wide eyes. He stared at her as though she'd admitted to having lost her mind.

"Of being a disappointment to you. I'm not a faerie, or... Maybe I am. I don't know." Freya slid her fingers from his grip and tangled them in her skirts. "I won't be like anyone else you've ever been involved with. And everything I do will probably confuse or frustrate. I'm afraid you'll wake up in a few months, or perhaps years, and that you'll want someone else."

"Ah." He stood and sat down on the bench with her. Eldridge braced his elbows on his knees, stared off into the distance and nodded. "Yes, I suppose loving a mortal comes with its own complications."

At least he understood her thoughts. He would be disappointed eventually, in something that she did, or worse... who she was.

Freya swallowed hard and tried not to be too upset that he'd agreed so easily. But she had to expect that. After all, she was the one who had brought it up.

She opened her mouth to say she was going back to her room, only for him to interrupt her.

"Except..." He turned toward her, and the grin on his face didn't match what she had thought was running through his head. "It is rare for anyone to ever truly understand love. I know that when I look at you, I can feel my heart take flight. Every time you speak, my stomach lurches like I'm going to be sick, but it's an illness I desire. You touch me and I want to be a better man. Not just for you, but so I know that I deserve you in my life."

Tears built in her eyes again. How was she ever supposed to know how to deal with this man? He was trying so hard and she was struggling to even admit her feelings to herself. No matter how much she wanted to.

He cupped her cheek in his hand and grinned. "You don't have to say it back, you know. I don't expect that. But I want you to know and acknowledge that I would tear the stars from the sky for you. Every inch of your body is beloved by me. And I will rip apart anyone who dares try to take you from me."

Her lips parted in a sigh and he took advantage. Eldridge gently kissed her with all the passion he had kept in his heart.

She wanted to say it back to him. Every fiber of her soul screamed that she loved him too. Dearly. More than her own soul. But something stopped her. The words caught on her tongue and refused to come out no matter how hard she tried.

Eldridge slid his lips from hers, then pressed a kiss against her ear. "It's all right," he whispered. "I'll say it for you."

He kissed the highest point of her cheekbone. "I love you."

His lips glided down the sharp edge of her jaw. "I love you."

He pressed twin touches to her eyes. "I love you. I love you."

Freya kept her eyes closed and basked in the knowledge that not only was she loved, but she was safe here in his arms. And she might not be safe forever, but in this moment she was.

Tomorrow they would start figuring out how to save her father. Tomorrow she would walk into a room where her mother was alive with unfinished business between them.

Tonight, she would indulge herself in the delicious, forbidden touch of the Goblin King.

OF WEREWOLVES AND CURSES

CHAPTER 1

"What a lovely day to contemplate murder," Arrow snuffled, then plopped down beside her. His tail wasn't wagging and his teeth were bared in an impressive snarl.

Freya looked up from the map on the table. "And who exactly are we murdering?"

He stared her dead in the eyes and replied, "The Goblin King."

That would be rather problematic considering the Goblin King was very dear to both of them. She sighed and looked back to the map of the kingdom on the center of the gold table. Her father was out there, somewhere. And no one had a clue where the werewolf had fled. Someone had to have heard something.

But she supposed right now wasn't the time to figure all that out. She needed to help her friend rather than try to figure out where a wayward werewolf would run off to.

Sighing, she put her hand over the Summer Court and turned her entire attention to the handsome dog. They were in the castle's observatory, a rather strange room with swaying planets over their head. The two of them stood in the only section that was safe from all the flying projectiles.

A star circled overhead, the bright bulb casting shadows of planets and the metal arms that moved them. Freya adjusted her lavender gown, flipping the skirts over the small stool behind her while taking a seat.

Crossing her arms over her chest, she asked, "Why are we contemplating killing the Goblin King?"

"Because he refuses to see reason about anything. I told him the werewolf might be in the Autumn Court, but he's not talking with the Thief right now. I told him moving your mother in the western wing would be smarter, the view is nicer. Of course he won't move your mother farther away from Esther." He huffed out another angry growl. "I told him to put honey in his tea because he needs something sweet in his life, and he tipped it over onto the table and left breakfast without a word."

Freya winced. The Goblin King's horrible mood may have been her fault, considering she'd rushed up to this room to pour over the map for whatever details she could find. It wasn't like the map changed. No one had even spelled it to show what she wanted. But her heart told her to stare until something revealed itself. Maybe that was foolish.

"Ah," she replied. "Well, that horrible mood was my doing. I told him I would have breakfast with him because he had something important to tell me, and I forgot until this moment."

Arrow narrowed his eyes on her. "Right. So you were the one who unleashed the most terrifying goblin on us because you wanted to look at the map again."

"Apparently." She winced again, then cleared her throat. "I'm sorry?"

"No. No need to be sorry." Arrow stood up and walked over to the nearest window. Slashes of bright golden light illuminated the dust particles that swirled through the air. He hopped up onto a podium underneath a pointy star and stood in the light. "You have doomed us all to a horrible meeting. I will blame you when this is over."

"Meeting?" she asked.

The doors to the observatory busted open and a whole group of strange people walked in. Lux with his rat face and thin tail waving behind him. Esther, who was turning more faerie by the day. Her hands had already started growing pads on her fingertips. Her newly saved mother walked between them, eyes already sharpened with the wit and intent to save her husband.

Last, the Goblin King. He wore a glower that should have burned everyone around him to the ground. He squared his shoulders with aggression and stomped toward the table without even looking at Freya.

Right. So they were arguing.

She sighed and attempted a smile at the others. "Hello. It's good to see all of you."

Esther, as usual, was unaware of the tension that had entered the room with her. She flounced to her stool at the table, yellow dress billowing around her like a cloud. It perfectly matched her lovely blonde hair. "Morning, Freya! We missed you at breakfast."

Everyone in the room fell silent, holding their breath and staring at the Goblin King. He bared his teeth in a snarl and parroted Esther. "Yes, Freya. We missed you at breakfast. Where were you, considering you promised you would actually eat with the lot of us?"

Her cheeks burned. "I was here. Looking at the map and preparing for this meeting."

"Were you now?" He sat on his own stool directly across from her. "And did you find anything new? Anything worth wasting all of our time?"

She narrowed her gaze. If he wanted to play this game, then she would keep up with him. He could be as passive aggressive as he wanted. Freya had grown up with a little sister and she knew how to ignore children when they were being annoying.

Pointing to a small mark near the Summer Court on the map, she replied, "Yes, I think this is worth considering. There were a few books in the library that claimed the Summer Court was a home of sorts for the werewolves before the fae killed them all off. I think it would be interesting to research this place."

"The Summer Court is not where he would go," Eldridge snarled. "The curse wouldn't let him. He would know how dangerous it was to go there."

"Are you so sure of that?" She stood and slapped her hands down on the table. "I think you don't want to agree with me this morning. You know that it's a perfectly acceptable place to look into, and the more places we research, the better. It's not like the Summer Court is that far away."

"I think you need to be better about remembering promises!" He stood as well, mirroring her position with his fingers a hair's breadth from hers. "I forgot how frustrating it was to have mortals around when you can all lie through your teeth."

"Are you calling me a liar because I forgot to have breakfast with you?" She leaned so close she could see the sparks flying in his eyes.

This was ridiculous. He couldn't claim she was a liar because she wasn't catering to his every whim. She had a life outside of him, no matter how much he didn't want her to.

Her mother cleared her throat, interrupting them. "I understand that you two may be a little frustrated with each other, but can we please focus on finding my husband before you tear each other's heads off?"

Eldridge snarled. "I don't want to rip her head off, I want a few moments of her time, which is apparently very precious these days."

"We sleep in the same bedroom," she gritted through her teeth. "If you had something to say, then you can say it when we're there."

"Our bedroom should be a place of happiness and rest. I refuse to talk about anything but joyous things within those walls."

"Ah ha!" She snapped her fingers and pointed in his face. "I knew you had something bad to tell me! Why would I want to hear even more bad news when that's all we've been talking about these days?"

He mirrored her action, pointing at her with a clawed finger. "You should want to talk to me about anything! That's what a team is. That's what people do in a relationship!"

Arrow hopped up on the table in between them and shook hard. Water went flying throughout the room, soaking both Freya and Eldridge. She backed away from the table with a shriek.

"What in the world, Arrow!" She wiped water off her face before glaring. "How did you even get wet?"

Ah. That would be her sister holding an empty bucket in her hands that Esther quickly tossed to the side.

Freya glared at both of them.

Eldridge wiped water off his fine suit and grumbled. "You two with your pranks. Why were you getting involved?"

Neither of them knew how to answer their king. They looked at each other, then back to the table, then back at each other.

With a heavy sigh, Astrid stepped forward and answered his question. "We all understand the two of you are tense. A new relationship on top of all your responsibilities is particularly stressful. No one could ever say otherwise. However, you are both letting your stress get in the way of many things these days. We need you to focus on the task at hand, which is finding out where the wolf might be hiding. Whatever tiff you're in can wait until after that."

Had they poured water over Arrow just to cool Freya and Eldridge off? That seemed rather overkill.

Frowning, Freya pointed back to the map in the center of the table. "I already know where Dad is. I told you, this is the summer home of the wolves and he would return to it. There's no way he's anywhere else."

"And you know the faerie realm so well," Eldridge scoffed. He leaned over the map and read the name of the mark she'd pointed at. "Actually..."

Freya let out a grunt as he rounded the table and pushed her aside.

"Move," Eldridge said after shoving her.

"I didn't really have a choice not to," she grumbled. Freya jostled back to her position in front of the map, hip checking him out of her way. "This is the spot I read about. You gave me the book on the werewolves, you know."

"Yes, I remember." His brows furrowed in concentration, he looked over the roads that were near the small town of Sunhold. "I remember this place from when I was a boy. It's near the Summer palace."

"I must have missed it on my travels throughout all the kingdoms," she snarled.

"Easy, now you sound like your father." He tapped his claw against the mark on the map and gave a quick nod. "I take back what I said. You were right, this is a good place to start."

Freya could have flipped the table; his words made her so angry. Of course it was the right spot. She was the only one who had dedicated every single day to researching the wolves and their history. She'd read countless books, at least twenty, recounting the wolves' movements, the battles, even the interviews the fae had conducted on the wolves they had captured.

Her mind was painted with bloody battles and horrible endings for people like her father. Sometimes it felt like she had lived through the moments with the wolves themselves, and that was difficult to think about. The stories had even slipped into her dreams until she was frightened to fall asleep.

In short, if anyone knew where the wolves were, it was Freya.

She balanced her hip on the side of the table and eyed him with a lifted brow. "And?"

"And what?"

"Are you going to apologize for automatically thinking I was wrong? I wasn't. I want to hear you say it." Maybe that was because she found it ridiculously attractive when he admitted she was right.

Eldridge snarled and bared his teeth.

Astrid rolled her eyes and held out an arm for the others, gesturing toward the door. "Come on, then. Now that we have a clue, we'll all research Sunhold. In the meantime, I suggest you two get your argument over with. Otherwise, you're going to annoy the rest of us. Come, children. Now."

Though she might have expected Lux and Esther to balk at being called children, everyone filed out of the room with surprising swiftness. They raced to the door and quietly closed it behind them, leaving Freya alone with a very angry Goblin King.

She shrugged, arms still hugged tightly over her chest. "What? What could you possibly need to tell me, Eldridge? You made us look ridiculous in front of them."

"Oh, I made us look ridiculous?" He pressed a hand over his heart. "That was me doing that? Not you?"

"Well, it couldn't be me. I can't look foolish, that's your job."

The growl that erupted from his chest would have put a werewolf to shame. Eldridge lunged for her, hands tunneling into her hair, and yanked her forward.

He kissed her with all the anger that he was feeling. Lips hard and unyielding, teeth nipping at her mouth, and tongue demanding to be let in. For all that she was mad at him, Freya was more than happy to let him take out his frustration like this.

She grabbed him by his waistband, tugging him closer to her with a grunt. "You make me so angry," she hissed against his lips.

"And you drive me mad," he growled. With a swift movement, he scooped his arm underneath her bottom and tossed her on top of the table. Map be damned, she would let him do whatever he wanted.

Eldridge returned his hand to the back of her neck, forcefully holding her in place and locking her lips to his. He ground himself against her hips. Every rolling movement sent her closer to the edge. He consumed her. Devoured her whole and she could think of nothing but him.

The Goblin King who wanted her even when he was angry. Even when he wanted to yell and scream and shout. Instead, he channeled all that energy into kissing her. Loving her. Turning her thoughts away from anger.

His hot breath echoed in her ear. His body moved with power and barely leashed rage. And she wouldn't have it any other way.

He made her entire body ache, tense, and release more times than she could count. He took magic from her body until it felt like all her energy was rolling off her in waves.

Finally, he stopped. She pressed her hands to his sweat slicked back and held on for dear life. Freya wanted just a few more moments when they were one, not two.

Eldridge leaned down and pressed his lips to her shoulder. "I should have apologized before we started all that."

"I think it was apology enough." Goodness, her voice was raspy. She finally released her hold on his muscles and leaned back. "I think we ruined the map, though."

He leaned to look at all the drops of sweat they'd left in the smudged ink. "Ah well." He shrugged. "I have more."

She moaned as he pulled away from her, leaving behind a sense of emptiness. "No. You know I hate it when you do that."

Eldridge tugged his pants up but grinned at her with far too much male pride. He leaned toward her again and tugged her in for another hard kiss. "I know, darling, but we both have to start our day."

Oh, if only he wasn't right. They had a lot to do, and not enough time for either of them to do everything.

Sighing, she hopped down from the table and tugged her dress back into place. Her hair, however, she could do nothing to save. "I suppose you're right. And you know how much I hate it when you're right."

"As always." He pulled his pale shirt back over his head. "But a king has many responsibilities."

"Mm." Running her fingers through the tangled mass of her hair, Freya paused and looked at him. "What did you have to say, anyway?"

A small flicker in his eyes gave away that he wasn't telling her the entire truth. Or that he was spinning words when he replied, "It's not important anymore. I'll tell you later, my love."

He silenced her with another kiss before walking away, whistling as he went.

Freya wondered if he'd ever tell her. Obviously he had something on his mind that was important enough to put him in a foul mood. And she wouldn't always be around to entertain him on a table.

Although it had been entertaining.

No, she had to stop thinking like that. After all, there was a job to be done.

A king had to be a king, he was right. But a hero also had to save. She needed to find her mother and the others so they could figure out the next steps in finding her father.

Sunhold. Perhaps another adventure awaited them already.

CHAPTER 2

Freya found her family in the library with their noses stuck in books. That was... odd. Her family rarely wanted to read about the lands they needed to go to. They were action people, not readers.

She leaned against the door frame and watched them with a careful eye until Esther looked up and yawned.

"Oh, Freya," she said. "We wondered when you would finish with your argument. Did you tell the Goblin King to stuff it?"

Lux snickered and pressed his hand to his mouth.

Oh, they were all children. Rolling her eyes, she walked into the library and sat down in the empty chair. "You were all listening at the door, weren't you? That's disgusting."

"You're telling me." Arrow grumbled from his seat on a pile of blankets next to the window. He turned the page of his open book. The worn red leather gleamed in the sunlight. "I could have gone my entire life without hearing what I did. The others might be able to run and not remember it, but it took forever for me to get far enough."

"That's gross." Her cheeks burned so hot, she thought she might burst into flames. "You shouldn't be listening at doors. You got what you deserved."

He shuddered. "Nightmares. Nightmares for life."

Lux finally couldn't hold his laughter in anymore. He set his book on his lap, the book Freya now realized was upside down, and tilted his head back with roaring laughter. He didn't even try to hold in the mirth that shook through his shoulders and entire form. The rest of the room dissolved into laughter as well.

Her mother was clearly trying to pull herself back together, and Astrid held up her hand for them all to stop screaming. "All right, everyone. That's enough teasing. I, for one, am glad that the Goblin King and his hero have given up being angry with each other. It makes everything else so much easier."

"Thank you, Mother," she said.

It was the first time she'd said words like that since she had gotten her mother back. They felt odd to say, but somehow right at the same time. Maybe someday it would get easier to talk to the woman who had birthed her. Maybe. She hoped.

Clearing her throat, she pointed to the book Arrow was actually reading. "I'm guessing that's the only book in this room that will give us more information about where Dad is?"

Arrow looked up from the pages, obviously bored with them all. "You are correct. No one else is working but me."

"Right." She bit her lip. "I suppose that makes sense considering everyone else was more enamored with gossip. What have you found?"

He stood up and shook himself, then pinched the book between both paws and walked it over to her. "Sunhold was the summer home for most werewolves, as you said. However, I think there are a few distinctions that you should know about. Namely that the wolves chose to go here. They weren't called like turtles to their birthplace. He might have gone somewhere else because he knows how dangerous this place is for his kind."

Astrid straightened in her chair, her amused expression changing to one of severe worry. "I wouldn't discount that, but I think it's unlikely he'd think that far ahead. Your father knew little about the were-wolves. He stayed with us because he could. Leaving them was an easy choice for him, so he wouldn't know their history."

A low hum vibrated in Freya's throat as she thought about those words. "You said Dad was bitten when we were young?"

"Yes."

"How young?" She gestured to the red leather book in Arrow's paws. "This claims the wolves were all killed off. And where was he when he was bitten? That... It doesn't make a lot of sense, is all."

Astrid shook her head, brows furrowed. "I don't know the answer to that. Your father said he had to go home. He never told me which court his family was from, and I never met them. He might have come from the Summer Court, and maybe that's why he went there? If the wolves were even there to bite him. You said there weren't many left."

Wincing, Freya shook her head with disappointment. "There are too many holes. We would only be able to guess that he might be here."

"I can send some messengers and see if they find anything," Arrow said. He patted the book and placed it in her lap. "This might help with understanding the wolves better, if you haven't read it yet. But I think we all need to understand that he isn't in his right mind. He's not your father at the moment."

She remembered reading that. Freya looked down at the book and wished it would reveal further secrets to her.

Esther asked, "What does Arrow mean? Not in his right mind?"

"He wasn't killing pixies only because he wanted to help Mom," Freya replied. "The wolves have three forms. Human. Wolf. And then that twisted being we saw in the Spring Court. He doesn't know what he's doing, and he doesn't understand us when we're talking to him. Maybe a little, but they aren't... Well, they aren't human when they're like that."

Arrow coughed. "It's a cursed form, Miss Esther. Painful to be in and even worse on the mind. Your father probably doesn't remember who he even is. He just knew that the human inside him was tied to your mother, and he couldn't leave her side for that reason."

She hated seeing her sister's expression twist to sadness. Esther wanted everyone to be happy and together. She wasn't built for a life like this, with their family fractured into pieces.

Freya could only hope that they got him back quickly. She also wouldn't mind having them all back together again. It might be nice to have a family unit in the faerie realm.

The book in her lap held some answers she searched for, and that was a start. Freya palmed it and stood up again. "All of you keep looking for anything that might help in the long run. Nothing is too vague for us to take seriously. I hope you understand the urgency of this."

Lux saluted her. "You've got it, Queen Killer."

She pointed at him with a frown. "Don't call me that."

"Sorry, it's the name you've been given." He reclined in his chair, hands linked behind his head and ankles crossed over each other. "You can't undo a nickname once it's given to you."

"Watch me."

Freya left the library, battling hope with every step. She knew better than to let herself get excited about the opportunity this might provide. Her father could be exactly where she had pinned him down to be.

Sunhold. The town that the fae had abandoned all those years ago and then taken over by werewolves. It was the perfect place for them to enjoy the heat for a little while. She knew why their kind would want to stay there.

But now she had to face the Summer Lord again. She wasn't looking forward to going back to the Summer Court and seeing all those masked elves. They had made her intensely uncomfortable.

Freya didn't know where she was going, only that she had to go somewhere. She found herself back at the room she shared with Eldridge.

Her heart knew who she wanted to talk to. The only man who had ever understood the wild need in her heart to be more than what she was. The only man who had given her permission to be herself. Even when she was being hard headed.

Freya nudged the door open and found Eldridge waiting for her. He stood in front of the floor to ceiling window, hands held behind his back. A galaxy swirled in front of him, the stars glowing brightly and then disappearing as they faded from life.

She didn't know how she always found him so easily in this palace.

The hallways were difficult to maneuver, and Eldridge never told her where he was going. But no matter how challenging it should have been, if she wanted to find him, then she could.

"Ah," he said as she closed the door behind her. "That didn't take long."

"Well, they weren't working all that hard." She waved the red leather book in the air. "Arrow was the only one to find anything, and it's not exactly helpful."

"How so?"

She sighed and tossed the book onto the bed. "It's mostly about how the werewolf mind thinks, and the history of why they went to Sunhold. I'm sure I've read it already, but I've read so many of them all the words blend together."

He turned around, and she was enraptured with the sight of him all over again. Those broad shoulders had filled out after his torture in the Winter Court. His glossy dark hair fell over his shoulder and those pointed teeth gleamed in the dim light of the stars. His silver skin reflected the light as though he really were made of metal, and every fiber of her soul wanted to jump on him again.

It had been like that ever since they returned to his kingdom, though. They couldn't keep their hands off each other. Even when they tried.

She shook her head to dispel the hungry thoughts from her mind. She needed to focus, not lust after the Goblin King. "I still think Sunhold is our best bet. My mother doesn't think he would avoid the location because he knows next to nothing about werewolves."

The bright heat of passion faded from Eldridge's eyes. "Are you so sure about that?"

"Why would he know anything? He'd grown up here, yes, but the fae don't consort with werewolves. You said so yourself." She tilted her head to the side. "Or do they?"

"It depends on who his family was." He released his hands and raised them in a gesture of disbelief. "I know there are a few fae out there who have surprised you, my dear. Some of us aren't as... hateful as others. If they thought the werewolves were useful to whatever cause they had, then it is likely someone might have taken a few of them in."

She narrowed her eyes. "That sounds like an Autumn Court choice to me."

"What would make you think a goblin would be interested in a wolf?" He scoffed, but she saw the nervous glint in his eyes. "None of us would take a werewolf under our wing."

"Look at Arrow." The more she thought about it, the more it made sense. "He looks like a dog. Logic would bring me to believe there are more goblins who look like wolves than dogs. It's not impossible to think that someone who looks like them may have been interested in helping someone who shares the same features."

"It's a start to finding your lineage." The Goblin King looked disturbed.

Freya couldn't stand that expression. "What? What are you thinking?"

He pressed a hand to his mouth but didn't hide his smile fast enough. "I hope we don't find out that we're related."

"Eldridge!" All the blood drained from her face. "Please tell me you don't believe there's a chance of that."

He burst out laughing. But that still didn't make her feel any better. Could they really be related? She was already turning green at the thought. She couldn't let him go. He was everything to her now, even if she wasn't very good at telling him that yet.

But related?

Eldridge reached for her and tugged her into his arms. "No, my love. We can't be related."

"But if you're from the Autumn Court, and I'm from the Autumn Court, then how can you be so sure?" she asked, her mouth mashed against his chest.

"Because otherwise I would have heard of your father. There is no one in my family who went missing, and we did not partake in any changeling swaps of children." He leaned back and brushed his hands over her head, smoothing her hair back from her face. "And my darling, your father grew up here, but that doesn't make him related to any of us. Changelings are different, remember?"

Right. Even though she could perform magic, her father wasn't fae.

They didn't know how all that would have affected his children, but he still wasn't a faerie.

Thank goodness.

Blowing out a long breath of relief, she nodded. "All right. Well, don't scare me like that next time."

"Why not?" he arched a brow. "I've heard there are quite a few mortals who like keeping everything in the same bloodline. We'd create a noble family lineage no one could deny."

Freya pulled herself out of his arms and slapped him on the shoulder. "Stop it. It's not funny."

"It is a little." He held up fingers and pinched them together. "Just a tiny amount, maybe?"

"Not at all," she scolded. But she couldn't stop the grin from spreading across her face. "Fine. Maybe a little. But can we focus, my Goblin King? What are we doing now?"

He rolled his eyes and backed her toward the bed. "First, I'm going to enjoy an afternoon with my dear hero that I used to dream about when I was a boy. And then we're going to start packing for a trip to Sunhold."

"Another trip? So soon?" She veered away from the bed. "I should probably start packing now, then."

"Oh no, you don't." He caught her around the waist and tumbled with her onto the mattress.

They didn't start packing until very late that night.

Eldridge opted for horses this time, and Arrow was less than happy about it. He grumbled from the back of Freya's horse about how horrible the travel conditions were. He was more a cart kind of goblin. Or at the very least, a goblin who would ride in a carriage.

Not a horse.

Never a horse.

If she had to listen to him complain any more, she would explode. The goblin seriously underestimated how much patience she would have during this trip. If he said one more thing, she was going to dump him off the saddle and ride off into the sunset. He could walk to the Summer Court.

Eldridge kicked his horse until they were walking side by side. "Arrow, you can always walk if this is such a great inconvenience."

The goblin dog snapped his jaw shut and glared at the Goblin King. "You know I can't keep up."

"No, I wouldn't imagine you could. But I'd give you a map."

Arrow grumbled and settled back down on the pack he was holding onto for dear life. Freya couldn't say she was the biggest fan of the horses, either. They weren't normal creatures like she was used to in the mortal realm. These horses were larger, nearly two men tall and wide enough that she had to sit side saddle.

She glanced over at Eldridge, who looked too pleased with himself.

"You know," she started. "We didn't have to take the horses."

"Of course not, but I enjoy riding them." He patted his own horse on the neck. "Don't you?"

She wasn't going to answer that. He already knew what she was going to say, considering the bright glint in his eyes.

The horses weren't all that bad, but their travel was now uncomfortable and she also would have preferred the carriage. Though, they had lovely fresh air to breathe on this journey, rather than a stuffy box with all three of them packed inside.

"Fine," she admitted. "This is a lovely way to travel and I do feel better for having all this air around us."

"I thought you might."

Arrow snarled from behind them, but didn't chime in with his opinion. They both knew what it would be, anyway.

She let them travel in silence for a few more moments. Tilting her head back, she let her horse walk as he wished and enjoyed the sun on her face. A slight breeze toyed with her hair, tangling in the long strands and brushing them off her shoulders. Every step brought them farther from the chill of autumn and into the heat of the Summer Court.

"You know," she said, starting the conversation that they needed to have, even though she didn't know if he would tell her the truth. "When I was first in the Summer Court, it appeared that you knew the Summer Lord well."

"Did I?" Eldridge asked, playing dumb to her question. "I don't know why you'd think that."

"Well, because you were sitting on matching thrones, for a start. But also because there were a few jabs that each of you flung at each other that were more brotherly than they were noble." She frowned, trying to remember the exact words.

Strangely, she couldn't. There were so many moments between the Summer Court and now that she honestly remembered little other than the highlights of that journey. The elves without faces. The beautiful castle with all its seashell glory. She even remembered the Summer Lord himself, wearing his pressed white suit and the gleam of his skin like a rare pearl. Even the labyrinth where the Goblin King had tried to trick her into getting lost.

But that was it. She didn't remember what was said or even how she had gotten there.

Eldridge shrugged and then relented to her questioning. "The Summer Lord and I were childhood friends. Both young noblemen who had no right to be nobles at the time. We were wild and perhaps a little too... aggressive with our tactics in learning how to be men. We were friends for a very long time and then had a falling out."

Oh, she had so many questions. Freya shielded her eyes from the sun so she could look at him with a little more focus. "You were friends? And aggressive tactics? What on earth are you talking about?"

Arrow poked his head around her shoulder, resting his chin against her arm. "He means they were idiots back in the day. My father used to tell me about those foolish things they did when they were young. Both of them were trying to prove themselves worthy of a throne so they went off gallivanting around the countryside trying to bring back the most impressive kill. Or woo the most beautiful lady."

Eldridge was quick to interrupt his friend. "We never did any of that. Most of the court thought we both were unfit for a throne and ignored us. We were just children trying to prove ourselves."

"What kind of kills did you think you were going to bring back?" she asked. Freya tried very hard not to focus on the latter because that would only make her frustrated and jealous.

"Mostly the heads of fabled beasts. A few stag were known to glow in the dark, their hides were so white. And there were a couple..." He paused, then sighed. "Werewolves back in the day. They were menaces to all faeries, and we wanted to take care of that issue for our people."

"Ah." So that was why he hadn't wanted to tell her. "You were worried I wouldn't like that you hunted the wolves. I assumed you did, Eldridge. You've been around much longer than my father has been alive."

"Perhaps." He shifted on his horse, gripping the reins too tight.

"But that doesn't make me any less ashamed of my actions. Even back then, I knew it was wrong to hunt them."

As much as Freya wanted to say he was right, she wasn't so sure. What she had read in those books made her think the fae had no choice in the matter. The wolves, like her father had proven, were too strong. They hunted the poor faeries down and pulled them apart. Rarely did they eat their prey, they simply wanted to feel flesh beneath their claws.

But his brows were furrowed, and she knew he was already slipping into those dark memories that made him feel like a monster. She couldn't let him linger there. Not in the war, not with the death of the wolves that were now too close to her father. He didn't deserve that.

She changed the subject to something she really didn't want to talk about. "And the ladies?"

Arrow ducked back to his spot on the horse.

At the same time, Eldridge turned to look at her with a shocked expression. "The who?"

"The ladies you were attempting to woo. The most beautiful women in the court, I assume. Who were they?" She looked straight ahead and tried not to give away the anger riding her shoulders. "I can't imagine what the lovely women of the faerie courts must look like."

"Oh, they far surpass any creatures you may have seen in your life. Their skin is made of moonlight, some of them of darkness. Their hair is spun sun rays and their eyes are chips of gemstones. No one is more lovely than the ladies of the faerie courts." He sighed dramatically.

She wanted to hit him. Freya knew that this would be the answer, of course, but it still stung. She would never be one of those faeries made of the elements and most beautiful places in the realms.

Eldridge chuckled.

"What?" she asked, refusing to look at him still.

"Freya."

"What do you want, Eldridge?"

He snapped his clawed fingers in front of her face, forcing her to look at the laughter dancing in his eyes. "None are as lovely as you, my dear. I would never be so foolish as to compare you to the fickle and far off fae. Not a single one captured my attention as you have, and none ever will again."

If she blushed any harder, Freya would set her horse on fire. It was so easy to get caught up in those jealous thoughts that she would never be enough compared to the faeries he'd been with before. But she also knew the reality of their story.

He had chosen her. Not one of them. And Eldridge could have chosen one of the fae at any point. Every single day he reminded her that he had and would continue to choose her. She needed to remember that a little more.

Sighing, she tucked a strand of hair behind her ear and nodded. "Right. Well, I suppose the only other thing I want to know is why you and the Summer Lord are no longer friends. And don't try to get around it by saying you lived different lives and drifted away from each other. I saw you two together, and there were no remnants of fond memories."

Eldridge stiffened. He gripped the reins a little too tightly again, uncomfortable with this question. "The Summer Lord and I had a difference in opinion."

Freya waited for him to continue, but he didn't. He let the conversation end there and would have kept on with their journey without ever explaining himself.

She huffed out an angry breath. "Well? What was the difference in opinion?"

"Do you really need to know?"

"What if it's important? Yes, I need to know!"

Eldridge threw the reins down and tossed his hands up into the air. "I didn't think he should become the Summer Lord. I thought it was too much pressure for him, and I didn't see his ability to be a good leader. And when I told him that, he threw me out of his court and vowed I'd never set foot in it again."

She could understand how that would be hurtful, especially from someone who the Summer Lord had thought was a very close friend. "But obviously you did visit the court again."

"I did." His eyes narrowed on the road ahead of them. "When I surpassed them all and became the Goblin King."

Ah, and she supposed that was also a pain point between the two of them. They had both wanted a throne, although Eldridge had only wanted to be the Autumn Thief. And he had been for a time, before it was revealed just how truly powerful he really was.

She could only imagine that stung when the Summer Lord had wanted to prove himself alongside his friend, who was no longer his friend at all.

Sighing, she kept her eyes on the road as well. "I hope that won't sting in his mind for too much longer. After all, he has a court just like you."

"And I rule over him. The friend who betrayed him when he needed me most."

Right. That didn't bode well for the end of their journey.

Freya waited until she saw the Summer Castle appear on the horizon. It was beautiful with its abalone shell walls and the whirling towers that rose like pointed seashells. White sand spread out around the base of it and the gardens were lush, deep emerald that spread around the entire land like everything could grow in this soil.

Elves dotted the distance. They wandered through the gardens and pet the plants as they went. They lived in a jungle of greenery and blue skies.

She had the strangest thought: that no one here had ever experienced hardship. They had never gone hungry and they likely never would. If only they could understand what it felt like to have their stomach crawling with hunger, then they might understand humans a little better.

Maybe they would all get their faces if they did that.

"Here we are," Eldridge said. "I hope you're ready for what we're about to do."

"I suppose I am. I haven't ever been to a court I couldn't handle yet." Freya straightened her posture, hoping she looked intimidating and prepared for this moment. "Are you ready?"

"I'm never ready for a trip to the Summer Court." His haunted expression darkened as they got even closer to the castle. "I know he'll help us. He's never been able to stop himself from being called to the hunt. I'm just not certain where he'll go from there. He's unpredictable at best. Always be on your guard."

She remembered. The Summer Lord had made an impression when she first met him, and not in a good way. The man had been mostly disappointing. Freya would never forget the acrid scent of alcohol on his breath, or how she had gotten him so drunk that a mere mortal had stolen from him. It wasn't impressive.

It was downright sad.

One of the elves caught sight of them and ran into the castle. She knew this was the moment when they had to look their best. Freya squared her shoulders, smoothed her pale blue riding outfit into place, and kept her eyes straight ahead. She didn't look at any of the elves, because she didn't want them to see the fear behind her visage of bravery.

The doors to the castle opened as they rode up to the front gates. The Summer Lord looked exactly as she remembered him.

He wore a gold suit this time, and Freya knew it wasn't meant to be mistaken for yellow. He glowed like some kind of Sun god. The fabric appeared to be stitched with actual metal because the collar was stiff as he walked down the steps and approached them. His dark skin was glorious, oiled to perfection and highlighting the vivid darkness of his eyes. The entire sea was contained in the depths of his eyes. But not a kind sea.

"Welcome back to the Summer Court," he called out, opening his arms wide even as his eyes narrowed on them. "To what do I owe the absolute pleasure of the Goblin King and the Queen Killer's presence?"

If Eldridge replied, she feared they would lose all chances of getting the Summer Lord to help them. Freya cleared her throat and answered for him. "We're looking for my father, and considering the tale is one of intrigue and magic, we thought you may like to help."

"Your father?" He tilted his head to the side and pursed his lips. "I don't think I'm very interested in hearing that story. Mortals are so tiresome."

"He's a changeling," Freya replied. She knew that word alone would capture his attention, but she had no fear of saying who her father really was. "And then he was bitten by a werewolf when I was young."

The Summer Lord's eyes lit up with a burning passion. "Did you say werewolf?"

She nodded. "I did."

He looked at the Goblin King, then back to her. With a sigh, the Summer Lord gestured for them to get off their horses. "Fine, then. I'll suffer the Goblin King in my court for a little while. I'm curious to know more about your werewolf father and why you think he might be here."

Well, it was a start. Freya made eye contact with Eldridge and shrugged. At least they'd gotten the Summer Lord's attention for the time being.

They trailed the Summer Lord into the Summer Castle, past the giant stairwell overrun with flowers. Freya stared up at the mosaic on the ceiling as they passed, and she remembered the fear she'd felt the first time she was here. Sneaking through the palace and hoping that no one would find her.

The elves were terrifying to her then. Their masks didn't cover enough of their smooth faces. And she so greatly feared what they would do if they found her.

Of course, none of them had. It had been the Goblin King to find her in that strange room with its single stairwell leading to nowhere. How could she ever forget his fingers trailing up her spine? It was the first time they'd ever touched skin to skin.

A tremble shook through her shoulders. Without even looking at her, Eldridge put his hand on her back and mimicked the movement he had used when he helped tighten the corset. Almost as though he knew what she was thinking about.

He distracted her the entire time it took them to get to the small office. The warm colors of blues and golds caught her attention, but she couldn't stop thinking about Eldridge's hand. He smoothed his thumb at her waist and she couldn't focus. Not on the Summer Lord. Not on what they had to do. All she could think about was him and his damned fingers.

Eldridge had to tell the entire story to the Summer Lord. And when he was finished, they were dismissed to a private room until the Lord decided whether or not he wanted to help them.

She was just pleased to get out of everyone's eye. She was going to combust if they didn't give her a little privacy with the man she loved.

The man she loved whom she hadn't told yet. But someday soon she would say it. She would tell him how much she loved him and just how much he meant to her happiness.

When they finally got into the room that looked like the inside of a clamshell, Arrow snarled. "I'll be back. You two obviously need some time with each other and I can't stand it any longer. You were much more fun when you weren't..." He gestured up and down with a paw. "This."

The dog left the room and then she was alone with Eldridge again. She stared up at him, silhouetted by the bright sun through the glass doors that led out onto their private balcony. It wasn't fair that he looked so good. Like he was still put together while she was falling apart.

"Were you distracting me on purpose?" she asked, her voice wavering.

"Maybe. I enjoyed your reactions." The expression on his face was far too smug. "Besides, I know the story as well as you do. I could tell it while you were trying to hold yourself together."

Freya stomped her foot in frustration. "How dare you? I should have been the one to inform him about my father!"

"You were preoccupied with your thoughts." He shrugged and reached for her like he was going to tug her into his arms. "And I find that I quite like you when you're distracted. You're adorable when your cheeks are that red, you know that, don't you?"

She slapped his hand. "What did you even say? And did you cast some kind of spell on me or something? I don't remember any of it."

And that was terrifying. Freya didn't know why those memories or thoughts were gone, but they absolutely were. She couldn't remember a single thing Eldridge had said, only that he was talking about her father and slowly tracing the bumps of her spine the entire time.

"I told him all he needs to know, and that was it. You can tell him more later if you want." Eldridge walked over to the bed and laid down, lifting his arms over his head as pillows. "But I thought maybe you would want a diversion in the meantime."

"I think I've been distracted enough for one day, thank you very much." Although, he was very tempting all laid out like that. She wanted to lick him from his knees all the way to the top of his head, but they didn't have time. "How did the Summer Lord respond, though? Does he have any idea where my father might be?"

Eldridge sighed and scrubbed a hand over his face. "No, Freya. No one knows where he might be, but that's all right. We know the greatest likelihood is that he's here, isn't it?"

She supposed. But that wasn't quite good enough for her. Not when there was an opportunity here to meet with the Summer Lord and find out so much more information than they already knew. If the were-wolves used to live here, then surely the Summer Lord had texts that were filled with more knowledge.

"Are you going to sleep the day away?" she asked. "What about finding the Summer Lord's library? We could at least see if he has any more volumes that might give us a few more clues."

"You can try to leave if you want. He made it very clear that we weren't wandering about his castle when he didn't trust us." Eldridge gestured toward the door. "Go ahead, though. Be my guest."

Ominous. Freya strode to the door, opened it, and nearly bumped into the back of the giant elf who stood on the other side of the door. He turned back to stare at her, his mask covered in the scales of a lizard. His eyes were blank from emotion and the terrifying mask was enough to send her back into the room with a swift slam of the door.

"Right," she muttered. "Apparently I won't be going to that library after all. But really, what is a room full of books going to do? It's not dangerous for me to be in there."

She turned around, wondering whether there was another exit, only to find that Eldridge had disappeared. There wasn't even an indent on the bed where he had been lying.

And had the room changed? The walls weren't quite right. At least, not like she remembered. Perhaps it was the sheen of color that was different.

The most glaring change, however, was the balcony itself. No longer were the windows looking out toward the sea, but into another room. The seashell quality of the walls changed to a shimmering green, and she didn't think it was a bathing area.

"Eldridge?" she whispered. The magic inside her stretched, seeking him out because she feared losing him forever if she didn't. "I need you here with me, now. I think something in this room is trying to hide you from me."

She felt him trying to find her. His magic was just so far away from her that it was hard to latch onto. But he'd taught her how to find him. No matter the cost to each other.

And in this strange, shimmering room, Freya feared she was in a lot more danger than she realized.

She reached out in her mind's eye and tugged hard. She pulled him through whatever barrier stood between them and felt him doing the same. Together, hand over hand, they fought to be beside one another again.

Finally, she saw the faint outline of his shadowy form. Freya held out her hand and felt him touch her fingers. With one final heave of energy and power, she pulled him through the veil and into the room she'd been transported to.

Eldridge was breathing hard, sweat slicking his brow. "What was that?" he snarled.

"I have no idea. One moment I was in our room, then I closed the door and suddenly, I wasn't there anymore." Freya turned fearful eyes toward the balcony that should have been looking out to see. "And the room changed. Quite a bit, actually."

He followed her gaze and blew out a long breath. "That's not supposed to happen."

"I can't imagine magic is ever supposed to happen. But what do you think it is?" Freya touched a hand to his shoulder. "Did the Summer Lord curse us?"

"No," he replied. Then he shook his head and cleared his throat as if he were trying to pull out of a memory. "I mean, I don't know if he cursed us. He might have. But the forest, Freya. That's what is not supposed to happen. The forest is part of the Summer Lord's magic. It's an advisor, of sorts. And it isn't supposed to appear for anyone but the Summer Lord himself."

"Oh." She looked to the trees and fear made her heart race again. "That doesn't sound good."

"It isn't." He took a step toward the balcony, only to be shoved back by the same magic that had tried to hide from him. "I don't know why it's fighting me. I'm the Goblin King. I'm here to help the forest and those it serves. I don't..."

Freya understood.

It was plain and simple. The forest didn't want to speak to the Goblin King. No one could argue the truth of that fact as the forest shoved him back yet again. The trees wanted to speak with someone. They had a story to tell, but it was not the Goblin King who should hear it.

"I think it wants to speak to me," she whispered.

A sudden wind caught her words and echoed them back through the air. But this time, the sounds were warped. "Speak to her," it whispered.

Eldridge looked at her, then the balcony, then shook his head. "No. You can't go in there alone. I've never even been inside that forest, and I have no idea what might wait for you through those doors. It's too dangerous."

"As dangerous as fighting the Goblin King? Or killing the Winter Princess? Perhaps as dangerous as finding out the Spring Maiden was lying?" Freya approached the doors, completely unhindered by the magic. She gave Eldridge a sad smile. "Or maybe you meant it's more dangerous than seeking out a werewolf."

"Freya." He reached out his hand for her, struggling to lift it as the magic shoved him again. "I'm begging you not to do this without me."

She looked back to the room beyond the balcony that turned more green as she watched. Leaves broke through the seashell texture of the walls, and she could almost hear a voice calling out to her. It wanted to speak, and she didn't think denying the forest what it wanted was all that smart. In fact, she'd argue it was rather foolish to deny the trees anything. After all, they'd been here a lot longer than either Freya or Eldridge.

"I don't have a choice," she whispered.

She gave him one last look, just in case it was the last time she saw him. She could see how much this was killing him.

"Freya," he growled one last time. "There's too much left unsaid between us. Let me come with you. We can fight against this magic if we're together."

She felt the power of that forest pressing against her back. It was shoving her toward the doors, pulling at her very soul until she felt it slip underneath her tongue and waggle the appendage for her. "I don't want to fight it," she whispered. "I want to hear what it has to say."

"Freya!"

His shout echoed in her ears, but she couldn't stop herself. Freya reached for the handles of the balcony doors and pulled them open. They were light in her grasp, oiled perfectly so there wasn't a sound at all other than the Goblin King's shouting.

And then the doors were open and she couldn't hear him anymore. All she could hear was the sweet song of birds in the distance. The calm sound of wind rushing through leaves. Golden light spilled through an emerald canopy, and the whispers of the trees could barely be heard.

"She's coming," they said. "She has to take one more step and then she'll be here. Hush. Don't say too much. Not yet, he might still hear us."

These ancient beings desired to speak with a girl from the mortal realm. Such an honor couldn't be ignored. Freya looked behind her at the chaos in that in-between place.

Eldridge fought against the magic with everything he had. Shadows coiled around his fists and undulated like waves behind him. Lifting a hand, he pounded on the invisible barrier that stood between them.

If she gave him enough time, she knew he would shatter the forest's magic.

The Goblin King was a powerful man. He wielded magic with an iron fist.

She couldn't give him that choice. Freya took one more step, felt moss squish beneath her feet, and closed the doors firmly behind her.

CHAPTER 5

The trees heaved a sigh of relief when it was just Freya and them. They waved their leaves in the wind, and all was calm. Their magic fell away from her shoulders and apparently she was free to wander wherever she wished to wander.

Freya hadn't been in the woods for what felt like years. The Spring Court was full of gardens and the deep depths of the mines. The Winter Court was all icy tundras and forgotten ice caves. And of course, Eldridge's kingdom was a galaxy of possibilities, but no trees.

And heavens, she had missed the trees.

Freya walked past their thick trunks with roots stretching deep into the ground. A knot inside of her untangled. Almost as though she recognized the forest she was in. As if she'd been here before.

She stepped over a fallen tree limb and froze when she saw two initials carved into the base of the nearest tree. She reached out and ghosted her fingertips over the carefully scratched letters. F and E.

Maybe she had been here before then.

"You've been in my life for longer than I realized, haven't you?" she asked quietly.

The tree bent into her touch, the bark shifting and moving. She thought she would have remembered a forest like this. But if this one had been leaking into the mortal realm, then maybe she wouldn't have known. They'd lived so close to a faerie portal, after all. It wasn't such a stretch to think that there might have been more that surrounded their home.

"My father used to live here, didn't he?" Her voice floated through the forest and tangled with the birdsong.

Freya didn't really think the trees would reply to her. They had more important things to do than listen to the mortal girl asking questions. And they had asked her here for a reason. They wouldn't care about her desire to find her father, and yet, she had hoped this journey would be the first step closer to him.

Rather than give up, she continued wandering underneath the giant branches, talking as she went.

"My father came here as a changeling child a long time ago." Freya carefully brushed a branch away from her face. "He loved the forest near our small cabin in the mortal realm. He said the world was empty without the scent of leaves on the ground and the wind rustling through the forest. If he didn't have that, then he surely would have wasted away."

The rattling branches over her head moved a little faster. As if they wanted her to keep telling them the story about her father. And if that's what they wanted, then Freya was all too happy to oblige.

She stepped over another log and felt her feet sink down into the ankle thick moss. "He used to call the forest the place where souls went to heal. Did you know that?"

The tree nearest to her rattled its branches ever louder. She'd take that as a yes.

"I'm looking for him," she admitted. "He lost himself for a bit, but I think he'd like to find his way back home. To me. To my mother and sister. Family was everything to him. At least, it was when I knew him."

Freya heard the deep hum of magic long before the trees shifted. She stopped and held out her arms as the world seemed to stretch and pull. The trees reordered themselves, first backing away from her and then snapping back into place. She blinked, and they were in a different spot than before.

The trees now created a row for her to walk down. The path was devoid of moss or greenery. And golden light speared through the suddenly much taller trees. The path led to a silver gate at the very end, with twisting coils silhouetted against the bright light.

"Ah," she mumbled. "I'm going to assume that is where you want me to go?"

That deep sound echoed through the forest again. It was a rumble of earth and loam. The voice of the land she walked upon.

She wasn't sure why she was listening to its whims. This was part of the faerie realm, and obviously this place could be leading her into a trap. Eldridge had thought that was what it was.

But this place felt like home. She'd been here before. She'd walked through these moss covered glens and she knew deep in her heart that this place would never try to harm her. It wanted to help.

She reached the gate and eased it open. It squealed loudly. Rust turned the hinges bright green, and moss grew up the edges. When was the last time someone had been here?

If this forest was supposed to be only visible to the Summer Lord, then she would have expected to see some movement. Wasn't it his duty to speak with the forest? Or was this merely an advisor who had remained silent for all these years?

She stepped into the hidden glade in the center of the forest. A small cage sat in the corner, made of roots and tangled vines that hung down from the branches of an impressively large tree. This great oak was covered in moss and lacked any leaves. But Freya could still feel the strength that emanated from the beautiful, ancient being. It was still alive.

Movement behind the earthen cage caught her attention. At first, she thought it was nothing more than a squirrel or some other woodland creature. Then, the dark fur brushed up against the tangled roots and she recognized the color.

"Dad?" she whispered.

The movement within the cage stopped, and then a red eyed gaze turned toward her.

Freya lunged forward, reaching out her hand but not knowing if she should stick her fingers through the wooden bars. What if he didn't recognize her? The wolf could take off her fingers and those red eyes didn't seem to know who she was.

Her father continued his pacing. She peered through the shadows to see a sort of cave created deep in the hollow of the tree. This was more than just a cage, it was a prison meant to keep others out. Or something in.

"You're alive," she said, her voice breathy with relief. "I didn't think we'd find you so easily. But I'm so glad to see that you're alive."

Another voice interrupted her, and it was the strangest sound she'd ever heard. Like someone was taking their dying breath and speaking the words with lungs overfilled with air. "He's alive, but barely."

Cold chills rose up her arms. All her hairs lifted in fear and Freya had to talk herself into turning around. Whatever stood behind her was bound to be a terrifying monster, of sorts. She hoped it wasn't what she feared most. Some kind of spider or mashup of woodland animals that lived in the shadows.

Her imagination really was getting the best of her these days.

She stood and put her back to the cage, keeping far enough away that her father wouldn't be able to nip at her through the bars. At first, she didn't see the speaker at all. There was nothing behind her but trees covered in moss.

But then she realized that the voice had come from much closer to her. The tree was the one that had spoken, but not quite the tree itself.

She looked to her right and stared down into the roots. There, underneath the thick cover of leaves and moss, was a person. He had been buried deep in the ground, although the shifting of time had brought his body up through the soft earth. His hair was stuck to the tree, growing into the moss as though he were part of it. Even some of his skin had attached itself to the bark, turning green and brown with age. But his eyes were still vivid blue, even though tiny sprouts of grass were growing where his eyelashes should be.

"Hello," she whispered. Freya hoped her horror didn't come through in her tones.

"You shouldn't be here," he said again, struggling for breath and heaving air back into his lungs.

She looked closer and realized there were twigs sticking through his torso. They created a mockery of a ribcage, and she imagined struggling to breathe was difficult. Hence the wheezing tones of his words. "I didn't have a choice," she belatedly replied.

"Ah." He forced more air through his throat. "The trees wanted you here, then."

The trees suddenly seemed far more ominous than before. She was afraid of them now, if this was what they wanted to do to visitors.

"Why are you here?" she asked. "It seems like a poor resting place for one such as you."

"Such as me?" the creature looked down at itself then back at her. "Oh, missing limbs and all. I suppose that does look a little... strange."

Strange wasn't even the word for it. She didn't know if she would even consider him to be alive. Magic was strange. A forest that moved on its own. That was strange. But a man stuck to a tree with moss growing all over his body, or at least what parts of his body that she could see?

That wasn't strange. That was a nightmare come to life as she talked with a corpse.

"Um." Freya glanced over her shoulder at her father, who was still pacing in his cage. When she made eye contact with him, he snapped his jaws. And he was entirely a wolf at this point. There was no cursed figure, which she thought was maybe a good thing.

Was she supposed to talk with this dead man about how to get her father out? Maybe that's what the forest wanted. She was supposed to ask her questions here and now, and that would get her pointed in the right direction.

Freya really didn't want to. The heaving sound of his breath terrified her, and she knew it would stick in her dreams for months to come.

Staring up at the sky, she watched the light filter through the branches over her head and chewed on her lips. She'd always said there was no time to waste when she had to get something done. After all, a hero didn't hesitate. A hero charged forward to help.

"Am I supposed to speak with you about getting my father back?" she asked.

"Maybe." The man shifted again. This time, she watched as he lifted an arm out of the moss. Giant mushroom caps grew from his bicep down to his elbow, though the appendage was very thin and almost mummified. "The trees talk through me, sometimes."

"Are there more like you?"

"Hundreds." He met her gaze with those horrible blue eyes. "You didn't notice all of us?"

All of them? She turned her gaze back to the forest and this time, yes, she saw all the bodies. One for each tree. People growing into the bark, into roots, tangled in moss. Some of them were so much a part of their tree that their skin had turned rough and ashen. A few of them lifted their arms when they saw her looking at them, beckoning for her to come forward and speak with them as well.

Magic pulsed in her heart and told her to stay right where she was. Now was the moment where danger ran hot. She had to stay safe, and that meant speaking with the only tree who mattered.

She looked back to the giant she stood beside, the one who had nearly died to create a prison out of its own body. "You wanted to see me, didn't you?"

The tree shuddered. The body at the base of its roots suddenly quaked as though having a seizure. The man's eyes closed, and his mouth opened wide. His lips didn't move at all as another voice spoke through him. It was the ancient sound of a madman and a healer all wrapped in one. Deep and echoing through the throat of the dead man. "I did."

"Why?" She tried very hard not to shiver in disgust.

"Poison spreads through the Summer Court. A monstrous poison that cannot be contained by any root or poultice we make. You must help us." A small green beetle crawled out of the man's mouth, shook its body, and then flew off into the golden light of day.

Freya swallowed hard. "What can I do to help? I'm just a mortal."

"You're more than that. You're this changeling's child and he came to us seeking help. As the wolves did in the old days." Perhaps the tree sought her out because it didn't have leverage on anyone else. Freya was the only one it could speak with at this point in time. Whatever the reason, the trees knew they had her by the throat.

She would do anything to help her father. Even make a deal with a forest.

Sighing, Freya nodded. "If I find out what is harming the Summer Court, will you let my father go?"

"I'll do better than that." The forest sighed with her, every tree shifting with a breeze that tangled in Freya's hair. "I will heal your father of his curse, but you must save the Summer Court from itself."

"Are you going to tell me what needs saving? Or why it's poisoned?" Freya lifted her hands, knowing that she'd get no answers. "Perhaps who is poisoned or where that came from?"

The tree laughed, and the sound was horribly eerie coming out of a mouth that didn't move. "No, Freya. You've been in the faerie realms long enough to know that I will give you no help at all. Save us and I'll give your father back as he once was all those years ago."

Of course it couldn't be that easy. Freya turned to give her father one last look, but the forest warped and stretched again. The ground shifted underneath her feet and she had the awful sensation of something picking her up and throwing her through the air. Her stomach leapt into her throat and then she slammed down onto a cold seashell floor with balcony doors just behind her.

Birds chirped in her ears. The sun warmed her back. And the forest disappeared with the faint sound of laughter dancing in her ears.

She stood up carefully, wincing at the aching bruises on her knees from where she'd hit the balcony too hard. She dusted off her skirts and planted her hands on her hips. "That wasn't very friendly, you know!"

The doors behind her slammed open so hard the glass shattered. Freya whirled around to see a furious Goblin King standing in their bedroom.

"How dare you put yourself in danger like that?" he snarled. "Get in here."

CHAPTER 6

CHAPTER 6

Oh, she was in so much trouble. The angry glower on his face didn't budge, even when she skirted past him into the room beyond.

Freya walked into their bedroom like a child who was about to get scolded by her parent. And she knew he had every right to do so. He didn't know where the portal had taken her, only that it didn't want her with him. No way to know if she was even alive. If that had happened in reverse, then Freya would have been an absolute mess.

He could yell at her all he wanted, she supposed. That was fair.

Freya sat down on the bed, tucked her hands underneath her bottom, and squeezed her shoulders up to her ears. She was ready to be shouted at, and he could take his time. However long it took for him to feel better, that was how long she would sit here and listen.

She heard the pounding of his footsteps as he started pacing across the room. Each thud mirrored her heartbeat. Eldridge lifted a finger, opened his mouth, then closed it again. He continued pacing and trying to speak for long moments before he finally sighed.

His long legs ate up the distance between them and he sank onto his knees before her. Gently, ever so gently, he laid his head down in her lap and surrounded her hips with his arms. "I thought I had lost you," he muttered. "That magic was old and powerful. I fought against it for hours and it didn't budge. I could have done that for centuries and not known if I would ever get you back, or just your corpse."

She shouldn't tell him about the dead things in the forest. And some other voice whispered in her mind that she shouldn't mention her father, either. Eldridge would want to rush into the trees and free her father, tearing this court down around their ears in the process.

They couldn't. This game had to be played the way the forest wanted, or they would all end up tangled in the roots like those other elves.

Freya combed her fingers through his hair, scraping his scalp with her nails and easing her fingers down the back of his neck. "I didn't die, you know. I was fine."

"Yes, I see that. But I realized in the time that you were gone that the thought of losing you wrecks me. I couldn't use my magic in the right way. I couldn't even think about what would happen if you didn't return." He lifted his head, eyes more serious than she'd ever seen before. "You give me a reason to live, Freya. A reason to be a better version of myself."

"I'm sorry I made you so worried," she whispered. Freya traced his eyebrows with her fingers, following the strong, sharp lines to the edges of his eyes. "I wouldn't have taken the risk if there was any other way. I had to know what was happening."

"And what happened?"

"That place... Those trees." She swallowed hard. "They were the same trees that were behind our house, Eldridge. The same ones that were in the mortal realm."

His hands flexed on her hips and he lifted himself onto the bed with her. Eldridge threaded his fingers together, pressed them to his lips, and frowned. "The same trees? My darling, that's not possible."

"Apparently it is. They even said they were. But they..." She paused, trying to figure out a lie that was not too far off from the truth. "They knew something about my father. Some detail that will solve all of this.

They said they would tell us, but in return, we have to help the Summer Court."

Eldridge rolled his eyes in frustration. "Of course we do. It's never easy in the faerie realm, and apparently even the trees won't do anything for free. What do they want?"

"They said there's a poison spreading through the Summer Court. We have to find out what it is and how to stop it." She shook her head and frowned. "I'm not sure how clear that direction is, though. The Summer Court seems fine to me. It's exactly like it used to be."

It didn't seem that Eldridge felt the same way. His expression darkened, and he stood. He made his way to the balcony where he could stare out over the ocean beyond. "The Summer Court wasn't always like this. The elves weren't always faceless and searching for the next beautiful thing. The Lord was the one who helped people find themselves. They settled into what they should look like so they could understand themselves better. Finding a face was like finding your soul."

Perhaps that was why all those people who were stuck to the trees had faces, then. They were the older elves who had lived in a time that was gentler on their kind.

"Ah," she replied. "So maybe that's the poison?"

"It's too easy." He took a deep breath, shoulders moving with the slow movement. "There's only one person who would have felt a poison spreading through this land, and that would be the Lord himself. But he should have told me if there was something wrong here. No court leader is supposed to handle something like that on their own."

She stood up, followed him to the window. Freya put her hand on his back and rubbed the tension there. "But you two have a strained relationship at best. Perhaps he didn't feel comfortable talking to you."

"Perhaps not." He reached an arm out for her, tucking Freya against his side and holding her close. Eldridge pressed a kiss to the top of her head. "Very few people actually liked me until you."

"Is that so?" She smiled against his side, listening to the beat of his heart against her ear. "I can't imagine why."

He snorted. "Right, I'm sure you can't. But we may as well take our chances while we can. Look." He pointed below them toward the sands that spread out toward the sea.

The Summer Lord strode across the white sand beach with three elves trailing along behind him. His bright white suit almost blended into the setting, but he was relatively alone and yes, this was a great opportunity for them to speak with him. No guards to stop them. Other than the one at their door, that was.

She looked up at Eldridge and lifted a brow. "The question is how we're going to get out there before he leaves. The guard was much larger than most elves. I know you're powerful, Eldridge, but he's pretty big."

"First of all, I don't appreciate the suggestion that I couldn't fight someone much larger than me." He scowled at her. "Second, what makes you think I planned on walking?"

"Well, most people do need to walk. It's not like we can float through the air." She regretted saying the words as soon as they came out of her mouth.

Eldridge tightened his grip on her and his face twisted with a mad smile. "Oh, my darling, I so enjoy proving you wrong."

His magic whipped around them, hugging her tightly and dragging her off the balcony. Eldridge walked through the air like it was solid. He strode without purpose or haste, just a few steps here and there while he watched her expression change from horror, to fear, and then laughter as Freya finally let go and realized they would not plummet to their death.

They strolled like a couple who had done this a thousand times before. Like they were walking beside a pretty river and he was pointing out a view for her to admire.

Eldridge nudged her to look to their left. "That's where Leo and I used to hide from his parents. Dreadful people. They were so stuffy and we always wanted to go on adventures. They wanted us to learn which fork to use."

The small building was likely used by the gardeners to store their tools. "A rather dangerous place for children to hide. How did you keep all your fingers and toes?"

He snorted. "The same way I do now. Practice and hoping no one notices if I lop one off and stick it back on with magic."

That fit her description of him quite nicely. Eldridge apparently had always been the kind of person to take the risk first and then wonder if it was the right decision later. She could imagine him as a little boy, running wild through the Summer Court with his dear friend at his side.

"I'm imagining you as a little terror," she said with a laugh. "How accurate is that?"

"People screamed when they heard my name." He smiled at her with a sharp-toothed grin. "They still do."

Yes, she was certain that was true as well. There were very few faeries who wanted to risk angering the Goblin King. The man was terrifying when he wanted to be.

They landed on the sand behind the group of elves and their Summer Lord. None of them appeared to notice the couple that had floated down from the sky, nor did they react when the two of them started walking nearer.

"Leo!" Eldridge called out.

The Summer Lord flinched so hard that he almost fell onto the sands. He righted himself and spun around with an angry glare. "You're supposed to be in your room!"

The thunderous sound of his voice was impressive. Even the sea seemed terrified of the Summer Lord, because the waves froze for a moment before they kissed the shore once again.

Each elf retreated to a safe distance away from their Lord. Freya wondered if that was a warning. Was this court leader known for exploding? Considering how much she'd seen him drinking when she was here, she wouldn't be surprised if he did.

His anger ruled his actions rather than logic. And it was such a shame, because he really was handsome. Someone had braided his hair tight to his head, and the long tails looked like that of a squid that flung around him as he moved. The sheer amount of time it would have taken to make him look like that made her think him even more attractive. The golden buttons on his suit gleamed in the sun. Tiny aquamarine gemstones were inlaid in each button.

"Yes," Eldridge replied, looking at his fingers as though he were already bored with the conversation. "You know I don't like being locked up. I get too bored."

"I don't care if you're bored," the Summer Lord snarled. "I care that you stay where I put you. You're not allowed to wander through my court without an escort, Eldridge."

"Not allowed?" Eldridge lifted his brows in fake surprise. "I'm the Goblin King. There is no part of this court or any other that is off limits for me to visit. Or have you forgotten that?"

The Summer Lord's expression darkened. Clouds appeared over their head and Freya heard thunder in the distance. This faerie lord was extremely powerful. She wondered how close he had been to getting the Goblin throne himself.

And they didn't have time for the two of these men to butt heads yet again. She wanted to confront the Lord and get this over with.

Stepping in between them, she forced the Lord's attention onto her. "I met with the trees," she said.

Her voice rang through the air and suddenly the skies were bright blue again. The Lord stared at her with a shocked expression, mouth open and brows furrowed. "You what?" he asked in hushed tones.

"I met with the trees," she repeated. "They said I needed to help rid this land of a poison. And I think you know what that poison is. Let us help you, Leo. Take a step back from being the Summer Lord or having old prejudices. This isn't about us, anymore. This is about your court and the safety of your people."

He took a step away from her, shaking his head. "It's not possible." The horror in his expression told her everything she needed to know.

"The poison has affected you too, hasn't it?" She trailed him through the sands, matching his every step. "You know exactly what I'm talking about, and you haven't tried to stop it at all. Do you even want to stop it?"

"Eldridge," Leo growled. "Get your woman and make sure she stays away from me."

Freya felt the grip of the Goblin King on her arm, but she wasn't pausing now. She couldn't. Not when they were so close. "Tell us what it is and we might be able to help. Why wouldn't you want someone to help you?"

The Summer Lord lifted his hands, the rings on his fingers glowing with power. "Get her away from me before I do something I regret."

Without question, Eldridge scooped her up by the waist and dragged her away. "Freya, we'll talk to him another time."

She struggled, although she knew it was a waste of energy. "But he knows! Eldridge, he knows what I'm talking about. Let me go!"

The Summer Lord turned away from them and walked back down the sands. The elves looked between the three of them and then continued to follow their master. Though, this time they stayed a lot farther back.

When Eldridge finally released her, she whipped around with an angry snarl. "How dare you? I was so close!"

"To getting killed." He ran his fingers through his hair with a frustrated sound. "Listen to me. Leo has never been good at controlling his emotions. It's the main reason he didn't get the goblin throne when we were all competing for it. There's something missing from him. Compassion has never been his strong suit and if you had pushed him any farther, he would have killed you."

"With you standing right here?" She pursed her lips. "I doubt that."

"You shouldn't." The haze of a haunted memory ghosted over his features. "I've seen him do it before, Freya. Just because I'm standing here wouldn't stop him. And I don't know if I'm quick enough to prevent that gesture of anger from hitting you."

Well, that would make this all much more difficult if the Summer Lord refused to help them.

Tossing up her hands, she gave in. "Fine, then. If we can't talk with him about it, then what do we do next?"

He shrugged as if he didn't know the answer to that either. "I suppose we try to talk to the elves."

She stomped through the sand back toward the castle, muttering the entire time. "Talk to the elves. Like that will be so easy. None of the elves like to talk, and if they do, they only want to talk about dresses and parties. Talk to the elves. Sure. Let's see how far that gets us."

CHAPTER 7

Freya pinched the bridge of her nose and stared down at the small journal in her hand. She'd taken notes every time she talked with each elf, but that wasn't helpful at all.

This one had talked about the various plants that were in the Summer Kingdom for about an hour. And while these details would be interesting any other time of the year, she didn't really want to hear about this right now.

"Right," she repeated. "So I just want to clarify, please. We're asking about any poison you might feel in the area. A sickness, perhaps? Or maybe some of the plants you've taken care of happened to have died recently?"

The elf tapped a finger to its butterfly mask, then shook its head. "No. I don't think I've seen any of that."

"Really?" Freya pushed a little with this one because she couldn't believe that no one had seen any sign of poison. "Not a single note of concern in any area of the entire court?"

The elf shook its head and shrugged. "We're quite happy here. It's the best court to live in, you see. Summer is the most comfortable season, and the Summer Lord is a wonderful ruler. I'm happier than a clam."

Freya just didn't believe it. She couldn't imagine any of these people were happy when there was something insidious growing within their court. There had to be something someone wasn't telling her.

But that person wouldn't be the elf standing before her. She snapped the journal shut and gave the creature a sharp nod. "Thank you for talking with me. It's been a pleasure."

The elf waved and walked away, back into the lush greenery that it had been grooming. A few leaves stuck out of the elf's hair, and Freya had the distinct impression that they were actually growing out of the elf's head.

That one would end up in the forest before long, a voice whispered in her head. Soon it would be absorbed, just like the others.

Shivering, she stood up and walked back toward the castle where the others should be waiting for her. They had all split up to talk with as many elves as they could. All she could hope was that one of them had found out more information than she had.

Both Arrow and Eldridge stood to the side of the castle, nearer to an area that was currently undergoing construction. The gardens had all been ripped up, and none of the elves would go near it until someone had finally planted something there. Freya just wasn't sure who was supposed to do the planting.

She tromped up to them and waved the journal in her hand. "I've got absolutely nothing. It's like all the elves in this place lost their brains out their ears. Not a single one is aware of any poison, anything spreading, and all of them say they're perfectly happy. Why in the world would I want to meddle?"

Eldridge held up his own pale white leather notebook and grimaced. "I'm afraid my experience has been much the same. The elves aren't interested in talking to us, if they have any idea what's going on at all."

She turned toward their only hope, the little goblin dog who always wiggled underneath people's skin. "Please, Arrow, tell me you found out something about the curse affecting this court?"

His ears went straight up and he took a deep breath as though he were about to tell them the greatest information of the century. But then his ears flattened to his skull again, and he tucked his tail between his legs. "I'm afraid not, Miss Freya. The elves wouldn't even talk to me. It's like they live in a different version of this court than we see."

Freya puffed a breath at the hair in front of her face and wished there was something stiff to drink. "Of course they wouldn't," she grumbled.

The elves were loyal to their Summer Lord. Freya and her companions were utter strangers, and they stood out among the crowd. If they wanted to get information out of these people, then they needed to seem like they were one of them.

Or find out information from the Summer Lord himself. But that seemed even less likely.

She tucked her journal into her pocket and crossed her arms firmly over her chest. "Well, do either of you have any ideas?"

Both Eldridge and Arrow shared a look, then turned back to her with blank expressions. Freya was so tired of doing everything, especially when she had no idea where to go with this one. Staring out into the pavilion and the beautiful gardens beyond, she finally just shrugged.

That was it, then.

She'd failed her mother. Her father would remain trapped in those trees, and she would be stuck here. Trying to mend the bond between a family that had lost a very dear member.

Her father used to swing her up over his head until she screamed in the sunlight. Freya remembered him as an overly large man with a laugh that boomed like thunder. He was too loud. Too opinionated. Everyone had thought him to be a bear of a person, but they'd still liked him.

It was hard not to like her father. He had a pure heart and that shone through everything he did.

Arrow stepped forward and tucked his nose underneath her hand. "There's one more person who might help us. I don't know if she'll answer, but..."

Eldridge snapped his fingers forcefully. "Arrow, you genius! Why didn't I think of that?"

"Of what?" Freya looked between the two of them, trying to guess who they might be talking about. "We already know the Summer Lord won't give us a hint at all."

"But there was another person who stayed with us every summer I visited here." Eldridge's eyes glowed with excitement. "I need a pool of water. Come on, you two."

He raced away before Freya could get anything else out of him. Arrow was quick to follow, and if she didn't hurry, then they would both leave her in the dust. She tilted her head back to stare up at the clouds above them. "I don't understand a thing about these two," she muttered. "Why can't they just tell me what's going on before they race off into the distance?"

Shaking her head, she ran after them through the lush forest beyond. Freya slapped large monstera leaves out of her way and tried her best not to step on the flower gardens that the other two were so carelessly trudging through. The elves were still dangerous and territorial about their land. The last thing she wanted was to make these masked creatures angry enough to hunt her and her companions down.

She burst through the undergrowth out into a small glenn in the middle of this terrifying garden. A vernal pool waited in the center, tiny clusters of algae and lily pads making the edges difficult to tell what ground was solid. Some of the earth disappeared into the aquamarine waters.

Eldridge stood at the edge, holding out his hand above the water. He squeezed his eyes shut and muttered words she couldn't quite hear.

A furry paw stopped her from stepping any closer. "Don't interrupt him when he's casting spells," Arrow said. "We wouldn't want the whole thing to go awry and then end up with our feet as hands."

Freya didn't want to know if that was actually a concern. She didn't plan to risk it.

They both waited and watched the Goblin King as he worked. He moved his hands in strange patterns over the waters, muttering those words in a certain cadence that started to sound like a song. The more she listened, the more Freya wanted to walk closer to him. To step into the pool of bubbling pond water...

"Freya," Arrow hissed. "He's almost done. Just stop moving, would you?"

She snapped out of it and suddenly, Eldridge stopped speaking. He spread his fingers wide and dark magic sank into the water from his fingers. It spread through the very air like drops of ink, and the pool stopped bubbling. All sound in the glen silenced as the water turned into a solid mirror.

Freya gulped. What had the Goblin King done with his magic?

Eldridge held out his hand, gesturing for her to step up to his side. "Come here, Freya. I want you to look at this."

Had he created some way in the water to see the future? Freya wasn't sure she'd ever want to see that. The future was meant to be unknown and if she knew it, then would it ever come to pass?

Yet her feet brought her to his side without argument. Eldridge slid his arm around her waist and tugged her to the mossy edge of the pool. Their reflections were perfect on the glassy surface. And then he lifted a hand and pointed. "Look."

Just behind their image, another appeared. Horns silhouetted against the sky, and a bell skirt swaying around her hips, the Autumn Thief was lovely as ever. She wore bright red lip paint today, and her eyes were dramatically ringed with kohl.

Freya looked behind them. But the Thief wasn't in the glen. She was only in the water. "How is that possible?" she asked.

"Magic," the Thief replied with a laugh. "You've forgotten how much is possible, my dear. And how little you know."

A knot of tension eased in her stomach at the sound of the Autumn Thief's voice. Somehow, this woman always made Freya feel safe. No matter what circumstance they were in.

Freya glanced over at Arrow. "This was your plan? Ask for help from the Thief?"

"She knows more than most." He trotted to their side and stood up on his back legs. With a sheepish smile, he waved into the pool. "Hello, darling."

"Arrow. I see you've at least been able to dress to your standard on this adventure." The Thief crossed her arms over her chest and glared at them severely. "I was busy, Eldridge. You know I cannot be summoned without warning. There's too much to do here."

"Yes, yes." He dismissed her words with a wave of his hand. "Whatever you need to do can wait. We've something a little more important to deal with here."

Freya rolled her eyes at the same time as the Thief. "Eldridge," she scolded. "Just because we have issues here doesn't mean the Thief's are any less important. We thank you for your time, Thief. Really. We didn't know who else to turn to."

A breeze kicked up and swirled the skirts around the Thief's legs. She nodded, and a small green snake curved around one of her horns. "Then how can I help?"

Eldridge was quick to answer this time, and Freya supposed he was the one who knew best how to ask questions. "Do you remember when we were young and used to spend our summer here?"

"Of course I do." The Thief shrugged. "I was a very different person then, but that doesn't mean I have banished the memories from my mind."

"Good. Because apparently there's a poison spreading through these lands, and I have a gut feeling it has to do with something we saw when we were here. In the isles after all that time." He shook his head. "There's something warning me to look further, deeper into our history, but I cannot put my finger on why. Or how."

"Might I suggest that's because you and the Summer Lord were always running around seeking out new adventures? You wouldn't remember something important if it bit you in the ass, because you would find the next thing to bite in the same spot." The Thief heaved a sigh and then pointedly stared at Freya. "You're the one who took this on, you know. You must have the patience of a saint to deal with this one."

"To be fair, I don't really know what I'm getting into," Freya replied with a laugh.

"Hm." The Thief turned her attention back to the Goblin King with pursed lips. "I don't know everything you're looking for, but I remember that we found a book that warned the Summer Lord could grow ill. And it wasn't something he could catch, but was entirely related to the forest. Remember?"

"Not really." Eldridge's hand flexed on Freya's hip and he stepped away from her. Closer to the pool so he could see the Thief easier. "Was it a book that you and I found?"

"A scroll. Some story on it had said the Summer Lord wasn't the true ruler of this court. That he never would be, because the forest and the plants make the decisions for the Summer Court. I remember Leo was horribly upset about it." She turned her face from them, clearly listening to someone they couldn't see. "I don't have a lot more time, my dear. All I can say is that I know the forest can take back the right to rule its court if it's disappointed in the Lord. That's as good a place to start as I can think of."

The pool shuddered with a wind that brushed over the surface, and then the Autumn Thief was gone. All three of them stared into the shimmering, algae tinted water as if she might return.

Freya was the first to speak. "Well, that settles it."

Her two companions looked at her as if she'd grown a second head. Eldridge cleared his throat and asked, "Settles what?"

"I have to go back to the forest, clearly. It didn't give me all the answers I need to figure this all out. And if the forest is disappointed in the Summer Lord, then I need to figure out why." She shrugged. "Disappointment is one thing, but poisoning the entire court because it's upset with a single person? That's just immature."

Eldridge lunged toward her and slapped his hand over her mouth. Frantically, he stared up at the trees, eyes wide and flicking through the canopy. "She didn't mean it. She's just a mortal and has no idea what you listen to. Please don't punish her for ignorance."

What was he talking about? Freya glared at him, wiggling to get out of his grip.

Finally, she pulled herself away from him and took a deep breath of anger. "Excuse you! Eldridge."

"I'm not saying you shouldn't," he rushed to say, holding his hands up for peace. "Just... Be a little more careful about the words you choose. Would you?"

She supposed he might be right. After all, if she was going to converse with those trees again, she needed to have her wits about her.

CHAPTER 8

Their bedroom filled with dread as Freya readied herself to return to the forest. Even she was starting to get a little nervous.

Eldridge held her face in his hands and squeezed a little too tight. "Be careful."

"I plan on it," she replied with a soft laugh. "You don't have to worry so much, you know. I made it there and back the last time without a scratch."

He pressed his lips to her forehead, drawing her in for another long hug. "Yes, I know you did. I hope that the forest doesn't want to hurt you, and that it won't think this second visit, uninvited might I add, is the opportunity to amend its previous mistake."

Freya didn't think the forest would mind at all. After all, it was keeping her father locked away from her and her family. And it wanted to heal her father. It had made that very clear.

But Eldridge didn't know that her father was in that magical forest, locked away in a prison made of roots. She should have told him by now. The same voice kept whispering in her ear that now wasn't the time to tell Eldridge. He was rushing too much through this quest, as he usually did. His attention to detail just wasn't there yet. Soon, she could admit that she already knew where her father was. Not yet, though.

She pulled away from his grip and nodded. "I'm going to be fine, you know. Nothing bad is going to happen. I'm going to get more information out of the trees, then I'll be right back here and ready to take on more questions with you. All right?"

He stepped away from her, but the expression of worry never left his face. He didn't think this trip would be as easy as the first. That much was clear in his expression. "All right. Just..."

She smiled. "Be careful. I know, my Goblin King will be worrying on the other side of this door."

"And if you think for even an instant that the forest wants to hurt you, call to me."

If it wanted to hurt her, then no one was getting through that portal until it was finished with her. Freya didn't have to understand magic better to know that without question.

Still, she nodded to make him feel better about the whole situation. If she could ease his worry with her false bravado, then so be it.

Freya turned toward the balcony doors and put her hands on the bronze knobs. She did exactly as Eldridge had told her to do. Envision the doors opening into the forest where she wanted to go. She'd already been there, so this kind of portal should be very easy. All she had to do was let the magic do what it wanted to do.

And he'd insisted her magic wanted to help her. That was the function of having magic, or at least that's what he claimed. It would bring her from the Summer Court and into that secret place, if only she would let it.

The magic uncoiled deep in her belly. She'd finally given it a personality or a visage inside herself. Freya imagined her magic like a snake that twisted through her veins. Sometimes it was nice and only wanted to be held high in the sun. Other times, the magic wanted nothing more than to bite down hard on someone else.

She exhaled and opened the doors. Freya didn't open her eyes until she felt the soft breeze on her face and smelled the dark, earthy scent of moss and wood.

Blinking, she stared up into the golden sun and smiled. It had worked. If only she could turn around and tell Eldridge that he'd been right. She would have enjoyed sharing this moment with her Goblin King, who so loved teaching her how to use her magic.

Instead, she was alone with the trees.

Or rather, not so alone. This time, the bodies were far more evident, each of them reaching out for her with their mossy hands and bony fingers. She strode by them very carefully, making sure none of them caught hold of her pale yellow skirts. They would drag her into their prison with them. She was certain of it.

Even the trees seemed more sinister this time. They loomed over her head and their branches were too heavy with moss. Dripping wet plops of green down on her shoulders and head.

"I'm here to ask questions," she said firmly. "You will not frighten me away."

The forest shook with a sound that was almost laughter. Like the trees thought her bravery was adorable, but that she would not get far with that kind of ridiculous thought. She was just a mortal in a forest of ancient trees who could tear her limb from limb if they wanted to. Even the roots were rolling in the ground. They were ready to pull her into the moss where she would stay forever.

Freya carefully picked her way over the wet ground and headed to the same tree where she knew her father was. The giant tree that was hidden behind gates because apparently someone had thought the beast was dangerous enough to keep under lock and key.

Although, she didn't know where that key was.

Dust motes swirled in the air like tiny glowing faeries lighting her way. It was almost beautiful enough to make her forget the bodies that were still dragging themselves closer to her. They reached with skeletal fingers, trying to touch the trailing edge of her skirt.

No, she wouldn't focus on the dead things. The forest was trying to scare her away, and though it could do its best to try, she would not allow it to have space in her mind. Fear had no place here.

She walked through the iron gates and into the glen where the tree grew. It was larger than she remembered, or perhaps she was looking at it through a healthy amount of fear. Either way, she knew to tread more carefully now.

"I have questions," she called out again. "And I would like to see my father. Please."

Freya threw the last word into the air, hoping the tree would see she didn't mean any harm. She wasn't demanding for its attention. She was a girl looking to see her father one more time.

The tree heaved another sigh, and suddenly, the dead man in the roots came to life again. He opened his eyes and yawned, then met her gaze with one as green as the leaves above them. "You shouldn't have come back here without an invitation, girl."

"I know that." She stepped closer, holding up her hands. "But I had to know you were making good on your own bargain. I had to know he was doing better, or at least that my father was still alive."

"You don't trust us?"

No. Of course she didn't trust the trees. Freya frowned at the question and tried very hard to find words that weren't insulting. But her answer couldn't be dulled when she only had sharp anger in her chest.

"No," she replied. "I don't trust you at all. I think you have your own reasons for calling me here, and that I would be a fool to ignore that truth."

The man's face twisted with mirth. He opened that cavernous mouth and laughed. A tooth fell from his skull into the moss that covered the remains of his legs. "I had forgotten how lovely it was to see a mortal brimming with honesty. You're smart to not trust us, but you are also a fool for coming here. What a strange mixture brews inside that head of yours."

Freya didn't think she was all that strange. Most people were intelligent, but they made foolish decisions all the time. Usually in the name of love. As she was doing now.

She took a step toward the prison of roots. "May I see my father, please?"

"Do you think he'll be so changed? He was nothing more than a wolf when you saw him last, child." The man in the moss grinned, his eyes still wild and teeth glowing bone white in the moss of his skull.

Freya thought about how to answer that one. She could lie and question the tree's integrity. Perhaps making it angry would get her what she wanted faster. But Eldridge's words still rung in her head.

Sometimes she didn't have to fight with another to get what she wanted. Maybe she could ask for it.

"I do think you'll have changed him. You love him as much as I do, although I don't understand why. Was he a child in these forests? Was that when you first met him?" She took another step toward the prison where the tree was keeping her father. "He's a very good man, I know that. And I can only imagine you had some part in ensuring he grew up like that."

The dead man sighed. He closed his eyes, and she thought for a moment that the tree would let her go to her father. Instead, he talked with his eyes closed. Like he was remembering the past. "He was a good little boy. Where the other faerie children ran through the forest without care, he picked up sticks in their wake and lay them back in our roots. He used to think if things broke off of our branches, that we would miss them until they came back to us. A kind heart in that one."

Freya smiled. That was exactly how she remembered her father. He took the time to notice the little things that made other people's lives easier.

She inched to the side until she was right in front of the cage. Peering into the shadows beyond, she could see him standing. Though this time he was in that strange form, mixed man and beast, she knew that meant he was a little more like himself.

"Look at that," she whispered. "You were healing him the whole time."

"I wasn't going to let him rot in there. He never liked being a wolf." The tree shook its branches over her head and a rainfall of leaves dusted the prison. The thick layer hid her father from her gaze. "Now you are going to ask me your question and leave. Too much stimulation would only make him turn back into the wolf and then all our work will be for nothing."

She wanted to see more of her father. Just a little. Every glimpse healed a painful ache in her chest that wouldn't go away, no matter how hard she tried to ignore it.

But she wasn't here to see her father.

Not yet, at least.

"I spoke with a friend to figure out what the poison in this land might be. You've been going to great lengths to hide that information from me." She turned back to the man tangled in roots, planting her hands on her hips and hoping she looked like her mother when it was time to scold the children. "If you want my help, why are you doing everything in your power to hide the truth?"

"A quest, once given, cannot be made easy." The tree said the words like they were something she should have known. As if everyone in the faerie realms knew that this was the truth. Plain and simple.

Freya furrowed her brows. "That's not the way of it, though. If you want to change things, then why wouldn't you help?"

"The rules of the game have always been clear, Freya."

Clear as mud, as they were.

"Fine," she grumbled. "I want to at least be clear. I know you're the one who caused all this pain and suffering. The poison you spoke about is erupting from the very trees, and that I don't appreciate not knowing this from the start."

The man shifted, lifting an arm and pointing at her. "You're smarter than you look, Miss Freya."

She hummed low and under her breath, but nodded her thanks. "You're unhappy with the way the Summer Lord is ruling this court. That much is very obvious. But I want to know why."

This perked up the man in the tree. He moved his bony arms, his whole body shifting and rolling with moss that grew and died within blinks. He rose to the trunk of the tree, still stuck to the bark and hanging limp. Somehow, he was ominous to look at. "The Summer Lord mocks this court with his parties and his drink and his foolish nature. He knows what we've asked of him. He knows exactly what he has to do to make this throne his. And until then, I will continue to eat away at his court until it is buried beneath my roots. The age of the elf is coming to an end, and he knows how to stop my reckoning."

A chill swept down Freya's spine as he finished the speech. If this tree wanted to murder everyone in this court, she didn't question that it could. This wasn't just a forest, this was a creature who was living and breathing. Through dead things, sure, but still alive in some way.

"I understand," she said, ducking her head low. "My only challenge to you is to understand that no one can fix something they don't know is broken."

"Oh, he knows," the tree snarled. "He is aware of what he has done. The Summer Lord continues to refuse our requests. If you want to know as well, then I will tell you this. Go to the isles off the coast. The ones he told your Goblin King that no one travels to any longer. See the truth for yourself."

Freya shivered, fearing for her life and that of her father's as well. "Thank you," she whispered. "I am very grateful for your assistance in this quest you've sent me on."

"Please." The man drifted down the trunk and landed back in the mossy roots. "You are not a meek creature, and it doesn't look good on your frame. Pick your chin up and be the terrifying woman I first met. The one who I knew could turn this court around if she wished to."

At least the compliment boded well for later on. Freya nodded firmly and turned to leave. She squared her shoulders and forced herself to look brave as she wandered past those dead things that wanted to clutch onto her. She kept her chin up even as she reached the doors that would lead her back to her private rooms in the Summer Court.

But inside, she was so frightened that all she could hear was her own screams.

CHAPTER 9

"You think the trees want to help us?" Eldridge shook his head while he flipped the covers back on their bed. "I really don't think they want to do anything like that, Freya. They aren't giving beings, if you hadn't noticed."

"Oh, I noticed." She pulled her hair from its braid and let it fall loose down her back.

Now that they were sleeping in the same bed consistently, she'd taken to letting her hair get wild. As much as she hated the long length of it getting tangled, she very much enjoyed waking up every morning and having Eldridge there to brush it for her. And he liked brushing it. Every morning they got up and had their own little routine to start the day.

He frowned and punched his pillow, fluffing it for the night. "Why do you think they want us to go to the islands?"

"We've already been over this multiple times. I don't know why." She crawled onto her side of the bed and motioned for him to get in with her. "But arguing about it repeatedly will not get any more information into our heads."

"I think if we talk through it, we might at least be able to understand why the trees are so frustrated." He glared at her.

Oh, he was so handsome. Freya loved it when he glared at her like that. His brows furrowed in the same way they did when he was in the throes of passion. Not that she'd ever tell him that. His ego was already too big.

One last time, she waggled her fingers for him to get into bed. "We can't do much more until the morning, Eldridge. Even if we both bang our heads against the walls. I don't think we're going to figure this one out. The trees said go to the isles. I don't see another choice. Do you?"

He grumbled but crawled into bed with her. Hand over hand, he dragged himself closer and dramatically fell on top of her.

All the breath whooshed from her lungs. She curled her arms around him, holding his head close to her heart, but she still wheezed, "Was that necessary?"

"Yes. You disagreed with me and I don't like it," he muttered, his mouth mashed against her neck. "You don't have to be right all the time, you know."

"Yes, I do," she replied with a laugh. "Otherwise no one would ever be right, and then where would we be?"

Eldridge curved his arms around her, holding her as tightly as she was holding him. "I suppose we'd be in the same place as we currently are, my love. Fumbling around in the dark because damn trees won't tell us where to go next."

She laughed, bouncing his head on her chest with the sound of her mirth. "Eldridge! We know where we have to go next. We have to go to the isles, because that's where the trees told us to go."

"And we can't go there without the Summer Lord's permission." He pressed a kiss to her throat. "Which means tomorrow we have to beg him to give us that permission."

"Ah." And she assumed that wouldn't be all that easy. "What are the chances of him saying yes without asking questions?"

"Zero to none." He pressed another kiss to her skin, this time lingering on her jaw. "But I don't want to talk about him right now."

A blush spread across her body and suddenly she didn't want to talk about the Summer Lord either. She wanted to focus on the Goblin King in her bed, who commanded every ounce of her attention. "Oh," she whispered, cupping the back of his head and drawing him up her body. "What do you want to talk about then?"

"Nothing," he growled against her lips. "Nothing at all."

It took them a very long time to fall asleep.

The next morning, Freya felt like she was walking on clouds. She'd spent the night in his arms, in the most warm and wonderful place they'd traveled to so far, and the sun was shining. She stretched her arms over her head, reveling in the sunlight on her body. Finally, this was a place in the faerie realm where she would stay for a while.

"Up!" Eldridge's voice sliced through the air. "We don't have time for you to be lazy this morning."

Well, that would ruin the mood in a heartbeat. Why wouldn't they have time? They knew what they had to do today. She'd spoken with the trees and they were healing her father step by step. Why couldn't she enjoy herself for a morning?

Grumbling, she sat up in bed with her hair wild around her face. Blowing at one of the frizzy strands, she watched as he paced from one end of the room to the other. Eldridge lifted his hands up and down, summoning things as he went.

A vanity appeared directly across from her with a sparkling cushion that was clearly from his own court. Then dresses popped into view to her right. Too many of them to count, but they were all hung rather daintily on their hangers. Another crackle of magic revealed a stand that was where she should get her makeup done, considering the many pots of paint and rouge.

"What is all this?" she asked, stunned that he could bring so many things into their room with so little thought.

His magic was impressive. And she wondered if there was a limit to his abilities.

"This is everything we will need to get you ready to talk with the Summer Lord." He paused and stared at her with a critical eye. "Leo only likes pretty things, and if you aren't up to his standards, then you won't get the permission we need out of him."

"Excuse me." She stood and stretched her arms up over her head with another yawn. "Why am I the one who's convincing him to help us? Shouldn't that be your job?"

"Absolutely not." He snapped his fingers and the remnants of her nightgown disappeared from her body. "I cannot lie, but you can. Thus, the only logical conclusion is that you will lie to him and say we want to go to the island to spend a little time with each other. Alone. Far away from the prying eyes of the elves. He will give us permission, and then we'll be on our merry way without him being any the wiser."

Right, because that was so much easier than telling the truth.

Freya lifted a brow. "Then why aren't you magicking me pretty like you've done so many times before?"

"Because the Summer Lord will notice that I've done that, and then he will get suspicious. We can't do anything that would make him question our intentions. He must believe that we want to get away for a while because we are desperately and wonderfully in love." He gestured with a hand and a sheer robe floated over to her. "Now, put this on."

She took the robe and stepped into it while still rolling her eyes. "That shouldn't be too hard to pretend that we're in love."

"Shouldn't it?" He paused in his spell casting to stare at her with eyes that saw right through her. "I would have thought it would be a little difficult for you. Considering you haven't said the words yet."

That stung. She knew she should have said them. Freya also was certain that she loved him with every fiber of her being. But that didn't make saying the words easier.

Freya tightened the ties around her waist and blew out a long breath. "I don't want to say it too early."

"We basically live together and sleep in the same bed every night. How much more serious do you want it to be?" Eldridge pinched the bridge of his nose, then shook his hand in the air. "No, wait, don't answer that. I'm not pressuring you to say the words before you're ready. That is not who I am."

Freya wanted to reassure him. She wanted to say that she intended to say them when the time was right, but...

Well. She didn't know what was holding her back.

But she knew that she shouldn't take this long. That their relationship was as important, if not more important, than finding her father. She had to take the time to tell the Goblin King how she felt.

Freya opened her mouth and resolved to let the words pour out, even if she wasn't quite ready to say them. "Eldridge—"

He lunged forward and put his hand over her lips. "I'm not rushing you. I don't want to remember this moment for the rest of our days as the time when I pulled those words from your lips. Listen to me, Freya. I will wait a century if I must to hear you say the words that I so desperately want to hear. A thousand days, a thousand lifetimes, the wait would be worth it." He let his hand drop from her lips and gave her a wry smile. "But not a moment longer than that, my love. A man has his limits, after all."

She smiled and tried to remind herself that this was all right. She shouldn't feel rushed to tell him how she felt, even though she knew the feelings were mutual.

Freya sat down at the vanity table he'd set up, ready to prepare her makeup, and placed her hands on the wooden top so she wouldn't meddle with his design. "I do feel that way, you know. I don't know what's holding me back from saying it."

Eldridge approached her from behind, his expression calm in the mirror. He put his hands on her shoulders and squeezed. "I know you do, Freya. Otherwise, I wouldn't be waiting around for so long. I know when I'm not wanted, and you? You want me more than breath."

"Well, that's a little arrogant."

"We share the same vice." He leaned down to peck a kiss to her cheek, then grabbed his weapons of choice. Brandishing a brush at her, he started in on creating a perfect woman who would tempt the Summer Lord, and yet still be strong enough for the other elves to not mess with her.

Maybe it would take a lot of work, Freya didn't know. The last time she'd been here, all she had done was put on a fluffy dress and run out with the other elves.

But then again, last time the Summer Lord had known the elves he summoned to his dance were going to tempt the Goblin King. Perhaps this Lord had different tastes. And the longer Eldridge worked on setting her figure and features to right, the more she realized just how difficult it would be to please this Summer Lord.

The makeup changed the very shape of her features. He made her nose thinner, her cheekbones higher, and the hollows a little deeper. Her jaw suddenly appeared sharp enough to cut, and the wings he put on her eyes in dark kohl made her eyelashes look much longer. Eldridge even spent a ridiculous amount of time carving out the shape of her brows until they were so pointed, they almost touched her temples.

Then he set about on her hair, smoothing it down with a warmed pole that he'd set in the fire. The metal shape allowed him to create perfect, soft curls that she'd never be able to create on her own.

How in the world had he made her look like another person? She turned this way and that in the mirror, then made a tsking sound. "I don't even look like myself."

"No, you don't. But that's the point." He pointed to the rack of dresses. "Pick one."

"Oh, I get to choose what dress I wear? What if I wanted to show up like this?" She lifted her arms in the sheer fabric robe. "If we're selling my looks to the Summer Lord, wouldn't this intrigue him?"

"You aren't seducing him," Eldridge snarled. "I know you're trying to get a rise out of me, and it's working. Pick a dress."

Freya was goading him, but he was really enjoying this process a little too much. Knowing that this was what the fae thought of as pretty stung. Freya wasn't going to waste time every morning doing this to make herself presentable for him. She couldn't.

She walked over to the dress rack and picked the first one her eyes landed on. It was the color of seafoam and summer. A pale green with blue edges that fluffed like the tide kissing the land. The deep neckline pointed to her navel, but the rest of the dress was very modest. It clung to her form, certainly. But the sleeves were long, and the skirt touched the ground. Yet again, this was something Freya would never wear on her own. She wasn't this woman. At least, she wasn't sure that she was.

But she'd admit it felt amazing when Eldridge stared. His eyes heated with passion and his jaw dropped a bit before he shook himself.

"Wow," Eldridge whispered. "You look amazing."

"Thank you." She lifted her arms and did a tiny spin for him to get a good look. "Do you think I can convince the Summer Lord to let us go to the isles while I'm dressed like this?"

"I think you could convince him to kneel at your feet and worship the ground you walk on." Eldridge closed the distance between them and tugged her against him.

One arm banded around her waist like a bar of steel. The other he lifted to scoop his hand into her hair and hold her firmly in place for a kiss that stole her breath away. He branded her with his lips, teeth, and tongue. Like he was trying to remind her that no other faerie would ever satisfy her as he did.

Freya wouldn't deny that. The Goblin King was the only man she wanted and the only one who haunted every waking moment of her dreams.

She was breathless when they parted. Her words shook slightly even as she resolved herself to focusing on the task. "Well, then."

He grinned, lips bright red. "Is that all you have to say?"

"I'll find my words by the time I speak with the Summer Lord." Freya stepped away and hoped she wasn't lying.

The longer she was around the Goblin King, the harder it was to focus on anything other than him.

CHAPTER 10

"Freya," Eldridge grabbed her arm just as they were leaving the castle. "Wait a moment, please. There's something I want to ask you. Tell you, I suppose. Before you go in there. That is. You should know it."

Since when did the Goblin King stammer? Freya looked over at him, bemused and wondering why now was the most important time to tell her anything. But then her stomach sank as she saw the expression on his face.

He was nervous. Anxiety nearly swallowed him up, and she couldn't imagine what he had to tell her that would make him so uncomfortable. He knew that she loved him, and he knew that she wouldn't fall under the Summer Lord's spell because she hadn't before with him. So why was he nervous now? Of all times?

"Eldridge?" she stepped closer to him and touched her hand to his cheek. "What's wrong?"

"Ah." He shook his head and forced a smile. "I've made you nervous, too. That wasn't why I wanted to talk with you."

"I always have time to talk about what you're feeling. Out with it."

He shook his head again, but at least cupped her hand with his own. Holding her against his cheek and inhaling as though he could smell her scent on the inner part of her wrist. "Just be careful. That's all I wanted to say. I know the Summer Lord is a handsome faerie, but he's no good."

She rolled her eyes and drew away. "That's what you're worried about? There's only room for one handsome faerie in my life. I couldn't handle two of you at the same time."

"No, of course not." He squared his shoulders and all the nerves fell away underneath the mask he wore. Not a real one made of metal or gemstones. The Goblin King's mask was one of flesh and years of experience. If he didn't want anyone to know what he was thinking, then no one would.

Freya could only hope she was so talented at hiding her emotions someday.

Together, they strode out of the castle and followed a white sand path. It was covered with tiny seashells that crunched beneath her feet. Not a cloud darkened the sky, and she knew this wonderful feeling wouldn't stay for long.

They followed the path all the way to a smaller garden, though still as lush as the others. This jungle setting was the perfect place for the Summer Lord and his veritable army of elves that draped themselves at his feet. A giant marble fountain sat in the center of the small pavilion. Two elves were seated on the edge, delicately sprinkling bits of bread into the water. Freya peered into the azure depths and saw bright orange koi fish swimming lazily to get their food.

She understood why the elves were so in love with this place. It oozed beauty and brilliance, but she also understood why the trees were mad.

There was a time and place for relaxation. Then there were times for action and purpose. What were these elves doing to better the world around them? Other than lazing about all day and indulging in their every whim?

The Summer Lord sat on a large couch they had brought into the jungle. Two elves fanned him with giant leaves.

He looked different from what she had grown used to. He had favored suits previously, just like Eldridge, who stood beside her in his classic black velvet suit with the gold embroidered edges.

The Summer Lord wore nothing more than white linen pants. The billowing fabric cinched tight to his waist. He wore many long loops of gold necklaces over his bare chest. Sweat slicked his skin and gave the dark color a sheen like oil. Rainbows danced over his chest every time he moved.

He lazily turned his gaze toward them and smiled, bright white teeth brilliant in the sun. "Ah, look who it is! The lovebirds I said weren't allowed to leave their cage. How do you two keep escaping?"

Eldridge bristled at her side. She knew he was about to argue, and that was the exact opposite of their plan.

She cleared her throat and stepped in front of him, purposefully twisting her body so the Summer Lord was looking at what she hoped was her best angle. "My Lord. You can't expect us to stay cooped up in the same room for days upon end while we're here. The Summer Court should be explored, don't you think?"

The words were supposed to make him think of all the lovely areas of his court. Freya had hoped he would wax on about the things that he loved. Eldridge certainly would have.

But the Summer Lord wasn't like the Goblin King. Instead of talking about all the things he loved, Leo narrowed his eyes at her. "What's that supposed to mean, little dove? You haven't fallen in love with this court, that would be a lie. If you're interested in Eldridge over here, then you would hate every aspect of my kingdom. Right down to every tiny seashell on my beaches."

At least Eldridge had calmed down enough to sound jovial when he responded. "You know that isn't true, Leo. I used to enjoy every summer that I spent here with you, and you remember that as well as I. Just because I haven't visited in a while doesn't mean I don't want to show Freya all our usual spots."

Leo's suspicious gaze turned to the Goblin King. "Usual spots? You hated every single one of them. I remember how often you used to complain here. It's too hot. It's too sticky. How could anyone live here when they could see the vibrant reds and oranges of the Autumn Court?"

Freya had worried the conversation would turn ugly. The two of them were incapable of being close to each other without a shouting match. If only she could get them to talk like civil men.

Once again, she stepped in between them and tried striking a pose. "Perhaps you would share your refreshments with me, my Lord? I quite enjoy being here and I remember the last time I met you, you had a wealth of delicious drinks."

Wrong thing to bring up.

Leo's cheeks darkened, and he sat up from his reclined position. "The last time you were here, you stole a very valuable magical item from me."

Oh no. Yes, she had stolen something from the Summer Lord, and she'd been trying to avoid that fact. Stealing wasn't something that the fae were particularly fond of, and most of the court leaders would have something to say to her.

She cleared her throat aggressively. "And I'm very sorry for that."

"I'd like it back."

Could this get any worse? Freya didn't have the little vial, at least, not with her. She assumed it was still in her things somewhere at the Goblin Court, but the vial with a lavender sprig in it hadn't exactly been her primary focus while traveling here.

She looked at Eldridge for his support, but he wasn't even looking at her. He was still glaring at his childhood friend as though his eyes could bore holes in the Summer Lord's shoulders.

Right, so she'd have to answer to the Lord on her own.

"I don't have it with me," she started, slowly saying each word. If she wasn't speaking quickly, maybe he would forget that they were trying to trick him. "But I'm happy to go get it later. I'm afraid I didn't realize how important it was to you."

"It's the only thing that keeps me calm." He gestured for one of the elves, and the lovely lady with the mask of a cat brought over a full goblet to him. "And no. You aren't getting any of my drink while you're here. The last time you drank me under the table, and the more I think about it, the less likely I believe it to be possible that you actually did that."

Maybe this was the game she had to play. If she revealed her tricks, perhaps he would be more inclined to speak with her.

Freya took another step closer and nodded. "I lied. I'm sorry for that, too. But I needed the vial to beat Eldridge and then discovered I like nothing more than doing that."

"Doing what?" Wine sloshed over his hand as he wildly swung the goblet around. "Lying?"

She rolled her eyes. "No. I don't enjoy lying, and I don't like to trick people as I did you. That's a faerie's game, not a mortal's."

"Exactly." The Summer Lord leaned forward, weaving slightly to the side before he gave her a half grin. "And yet here you are, with a faerie, lying through your teeth. How strange to think that you've learned your tricks from the Goblin King, while still being able to lie. You're a dangerous little creature, aren't you?"

Even like this, Freya was struck by how handsome this man was. In his suits, he looked stuffy and broad. But without the tight expectations of being the Summer Lord wrapped around his neck, he was a lean man with a crooked smile that lifted at the ends into dimples. He looked like the kind of man she'd find down an alley, ready to sell her dark magic spells for the cost of her soul. And she'd sell that soul to him, without question. A man like this could charm her into doing anything.

Well, almost anything. The thought of the Goblin King would prevent her from doing too much more than selling him a soul. But it was still enough to be frightening.

"I don't want to lie or deceive you today," she replied.

"I don't think you know how to not do that. Why should I ever trust you?" He leaned back in his chair, that crooked smile still locked on his face. "Freya. You want something from me. Why else would you be here? That puts me in a position of power, and I think you've realized how little you want to do that. Because if I'm the one making all the decisions, then I will never make them in your favor."

"Then get us out of your hair." Freya quickly pulled back the bow string of her words and loosed an arrow she knew he would bite on. "We want to travel to the isles. Now I know you won't give us permission to do that, but at the very least you should consider it. Then we won't even be here. We'll be all those waves away from you."

At her words, his skin turned ashen and his eyes widened in fear.

The goblet dropped from his hands, slipping to the floor and spilling red wine across the ground like blood. "You will never go to the isles. No one goes to the isles."

So something there was important to him.

Considering the way his hands shook uncontrollably, she would assume there was something on that island that could destroy him. Now, she very much wanted to go.

"I'll trade that vial back to you," she said. "All I want to know is how to get out there. That's all."

"On the back of a sea serpent," the Summer Lord snarled.

Eldridge put his hand on her shoulders and tugged her away from Leo and his elves. "Freya, we're not going to get his permission. I knew better than to ask this fool if we could have an afternoon away from all this."

She stared up at him with a frown. Freya was certain she was getting somewhere! All she needed was a couple more minutes and then she'd have him. Sure, she might be brow beating him into giving them permission, but she would have gotten what they wanted.

"Eldridge," she argued, but he put his finger on her lips. Silencing her.

The spark in his eyes was one of mischief. The Goblin King had a plan. She snapped her jaw shut and nodded ever so slightly.

"Be sad or angry," he muttered out of the corner of his mouth.

There was only one emotion that she could be convincing enough to act. Sad simply wasn't in her ability to fake.

Freya slapped her hand to his chest and shoved, hard. "Let go of me. I wanted to get out of here for a little while, and you promised you would see if you could make that happen."

Eldridge drew her farther away as he answered, "And I tried! I brought you to the Summer Lord, we talked with him, and he won't give us permission."

"You didn't even try to speak with him! All you wanted to do was argue!" She would have slapped him if she could bring herself to do it, but that felt too far. Besides, leaving a mark on his perfect face was more than a little wrong. She'd never forgive herself for it.

Soon, they were out of the Summer Lord's sight and nothing had changed. Freya looked around them, expecting something to happen and yet... nothing.

"Why did you want me to make a scene?" she asked, drawing away from him while crossing her arms over her chest.

He pressed a finger to his lips and grinned. "Wait for it. Scold me a little more, your shrewish voice is amazing."

"Shrewish!" she shouted, then immediately quieted down when he gestured with his hands. "I don't understand why we can't have private time together, that's all. I feel like the walls have ears here, and I wanted to get away. Just you and me."

The bushes rattled behind them. Freya lifted a brow and Eldridge mirrored her action, then waved a hand in the air for her to continue.

"I—I—" She decided to go for it. If they were supposed to be acting like they were in a fight, then she'd really sell it. "If we don't get some time together alone, then I don't see why we're even continuing this charade together. I'm done, Eldridge. Done."

An elf burst out of the greenery. "Wait! My lady, please wait. Don't say any words you can't take back until you listen to me."

Apparently, Eldridge had been right. They were being listened to and somehow their fight had swayed one of the elves. She put her back to the elf and mouthed, "Bravo," at Eldridge, before turning back around.

"What?" she grumbled. "I don't think you could say anything that would change my mind."

This elf was smaller than the others. Her delicate hands fluttered like birds at her side, and the butterfly mask on her face shuddered with the strength of her emotions. "You're such a lovely couple. I would hate to see the Summer Lord's cruelty ruin the beauty between the two of you."

Eldridge must have sensed weakness in this little elf, when Freya had been focusing on the Lord. Interesting.

She looked at Eldridge, then back to the elf. "That doesn't change the fact that I'm stifled here. I cannot be alone with him, and without that time, I will not be able to love him as before."

"Then go to the isles!" The elf stepped even closer to them, lowering her voice to a mere whisper. "There is a cavern down the beach. You can't miss it. Enchanted boats wait within and they will take you to the isles themselves. The Lord doesn't like anyone knowing they're there. But I know."

Freya reached out and patted the elf's shoulder. "You may have saved our relationship, my dear. Thank you."

The elf's gaze fell to the ground, and Freya was certain there was a blush underneath that mask. "It's my honor, Lady Freya."

She waited until the elf disappeared into the bushes again before turning to Eldridge with a shrug. "Well played, Goblin King. Well played."

He dusted his knuckles off on his jacket. "I've had a few centuries of trickery to learn how to manage these people."

"Apparently so. Shall we gather up Arrow and see what is on those isles?" She held out her arm for him to take.

"We shall."

CHAPTER 11

Freya watched as Arrow picked his way over the sands. Every now and then he would stop, stare at the sticky grains on his foot, and then shudder. He had forgone clothing this time, certain the salt would destroy his precious and luxurious fabrics. Freya and Eldridge had chosen matching brown linen pants and white shirts that should keep them cool in the hot sun.

Thankfully, Arrow wasn't complaining. The goblin dog was more likely to do that than breathe, so she was automatically suspicious. Even Eldridge was quiet when he should have been waxing on about wherever they were going.

The cave appeared on the horizon, plunging into the white cliffs and erupting with shadows that stretched out onto the sands. Both Eldridge and Arrow stiffened at the sight.

Freya planted her hands on her hips and stopped walking. "All right then, spit it out. You two know something I don't know."

They froze, each looking over their shoulder at her with a guilty expression that would have rivaled her sister's when she was a child. They thought they could wander through this place without her noticing their fear?

Men.

Freya stomped toward them and pointed severely. "You two are worried about something. Why wouldn't you warn me we were going into a dangerous place? Here I was thinking it was just a cave, and instead, you're both planning for a fight!"

If either of them looked at the other one more time for information, she was going to explode. Freya crossed her arms over her chest and glared. They had no right to keep her in the dark on anything.

"Fine," Eldridge muttered. "I'll be the one to tell her. You owe me one."

"I'm aware," Arrow replied before trotting off into the distance.

Freya waited until Eldridge broke. She would say nothing until he gave her the entire truth. He owed her that much.

"Look, neither of us are certain there will be any danger in there. The Summer Court is relatively safe, but we're both worried that there might be some creatures in that cave that Leo has placed to keep people away from the boats. That's all." He held his hands up in a peace offering. "Since we weren't sure if there were actually going to be creatures, we thought it was smarter to not worry you."

"I completely disagree."

He rubbed the back of his neck and gave her a sheepish grin. "I thought you might say that. Look, I understand your hesitation and that you disagree with me. But can we go into that cave with our wits about us? We can always argue later."

She stomped past him, shaking her head in disapproval. "We could have walked into a trap and I'd be clueless."

"I didn't want to worry you!" he called after her.

Right. Or he didn't want to be wrong and then look like an idiot when nothing happened. Or when something actually happened, being embarrassed that he hadn't made a big enough deal about it in the first place. She should strangle him. It would save her trouble in the future.

She'd go in on her own if they insisted on being so ridiculous. Without the two of them, she could focus on taking care of herself. Obviously she had to do that on her own, even though the two of them were supposed to be her dearest and closest friends.

Freya supposed they still were, even if they were a little ridiculous in their methods of taking care of her.

Sighing, she strode to the mouth of the cave where she waited for the two men to catch up to her. Sunblind, she stared into the darkness until it undulated like it had a life of its own.

Freya was used to that happening. The Goblin King's magic had prepared her to not be scared when the darkness moved. However, she was quite sure that the darkness wasn't expected to move in this case. Better to be safe than sorry.

By the time Eldridge caught up to her, Freya's eyes had adjusted. Large stalactites hung from the ceiling and dripped water down onto the stone floor. There was an impressive stairwell leading to a hidden place where the sea snuck underneath the cliff's edge. The water glowed bright blue with life.

How was this supposed to be scary?

She pursed her lips and waited for Eldridge to look over everything before she decided it was time to rub his fears in. "It's really terrifying," she said as she made her way down the steps. "I never would have thought you would be right, but look at all the terrifying creatures just waiting to take a bite out of us."

He watched her with a grin, letting her get her jabs in. Until he pointed to her right. "Like that creature, you mean?"

Freya turned and saw a giant crab latched onto the wall. Its legs were as long as her arms and spines grew on the sides of its shell. Tiny arms next to its mouth were working hard, picking at something it held clutched in its arms. It shifted, and she realized it was devouring a large meat rabbit that looked so small in the crab's grasp.

Fear zinged like electricity down her arms and she gasped, falling backward. She would have fallen to the ground if Eldridge hadn't caught her by the waist. "Careful," he muttered, staring behind her. "Apparently there's more of them than I thought."

She looked over her shoulder and a scream caught in her throat. There was yet another, this one standing on its legs, waiting for her to fall into its outstretched claws. The crab was four feet tall and could tear her apart if she slipped into its clutches.

Arrow carefully stepped next to them, his lips curled in a snarl. "I hate these things. Terrible monsters. Keep on the path you two, I suspect it's been spelled to protect anyone on it."

"Why would anyone ever step off this path?" she muttered.

"For those." Arrow pointed at the wall.

Gemstones were encrusted within the stone. Thousands of them, and likely worth a king's ransom. Rubies. Emeralds. Even clear chipped diamonds that should never have been able to grow where these were. And yet, here they were.

"Ah." Freya muttered. "Yes, I suspect many people would be enamored with those."

Eldridge squeezed her waist a little tighter. "Thieves fall under the spell of riches. Unfortunately for them, these guards are all too happy to pick them apart should they try to steal from the Summer Lord."

Suddenly, she was very grateful he'd asked her to steal off the Summer Lord's neck and not something down here. Freya wasn't so sure she'd have succeeded if he'd wanted her to bring him a gemstone.

They walked through the lines of crab sentries, and Freya tried her best to not anger them even further. By the time they all reached the boats at the bottom of the stairwell, the crabs were clacking their claws angrily. Each one she swore was glaring, threatening the intruders with the sharp edges of their claws.

Steadying herself with a hand on her hip, she looked at the first boat and pointed to it. "I think the one with a sun painted on it looks like good luck. What do you think, boys?"

Eldridge didn't even respond. He clambered into the wooden vessel and held out his hand to assist her in as well. "I'm not sure we have a lot of time before the spell wears off and those crabs attack. I'd rather be rowing away when that happens, rather than standing here."

She hopped into the boat. He didn't have to argue with her about that any farther, and Arrow was quick to leap at her heels. Together, they pushed the boat away from the small dock and out into the glowing waters of the sea.

Eldridge settled himself on the bench where twin ores were notched in the side. He set his hands on them and they flew out of the cave. The opening to the sea was so low they all had to flatten themselves into the body of the small craft, but then the sun struck their faces with a wave of heat that slicked her skin with sweat.

But, oh, the sun was beautiful.

After the nightmarish creatures that lived in that cave, the sight of a cloudless sky was more than welcome. She leaned against the boat's side and stared down into the crystal clear waters. Tiny shells dotted the sand. Starfish the size of her head drifted across the ocean floor, while brightly colored fish flashed their scales and swam by.

This was the Summer Court she had expected to see. The entire ocean came alive with color and vibrancy that she'd never seen in her life. Compared to the other courts, this one was a veritable wealth of luxury for her eyes. She felt blessed to see any of the creatures here.

Except, of course, those horrible crab things.

Shuddering with the memory, she leaned back into the boat and eyed her companions. "How many other faerie creatures like that are there?"

"Plenty." Eldridge's shoulders flexed as he rowed, his arms moving them through the water with powerful strokes. "Wait until we get out into the open sea. I'm sure there are more creatures like that before we reach the isles."

She hoped not. Freya didn't want this feeling to be ruined by yet another monster.

Thankfully, they had time before any monsters attacked them again. The sun teased her face with warm kisses. Eldridge removed his shirt so he could row faster and easier. The glistening silver tones of his skin made him even more otherworldly, but still handsome. She'd never seen someone quite so inhuman, but still so tempting.

She wanted to lick every drop of sweat off his chest.

Arrow grumbled and turned away from her. "I can't stand it when you look at him like that. He's not a meal, you know."

"He kind of is." Freya lifted a brow and watched as Eldridge's cheeks darkened. "Wouldn't you say, Eldridge? Nothing wrong with making a meal out of a man."

"I'm trying to focus, love." Though his tones were scolding, his eyes burned with passion. "We'll take up this conversation again soon, but let me get us to the isles. Then we'll embarrass Arrow even more."

"I'm certain he doesn't mind." Freya had no intention of continuing the conversation, but teasing Arrow was too much fun. "We could continue in whatever way we want."

"Do you think?" He eyed Arrow as well, clearly understanding that she wanted to poke fun at their small companion. "I'm happy to go over the details of our nights together, however, I think the goblin is turning a little green."

Arrow burped, and the sound was horribly wet. "I don't do well on boats."

"Is that so?" Freya lifted a brow. "How interesting. And yet you do so well on carts."

"Not really." Arrow lunged for the side of the boat and threw up into the water. His retching echoed across the waves so loudly she was certain he could be heard from land.

Oh, the poor dear. Freya stopped teasing him and rubbed his back. "It's all right. I can see the isles! We can't be that far away from them. You'll make it."

Eldridge made eye contact with her and shook his head. Apparently the distance was more than she realized. Freya hadn't been on the water since she was a little girl, though, so she knew very little about their journey. Her father used to row her around a lake, but that wasn't the same as the sea.

The waters darkened as they grew deeper. Freya watched the waves get larger and felt her own stomach flip as they continued through foaming swells. Not once did Eldridge hesitate. His arms flexed. His back worked hard. And they didn't stop even when the waves were concerningly large.

"Eldridge?" she asked, yelling so he could hear her over the crashing water. "Should I be worried, yet?"

"Yes!" he shouted back. "Definitely worry!"

Well, that wasn't very reassuring. The boat they were in was small and the waves were large. She feared they were going to tip over, and Arrow wasn't helping the situation. He kept leaning over the edge of the boat, tilting them dangerously close to the water. His retching couldn't be controlled, but she also didn't want him toppling into the waves. Freya wasn't confident they'd ever get him back.

"Arrow," she said, exasperated. "Get back into the boat."

"I can't!" he moaned. "I can't stop throwing up and I'm afraid what will happen if I'm not near the edge!"

"Oh, you'll be fine." Freya picked him up and set him down on the floor of the boat. "Throw up on the floorboards, no one will mind. It's a boat. We can wash it."

"But then I can't see the isles!" He stayed where she put him though, dramatically moaning and holding his head between his paws.

If they could still see the isles, then she would have let him look. But Freya stared up at the waves and realized she had no idea where they were going anymore. The walls of water were so tall, all she could see was the darkness and foam.

The next wave swelled and a flash of teeth came with it. The shadow of the monster was larger than their boat. A sharp tipped fin and angular features warned Freya that this might be a shark. But she'd never seen one so big.

"Eldridge?" she called out again. "Please tell me you saw that!"

"I did," he said with a grim expression on his face. Eldridge released his hold on the oars and let the boat guide itself. "The best we can do is ignore the monster and hope for the best."

Right, ignore the giant shark that was in every single wave they rode over. She gulped and looked down, only to make eye contact with a black, soulless gaze.

Two sharks. There were more of the monsters. Lovely.

Freya reached for Eldridge's hand and gripped it tightly in her own. "If you aren't rowing the boat, how are we going to get to the isles?"

"I was never really rowing it." He lifted her hand and pressed a kiss to her knuckles. "It's magic. It'll take us to the isles no matter what. I just wanted to impress you in case things went poorly."

Somehow, even with fear turning her stomach, Eldridge made her laugh. Freya chuckled and pulled him closer, pressing a swift kiss to his lips. "Why? So I could see your bare, sweaty chest?"

"You enjoyed it."

"I did." Her heart swelled with the next wave and for a moment, she felt like she wanted to say "I love you".

Freya opened her mouth to let the words fall from her lips, but never had the chance. Eldridge put his hand on top of her head and shoved her into the deep belly of the ship. Flashing teeth snagged a few strands of her hair, and then the shark sank back into the waves without its prize.

"That was a close one," she whispered.

"Let's stay low until the ship makes it, shall we?" He sank down with her and pulled her against his heart. "We'll make it, Freya. I'm certain of that."

She wasn't, but Freya was glad he had faith. She didn't know how long it took for them to reach their destination. All she could focus on was the horrible sound of gnashing teeth scraping the bow of their boat and the splash of sharp tails striking the surrounding waves.

But eventually, their boat bumped against something that wasn't a shark's flesh. It was sand.

Freya was the first to look up and there was the isle. Right in front of her. They'd reached the singular point they needed to go to. And they'd made it alive.

CHAPTER 12

She staggered out of the boat and landed feet first in the clear, salty water. Gone were the raging waves and the cloudy sky overhead. This island was an oasis of beauty, peace, and lovely bird song. A small slope led up to the grassy area of the island that disappeared into a forest of lush trees and a brightly colored rainforest.

It was very similar to being on the mainland in the Summer Court. No sharks. No crabs. Nothing to deter anyone who had made it to the island.

Eldridge hit the sand beside her, tilting his head back and breathing in the clean, fresh air.

Poor Arrow wasn't doing well at all. He shambled on all fours toward the sand, threw up one last time, then buried his face in the cool water. A few bubbles erupted from his nose before he finally lifted his face with a gasping breath. "I can't do that ever again."

"I hate to break it to you, my friend, but we have to go back that way." Eldridge flopped his arms at his sides and chuckled. "There are no portals on the isles. We'll be back on that boat in no time."

Arrow groaned, then dramatically laid down in the sand. He rolled onto his back, legs splayed in all directions, and then crossed his paws over his heart. "Then I will die here."

The dramatic goblin dog was exactly the relief she needed. Freya bent over, put her hands on her knees, and burst out laughing.

They had made it. They had traveled across that terrible ocean with all those sharks who had wanted to swallow them up. And they'd succeeded in getting to this damned island. Now, there better be a worthwhile secret that the Summer Lord was keeping from them or she was going to start breaking things.

When she caught her breath, Freya straightened and eyed the mysterious land. Where was the secret? What did she need to find that would be the thing the Summer Lord wanted to keep from them?

In one of the cliff edges she noticed there was a strange carving. The smoothed stone was a little too far for her to guess what it was. Squinting, she pointed over to the strange sight in the cliff. "What do you suppose that is?"

Eldridge looked the way she was pointing. He let out a little scoff. "Well. Would you look at that?"

"I can't," Arrow called out from his spot in the sand. "I'm dying."

"You are not," Freya scolded. "Eldridge, what are you seeing that I'm not?"

"I'm quite certain that's a house." He shaded his eyes from the sun, peering toward the strange carvings, but his eyes blurred. He stared as though he was looking into memories. "I had forgotten the Summer Court used to live in rooms like that. There were thousands of elves that lived all throughout the cliff faces, like pearls living inside clams. Why didn't I remember before now?"

She suspected it had something to do with magic. Why wouldn't it? Their entire lives had been molded, shaped by the ephemeral strangeness of powers that were beyond their control. At least, sometimes. Unless one was the Goblin King, and then most magic was at his fingertips.

Shaking her head, she pushed for a little more information, wondering if he'd even remember such things. "Was there some kind of curse put on those who lived within the Summer Court?"

He shrugged. "I have no idea. But I'm curious to find out if there's someone within those walls who knows the answer."

Freya was just as curious. If the Summer Lord was hiding someone like that from the court, then he had a bigger secret than she imagined. What else had his powers hidden? Perhaps they were very close to what the forest wanted them to discover.

"Let's head into the house, then," she said with a bright smile. "One step forward, and an impressive one at that. Don't you think?"

Eldridge nodded, but his attention was still far from her reach. He walked across the sand toward the home like he was wandering through a dream. His eyes unfocused, his hair blowing in the wind. Sweat still glistened on his bare chest. Eldridge looked like some silver god of the sea who had strode out of the waves.

She would have followed him to the ends of the earth if he asked her to. And that terrified Freya to the very core.

They walked through the sands to the small home hidden in the side of the cliff. Or at least, Freya had thought it would be small until she saw how many small crevices opened up and disappeared into the stone. It seemed like there were hundreds of openings large enough for a grown man and woman to walk side by side through. The white stone cliff became a seashell with swirling secrets.

Eldridge peered into the first cave and braced an arm over his head on the stone. "I never thought to see a place like this again. Now that I can remember what happened when I was a child, the Summer Lord before Leo got rid of all these. He said they were dangerous."

"Why?"

He shrugged. "They aren't. No one could ever give a real reason for any danger. I suspect that the Summer Lord didn't like how easy it was for people to hide in them."

"Ominous," she muttered.

"It was." He stepped into the cave and disappeared from sight.

She didn't know if she should follow him or stay here. What if there were more crabs waiting for them? And this time there wouldn't be the added help of a spell keeping the creatures at bay.

Eldridge popped his head back into sight, glaring at her. "Are you coming or not? We have to see if there's anything in here for us to find."

Right. Of course they did. She wasn't supposed to be afraid when they'd just seen monstrous beasts from the depths of the sea that shouldn't exist.

Rolling her eyes, Freya walked through the small doorway and waited for her eyes to adjust. It didn't take very long, namely because the tunnel through the cliffs was very short. It took her ten steps and she was back in the sunlight.

Gleaming white rooms filled with light that spilled from holes in their roofs. Everything here had been painted with scenes from the ocean. Some murals were bright blue rolling waves, others were yellow like the sun. The room opened up to several others, creating a home out of carved spaces. She hadn't expected the inside of a cave to be so… welcoming.

Eldridge walked over to one of the small windows that looked into the other bright rooms and put his elbow on the edge. "Now I remember. So many elves used to live here, you know. So many."

"And they all left because one selfish man didn't want them here anymore." Freya shook her head. "That's a damned shame. I know many people who would be honored to live here. It's so beautiful."

Though there was a lived in nature to this home that felt strange. If the elves weren't supposed to be here anymore, then why did it feel like the cups were too clean? The silverware had been laid out on the table as if someone was going to eat. And, strangely enough, it smelled like cinnamon.

Freya watched the area behind Eldridge, a small cozy room, and swore she saw the shadow of a person pass by. It stood to reason that they weren't alone, but she didn't know why anyone would hide. Unless they were afraid of the Summer Lord. Which, now that she thought about it, was entirely possible.

Strange, but not unexpected.

"Do you think this room is connected to others?" she asked, walking toward the other room and searching for the owner of the shadow. There was no one in the next space, but that didn't deter her. Freya knew in her gut there was someone to find.

"They all connect, yes." Eldridge looked around them. "Ah, there it is."

He touched his hand to a small glass knob on the wall that blended into the blue mural of the sea. The simple action very quickly opened a door she hadn't noticed that was perfectly painted into the blue coloring.

"Ah." Freya smiled and strode toward it. "So is this another room they would have used?"

"This would be their neighbor's home." He seemed to enjoy talking about the oddities of this place. "The elves aren't much for privacy, if you haven't guessed."

She'd assumed. Their homes were connected to the other families they lived near. She'd never wanted to be that close to the other people in her village. Freya was certain that would have driven her insane.

"Huh," she said, stepping into the other home. "How many homes do you think there are?"

Eldridge walked past her into the kitchen of this new home. This one was decorated with tiny daisies painted on the white walls. The oven was an ancient carved place in the wall, and now sunlight spilled through the chimney. He touched a hand to the carved name over the oven's opening. "Hundreds. More families than in the Summer Court now. There aren't as many elves as there used to be."

And what a horrible thing to think. All because one man had been so stubborn that he didn't want his elves to live here when they could live on the mainland with him. That sounded like her image of the Summer Lord. Including the current one.

Yet again, she saw a shadow streak by the white-washed wall. If there was a person here, then where were they hiding?

Maybe the person feared approaching such a large group. Freya had never been overly intimidated by one of the elves, so she couldn't imagine they were in any significant danger. Unlike the pixies, these were not a warring people. They were kind and shy, hiding their faces from the world because they worried about what would happen if they chose a face that someone else didn't like. The elves were not intimidating.

They were afraid, Freya realized. The elves were terrified of their Summer Lord, and that was why they wouldn't talk to her or her companions.

The last Summer Lord had taken them all from their homes, forced them to live where they didn't want. They had gone to the mainland when they were creatures of the sea.

Maybe the elves who currently lived on the mainland didn't remember their life here, just as Eldridge had forgotten. But she was sure they remembered deep in their soul their love of this place. And that they missed it more than they realized.

"Do you mind if I peek in this room?" she asked Eldridge. "I want to cover as much ground as we can."

"Do you think that wise?" Arrow sat down on her foot and stared up at her with disappointment. "Splitting up has only caused us trouble in the past."

"Splitting up saved us in the mines of the Spring Court, I'll remind you." She couldn't risk Arrow ruining her plan when the elf likely wanted someone to be alone so they could talk. "Why don't you go with Eldridge if you're so worried about being left behind?"

"He's right." Eldridge frowned, and she worried he'd already seen through her words. "If we split up in a place like this, we might never find each other again."

"We'll only go into a few rooms and then come right back here. Every room looks like it's painted differently, so I can't imagine they would be easy to forget." Freya flipped her hair over her shoulder and tried very hard to look like she knew what she was doing. "Besides, this is a ghost town in the wall of a cliff. There's no way anyone lives here. The Summer Lord made sure of it."

Eldridge hesitated, but eventually gave in. He grumbled something about headstrong women, but then scooped Arrow up under his arm. "Fine. I'll take the frightened dog. But don't go too far, and if anything happens—"

"I'll yell." She reached up and kissed his cheek. "You stay out of trouble too. I won't be there to save you this time."

"Ha. Ha. Very funny." He motioned that he was watching her before rounding the corner and heading into the next room on his side.

Perfect. Now her plan could work.

Freya darted into the next room and pitched her voice low. "I know you've been watching us. I saw your shadow a few times. It must be very scary to have three strangers walk onto your island after being on your own for so long."

There was no way to know if anyone was listening to her talk, but Freya was certain someone was watching her. The hairs on her arms were standing straight up.

She walked into the next room that looked like a bedroom. This one was painted with tiny elves dancing on every wall. The artist had spent many hours painstakingly perfecting each and every face. Even the dresses the elves wore swirled around them, appearing almost to move on their own even though they were painted.

Freya could stay in this room forever, but she had to find out who was in this abandoned place.

A gemstone had been stuck into the wall, held aloft by a painted elf who stood above the rest. She could only assume that was the button to get into the next room. Without thinking, she reached out and thumbed the small gemstone.

Well oiled and silent, the door to the next room swung open and revealed a garden waiting for Freya. The ground was covered in moss and tiny rivers that flowed to the center where a small pool held countless colorful fish. But Freya's eyes weren't on the greenery, the fish, or even the rivers that sloshed over her ankles. No, she was staring at the young woman crouched in the corner, staring at Freya with horror in her eyes.

She was beautiful with skin a deep umber. Her eyes were dark as midnight and glistened with unnatural light. Her hair was braided tight to her skull, individual strands standing out amongst the rest and nearly reaching her waist in length. Her clothing was old, outdated but still lovely, clinging to her strong, lean form.

But what shocked Freya the most was that this woman, this elf with her lovely pointed ears, had a face. She wasn't wearing a mask, but instead, she had a real face.

Just like the Summer Lord.

Freya stopped in the middle of the room and hunkered down on her haunches. "I'm not going to hurt you."

The woman's eyes only got wider. Clearly, she didn't believe Freya at all.

"Really, I'm not. I only came here to get some answers to questions that I cannot even begin to understand." Freya knew she was pushing this woman too fast and too far. But she had to try. "May I sit? I won't come any closer."

The woman shook her head, and Freya decided to take that as the other, not minding if she sat. The other option wasn't acceptable.

Obviously the woman didn't trust her at all. Her eyes flicked to a blank spot in the wall that could be a hidden door. Freya had to distract this stranger, or at least entertain her long enough to win her trust.

Shifting, she sat down onto the wet floor, crossed her legs, and sank her fingers into the watery moss. "Now. Let me tell you a story about a mortal woman who fell in love with the Goblin King. That'll help us get to know each other. What do you say?"

Fear was pushed aside by curiosity, and the woman relaxed against the wall. Freya took that as her opportunity, and so she began to tell her own story with all its strange and magnificent events.

CHAPTER 13

It didn't take long for Eldridge and Arrow to find them. Freya figured they'd only have a few moments alone, and she used those moments wisely. She spun a web of a story that would ensnare even the hardest of hearts. So by the time Eldridge walked into the room, she had already prepared the young woman to know who the Goblin King was.

Apparently, she didn't need to waste her time.

Eldridge walked through the door and his eyes grew wide. "Cora?" he asked. "What in the world are you doing here?"

To the other woman's credit, she didn't react at all to Eldridge's presence. "I should ask the same of you. You brought a mortal here and fell in love with her? That's not the Goblin King I remember."

He sheepishly rubbed the back of his neck. "I was a boy the last time we saw each other."

"Yes, you were. And you didn't yet know what it meant to be a king." The woman sighed and smiled at Freya, though the expression was sad. "I'm sorry I didn't speak. I thought you were lying. It's an incredible story you told and very few would believe the words true."

Freya shouldn't be so uncomfortable meeting someone Eldridge used to know. She'd met countless others in the faerie realm, and yet this one unsettled her. Perhaps because the faerie woman was far more beautiful than the others.

Was this what jealousy felt like? Freya had tasted the emotion before, but only in small doses that hadn't felt like this. She could hardly think through the panic in her chest that warned she shouldn't let Cora and Eldridge anywhere near each other.

But that was silly. They were childhood friends, nothing more, nothing less.

"I wish you'd told me before my throat went raw," Freya replied with a small laugh. "But I'd like to know what you're doing here. Alone. Eldridge said this place was abandoned a long time ago."

"It was." Cora stood up and dusted off her sheer cream skirts. "Until the forest named me the sea. And after that, I was sent to live here by the Summer Lord. Far away from anyone else's gaze."

"The sea?" Those were strange words to use. The forest naming a person after the other element that made up summer? It sounded like what Cora had told them was important. But she couldn't make hide nor hair what it meant.

But even Eldridge appeared confused. His brows furrowed in concentration and he shook his head. "I think my mind's still foggy. I didn't remember what happened here until I stepped foot on the isles. I assume that's someone else's doing in wanting to hide whatever knowledge is kept here."

"The forest and the sea cannot live without each other," Cora said. She tucked her hands together in the picture of poise and delicacy. "The Summer Lord is no one without his lady, you see. So I've been here. Waiting for him to come to me so we can finally put the court back together. It's been a long time of being alone, but I know it's a matter of when he'll show up. Leo was always so late to everything that was important."

Freya's heart broke for this poor woman who was still holding out hope that Leo cared at all. In Freya's limited experience with the man, she wasn't so sure he was ready for a serious relationship. He seemed to hate himself a little too much to bring another person into his life.

She glanced over at Eldridge to see him staring at her with a thoughtful expression. "What?" Freya asked. "Why are you looking at me like that?"

Eldridge shook himself out of whatever thoughts had taken over. "Nothing. Cora, how long have you been here?"

"I don't know." She walked toward the small pool in the center of the room and sat down on the edge, swirling her legs in the water. "A while, I suppose? The last Summer Lord was the one who said I should stay here. And Leo was supposed to come get me when he took the mantle from the other. I didn't expect it to take this long, but I'm not surprised. The Lord was always a healthy man."

Oh, but it had been much longer than that. Did this poor woman not know how many years had passed since Leo became the Summer Lord?

"I—" Freya didn't know if she should be the one to tell this poor woman that she'd been here for a very long time. She wanted to go get the Summer Lord, drag him back to this isle, and force him to talk to Cora. Obviously, there were a lot of words left unsaid between the two of them.

If the Summer Lord was supposed to marry this woman, or unite with her, then this was the secret that Leo had been keeping. He wanted nothing to do with this picture of perfection, and Freya couldn't understand that. What man wouldn't want to be married to a woman like this?

She took a step toward the pool and crouched down once again beside Cora. "I think you've got the story mixed up, Cora."

The elf furrowed her brows and smiled at Freya with confusion in her eyes. "I'm sorry, I don't know how you'd know that? You're a mortal. The Summer Court's history has been hidden from your eyes."

"It's just that... Well. Leo has already taken the throne." She looked over her shoulder at Eldridge for some help. "It's been... How many years since he's been the Summer Lord?"

Eldridge's gaze darkened with anger and rage. "Nearly two hundred."

Cora's eyes widened with every word. Her feet stopped swirling in the pool and an unsettling quiet fell over the small garden hidden within the cliff.

What was going through this woman's head? Freya would have throttled Eldridge if she were in Cora's place. She would have put her hands around his neck and demanded to know why he had put not only their own relationship in peril but also the lives of so many others. The Summer Lord had a duty to take care of his court, and that duty was sitting right here.

Instead of doing any of that, Cora merely put a hand to her cheek and caught a single glistening tear that had slid from her dark eyes. "Oh." She looked down at the glittering droplet of saltwater and then smoothed it into her skin. "I suppose that means he doesn't want me."

"No!" Eldridge rushed forward and sat down on her other side. He reached for Cora's hands and gripped them in his own. "I remember you very well when we were children. Leo always tugged on your braids and chased you through the sands. He was very much interested in you, and I cannot imagine why he hasn't rushed to your side, even now."

"Because he doesn't want me." The smile on Cora's face was horribly sad. "It's all right, Eldridge. The forest picked us to be together, and I understand that's not always what the other person wants. I should be happy that I have lived my life out here, and not in the Summer Court while it collapsed without both of our attentions."

The two of them began speaking of their time as children. Eldridge reminded her of the small set of caves they had found that were filled with flowers no one had seen before. Cora giggled a memory of a grotto where mermaids lived, if only they waited long enough.

And suddenly, Freya felt as though she were intruding on private time between two friends. She stood up and made her way back to Arrow, who had laid down in a bright spot of sun.

She sat down next to him, beyond caring that the ground was wet. She had already soaked her bottom when she first came into the room.

"So they know each other, then," she murmured, pitching her voice low so she wouldn't interrupt the faeries at the pool.

Arrow snuffled and lifted his head from the soft moss. "Oh, yes. They were the best of friends back when the faerie courts liked each other. They spent every hour they could with each other until their parents wouldn't let them anymore. Sad stuff, that. Most people thought they would end up together."

Jealousy burned again. And she knew it was ridiculous to feel like that. People changed as their story changed, and the two faeries sitting next to each other were no longer the same children they had once been.

Still, it made her sick to her stomach to think she could lose him. "Is that so?" she gritted between her teeth.

"No." Arrow chuckled, sitting up so he could look at her better. "I wasn't even alive when they knew each other, Freya. You know when I was born. I imagine they were just good friends. Listen to the way she talks about Leo. Cora would do anything to have him in her life. She's in love with the fool."

It was hard to listen to the tones of love when she was so worried the other woman would take one look at the Goblin King and realize she'd picked the wrong friend. And maybe that was a ridiculous worry. She wasn't so caught up in her jealousy that she couldn't see that. But what if?

Again, Arrow made a snuffling sound and nudged her with his paw. "Freya. This look doesn't suit you. Jealousy is a poison as bad as what the forest is spreading through the Summer Court."

She sighed. He was right. Of course he was right when she was sitting here, green in the face, just because she didn't have the undivided attention of the Goblin King. Freya was acting like a child, and unlike herself when all she had ever wanted was to be an independent woman who took care of herself.

Shaking off the emotions with a quick jerk of her neck, she put her attention to fixing the problem laid out before them. The forest wanted the Summer Lord to do what needed to be done. And clearly, that was this woman in front of them.

Cora was the personification of the sea. And the Summer Lord represented the forest itself.

Frowning, Freya stood back up and interrupted the two of them as they continued talking about their childhood. "Cora? Might I ask a question?"

The beautiful woman looked over her shoulder and smiled. "Of course."

"The forest is punishing Leo for not joining with you, or whatever it was you said needed to happen. What happens to you if you don't become the Summer Lady?" Freya feared the answer would be just as bad as Leo's fate.

"Then the sea will take me back," Cora replied. "That's the way of the Summer Court."

The sharp edge of Eldridge's gaze bored into Freya's own. They couldn't let that happen. Neither she nor he were the kind of people who would let an innocent woman die without trying to save her. That was part of what made Freya fall in love with him so thoroughly. So dangerously.

Even with jealousy still bitter on her tongue, Freya hated to imagine Cora as the cold, still body she had seen so many times since coming to the faerie realm. This vibrant woman deserved to live, not die as the Summer Lord had resigned the both of them to.

"We won't let that happen," she replied. "Right, Eldridge?"

"We'll try to stop it," he corrected. "Leo is the only one who can save the both of you, and he isn't as you remember, Cora. Time has taken its toll on the Summer Lord."

Freya wanted to laugh, but she smothered the noise before it could burst free from her throat. Cora needed to remember Leo with all the possibilities of their future that she had been nursing for all these years. If this elf still thought there was a chance for her love to grow even stronger, then that made their task even easier.

"We'll need time to plan," she said. "I don't think we can go back to the Summer Court and demand that he come back here and take his bride home. Leo barely even speaks with us."

Eldridge stood and held out his hand for Freya to take. "We'll stay here for a few nights. I'm sure Arrow would appreciate the respite from all those horrible waves."

The goblin dog groaned from his corner and pressed a paw to his mouth. Apparently, the mere idea of waves made his stomach roll yet again.

Freya nodded. "All right. We'll stay for a little while and figure all this out."

They tunneled deeper into the cliff until Eldridge found a room he thought was satisfactory. Freya noted how far that room was from where they had seen Cora, and where they had left Arrow.

The goblin dog was more than happy with the bright, sunny room painted with even more rays of sunlight. He'd laid down in a beam and said he was going to sleep until he forgot that adventure existed. Freya wasn't so sure why he had become so dramatic lately, but having a little time with the Goblin King to herself sounded like a good idea.

She wanted to kiss him. She wanted to run her hands over his shoulders and press her fingertips into him until he forgot all about Cora and her beauty. She still thought the jealousy was poisonous. Arrow was right in that.

But she couldn't shake free.

Eldridge chose a room that was darker than the others. It might have been the last room before they had stopped tunneling into the cliff. The walls were painted with deep blues and scenes from the depths of the ocean. Brightly colored squid with glowing tendrils. Fish with lanterns on their heads. And sometimes, if she looked closer at the dark paint at the bottom, she could see there were shadows of sharks added into the depths.

Beautiful and deadly. Just like her Goblin King.

He sat down on the edge of the bed and lifted his arms over his head with a yawn. "I am exhausted, aren't you?"

No. She wasn't exhausted in the slightest. She had a thousand questions running through her head and a million worries that he needed to ease. Why would he even think about sleeping at a time like this?

"We should talk about Cora," she said, approaching him with single-minded intent. "We should plan out everything that we intend to do. The Summer Lord won't be easy to convince that he should come back to the isles. Let alone that he should take a bride."

"I think we should get some rest and talk about it in the morning, when our minds are fresh." But his eyes glittered the closer she got to him.

Eldridge reached for her when she straddled his waist. Freya sat in his lap, wrapped her arms around his shoulders, and relaxed into the confident grip as he held her tight to his heart.

Maybe she didn't need to brand him with her touch. She didn't have to force him to be interested in her because of how many times she could pleasure his body. All she had to do was sit in his arms, listen to the beat of his heart, and shift her breathing to match his.

He rubbed her back with his hands, gently putting pressure on the tense muscles surrounding her spine. "You did good today," he murmured against her neck.

"Did I?" She pressed a kiss to his shoulder, inching a little closer as she did so. "I feel like I wasn't myself."

"Oh, because you turned green the moment you realized Cora and I knew each other?" he chuckled. "I saw how frustrated you were getting, my hero. Did you think I would miss that detail?"

Yes. She had thought he would miss her reaction to the two of them. In fact, she had very much hoped he wouldn't notice at all.

Pulling back from his grip, she stared down at her hands. "I'm not proud of it. I know you're in love with me, and that you'd do anything to keep me in your life. There's no reason for me to be so jealous."

"No, there isn't." He reached up and brushed a strand of hair behind her ear. "But I know that this still feels very novel to you. As if our story is a fairytale you were sucked into, and someday it's going to spit you back out in your boring life by the forest. Isn't that right?"

To her great embarrassment, tears burned in her eyes. Freya refused to let them fall because crying right now would be utterly ridiculous. She had nothing to cry about.

So instead of letting her emotions get the better of her, she nodded.

"Oh, Freya." Eldridge stroked her jaw with a single finger, forcing her to look up at him. "I wish I could tell you in words how I burn for you. Every moment of every day I fall deeper in love with you. When you are at your worst and when you are at your best."

This man made her melt. He never failed to ease all her worries and remind her how much she loved him. And she wanted to say it. She wanted to tell him that her heart beat for him and that no matter where she was, she always thought of him.

But she couldn't. Not yet. Not when he knew how jealous she was of his relationship with Cora. If she said the words now, then he would think she was only saying them because there was the possible threat of another woman.

And that wasn't how she wanted him to remember this moment. She wanted Eldridge to know that without a doubt in her mind, she loved him. A thousand times more than there were stars in the sky. Regardless of old flames.

She settled back into his arms and let him draw her into the bed with him. Eldridge tucked her head into the crook of his shoulder with a happy sigh. "You and me, Freya. We're the same kind of creature, you know that? Adventurers at heart. We don't stay in the same place for very long, and I've always admired that about you."

What if she wanted to stay in the same place for a while, though? She hadn't been this person before she met him, and Freya worried he'd get bored with her.

Eldridge's breath evened out into the deep rhythm of sleep. But while the Goblin King found himself in the dreaming world, Freya couldn't even consider sleeping. Her mind was racing with all the things that she needed to get done. To think about. To understand.

Cora was the personification of the sea in this equation. And she could understand that there was a connection between the land and the sea. They were two elements who were constantly touching, but never existed in the same plane. They were the perfect symbols for magic to grow and develop.

What she didn't understand was how a person could be on an island by herself for over two hundred years and never realize how fast the time was passing. Freya would have been counting the days on the walls. Every room in this cliff side town would have been painted with tiny numbers as she waited for someone to come and get her. Wasn't that the same feeling Cora must have had?

Two hundred years alone was a very, very long time.

And then there was the reasoning why the Summer Lord didn't want to make her his Lady. After all, Cora seemed to be the perfect choice for such an illustrious position.

Mortals did this all the time. Nobles married people they weren't in love with, but who were good political matches. They made it work. She was certain they didn't exactly enjoy the company of each other. Most likely they focused on their own lives, and that was that. Why wouldn't the faeries do the same thing?

Rolling over in bed, she planned to ask Eldridge what made the faeries so different from the mortals. But he was sleeping. His features were smooth as glass, relaxed as she hadn't seen him in a very long time. She shouldn't wake him when he had fallen into a deep sleep.

Freya inched herself closer and closer to freedom. She tried very hard not to jostle the bed with her movements, and made it out of the covers, then to the very edge of the room. She spared a single glance back to look at her handsome Goblin King one more time.

"I really do love you," she whispered, letting the words float into the shadows and hopefully into his dreams. "And when the timing is perfect, I will tell you that with so much certainty that you will never question it again. My love. My life. My Goblin King."

Slipping out into the hall beyond, she weaved through all the homes of the neighborhood. Freya understood Eldridge's fear that she would get lost in the countless rooms and then no one would ever find her again. But she didn't share the same concern.

Each home was distinctly different, but there were markings. The elves had gotten in and out of these cliff side homes with ease, and that wasn't because they knew every single neighbor and where that neighbor lived. They had a pattern. A tool to getting out even while they marched through the living space of another.

She put her fingers to the frame of a door and thumbed the markings carved there. Three lines, each one distinct. One wavy, two straight but a little shorter than the other. Strange markings, but ones she was certain had to do with the direction to go in.

And she had all night to figure it out.

Freya strode through colorful rooms and made up stories in her head about the elves who used to live here. The ones who painted flowers on their walls missed living on the mainland, but they were happy here on the islands as well. The ones with dolphins were the funny family, the tricksters who always played pranks on their neighbors. Her favorite, though, were the ones who painted elves on their walls. Those were the artists she fell in love with. The elves who had stories to tell and didn't want to forget them no matter what.

Eventually, she figured out what the lines meant. The waves were directional, telling someone to go left or right depending on the direction of the pointed crests. And the other two lines were how far to go. The top line was the distance to the sea. The bottom was the distance to the end of the neighborhood.

In very little time, Freya stood on a balcony overlooking the sea. A full moon illuminated the white sand beach, and the stars were so bright, it looked like the sea sparkled with a thousand glowing fish. Perhaps this was how Cora had stayed here all these years and never once questioned how long it had been. With a sight like this every evening, Freya didn't think she'd want to leave either.

The shadows to her right shifted, and Cora appeared out of the darkness. This time, the lovely woman didn't speak at all. She watched Freya with hope in her eyes, and a sense of oddness that could only come from a someone who had spent very little time in the presence of others.

"You and Eldridge share that ability, you know." Freya smiled. "The two of you are always popping out of shadows and startling me."

"Oh." Cora looked behind her, and then a sheepish grin crossed her face. "I forget that mortals can't see very well in the dark. I thought you knew I was here."

She hadn't, and the excuse was a foolish one. Freya used this chance to get to know the other woman, however awkward that might be. The more she knew about Cora, the easier to convince the Summer Lord to come to the isles.

Freya leaned against the railing of the balcony and crossed her arms over her chest. "Why do you want to marry the Summer Lord?"

The elf's eyes widened in shock before she stammered, "Well... I... I..."

Yeah, Arrow was right. The woman was madly in love with the idiot, and Freya understood the fear that came with that realization. It was a bone deep need that never went away, no matter how hard they wanted to be their own person. Both Eldridge and Leo had wiggled into their very souls. The fiber of who they were.

Freya sighed and reached out to take the other woman's hand. "Is there a kitchen where we can talk? I think I'd like a cup of tea, if you have any."

"Oh, I have more than enough tea to satisfy both of us." Cora squeezed Freya's fingers with a radiant smile on her face. "Come on. We'll have a chat. I'm afraid it's been a very long time since I've had another woman to speak with."

Freya suspected that was very much the truth.

The kitchen Cora brought her to was warm and inviting. A fire crackled in the oven that was inlaid into the wall, and the table was filled with dirty dishes, food, and countless other objects from the sea.

Freya picked up a dried starfish and held it aloft. "One of yours?"

"I like to collect things on my walks. Sometimes I find items from the mainland that people have set adrift." Cora reached for the starfish and gently set it back down on the table. "Other times, I find treasures that the sea sends me."

A treasure. Freya looked down at the small dead creature and supposed it was a bit like a treasure. Esther had once gone to the sea with Freya and their father. They had collected sand dollars to put in a jar, and Esther had loved looking at them.

"Treasure," she repeated with a soft smile. "That's a lovely way to look at it."

Cora spun around and grabbed for teacups that hung from tiny hooks on the wall. She set about putting a large metal teapot directly into the fire and then filled her arms with a mound of dirty dishes that likely should have been cleaned weeks ago. "Lovely is correct! Just don't look at my mess. I'm afraid living alone has made me... well."

Freya reached out and grabbed a plate before it fell out of Cora's arms. Though there were likely plenty of plates to steal from other homes, she suspected Cora liked these the best. "You've only had to take care of yourself and not had to worry about the opinions of others. I completely understand."

She'd get messy too if she didn't have to clean every single day. It was so much easier to let things be as they were.

"Exactly." Cora precariously took the dishes over to the corner where she laid them down into a box. "I usually wash them in the ocean, you see. I just haven't had time lately and..."

No more words came out to explain her predicament away. Freya grinned and lifted her teacup. "We have two clean teacups! That's all we need right now."

The expression on Cora's face brightened once again. "I like the way you think, Freya. You're a good friend, I can tell that already."

As Cora bustled about the kitchen, searching for tea, Freya suspected, she peered into the teacup. There was a giant stain on one side, and the other was still muddy with soot. At least, she hoped the black substance was soot. Making a disgusted face that she couldn't suppress, she picked at the black goo and pulled it off with her finger. Maybe that wasn't soot. It was a little too thick.

"Here we are!" Cora exclaimed.

Freya wiped her expression clean of any expression. "What kind of tea did you find?"

"It's only earl grey, but it's something. I hope you like strong tea?" Cora asked, then emptied the entire container into the teapot.

Freya could only hope there was a strainer in all that, or they would both be picking tea out of their teeth for weeks to come.

"I love strong tea." She gestured to the holes in the ceiling where sunlight would normally filter through. "Especially when it's nighttime. If I'm going to stay up all night, I might as well have a good cup of tea to help keep me awake. Don't you think?"

"I do." Cora sat down in the chair on the opposite side of the table and put her chin in both hands. "You wanted to know why I hope to marry the Summer Lord?"

Here they went, telling each other stories as women often did by candlelight. At least she'd get a few secrets out of this strange and messy ordeal. "I do. I know you haven't seen Leo in a very long time, but I can't imagine he's the same boy you remember."

"Probably not. But I'm not the same girl I was back then, either." Cora gestured around at the mess. "Believe it or not, I used to be very clean."

Freya snorted. "This mess doesn't come from a couple hundred years on your own. I don't think you ever were the tidy woman you describe yourself to be."

"No. But I did at least have servants to pick up after me." The elf shifted on her seat, obviously uncomfortable that the mess was so uncontained. "I just... Look. I remember Leo when he was a boy, and there was always an edge to him. He was a little dangerous, and someone that a girl like me would fall head over heels for. I always knew there was a level of uncertainty in our relationship. But I never questioned that we could and would get married."

"So you knew?" Freya moved the cup into her lap as though she wanted to hold it. Instead, she used the edge of her shirt to clean the interior. "You knew that you were going to get married to him, that is."

"We both could guess. The titles of Lord and Lady always goes to the strongest of the fae in the court. He and I were the obvious choices." Cora leapt up at the scream of the tea kettle. "I was much more interested in the possibility than Leo, as you must have guessed."

Freya assumed. She held out her cup and let the conversation fall silent as Cora poured the mixture of tea leaves and liquid into Freya's teacup. The silence wasn't awkward between them, though. It was simple and quiet. Like two friends who hadn't been able to talk together for a very long time.

Sipping carefully so she didn't get any leaves, Freya cleared her throat. "Can I ask you a question that might be rude, but I honestly don't know if it is?"

Cora grinned into her cup. "Those are my favorite kinds of questions. By all means. Ask away."

"Why do you and the Summer Lord have faces, but no one else in the Summer Court does?" Freya didn't know if that was overstepping her bounds. After all, the ownership of a face seemed like a very personal thing. Even if it was just a choice, she assumed that still meant it was personal.

"Oh." Cora laughed a little and set her cup down. "That's not so hard to answer. Surprisingly, the Lord and I picked our faces together when we were children. Usually an elf would take a long time to decide what face they wanted to commit to. Neither of us saw the reason for that. So we went to the mortal realm, tried on more faces than I can remember, and then we both settled on these."

They tried on mortal faces? Freya didn't like the sound of that, but her curiosity burned ever brighter. "Whose faces were they? Or do you not remember?"

"Of course I remember. A face is a thing that is freely given by mortals, even when they don't realize it. But they mean so much to the elves." Cora touched a finger to her cheek. "They were a young couple, very much in love and so looking forward to the rest of their lives together. I knew when I saw her face that she loved her husband more than the sun loves the moon. I had to have that expression when I looked at Leo on our wedding day."

Freya's heart melted. "What a lovely thing to desire. And Leo must have felt the same if he took her husband's face?"

"We thought it would be poetic. We'd tell the story to the other elves, they would all melt at the story of our young love, and the entire court would fall in love with our own story." She shrugged. "I guess it just wasn't meant to happen like that after all."

This poor woman shouldn't feel like she had done something wrong just because a man hadn't chosen her. The Summer Lord's adoration was no more impressive than that of a simple farmer's love, and Cora would have made a thousand people fall in love with her in the mortal realm.

She reached across the table and grabbed onto Cora's hand. "I don't think that anyone's love is lesser because of a choice they made. It sounds like the Summer Lord had intense feelings for you, and I don't know why he decided not to act on them. But before I leave this court, I promise you, I will try to find the answer for you."

Cora squeezed her fingers in return. "I don't know where you came from, or why you're helping me, but I can see why Eldridge loves you so dearly. Your heart is more pure than anyone I've ever met. The fae are not..."

"Like the mortals?" Freya grinned and shook her head. "I assure you, there are a million people in the mortal realm who are kinder and more giving than me."

She could list off a handful of priests who would be horrified to know that any faerie thought Freya was a good person. After all, she had been the one to skip mass more times than was acceptable. But the reality was that she was trying to be a good person, and perhaps that was where so many of the fae failed. They were selfish creatures by design. They expected other people to take care of them, but all the fae were like that. When there were a hundred takers, and only one giver, she could only guess that faerie would end up in the mortal realm.

Her grin nearly splitting her face, Freya leaned back and released her hold on Cora's hand. "If you weren't so dead set on winning Leo back, I'd tell you to run to the mortal realm. You might meet some fisherman who steals your heart and thinks being married to the sea would be the best thing that ever happened to him."

"Oh, I doubt that." Cora's cheeks darkened. She sipped at her tea and made a face. "This is horrible."

Freya sucked in a deep breath and nodded, gently nudging her tea away from her. "Yes, yes, it is quite bad. I think there was something in the cups that gave the tea a distinctly fishy flavor."

"I'm so sorry." The laughter in Cora's voice was everything that Freya needed to hear. The bubbling sound was so wonderful, so heartfelt, and it was the first time she'd heard Cora's happiness.

And that was all Freya wanted for this kind, sweet woman who had been locked away by everyone who mattered. She deserved to be happy, even if Freya had initially been jealous of her beauty.

"That's quite all right," Freya said with a chuckle. "Just don't make me drink it anymore, and I'll forgive what horrible tea making skills you have."

"I would not be a very good lady's maid."

"No, but I can't imagine the Lady of the Sea requires such a skill set. There are quite a few women who will be ready to wait on you when you return to the Summer Court." There had to still be people there who remembered Cora, like Eldridge had. And what a welcome surprise that would be.

At least, Freya hoped that was the welcome this wonderful young woman would get. Even though the Summer Lord hadn't wanted her as his bride, that didn't make Cora any less worthy. It wasn't like Leo was going to pick one of the other elves in his court. Freya didn't think he wanted to be married at all, and that was the problem here. Not that he didn't want Cora.

She hoped.

Heavens, she hoped that was the case because otherwise she and Eldridge had their work cut out for them.

Patting Cora's hand one last time, she stood up. "I should get back to the room where I left Eldridge. If he wakes up and I'm gone, I'll never hear the end of it."

Cora stood with her, a swift smile breaking out over her features at the mention of the Goblin King. "He'd like that. Knowing where you are when he wakes, that is. He's very protective of you. I could see that in the few moments we were all together."

That jealous knot in her stomach twisted yet again. And it shouldn't. She knew it shouldn't.

Cora was being kind. She wanted Freya to know that as a friend of Eldridge's, she could see how strong his reaction was when Freya was around. Yet, it was still hard to stomach that Cora could see what Freya still had a hard time seeing.

Giving the other woman one last smile, Freya nodded again and left the room. She hoped that in leaving, she wasn't giving the wrong impression.

She just couldn't stay a single minute more while her mind whispered a mortal would never be enough.

CHAPTER 16

Together, she and Eldridge pushed the boat back into the waves. The small vessel had done them well on the journey to the isle, although Freya wasn't looking forward to whatever waited for them in the deep seas again.

Cora stood on the beach, wringing her hands with worry marring her usually pretty expression. "Do come back!" she called out. "The sea won't make it difficult for you this time. Everyone wants the elves to be on the mainland. Even the ocean."

"We'll come back!" Eldridge called out. He deposited Arrow in the bottom of the ship. The poor dog already looked green in the face. "And next time, we'll bring Leo to see you!"

Freya smiled but couldn't stand to see the frantic waving of the lovely woman for a moment longer. She needed to get back to the mainland and center her mind before charging into Leo's room with a single-minded intent. The man would return with them to this isle and he would give Cora a chance. Even just to talk.

The entire court depended on it.

She clambered over the edge of the rocking boat and waited for Eldridge to slip in as well. Saltwater clung to her legs and a cold chill danced down her spine. Leaving Cora behind felt wrong, but the elf

740

had made it very clear that she was to stay on the island. Even if she wanted to go with them.

Eldridge picked up the oars, and they were off. Flying through the sea surf as though the boat had wings.

"You don't have to row, you know," she said with a quirked brow.

"I know." He heaved back, the muscles of his biceps rippling. "Feels good to use my body, though. Wouldn't you agree?"

His waggling eyebrows suggested she should be warmed by the sight of him. But there was too much on Freya's mind to enjoy the look of her Goblin King. And he was hers, even when she was second guessing herself.

Sighing, she dropped her head into her hands and let out a long groan. "How are we going to get the Summer Lord to come back here? I think he's quite happy in his choice that he isn't interested in whatever Cora can offer him. In fact, I would argue to say he's going to banish us from this court entirely at the mere suggestion that he should return here."

The sound of oars striking water continued for a few moments before Eldridge replied. "We'll find a way. We always do. He'd be very lucky to have Cora at his side. And from what I remember when we were young, he was also very interested in having her. I don't know what changed."

Arrow nosed his way underneath her legs and stared up at her with big, brown eyes. "If there's one thing I know, it's romance. The Summer Lord is afraid of what a life with Cora might look like. And that kind of fear is normal, but we need to remind him that it doesn't have to be an awful life."

"And?" She wanted more than that. She knew the concept of love was terrifying to some, especially the idea of marriage. Even Freya hadn't wanted to consider herself shackled by a man.

Until now, she realized. If the Goblin King had wanted to spend his life with her, then she would say yes. But it would be a brief life for him, and Freya couldn't imagine why a faerie would ever tie himself to a mortal who could die at any moment.

Shaking herself out of such thoughts, she sat back up and stared out over the ocean. The shore was much closer than she expected, and the seas weren't quite so deep. Almost like they were traveling through an entirely different ocean. "I think we need more of a plan than simply talking about Cora."

"I think talking about Cora is the first step." Eldridge set the oars down and braced his arms on his knees. "He has to remember her. The feelings she inspired in him. How wonderful being in her presence made him feel. All of those things are the first steps toward convincing him to at least see her."

She had a feeling he was speaking from experience. That at the sight of the person he loved, the Goblin King could only think of the good memories. She hoped, at least.

Freya nodded and tried to release some of the tension in her shoulders. "We'll run with that. I hope he understands and wants to see her. He's a good man. She's a good woman. They would make a suitable match."

As Eldridge turned his attention back to the mainland, Arrow touched his cold nose to Freya's hand. She glanced down at him to see worry reflected in his eyes.

"It's just..." Arrow pitched his voice so low, she almost didn't hear him. "What if he doesn't want her because she was picked for him? What if he wanted to choose for himself?"

"Then that's a hurdle we'll have to overcome when we see him." Freya feared the same thing. The Summer Lord could dig his heels in for any reason, and they had to be prepared for any reaction.

Before she knew it, they hit the mainland. The boat rocked gently, not a single monstrous creature having disturbed them, and she was shocked to realize that this journey had been easy.

Turning around, she stared back toward the isle where she could see dark storm clouds gathering. It was impossible that they had traveled without touching that storm, or those horrible sharks that had wanted nothing more than to chomp through their flesh. But they had journeyed with no issues back to the mainland. Likely their next visit to Cora wouldn't be so easy.

Frowning, she left the boat and stood in the sands, waiting for her companions to join her.

Eldridge already scowled, staring up at the castle of the Summer

Lord with anger in his eyes. "This will be an argument unlike any I've ever had before."

"Most likely."

He shook his head. "I'm going to see what I can find around the castle that might help us."

"Oh." Freya had hoped they might have a few moments together before they started this insane plan. She wanted to reconnect with him, to breathe in the air of his lungs, so she could be sure that none of what was in her head was real.

But she hadn't asked for that, and now he already had another plan. She knew he was right, as well. They would need more than a memory to convince the Summer Lord to go to the isles with them. And even though that memory would be a major part of their plan, they might need a few additional tricks up their sleeves.

Not a single thought trickled from her mind to her tongue. Instead, Freya nodded and took a step away from him, down the beach and toward the caves where they had first searched. "I understand. I'll do the same."

He looked over at her with a frown. "Shouldn't you search through the castle, too?"

She tried a bright smile, but feared it wasn't very convincing. "I'm going to start on the beaches. It's where it all started, didn't it? There has to be something, or someone, I can find down here."

Though obviously suspicious, Eldridge didn't argue with her. He made his way up the beach toward the stairs that would lead him to the castle. Arrow tottered off after him with a sickly smile and a quick, "I'm going to clean myself up."

Why couldn't it be easier? This relationship between herself and the Goblin King? Freya wanted to let go and love this faerie man who so dearly wanted to wrap her up in his love. The warmth of his affection should have been enough for the fear in her chest to dissipate. And yet, it wasn't.

A deep hum in the earth beckoned her toward a small crack in the cliff's wall. Just large enough for a woman like her to fit through. Eldridge would never have managed to follow her. She already knew who wanted to speak with her.

Freya didn't argue or hesitate. She squeezed through the crack and emerged into the emerald forest beyond. The trees swayed at her presence, their branches leaning down to touch her hair and her shoulders.

They didn't speak this time. The dead things in their roots didn't move. She was allowed to walk all the way to the largest tree in the forest where the man with vivid green eyes waited for her. He opened his arms, gesturing for her to enter the grotto without hesitation. "So you found her."

"I did," she breathed. "I think Cora is an excellent match for him, although I don't know why he would defy you in this."

"Simple," the tree replied. "He doesn't want to do anything we tell him to do."

"Sounds like a spoiled child." Freya remembered Esther going through the same phase. Freya would tell her to wash, and the answer was no. Eat. And again, the argument would continue. Whether she wanted something from Esther or not, the child would never do what Freya wanted because it was Freya who had asked.

The tree nodded the dead elf's head, expression wise and sage as an ancient being should be. "You understand. He is an exceptional boy, and we raised him well when he was first given to the forest. But faeries age a lot slower than mortals."

"Hundreds of years in the teenager stage." Freya shook her head and sighed. "I pity you."

"Pity." The man tilted his head back and burst into laughter. "That's the first time anyone has ever said that to me. You are a refreshing distraction, my dear Freya."

She supposed no one was likely to pity someone like this. An all powerful being who used the dead to speak. She understood how her statement must have been a novelty.

But she really did feel for the tree. She knew what it was like to give and give, only to be certain that the person you're giving to would not appreciate all the work.

Freya wished she had more time to commiserate with this powerful being. It was making her feel better. However, she had to work on convincing the Summer Lord to do what the tree wanted, and that was going to take a very long time.

"You asked me to come here," she said. "What else do you need?"

The man shrugged, and the tree lit up with bright, golden lights that swirled around the base. "I didn't ask to see you, Freya. You wanted to come here. You wanted to see us, or perhaps there was someone else you desired to speak with."

"Speak?" Words stuck in her throat at the mere thought of speaking with her father. He had been gone for so long, she didn't know if she had anything to say to him. Would she get angry like she had her mother?

Freya still didn't know what to say to the woman who had raised her. Her mother was the one who was supposed to take care of both her and Esther, but her father? He was the flagstone that anchored their family down. And all of this was his fault. That damned werewolf should never have bitten him, but because it did, her entire life had turned upside down.

The man nodded toward the cage of roots. His eyes darkened with magic. "See for yourself. Magic can do a lot of good as well as a lot of harm, but you know that already."

Heart pounding, she stepped toward and peered into the shadows of the root prison.

The fur had almost entirely left her father's body. He sat in the back corner, as a man might sit. His head in his hands that were still lightly furred. But his feet were human. And the baggy pants that didn't quite fit his thighs weren't ripped. He was more a man than she had seen in a very long time.

"Father?" she whispered.

He looked up, and those eyes weren't his. Not yet. He was still a beast inside the body of a man. But the werewolf had recognized her, and this creature lifted his head, sniffed the air, and she knew the moment he realized that Freya was his daughter. His eyes brightened. His shoulders squared more as though the presence of his own family gave him strength.

Her bottom lip quivered. Her father was looking at her as he used to. With so much love and pride in his eyes, even though she knew this wasn't really her father. He was a beast in a man's body, but that didn't matter.

They were so close to saving him.

She reached out her hand, slipping it through the roots and waiting for him to approach. "Hi, Dad."

He stepped closer and reached out. His fingers were calloused and rough as he wrapped her hand in his. She remembered his hands feeling like this. Not a single day had passed when he wasn't working in the woods or using his hands to do something that would leave tiny cuts and scrapes all over him. Such hard labor had turned his grip into iron and his skin into leather.

Tears blurred her vision and she let out a little laugh, staring up at his face that was wrinkled with concern. "You grew a beard," she whispered with a small chuckle. "You look awful with a beard, you know. Mother always hated them."

He tilted his head to the side and frowned. "Daughter?"

"Yes." She nodded, not wanting to lose this moment and watch him trail back into those beastly ways. "I'm your daughter. Freya."

This time, there was even more recognition in his eyes. He looked at her as a father did a child, with a soft gaze and the knowledge that he had created someone who was the spitting image of himself. "Freya," he repeated. "Yes. That is your name."

She wished she could believe he remembered more than that, but Freya knew that was unlikely. He only knew of her as Freya and that she smelled like him. It was enough for now, because rushing the process of healing could take more of her father away from him. Memories took a long time to return.

Squeezing his fingers in hers, she pressed her forehead against the root bars. "I wish I could ask you how to get the Summer Lord to the isles. You always had the best ideas."

"Summer Lord?" The frown on his face deepened. "He fears the isles."

It was surprising that he knew. Perhaps she wasn't giving her father enough credit, even though it was still the wolf looking back at her. "Yes, I suppose he does fear the isles. There's a woman there who waits for him, and he doesn't want to see her."

"Ashamed."

She jerked her head back up and stared into her father's eyes. "What did you say?"

He released his hold on her hand and retreated into the shadows of his prison. "He's ashamed to see her. To let her see who he has become."

Freya wasn't so sure if her father was talking about himself, or if he was talking about the Summer Lord. She supposed the words were meaningful for both of them. If the Summer Lord knew that his drunken nature was an embarrassment, but couldn't stop, then why would he want to see Cora? He'd been the strong, handsome elf ready to take on the throne. Now, he was nothing more than a drunken fool who threw parties for a dying court.

Was he embarrassed to let the woman he loved see who he had become?

"You might be onto something, Dad," she whispered. "And it's a great place to start a conversation with the elusive Summer Lord."

CHAPTER 17

Freya emerged from the cave hours later, certain that she was on the right track. Though her father wasn't even close to human yet, he was making progress every single day. The trees were making good on their promise. Now, it was her turn to show that she had what it took to convince the Summer Lord to take up his rightful position.

She stepped into the sunlight, blinking away the sudden blindness from the white sand beach. She would never get used to the sun here. Everything was so bright and vivid, no matter which direction she looked.

But when she could see through the stars in her eyes, she noted a figure standing in the middle of the beach. A dark figure, outlined by the sun itself, staring out to sea as though there was something there waiting for him.

She supposed there was, although she would be surprised to hear that he cared.

The Summer Lord stood in loose pants made of silk and chiffon. They blew in a light breeze and the tails of the band at his waist whipped. His chest was bare other than a few symbols painted in bright gold. He was handsome in a way that was breathtaking sometimes.

She walked up to his side and was shocked to realize there wasn't even the hint of alcohol in the air. She didn't smell beer or wine or mead. Just the barest scent of lemongrass.

He was sober. She didn't think she'd ever seen him sober.

She mimicked his posture and tucked her hands behind her back as well. "Leo."

"Freya." He glanced down at her with a curled lip. "I don't like you using my name."

"You don't like me at all. So it wouldn't be the end of the world if I used your name. It's not going to change how you feel about me." She stared out to sea, even though she could feel him looking at her. "Besides, we have more to talk about than if you want me to use your given name or your title."

"More to talk about?" His voice betrayed not a single emotion, but he shuffled his feet in the sands like he was uncomfortable.

Freya had learned how to read the fae. She knew when they were trying to get around a subject that they didn't like. She knew when they felt like she had pushed too much. Leo was feeling all of these things and more, because he was afraid of so much. Fear rode his shoulders, and she didn't know how he even breathed.

Still looking out at the islands, she replied very quietly, "I met her."

Silence stretched between them like a taut string. If either of them was careless, this conversation would snap back and strike them in the face. Leo would not be the first to respond to such a ridiculous comment. He must fear if he said anything that would betray Cora's presence, then he would fall right into Freya's trap.

He cleared his throat and replied, "Met who?"

"Cora."

The physical reaction to her name was violent. He recoiled from the word as though the sound was a poisonous snake. He feared even hearing the name of the woman he had once loved.

What a horrible way to live.

He struggled for long moments, opening his mouth, then closing it again. His beautiful smooth brow furrowed with the weight of his emotions, and Freya knew this was more difficult for him than any of them had imagined.

Her father was right. The Summer Lord was embarrassed and ashamed to have Cora see him like this. He was supposed to be this powerful being who could take on anyone that threatened the Summer Court. And instead, he had turned to alcohol to ease the stress of his responsibilities.

Finally, Leo found the words he wanted to say, and they weren't at all what Freya had hoped. "There are many Elven women by that name. I'm afraid you'll have to be more specific than that."

"We both know you're being deliberately obtuse. We found a way to the isles, and we survived all those horrible creatures you placed in our way. And then we met Cora. She's a beautiful woman now, and she's been alone for a very long time." Freya squeezed her hands together, so she didn't slap Leo at the thought of how long he'd made Cora linger. "She doesn't want to live there anymore, and she's feeling the same thing you are. The elements are going to take back what they gave you, Leo."

"Then let them," he snarled. "Maybe she deserves the title. I could see her ruling this land well, but not me. I wasn't cut from the same cloth as the other Summer Lords. Never have been. And as such, I have been nothing more than a disappointment to this title. They will wipe my name from the history books when this is over."

"When it's over?" she repeated, her voice a hushed whisper. "You are giving up your own life and the woman you love, simply because you are not willing to rise to the occasion?"

He looked at her, then. His feet whipped through the sand that sprayed up behind him in a beautiful golden arc of color. The sun struck his handsome face, his dark features like something out of a storybook. The Summer Lord was one of the most handsome men she had ever met, and that included Eldridge. So why wouldn't Leo just accept that he had a place in this world?

This injury to his soul was deeper than she thought. Freya would need to find out where it had stemmed from. Why he drank. So many questions that needed answering, but this was her moment alone with him.

He stared down at her with spite in his eyes, jaw set, and hands fisted. "I cannot rise to this challenge. It's not as simple as you think."

"Because you are afraid." Freya nodded. "I know what that fear feels like."

They weren't the words he'd expected from her, clearly. Leo opened his mouth, ready to argue with her, but then all the wind in his sails died. "What did you say?" he asked.

"I'm the Queen Killer," she replied with a chuckle. "I defeated the Goblin King, then the Queen. And then I went to the Spring Maiden's court, and I caught her in an elaborate lie to prevent my family from ever finding each other. The expectations of what I will do next are infinite."

"I don't understand why that would make you feel fear." He glared as only the fae could. Leo obviously believed his issues were far more difficult than hers, and maybe they were.

But that didn't mean she couldn't sympathize with him.

"All of these titles are adding up. I have become something of legend to some people I meet, and all the court leaders are afraid of me. Because I did run through your courts and dismantle everything that you knew and loved." Freya opened her hands wide, palms facing him. "But I am a mortal woman. I grew up as a peasant on the edge of the forest, worrying about what I would eat the next day. I don't know how to be this terrifying creature all of you seem to think I am. Luck is on my side. Most of the time. That's the only way I've gotten to where I am."

Leo's eyes widened, then turned into a deep golden hue. "You fear everyone will soon think you are a fraud."

She nodded. "And now you know my secret, Summer Lord. I understand that you are afraid of what she will think when she sees you again. And that someday, she might wake up and realize that you are nothing more than what she feared you were. The terror of your loved one suddenly becoming a stranger is a horrible one to face."

And there was the real secret. Someday, perhaps in a few months or in a few years, Eldridge would roll over and see that she wasn't what he thought she was. That she was an unimpressive woman who had stumbled into the faerie realms, and who had no right to remain.

The Goblin King had helped her every step of the way, and without him, she would still be under the Spring Maiden's spell. And no one would ever have found her.

"Then you do understand." His gaze saw too much. The Summer Lord looked right through her and into her very soul.

He saw that she feared losing the man she loved, and that she wasn't good enough for the person who loved her. He must have known that from the very first moment he saw her. She wasn't a faerie. She wasn't anyone other than Freya, and someday that might not be enough to keep Eldridge at her side.

Leo reached for her hand and grasped it in his own. "We have had our differences, Queen Killer, Defeater of the Goblin King, and Spring Maiden Truth Sayer. But hear me when I say this now. I will put aside what happened in the past because we are so similar in the present."

Goodness, he was a compelling man when he wasn't soaked in alcohol.

To her great embarrassment, tears built in her eyes. Freya realized that this was the first time any faerie had ever forgiven her for what she'd done. And she was intensely aware that her first trip through the faerie courts had been anything but polite or helpful. She had wreaked havoc throughout all the courts. To hear that he forgave her for that, for stealing from him, lying to him, manipulating his court...

It healed a hole in her heart.

She squeezed his hand in her grip. "Good. I'm afraid I needed to hear that more than I want to admit."

"That is quite all right," he replied, releasing her instantly. "Now, if you don't mind my absence, there are a few bottles of wine in my room that are waiting for me."

He turned to leave and Freya's jaw dropped.

That was it? He was going to walk away from her and get drunk after all that had been said?

"Where are you going?" she asked, clarifying, because he couldn't have said what she heard.

"To get very, very drunk, Freya." The Summer Lord's shoulders rounded in on himself, as though he knew what he said was wrong.

That the alcohol wouldn't help his situation and only bury these emotions under deep layers of wine and mead.

"No, you aren't." She planted her fists on her hips and drew on every motherly instinct inside herself. "You're going to stay here and talk with me. You need to go see Cora. She's been waiting for you for two hundred years, Leo. You owe her at least a single meeting."

He shook his head. "No. No, I will not be doing that. She will stay on that isle, far from where I can harm any remaining memories of what we once were. What we could have been."

"You deny yourself happiness, and for what?" She threw her hands up in the air. "Because you don't fully believe that you're worthy?"

"Yes!" He spun around again, shouting the word so that it echoed over the waves. "I am undeserving! For what I have done to this court, to her, to myself! She would be better off dead then shackled to me for all eternity."

Freya refused to believe him. Not when she had gotten a glimpse of the man he could be, the one who had so much potential. "At least send her handmaidens, damn it! She's been living out there on her own for far too long!"

Though his eyes widened at the thought, he at least nodded. "Sure. If that's what she wants, then she can have that. But she cannot have me."

The Summer Lord walked away. And though she should have been disappointed, Freya felt as though she had won.

CHAPTER 18

Freya made her way back to their room, hoping that Eldridge would be there so she could share everything that happened. Of course, not the conversation with her father. Eldridge still didn't know she'd found her dad, and that made things even more difficult.

Leo was ashamed to see Cora, and that was an emotion both she and Eldridge could work on. Leo was a decent man. He had grown up in strange circumstances, certainly, but that didn't mean he was any less worthy of a wife.

At least he'd agreed to send Cora handmaidens. And the more Freya thought about it, the more that sounded like the best plan. Two hundred years alone on an island was bound to make a person a little unusual. It would be easier for Cora to dip her toes back into being around this many people. A few handmaidens would ease her into being around others before she dove headfirst back into the life of the court.

Pushing open the door to their room, Freya thumbed her bottom lip in thought. "Eldridge?" she called out. "I have developments I think you need to hear."

He was sitting on the corner of the bed, hunched over something he held in his hands. It looked like a child's keepsake, something he might have found in the library. And if that tiny box held the key to everything, perhaps the reason why Leo had decided to drink his feelings away, then that was the greatest find they'd have.

"What did you get?" she asked, taking a few rapid steps forward.

Eldridge flinched in on himself and pocketed the item. "Nothing."

"What do you mean, nothing? I just saw you holding it." She held out her hand, fully expecting him to set whatever magical item he'd found in her palm. "Let me see! Did you find something in the library that might help us?"

"No. I found something that means a lot to me, and me alone." He furrowed his brows in a glare. "And perhaps to Cora, if I think about it hard enough. She'll need to see it before you do."

Why wasn't he including her in this? Freya thought they had already worked through him, telling her all the things that she needed to know so they could continue working together, and not apart.

Her heart stuttered in her chest. This was an item that meant a lot to both Eldridge and Cora. So it was something from their childhood, but something that Eldridge didn't want Freya to see. He wanted to share that first with the young woman on the island.

It shouldn't have stung so much. Freya knew that a childhood friend might reminisce easier than her. And that wasn't all so surprising. If she'd found a toy that she and the local boys in her village used to play with, she wouldn't want to talk to Eldridge about it. Such a conversation would feel foolish.

But she still very much wanted to know what it was. She wanted to share her life with Eldridge and every bit of what he'd experienced.

Apparently, he didn't feel the same.

Licking her lips, she tried to distract herself by telling him what had happened. "I, um... I spoke with Leo."

"You what?" His shuttered expression narrowed in on her, the sharp focus sending her back a few steps. "What did he say? What did you say?"

Well, now she couldn't tell him what she'd said. She didn't want to share those personal feelings in her chest when he was already hiding what was in his pocket from her. Though, apparently, Cora was good enough to know what the item was.

Bristling, Freya ground her teeth together before responding. "It doesn't matter. The conversation didn't go as planned. He's still refusing to see her, but he has agreed to send handmaidens to the island. In the long and short of things, I figured that was best. Then Cora can get used to being around so many people again."

"That's genius." He reached for her and swung her into his arms. Eldridge lifted her into the air by the waist, then tucked her against his heart with a spin. "You are a genius. Yes, that's what we need. Leo needs to send some people for her to get comfortable, and then with his court returning and speaking of how kind she is, he'll eventually be tempted enough to return to the isle."

How kind Cora was?

Yes, Freya knew that was the truth. Of course it was. She needed to step away from all this so she didn't turn into a green goblin from the jealousy, however.

She knew he didn't mean to make her jealous. Cora was a dear friend, and that was all. But she still was aching to know what he hid in his pocket, why Cora needed to see it, and why Freya couldn't.

Freya pulled herself out of his arms and smiled at him, although the expression felt as fragile as a spiderweb. "I didn't get through the entire faerie realm without learning to keep a few tricks up my sleeve."

"And don't I know it. You magical woman." He pressed a hand to his chest. "I'll go with the handmaidens and Arrow to help prepare Cora for what she should expect. You know the dog is so good at wooing the women. And since you've already worn down Leo's defenses, you can stay here and keep working on convincing him to see Cora. Everything is falling into place."

Was it?

Freya wanted to argue with him, but Eldridge was already leaving. He strode out of the door while waving his hand over his head.

He called out one final time, "I'll take care of gathering the handmaidens! We'll return in a fortnight, my love. Don't you worry about a thing!"

And then he was gone.

Two weeks.

Two weeks without him, all because she'd told him what had happened between her and Leo.

"Wait, Eldridge, I thought..." He was already out of the room by the time she found her voice. The words fell flat with no one to hear them, and anxiety melted over her entire body in a wave of sudden discomfort.

All she wanted was to feel a little more confident to let him go. And she realized that was a lot to ask. He was a busy man and wanted to get this over with so they could return to his court. Really, she should be thankful that he was here at all. Everyone needed help from the Goblin King. Or at least, she supposed they would. He'd never told her about what he did as the king.

She stared around the empty room and a horrible sense of foreboding shadowed her mind. She was going to be the only person in this room for two weeks. Two weeks of rolling over and reaching for him in bed, finding only the cold, empty space where he once had been. Two weeks of wondering where he was, if he was missing her too, and if maybe he wasn't.

Heavens above, she was going to lose her mind without him. And that was even more terrifying than knowing he wouldn't be with her. Since when was she afraid to be alone?

She couldn't stay in this room and wonder what was going to happen next. She just couldn't. Freya had to get up and do something, or she would sit here in the shadows and berate herself until the sun set.

So she fled. Her feet took her through the hallways of the palace in a near run. Flower petals fell on top of her head as if the very soul of this castle was trying to make her feel better. All the hydrangeas that grew up the walls glowed brighter blue in the hopes that their pretty colors would make her smile. Instead, all she could feel was a sense of numbing pain that drowned out everything.

She burst out of the castle to a large room that opened up in the center. It was the floating staircase that led to a crumbling part of the castle. The same place where she had first felt something other than hatred for the Goblin King. He'd dressed her up there in a gown the color of the ocean, and he'd made her feel like someone important in his life.

Of course her feet had brought her here. This was where she had felt the closest to the man she loved.

Sighing, Freya strode around the crumbling structure and realized there was already someone here. A dark skinned someone who was tucked into the moss at the base of a half wall with three bottles of wine situated next to him.

The last person she wanted to see was Leo. He was the reason she was here, and they were all in some sense of turmoil. The ridiculous Summer Lord couldn't pull himself together, and that somehow had translated into her own relationship falling apart.

But those bottles of wine could tempt her. Even a single sip from one of those might make her feel a little better.

"Leo," she said with a grumble.

"I don't care to see you again so soon after our last conversation." He gestured at her with the bottle of wine, swinging it around himself. "You are not my favorite person. If you're having trouble, you can find somewhere else to mope."

"I don't care that you feel that way." She crossed her arms over her chest and tried to look anywhere but at him. Unfortunately, that wouldn't get her anywhere considering they were in a small mossy garden and the only thing in this room was the structure he leaned against. "Besides, I'm trying to hide too."

"Then get your own castle." The sound of a deep swig of wine followed his words, then the faintest smack of lips. "I'm trying to drink in peace."

"Why? Will your own court not even drink with you anymore?" She wouldn't be surprised. The elves could only condone his behavior for so long before they too would grow weary.

"Something like that." There was a tone in his voice that made her turn around. A sadness that leached through every word and a self hatred that made her concerned.

Freya looked him over and realized the Summer Lord looked worse than usual. His clothing was rumpled, his pants creased beyond fixing and his shirt hanging ripped over one shoulder. His eyes were bleary, as if he'd already been drinking for far too long.

She heaved a great sigh and walked over to his side. "You know, it doesn't matter if you want me here or not. I am, and I suppose you'll just have to deal with that."

"I wanted to be alone." He touched the mouth of the bottle to his lips, but this time he didn't drink. "Privacy is impossible to find in this castle, though."

"Privacy? As the Summer Lord? That sounds like a novel idea, but a fantasy nonetheless." Freya wiggled her fingers in front of him, gesturing for him to hand her a bottle. "Give me one."

"They're all mine."

"And yet, you are going to hand me one because I have also had a very difficult day." And if he didn't hand her one, she planned on lunging for a bottle and then he'd have to fight her. Considering the state he was in, she thought she had a good chance of beating him.

Leo eyed her and seemed to understand that was the case. He sighed and handed her a bottle. "What happened to you, then?"

"Do you care to hear?" She took a deep drink of the wine and tried very hard not to cough. What was this oil slick fluid? It was disgusting but burned quite satisfyingly on the way down.

"I find that I'm interested." At the sound of surprise that crossed her lips, Leo looked over at her and shrugged. "I don't have to wallow in my self pity all the time, you know. Maybe I'll feel better if I hear someone else struggling as horribly as I am."

"Struggling?" She wanted to argue that she most certainly wasn't, but look at where she was.

Freya had wandered through the castle to this forgotten place because she wanted to cry over the memory of what she and Eldridge had once had. Like a sad sap of a person. She took another deep swallow and then nodded.

"I suppose I am," she muttered.

And that was the worst thing about all of this. She should be able to be fine without him. Eldridge hadn't come into her life until she was much older, and yes, that was probably a bad thing. She should have gotten married to some lonely farmer who wouldn't have given her any adventure, but he at least would have left her alone to do whatever she wanted.

Instead, she had to find herself in the faerie realm where she shouldn't be. No husband. No family that still relied on her. Instead, she was going to wander through this magical world until she died.

"I'm going to be alone forever," she muttered into the bottle. "Eldridge is leaving with the handmaidens to go back to the isle with Cora. He had something in his hand when I walked into our room. No idea what it was, but he said Cora had to see it."

"She has that way about her, always has. Even when she was a child, she would end up convincing everyone around us to love her more than anyone else in the room." He shook his head, eyes still unfocused with the memory. "It was why I fell in love with her back then, you know. She captured my attention just as she did everyone else."

"I worry that he's going to be on that island without me and forget. That's what he said we needed to do with you. Get you to Cora so you would be in her presence and all those emotions would come back." She swallowed the bitter taste of her fear. "What if two weeks away from me makes him forget how he feels?"

"I never forgot. Not even for a second. I dreamt about her for the first hundred years, and even now I feel like I see her out of the corner of my eye sometimes. You don't forget someone you truly love." Leo tightened his hand so much around the neck of the bottle that the glass shattered with a stunning crack.

They both stared at the mess and the blood leaking between his fingers in silence. Freya knew she should jump to help him and insist that he get the cut cleaned. But she stayed frozen, instead.

"We're both a sad pair," she muttered. "No one should be able to make us feel like this. Not without our permission, at least."

"That's what love does." Leo dropped the shards in disgust. "It twists your damn mind and convinces you that life isn't worth living without them. When in reality, we're better off on our own."

No, she couldn't believe that. No matter how badly this stung, she also realized what a blessing it was to have Eldridge in her life.

Reaching forward, she grabbed his hand and dabbed at it with the tails of her shirt. "You don't actually believe that."

He looked up at her and the sadness in his gaze made her heart ache. "No, I don't. I still love her more than life, but that terrifies me."

She sighed. "Me too. Love is terrifying and wonderful and horrible all at the same time."

Without hesitation, Leo reached for another bottle and clinked it with hers. "Then I suppose all we can do now is drink."

"I suppose you're right." But it sure would make for a very long night.

"My answer is still no," Leo snarled.

And that wasn't a satisfactory answer, nor the one Freya wanted to hear. She pulled harder on his arm and continued dragging him through the halls to her private rooms.

It had been one week since Eldridge left with the handmaidens. An entire week of horrible conversations with Leo that ripped at every insecurity the both of them had. She didn't know if they were healing with each other, or just digging knives into each other's wounds. But whatever they were doing had worked on bringing the two of them a little closer together.

Close enough that she felt comfortable dragging him through the hall like an infant while she argued that it had been far too long since he'd talked with the trees. That was all they wanted from him. A conversation. A chance for him to listen to what they had to say without alcohol running through his veins and making him an insufferable ass.

Yes, she had called the Summer Lord an ass to his face. And she was proud of it.

Leo grabbed onto the doorframe and dug his heels into the floor. "Absolutely not! Freya, would you listen to me? The moment I step foot into that forest, the trees will string me up with their roots and add me to their collection of dead things."

"How do you know that?" She tugged harder on his arm. "I think they want to talk with you, otherwise they would have killed you a long time ago!"

"They have been biding their time for the right moment. And apparently the right instrument of destruction came in the package of a mortal woman." He tugged back, dragging her across the floor toward him. "You're going to get me killed."

Perhaps there was the slightest chance of that happening, but Freya was pretty sure she had a good handle on what the forest wanted. It didn't want to kill Leo, otherwise it never would have sent her on this wild goose chase to convince him to be a better man. If the forest had wanted him dead, then he would be dead.

To her, it sounded like the forest was a lot more interested in getting to know Leo. It wanted him to find out who he was, and to rejoice in the man he could be. Sure, it would be a lot of work to pull himself out of this hole that he'd dug. But that didn't mean it was impossible to do.

She tugged again, much harder this time while throwing her entire body weight into the movement. "I'm right. You're wrong. You're coming with me no matter what."

The veins in his arms stood out as he forcibly held himself in place. "That's hilarious, but no. I'm not. You are but one tiny woman and I am the great Summer Lord. You will not force me to go anywhere with you."

Like the forest had been waiting for his words, the floor opened up beneath them and swallowed both of them. Freya tumbled through the dark, clutching his arm with an iron grip. She wouldn't lose him even when her stomach had shoved its way into her throat. She would hold on until they both struck the ground.

And they hit hard.

All the breath whooshed out of her lungs in one great heave as they struck the earthen floor near the great tree. Wheezing, she pressed her hands to her chest and forced her lungs to inhale. She had to breathe. Why couldn't she breathe?

Leo was making similar horrible sounds, but he at least reached over and slapped her back three times. At the impact, her lungs heaved in the air finally.

She staggered to her feet and held her hand out for him to take. Leo glared at her, choosing to remain on the ground.

"See?" he gasped. "The forest wants me dead."

A stirring at the base of the tree revealed the moss covered body that the tree used to speak. The man's angry expression was only the beginning of a scolding Freya was certain would make her cheeks burn. "If I wanted you dead, then you would be. You stupid little boy. But you deserved to be rattled around before you talked with me again."

Leo's cheeks darkened with what Freya could only hope was embarrassment.

Before he could say something insulting and get himself killed, Freya stepped in front of him and bowed to the dead man. "As always, it's a pleasure to see you."

"The taste of your lies is very sweet, Freya, but we both know it's no sweeter to me than a rotting pumpkin." The man still grinned, however. "Thank you for bringing my boy to see me, though. It's been a very long time since Leo and I have had a conversation."

"For good reason!" Leo staggered to his feet and wiped a hand across his mouth. "You'd rather have me dead than on that throne."

"You know that's not true. But it's easier to say that than to admit you've disappointed me." The man struggled in the roots of the tree, then yanked a skeletal arm from the thick moss. He pulled away from the bark and the rubble until he ripped himself to standing.

Freya tried very hard not to shudder at the sight of a corpse walking toward Leo with single minded intent. The man's bright green eyes glowed as he reached his fingers for the Summer Lord.

"Wait," she croaked. "You aren't going to kill him, are you?"

The corpse turned its head and stared at her with an unimpressed look. "After all the talking we've done, Miss Freya, do you believe I want him dead?"

No. She didn't. Otherwise, she never would have brought the Summer Lord here. This tree wanted to talk with someone it loved very dearly.

She gulped, then replied, "No. I don't think you want to hurt him."

"Then go talk with your own father. He's been waiting for a while to speak with you."

To speak with her? All the blood drained from her face at the mere thought. He was ready to talk? Had the tree healed him so thoroughly?

Summer Lord forgotten, she turned away from the corpse and the faerie. Instead, her eyes found the prison and the dark form hidden in the shadows. She walked toward the small room as though she were in a dream.

What would she even say to her father? That she'd missed him? That seemed too easy. Of course she had missed him. How many years had it been since she'd seen him or her mother? Ten? Eleven? Freya couldn't even think through the passage of time and the worst of it all was her fear that he didn't remember any of the time being gone?

Tears gathered in her eyes. She wrapped her hands around the roots of the prison and watched as a man stood up in the back corner. He turned around and all parts of the wolf were gone. It was her dad staring back at her with a hesitant smile on his face.

He didn't know what to say either, it seemed. For a while they just stared at each other.

Finally Freya croaked, "Can I come in?"

"I think the tree will let you."

The roots shifted, and she flew across the small room. Freya threw her arms around his neck and buried her face in his chest. He still smelled like her father, with the sweet scent of hay and fresh grass. His arms were strong as they wrapped around her, clutching his daughter to his chest.

The sound of his heartbeat was all she'd ever wanted to hear again. This was her father, finally, alive and well when she had been so certain he was dead.

"Dad," she whispered again. "I didn't think I'd ever see you again."

"I was certain you were right only a few days ago." He pressed his lips to the top of her head, tightening his grip on her. "Oh my sweet, brave Freya. You've grown so much."

Goodness, she must have. The last time he saw her, she was nothing more than a teenager. The same age as Esther, who still had more growing to do. Freya pulled away so she could look at him, reaching to pat her hands on his cheeks. "And you got older."

The silver streaks at his temples looked handsome, though. She thought her mother would very much like the change when she saw him again.

Her father tilted his head back and let out a clap of booming laughter. She'd forgotten how loud the sound was. How he could fill a room with happiness with the sound of his laugh. "Oh, I'm sure I look older. You don't have to point it out though, darling."

She laughed with him and it felt like the most natural thing in the world. They spoke as if no time had passed between the time they had last seen each other, and it felt like she had seen him yesterday. All the anger she might have directed at him melted away, knowing that he was alive. That he wasn't the werewolf any longer.

The werewolf. A shiver ran through her with the knowledge that it might not actually be gone. She had to ask. She had to know.

"Is the wolf..." Freya cleared her throat and took a step back. "Is the tree holding the wolf at bay? Or do you have it under control?"

The frown on his face suggested she wouldn't like the answer he was about to give her. "Both," he replied. "The tree is helping me keep control, but I am learning how to hold it back. The wolf is difficult to understand. And I grew up with people like this. Wolves who lived in hiding and no one would ever have guessed they were afflicted by this curse but... I didn't realize how hard it was for them."

She could only imagine it would feel like denying himself food or water. The wolf was a part of him, not just another being.

He shook his head and held out his hand for her to take. "Come here, darling. Tell me what I've missed and then we'll talk about the wolf. I'm not leaving here for a little while longer, and I need to know how you found me and if... if..."

He couldn't say her mother's name. She knew that would be difficult for him, but she hadn't guessed how choked up it would make him.

Freya took her father's hand and let him guide her to the back of the prison where he'd set up a small table and some chairs. A cot rested in the corner, all human furniture now that he wouldn't destroy them in the form of a wolf. "Mother?"

Her father sat down and briefly nodded. Although, he couldn't look her in the eye now that he thought of the woman he loved.

"She's alive." Freya joined him at the table. "I found her first. You led me to her."

"I did?" He breathed a long sigh of relief. "I thought I remembered seeing her while I was the wolf, but sometimes that's not a good sign. I had hoped... Well. I had hoped that she was still alive and that the wolf hadn't done something we both would regret."

"No. You saved her. You saved all of us."

Freya let the story pour out of her lips like a dam had broken open. She told him everything she and Esther had done when they realized their parents were gone. She told him about Esther and that stupid necklace, and how she'd beaten the Goblin King. She told him about saving the faerie courts and bringing back their rightful ruler, only to realize that her mother was under the Spring Maiden's thumb.

Not a single detail was spared, and she probably told him too much information by the end. She feared his head would spin with all the stories she'd told him, but instead, her father stared at her with wide, proud eyes.

"You did all that in my absence?" he asked.

"I did." She tucked a strand of hair behind her ear and tried not to let exhaustion overwhelm her. "It wasn't easy. I'm sorry if I told the story wrong and made you think that I could do it all on my own. I had a lot of help along the way."

"Yes, you did. I think I'd like to meet this goblin dog. He seems like my kind of person." Her father tapped a finger to his chin. "Although this Goblin King... I'll wait to decide if I like him."

She wouldn't expect any different. Freya chuckled. "He's a good man. I don't know where I stand with him right now. That's not his fault, that's my own."

"Is it?" Her father reached across the table and caught her hands in his. "I know you will do this, and you will succeed. Because you're my daughter. There is nothing in this realm that could stop you."

His words lifted her up and gave her a confidence she'd been missing. Freya straightened her shoulders and felt power return to her veins. "I can. And I will."

"Good girl." Her father released her hands and nodded back toward the Summer Lord. "You might want to gather him up now, child. He looks well and thoroughly scolded."

She looked over her shoulder and thought Leo looked a little green. He might have looked drunk if she didn't know he was stone cold sober.

Sighing, she stood up and dusted her hands off on her hips. "You're right. I need to take him home. But..."

What words could ever explain how she felt? How her heart was healed at the sight of him?

He smiled at her. "I'll see you again, Daughter. I have no doubt in that."

Freya pressed a hand to her thundering heart. "I'll see you soon, Dad. I swear it."

CHAPTER 20

Freya teleported to her room in the Summer Palace and landed on her back hard with the Summer Lord at her side. She wore a dazed expression that she wasn't proud of. But what was a girl supposed to do?

Her father was not only well and alive, he was talking to her like a normal father would. He had laughed with her, joked, and listened to her stories. Freya was elated that he was back to himself. Except now there was a whole new host of issues that she had to overcome. What would her mother think when she saw her father again? Would Esther even remember him?

Why wasn't she angry at her father the same way she had been angry at her mother?

Huffing out a breath, she looked over at Leo to see how he was handling things. Considering his face was ashen and his brows furrowed, he appeared to be handling his own situation even worse. Good, at least he was in the same place she was in mentally.

Freya reached out and patted his shoulder. "How are you holding up?"

"Not well."

"That tree really gave it to you, huh?"

She waited for the words to sink in before tilting her head back and laughing. They both chuckled through the pain until they settled back onto the floor in twin heaps.

"Yes," Leo replied. "The tree really gave it to me. I haven't been scolded like that since I was a child, and the last person to do it was..."

At his hesitation, Freya filled in the blank for him. "The tree?"

"The tree. I suppose there's only been one person daring enough to scold me like I was a petulant child." He touched a hand to his chest, right over his heart. "I suppose I still am that angry little boy who wanted to yell at his parents for not giving him all the things he wanted. That's rather frustrating, you know."

"No personal growth is simple." She pillowed her head on her arm, rolling so she could stare at him. "I know it's not easy, but change isn't something to fear. You could be someone great. Someone better."

"What if I don't like that new version of myself?" His troubled expression deepened. "What if that person is someone I don't recognize?"

"I think if you met yourself when you were a child, you'd be annoyed to see that you were a very different person then as well. We all change and grow. That's how life works." Even she had changed, drastically.

Sometimes it still startled Freya to think about how much she had changed. But then again, that was the same situation Leo was having. He didn't want to believe he wasn't the same person he used to be.

He hummed deep in this throat before nodding. "It's something I'll consider, mortal. Thank you."

Well, she hadn't expected his thanks. But she'd take it.

Freya pushed up onto her hands and knees. "That's that, then. I suppose we have to find something else to do to bide our time. I'm ready to have Eldridge back, and I'm sure you're dreading the stories from the isle."

"The tree wanted me to tell you something, too." Leo put his hand on her arm, forcing her to stop and look at him. "There is a method of finding out the secrets of others. It's... Well the fae don't use it. It's backfired one too many times for us. But the tree said you might need it."

"Excuse me?" She didn't want to admit that made her frightened. All the blood drained from her face and she felt light headed.

Why did the tree think she needed to reveal someone's secrets? Why would it even want her to have that ability?

"Water in the Summer Court holds an immense amount of power. And since your father was a changeling here, and absorbed some of that magic to pass down to you, there is a chance you could use the pools to see what you want." Leo released her, and his expression said he was uncomfortable even telling her this. "It said you have already seen how some might use their magic in the pools to communicate, or perhaps see the future. But the tide pools can also be used to spy."

The temptation was so great it made her fingers curl into her palms. No, she wouldn't entertain this thought at all. Eldridge wasn't doing anything that he shouldn't and even assuming he might be was the greatest betrayal of their relationship thus far.

She clenched her jaw so hard it made her teeth hurt. "I don't foresee myself needing to use that."

"Regardless, if you wanted to spy, all you would have to do is find a glassy surface of water and ask to see what you wanted to see." He rolled onto his feet and then held out his hand for her to take. "Come on. Considering the warning, I thought you might like to go to the isle now."

"I don't want to go across those waters alone." She took his hand and let him drag her to her feet. "I will wait for Eldridge to come back."

"Then don't." He sheepishly ran a hand over his head before gesturing for her to follow him. "I should have told you a long time ago, but there's another way to get to the isles. It's just... not well known. I'm the only one who's supposed to use it."

Curiosity would always be her downfall. Freya followed him all the way through the halls, touching her fingers to the glowing plants that lit up the hallways. They reached for her now with friendly whispers, unlike the first time she'd been here when she was certain the plants would kill her if she touched them.

They were kinder. Softer. More likely to give her a little room to breathe if she needed it. Although, she hated to think that was all changing simply because she'd created a tentative friendship with the Summer Lord. She still planned on making him marry Cora. For the good of the court.

Leo stopped in front of a door hidden in the wall. Ivy covered it so thickly that she would have walked past it if she hadn't been told it was there. He reached into his pocket and drew out a small skeleton key. "This will only open the door once every five days."

Surprising. If this room held a portal, then why wouldn't it open as many times as he wanted?

Freya stayed quiet as he swung the door open and revealed a hidden pool of water. Light glowed from deep underneath the still surface, spilling out over the mossy floor and up into the tendrils of ivy hanging from the ceiling.

"What is this place?" she asked.

"A portal room." Leo tucked his hands behind his back and strode toward the water with a slight saunter to his step. "I'm certain you've never seen such a thing before, and that's unsurprising. After all, the Summer Court is so much more beautiful than the other courts. We know what it means to have some sense of aesthetic."

She didn't agree with him, but she couldn't argue over the beauty of this place. All the other portals she had seen were built out of wind and magic. But this one? This was the very ocean waiting to be used at the whim of the Lord.

She stepped close to the edge and peered into the water. "Where does it go?"

"There's another one on the isle, within the cliff side village that I'm sure you visited." He joined her hesitantly, almost like he was afraid of what he would see staring back at him. "All you have to do is step into the water and then you'll be there. It's that easy."

Sure. Easy to him. But Freya feared what would happen if she walked into the water and the magic realized that she wasn't the Summer Lord, or even fae.

Gulping, she stepped onto the edge and held out her arms for balance. "It's not going to spit me back out because I'm not you, right?"

"There's only one way to find out. Oh, and tell Cora I'm coming to visit her soon. It's long pastime we met again." Leo's wicked grin only served to make her even more nervous. He stepped up to her side, planted his hand on her back, and shoved.

Freya fell into the water with a horrible belly flop that stung her skin even through the thin skirts she wore. The water rushed up her nose and pressed into her lungs. She floundered for a second underneath the water, not knowing which way was up. Blinking through the saltwater, she searched for the light of the portal room.

Her gut said this was no portal. Leo had played a grand jest, but she didn't want to drown before she made it to the isles. Swimming to the surface, she spluttered as cool air blasted her face.

"Damn it, Leo!" she snarled, blinking through the painful drops of saltwater. "I didn't want to get wet!"

But Leo never responded.

Freya swam to the edge of the pool and hauled herself onto the lip. Sitting, she scrubbed her eyes to clear her vision and was shocked to see white-washed walls and sunlight glittered through the tiny chips of seashells embedded in the stone.

She was on the island. And without having to go past those terrifying crabs and sharks again.

This would have been so much easier to get to their destination the first time. Poor Arrow. There was no need for him to be as sick as he had gotten, and the days of complaining she'd endured afterward.

Freya swung her legs over onto the floor at the same time the doors slammed open and Cora came rushing in. Half her hair was braided, the other side a plume of dark curls that coiled around her skull. "Leo? Leo, is it really you?"

The other woman's expression fell when she caught sight of Freya.

"Sorry to disappoint." Freya lifted a wet arm and waved. "He sent me."

Cora sighed and crossed her arms over her chest. "Why am I not surprised? Of course he sent you. He'll do anything to avoid seeing me again, won't he?"

Freya stood and wrung the water out of her skirts. She'd need something else to wear, and fast. Her teeth chattered already. "He said to let you know that he is coming soon. He wants to see you, Cora. He's just scared."

"Of what?" Cora threw her arms into the air. "Never mind, I don't want to know. So much has happened since you were here last, and I think you should see it all. Your Goblin King is a resourceful man, and the handmaidens are hard workers. We're all ready to welcome the Summer Lord should he ever decide he wants to see me. Or even step up to the throne the trees gifted him."

Apparently Cora had been talking with Eldridge too much. The sting of her words would be heartbreaking if Leo heard them. The poor man needed someone who would see him and forgive all the actions he'd taken. Or at least set them aside until he grew more confident. His misguided choices were the very reason he had avoided seeing her for such a long time.

"He's trying his best, Cora. You need to be gentle with him when he does come to see you." She padded over to the elf, wet footsteps slapping the stone. "The last thing he needs is to think his wife is a harpy."

"A harpy? No, of course not." Cora sniffed and ran a hand over the side of her head that was braided. "He'll be married to an Elven princess, and he better remember that."

Oh no. She had been talking to Eldridge far too much. Freya trailed after the elf, who had suddenly found her aggressive side and wondered how she was going to fix this.

Yes, it was very important that Cora be confident and able to call Leo out when he was doing something that she didn't like. She absolutely should, as well. A partnership was just as much about helping the other person become a better version of themselves as it was supporting each other. However. There was a correct way to do that, with gentleness and understanding. It seemed like Eldridge had convinced Cora to beat Leo over the head with a stick until the Summer Lord broke under the weight of her disappointment.

And that simply wouldn't do.

"Cora," Freya called out. "I think we should talk about Leo before he gets here. There are some things you should know, and understand..."

"I think I understand him perfectly after talking with Eldridge."

Freya muttered under her breath, "You don't. I'm trying to help you, woman."

But of course, she couldn't say that too loud. Not when Cora was clearly happy with this new, confident version of herself. Softening this woman would take time and energy that Freya didn't have right now.

All she wanted was to see Eldridge. That was it.

"Cora, where is Eldridge?" she called out.

The faint discomfort she'd felt when the trees told her to scry came back. What if Cora acted strangely? What if...

The elf flippantly waved over her shoulder. "Oh, he's around here somewhere. Probably with the handmaidens knowing him. He hasn't left their side since they got here. Everything has been about preparations and I have no idea what he's been planning. The man has been running around here like he's decided to quit being the Goblin King and change his profession to head of household."

That... Didn't sound like Eldridge at all.

Frowning, Freya glanced down one of the village hallways and cleared her throat. "Do you need me now, or might I find the Goblin King?"

"Well, you are here for me, aren't you?" Cora looked over her shoulder and must have seen Freya's expression. The odd, new personality fell from her shoulders. Cora's face softened, and she smiled. "Oh, right. Of course you'd want to see him. It's been a while, hasn't it? Time passes differently for me, and I forget that. Please, Freya. Go steal him away from the handmaidens for a little while. Walk the beach and reconnect."

"Thank you," she whispered, then ran through the nearest home to find her Goblin King.

CHAPTER 21

She found Eldridge in the garden of tide pools outside the cliff village. He was surrounded by jewels of the Summer Court, each handmaiden more beautiful than the last. They were almost blinding in their stunning nature, but Freya didn't want to look at them.

She wanted to look at her Goblin King, who stood in the center of all the chaos with his hands clasped behind his back. His eyes were narrowed on their work, his voice sharp and critical. It almost looked like they were gathering things from the pools, but what could he have found?

"Eldridge!" she called out.

His gaze traveled up to the village, and he stared at her for a few moments before a bright smile crossed his lips. "My darling! What are you doing here? How are you here?"

The steps to walk down were slippery with saltwater and a sticky residue she couldn't name. Freya clambered down them, less than gracefully, but she didn't care who saw her stumble. She wanted to throw her arms around the Goblin King and not let go.

Two weeks had been far too long. And she didn't intend to do that again anytime soon.

With one last trip, she tumbled into his arms. It didn't matter that she wasn't very graceful, or even that she must have looked ridiculous. All that mattered was the way his warm, strong arms came around her and held her close to his heart.

He still smelled like sweet apple pie and cinnamon. Even surrounded by the ocean. And the tittering elves that held their hands to their masks didn't bother her, even though she knew they were watching.

Freya tilted her head back and wrapped an arm around his neck. She drew him down for a deep, long kiss that fueled her soul with each lingering press. "I missed you," she whispered. "I missed you so much."

He drew back with a bemused smile, clearly not sure why she was so clingy. "I missed you as well, my love. But what are you doing here? We had a plan."

"We did." Freya looked around and noted how lovely the sun reflected on the metallic shimmer in the handmaidens' gowns. "I already spoke with Leo, he's coming to visit soon."

"Soon or tomorrow?"

"Soon." She glanced up, then frowned at his expression. "What?"

"Leo is a very good manipulator. He twists words with the best of us and I just... I don't think it's likely that he'll be coming as he said." Eldridge released her and stepped back toward the handmaidens. "Perhaps you should return and force him to come here."

"I believe him." And it made her cheeks heat with anger to think he didn't think she was capable of convincing Leo to come here when that was the only job she'd had. "We struck up a strange sort of friendship in your absence, and I know he's going to come to the isles. He wouldn't have said so if he didn't have the plans in his head."

"Freya, I know you made some kind of friendship, and I'm not surprised by that. The fae seem to love you." He rubbed his cheek, clearly uncomfortable. "But I don't think you know him as well as I do."

"A person can change." She didn't understand why he was so determined to not believe her. Or Leo.

It was like Eldridge had some vendetta against the man. He was so certain that Leo was the same boy who had so disappointed him long ago, that Eldridge couldn't see through the visage Leo had built around himself.

The Summer Lord was a decent man with a weak spirit. But that didn't mean he couldn't change or grow with the right help. Like any tree, he needed a place to put his roots, and then he could flourish with the support of family and friends. Without that support, he would continue to topple over and have to start anew.

"I—" Freya started, only to be interrupted by one of the handmaidens.

"My lord! We've finished gathering all the crystals you requested in the water. What would you like us to do with them?"

Eldridge turned toward them with a bright grin on his face. "Excellent! Bring them to the section of the village we've taken over and we'll start enchanting them. Soon, this isle will glow with lights like the stars!"

The women teetered off, all of their arms overladen with bags of tiny crystals. So that's what they had been gathering. Why there were crystals in tidepools, Freya would likely never know.

"I thought maybe we could take the afternoon together?" Freya was very aware of her sodden dress that likely smelled of seawater. She'd need a bath before they did anything, but she could dunk herself in the ocean again. Or maybe they could swim together.

She would love to have an afternoon swimming in the magical waves with the man she loved. Maybe this was the perfect time to tell him that she was madly, deeply in love with him.

But Eldridge wasn't even looking at her. His eyes were on the handmaidens as they raced toward the opening in the cliff. A thousand thoughts danced behind his eyes and Freya already knew his answer long before he opened his mouth.

"If Leo is coming soon, then we have less time than we thought to prepare. This is the first step toward getting your father back, Freya. The first step toward our future. We can't slow down now." He reached for her hands and squeezed her fingers. "I know it's tough, my love. I also want an afternoon with just the two of us, but we have too much to do."

And then he raced off after the other women without even a second glance back at her.

What was she supposed to do? Freya had nothing that was under her control here. She was left standing on the rocky beach, wondering what had happened that made her feel so... alone.

Wrapping her arms around herself, Freya turned down the beach and started walking. She didn't know where she was going or what plan was in her head. All she knew was that she had to keep putting one foot in front of the other. For a little while at least. Otherwise, all those horrible thoughts would spew out of her mouth.

Logically, she knew Eldridge was right. They needed to figure out this riddle in the Summer Court, although Eldridge had no clue that she'd already found her father. The forest had to be appeased or they would never get him back. And the forest wanted Leo and Cora to accept their rightful place in the court.

And if they didn't, then she might as well give up now and head back to the Goblin Court with her proverbial tail tucked between her legs. She didn't have a luxurious one like her sister, but that didn't mean she wouldn't feel it when she returned to her mother and told her that she'd failed. Her father would likely go back to being a mindless beast slathering in that prison for the rest of his life. And she would never let herself live this down.

Which meant she had to follow the plan. She had to focus now, and then she could figure out what she was doing with her relationship later. It wasn't like they didn't have all the time in the world.

Except they didn't.

She touched a finger to the corner of her eyes where she'd noticed a few crow's feet were already showing. She wasn't that old yet, but she could already see the signs of age. Eventually she would be this ridiculous, old woman limping after a handsome Goblin King. Maybe he would still love her when she looked like that, but maybe he wouldn't want to deal with the pain and discomfort that came with old age.

Freya knew she was spiraling. But she couldn't stop.

She paused next to one of the tide pools and stared down into the crystal clear water. The surface was so smooth it was like a mirror, reflecting her own wide-eyed stare back at her. She looked manic. Mad.

Crazed knowing that she couldn't stop the aging that would divide her and the man she loved.

No, she couldn't think like this. Freya tapped the surface of the water and watched the ripples spread from the single tap. If only she could make sure that she wasn't crazy. That he loved her still as much as he said he did.

The temptation to scry rose again. The trees wouldn't have told her to use that magic if they hadn't seen that she would need it. What if they were warning her to look, because something important was happening right underneath her nose?

It was a bad idea. The Goblin King might even feel that she was spying on him, and then how would she explain herself?

Freya still let all the thoughts trickle from her mind and whispered, "Can you show me the Goblin King?"

Guilt already gnawed on her conscious, but she was given the opportunity to prove to herself that the whispers in her mind were nothing more than anxiety. This was all in her head, she had nothing to worry about.

The water shimmered with magic. It wasn't her magic. Freya didn't feel that strange pull on her very life force like it had the few times she'd used her power. This was almost like the Summer Court was showing her what she needed to see.

Suddenly, she wasn't looking at the tiny stones at the bottom of the pool or the crab picking through kelp. Now she was looking at Eldridge as he strode into a room where Cora stood in the center. He held out his arms for the beautiful woman and tucked her against his heart, as he did to Freya when she needed someone to lean on. He whispered something to Cora, who laughed with her entire body.

The scene was innocent. She shouldn't read anything into the body language that they exhibited and yet, she did. Cora was too comfortable. Eldridge was too happy. And she was standing alone on a rocky shore covered in seaweed and saltwater.

Swallowing hard, she whispered to herself, "It means nothing. They're friends. You know they're friends."

But it still hurt to see him hugging Cora. Her heart twisted in her chest knowing that even though this was an act of comfort and excitement that the Summer Lord was finally going to be here, it didn't matter.

Jealousy was a wicked poison that spread through her chest like a wildfire through a dry forest. She couldn't think. She couldn't breathe. All she could do was stare down at the water in shock and horror.

She had to stop or she would surely go mad. She'd rush to the room they were in and slap both of them, making a scene out of nothing.

Freya dashed her hand over the water, slapping the surface so it wouldn't show her that horrible image any longer. If only she could get clarification, hear what Eldridge had said...

She stood back up and pressed a hand to her chest. This was the poison the forest was talking about. The Summer Court was sick, and it was affecting her. She'd never been this jealous woman who wanted to follow her significant other around and limit what they could or could not see.

Freya had never once questioned his adoration or his intention with her. Eldridge was a doting, loving partner who had seen that she needed more reassurance than most. He'd given her that and here she was. Spying. All because there was another beautiful woman around him and she couldn't stand it that she wasn't the prettiest girl in the room.

Freya had never been the prettiest girl.

"You have been surrounded by fae this entire time," she reminded herself. "And he still picked you."

The grubby, strange, arrogant mortal woman who had been bound and determined to hate him no matter how hard he tried to convince her otherwise. Their love hadn't bloomed suddenly or without work. They had struggled through the courts together and...

No. She couldn't do this anymore. She needed to clear her head.

Staring up at the cliff's edge, she resolved herself to being better. She would go back into that village and she would help Cora get ready for the moment when Leo arrived. Then the Lord and Lady could reconcile their broken relationship. The forest would be happy and it would release her father.

Then and only then would she focus on fixing her own relationship with the Goblin King.

CHAPTER 22

"When do you think he'll get here?" Cora asked.

The pretty elf looked over her shoulder at Freya, who sat on the side of her bed. Cora was delicately twisting the braids on her head into little bubbles that were both gorgeous and strange to Freya.

She'd offered to help prepare Cora for when the Summer Lord would get here, but Cora had laughed and said Freya wouldn't know how to do her hair. Watching now, Freya realized the other woman was very correct. She had no idea what to do with hair that curly.

So she'd sat on the edge of the bed with her hands under her bottom so she didn't touch anything.

What had Cora just asked? Oh right.

"He didn't say, but considering the rushing handmaidens that keep running through the room, I'm going to guess he's informed them that he'll arrive today." She tucked a strand of hair behind her ear. "He said to tell you that he was coming. I think that bodes well."

"I'm not getting my hopes up." Cora wrung her hands, then finished up the last braid. She kept touching the bubbles on her head, then turned toward Freya with a frown on her face. "Do you think he'll like this? Or should I do something else?"

Considering it had taken many hours to do what she'd already done, Freya wasn't sure she'd have the opportunity to do something different.

But she couldn't tell Cora that. The poor woman would fall into a dead faint.

She stood up and approached Cora with a soft smile on her face. Gently, Freya turned the elf to look into the mirror at her own reflection. "You're a beautiful woman and he loves you already. The sight of you is going to take his breath away, even if you were wearing a burlap sack."

Cora stared at herself and touched a finger to her glistening cheek. "Do you really think that?"

How had Freya ever thought this woman would entertain a relationship with Eldridge? Cora continually made it so very clear that she was in love with Leo. That she would wait for ages until he came to his senses and saw the stunning woman who was in front of him. Waiting for ages so that he would love her the way she loved him.

Freya smiled and patted Cora's shoulder. "I do. I think he's going to walk over the beach and fall to his knees in the sand because he's a fool for waiting this long. You're going to make him so happy. And not by listening to whatever Eldridge told you to do. You'll make him happy just by being yourself."

And there it was. Cora's expression crumbled, and she stared down at her fingers in her lap. How dare Eldridge make her feel like she couldn't be herself!

Freya retreated to the bed and sat down with a hard thump. "What did Eldridge say?"

"He said to be harder than I normally would because it's been two hundred years and I have every right to be angry." Cora met her gaze in the mirror, her expression filled with rage. "And I am furious, Freya. It has taken him this long to come here and... well. What is different this time?"

"The world as the two of you know it might end?" A thousand possibilities came to mind on why he was doing all this, but Freya realized that Cora's anger was justified as well. "I think you can be angry at him and kind at the same time. You don't have to attack him the moment he steps on this isle just because he's made mistakes. He knows that. What he's doing right now is holding out an olive branch so you two might talk about everything that's happened and figure out a way to fix it."

"I don't know how to fix it." Cora lifted her hands as if she had hoped she could grasp something in them. "The threads of our lives are intertwined as no other lives are. I feel the forest wanting to throw him into the ground and I know the sea is angry with me. But what if all this time apart has turned us into very different people? What if neither of us want to be with each other?"

"Then you won't." Freya knew that to be the truth, at the very least. No matter how hard she wanted them to be together, the reality was that no one could force them to fall back in love. "A lot has changed, I agree with that. But if you listen to Eldridge's advice, the first thing that Leo will see is an angry woman who cannot forgive him. That's a lasting memory that will take years, or perhaps centuries, to heal."

"You're right." Cora nodded firmly. "You're absolutely right. I should be myself."

"I think once you two get some time alone, you'll be surprised at how much hasn't changed. Sure, there are a lot of experiences that have made the two of you different people. But I know the children you once were are still in there somewhere. You'll know what to do when you see him."

Freya would have said more, but a pounding knock on the door interrupted her. A handmaiden burst in without waiting for them to call for her.

"The Summer Lord approaches!" she said excitedly. "He's here! He's coming on a ship, with countless other elves from the court behind him!"

Right, well, she should have told him to be a little less showy than that. Poor Cora already looked like she was going to faint.

Freya rolled her eyes up to the ceiling and tried very hard to stay calm and collected. Both fae were centuries older than she was, and they needed their hands held for love. Romance should have been easy for them by now, and instead, they only excelled at mincing words and twisting the truth.

"Everything is going to work out," she said again. "Cora. Listen to me, we need to get you dressed and ready to see Leo. Do you think you can do that?"

Cora's face said she couldn't. Her entire being radiated with fear and discomfort. And Freya didn't blame her.

After all, Cora had been on this isle for two hundred years by herself. Now she had a few handmaidens, and that was likely fun at first. Finally, some people for her to talk to. But the reality of having an entire court on her doorstep, with the man she was supposed to marry... That was a different story.

Freya pinched the bridge of her nose. "You stay here. Get ready and when you are finished, talk with Eldridge. Let him know that I went to greet Leo and I'm getting him settled. We will not push you, Cora. You need to do these things on your own, and only when you are ready."

In the meantime, she had to be the one that raced down the beach like a crazy person. What was Leo thinking? He was going to overwhelm Cora and then they all were going to be sent from this shore. She would end up having to start this process all over again and honestly, Freya was about done with these two lovebirds who had no idea what they wanted out of life. Or each other.

"Wait!" Cora called out. "Wait, Freya! I'm coming with you."

Cora stood up and Freya turned to see the Summer Lady standing behind her. And that was exactly what Cora was.

With a simple hand flick, magic poured a golden dress over her skin. The sheer fabric was stunning and looked like molten metal had been formed in the shape of her body. The dress hugged her curves, accentuating her hourglass waist. Her hair was done perfectly, not a strand out of place, and her expression was one of serene confidence.

This was exactly what Freya had thought to find at the hand of the Summer Lord. A Lady who commanded attention, and if a person didn't bend their knee to her, she would summon a storm to sweep them away.

Her eyes must have been bugging out of her head, and maybe that was rude, but Freya couldn't stop staring at Cora.

"My goodness," she whispered. "Look at you."

"Does it look silly?" Cora brushed a hand down her stomach. "I always thought this would be what I wore, but I can change it."

"No. Don't you change a single thing. You look like a goddess." Leo was going to trip over his own tongue when he saw what he'd been missing all this time. The fool had taken far too long, but thank goodness their kind was long lived.

At least, Freya assumed they were. Were the fae immortal, or did they have only a certain length to their life?

She'd have to ask Eldridge. The answer seemed rather important, she'd just never wondered what the truth was before.

Cora swept out of the room with Freya on her tail. Almost all the handmaidens were waiting for her, holding glowing crystals in their hands. "My Lady," one said, holding out a crystal for Cora to take. "We've decorated the entire village with these. It will look like the sun itself shines from your home. He will be so pleased when he sees you."

Though Cora took the offered crystal, there was a darker expression on her face. "Good. I want him to think this isle is beautiful."

Freya read between the lines. The Summer Lady worried that her Lord would find her wanting. And that wasn't fair. Not when there was so much good in her.

She reached out and touched a hand to Cora's back. Whispering so the handmaidens didn't over hear, she said, "You're going to make it through tonight. And then, when it's all said and done, I'll think you'll have found this all very easy."

"Thank you, Freya," Cora replied. "I couldn't do this without you."

They walked through the halls until they met Eldridge, who waited for them at the entrance to the village. He wore his customary black velvet suit with the gold foiled edges, bowing low as they approached. "My Lady. You look exquisite, as always."

"And you flatter me, Goblin King." Cora's cheeks darkened. "But thank you. I believe the Summer Lord will be impressed with the show you have provided."

"It has nothing to do with me, and everything to do with you, if he's impressed. His Lady has been waiting for a very long time, and he needs to see what a fool he was to keep you on this isle when he could have had you by his side." Eldridge's gaze met hers, and he grinned. "Like I feel every time this one lingers too far from my gaze. Freya? A moment, if you would."

Though a part of her very much wanted to hear what he had to say, Freya also feared they would get in an argument. And the frustrated part of her also realized that she was still angry at him for leaving her on the rocky shore when he could have been with her. Just as he wanted to be now.

Instead, she shook her head and nodded toward Cora. "They need us to be there when they finally see each other again, Eldridge. Isn't that what you said when we last spoke?"

His brows drew down as he thought through her words. She could only hope that he wouldn't realize her frustration about how he'd treated her. Because then he would drag her to the side and make her talk about how she was feeling.

Freya wasn't ready to talk about that, yet. She was still frustrated. Angry. Upset. And some of those emotions were her own doing because she had scried and seen them doing things that she didn't like. And sure, that wasn't fair of her to put that on him. But it didn't make it any easier.

"Well," he said, clearing his throat. "Then hold on a second and let me make sure you're presentable to the Summer Lord."

She tried to ignore the disappointment in his eyes as he waved a hand. The magic settled over her shoulders in a wave, and the gown that appeared on her body outdid any magic he'd performed thus far. Like him, she was in dark clothing, but he'd covered the fabric with tiny diamonds that sparkled as she moved. The low neckline was tasteful but still showed off an ample amount of her chest.

She lifted a brow and stared at him, wondering why he'd chosen this dress for her. It certainly showed more of Freya's skin than she was comfortable with. And bare arms?

Cora started off ahead of them as Freya took Eldridge's offered arm. He leaned down and whispered in her ear, "I know this is Cora's moment. But I intend on reminding the Summer Lord that while his bride is beautiful, mine is far more powerful."

She blushed, her cheeks heating unbidden at his words. And it was entirely natural for her entire body to flush when he was that close to her. She missed the feeling of his skin against hers and the way he would chuckle in her ear as he moved above her.

But now was not the time for such thoughts, not when she was already too nervous to think straight.

Freya sighed and tugged him toward the walkway that would lead them to the ocean. "Come on, Goblin King. We need to greet the Summer Lord and make sure these two lovebirds don't kill each other when they do meet after all this time."

He wrapped her hand in his, linking their fingers even as she tugged him to move faster. "The lovebirds should be able to handle themselves considering their advanced age. Are you sure we can't have a few moments to ourselves? I need to talk with you Freya."

And she needed to chew his ear off in anger when they were finally done with this mess. Didn't he see how mad she was at him? Surely he could sense the anger radiating through her entire body.

"Soon," she replied. "You can have your moment soon, Eldridge."

CHAPTER 23

Freya and Eldridge walked down the beach, hand in hand. She watched the small boats approach in the distance. The Summer Lord had hung lanterns from the bow of each boat, and the bright lights lit their way as the sun set on the horizon. The stars twinkled and all the crystals Eldridge had enchanted gave the entire beach a lovely glow that could not be beaten by any fairytale.

Cora waited at the edge of the shore. The waves kissed her toes with every small movement and she held the crystal in her hand like a candle. This was the kind of scene that inspired artists to paint, Freya was certain of it.

The boats hit the sand and Leo remained standing at the bow. He wore billowing white pants and a golden vest, lacking a shirt. Freya knew he'd done that to show off the muscles of his arms and chest.

Someone had painted gold symbols all down his arms in tiny, decorative marks. She leaned over and whispered, "Do the marks have meaning?"

"They're runes." Eldridge squinted, then smiled softly. "They're for good luck. Clever man, I'm certain she'll remember those."

Freya hoped Cora did. The runes were a cry for pity, or perhaps for the chance to make up for what he'd done. With a swift leap, he struck the waves and waded through them to Cora's side.

No one could say Leo didn't have a flourish in his movements. And the tactic was working on Cora. Her eyes were wide and her mouth dropping open as she watched this prince from the storybooks fall onto his knees before her. Exactly as Freya had said he would.

"My Summer Lady," he said, his words quiet though somehow ringing over the sands. "I have made you wait for too long. I beg your forgiveness, and for a single night to convince you that I am still worthy of your grand attention."

"Is that so?" Cora held the crystal higher so the light could bask on Leo's handsome features. "You have a lot of explaining to do, Summer Lord."

"And anything you ask of me, I will tell." He lifted his head and stared up at her with so much love in his eyes all the women in the crowd swooned. "My greatest mistake was in not finding you sooner, Cora. I'm ashamed to admit I've been hiding. Afraid of what you think of me."

"What changed?"

Leo glanced over at Freya and Eldridge, the flick of his gaze telling in the movement. "A very dear friend reminded me that people can be forgiven, and that sometimes change isn't as hard as we make it out to be."

Freya's heart twisted in her chest. Apparently her words had sunk in, and that meant all the difference to her. She truly believed he deserved a second chance.

"I'm willing to listen," Cora replied. "Because I believe a similar friend convinced me that a future without someone to love is a bleak future, indeed."

Eldridge squeezed her tight to his side as the Summer Lord and Lady led the other elves down the beach. Their entourage trailed along behind them, farther than the others but still close enough. The elves with the Summer Lord all jumped from their boats into the ocean, then raced down the beach to join the handmaidens.

Now that she was looking at them, there weren't as many elves as she had thought. The boats were small, so they couldn't fit so many people without the entire thing sinking. The Summer Lord had brought roughly fifty elves with him. Only a small fraction of the Summer Court.

She'd have to track down the handmaiden who'd said he brought everyone with him and scold her.

"Where are we going?" she asked. Sand slipped into her shoes and slid between her toes. Though the grit should have annoyed her, she didn't mind it so much. Not when the moon was lighting up the entire beach with a lovely silver glow, and the elves were already singing even though they hadn't reached their destination.

"We set up a small area for them to all enjoy each other's company." Eldridge twisted their fingers together again, linking them even closer if that was possible. "I thought it might be smart if they were all together. Even the other elves."

She wanted them to have a few moments alone, but he might be right. The Summer Lord and Lady weren't exactly friends. They had a lot of catching up to do, and two hundred years of heartbreak and disappointment was a lot to cover. They might have forgotten who the other was, and they needed those moments to grow and learn from each other.

"Probably a good idea," she muttered. "Are we going to watch them all night?"

Eldridge lifted his brows and bit his tongue before replying, "Do you think they're both mature enough to be left alone for a while?"

She wished she could say yes. But already she could see Cora's shoulders lifting to her ears. Leo took yet another step away from his intended bride. Freya sighed and shook her head. "No. No, I don't think they're ready for that just yet."

"Shall we go babysit the children, then?" He lifted her hand to his mouth and pressed a kiss to her knuckles. "All we have to do is get tonight over with. Then we can finally have an evening to ourselves again."

Yes, that's exactly what she wanted. A quiet evening by a fireplace with a bottle of wine and her Goblin King stretched out on a sheepskin beside her. That's it.

But she didn't have that yet. And she was damned frustrated.

She sighed and started toward Leo. Eldridge framed her other side, his eyes set on Cora. They had to fix this before the two of them ruined it again.

Maybe that was a sign that they didn't belong together. Freya knew there was no one keeping Eldridge and her together. They figured out their relationship on their own, even though it would be easier to have a go between.

Speaking of.

A little black and white body weaved through the throngs of elves to reach her side. Arrow was out of breath. But he had made it here when she needed him most. "At your service, Miss Freya."

"Where have you been?"

He nodded toward the handmaidens, baring his teeth in a nasty snarl. "I don't trust any of these elves. I've been keeping an eye on the servants to make sure no one decides to poison the food."

Freya dropped onto a knee and patted his head gently. "We don't deserve you, Arrow. You're a faithful companion that no one could ever beat."

Arrow straightened his shoulders, sitting regally in the sand. "It's my pleasure. How might I help?"

Pointedly staring at the couple awkwardly lingering beside a table of golden refreshments, she sighed. "These two are bound and determined to make this meeting as awkward as possible. And Eldridge made certain that meeting was public."

"Why would he do that?"

She turned that stare to him. "Why do you think?"

"Right." Arrow sighed and snapped his jaws at the Goblin King who passed by them. "Ridiculous man. He seems to think his way of wooing is the only way to romance, and he knows much better than that."

"Apparently not." She stood and started toward the Summer Lord, knowing that Arrow would follow her. "Let's not interrupt at first. We should listen and see how they're doing. Maybe they'll surprise us."

And considering they were next to the refreshments, she didn't have to worry about looking suspicious. She did want a drink to soothe her parched throat. The sand was dry this evening.

Leo's voice was easy to hear, even over other conversations and the faint sound of musical instruments being tested for tuning. "I'm just saying, I think it's fine for you to stay on the island if that's what you want. I have a life on the mainland. You have a life here. It's okay if you don't want to return."

The look she shared with Arrow was one of complete and utter disappointment. What was the Summer Lord doing now?

She turned around and bumped into Leo's back, almost spilling her drink all over him. "Oh! Leo, I'm so sorry."

He spun in surprise, then softened when he saw her. Leo caught the drink in her grip and helped her still the wildly swinging liquid. "Please, don't apologize, Freya. There are many people here and anyone might bump into someone else."

Freya caught his hand and tugged him close so she could hiss in his ear, "What are you trying to do? Scare her off?"

"I'm trying to tell her that whatever speed she is comfortable with is how fast we'll go," he whispered back. "Was it not coming off like that?"

"No. It was coming off like you wanted her to stay here."

"But I don't!"

Freya pulled away with a bright grin on her face, even though she was grinding her teeth. "Thank you so much, Leo. I'm so sorry again. I'll leave you two alone now. Be nice!"

She realized her voice was far too high pitched for anyone to believe she meant what she said. But how else was she supposed to get her point across other than with waggling eyebrows and overly emphasized words?

The foolish man was going to run this woman off because he didn't remember how to be kind to someone other than himself. Maybe she should have asked Eldridge to talk with Leo as well. Cora's predicament was rare, and she imagined it was difficult for anyone to put themselves in her shoes. Leo needed to know how Cora was feeling. Really feeling.

God, she hated admitting Eldridge was right.

Freya picked a place far enough away from the other elves that they wouldn't bother her while she sneakily watched the couple in the distance. Arrow sat down on her foot and surveyed with her. "How bad was it?"

"Bad." She sipped her drink, then winced. "And this liquid is awful. What even is this?"

"Probably a honey wine that the fae make. Humans find it very sweet. Is it?" He reached for the cup and then took his own sip. "Yes, this is the good stuff. Eldridge wanted to impress Leo, apparently."

"Good?" She looked back at the crystal glass and frowned. "It's awful. I don't know how you all drink this."

"Well, it's not for humans, is it?" Arrow grabbed the cup from her and drank again, grumbling about mortals that didn't know what tasted good and what didn't.

For a little while, it seemed like Leo and Cora were enjoying themselves. They laughed together and meandered from the crowd. They sat down under a pagoda that Eldridge and the handmaidens had built, with twinkling crystal lights and white fabric that billowed in the warm summer breeze. Cora even scooted closer to Leo for a few seconds, their fingers nearly touching on the bench.

Freya was comfortable enough to wander through the crowd and take her eyes off the couple. Another table had been set up a little farther away and laden with food. Freya's stomach grumbled, and she realized she hadn't eaten in quite some time.

She loaded a plate with bread, cheese, and honey. At least that would give her a reason to not talk with anyone. Even the elves wouldn't speak to someone stuffing their face with food.

But only a few bites in, something happened with the couple. She didn't know if one of them said words that were hurtful or what. Cora jumped up and stalked away from Leo, who stared after her with wide eyes.

"Damn it," she muttered. "What now?"

Eldridge appeared from the shadows behind her. "I'm on it."

"Good," Freya grumbled, leaning back against the table of food she'd commandeered. "It's your turn, anyway."

She waited until he was far enough away from them before flicking her gaze at Arrow. The goblin dog immediately trotted off to "help his king", when in reality he was spying for Freya. At least their connection was tighter than Eldridge and Arrow. She wanted to know everything the King said to Cora.

Arrow returned in no time, but Eldridge and Cora were still lost in the shadows somewhere.

"What happened?" Freya asked, setting down her plate of food. "Things looked like they were going so well."

"Apparently Cora thought she was getting too close to him and then she thought he must think she was a harlot or something ridiculous like that. Being that close to someone else after so long has been messing with her head." Arrow shrugged. "Eldridge has it under control. Surprisingly, the Goblin King has a lot of good advice for someone suffering from that."

Did he? That was surprising. He had never cared about touching her, even when they didn't know each other well enough for those touches to be warranted. She still vividly remembered him dressing her in this court the first time they were here, and how that had made her entire body tingle.

Cora returned, this time with darkened cheeks and a sheepish smile. She tucked a loose curl behind her ear, though it popped out again. Leo appeared to think that was quite captivating because he reached forward to tuck it himself. Obviously, that didn't work.

The couple shared a small smile and then returned to the dance floor where many of the elves were already dancing. They were swept into the sway of bodies, curling into each other as though no one else existed on the beach.

How lovely.

She pressed a hand to her chest and sighed at the romance of it all. They might not be in love with each other again, but they were on the right road to becoming head over heels just like they were when they were children.

A warm hand tucked into the curve of her waist. Eldridge tugged her closer to the comfortable haven of his arms and murmured in her ear, "I think they're on the right track enough for us to dance. What do you say, my love?"

"Yes," she replied, staring up into his handsome silver features and seeing the stars in his eyes. "I think we could manage."

He swung her into his arms and spun her through the crowd like she was lighter than a feather. He held her in his arms with utmost care. And Freya knew with every spin that she didn't have to fear or lead in any step. While she was in the Goblin King's arms, she was safe.

In return, his gaze warmed, and he stared down at her like he'd seen nothing so beautiful in his life. His hands flexed on her back and his lips curved into a warm smile. "Freya, there's something I've been meaning to talk to you about."

A hissed, "Hey!" interrupted them.

Freya glanced over her shoulder as Leo and Cora spun by them. Leo gave her a thumbs up with a wild grin.

She chuckled and shook her head, "Well, I'm glad they're getting along. I thought we'd have to follow them around like two lost puppies tumbling over each other."

Eldridge sighed, but still managed a sharp smile. "They're adults. They will either figure it out now, or they won't. But I believe they have a good chance. Look at them! They haven't been happier since we arrived in the Summer Court."

He was right. Both of the Summer Court leaders wore smiles that were brighter than the sun. And when they snuck off the dance floor and down the beach with each other, Freya gave a long, relaxed sigh. "Finally. I think they'll be fine."

"I do too." Eldridge tugged her in the opposite direction. "Now, perhaps we can sneak a few moments together?"

That sounded like everything she'd been wanting for a long time. "Maybe for a little while."

As they strode away from the crowd, Freya gave Arrow a quick wink. He waved a paw and toddled off to the drink table once again. At least he'd enjoy himself while they stole a few moments together.

Now, she could only wonder what Eldridge wanted to talk to her about that was so important.

The breeze shifted with them and tangled in the sweat at the base of her neck. Finally, Freya felt like she could breathe again.

Eldridge held her hand in his, tangled their fingers together and tugged her this way and that. Sometimes he tried to throw her off balance and she'd immediately bubble with laughter.

They didn't talk for a while. Instead, they enjoyed each other's company in silence under the stars. And what a lovely silence it was.

A thousand twinkling lights danced above them. The waves crashed on the shore. white foam lingering on the sandy beach that cushioned her toes. She'd so rarely been to the beach growing up. As an adult, she didn't have time to wander the sand like this. Let alone find someone handsome to walk with while the moon lit their path.

Eldridge lifted her hand and pressed a kiss to her palm. "It's been a long time since we had a few moments to ourselves."

"It really has." She danced away from a wave that got a little too close to her legs. It would have soaked the hem of her dress, and Freya wanted it to be preserved for a few moments longer. After all, this was a rare moment when she felt beautiful. "I've enjoyed being here, though. Sure, there's been some struggles and frustrating things that have happened, but I like it in the Summer Court."

"Everyone does," he said with a scoff. "That's why I spent my summers here as a boy."

She frowned, a question popping out of her lips before she could stop it. "I meant to ask. If you're from a certain court, how do you have seasons here? You keep saying you spent summers here, but there are no summers in the Autumn Court. Are there?"

Eldridge quirked a brow and the small smile on his face was one of complete and utter mischief. "I was wondering how long it would take for you to pick up on that. No, we don't necessarily have seasons. But we still like to pretend we do. I'd spend four months here every year, and then rotate to the next. The children of royals can choose to do so."

The children of royals.

She forgot that not only was he the Goblin King, but that he had been a noble his entire life. Sure, it wasn't the same as being the king of the all the faerie courts. But royal blood ran through his veins.

To her, he was just Eldridge. A rather unconventional and strange man who had found her at a time in her life when she needed someone to force change upon her. And he had. Even though she had fought him tooth and nail every single step of the way.

Biting her lip, she ruefully smiled. "Well, there's the answer to that, then."

"Freya." Eldridge tugged her to a stop, still holding her hand in his as if she were made of glass. "I know things between us have been strained since we came to the Summer Court. I thought we were getting along well, but then something happened while we were here. Care to explain what that was?"

Oh goodness, there were a hundred things she could tell him.

That she was jealous because he'd given Cora a lot of attention. But in contrast, she'd also given Leo more attention than he deserved. She supposed Eldridge could have gotten jealous about all that, but he hadn't. Likely because he trusted her more, and he was very secure in their relationship.

She'd also lied about finding her father. She should have told

Eldridge the moment she found him in the trees and that the reason she wanted Leo and Cora together wasn't entirely to save the Summer Court.

Or perhaps that the trees had told her to do all this, and not that she had pieced together the entire story on her own without their help.

Maybe she should start with the fact that she was feeling insecure and then the rest could come out on its own?

Freya released her hold on his hand and ran her fingers through her soft curls. "Listen, there's so much that I need to tell you. I haven't been entirely truthful this whole time. I know that Leo and Cora getting together again is very important for this Summer Court, but I... I... I'm afraid that in doing so you'll be reminded just how much you love the faerie courts. And how little I compare to the beauty here and all around us."

His eyes grew wider with every word she said, and Eldridge seemed to fall apart right in front of her. His shoulders curved forward, softening in a movement that she hated to see but also loved. It was times like these when she knew he wouldn't berate her for her thoughts. Instead, he would listen to what had made her so uncomfortable.

"My darling," he muttered, reaching for her hands again so he could hold them in his own. "Is all of this because you saw Cora's beauty and you feared that I wouldn't want you anymore? Because you aren't a faerie?"

In the simplest way of saying it, yes. That was correct, even though she hadn't voiced the fear to herself. She worried that he was going to wake up someday and realize she wasn't the faerie partner he'd always seen for himself.

But this was too close to peeling open her many layers and revealing the horrible wound in her heart. The wound that had always whispered she wasn't as good as others. The wound that made her aggressive and push people away so that she was safe from their love. Just in case they wanted to take that love away.

She recognized when she was doing it, but Freya had never stopped herself from shoving people out of important positions in her life. Esther was the only one she loved with her whole heart, even though sometimes she was controlling over her sister as well. Because Esther was family. She couldn't leave.

Until she did.

Sighing, Freya changed the subject to something even worse. Something that she knew would turn Eldridge's mind away from this conversation and to another. "I found my father," she blurted, deliberately ignoring the question he'd asked her. "I didn't tell you, and I feel awful for it. But the trees have been keeping him, healing him, in return for getting Leo to do the right thing and take control of the court."

Eldridge's eyes widened even farther, if that was possible. "Your father?"

"Yes. Nearly the very first day we were here. I didn't tell you because the timing didn't feel right, and he wasn't in his right mind, anyway. I thought you wouldn't let me go back to the forest if you knew a wild werewolf was being kept in a prison there. But he's better now. I spoke with him." She pressed a hand to her stomach that rolled with the truth. If she kept talking, it would keep spewing out of her.

She stopped talking. She stood silently in the sands, watching the many expressions play across Eldridge's face.

First disbelief. He couldn't understand how she'd kept all this from him, and she had known that would take a while for him to accept. Then frustration, likely because it would have made everything easier if he'd known this from the start. Freya winced to see betrayal on his face when that was the last thing she'd wanted him to feel.

But she'd known he would. Of course he would feel like she was keeping him out of things. Hadn't that been why she'd been so angry at him and Arrow this entire trip? They made decisions without her. And here she was, making decisions without him.

Eldridge licked his lips and took a deep breath. "You should have told me he was here. I could have helped."

"I know," she replied. "I know you could have, but it didn't feel right. My gut screamed to wait. That you needed to do this without knowing where my father was. I don't know why."

A low growl rumbled through his throat, but he eventually shook his head and seemed to dismiss the conversation. "We'll talk about that later once we finish this quest for the forest and put the Summer

Court to rights. After that, we will pull apart why you decided you had to do this all on your own. Again."

Well, she already knew the answer to that. Freya was a control freak and when things were out of her control, then she didn't know what to do. Her heart pounded in her chest and her mind raced at all the possible endings if she wasn't the person controlling every step of the way.

And if he loved her as he said he did, then Eldridge would have to get used to that.

Then she remembered the worst lie she'd been telling him this whole time. The lie that had broken her very soul every time she saw him.

The timing wasn't right. She shouldn't have even thought about it, but the stars were shining overhead and the moon glittered in the sky. And Eldridge looked so handsome standing there in the sands, ready to forgive her for the grievous mistakes she'd made.

"I love you," she whispered. The words ripped out of her soul and flew into the air like an arrow seeking its target. "I don't know why it's been so hard to say, but I do. Every part of me aches for your presence. I love you with every waking breath and with every sigh of sleep. I dream of you, and I can't imagine living in any other way than worshipping the very ground you walk on. It has plagued me that I haven't told you sooner, but then we were here and you were so focused on..."

"Cora." Eldridge stepped closer, tugging her close with their hands raised between them. Love burned in his gaze. "I have waited so long to hear you say those words."

"Sorry if they feel a little strange," she replied, looking down at their clasped hands and knowing she would never feel more loved than this moment. "I know it's been difficult for you to be in the Summer Court, and I haven't made it easier on you. But I do love you. I prom-ise, from now until the day I die that I will say those words every single morning and every single night."

"I'll hold you to that." He leaned down, closer and closer to her lips. "You are the other half of my soul, Freya. My heart beats for you and you alone. I hope, in time, you will believe that."

"I do." Really, she did. She believed he loved her and that the world stopped spinning when he looked at her. "Should I say it again?"

Eldridge stole a kiss, his lips lingering on the corner of hers. "Yes."

"I love you," she whispered against his mouth.

He moved and pressed a chaste kiss to the other corner.

"I love you."

With a slow glide, he eased his mouth to hers and devoured her lips. Soft velvet and a tongue that tasted of sweet faerie wine turned her senses to madness. She couldn't think of anything but him. Her entire being shifted toward him, wanting more than anything to be one with him. The Goblin King. Her strange villain in a story that had turned him into a hero.

When she pulled away, Freya blinked up at him with heavy-lidded eyes. "I really do, though. I love you."

"I know you do." He kissed her forehead. "There's still something I need to talk to you about, though. Before we continue this conversation or get lost in each other's bodies. I need you to know something, to hear these words and think about them."

Her stomach clenched. Words that she had to think about before they went any further? What could the Goblin King possibly have to say?

Before he could even speak, a scream rolled down the beach like a thunderstorm. The deep, echoing call was one of pain so biting that it would kill the person who cried out for help. A man's scream.

She released her hold on Eldridge and peered around him. All the elves had frozen, staring down the beach before a few of them screamed as well.

"Leo?" she asked, looking back at Eldridge.

"This can wait." Again, he kissed her forehead before turning with her hand in his. "Run."

Together they ran down the beach. She could only hope the Summer Lord was still alive when they arrived.

CHAPTER 25

Freya's feet pounded across the beach. The screams never stopped for the entire journey as they raced toward the sound that echoed in her ears.

Please don't let him die. She sent the prayer out into the realm and hoped that someone heard her. The forest must be listening. It was always listening and if she begged hard enough then maybe, just maybe, she could save him before all this went wrong.

They hadn't had enough time. The forest should have seen that he was doing better. That he was so close to taking control over all those things that had been thrust upon him at too young an age. And, if they just waited a few more days, then maybe Cora and Leo would have done the right thing. They would have fallen in love all over again.

Breathing hard, they rounded a corner of the cliffs and Freya nearly fell onto her face. Leo and Cora had indeed been enjoying each other's company, but that had all ended in pain.

He knelt in the sands with his hands pressed deep into the white chips of seashells. His head hung low and sweat already slicked his bare back. The vest that had covered him, the one covered in gold, lay on the ground next to him.

As she watched, his skin seemed to roll. Not as if he were curving his spine, but something inside him moved. Like snakes slithered under the thin layer of his skin.

Leo threw his head back and screamed again, though at least he didn't try to dig out the curse that affected him.

"What happened?" Freya gasped, racing to Cora's side.

The beautiful woman had tears streaking down her cheeks. Cora pressed her hands to her face and shook her head, eyes watering still. "I don't know. I don't know! We kissed and then he fell like this."

They'd kissed? If the situation had been different, Freya would have crowed in happiness. But that kiss had caused pain while they were all hoping that it would fix everything.

Tugging Cora into her arms, Freya pressed the other woman's face into her shoulder as Leo screamed again.

Eldridge walked toward his friend, hands outstretched. "What can I do? How can I help you, Leo?"

The Summer Lord was incapable of speech. He opened his mouth. No sound came out other than a horrible groan. It wasn't a good sign. Freya knew next to nothing about magic or the properties that clearly affected the Summer Lord, but she knew this wasn't good.

Eldridge dropped to his knees and lifted his hands. The strange language of magic spilled from his tongue, and dark shadows erupted from his fingers. They slithered across the sands and tangled around Leo's wrists like manacles.

Freya couldn't stand to look at his rolling skin any longer, so she pulled Cora toward the cliff where she sat the shivering elf down onto a rock. She knelt in front of Cora so the poor woman wouldn't have to look at the two men struggling to beat back the curse.

"Look at me," she said, snapping her fingers in front of Cora's face. "Don't look at them."

"But he's in pain." Another scream echoed across the sands, and the Summer Lady flinched. "I should do something, shouldn't I? I was the one who hurt him."

"No, Cora. Listen to me. That is not your fault. You know what the curse is, and you've seen the effects on yourself as well as him. His pain has nothing to do with you and everything to do with the forest taking its price." She smoothed her hand down Cora's cheek and pinched her chin. "You look at me, and not them. Eldridge is a very powerful fae. If anyone can fix Leo, it's him."

"I don't know if he can." Cora's eyes were wide and brimming with sparkling tears. "What if we're too late? What if no one can save him?"

That was Freya's fear as well, but she would not entertain the thought. Not now when she knew how much pain Leo was in. The forest needed to give them a chance, and all it had done was try to stop them at every corner.

But nothing could ever be easy in the faerie courts, could it?

Taking a deep breath, she patted her hands on both Cora's knees and pushed herself back up. "I'll go check on them. You stay here and please, whatever you do, don't look."

The last thing Freya wanted was for this memory to be burned into Cora's mind for the rest of her days. She could never look at Leo again in the same way.

At least, if he survived.

She crossed the sands back to the two men. Long lines had split open down Leo's spine, like someone was whipping him. She sucked in a breath through her teeth and knelt beside them.

If she could have put her hand on him without causing even more pain, Freya would have. Clearly Leo needed someone in this moment. His handsome face was unrecognizable and twisted. She wanted to help heal him, but how?

"What's happening?" she asked. "What do we do?"

"Nothing." Eldridge lowered his hands and sighed. "We're too late. The forest is taking its price and nothing will stop it now that it's started."

No, that couldn't be right. They'd worked too hard and now the forest would what? Ruin this moment? They were closer now than they had ever been!

"We aren't too late. I refuse to accept that." Freya reached out then, taking the chance to hurt Leo and putting her hand on his shoulder. "You must know a way that can stop this. I know you think you deserve this, Leo, but how can we stop this?"

He met her gaze, and she saw all the blood vessels in his eyes had popped. Those beautiful green eyes were now ringed with red blood.

"We were too... late." He stuttered over the words, each one ground through his teeth as he fought to speak.

Freya pursed her lips and patted his shoulder. "You're wrong. I know you're wrong, and you're thinking that you deserve this. As your friend, I will not let you make this mistake. So you tell us how to fix this."

Soft footsteps approached them through the sands. Cora stood beside them, and a slight wind ruffled the curls that had escaped her carefully laid braids. "I think I might know how to help him, but none of you are going to like it."

Of course. Why hadn't Freya thought of asking Cora first? This was the woman who was meant to be the Summer Lady. And though she had been absent from the court for a very long time, all the secrets Leo wanted to hide were surely known by this lovely lady.

Freya whipped around, sand blasting from her movements and dirtying the hem of her dress. "Tell us. You know we'll do whatever it takes."

But a frown marred Cora's face. "The forest wants to take him back. It's disappointed that it has taken him this long when it already gave us all the opportunities we needed."

"Yes, we understand that part."

"The only thing I can think of that might stop this is bringing him to the forest." Cora wrung her hands and stared out to the sea. "But that would take a very long time to get back to the mainland. And worse, I don't think he'd make the journey."

Freya snapped her fingers. "But there's a portal that goes back to the mainland. That's what I came through."

"It only goes in one direction. The portal was meant to give the Summer Lord a way to come and visit me whenever he came to his senses." Cora's expression saddened, and she curled her shoulders inward. "I don't think he'll make the trip, Freya. The forest is plaguing him. All that movement underneath his skin? It's turning his blood to roots. Soon, he will attach himself to the nearest tree. Just like all those other faeries who ended up stuck in the forest."

Freya remembered them. How could she ever forget?

Those dead beings in the roots of the trees had reached for her every time she walked by them. And though she'd thought they were being punished by the trees, she wondered if they were the disappointments. The cast offs that the forest had thought might entertain, but then decided weren't worthy of so much attention.

She licked her lips and whispered, "The trees keep what they love, even after they are no longer useful."

Leo flung out his hand and latched onto Freya. His wide, bloodshot eyes tried to convey some fear that she didn't need him to voice. He didn't want to go to the forest. Leo feared staying there for the rest of time, alive but not. Dead, but not.

If he was going to suffer, then he wanted to be here. Out in the open where the forest couldn't reach him other than to kill him. Maybe that was the merciful thing to do. Maybe Freya should let him fall onto his stomach, roll him over, and then watch as a small grove of trees grew from his body.

She looked over to Eldridge and saw tears in the Goblin King's eyes. Even he didn't think they could save the Summer Lord. She knew that guilt would gnaw and bite. Though their relationship had dimmed in recent years, Leo was still important to Eldridge.

Faerie realms, he was important to Freya too. She'd struck up a friendship with this ridiculous, foolish man who would sacrifice so much because he feared the unknown.

Freya covered Leo's hand in her own, squeezing his fingers as they spasmed with yet another spike that rocked through his entire body. "You want me to let you die," she whispered. "You are fine with sinking into the sands and disappearing from this world."

Though his features were strained, Leo nodded.

She looked up at Cora. The Summer Lady pressed a hand to her mouth and barely caught a sob. She didn't need Cora to say anything to know what was going through the woman's head.

Cora was so sad that she had only had enough time to remember that she did love him. That the feeling in her chest wasn't something that she'd imagined or forced herself to feel, so she didn't forget what love was. Their lives were intertwined and now someone wanted to rip them apart again.

Freya should step away. She should let the Summer Lady have a few moments with the man she loved, alone with only the sea and the stars to share in their sadness.

But she couldn't do it.

Unlike the faeries with her, Freya wouldn't give up.

"No," she growled. "I won't let you die, Leo."

She planted her hands in the sand and poured all her rage into the white sand beach. She let the ancient being deep in the earth feed upon her emotions. It ripped from her lungs anger, rage, sadness, and fear. It pulled all emotion until she was little more than a husk. And when she had satisfied the gluttonous creature that had named itself "ocean", Freya told it to slow down time.

A mortal telling the sea to help them was a ridiculous request. Even Freya knew that. But she didn't have enough magic to do it herself.

The forest had taught her to ask. The very fabric of the world wanted to help if only the person in need knew how to ask. So that's what Freya did. She made the sea listen to her, and she begged it to give these lovers a chance. All of her concentration and energy went into this singular task that might have taken all but a heartbeat, yet felt like a lifetime of battling with her will alone.

The argument was always the same. That the Summer Lord and Lady took too long.

What were a few more heartbeats? A few more days when the sea was inevitable? The oceans would never die in this place. It would exist long past the ages of fae and man. The waves would see new people take over the earth. The water would still kiss the sand even when time itself had ended.

A few days.

A few weeks.

Such bartering tools were not waiting for the ocean. It was a small rest and when it finally woke, the Summer Lord and Lady would be ready to take their thrones and lead this court into a prosperous age.

The sea didn't agree with her. But the more she argued, the more it softened. Like dripping water on a stone over centuries of time.

It refused to lessen Leo's suffering, but it agreed to slow time. Just enough for them to get to the mainland, and then she could argue with the forest.

Freya opened her eyes again and could hear a soft chuckle in her mind. The conversation with the sea had been entirely in her head. There were no words, only emotions and an argument that played out as though she were watching someone else speak.

This time, the ocean finally said words. "I will enjoy hearing about your argument with the forest," it said. "You're a persuasive little thing for a mortal."

Whispering under her breath, Freya replied, "My father was a changeling. I know the ways of the fae."

"You do." The sea chuckled again. "But not because of your father. You've taken on many of the Goblin King's qualities, but you have more hope than he does. It is a good thing, Freya of Woolwich, Queen Killer, and Lover of the Goblin King. Welcome to the faerie realms."

She blinked and the presence of the ocean was gone. Time had slowed, just as the sea had promised. The waves moved at a snail's pace now, and that would give them the chance they needed.

"Come on," she said, darting up from the sands. "Eldridge, pick him up. We don't have long."

The Goblin King stared up at her with wide, horrified eyes. "What did you do?"

"I begged for time," she muttered. "And we have little of it. Let's go."

CHAPTER 26

Eldridge hauled Leo to his feet, though the Summer Lord groaned like the hounds of hell gnawed on his bones. And perhaps that's what it felt like. Freya didn't have time to pity him.

She raced ahead of them with Cora on her heels. Freya tossed words into the wind and hoped the other woman would hear them. "We need a boat. A fast one that will fly through the waves."

"I have a better one than he does." Cora's brows were drawn down in concentration. "The Summer Lady is always gifted a boat that has wings across the waters. The ocean will let us use that one."

Freya wasn't so confident. She had just spent a lifetime arguing with the sea, and maybe the great being would rather not help them any more.

With a flourish, Cora raced into the waves and raised her arms above her head. Sparkling gold cascaded from her fingertips and sank into the slow swells. The glitter spread over the surface of the water, reaching out into the sea where it disappeared into the depths.

Long heartbeats passed and Freya held her breath. Please let the sea help them this one last time. All she wanted was the chance to get Leo into the forest. The chance to get her father back.

A longship rose from the depths of the ocean. Its hull was solid gold, and though it shouldn't float, it did. The sides were carved with swans, their wings outstretched and their necks creating a bannister on the edges. This was a beautiful craft that Freya could only hope would get them to the mainland faster.

Cora looked over her shoulder with a grin. "Will this do?"

The sparkling lights of her magic still surrounded the boat. Freya thought the entire thing looked like it had emerged from a dream. All she could stutter was, "Yes. That will do."

They still needed to load Leo onto the boat and then get to the mainland, however. And though she'd argued well, and the sea was happy to give them the time they needed, she didn't think that included stopping the sea monsters from their hunt.

Nothing was ever that easy in the faerie realms. Never.

Freya turned and watched as Eldridge dragged Leo down the beach. The Summer Lord was slowing with every step. When he reached their side, she could see moss had grown on his shoulders and reached for his neck.

"Not yet," she snarled. Freya plucked it from his skin and tossed the moss into the sea. "I still have words to say to you, forest. I'm coming and you will not take him before we meet again."

Eldridge lifted his brow as she met his gaze.

"What?" Freya asked.

"You're impressive, that's all. I wasn't aware you were so... so..." He shrugged. "Feral."

She pondered the word, rolling it over in her mind before nodding sharply. "I like it. Feral suits me well."

"Indeed."

The burning edge of his gaze was one of pure passion. Though they didn't have time to entertain such thoughts, Freya was pleased to see she could still tempt him even when the world was falling down around their ears.

Eldridge's lips spread in a wide smile. "Let's get him in the boat, and then we'll argue with the forest as you seem so dead set that we need to do."

"We do," she grumbled, though she wasn't looking forward to it.

It took all three of them to load Leo into the boat. He couldn't help at all. His arms flopped at his sides and his legs refused to hold his weight. Freya grunted, shoved his legs over the edge and winced when he struck the bottom of the metal boat hard.

"Step two, complete," she muttered.

Eldridge helped her get into the boat. Cora leapt in gracefully and with no assistance. All the damn fae moved like water flowing through the world, while Freya was the awkward mortal that couldn't manage without their help. Eldridge vaulted over the edge and took a seat at the helm.

"So," he said, clearing his throat. "We're off. Just how many monsters are going to try to stop us this time?"

Hopefully none. Although Freya knew that was wishful thinking. There were going to be a thousand monsters rising out of the depths with gnashing teeth, ready to tear this boat apart if they were given the chance. The sea wouldn't make it that easy for them.

Cora leaned over the side of the boat and stuck her hand in the water. Her brows furrowed in concentration before she leaned back and flicked water from her fingers with the grace of a dancer. "Many. I didn't even know some of them existed. The sea will make this a battle and I fear we will need your magic, Eldridge. Otherwise, this ship will sink."

Right. This was Freya's nightmare.

Loud barking echoed across the sands, and Freya turned at the last second to see a black and white body dashing toward them. "Don't you leave without me! Don't even think about it!"

Arrow darted toward the water and leaped. His body arched gracefully, but then landed in a smacking belly-flop that looked horribly painful. Still, he swam through the water to the side of the boat where he scrabbled with his claws to get in.

She should have known he wouldn't let them leave without him. Freya reached into the water and scooped him into the boat. "This isn't going to be an easy journey, my friend. We're about to battle sea monsters and we can't have you getting sick."

"I'm stronger than I look," he snarled, although he already

appeared to be woozy. "I will muster my strength for this. My place is with you."

Eldridge forced Freya to sit at the back of the boat. "You'll have to steer, Freya. I need to be at the bow so I can use whatever magic might stop them. Arrow, you sit with Freya and let nothing touch her."

The goblin dog straightened with pride. He puffed out his chest and took a very prominent seat directly in front of Freya. His legs were spread wide, ready to battle whenever the time came.

She didn't think he'd do much against the sea monsters. They would probably look at him and chuckle in the way only sea creatures could. Then they would chomp him in half and dive for Freya next. But it's still nice to know she had someone who would at least try to save her.

Eldridge gave her a sharp nod, and they were ready to fly across the waves. Freya hoped the sea monsters were also slowed by time, but that wasn't likely. The sea had given them one boon. It wouldn't give them another.

She steered them toward the mainland and into the storm clouds overhead. Thunder rumbled, but no rain fell on them. Almost as though the sea wanted them to see they were being hunted. And they were.

The waves were taller than ten feet high. The white foam at their crests bubbled like a witch's cauldron. Freya took them over the first dark swell and lightning struck nearby. The flashing light blinded her for a moment. When she opened her eyes again, the entire sea had come alive with sharp teeth.

A shark swam directly next to them and hit the boat with its tail. They rocked dangerously to the side. Freya made the mistake of staring into the water and made eye contact with a beast that looked like a squid. But its eyes were larger than her head, and its tentacles were tipped with sharp barbs.

"Freya!" Eldridge shouted. "Turn the boat!"

She threw her weight in the opposite direction and turned the rudder with a wild jerk. They narrowly missed a giant whale with teeth as sharp as a shark. It blew air from the top of its head and sharp shards of ice rained down from above.

Eldridge threw his arm around the swan figurehead, holding on for dear life as he spun his first spell. Shadows gathered around him, yanked from the very sea itself before he unleashed his magic. Each of the shadows took on a life of its own. They sank into the waves and darted toward creatures where they wrapped around each one like chains.

For a brief moment, the sea was quelled.

Then they heard a deep rumble. A scream that echoed and something massive rose from the deep. Freya swallowed hard and stared wide eyed at the giant wave that rolled toward them. Lightning flashed again. The entire wave illuminated, revealing the silhouette of tentacles as large as a ship, each one reaching for their tiny boat.

"Turn!" Eldridge shouted. "Freya, turn!"

Where was she supposed to go? There was no where for the boat to turn. Those tentacles were everywhere. The beast was larger than anything she'd seen before. Larger than a city.

She couldn't turn the boat because then they would head right into the mouth of the beast. Craning her neck to look behind them, she stared in horror at the rest of the creature's body that had risen from the waves.

It was a monster from the ancient stories. A creature made of nightmares and sea barnacles. The mouth opened wide, jaws filled with a hundred rows of teeth. She didn't know where its eyes were, or if it even had eyes. But the creature would not stop until they were in its belly.

"Freya!" Eldridge shouted again.

What did he want her to do? If they hit those tentacles, then the creature would devour them whole. It would drag them toward its mouth, and then they would never get out of its clutches.

Unless she slipped between the tentacles. And the only way to do that was to sneak up that wave and be quick.

Their boat was the fastest in the Summer Court. She narrowed her eyes and drew down her brows in concentration. Perhaps it was her imagination, but it seemed like the golden swans did the same. "Everyone hang on!" she shouted.

Cora dove for the bottom of the boat and wrapped herself around

Leo. Eldridge sat down hard and hung onto the sides, though he glared at her for taking such a risk. She already knew he was going to shout at her.

And why shouldn't he? She was jeopardizing all of their lives in doing this.

Freya directed the boat at the small gap where it seemed like the creature was missing a tentacle. She thought maybe she could sneak through. Maybe.

It was a ten percent chance they'd make it, but that was more than what would happen if she turned around.

Every muscle in Freya's body locked up tight, and she guided the boat up the wave. "Slowly," she muttered. "Take your time until the last second. Surprise the beast."

Arrow pressed his face against her knee and Freya touched her hand to his head. Grinding her teeth, she shot the boat diagonally across the wave. It moved with all the speed of a flying beast, and then the tentacles came out of the water.

Great, meaty appendages swung over their head. As if the creature was trying to terrify them into hesitating. But Freya refused to let it scare her, not when she had conquered so many beasts here in the faerie realms. No sea creature was worse than what she'd faced thus far.

There was the gap. The smallest gap and she couldn't move until the right moment. She blew out the breath she'd been holding slowly, letting it leak out between her lips so all the sound in the world disappeared other than the next great inhalation she sucked into her lungs.

"Now," she whispered.

The boat careened up, up, up the wave and the beast let out a scream that rocked the slow moving crests. She set her grip hard on the handle that guided the ship and closed her eyes.

Perhaps it made her a coward to not see what happened. But in that blissful moment of darkness, Freya watched all the memories she loved play behind her eyes.

Death had come for her many times, and Freya had slipped away from its cold clutches every single encounter. If a giant sea monster was what finally claimed her, then so be it. She would gladly accept that heroic death.

But that death did not come.

They darted between the tentacles and slid out into a calm sea. The storm disappeared behind them with the call of the ancient beast as it sank back into the depths.

The boat moved with grace and calm ease. No more waves rocked the gull. They skidded across a mirror-like surface of water so pure that she could see the bottom. Azure light glimmered in the depths, and only kind creatures watched them as they passed.

The time for death had ended. Freya took a deep breath of salty, warm air. They had made it.

None of them said a single word until the boat hit the shore of the mainland. The soft crunching of seashells seemed to break the spell of silence they all had upheld.

Arrow was the first to speak. He snuffled loudly and then declared with confidence, "I will never step foot on another boat in my life."

A chuckle burst from her lips and then once it had been released, she couldn't stop laughing. The other two faeries joined her. Their laughter rose into the air, and all the last remnants of tension and fear drained from Freya's body.

"You know," she said, still laughing with tears streaming down her cheeks, "I don't think I want to get on another ship any time soon."

"Neither do I," Eldridge replied. He leaned down and picked up Leo's limp body, throwing him over his shoulder. "Now, why don't we go convince a forest that this lump of flesh is worthy of being the Summer Lord?"

Of course, they still had work to do. Freya catapulted her body from the ship and splashed onto the sandy beach. "I think that's a grand idea. It's been a while since I've shouted at an ancient being."

CHAPTER 27

Their travels would have been easier if there was a portal, but Freya didn't need a portal. She knew where the forest was now. If it hadn't wanted to be easily found, then it shouldn't have brought her within its glen so many times. Freya could get there with her eyes closed.

"This way," she said.

They all ran toward the small hole in the cliff where she knew there was a gap. They might all be able to fit, although it would be difficult with Leo. She pointed and made a small, disappointed sound.

"That's how I got there last time. But with Leo being like he is..." She didn't see him waking anytime soon, nor capable of walking on his own.

Eldridge grunted. "I can get him through. If this is the only way, then that's the way we'll go. Lead, Freya. I will follow you."

To the ends of the earth. She knew that was the end of that statement. He'd follow her through whatever adventure she led him on because he knew she wouldn't lead him wrong. No matter what feat, the Goblin King had always known she would keep him safe.

And she knew he would give his life for her if that was what the journey needed. Though she'd never let him.

Freya nodded. "Come with me, then. Let's go to the trees."

It was a lot harder to squeeze through the tunnel of rock this time. Every breath pressed her chest against the stone. And when she looked back, it appeared to change and warp for each person. It was trying to make everyone feel claustrophobic. Such a deliberate magic could only be the trees trying to slow them down.

But Freya would not be slowed.

She moved through the crag with purpose and determination running through her veins. No one would stop her. She would continue without question because this was the right thing to do. Even if the trees disagreed.

Freya popped out on the other side of the stone with a wet sound, as though she were birthed into the forest. Freya fell onto her hands and knees, already bowing to the trees without realizing what she was doing.

She would have bowed on her own, if they'd given her the chance. But they didn't.

The forest had expelled them right in front of the ancient oak that stretched its roots deep into the ground. The dead man looked at her with a maniacal grin on his face. "So, Freya of Woolwich, you're determined to become a hero once again."

"Of course I am," she hissed. "Why would you rush him like this? Even you could see that love was blooming between them again, and instead, all you want to do is hurt them. This was not our deal."

"We never had a deal. You were supposed to help me, and then I would help you." The dead man yawned. "I grow weary of your games of matchmaking and love. I wanted it to go faster, and since it didn't, I'm ending this game."

Cora wiggled out from between the stones and then dropped into a low bow. Freya wasn't even sure the other woman had looked around herself, she'd just fallen into a bow knowing that the trees would be watching. Arrow came next, his pointed nose lowered to the ground while holding his ears flat against his skull.

How ridiculous. This forest was trying to renege on their deal, and that made it unworthy of anyone's honor.

The dead man's eyes flicked to Cora, then back to Freya as though the faerie wasn't all that impressive. "I'm disappointed in you, Freya. I thought you would understand our need to see something happen quickly. Instead, you're arguing that we need to have patience. To show virtue where there never has been."

Freya scoffed. "Virtue? Patience? You're an ancient being. A lifetime of a mortal is merely a breath for you. I'm not asking for patience. I'm asking you to wait a few heartbeats so they can fall back in love again and give you what you want."

A single eyebrow rose and an emerald beetle crawled out of the man's mouth. "I'm unimpressed. Your fervor for the fae is unfounded. Give up."

Eldridge slid out behind them and yanked Leo's limp body through the portal. They both flopped onto the mossy ground, too hard. Eldridge winced but crawled to her side while still dramatically holding himself in a low bow. "Great tree of the ancients. It's an honor to see you again."

"Goblin King." Tree branches over their head shook and leaves rained down on their shoulders. "The pleasure is all mine. But, as I was telling your mortal lover, you are far too late."

They couldn't be. Freya wouldn't allow that to be the truth, because that meant her father was trapped here.

She had to save him. No other ending would satisfy her.

She straightened her shoulders and glared at the dead man. "You keep saying that we're too late, but I know that's a lie. We are here right when we were supposed to be. And I'm not going to take no for an answer, so you'd best change your words."

"Or what?" The dead man sat up, pushing his arms into the mossy bed and tilting his head to the side. Obviously the tree was intrigued.

Good. Let the tree be curious. Freya was going to sit here until the sun set on the world, if that's how long it took. "Give them a chance. That's all any of us are asking for. And all you asked for. You want them to be together, because you told me that was what you wanted. What changed?"

"Why are you fighting so hard?" He lifted a fist and opened it to reveal a tiny, glowing lightning bug. "Is it only for your father, or for some other reason?"

She wanted to argue that of course she wanted to help the Summer Court. At no point in this journey had her reasons been entirely selfish. Even when she saved her sister, it hadn't been just for her. And yet, she couldn't look away from the glowing light.

The light rose into the air and glittered like a mini sun that the tree had conjured up. She took a shambling step forward, lifting her arms with her fingers outstretched. Like she could somehow hold the light.

And she wanted to. What would it feel like to hold a tiny faerie in her hands? Would it make her like them? Ethereal and beautiful?

"Stop it!" Cora's voice cut through the magic of the orb. "Stop teasing her! We aren't monsters. We don't do that anymore."

Faintly, Freya heard the tree respond. "You think wisps no longer lead mortals to their doom? That kelpies no longer drown poor men who should never have tried to tame a beast? Do sirens no longer sing ships into rocks so their sailors won't fill the ocean with blood? Cora. You've been on that isle for too long."

The light was still so pretty. Freya's entire face and body were lax, comfortable finally and at ease. She couldn't remember the last time she'd been so relaxed. All her life she'd been tense, angry, looking for something that would make her feel strong when she wasn't. The orb pulsed and her attention focused on the light.

"You will not take her from me," a snarling voice echoed through the clearing and, in a blink, the light went out.

Dark shadows wrapped around it, holding on for dear life even as spears of brilliance broke through the magic. But the spell was broken at that moment. Freya spun away from the orb, shivering in the suddenly frigid air. Why was she so cold?

Blinking through the confusion, her vision cleared, and she saw Eldridge with his hands outstretched. His fingers had turned to black claws as he struggled to contain the ancient magic of a being far older than him. His expression twisted with rage and he shouted again, "To your father, Freya!"

She didn't need to be told twice. Freya dove for the prison of roots and branches. Even though it was made of the tree, she didn't think the tree itself could move. It relied on the dead things to be its voice and its armor.

Her father emerged from the shadows and caught her to his chest. "My girl," he whispered. "What have you done?"

All the faeries in the clearing gathered together. Eldridge still held his hands in front of him, muttering words that would turn into a spell at some point. Arrow stood on his back legs, ears still flat against his skull and his teeth bared, ready to bite. Cora stood with Leo's arm wrapped around her shoulder, and surprisingly the Summer Lord woke. Together, they weren't exactly the most intimidating of groups, but they were all together. Standing at the ready to take on a tree that she should have stopped.

Freya pressed her palms against her father's heart and swallowed hard. "I don't know. I thought bringing the family together might help them talk about their differences. It would force them to listen to each other."

"Or it will bring about the end of the Summer Court."

They looked at each other. Two mortals stuck in the quarrel between faeries and Freya realized she should have asked her father's opinion about all of this. He was a changeling. He'd been here far longer than she had, and he knew the fae like they were his own family.

"Did I make a mistake?" she whispered, eyes wide as she stared up at her father.

She felt like a little girl again. Freya needed her father to tell her everything was going to be alright. That she hadn't made that big of a mistake, and look, he'd fix it for her. Just like he used to do when she was a babe, and could still fit on his hip.

But she was an adult now, and running to her father to fix her mistakes wasn't an option.

"I don't know," he replied. "I suppose we should watch and see. But let's not look at any of those glowing lights anymore."

She had no intention of doing that again. The magic still lingered in her head, like the tree still had some control over her. Freya shuddered and stepped out of her father's embrace. She wrapped her hands around the bars made of roots and watched as her dearest friends fought an ancient power without her.

"You will take none of them," Eldridge called out. "You cannot force the Summer Lord to leave the throne. It was his by right."

"I gave it to him," the dead man snarled. "And if I want to take it away, then I will."

To her horror, the man shifted. He reached his arm underneath him and shoved with a bony movement that should have been impossible. The corpse lifted itself out of its permanent resting place and suddenly, it was a shambling, rotting mess of a person that stepped toward the group of faeries.

The dead could walk in this forest of nightmares. And they did.

Hundreds of bodies that had once been nestled in the roots of the trees stood. They all stretched out their arms for the faeries, muttering words that sounded similar to the language Eldridge used. A spell? What kind of spell could hundreds of elves cast at the same time? Considering they were using the power of the trees, Freya could only guess that such magic would be terrifying and powerful.

The Summer Lord shook his head, casting off the curse that pained him. Or perhaps convincing himself that pain would not keep him out of this battle. Either way, he untangled himself from Cora's arms and took a shaky step forward.

"Stop," he called out, holding his hands out as if he alone could hold back the horde of dead. "It's me you want. I know that. You do as well. Take me and let the others leave."

The dead man who had been in the base of the biggest tree laughed. He still stood behind the others, either too rotten to walk or more interested in watching what was about to happen. "They came here of their own free will because they wanted to save you, Leo. I will not let them go! You did this and you will be placed in the roots of a tree where you can watch them slowly rot. I'll make sure you have a good view."

She couldn't just stand here and let them argue like this. Shouting from the relative safety of her prison, Freya pleaded, "You didn't give him enough time! This isn't about punishing him. This is about proving you were right!"

With a flippant gesture over his shoulder, the dead man ignored what she said.

Freya knew she was correct. The tree didn't want to be wrong, and in this instance, it was just as bad as the Summer Lord had been.

Leo took a step forward again, closer to the rotting corpses. "These are my friends and the woman I love. I will willingly give myself up to know that they are safe and alive after this is all said and done. I won't let you take them from me."

"You *will* all be together."

"That's not good enough." Leo took another step, so close that one lunge would have him in the clutches of the dead. "You wanted me, and now you have me. This is my deal, or I will fight with every last bit of my magic until I die. And then you won't get what you want after all."

All the dead seemed to hesitate. They looked over their shoulders at the larger tree, who was suddenly very upset. The man's face twisted in denial. "No. You can't do that. You won't."

"I will," Leo corrected. "If I don't have them, or if Cora is to suffer this fate as well, then this isn't a life worth living. I'm happy to take myself out of this game you so dearly love to play."

The dead man growled, but he looked to branches overhead and sighed. "Fine, then. If that's the deal you want, then that's the deal you shall get."

He snapped his fingers, and the dead moved to take Leo to his new prison. Freya couldn't watch the man she thought of as a friend suffer that fate. He'd given himself up for all of them. If that didn't prove he'd changed, then she didn't know what would.

A scream blasted and Freya turned in time to see Cora throw herself in front of Leo. She held her arms outstretched, face turned away from the dead.

Everything in the clearing stopped. Time held still. Even the motes of dust stopped spinning in the air.

Freya held her breath with everything else in the clearing. She stared at the lovely Cora, who intended to sacrifice her own life for the man she loved. Just as Leo had tried to do for her.

A great sigh echoed from the tree. And suddenly all the dead turned and shambled back to their places in the trees.

What was happening?

The dead man heaved another sigh and inclined his head. "Summer

Lady, you were the one I was waiting for the longest. I see you've made up your mind."

"I will not let him die, if that's what you're asking." Cora straightened her shoulders and looked every inch like a lady of this court. "He doesn't deserve it."

"Neither do you." The dead man turned and staggered back to his own tree, where he laid down like the ancient being he was. "That's all we wanted. To know for certain that you and the Summer Lord were truthful with each other. A party on a beach means nothing. But being willing to give up your life for each other? That's a good sign."

Angry visions flashed in front of Freya's eyes. She wanted to take an axe to that ancient tree and force it to feel the same fear she and her companions had shared. This cruelty was uncalled for. Entirely.

The roots of the tree lifted and freed her and her father. They both took each other's hands and approached the waiting faeries.

Arrow walked over to her side and held out a paw. "Sir. I'm afraid I don't know what to call you."

Her father smiled and took the dog's offered paw. "Henry. You can call me Henry."

Arrow nodded. "Well then, Henry. Why don't we get you out of this prison and back into the sun?"

CHAPTER 28

They didn't leave for another week, even though Freya wanted her father home as soon as possible. But Eldridge reminded her that they needed to stay and help. Two court leaders needed guidance, and they were the only ones who could provide that direction.

Or, well, Eldridge was the only one who could provide that. And no one else could return home without him. Apparently.

Freya packed her last item into the trunk and sat down hard on it. The clothing within might be a little wrinkled when they got home, but she was returning with so much of it. The elves had made certain she had all the beautiful dresses she needed for giving them back their Summer Lady.

Not that Freya had wanted any of it. She'd go right back to wearing pants when they returned to the Goblin Court, though she appreciated their candor. At least they were kind enough to see what she'd done for their court.

The door to their room opened and Eldridge strode in. He held a pile of papers in his hands, then set them on her vanity with a heavy thud. "These all need to go with us, apparently. Is there room in your trunk?"

She looked underneath her, then back to him. "If I stand up, the trunk will open on its own. I can't latch it."

"They gave you that much, did they?" He shook his head with a wry grin. "Elves."

"They're very kind," she corrected, but then smiled as well. "But maybe a little overzealous in their gratitude with what we did. I don't think I need any of these dresses. They wouldn't take no for an answer."

"Rarely does any elf even know the word no." He glared at the papers and then shrugged. "They'll stay here, then. I don't need them, but Leo insisted I take them and look through all his accounts. Apparently he's not very confident as a capable leader."

"That's why he has Cora. I think she'll round out his weaknesses rather well." She hoped, at least. The both of them had a lot to learn about ruling an entire court.

But if Eldridge could do it with grace and poise, then so could the new leaders of the Summer Court.

She sighed and stood up, holding out her hands in case the lid to her trunk popped open again. The last time it had blasted open like something within had exploded. This time, thankfully, it stayed down.

"If we're lucky," she muttered, "We can escape before the clothing attacks again."

"Again?" Eldridge gave her a bewildered look.

"Yes, again. It's already tried to take over the room like it was spreading. I don't believe this is the same amount of clothing the elves gave me, and such a curse could be quite dangerous." She hoped her joke was landing, but of course, the Goblin King took everything rather seriously.

With a burst of movement, she grabbed his hand and ran from the room. He sprinted with her, concerned at first, but then laughing as they raced down the stairwell covered in flowers and sunlight. Freya wanted to sneak a quiet moment before they went back to the real world where they both had a lot of responsibilities.

For now, the sun was shining, and the beach waited for them.

She slowed down when they exited the castle, breathless with laughter. "I'm sorry, Eldridge. I didn't mean to scare you. I thought maybe we could enjoy a little sunlight before we left."

"How strange, I had the same thought." He placed her hand on his forearm and guided her down a stairwell to the garden that led to the beaches. "I believe this is the last task we have before we return to our actual lives."

"I suppose so." She tilted her head back and let the sun play over her features, eyes closed with the confidence that Eldridge would guide her around any obstacles. "Have you seen my father today?"

"I have." His arm shifted in her grip as he guided her around a fallen log in their path. "He's in good spirits, although a little nervous to see your mother."

"If I remember right, they had a love that burned hotter than the sun. I don't think he'll have any issues when he sees her again." She opened her eyes and blinked at the bright light. "Although, she might slap him the first time she sees him. She's quick to anger, but at least she'll be nice after that. He made her run around the entire faerie realm to save him, after all."

"Sounds familiar." He walked down a few stairs and paused at the bottom, just before the longer stairwell that led to the beach. "Arrow has taken good care of introducing your father to this realm again. He said it was the least he could do for you, so you don't have to worry about your father any longer."

Freya sighed. "I don't know what I'll do next. First, I was worried about Esther, then mother, then father. Who will I worry about now?"

The sunlight played in the dark strands of his hair. He looked so handsome standing a few steps down from her, with his finely pressed dark suit and silver skin that the sun had burnished. Even his eyes seemed a little brighter. They twinkled with lights that never failed to capture her attention.

He reached out and tucked a strand of hair behind her ear. "You could worry about yourself for a while. After all, you've saved everyone you love."

Ah yes, she had told him that she loved him. The words danced between them, as if he feared she would try to take the statement back. But of course she wouldn't.

Freya wanted to shout the words to the high heavens and let no one take them from her again. She placed her hands on his shoulders and dipped low to press a kiss to his plush lips. "I do love you, Goblin King. With all my heart and soul."

"Good," he muttered against her mouth. "Because there's something I have been trying to talk with you about since before we left the Goblin Court, but things keep distracting us."

Her stomach tied into a knot. She'd been avoiding this conversation for so long because she was so afraid it would be something that tested her love for him. What could he possibly have to say to her that was so important? She didn't want to question her choices now, not when there was so much love in her chest that beat only for him.

Damn it. She'd been having such a good afternoon.

Freya supposed she owed him this, though. If the Goblin King thought there was something so important that he needed to tell her this now, then she had to listen. That was the way of things.

"All right," she replied with a shaky smile. "What is it then?"

He looked around them and a muscle jumped in his jaw. "Not here. I don't want anyone to hear this."

Right, because that eased her fears so well. She was going to fall apart at the seams. Hadn't he just said she could worry about herself for a while? What insane quest were they to go on now?

She didn't say any of that, though. Freya allowed him to guide her down the stairs to the sandy beach. She licked her lips and went over and over in her head how she would respond to something bad. That she would always love him, no matter what the cost might be. That he didn't need to worry about her leaving him in difficult times. Their love was strong enough to last through all that.

"Freya," Eldridge said with a chuckle. "You don't have to stare at your feet. I'm not leading you to your death."

Of course she was staring at her feet. She wasn't focused on where they were going. She was bracing for the moment he'd open his mouth and let out all the things she feared. "I'll keep staring where I want, thank you."

"Yes, but if you don't look up, then you won't see what's in front of us."

"Is that so important?"

Eldridge snorted. "I think you'd like to see it, yes."

Oh god, what had he sprung on her now?

Freya looked up at the beach and her heart stopped in her chest. Someone had opened a portal on the beach, that's the only way she could describe it. A giant circle of green grass filled with butterflies had appeared in the center of the white sand. Edges of magic fluttered like sparkling dust. Rose petals decorated the entire ground and floated through the air on a breeze that danced lazily with its prize.

She stepped up onto the grass, standing in the center of this magical summoning. A blue butterfly twisted in front of her face, then landed on her offered finger. Its wings were so clear, it looked as though they were made of crystal.

"This is beautiful," she whispered. "Eldridge, did you summon this?"

She couldn't imagine why. Freya turned around when he didn't answer, searching for her sweet Goblin King who had only wanted to make her day a little better. To remind her why they loved the Summer Court before they left.

Eldridge crouched behind her on one knee. In his hand, he held a tiny box made of a seashell. He offered it to her with a smile on his face so big, she wondered how it didn't split his cheeks.

"You kept running from me," he said. "I know this might not be the right time, but I fear no time will ever be right."

She let out a little shocked sound that sounded like a sob. Tears had already built in her eyes, which she dashed away because she wanted to remember every single detail of this moment. This perfect, wonderful, surprising moment that made her heart sing.

Eldridge opened the seashell to reveal a beautiful black ring. The twisted metal curved up to hold a dark orb that reflected a thousand colors wherever the sunlight struck it.

"I love you," he said. "From the very first moment I saw you, when you walked into my life like a storm. I knew that every day without you would be dull, colorless, and soul crushing. You reminded me how beautiful life could be, if I would only be courageous enough to leap into the unknown. You reminded me what it was like to not be the best at everything. But most of all, you showed me how my heart could glow in the darkness if I let someone be my light. Freya of Woolwich, Defeater of the Goblin King, Queen Killer, and all your other well-earned titles…"

He paused for a breath and Freya saw her entire life unfold before her. A life of happiness, love, and adventure.

"Yes," she blurted.

He lifted an unimpressed brow. "Let me say it first. That's how this works."

"Oh, sorry." Freya pressed a hand to her mouth and gestured with the other for him to continue.

"My love, my life, my Freya." Eldridge's lips twisted into a sideways smile. "Will you marry your Goblin King?"

"Yes!" she shouted again, then threw herself into his arms.

Eldridge caught her, tugging her against his heart and kissing her until she saw stars. And why wouldn't she? The man she loved, the one she would now marry, was made of galaxies and magic. She intended to spend the rest of her life loving him until she couldn't any longer.

Loud cheers interrupted their kiss. Freya broke away to see all the people in the Summer Court who had made her time here so dear and so wonderful.

Arrow shouted so loudly that people in the castle heard him, "Finally!"

Laughing, Eldridge released her to hold out his hand for Leo to shake. "Did you ever think we'd both get to this point in our lives?"

Leo shook his head, but pulled Eldridge in for an embrace. "No, my friend. I thought we would hate each other until we died, and then the both of us would die alone as old men."

She turned toward Cora, who was already reaching to hug Freya tight. "Congratulations, my dear. When Eldridge asked how he should do it, I told him something like this would make any woman fall madly in love with him. I hope it wasn't too much."

"It was perfect," Freya whispered. "Thank you for all your help."

Though guilt twisted in her stomach because she'd believed the other woman to be interested in Eldridge, too. She should have known better. Cora was too kind for that. Cora wasn't competition. She was a friend.

The last person on the beach stood apart from the others, but he was the only person Freya wanted to see. She walked away from the faeries to give her father a tight hug.

He sighed into her hair, then chuckled. "He asked for my permission this morning. I told him it was a little late to be asking, but that I'd come around to the idea of my daughter being married to a faerie. Besides, he seems like a good man."

Freya couldn't believe Eldridge had even asked her father's permission. He had been planning this for a very long time. "He is a good man," she repeated. "And I love him more than anyone I've ever met before."

"Good. That's how it should be." He kissed the top of her head, then pushed her away. "Go to your Goblin King, daughter of mine."

She didn't have to be told twice. Freya tucked herself underneath Eldridge's arm and listened to the faeries joke with each other. But it didn't take long for Eldridge to turn his attention only to her.

He kissed her again and whispered against her lips, "My Queen, let's go home."

CHAPTER 29

"You're getting married?" Esther's shriek echoed through the halls.

The ear piercing sound crossed Freya's eyes, but she nodded before wiggling a finger in her ear. "Yes, I am getting married."

"Why didn't I hear about this sooner?" Esther shouted again.

"Because we just got home. My god, what have you been doing since we've been away?" She tried to change the subject so her sister couldn't ask even more ridiculous questions. She hadn't even seen their father get out of the carriage yet. And then what sound would she make?

Apparently another scream that bloodied Freya's ears. She walked away from her sister's meltdown as Esther saw their father. Of course it was difficult for Esther to see him. Freya had cried when she'd seen their dad as well.

But, as callous as it might seem, she wasn't as interested in her sister's reaction.

Her mother walked down the steps of the castle in a pale yellow gown that made her hair seem like golden silk. She floated down the steps, approaching her husband that she'd braved the faerie realms to find.

Her mother hadn't even realized that Henry had been watching over her. While her father had spent what felt like two hundred years watching over his wife, she hadn't realized a single day had passed.

Henry broke away from his daughter and stepped toward his wife as though she were a dream. "Is it really you?" he asked.

"I'm awake, Henry." Her voice caught on a sob. "I'm really awake."

Their hands shook as they reached for each other, and Freya had to look away when they embraced. There was clearly too much to be said between them, but neither of them was interested in speaking. They just wanted to hold each other after so long away from their loved one's arms.

The picture they painted on the steps to the goblin castle filled her heart with hope for the future. She could see herself in a similar situation as them, finally having her entire family together and maybe adding more.

If only she could paint this moment. To forever have it saved in some hallway where she could look at it when she was sad. To help ease whatever torment she might face later on.

Eldridge hooked an arm over her shoulders and tugged her tight into his arms. "How does it feel?"

"How does what feel?" She looked up at him and grinned, knowing exactly what he was talking about.

"To have your family all back together again," he replied, giving her a little shake. "Plus one, of course. We can't forget the most important person in your new family, after all."

"Lux?"

Freya burst out laughing as Eldridge swept her off the ground. He lifted her up toward the lingering sunlight and wiggled his fingers on her ribs. "I can take it back, you know!"

"Take what back? Spending the rest of your life with me?" She kicked her legs, forcing him to put her on the ground. "Oh no, Goblin King. You can't take that back. You're stuck with me until the day I die."

"Oh, I think that would be the perfect ending to this story. A love that will last for a thousand lifetimes." He kissed her, then smiled. "I could get used to living like this. You, me, your family."

A cold nose pressed against her palm. "And Arrow. Obviously."

She snorted as her goblin companion referred to himself in the third person. "Yes, and Arrow. Obviously."

Freya started toward the stairwell with her heart filled with light for the first time in ages. When had she last been so happy? Certainly not when she'd had so many responsibilities. Finally, she could relax and rest in her newfound life.

But the faerie realm had another plan for her.

The faint popping sound of magic came before she smelled it. Blood. The metallic scent filled her lungs, and she knew that her time in adventure wasn't over yet. She had too much to lose this time, though, and her stomach turned knowing she had a choice to make.

She could walk into the castle, away from all this, or she could turn around and face whatever had come for her now.

Freya had never been selfish. She wouldn't start now.

She turned with Eldridge and cast her eyes on the bloody scene. The stairs they had just climbed were covered in blood, like a red carpet had been rolled down them. And at the very bottom was a familiar, limp figure.

"Thief," she gasped before racing down the steps.

Freya nearly tripped twice before she landed onto her knees beside the Autumn Thief. Gently, she turned the woman over onto her back. Something had snapped one of her antlers off her head and the other was missing its tines. Blood coated her chin and throat, spilling from her mouth where a few teeth were missing.

"What happened?" Freya asked, hovering her hands over the Autumn Thief's body but unsure if she should touch the wounds.

"Death," the Autumn Thief gurgled. "Death came to the Autumn Court."

OF FAIRYTALES AND MAGIC

CHAPTER 1

The rattling sound of death erupted from the Autumn Thief's lungs. She'd made that sound for days now, and Freya didn't know how to help or stop the sound. Instead, she merely sat beside the four-poster bed, holding her dear friend's hand. She thought of praying, but that didn't feel right. Would praying even work for one of the fae?

Freya didn't know what else to do. The faeries were working around the clock, trying to find some way to save this important court leader.

This important friend.

So far, no one had found anything useful. All they knew was that someone had slit the Autumn Thief's throat, and that poison ran rampant through her veins. At least that's what the fae thought. They didn't really know what was wrong.

Eldridge emerged from the shadows behind Freya and placed a hand on her shoulder. "You can't stay up with her all night again, my love. She doesn't even know you're here. "

"I think she does," Freya whispered. "I think she can hear us, and any kind of comfort is better than nothing at all."

Smoke curled from a candle on the bedside table. Eldridge insisted they keep the Autumn Thief in darkness because that was a natural state for those who ruled the Autumn Court. But Freya worried it was too much like death. Too much like the Thief was right on the precipice of never returning to them at all.

She wished they could put her in a room better than this dark dungeon of a place. The black curtains swallowed up all light, even from the flickering candles that cast an ominous red glow upon the fireplace that had never been used. Even the windows were darkened, revealing nothing more than a starless sky outside.

Freya touched a finger to the curl of smoke rising from a nearby candle. It coiled around her finger before funneling back into the air. Like a spirit she couldn't catch. "I can't sleep knowing she's like this."

"And you can't save her if you aren't getting any sleep. You know there's nothing more we can do, Freya." He squeezed her shoulder. "We have to rest or we'll fall to the same poison that is killing her."

Freya didn't know that. She still wondered if there was actually a poison in the Autumn Thief's veins.

She'd always thought there were signs of ingestion when a toxin was involved. Sweating being the first. Bodies tried to get rid of poisons that didn't belong inside them. Maybe the Thief's eyes would have moved beneath her closed lids. At the very least, Freya had expected vomiting.

The Thief didn't move at all. She stayed still, as if she were already dead. She didn't even flinch when Freya touched her brow with a cold, wet cloth. Droplets beaded down her temples and soaked her hair.

Eldridge sighed and put his other hand on her shoulder as well. "I know you want to save everyone that you possibly can, and you know I love that about you. But you have to come to bed."

"I don't think we're trying hard enough," she replied.

"She's my friend too, you know." His voice deepened with emotion. "I watched her grow when she was nothing like this. When she was stuck in a body that she didn't like, and people called her by a name that didn't fit. I walked through that life with her and I supported her every step of the way. It's killing me to see her like this, too, but I also know there is nothing I can do to stop it. Not until we find out what happened to her."

Freya knew that was the truth. She had seen how the Autumn Thief's state had affected Eldridge. Even in the mornings when they had breakfast together, he barely paid attention to what she said. They both stared off into the distance, fearing that even immortals weren't here forever.

Clearing her throat, Freya stood and turned into his arms. She wrapped her arms around his waist and drew him against her own heart. "We're going to figure this out," she said. "I know we are."

He wrapped himself around her shoulders and squeezed her tightly, but it didn't escape her notice that he didn't return her sentiments. There were very few things out of the Goblin King's control. This was apparently one of them. Of all the things he could do, he couldn't heal wounds.

They left that sad chamber with their arms intertwined. Freya and Eldridge wandered through the halls, back to their own room. They never released their hold on each other, not even when they clambered into their plush bed and tried very hard to rest.

Eldridge sank into a deep sleep, murmuring while he dreamt. The words made little sense to Freya, likely because they were spells he cast even while dreaming. Spells that were meant to protect those he loved.

At least he was getting some sleep. Freya was not so lucky.

She stared up at the ceiling, seeing stars shifting and morphing into new constellations as she watched. She counted up to a thousand and then decided she couldn't stay here any longer. No matter how much Eldridge wanted her to rest and get away from the sounds of death in that room, she couldn't leave the Thief alone.

Not when there was a chance that this could be the day it all ended. She refused to let the other woman die alone.

Slipping out of their bed, she wandered down the halls until she arrived at the dark door that led into the Autumn Thief's rooms. She listened intently, waiting to hear if someone else had beaten her. There were many people who wanted to sit with the Thief. The impressive faerie had helped entire villages of goblins in her time leading her court.

"No one's in there." The familiar voice came from behind her.

Freya turned and smiled at Arrow. He stood with a tray of tea in his hands, the steam coiling like the smoke from the candles in the Autumn Thief's room. A small plate filled with pale yellow macarons sat next to the tea pot painted with leaves.

"That's an odd thing to bring for dinner," she mumbled.

"I didn't want dinner. I wanted sweets to make this entire ordeal better." He sniffed, then nodded at the door. "If you're insistent on being such a bothersome creature, at least open the door so I can put all this down."

Freya noted there were two teacups on the tray, and she doubted one of them was for the Thief. Arrow had known he would find Freya here. And he'd come to keep her company.

Her companion was always looking out for her. This goblin dog had seen more than most, but he'd always been her loyal friend. No matter what they were going through.

Together, they walked into the darkness and prepared for another night keeping vigil. Just in case.

Arrow dragged an extra chair to the bedside and then set up his tea on the bedside table. He popped a macaron in his mouth and stared at the Autumn Thief while chewing thoughtfully. "I don't think it's a poison either, you know. I don't even think anyone tried to kill her."

The mere idea of what he was suggesting was too much for her to think through. Freya shook her head, cleared her throat, and then croaked, "What?"

"I think she did this to herself. Something was happening, or maybe she foresaw a future that she didn't like. She always was poking around in divination when she shouldn't. But I think she wanted this to happen." He swallowed hard. "I just can't figure out why she would think this was the only way out."

For the first time in over a week, the Autumn Thief stirred. Her hand shifted on top of her chest, and the rattling wheeze slowed enough for Freya to hear her whisper, "Water."

Shit.

They didn't have any water. Freya frantically looked around them, then decided tea would have to do. She brought her own cup with her, sat on the side of the bed, and helped hold the Thief's head up.

Though her eyes were watery and bleary, the Autumn Thief had awakened from her healing slumber.

Arrow hopped up onto the bed and watched every hesitant gulp of the warm water. Finally, he laid down with both paws on either side of the Thief's legs and hummed a long, low sound. Glowing energy spread from his paws and sank through the sheets that covered the Thief's legs.

"Thank you," the Thief muttered while leaning back into the pillows with a sigh. "And Freya, just call me Lark. It's easier."

"Of course." Freya hadn't known the Thief's real name, but Lark fit her well.

Both Freya and Arrow waited for more things to be said. But Lark leaned against her pillows and closed her eyes again, even with Arrow's healing magic pouring into her body. Assisting her to stay awake.

Freya whispered, "Did she go back to sleep?"

"No," Lark muttered. "I'm trying to gather enough energy to tell you what needs to be said."

"Right." Was she supposed to move, then? Should she open the windows and get some fresh air into the room?

The latter seemed like the best option. Freya rushed to the window and threw open the dark curtains. The floor to ceiling windows were well oiled as she opened them and hooked the fabric onto the metal clasps on the balcony outside. Cool, crisp air rushed into the room. Smoke billowed out of the room and poured down the side of the castle.

With a soft smile, Lark turned her head to stare out at the galaxies in the sky outside. "I always loved this kingdom," she whispered. "It's so beautiful."

Freya didn't want to push the dying woman, but there was a certain detail they were all waiting to hear. So she took a step closer to the bed and cleared her throat. "Lark, do you think you're ready to tell us what happened?"

She hoped it was nothing horrible. That maybe this was all a mistake. A disgruntled faerie who had taken it upon themselves to attack a court leader. She could work with that. Eldridge could find that person, and then they could all move on with their lives.

But when Lark sighed and turned her face away from Freya, she already knew the Autumn Thief had nothing good to say.

"The magic that made me the Autumn Thief is turning against me," Lark whispered. "I am no longer worthy of this throne."

"No," Arrow blurted. "You're the only person who is strong enough to have that magic. You're the only one who has guided us through so much hardship. The magic cannot turn its back against you."

"I'm not sure if that's it. I think the magic is restless. My purpose and use cannot grow the court any further." Lark turned her gaze to the dog, who still laid on her legs, and her eyes welled with tears. "I saw them again, Arrow. The triad who decides the fate of all in the Autumn Court. They turned their dark gazes upon me and then they looked away."

The goblin dog gasped and turned pale, if that was possible beneath the thick layer of fur.

Freya didn't understand any of what they were saying. All she knew was that Lark was awake, and that meant they could move forward. She had a goal she had to reach, and she didn't care if some godly figures were standing in her way.

"Well," she interrupted, sitting on the edge of the bed. "I've faced worse than three people who are disappointed in the most talented of court leaders. Sure, the most unconventional. But the Autumn Court runs better than most."

"Eldridge has fed you that untruth," Lark laughed. "The Autumn Court is dying. Our people have been forced into an ancient custom of selling cursed objects, but we can't sustain this kingdom without the kindness of the Goblin King or the other courts. I was supposed to find a way to fix it. And I didn't."

Freya frowned. "This isn't another situation like in the Summer Court, is it?"

"No. The magic is already leaving me. It's too late for anyone to save my position now." Lark touched a hand to the mark on her throat. "I tried to rush the process, but obviously that failed."

So she had tried to take her own life, then. Arrow had been correct.

With a brief hesitation, Freya reached out and took Lark's hand. "For what it's worth, I'm glad you failed."

"You might not be when this is all over." Lark sighed. "The magic will eventually leave me as nothing more than the woman I was before all this. It will seek out the strongest person in the court, take over their body, and then they would go through the trials. Just as I did. Everyone will know that I failed."

"They won't." Freya's words were harsh and sharp, but she refused to let Lark think less of herself. "I refuse to let them. You will forever be remembered as one of the best Autumn Thieves who ever lived. I promise you that."

Lark clutched Freya's fingers, squeezing them in her own and drawing Freya onto the bed with her. Together, all three of them snuggled into the plush pillows.

"You can't promise that, you know," Lark whispered as they all drifted off to sleep. "You can't control what people remember."

"Watch me," Freya replied.

In her heart, she knew she would stop at nothing to ensure everyone remembered how beloved Lark was. And that Lark survived losing her magic. There had to be a way. There was always a way.

CHAPTER 2

"Freya."

The whispered word threatened to pull her out of a lovely dream. A dream filled with magic and light, where she laid in a field with her Goblin King, and the only thing they had to worry about was how much wine they had brought with them.

"Freya, wake up."

Fingers touched her cheek, gently drawing her from the comfort of the dreaming realm and into the waking.

Freya awoke slowly. She laid propped up against a headboard, her hands folded on her chest. Embarrassingly, her mouth had fallen open and there was a sticky trail of drool dripping down her chin. Snapping awake, she wiped at the drool. How long had she been asleep? Did the Autumn Thief need something?

"Lark," she muttered, rolling off the bed as if she had to race off to get whatever her dear friend needed. "What can I get you? Do you need more water?"

"No, Freya. Come back." Lark kept her voice low, still whispering, as if she didn't want to wake Arrow. "I want to talk with you, dear. And Arrow cannot hear, so please, keep your voice quiet."

Where was this going? Arrow was one of the few dependable

faeries in this castle, and she considered Eldridge to be under that same umbrella. If the Thief had something to say, then either of her companions were more than capable of hearing it. The same as Freya.

But she wasn't about to argue with a woman on the brink of death.

She climbed back onto the bed and settled into the pillows. Lark held her hand immediately, as if they were two young women who had stayed up far past their bedtime and were hoping their parents didn't notice. But they weren't. As wonderful a fantasy as that might be, Freya knew whatever the Thief had to say was going to be something that kept her up at night for many months to come.

"I wasn't entirely truthful with Arrow," Lark whispered. "Or, at least, I didn't tell either of you the entire story. I knew I couldn't tell anyone other than you, but I don't know how to begin. You see, the magic draining out of me will go to whomever is the strongest faerie in the Autumn Court. You know that, don't you?"

Freya had heard the story before. Magic left the court leader and then it found the next best person. That's what had happened when Eldridge became the Goblin King. Though, in giving up the power he once had, he'd been gifted with magic even greater than all the court leaders combined.

"Yes," she replied, fluffing the pillow behind her and trying her best to concentrate. "I've heard that's how it works. The magic leaves the last leader and then finds someone else. Most of the time the courts have an idea of who it's going to travel to. Right?"

"That's the problem." Lark touched a finger to the tip of her nose and then pointed at Freya. "I always knew you were a smart one."

The problem? Lark must know who the next Autumn Thief might be, and that was part of her hesitation. Although Freya had met a lot of the people in the Autumn Court and most of them were quite lovely. They were all capable of leading if they had to, although no one could ever fill Lark's shoes. She was a figure in the Autumn Court's history that had changed time itself.

Freya pieced together the Thief's issue and sighed. "You don't like who the magic is going to go to."

"Power doesn't mean they are the right person to lead." Lark struggled to slide up the headboard, easing her leg out from under Arrow so she didn't wake up the goblin dog. "There are some in the Autumn Court who wouldn't mind a leader who rules with an iron fist, or a man who has a heart as hard as stone. But I do not want my people ruled by some imbecile who thinks that power is the only important thing in this realm."

Freya could see how that would be a problem. The goblins weren't fragile creatures, but they deserved someone who would see the strength in their weaknesses and teach them how to use that power without flinching.

She bit her lip, worrying at the flesh with her teeth. "I understand that, Lark, but there's nothing we can do. You want to control the magic and we both know that isn't how it works. If the magic needs to go to the most powerful person, then I don't think either of us can stop it."

Lark met her gaze, and Freya's stomach clenched. She knew that expression. She'd seen it on Eldridge's face more times than she could count. Lark had a plan that Freya would not like, and that was wholly because it went against the very fabric of their existence.

"What do you want to do?" Freya groaned.

"What if we didn't have to send the magic out at all?" Lark squeezed her hand, fingers shaking with excitement. "The magic only goes to the strongest person in the court if it is free to do so. It doesn't seek out an individual if it's in a body already."

But that... No. It made little sense. Free magic was dangerous, surely. Freya could only imagine that magic like that had a mind of its own, and trying to control such a thing would be impossible. Trapping it, however, sounded equally bad.

Power in this realm had a memory. A mind. And Freya knew from experience how frustrating and how horrible it was to be trapped. The magic could very easily burn up the body they tried to transfer it to.

Unless they transferred it to someone powerful enough to contain it.

"You want to give the magic back to Eldridge," she whispered. "Is that even possible? I don't know if he could control both the magic of the Autumn Court and the magic of the Goblin King at the same time."

If anyone could, though, that person would be Eldridge. He had also already had Lark's magic inside him before. He'd been the one who wielded the power of the Autumn Court for many years.

All this made sense. It was a solid plan, although she still didn't know why they were so afraid of who the power would go to. What goblin would take the Autumn Court's magic and then squander it so foolishly?

"No," Lark replied. Her antlers caught in the candlelight and looked as though they were burning. "I want you to take it, Freya."

Silence rang between them. All Freya could hear afterward was the horrible sound of ringing bells. Or maybe that was her own voice screaming in her head.

"Me?" She couldn't fathom why Lark would think she would be a good fit to take such magic. "Why would you think that I could contain the magic? I'm mortal."

Lark squeezed her fingers again, lacing their hands together until Freya's knuckles cracked. "There are so many words I could say to convince you, Freya. You're correct. Right now, you are mortal. And how long do you think it's going to take before Eldridge turns around and you're an old woman? A hundred years is a heartbeat to us, and we will live thousands. Losing you would kill him, you see, and I refuse to have the Summer Lord as our Goblin King."

So there were reasons behind Lark's choice. Reasons behind all this happening. Freya's mind turned with all the information suddenly thrust at her. All she could think to say was, "Did you try to kill yourself so Eldridge wouldn't end up alone? Or dead?"

Lark raised an eyebrow and licked her lips. "Among other reasons. I really don't like the person who is going to take the magic from me, Freya. This isn't all about you. Or Eldridge. And I do fear what would happen to my court if the magic was allowed to transfer to his body."

"Is it because he's a terrible person?" She eyed the Autumn Thief, knowing that this direct question couldn't be answered with a lie.

Lark grumbled a few times before muttering, "He'd probably learn how to manage well enough. But the man is a bumbling idiot when it comes to anything other than brute force, and I genuinely dislike him."

Right, so there was nothing wrong with this poor man. Lark simply wanted to use this moment to her own advantage, and that wasn't right.

Freya shook her head and drew her hand free from Lark's. "We can't take the magic from someone else who deserves it, Lark. He's the most powerful fae other than you in your court, and that means the magic is his."

"The magic belongs to whoever controls it. That's all. This could be the only way you and Eldridge can be together forever. Why wouldn't you take this moment and use it to your advantage?" Lark searched her gaze with frantic eyes. "Please, Freya. I'm offering you the chance to save yourself and the man you love. I'm offering you an infinite future with your soon to be husband."

At the words, Freya instantly touched a hand to her ring. She spun the metal as she thought, even though she already knew the answer. She couldn't. It wasn't the right thing to do, and Freya prided herself on making the choices that benefited everyone. Not just herself.

Eldridge and she hadn't even talked about her inevitable mortality. They had avoided the conversation entirely! Neither of them were interested in thinking about her death, or how he would handle such a thing. Besides, they still had at least fifty good years before they needed to have that chat.

Lark reached up and touched her fingers to the crow's feet at the corners of Freya's eyes. "You're already showing signs of age, my dear. I couldn't stand by and do nothing."

Her heart stuttered. Was she that old already? Did the fae look at her and see someone fragile, someone dying before their eyes?

She cupped Lark's hand against her cheek, and her hands shook. "You know it's not the right choice. If someone else is more qualified, more powerful, then it should go to them. I don't know the first thing about your court, or even being a court leader. The fae wouldn't look to me to be their Autumn Thief. And taking the magic would only make me even less worthy of the title."

"Taking whatever we want makes us goblins," Lark replied vehemently. "Seize the magic from me, Freya. Steal it away and everyone in the court will respect you. Goblin law rises above all fae law."

Freya waffled. She could take this magic, but then perhaps the fae would never forgive her. But in taking it, she would do the one thing that Lark wanted and perhaps save her friend in the process.

It was wrong. She would forever regret this decision if she did it, but she also knew that a part of her was tempted. A part of her wanted to become like them, just as she had desired for so many months since coming here. Taking this magic would make her formidable. But more than that, it would make her like everyone else.

She would no longer be a mortal woman with a little magic from a changeling father who wasn't quite mortal himself. She'd be a woman with more to her than some spells she shouldn't know and a quick witted mind.

Above all else, she would never have to wonder what would happen to Eldridge when she died.

Freya had already decided before the guilt could gnaw at her soul.

"How do I take it?" she asked. Her words echoed through her very soul as if she'd damned herself in even uttering them.

"You know how to sense when someone pulls at your life force, don't you?" Lark stared into her eyes. The black gaze turned even darker, somehow.

Freya nodded, entranced by the Autumn Thief's eyes. "Yes, I know that feeling."

"You need to turn it around. Look inside me, this time. Seek out the magic that boils in my veins."

"I don't know how." Freya sighed, nearly breaking her concentration. This was a futile lesson. Freya only used magic when she had to, and most of the time, that magic was from someone or something else.

"You do know how. You've just never done it before. All I'm asking you to do is to find Autumn inside me. Listen for the sound of crunching leaves and the bitter taste of an apple not yet ripe. Smell the bonfires in the distance and feel the cool breeze on your arms." The words were hypnotizing, and suddenly, Freya could use all her senses to feel exactly that.

The magic in the Autumn Thief danced in a joyous waltz underneath Lark's skin. It was stunning and beautiful and red as autumn leaves.

She reached out to touch it, feeling the magic ripple between her fingers and it burbled out a laugh like a child. It was a mischievous thing, and the idea of being stolen from the Thief was a grand adventure it wanted to partake in.

Freya didn't have to ask it to come to her. She didn't even need to convince all that power to touch her back.

It was almost as if the magic itself had listened to their conversation and it already knew what the plan was. All Freya had to do was reach for it and the magic... jumped.

It leapt into the air and pounded into her skin. Freya took a single sharp breath and then suddenly she wasn't herself anymore.

CHAPTER 3

The darkness in front of her eyes started to take on familiar shapes. A barren and dry landscape revealed itself, with dust that rolled in a cool wind. Freya tilted her face back. A slick layer of sweat covered her brow, and the breeze felt good on her overheated skin.

Where was she?

Her mind churned, tumbled, and rolled until she remembered that she'd taken the magic from the Autumn Thief. Stolen it. Ripped it away from the one person whom it really belonged to. Maybe this was her punishment for trying to take something that wasn't hers.

Swallowing hard, she let her eyes drift across the barren wasteland. She wasn't really here. Freya recognized the strange tingle on her skin, the way her body reacted when she was in a place between places. A land that was neither real nor fake. This place had been created by magic and then consumed by it.

Whispers floated on the wind, tickling her ears with words she couldn't quite make out. She cocked her head to the side and listened intently, trying to catch a few fragments of the conversation.

"Is this the one?"

"New."

"No, this cannot be."

"*Stolen.*"

The last word rang with so much rage that Freya feared she was about to be tossed from this landscape and the magic would then devour her soul. She didn't know how she even knew it could. A memory that wasn't her own played behind her eyes. The vision of herself being ripped apart by fire that burned from the inside out. Boiled alive.

No, she couldn't let that happen. Too much had already occurred in her life, and stealing the magic had been a momentary lapse in judgement.

"My name is Freya," she called out. The wind grabbed her words and flung them into the barren nothingness beyond. "I took the magic because the Autumn Thief herself thought I was worthy of it."

A voice whispered in her ear, "You aren't."

Freya flinched as an icy finger trailed down her spine. The sharp tip pressed against her skin, and it felt almost as though she split open in the place it had traced. Maybe this form of herself could cut much easier than the mortal flesh she'd left behind.

"I am." She put an impressive amount of conviction into the word when she didn't actually believe it herself. "I will not allow you to wriggle your way into my mind and convince me that I am nothing. I am more than you could ever imagine, and my deeds speak for themselves."

"A mortal woman walks upon our sacred fields, and you expect us to believe you are worthy of this gift? That you could rule as the Thief must rule?"

She licked her lips and dove right to the point. "I don't have to be mortal anymore. You have the ability to change me into something more than that. Don't you?"

Otherwise, the Autumn Thief would never have sent her here. The power that was now within Freya had more abilities than she could ever imagine, and that meant it could take a mortal sleeve and turn it into something else. Something more powerful and everlasting.

The voices whispered to each other once more, but Freya couldn't make out the sound. She did, however, get the chance to figure out where they were coming from.

These creatures had forgotten that she controlled the power. Yes, she was within the magic of the Autumn Court, but it was also within her. Freya could manipulate the enchantment, use it to her own desire, until they decided she was worthy of it.

She walked through the desolate landscape, turning left and right until the voices were at their loudest and directly in front of her. And once she finally reached them as close as she could, Freya lifted a hand and waved her fingers through the air.

The glamour that hid the creatures disappeared. It rolled away from their bodies, down from their heads to their feet, like she'd pulled a blanket from them.

They were made entirely of darkness. Dark, stretched creatures that were the embodiment of a long shadow. Their limbs were too long, their heads too narrow, their forms lean and impossible. Their fingertips touched their knees, and great horns stretched from the top of their skulls. They leaned together, away from her, ignoring that she'd revealed their terrifying forms.

One looked over its shoulder and she stared into glowing white eyes. Or perhaps not eyes, but pin pricks through the shadow body that light could break through.

She gulped. "I know where you are now."

"And we've always known where you were, Freya of Woolwich." It broke away from the others, looming over her and staring with that unblinking gaze. "We are the Midnight Monsters. You are in our realm now."

Yet something in her stomach claimed that she wasn't. These monsters were here to serve her, whether they wanted to or not. She had the magic, and these creatures didn't seem like the kind that could terrify the Autumn Thief. Lark was too strong and brave to think these creatures might end her life.

Which could only mean they were the gatekeepers. The ones who stood between her and those she actually needed to talk with.

"Lark claimed there were old gods. Those who used to judge the court leaders before they were given their power." Though she didn't want to say these creatures clearly weren't the old gods, she also didn't want to let them believe she was frightened of them.

Even though she was.

Freya had the distinct memory of long, clawed fingers reaching out from under her bed when she was little. The monster under her bed had grabbed the blankets and tugged them from her body. Leaving her shivering in fright for the rest of the evening. The hands had belonged to a monster like this.

A Midnight Monster. A creature who stood between the dark and the light. For they could not exist without light to give them form, but the darkness lived deep in their souls.

The creature's head split open where a mouth should have been, but it was the absence of a mouth that shaped the gap. The grin warped its face, and the creature chuckled. "The old gods only see those who deserve the magic. You will burn. Just like all the others who tried to take what wasn't theirs."

Fire bloomed in the distance. Figures standing on the horizon, each one aflame. Freya somehow knew they were all those who had previously tried to steal the position she now held. They were the ones who had failed.

She would not become one of them.

"I am meant to be here," she gritted through her teeth. "You cannot convince me that this wasn't some grand scheme of the entire realm moving me to this one moment. I was no one before I stepped into the faerie realms. A farmer's daughter who should have lived her life on the edge of the forest, afraid of every magical thing that might step out of it."

And since she'd come here, she was an entirely different person. Freya wasn't afraid anymore. Fear had no place in her heart when she could grow and learn from the things that lived in the dark. Just because the shadows might be unknown, that didn't make them dangerous.

Darkness was not evil.

It did not breed those who wanted to kill and maim. Most of the people who lived on the outskirts of the world were the kindest people she'd ever met. They wanted to be left alone, because they were afraid.

These Midnight Monsters would not convince her otherwise.

She drew herself up and stared the creature in the eyes. She didn't react when its mouth split open even wider, as if it found her defiance amusing.

The Midnight Monster hissed. "Yes, that is exactly how I would describe you as well. A molding little leech who has attached itself to the magic of this realm and now thinks to suck it dry."

"No," she stuttered. "That's not what I want at all."

"Then you wish to poison us with your fear and your mortality. You wish to spread that which is mortal into the very bloodlines of the fae. Allowing you to become the Autumn Thief would destroy everything we have worked so hard to build."

That wasn't right, either. This creature twisted her words into something dark and ugly. She didn't want any of that.

Still stammering, Freya tried her best to explain. "I don't want to hurt anyone. I want to preserve what I fell in love with. This world. These people. The goblins. All of it. I love it so much that sometimes it hurts my very soul to look at them."

The creature laughed, although the blinding light of its mouth never moved. "So you wish to hold something that was never yours. Like a treasure you found in the fabric of the earth. Is that how it is?"

"No!" She shouted the word, hoping that maybe the Midnight Monster would understand that she hated the words it put in her mouth. "I only wanted to be here forever. With you and the others. I don't want to harm your way of life. Magic could give me immortality. It could give me enough time to learn about this place and the people who live here. To rule in a way that does you all justice."

The Midnight Monster was apparently finished with her. It turned toward its brethren, and as one, they all strode away from her. And though Freya sprinted after them, her legs were not nearly so long.

Long, loping steps drew them away from her faster than she could run. If she didn't do something, anything, then they would get away from her. She'd lose this chance and then she really would boil up as they had threatened she would.

"Wait!" Her voice sounded like a croak even to her own ears. As though the strength of her very being weakened as they drew away from her. "Please, wait!"

They didn't stop. Their long legs drew them farther and farther away until she was certain she had lost sight of them. Any moment now she would be thrust back into her body. She could feel the heat already wrapping around her throat, threatening as a band of iron clasped at her pulse.

"No," she whispered. "Not like this."

Freya ran faster, harder, pumping her arms and legs. They would not get away from her. The Midnight Monsters had no right to deem her unworthy simply because they didn't want a mortal to have this power. They were the ones with the power to make her something else.

Words pressed against her lips. Words that weren't her own, but felt important. Words that demanded to take flight.

"I wish to see the old gods!" she screamed, falling onto her knees. She sank back on her haunches, arms limp at her sides and eyes staring wide into the vast darkness above. "Whatever they need me to do. Whatever proof they require to know that I will be the best Autumn Thief I can be, then I will provide it. But do not send me away from this place to die."

Shadows coalesced above her. They gathered like ink spilled on dark fabric. Pulling together, then ripping apart as someone tilted the very foundation of the world.

The same Midnight Monster leaned over her, his eyes now glowing bright blue. "If you wish to go through the trials of the Autumn Thief, then we will allow it. But know this, Freya of Woolwich. You will not survive them."

She looked it dead in the eye and laughed. "I will survive them. Because I am no longer Freya of Woolwich. I am the Queen Killer, Defeater of the Goblin King, Spring Maiden, and Summer Lord. I have made a name for myself in this realm and no new god or old will take that away from me."

A low chuckle erupted from the shadow creature's mouth. It nodded, then stepped away from her. "We shall see, Freya. I look forward to finding out how truthful your claim is. Now, you will return to the court you have claimed. The trials start soon, and you are nowhere near where they begin."

An icy hand pressed against her chest, and Freya's heart seized. She gasped, holding onto the black wrist and staring into burning eyes.

"Go," the Midnight Monster said. "You have very little time left, Mortal."

It drew its hand out of her grasp, then punched her so hard in the chest she felt it in her very heart.

CHAPTER 4

She fell out of that magical place and landed hard in her own body. Freya hardly had time to orient herself before she was jerked in yet another direction. This time, at least, she remained in her own body.

Hands clutched her shoulders and heaved her away from the Autumn Thief. Hands that came with the familiar scent of apple pie. An arm wrapped around her shoulders and braced her against a familiar, hard body.

"Freya," Eldridge hissed in her ear. "What have you done?"

She didn't know how to answer that. The Midnight Monsters sure seemed to think she had done something foolish. And she wasn't all that certain they were wrong. After all, the old gods didn't want her to have it. They had already deemed her unworthy because she was a mortal. She was lucky the magic hadn't already flared deep in her chest and started boiling her alive.

She looked up into Eldridge's enraged expression and opened her mouth. The only thing that fell out was, "I don't know."

And she didn't. Not really.

She should have asked him before she took the magic. But her own age had weighed her entire soul down until she couldn't think. Couldn't breathe. So many people were already looking at her as though she were ancient. Freya didn't want to die in front of their eyes.

His gaze widened in horror, and she thought maybe he could see the magic in her now. Magic that wasn't her own, but familiar to him.

"You stole her magic?" He whispered the question, as though he couldn't believe the words himself.

Lark coughed, then interrupted them with a wheezing sound. "Don't be too hard on her, Eldridge. I told her to take it."

"Why would you do that?" Eldridge snarled.

They both turned their attention to the Autumn Thief, and Freya watched in horror as one of Lark's antlers cracked in half. The sound echoed through the room, then the other mirrored the first. They snapped free from the top of her head, then fell onto the mattress on either side of her with quiet thumps.

She seemed to shrink on the bed. A smaller woman than she had been before. No longer imposing with threatening antlers, but a mere goblin woman with strange hands and hooved feet. So small the mattress swallowed her up, and the pillows were too large.

A once blindingly beautiful woman, Lark was now more human. Freya could look at her without flinching or wanting to shade her eyes. This was just Lark. The same woman that Eldridge had grown up with.

He let out a stuttering breath behind her. "Welcome back to yourself," he mumbled. "It's good to see you again like this. Even if it is under the worst circumstances."

Lark shook her head. She reached up and touched the soft nubs where her antlers had once been, and the sad expression on her face brought tears to Freya's eyes.

"Yes," Lark replied. "I'm sure you still think this is the worst thing that could have happened to either of us. Me losing my power. Freya taking over as the Autumn Thief. It all must pull at your very soul. But you know this was the only way."

"The only way?" he hissed, his emotions swinging to anger once again. "You put the woman I love in grave danger, and for what? Your own pride?"

"Because I didn't want her to die in front of you, Eldridge!" Lark pushed up on the bed, kneeling as if she were about to fly off the bed and wrap her hands around Eldridge's neck. "You and I both know that mortality is a disease that can't be cured. This way, at least she has a chance."

"If she survives the trials," Eldridge snarled.

His hands flexed on her shoulders, and the words reminded her of what the Midnight Monsters had said. They had talked about a trial, too. Their chuckles still echoed in her ears.

"What trials?" she asked.

Lark growled. The sound was unnatural from a throat like hers, considering Freya had never heard a deer make that sound before. "You foolish man. You know the trials are entirely dependent on the person that has the power. They will see her strength, her cunning, and they will create trials that won't cost them another Autumn Thief so soon."

He ripped his hands away from Freya's shoulders so he could point a long claw in Lark's face. "You're making assumptions and forgetting that they may take one look at a mortal and refuse to allow her to even go through the trials. Then what? Then you've killed her for a dream that we all knew could never come to light."

"Assumptions!" Lark tossed her hands in the air. Her rueful laugh filled the room with patronizing disapproval. "You speak of assumptions when you're making them yourself. The old gods are not so blind. They don't care if she's a mortal or if she's fae. They will turn her into whatever they want. Didn't they do the same to the two of us?"

Silence was her only answer. Eldridge glared at Lark. Lark glared back. Neither of them would budge because they were both doing the same thing. They both banged their heads against the other until one of them wore down enough to agree. Except neither of them would agree with the other.

Freya held her breath. She didn't know if she should try to speak, or if the two faeries might jump down her throat, considering they were ready to battle each other. But the question burned on her tongue, wiggling to be released.

If the magic had remade the two of them into what it wanted, or if the old gods had changed these two fae, what had Eldridge once looked like?

A furry body stirred on the bed. Arrow stretched, bowing low with his front legs and then wiggling each back leg as though they had fallen asleep. "I think the two of you are vastly underestimating Miss Freya. She's gone through every court in this kingdom but the Autumn Court. Perhaps she's already been completing her own trials."

Thank all the heavens and gods in the sky for her trustworthy companion. Freya grinned at Arrow, who gave her a sharp nod in return.

At least someone believed in her.

If Arrow thought she could do this, then Freya had no doubt she could. Clearing her throat, she forced herself to interrupt the two faeries that clearly had no interest in listening to the little mortal. "I want to go through the trials. I think I can do this. And Eldridge, I understand you don't believe in me. That's all right. I've proven you wrong before."

He pinched the bridge of his nose and blew out a very long breath. "It's not that I don't believe in you, Freya. These trials are meant for the fae. They were meant for the most powerful person in the court to be tested, weighed, and measured."

"Who says power has to be measured by how much magic a person can wield?" She had to believe this was the truth, or she really was walking to her death. "Power can mean so much more than physical prowess."

Eldridge turned toward her, and she knew all this anger was riding on the back of fear. His eyes were too wide. The set of his shoulders too shaky. He feared, yet again, that he was going to lose her, and there was nothing he could do to stop it.

"We don't have a choice now, do we?" he grumbled. "You took the magic from the Autumn Thief, and the only way to keep it is through the trials. I cannot save you from this, Freya. There is no way for me to take the magic away. I can't steal it like you did. That power is now locked inside you until you go through the trials or it eats you alive."

"I may not have understood the risk when I took this power." The words were an understatement. She already regretted her decision, but like he said, she couldn't go back. "But I am ready for what comes next. All I can hope for is that you are willing to guide me through whatever may come."

"Of course I will." He closed his eyes, took a deep breath, and forced his entire body to relax. Inch by inch, he drew the mantle of the Goblin King over himself until he looked completely and utterly unaffected by what had happened. "You would not be the first Autumn Thief I have mentored."

With a sharp bow, he left the room without another word. Though his movements were stiff and awkward.

Freya knew he needed some time to process all this. She couldn't race after him and beg his forgiveness, because she'd done all this without him. He hated it when she tried to wander through the faerie realm on her own, without his advice.

Now she understood why. Things like this happened when she didn't include the Goblin King in her decisions.

Touching a hand to her forehead, she winced and asked, "Did I do something horribly wrong? Again?"

Arrow snorted. "Probably, but you already did it, so we might as well move forward from here. I don't think you could back out now, even if you wanted to."

No, she didn't think she could either. Freya lifted a hand and chewed on her thumbnail. "Should I go after him? All of this was for us, after all. I don't want to make him think I decided all this without thought."

Which she had.

Freya continued, brushing aside her own reflections. "That is, I want him to know that I made this choice because I didn't want to put him through losing me. It wasn't some desperate bid for power or... Well..."

Maybe she was lying to herself. She had to work on not doing that anymore.

Freya wanted some kind of power. She wanted to be more like the fae who had little care in the world, or at least few worries. Every fiber of her soul wanted to know that her family and friends were safe because she was the one who could keep them like that.

And if that meant stealing a little magic, then she was willing to do so. She had to own that.

She sank onto the edge of the bed and pillowed her head in her hands. Groaning, she whined, "Why am I like this?"

Lark patted her shoulder and chuckled. "All the Autumn Thieves are. This is the one thing that makes you more like the rest of us than any other trait. We are selfish beings, my dear. To our very core. But that doesn't make us evil or dangerous. Merely that we are willing to do whatever it takes to get what we want. It's not a bad trait."

Yet every person Freya had ever spoken to would disagree with what Lark said. Women in particular were supposed to be kind, giving, willing to upend the world for the people they loved. But only at their own expense.

What was she supposed to do now?

Lifting her head, she met Arrow's gaze. The goblin dog had somehow gotten off the bed without her hearing and was now seated in front of her. Expectantly waiting for the moment when she would get over herself and look to him for guidance.

His tail swooshed over the floor, tossing a dust bunny back underneath the bed. "You're going to pull yourself together, Miss Freya. The magic that now lives inside you will take a while to get used to. And I'm sure it feels odd to have within your mind. However, we need to get ready for the trials and you need to pack your things."

"Pack my things?" She knew they would have to go to the Autumn Court, but so soon?

He placed a paw on her knee and sighed. "The trials start with or without you, Freya. The old gods don't care if you aren't in the Autumn Court right now. They just know that someone else has the power, and that means you need to prove your worth. We likely have until tomorrow, at the very latest."

So soon.

Freya nodded firmly. She could do this. This was the choice she'd made, and she had to continue forward. "All right. Do you think Eldridge will be in our rooms? Should I prepare myself for another argument?"

Lark wrapped her arms around Freya's shoulders and put her chin on top of Freya's head. "I think you should prepare yourself for quite the argument, my dear. Eldridge is going to fight tooth and nail, regardless of whether you already have the magic inside you. I think we can all safely assume that."

"Great," Freya muttered. "Just great."

CHAPTER 5

She dragged her feet down the halls toward their private chambers. Freya knew that an argument awaited her beyond the comfortable doors of their bedroom, and she didn't like to argue there.

But she also knew that Eldridge had every right to be angry with her. He deserved to shout and scream that she'd been foolish or rash in her decisions. And he would. She knew he wouldn't hold back a single second of his anger and fear.

Placing her hand on the door, she smoothed her palm down the warm wood. This was the one place in the entire castle that never got cold. Eldridge had caught her shivering the first few nights she'd moved into his bedroom, and that was that. He'd cast a spell to warm the room completely so she wouldn't be uncomfortable in their shared space ever again.

Damn it. She hated disappointing him.

She pushed the door and let it swing open before her. Eldridge had already started packing, it seemed. He'd brought out a majority of their clothing and tossed it at the bed. A single chest stood open at his feet and he angrily threw articles of clothing at it.

Walking onto the battlefield with no knowledge of what weapons he chose sounded dangerous to her. So instead, she leaned against the doorframe and crossed her arms over her chest. "You're packing already, I see."

"Someone has to," he snarled.

"I can manage packing on my own."

"Just like you manage everything else on your own. Yes, I'm aware." He threw a shirt into the crate without even attempting to fold it. "And yet, here I am. Still doing it for you."

They were definitely fighting, then.

Freya sighed and wandered onto the battlefield. She sat down on top of the bed, right in front of him, with a pile of clothing trapped underneath her hip. He huffed out an angry breath and turned away from her, obviously disinterested in the argument they were about to have.

But Freya didn't want to argue. She didn't want to go into this new quest, once again, without knowing that he was going to be there for her and not fight her. They had all the time in the world to fight with each other.

Right now, she wanted to talk.

"I don't think throwing clothes into a basket is going to make any difference," she started. "You're only going to wrinkle them."

"No one will care if your clothing is wrinkled where we're going." Eldridge raked his hands through his hair until the dark strands stuck up in all directions. "Do you have any idea what you did? I know the Autumn Thief is convincing, but I have always held your intelligence in high regard. You've proven me wrong today."

Low blow. Freya knew he was saying the words from a place of fear and worry. Still, they stung as they struck her with all the force of a falling mountain. She could play that game, too, if he wanted to make this personal.

"Do you want to watch me die?" she asked.

"No!" The word burst from his lips. "That's exactly why I cannot understand why you would take this risk! The trials are difficult for the most powerful of fae. For a mortal, I don't even know if they're possible to complete."

"I'm not asking about the trials. Everything in the faerie realm is dangerous. I know that." Freya threaded her fingers together and rested her hands in her lap. "I'm asking if you want to watch me get old and die slowly. Because that's our future. I'm a mortal, Eldridge. I will end up aging, as you've likely already seen. I will turn into an old woman right in front of your eyes, but for you, it won't be slow at all. It'll be in the blink of an eye and then you'll have to hold me in my last moments when I don't even look like myself."

His eyes widened with every word, and his throat worked in a hard swallow. "That won't happen. I'll find a way to make sure that doesn't happen."

"You know it's difficult to grant immortality. I have to become something more than what I am, and simply staying in the faerie realm won't do that. Look at my father, he was raised here, and he still aged."

"Because he returned to the mortal realm!" Eldridge threw his hands into the air. "I don't know what to tell you, Freya. You have to trust me that we'll figure this out without sending you to your death to take part in trials that you cannot defeat."

She wasn't so sure that the trials would defeat her. Freya had done a great many impossible things here, and she didn't feel any fear. She should. Everyone else certainly seemed very concerned on her behalf.

But she was confident right now. She knew what had to be done now. Go to the Autumn Court, prove she was worthy of this magic, and accept that being a court ruler of her own people would be the next stage. She could do this.

Even if Eldridge didn't believe that yet.

"I'm not so confident that's possible, and I think you know the same," she whispered. "I'm sorry, Eldridge. I know this isn't what you want to hear, but I don't think even the great Goblin King can save me from death itself."

"I would fight it for you." A lock of his hair fell in front of his eyes, but she could still feel the determined burn glaring at her. "Not even death itself could take you from me, Freya of Woolwich. You are the other half of my soul and I'll be damned if I will suffer being parted from you."

She wished it could end there. That her Goblin King could fight death and all its army until the end of time, but they didn't live in a romance novel. They weren't living legends that could battle against something nameless and faceless. No one had ever beaten death.

Freya patted the bed. "Sit with me, Eldridge. Talk to me without arguing like you are so wont to do right now. I don't want to fight before a battle as important as this."

Finally, he sighed. His spine curved, and he made his way to the bed, where he sat beside her. Listing to the side, Eldridge put his head on her shoulder and took one of her hands in his. "I am so afraid of losing you," he breathed.

"I know. I'm worried about losing you too, but the Autumn Thief is right. If there was ever a chance for me to live like you, this is it." She lifted his hand and pressed a kiss to his knuckles. "And if we're handed a chance, shouldn't we take it?"

He stroked his thumb up and down her hand. "I don't know. There has to be a better way to do this other than to risk our lives. Our happiness. I want to live a full life with you, Freya. Even if that is only the heartbeat of a mortal lifespan. Losing you any earlier than that..."

She knew why he couldn't finish the sentence. The thought of continuing on without him terrified her.

Tilting her head, she pressed her lips to the top of his head and sighed. "Eldridge, I don't think you're going to have to continue on without me. I don't think either of us is going to suffer that greatly."

"You know nothing about the trials," he grumbled.

"No, I don't. But that doesn't mean I cannot learn. I convinced an ancient forest to give a spoiled elf another chance. I talked the ocean into slowing time for us. And I convinced the Spring Maiden that I was a terrifying being worth fearing." She leaned back and grinned at him, even though she didn't feel the smile in her heart. "I am capable of a great many things. And you were the person who taught me that nothing is impossible."

Eldridge stared at her as though he'd never seen her before. As though her words filled him with a sense of hope that he hadn't realized he could feel.

She could only hope that feeling would bring them both a little peace. She needed him on her side through this insanity.

The door to their bedroom creaked open again, and the padding footsteps of a small dog filled the room. "I know this isn't the best time for me to join you," Arrow said. "But I think that the entire family should be together and if you thought you were going to make any plans without me, then you were both sorely wrong."

Freya tightened her arm around Eldridge's shoulders and waved for Arrow to join them. "Hop up, then. We're lamenting my mortality and the impossibility of the task I agreed to complete."

Arrow rolled his eyes dramatically, but he jumped up on the bed with them without complaint. "As if you'd let this be the task that kills you. The old gods have no idea what woman is coming to greet them, and if they did, then they'd all be blindly running for the hills."

He settled into the crook of her arm and placed his paw on top of theirs.

Freya stared down at their hands on hers, and she wished she could tell them they were the reason she could do impossible things. Every time she thought she might falter, they made sure to catch her.

And it was luck alone that brought her to their arms. These two goblins had gotten her so far in life. And they would continue to encourage her to be the best version of herself.

Freya kissed the top of both their heads one more time, then giggled.

"What?" Eldridge grumbled. "You can't laugh at a time like this. We're all worried you're about to die."

"I don't plan on dying." She didn't know if that was the truth, but she was going to put it out into the world that she wouldn't. "I'm laughing because we've never cuddled like this before. All three of us."

Arrow immediately wiggled in her arms, twisting to get free from this moment he no longer wished to be part of. "Let me go. We're not snuggling, woman, and if we were, then it certainly wouldn't be now. Release me!"

She only tightened her grip and forced him to stay where he was. Even Eldridge tried to get out of her hold, but she refused. They were right where she wanted them, and neither of them was going to get free from her love.

"Don't you dare," she said while still laughing. "The two of you are staying here and giving me the support I need!"

"We'll support you from afar!" Arrow growled, snapping his teeth at her. "But I will not be caught snuggling with the Goblin King and his fiance. Unhand me, I said!"

Finally she let go of the two angry men, still laughing until her stomach hurt. At least she'd gotten a small amount of time with her arms around the two of them.

Arrow stumbled off the bed, shaking his head and then his entire body, as if he wished to get her touch off of him. "Ridiculous woman," he snarled. "You two need to get ready for the Autumn Stronghold, and I need to prepare, as well. None of us have time to be..." He paused, swallowed, then said, "Cuddling."

He wandered out of their room. But now Freya had something to focus on.

The Autumn Stronghold.

The building sounded very different from the other castles she'd been to at the heart of the courts. "Ominous," she muttered, looking over at Eldridge, who had straightened.

His hands flexed on the mattress, fisting the sheets in his hand. "It is. The Autumn Court has ever been different from the others. You'll see when you get there, but the Stronghold is... is..."

Freya watched him visibly struggle to explain what his old home was like. She didn't want him to fear what she'd think, or worse, scare her even more than she already should be. She put her hands on top of his and squeezed his fingers. "I'll see it when I'm there."

He blew out a long breath. "Yes, you will."

But if he'd come from that Stronghold, if that was the place that had built the man she loved, then surely there couldn't be so much to fear.

CHAPTER 6

"I still don't know why we can't tell your family what is going on," Eldridge grumbled as he tossed their trunk up onto the small carriage. "They're going to think the worst if I return without you."

Freya refused to respond. They'd already had this argument, and she would not bend. Her family did not need to know what she was doing. If she succeeded, then it would be a nice surprise for them. She'd return a new woman, far more powerful and with a court at her beck and call.

If she didn't come home, then they would have blissful ignorance for a little while longer.

"Stop trying to change my mind," she said, looking over her shoulder as her mother approached. "Let them have a few more months of happiness."

Even if her mother would turn into a screeching harpy when she heard what Freya had done. She was going to hear this for the rest of her life, if they succeeded. And if they didn't, well, she wasn't so certain her mother was incapable of raising her child from the dead just to yell.

Spinning around, Freya plastered a bright smile onto her face and approached her family. "Thank you so much for letting us have some time alone. It's just that the castle and the... well. All of it. We need some time to ourselves."

Her mother matched her bright grin. "Of course! A newly engaged couple needs some time alone."

At least Freya could relax, knowing that her family wasn't worrying. Was that a selfish choice? Of course. But if Freya was the one risking her life, then she thought she had the right to be a little selfish.

Her mother squeezed her even tighter, then whispered in her ear, "I know something is going on, and I'm not going to ask what it is. Please be safe."

Freya squeezed her back but didn't respond at all. There wasn't any truth she could give her mother. No help to ease the worry that already grew.

Somehow, her family always knew when something bad was happening.

With a bright, fake smile on her face, she leaned back and shook her head. "I don't know what you're talking about, Mum. We're off for an early honeymoon, and we'll be back before you know it. Just keep everyone in line around here for me. You know how Esther can get. And the Autumn Thief is still healing."

The last bit felt wrong to say. After all, Lark was no longer the Autumn Thief. Technically, Freya was.

The rest of her family approached, and there wasn't another chance for her mother to speak. Esther and Lux gave out their hugs, arms squeezing Freya and Eldridge while hope glowed in their eyes. Freya assumed they were both thinking about when they could also have their own getaway. When they were finally old enough to enjoy escaping to the wilds of the faerie realms.

Her father glared at Eldridge with a fake snarl on his face. "You take care of my girl, you hear me?"

Eldridge rolled his eyes and clapped her father on the shoulder. "You know I always do."

It felt like they were lying to everyone. Maybe Eldridge was right. She should have told them what was going on, but now she couldn't.

She'd already fabricated this lie, and Eldridge was kind enough to dance around the topic since he couldn't lie at all.

Oh, she was an ass.

"I'll miss you all," she called out with a giggle that sounded fake, even to her own ears. "Don't burn the castle down while we're gone, please."

And with that, Freya clambered on top of the small cart they were using to travel and kept her eyes straight ahead. Eldridge finished up and joined her, though he kept giving her a strange look.

She knew her actions were suspicious. But if she looked back at her family, then she was going to cry. They would know something was wrong and she wouldn't get out of the castle for another couple of weeks. She didn't have a couple of weeks to spare.

With a final nod toward her family, Eldridge cracked the whip, and they started forward. The cart careened away from the castle, filled with all the people she loved. All the people who didn't know this was the first time she feared she wouldn't come back.

Freya couldn't speak for a while. She didn't know how to talk about anything other than the fear soaring through her chest. What was she supposed to do now? Should she plaster on a brave face and keep pretending that she wasn't burning up inside?

Rustling in the cart behind them made her turn around. Arrow poked his head out of a giant bag that was supposed to be filled with extra food for the trip. Instead, the sack was now covered in a fine layer of black and white fur. "That was callous, even for you Freya."

At least she knew how to deal with him. She could handle a grumbling goblin dog. "I didn't exactly have a choice, now did I?"

"We all have choices in this life. And I don't appreciate you worrying everyone."

"I didn't." Freya turned around and crossed her arms over her chest. "I did the exact opposite. They have no idea what's going on, and now they won't be worried while we're gone."

Arrow clambered up the cart and then plonked his bottom down between them. "And yet, they will worry because you are not with them. You can't stop them from worrying about you, Freya. That's what people do for those they love."

She refused to believe that, no matter how true it was. Squeezing her arms tighter around herself, she nodded at the road. "What villages are we going past?"

Unfortunately, they hadn't had a lot of time to explore the Autumn Court. It had been her favorite one all those months ago when she had fought the Goblin King for the very first time.

The cart rolled up to the edge of the boundary between kingdoms, and she stared at the line of wavering magic. It warped the sight of the kingdom beyond. Red and orange leaves blanketed the ground in a bright layer of color. The wind brushed crimson and ochre paint drops from branches and danced with fine ribbons of fallen leaves through the trunks of the trees.

Freya could already smell the crisp scent of apples and the cold bite of fall. She had loved this place so much. And now, she finally got to return and see the real Autumn Court.

"We're not traveling through any of the villages," Eldridge replied quietly. He cracked the whip, and the horses moved through the barrier into what was now Freya's kingdom. "We're going straight to the Stronghold. There's only one path to go now, my love."

The ominous words sent a shiver down her spine, as they always did. A stronghold didn't have a good connotation to it. The very word suggested it was a place meant to keep people out in case of war or famine.

Or perhaps it was a building meant to keep people in.

Freya kept her eyes on the dirt path that led straight through the Autumn Kingdom. It was the only path she'd seen in the faerie realms that didn't meander. This path was straight and narrow.

Scraggly trees curved overhead, their branches warped and odd. Everything seemed to get more terrifying the closer they were to the Stronghold. The ground darkened to an umber, like bloodstained earth. The trees leaned forward with the claws of their branches grasping at her hair. Even the birds stopped singing.

She held her breath, waiting for the first view of the Autumn Stronghold. The castle that should have housed the Autumn Thief and all her court, but seemed instead to have been left to ruin long ago.

And when she did finally see the vast expanse of that building, Freya's entire body clenched in fear.

The Autumn Stronghold was built to impose. Black water stains dripped down the gray stones of the boxy building. Not a single bit of the exterior had been touched by an artistic hand. Instead, it was rather like a mallet. Useful. Utilitarian. And completely without beauty.

It stood on the very edge of a cliff, surrounded by black water. Not because the water was deep. It bubbled, and thick inky balloons popped slowly. She couldn't guess what filled the moat surrounding the Stronghold, but she'd once seen oil billow out of the ground and destroy a small section of the beach where she'd once lived. The glistening surface was eerily similar to that experience.

Lines of cages that hung off the sides framed the square building. Freya squinted her eyes because surely she hadn't seen them correctly, but there it was. Skeletons still hung in the cages with vultures holding onto the metal rungs. They wouldn't get a snack off those bones, but she feared they would never leave the poor souls alone, regardless.

Exhaling long and low, Freya bit her lip. "This is where the Autumn Thief is meant to live?"

"A long time ago, when the courts weren't even a glimmer of a thought behind faerie eyes, this was where the old gods lived." Eldridge slowed the cart so they could all stare in horror. "They were not kind gods. They were punishing and cruel. Every single one of them believed fear was the best way to control their people."

Arrow shivered beside her, dread running through his body and lifting his hackles. "The old gods are a myth to our people now, even though we know they still live. The Autumn Thief is the only court leader who deals with them."

"Why would anyone?" She eyed a vulture as it screamed and took flight. The beast circled overhead. "You all left the castle to rot, didn't you? Why not leave them as well?"

Eldridge's brows drew down, and he lifted a hand toward the vulture. It screamed again, but wheeled away from them in the air. "Someone has to watch them. Someone has to make sure they're appeased, or we fear what they might do."

Yet again, Freya felt that twist in her gut that threatened she might not make it this time. The old gods wanted to punish, apparently. They wanted to hurt and maim and instill fear in the people who should worship them.

Those were not the kind of gods she looked forward to meeting.

Eldridge picked up the reins again and shook his head. "Let's go home, then."

Home?

She so easily forgot this was where he had spent many years of his life. As the cart lurched forward, she held onto the seat and watched the castle loom ever closer. Here she was. Finally, at the place where she would be tested, tried, and measured. But was she ready for any of that?

The cart wheels rattled as they struck the last bit of dirt that gave way into broken cobblestone. The Stronghold seemed to hold its breath and when they reached the front gates, that breath blasted out in a great wind.

Freya heard a voice in her head. A few whispered words. "And so the Thief returns."

It didn't sound happy. In fact, she'd argue the voice sounded very much like whoever waited for them within those walls had been hoping for a chance to punish the Thief.

She wasn't the same person they'd originally given this magic to, but she had stolen it. So, in a sense, she was more like the original Thief than many had been for years.

They stopped the cart in the courtyard. Great front doors towered over her head, but Freya stared up at them with her hands on her hips. The black wood with golden hinges had seen better days. The entire castle was well and truly abandoned.

"You know," she mused. "Leaving the old gods alone might have been a bad idea. From the stories you told me, they don't seem like the type who want to be ignored or neglected."

Eldridge hopped off the cart and made his way toward their things. He was clearly ready to unpack, but still grunted at her words. "I'm sure they hated being left alone. But they made their own bed."

The shattered windows of the Stronghold gleamed in the sunlight, reflecting the crimson forest beyond like a landscape of blood. "I don't think it was smart," she repeated. "After all, now I'm the one who has to suffer that punishment. They want someone to blame, Eldridge. And now I hold the title of Thief."

"And you actually stole the magic." He heaved a trunk off the cart and let it fall onto the ground with a solid thud. "Are you starting to understand why I called you an idiot?"

Arrow placed his paw over her shaking hands in her lap. "We're both here with you, Freya. The old gods can't send all of us away."

The ground rumbled beneath their feet. Stones shook free from the top of the Stronghold and rained down upon their heads. They were all very lucky that none of the stones struck them. However, Freya heard the warning loud and clear.

"I don't think they liked you saying that, Arrow," she muttered. "If they wanted to throw us out, they could heave us from this landscape with a single thought."

Eldridge snorted behind them, then returned to pulling their belongings off the cart. "You two will learn it's better not to insult the old gods. But everyone learns at their own speed, I suppose. Would you help me get everything off the damn cart so the horses can run off? Then I'll show you around the dusty old building."

She didn't know how he got away with insulting the gods, but she wasn't going to argue anymore. Freya clambered out of the cart and resolved to do whatever it took for them all to stay alive.

CHAPTER 7

Eldridge slapped the rump of the nearest horse, and both of the wild beasts wheeled away. They'd unhooked them from the cart, of course, so the creatures were free to go.

Freya hated seeing the wild look in their eyes every time they caught sight of the Stronghold. The horses knew something she didn't, and that was an unsettling thought she couldn't get out of her head. If the beasts wouldn't go close, what waited for her?

She didn't have a choice, however. The Stronghold contained the old gods, somehow. She turned on her heel, picked up one of their trunks, and started toward the giant set of front doors. The black wood hid much of the staining that covered the rest of the surrounding stone. The golden hinges were now covered in a fine layer of grit and what looked like moss.

"Open," she said as she strode up toward them.

Nothing happened.

The Stronghold remained locked and hidden from her eyes, as though it refused to deal with a mortal Autumn Thief. And yet, she was the only one with the power that controlled this court. A building would not be the first thing to insult her.

Growling now, she gritted her teeth and glared at the doors. "You will open for me."

They remained stubbornly shut.

Fine. If the Stronghold wanted to play a game like that, then she would play the game. Freya reached inside her and touched the burning flames that lingered in her soul now. The Autumn Thief's magic changed every time she thought to look at it in her mind's eye. First it was cold, then it was warm, then it was merely the faintest sound of crinkling leaves under her feet.

This time, a wildfire raged inside her. Almost as though the magic itself was insulted that the only home it had known refused to allow it entry.

Freya touched her mind to the magic and whispered a single word. "Go."

It flew from her body and slammed against the doors. They pounded open as though a troll had bashed through the gates of this Stronghold, and the wooden slats struck the interior walls so hard, the golden hinges snapped.

Dust and leaves blasted into her face, whipping her hair away from her face and jerking her skirts like a flag in a storm.

Freya pinched her eyes shut, only opening them once the angry roar of the Stronghold was finished. The damned spirit of this place didn't want her to come inside, and when she tried to force her way in, it wanted her to know just how unimpressed it was.

"That's fine," she grumbled. "I don't want to be here either."

Freya glanced over her shoulder for her companions, only to find the two men standing at the bottom of the steps with dumbfounded expressions on their faces. Even Eldridge's eyes were a little wide.

"What?" she asked.

"When did you learn how to use magic like that?" he asked.

"I didn't learn. I did the exact same thing I did in the Summer Court." She huffed out an angry breath, still ridiculously upset that the fae didn't understand that politeness got her farther than force. Ironically. "I asked."

They trailed her up the steps, Eldridge holding a trunk and Arrow holding a smaller basket. But all of them stopped where the doors had once been.

Freya could almost feel their anxiety. It bubbled in her chest, too. She was the mortal here. Of course she feared going into the haunted castle that clearly didn't want her to step foot inside the walls of its powerful, sacred place. Why were her companions so nervous, though?

She leaned over slightly and nudged Eldridge with her shoulder. "Go on, then."

"Excuse me?" He stared at her with wide eyes. "Why am I the one who has to go in first?"

"Because you used to live here."

Obviously. Freya expected him to guide them through the Stronghold. Preferably right out the back door and somewhere else, although she knew that was unlikely. At the very least, he could bring them to a comfortable bedroom where the spirits of this place might not prey upon their fear.

Instead, Eldridge did not do any of what she expected. He looked at her, then back at the Stronghold, then shook his head. "You were so dead set on being the Autumn Thief. I think you should go in first."

"Why do I have to? I've never been here before. I have no idea where we're going." The trunk was getting heavy in her arms, though. She'd have to put it down eventually, and if that was outside the Stronghold, then she fully planned on waiting Eldridge out.

They could stay here all day. She wasn't going in there first.

Arrow snarled, long and low. "I hate the two of you, sometimes. Fine. I'll be the one to go into the haunted castle first."

The goblin dog continued to snarl curse words behind him, but he strode into the Stronghold without a single issue. He left tiny paw prints behind him. Each pad left a perfect imprint in the dust covered floor. Then he disappeared into the shadows and all Freya could hear was the continual mutterings about royals who were supposed to be fearless and yet were cowards every time they were inconvenienced.

She shrugged and said, "Well, I suppose we should follow him."

"I guess so," Eldridge replied. He still leaned forward and peered into the shadows before he moved though. "I didn't think it would be this easy."

"I highly doubt it's going to remain easy," she grumbled, but then walked into the Stronghold before she changed her mind.

The interior lit up the moment she stepped inside. Countless sconces on the wall burst into flame. But there wasn't much left in the castle for it to be as foreboding as she had thought. Dust, grime, and leaves covered the floor in a fine layer. Like the earth was trying to take this place back after it had suffered centuries of neglect. There was no great hall to enter. Just a sitting room where people would have waited to be brought to the next person who desired to see them.

The furniture was all turned over. A small fainting couch lay in front of them, flipped onto its side. Shattered glass covered the floor near a fireplace in the back. But everything else was missing. This room was empty, dirty, and sad.

Even the walls were showing their age. The stone had yellowed. Smoke marks smudged the walls above the pronged sconces.

"Huh." Freya's heart twisted with sorrow. "No wonder it didn't want us to come in."

Eldridge placed his box on the ground and muttered, "What are you on about now?"

"It's embarrassed." Now that she said the words, she could even feel the old building's shame. "It doesn't want us to see it like this."

"It is a building. The shell of hidden magic, that's all." Eldridge reached for the fainting couch and gently set it back on its feet. But the way he smoothed his hands over the back made her wonder how much he believed his own words.

She didn't think this room was the shell of anything. Freya could feel that there were beings who lived here. Powerful creatures that were obviously the old gods they spoke of. But she could feel something else as well. A sentinel. A guard who made sure that the gods were safe.

That feeling was the building. It was the Stronghold that had soaked in so many years of magic that it had taken a breath and lived. Every room had a heartbeat and thoughts of its own. Judgements that it made without the impression or opinion of others.

But she wasn't going to convince Eldridge of that, or even pull his own thoughts out of his head. So she nodded and replied, "Where are we going now, then? I suppose we aren't going to stay in the waiting room."

His fingers lingered on the back of the fainting couch. "No, I suppose we cannot. I'll take us somewhere safe. But first, we have to pay our respects, my love."

She didn't need to ask what he meant by that. Of course she knew. The gods had to be spoken with long before any of them fell asleep.

The silence pressed down on their shoulders as Eldridge left their things and trudged toward the door in the back. He opened it gently, just a crack, then took a long time to inhale. Was he waiting for something? Did he fear some monster would pop out at them?

He opened the door with a jerk, and a black mass charged toward them. Freya shrieked and threw up her arms. Was the Stronghold not yet done? What kind of beast would choose to live in a place like this?

No claws raked down her arms. No jaws snapped at her flesh.

She let her hands drop and glared at Arrow, who sat on the floor, wiping at the tears in his eyes as he laughed so hard not a sound slipped out of his snout. "I got you both," he giggled. "That was hilarious. Did you really think I was some terrifying creature ready to gnash at your throat?"

"Arrow!" Eldridge snapped. "We could have killed you!"

Arrow shrugged and wiped one more time at his eyes. "I don't think so. You're both quaking in your boots so hard, you wouldn't be able to fling a spell at anything. Too bad, really. Come on, I found something the two of you need to see."

She'd yet to find her voice. Freya was so frightened that she thought her heart had stopped. She even pressed a hand against her chest, fully expecting to feel nothing beneath her ribs.

Still grumbling, Eldridge reached out his arm and gestured for her to tuck herself against him. "Come here. That damned dog is going to be the death of us both. I refuse to even call him a goblin at this point."

She wiggled until she was pressed against his heart, her hand moving to his chest. "I don't know why we keep him around."

"Because sometimes he's useful." Eldridge pressed a kiss against the top of her head. "He's lucky I didn't turn him to dust where he stood. I would do worse to anyone who dared to touch you."

A part of her wanted to ask why he'd held himself back, but she already knew.

The Autumn Stronghold was testing her already. The doors were the first bit of wondering if she was capable of holding this position. She'd passed that one, but no one knew what other tests she would have to forge her way through.

Any danger that Eldridge intervened with would only look poorly on her. And though he might want to protect her, at some point in this journey, he would have to stop.

"Let's go," she whispered. "Arrow tends to find useful things on our adventures."

Together they strode out of the room and into a strange central hall. She thought of it as central because the entire space was circular. Even the walls had been covered with some kind of smooth plaster, then polished to look like metal, though the years had taken their toll on that as well. The farthest side of the circle was painted blood red, with three metal faces emerging from the smooth surface.

Arrow trotted over toward the faces, nodding at them with no small amount of fear. "That's what I found. I don't want to scare you, but..."

"The old gods," Eldridge whispered. His voice rang with reverence. "I've never seen them show their faces so soon, or so blatantly."

A voice chuckled in her head and said, "The mortal wouldn't recognize us or know the tales."

She kept that bit to herself. Some of what these gods said seemed to be entirely for her, and it didn't matter if the others knew. Besides, this was her trial, wasn't it? And now she could see who was going to judge her.

Striding up to the metal faces with purpose, she stopped in front of them and pointed to the one on the left.

This face was the head of an owl, though attached to a particularly feminine body. A barn owl, if Freya knew her birds right. The circular moon shape was beautiful and eerie. "Who is this?"

"We call her the Owl Mother. She looks over lost and wandering souls." Eldridge stood beside her and tucked his hands behind his back. "It's said that she is the mother of all goblins. But, as such, she's the hardest on our kind as well. She has something to prove to the others, and her riddles are thought to be impossible to solve."

Riddles. Of course there would be riddles. What faerie test would this be if they didn't try her wit?

She turned her gaze to the next face, though she hardly thought of it as a face. The features were too long, the chin too pointed, the eyebrows too lifted at the end for it to seem anything other than demonic. The man's ears were tipped at the ends, and his grin was full of malice. Twin pointed horns erupted from his forehead and curved back into the wall.

Eldridge shuddered. "Now that I'm no longer the Autumn Thief, I can say he was my least favorite. He is the father of monsters, the Horned God. A lover of mischief and trickery, who feeds off what others love. He devours memories, sometimes. Other times bits of flesh. I remember him as being cruel, and reveling that he made people afraid."

That was the one she needed to be wary of the most, then. She should keep her eyes peeled every moment she was in his trial.

And the last. The last head was nothing but the skull of a deer. The coiled horns were jagged and raw, the eye sockets so dark she swore something moved inside them.

"And this one?" she asked quietly. "Who is this?"

"It merely asked to be called Death." Eldridge swallowed hard. "It is the end for all goblins. The face we see when our time has finally come and immortality fails us. This is the last trial for us all, not just the Autumn Thief."

"What does this one ask for?"

He met her gaze with haunted eyes. "I don't know. I don't remember. No one does after their trials. It's as if this third task never existed in our minds, and that's the way it should stay."

Why were all these old gods so cruel? Why couldn't this test merely be a moment where they looked inside her soul and saw whether or not she was worthy? Nothing was ever easy in the faerie realms, she reminded herself. Taking over an entire court couldn't be simple.

"All right." She returned her attention to the heads in the walls and took a deep breath. "I'll be seeing all of you soon, then. I'm looking forward to it."

Three chuckles echoed in her mind. Clearly the old gods thought those words were cute, but they didn't believe her for a second.

Honestly, Freya wasn't certain she believed her own words.

Eldridge cleared his throat and gestured for both Freya and Arrow to follow him. "Let's get our things and find somewhere safe to sleep for the night. After all, we have a very long road ahead of us."

Eldridge led them through long, winding hallways that seemed to have no end. Freya wanted to trail her fingers along the walls, marking their passage in the thick layers of dust. But something told her to keep her hands to herself. Sure, she might have proven herself strong by blasting the door open. But that didn't mean the Stronghold liked her just yet.

Besides, Eldridge knew where they were going. He walked through the halls with the confident stride of a man who had made this journey many times. Although the curve of his shoulders suggested he wasn't ready to do it again.

He paused and put his shoulder to a wooden door that was barely visible behind a thick layer of soot and smoke stains. "This is the room."

With that, he heaved his weight against the door and it swung open with an angry squeal of rusted metal hinges. Arms full, they all walked into a room that Freya could now call the great hall. For what else would this cathedral-like room be?

The ceiling stretched over three stories high above their head. Light filtered through the stained glass ceiling, though many of the marvelous pieces were shattered. Ivy dangled through any openings it could, and nature entered the room with wild abandon. Four massive pillars outlined the empty hall, each one carved with different symbols of the courts. Daisies for spring, waves for summer, leaves for fall, and snowflakes for winter.

Even the walls were painted with a thousand scenes, like they had walked into a secret chapel that honored the history of the fae. Battles with orcs wielding hammers the size of mortal men, and pixies floating in the air with sparks of magic at their fingertips. Quiet scenes of heartbreak as the fae knelt over the bodies of fallen heroes. Freya's eyes caught on a much larger mural depicting all the fae on their knees, worshiping three figures shrouded in darkness.

"Those are the old gods," Eldridge grunted as he placed his trunk down beside hers. "They always wanted us to remember that we were meant to bend a knee to them."

"Why did you? The fae are so powerful."

"They gave us life," he replied with a shrug. "And for all the power the fae hold in their hands, that magic was once living in one of the old gods. We worship them because they deserve it. Without them, we are nothing."

Arrow paused beside her and snorted. "Also, because the court leaders aren't sure if the old gods can take the magic back. What would the fae do without all the powers they were given? Better not to make anyone mad that gave us all we have."

Right, that made a lot more sense. Freya shared a knowing look with the goblin dog, before noticing even the floor was incredible.

Wide tiles of molten gold and silver had been strategically placed in a herringbone pattern. Each tile was inlaid with precious gemstones that gleamed even in the dim light of the room.

"What was this place, then?" she asked.

Freya had thought it was the great hall. She could imagine long tables here for feasting and parties. But now that she'd absorbed all the details, she wasn't so sure.

With a long sigh, Eldridge tousled his hair and ran a hand down the back of his neck. "I guess you would call it a church, but not really. The fae don't worship like you do. It's more a... a..." He struggled to find the word, then pointed his fingers at Arrow and snapped them. "What's that thing the mortals call it? The pagan ones."

"A shrine." Arrow nodded firmly. "That's closer, you're right. It's not the same as those mortals who insist on everything being so stuffy. This is more like the old ways of the mortals."

A shrine. That sounded right to her ears as well. And this room wasn't just for worshipping the old gods, but also for the very history of the fae. They mourned their fallen, because so few faeries ever died. Freya could feel thousands of years worth of emotions that had built up in the walls of this room. Heartbreak. Sadness. Guilt. It was a heavy place to even stand in, let alone sleep.

"And this is where you think we'll be safest?" She asked the question with no small amount of skepticism.

Eldridge nodded toward the back right corner of the room, the one with the autumn pillar. "I'm certain it will be safe. It's where I found my own solitude for the many years that I attempted to live here and appease the gods myself."

How had she missed it? The entire corner of the room had been turned into a makeshift bedroom. A small cot in the corner, with a desk and a wall plastered with paintings, notes, and what looked like ripped pages of books.

She stepped closer to the small area and pressed a hand to her heart. Freya hadn't realized how important it had become to see where he'd grown up as a child. She wanted to know his history, more than just described in words. And now she could really see what he'd been like for herself.

"I always wondered if you were the same when you were the Autumn Thief," she said with a soft chuckle. The sound carried through the room, a little too loud.

Eldridge paused at the old desk, leaned down, and blew hard. Dust burst into the air and danced in the thin beams of sunlight. "I suppose I was a little less confident."

"You were still cocky," Arrow corrected. He hopped up onto the bench that served as a chair for the desk and glared at the papers. "And perhaps a little obsessive in your research. But you were a younger version of yourself. Arrogant. Reckless."

"Fun," Eldridge added, then ruffled the fur on top of Arrow's head. "I was also very fun to be around and everyone enjoyed my presence."

Considering the look on Arrow's face, Freya wasn't so sure about that. She could easily imagine that Eldridge had been a little out of control in his youth. She turned away to hide the bright grin on her face. Instead, Freya focused on all the documents that Eldridge had pinned to the walls.

Some of them were histories of this land. Others were detailed descriptions of the old gods.

Leaning closer, she eyed a depiction of the Owl Mother with her eyes a little too realistic for comfort. "What were you doing here, Eldridge?"

"Researching the gods and trying to figure out a way to get out of the burden." Eldridge reached around her to trace the drawing with a finger. "I realized rather quickly that there was no way out of this. The Autumn Thief would always be tied to the old gods, and if we tried to sever that tie, all the other courts would suffer. Our line of rulers would suffer while the rest could flourish."

Maybe that was why Lark had given up. The old gods must have driven her to madness to cut through her own throat like that.

The thoughts were too dark. They clouded her mind and pressed against her lips and throat in a scream that needed to erupt. This was her future. She could so easily become Lark.

She turned her attention to the cot covered in yet another delicate film of dust. A blanket was folded at the foot of the bed, as if someone had been preparing to return but never did. She touched a hand to the plaid blanket, then looked back at the soft expression on Eldridge's face. "How old were you when you first took up the mantle of the Autumn Thief?"

He shook his head, eyebrows raising for a moment, before he shrugged. "I don't know. I was very young, certainly younger than any of the others. But my power was more than just the Autumn Thief, and the old gods knew it. They wanted to control me for as long as they could until I surpassed even them."

"I still don't understand why you are the Goblin King, or how that even came to be."

Eldridge looked a little awkward at the question. He shuffled his feet from side to side, looked at Arrow, then at everything but her.

It was Arrow who answered with a huff. "The Goblin King or Queen goes to the most powerful person in all the courts. We view them as almost godly. No court leader should be infinitely stronger than another. That would lead to war. Therefore, if someone gets too strong, they become the king."

"Who rules over all the others, but doesn't have a court of his own," Freya murmured. It made sense. It kept everyone in check. Even the most powerful.

Arrow huffed out another breath and scuffed his foot on the ground. "This place is dirty. I am dirty. And now I have to find a place to sleep that isn't this because if I have to sit in the dirt for one more moment, I think I'm going to lose my mind."

Freya flicked a dust bunny off his nose and wiped even more grime from his mouth. "I think you look cute while you're covered in dust."

Again, he snuffled something about rude mortals and how they were always happy to live in filth, but then slipped away. She should worry that he was going to get in trouble, but that sense of the Stronghold inside her didn't mind him wandering. In fact, if she stretched her awareness far enough, it seemed like the Stronghold was opening doors for him. Hurrying him into a part of the keep where he would be warm and clean.

So the dust and dirt could be a show then. Yet another way for the Stronghold to tell her that it didn't appreciate her being anywhere inside it.

Fantastic.

"I don't think the Stronghold wants either of us here," she said.

"No, it likely doesn't. But that's all right. The Stronghold doesn't get a say in who becomes the Autumn Thief, or whether they have a right to live within its walls." Eldridge tapped the stone for good measure before holding his arms out to her. "Come here, my love. How are you holding up?"

She wasn't. Freya felt a little like she was falling apart at the seams. Everything was going so quickly and she had been so certain that she wanted this, that she hadn't taken the time to think about what it would mean to be the Autumn Thief. Now she was thinking about it.

The Stronghold should be her home, now. She had an entire court of people to look after, and now the added responsibility of appeasing gods that could easily take away all the magic of the fae. She also had to figure out how to use this new power inside her, make it through the trials, and then somehow deal with the reality that she was immortal.

Or could be immortal.

Was she yet?

Brows furrowing, she looked up at Eldridge and asked, "Am I already fae? Or am I still a mortal with the Autumn Thief's magic inside me?"

He chuckled and tucked her head back underneath his chin. "The entire world falling down around your ears, and the only thing you're worried about is if you're still mortal."

"Well." Her words were garbled, mouth mashed against his collarbone. "I didn't exactly think any of this through. You know how I am."

"Yes, I do." Eldridge released his hold on her and took a step back, allowing them both a little space. "You run head first into danger without a care for yourself, as long as that danger benefits those you love. We're all very lucky to have you in our lives, even if you are a nuisance sometimes."

"A nuisance?" How dare he? She had spent too much of her life making sure everyone was happy to be called that.

Opening her mouth to argue, Freya stopped when Eldridge held his hands out to her. His fingers glimmered with power, then his skin darkened into a night sky. Just his hands glowed with all the power of a universe inside them. A million stars glittered on his skin, a thousand planets and so many lives all contained in a universe held inside him.

"This is how you know when your powers come in. You'll have an entire galaxy inside you, bubbling to the surface, incapable of being contained. It's like burning alive and falling in love all at the same time." He turned his hands over and the glittering magic intensified.

"I don't have that," she whispered. Freya told herself not to be too disappointed. Not yet, at least.

She couldn't wait until that magic burned in her, though. For the moment when she was the hero of the story one last time before responsibilities and the world pressed back down on her shoulders. Before she had to become someone else again. Someone that suited what the old gods wanted. What the Autumn Court needed.

"Don't you?" Eldridge asked. He looked pointedly at her hands.

Freya lifted them to his and watched as the tips of her fingers turned orange with bright, sparkling lights. Tiny pinpricks opened up in her skin, but they didn't hurt. They weren't wounds, after all. They were magic finally making itself known.

She pressed their hands together and her soul sang with an ancient song. Drums beat in her ears and the melody of a thousand voices lifted into a hymn she didn't recognize. All the Autumn Thieves who'd come before her were here with her now. They whispered ancient words, old spells, and power that could only be controlled by her will.

"As I suspected," Eldridge whispered. He brought her hands to his lips and gently kissed her knuckles. "It has already begun."

CHAPTER 9

She tried her best to get some rest. No matter how much her mind wanted to wander, Freya continually fought to still her thoughts. Relax. Do something other than ponder what was going to happen next and just how much she was about to go through.

But of course, the thoughts wouldn't stop poking their way through her relaxation. What if she woke up and one of those Midnight Monsters was leaning over her? Would she survive the heart attack?

Rolling over, she cushioned her head in her hands. The blankets underneath them didn't serve as a soft place for her head to land, and her back was already aching. But Eldridge looked like he was fast asleep. His dark lashes dusted his cheeks, the bags under his eyes a little too dark for her liking. He hadn't been sleeping much, clearly.

She wished she could take the worry away from him. She wished she could help ease the fear in his heart.

Freya knew what it was like to watch the person she loved wandering through all the dangerous situations that could rip him from her arms. They'd done this together for too long now, and all she wanted was to hold him against her chest and promise that everything would be all right.

It had to be. There was no other option.

He took a deep breath and shifted onto his back. Hand folded over his chest, he looked like a stone statue that belonged right where he was. The Stronghold finally had him back, and she could feel in her very bones that it was happy to have him home. Of all the Autumn Thieves, he was the one the Stronghold had missed the most.

Freya couldn't stay here when there was so much else she could do. If she tried to lie here and sleep, then all she would accomplish was staring at the ceiling until the sun broke through the ragged holes above them. She'd get herself all worked up in fear of what might happen in the morning.

And she was tired of being afraid.

Rolling over, she carefully slipped out from underneath the covers Eldridge had laid over her. On her hands and knees, she crawled over to the bench of the desk and leveraged herself to standing. Every movement felt like she was going to wake up everyone who actually had managed to rest, but no one shifted or moved. Even Arrow, who had taken up the cot that used to be Eldridge's. The goblin dog sighed in his sleep, snuffled a little breath, but then drifted back into the dreaming realm.

Good. She wanted to explore on her own for a bit. Maybe she'd have a heart to heart with the Stronghold that still hated her.

Padding barefoot through the shrine, she wandered through the strangely colored beams of moonlight that fractured through the remaining stained glass. Paintings of faeries at war blurred in front of her vision, though they weren't as terrifying this time. She'd stared at every tiny detail, and knew their warped faces weren't ones of anger or rage. They were of pain.

She touched a finger to the nearest one before slipping out of this holy place and into the hall beyond. Rather than the reverent, safe feeling of the room Eldridge had chosen, the hall felt hostile. She could still sense that the Stronghold wanted to throw a thousand trials in her way.

"I don't know why you hate me so," Freya whispered. "I took the magic from Lark. Perhaps you liked her a lot, but she was dying. Would you rather have me let the magic eat her?"

894

A rush of air barreled down the hall, blasting her hair away from her face and tangling in the skirts of her dress.

Apparently yes, the Stronghold would rather see an Autumn Thief die than a mortal take her magic.

"Fine, then," she muttered. "You could have that guilt on your mind with no issues, apparently. But I could not suffer through the rest of my life knowing I could have done something to help her, and I chose not to. Selfishly."

The last word seemed to subdue the Stronghold for a moment, although Freya had no idea if that was a good thing or not. It seemed to withdraw back into itself. No longer a magical home with thoughts and emotions. Just an empty building that had seen too many years of neglect.

She reached out and put her hand on the wall, trailing her fingers through the thick layer of dust. Ivy bumped over her knuckles. The sound of their rustling made it feel as though she were wandering through a forest rather than a building with such impressive stature.

And still, this didn't feel right. Something in her chest burned. Ached. Whispered for her to move through the shadows and keep going because something important was calling to her and she was still ignoring it.

Freya's feet moved through the hall on their own. Her body guided her to where her mind did not know to go. Heart thundering in her chest. Breath ragged with anticipation. She knew something was happening. Something important that would change her life forever.

She just couldn't guess what that something was.

Her feet paused in front of a wooden door. This one had long scratches down it, like a beast had tried to enter the room for many nights before it had given up on its prey.

What kind of creature wandered these halls? Eldridge hadn't mentioned that they needed to be frightened of any terrifying beast or anything that might hunt them. Carefully, Freya ran her fingers down the grooves, wiggling her nails underneath the chipped pieces of wood. They felt as though they were brand new, even though she knew that wasn't possible. The last Autumn Thief to be here had to have been Lark, and she had ruled the Autumn Court for a very long time.

Clawed silver hands came down over hers, pressing her palm flat against the door.

Eldridge whispered in her ear, "Every trial is different for every Thief. But no matter what the old gods throw at them, it remains here as though it were only a few days ago that it happened."

Shivers traveled down her spine. She should have known he would find her. That even if she tried to sneak off in the middle of the night, he'd know. She'd done it before to him, after all. And he'd always caught her.

She sucked air into her lungs and tried to find her tongue, even though she wanted to sink into the heat of his body and his arms. The Goblin King's confidence would be the only thing holding her up if she did that. Freya knew she needed to stand on her own right now.

Licking her lips, she asked, "Who was the Autumn Thief who defeated this beast?"

"I imagine that was Lark," he replied with a chuckle. The deep sound skittered down her back as though he'd stroked his hand down the bumps of her spine. "Although she never told me the story. I would guess she survived the night by locking herself inside this room."

"Is that an option?" She'd hide for months, if that's what it took. Freya knew how to be alone, and she certainly could use the rest.

"Hiding to defeat the old gods? No. I doubt they'd let you get away with that." He smoothed his hands down her arms, up to her shoulders, and then turned her around.

Freya looked up into his starry eyes and knew that she'd never feel this loved again in her life. Eldridge looked back at her with his heart in his gaze, and not a single thought hidden from her. Heavens above, he loved her.

She smiled, but the expression was as fragile as glass. "How did you know where I was?"

He pinned her against the door, shifting his hands to her wrists and clasping them above her head. "I've been following you for what feels like years, hero of mine. I would know where you were if I lost my eyes and ears. I will always find you, Freya. No matter how lost you are."

The words echoed through her mind as he leaned down to kiss her with all the ferocity of a storm. His confidence, pride, and love swelled in her chest. She kissed him back and let all her worry, anxiety, and fear bleed into him. He took it all. He shouldered the burden for her, knowing that she needed his strength, and he could take these dark emotions for now.

"Did you think I'd let you do this alone?" he whispered against her lips. "I can feel the old magic too, you know. I might not be the Autumn Thief any longer, but it still calls to me. The court would take me back in a heartbeat if I didn't have other obligations. I know when the old gods are calling to the new Thief."

So that's what she'd been feeling. Freya should have known, but perhaps she was more tired than she thought. "I didn't realize they would call me so soon. I thought we had more time to prepare. To..."

She didn't know what. Preparing for something like this was effectively impossible. They didn't know what the old god would throw at her, and she didn't know how to use the magic running through her veins.

The old sailors near her village would claim they were throwing her to the sharks. The old hunters would say they were throwing her to the wolves.

Freya thought these gods were infinitely worse than either of those fears.

Eldridge watched every thought in her head. She watched as his eyes filled with tears, though he refused to let them fall.

He took a step back, cleared his throat, and then dashed his hands over his eyes. "We shouldn't keep them waiting. The first test has already begun, and we have to make sure you'll pass it."

"I thought it was a test only for me?" Freya had been under the impression that she would be alone in this. That no matter how much she wanted the others with her, she would have to suffer without the support of her loved ones.

Eldridge cupped her cheek in his hand, stroking his thumb over the high peak of her cheekbone. "I'm the Goblin King, my love. Even the old gods cannot deny me what I desire. After all, I'm one of them now."

That shiver of fear trailed between her shoulder blades again. Months had passed with the man she loved, the one who had proven to her time and time again that he was trustworthy, but she still feared him sometimes.

Eldridge led her away from that horrible door with the claw marks of a beast. They walked back the way they'd come and past the door to the shrine where Arrow still slept. Somehow, she knew he was bringing her to the room with the three faces of the old gods.

The whole time they walked, she twisted the engagement ring on her finger. Over and over, as though the movement of the stone might settle the tension in her stomach.

It didn't, but a girl could hope.

She held her breath as Eldridge swung the door open and revealed all the metal faces waiting for her. This time, Freya swore she saw all of them blink. As though they were alive and ready to reach out with those cold hands.

Swallowing hard, she looked over at Eldridge and whispered, "What now?"

Even though she'd been deliberately quiet, her words echoed through the room. Lifting into the rafters and bouncing back to her ears. The words twisted in the echo, a mockery of what she'd said and the fear she felt.

Eldridge raised an arm and gestured to the three faces. "They are all waiting to meet you. Go with your heart, Freya. Choose the first one you want to see, and the first god whose trial you will face."

The words felt like an omen, as though her Goblin King was not the man she knew, but one she should fear as much as the old gods.

"I get to pick?" she asked. "Shouldn't there be a correct order of things or one of the gods that is more important than the others?"

"There's always a choice, Freya. No matter what stage of this you are in. You're the Autumn Thief for now, and though they want you to prove yourself, you will prove to them all that you are more capable than they ever dreamed." He smiled and bared his teeth. The sharp points of his canines glinted in the moonlight. "And if they dare think that you are weak, my love, my life, they will know how wrong they were."

With his confidence bolstering her courage, Freya stepped up to the metal faces and eyed them all. She looked into each of the eyes, and then finally settled on the Owl Mother.

"How do I choose her?" she asked.

"They're doorways," he replied. "You already know how to open them."

She wanted to reply that she didn't, but some age old knowledge bubbled in her chest. She did know how to open this door.

Freya lifted her hand, touched it to the owl woman's face, and pushed.

CHAPTER 10

The bronze owl woman's head depressed into the wall. Fine seams appeared around the edges of a doorway that Freya hadn't realized was even there. It swung open and revealed the strangest room she'd ever seen.

Moss and grass grew up to the edge of the doorway, and a slight breeze tickled the ends of her hair. Fog covered the meadow beyond, but there weren't any walls or ceiling. She leaned in slightly and looked up, peering into a gray, cloudy sky.

"It's a portal?" she asked.

"All the doors are strange," Eldridge replied. "I can't promise they won't take you somewhere else. And I certainly can't say they won't transport you to places where the old gods feel more comfortable."

"Right. Impossible things." Freya had always found a reason to love the phrase Eldridge had said when she first arrived in this realm. *Nothing is impossible.* But now, it seemed to have lost its luster.

She took a deep breath and stepped onto the grass. Somehow, she knew Eldridge followed her. She could feel him in the depths of her very soul, wandering next to her, never too far behind.

The air here was colder. She found herself slightly breathless with the ache of ice and the chilled bite of autumn. Though the grass was still lush, it already had brown patches where frost had killed it.

"Where do we go now?" she asked. The mist dampened her tones, making the words difficult to hear.

"I don't know," Eldridge replied. "You're the one undergoing the trials, my love. They will draw you where they wish you to go, and no further than that."

Right. Everything was on her shoulders right now, and she was realizing how terrible she was at listening to godly figures that wanted to order her around. She already thought to walk aimlessly through the fog if they desired to play this game.

Freya saw right through this. The Owl Mother wanted her to be disoriented. She wanted Freya to lose her way in the fog and then require a god to help her. That wasn't going to happen.

Lifting her hands, she blew into her palm and willed the magic to do something with the air. The power of the Autumn Thief knew exactly what to do. Her breath amplified into a wind that rivaled the misty air. It blew a clear path ahead of them and led all the way to the roots of a dead tree. The scraggly, gray bark rose into the sky like arms. Tiny circles hung from the branches, twisting in her wind.

"There we go," she angrily muttered. "Was that so hard?"

The ground rumbled as though it were responding, yes. It was hard. She forced the land to do what she wanted, and that was a cruel thing to do. The land hadn't bent to anyone's will in a very long time, and even if it had back when Lark first became the Autumn Thief, it hadn't done so willingly.

This place needed to learn that she wasn't like the other Autumn Thieves. Freya was more than any of them could have been, because she was mortal and she knew the value of life. She knew how hard it was to live, to love, to learn how to walk through each and every day with death dogging her heels.

That set her apart. The fear of death and the love of life would always make her more dangerous than any other fae who had walked through this place.

They approached the tree, footsteps quiet through the moss. She held her breath until they stood directly under the skeletal branches.

Circular stones hung from each branch, hundreds of them turning in the wind. Each stone was hollow in the center, tied with a leather thong, slowly spinning as though they all wanted her attention.

"What are they?" Freya asked, burning with curiosity.

Eldridge tucked his hands behind his back and watched them spin. "Hag stones."

She'd heard the word before, although Freya couldn't remember where. A memory bloomed. "Hag stones," she breathed. "Mother used to talk about them. She said witches used them to see the faerie realm."

"They do," Eldridge replied. "In your realm, they are the only way to see through glamour. Witches look through them to see our true form, and then they can tell if they're dealing with one of the fae, or perhaps another witch. It's a dangerous job to have, making magic for those you don't know."

"I suppose it could be." Freya reached up and stopped one of the stones from spinning.

With its slow, meandering journey paused, she could look through the hole into a world beyond. This one showed a shoreline with grey skies and foaming white surf. The pale sand almost melted into the sky beyond.

"What do they reveal in the faerie realm, then?" she asked.

"You always were too smart for your own good. This is a tree where we collect the matching pair to each hag stone in your realm. It shows what the witches are looking at." He reached up as well and stopped another, looking through it before letting it spin again. "They don't know the fae can spy on their every move, and we would like to keep it that way. Witches are so distrustful."

Considering the fae were spying on them, she thought they had a reason to be. Witches would likely lose their minds if they realized the fae used the hag stones against them. Magic was magic, after all.

Then his words rang in her mind like a bell. He'd said witches used the hag stones to see through a faerie's glamour. And she knew what that was. Her mother always said the fae never showed their true form because they were so ugly underneath.

Of course, the goblins didn't seem to mind. They were all some horrible mashed creation of man and beast.

But the Goblin King wasn't.

She'd never really thought about it, considering he'd always been so "other" to her. His title was the Goblin King, yes, but that didn't mean he was one of them. He had tufted ears and claws, which wasn't enough to make him a goblin, and she'd never once thought that strange. Until now.

Until he said those words that made her question if he'd told her the entire truth. Or, like always, if he'd hidden away a part of himself because he was embarrassed.

"What would happen if I looked at you through one of these stones?" she asked.

Freya remained frozen in place. She didn't want him to think she was about to lunge at a stone and immediately brandish it in his direction. If he'd hidden what he looked like from her, then perhaps that was for good reason. The Goblin King was many things, and vain was one of the most important.

He cleared his throat and awkwardly looked to the side. "I'd appreciate it if you didn't."

"That doesn't answer my question." Freya had to push. She couldn't let this go when she knew there had to be a good reason for him to hide what he looked like. This was yet another puzzle for her to solve, and one that was delicious.

This was better than the reality of having to face a god. Knowing what he really looked like would give her something to focus on, other than how her life might end very soon.

"Freya." He shook his head. "I don't want to talk about this right now. Look through the stones. See all the world through them and all the witches who know our powers. Experience mortal life for a little while longer."

"What if I was always bored with mortal life and I want to know the answer to this now?" She fiddled with the hag stone in her grip, ever so tempted to turn it on him.

What would she find through the small hole, bored by the ocean tide? Perhaps he would be more monstrous than any of the goblins she'd met thus far. After all, he was the strongest one. The most powerful faerie in all the realms. So surely he must look at least a little different from the others. He must be more ghastly. More dangerous.

But even knowing all she did about the fae, and about Eldridge, she couldn't imagine a version of him that she found ugly. He was the man she wanted to marry. The man who made her so happy and so strong, no matter what she faced.

She hoped that he would eventually show her what he looked like underneath all that magic. But she would also be satisfied honoring his privacy and all the anxiety he felt in knowing that she could choose to see him for who he truly was.

Freya dropped the hag stone.

A great sigh released from Eldridge and his shoulders curved him. Breathing hard, he chuckled and clapped his hands together. "For a moment there, I thought you were going to look through it even if I didn't want you to."

She waited until he caught his breath before she replied, "I almost looked."

The laughter in his chest died down, and he watched her with wide, bright eyes. Freya was more powerful than she'd ever been in this moment. She had faced the temptation of seeing his true form, and she had defeated it. But she had also proven how strong she was to him. She could have taken away all his safety. All his lies in one simple movement.

"I won't forget that," he breathed. His voice was a whisper in the mist, carrying with it all the bright tones of reverence. "I won't forget that you showed me mercy."

"If only that was the real test." Freya looked back up at the hag stones that spun above their heads. "I would pass with flying colors, I think. But mercy is not in the nature of the fae."

"You're right about that," another voice replied from beyond the thick white fog.

And so it began.

Freya turned on her heel and peered through the mist. It swirled as though something were alive within it. Everything in this cursed, holy place was alive. Even the ground they walked on.

Slowly the fog parted and revealed a person standing on a single dirt path that wove across the ground away from them. This person wore a black cloak, hood drawn over their head to hide their features from her sight. They stood with their shoulders and head lowered, staring at the ground.

"Who are you?" Freya asked.

She shouldn't have said the words. Obviously this was the person they were waiting for. The person who would either prove to be one of the old gods, or the person who would lead her to the place where she would finally be judged.

The figure lifted its hands and pushed back the hood. It was a woman with an owl's head. Though not the same woman that had been on the wall. This one was no barn owl, but a woman with tufted ears like a great horned owl. She stared at them with wide, yellow eyes. Her hands clutched the edges of her cloak as though she were ready to flee at any moment.

Freya didn't want her to be frightened. This obviously wasn't the godly figure that she was meant to meet, and scaring away a god's subjects seemed like a bad idea.

"My name is Freya," she said, trying again to get the woman to speak. "Who are you?"

"I am no one," the owl woman replied. "And everyone. I serve the Owl Mother and all who come into her kingdom."

"Ah." Freya awkwardly shifted her stance. "I assume I'm supposed to meet your Owl Mother, then?"

An awkward silence stretched between them again. Could she only say so many things and the rest had to wait until Freya saw the old god?

Huffing out a breath, she looked over her shoulder at Eldridge, who had frozen in place. He stared at the other faerie with a mixture of horror and sadness in his eyes.

"What?" she asked. "Do you know her?"

Before he could answer, the owl faerie giggled and covered her beak with a hand. "Know me? Yes, Eldridge. Why don't you answer that question? Apparently you haven't told her all that much, now have you?"

Freya frowned. "Eldridge?"

He didn't reply. His horrified expression never budged until the owl woman huffed out a disappointed breath.

"Fine," the new faerie muttered. "Follow me, Mortal. Oh, and welcome home, Brother."

CHAPTER 11

Brother?

The word tumbled through Freya's mind, even as the owl woman turned away from them. Eldridge claimed he had family, although he rarely wanted to talk about them, and she'd always respected his privacy. But this was his sister? This owl creature who lived not in the Autumn Court per say, but with the gods that had plagued the faerie courts for so long?

It didn't make sense, and yet it did. Eldridge had hidden so much from her, and this was something he'd be horribly embarrassed for anyone to know.

He wasn't just the most powerful faerie in the courts. He'd been given an advantage in becoming the Goblin King that no one could ever have guessed. Growing up under the wing of an old god certainly would have crafted him into a man far more deadly than the other faeries.

She looked over her shoulder and raised a brow. "Brother?"

Eldridge chewed on his lip. A muscle in his jaw bounced as he tried to figure out what to say that could make this all better. Part of Freya wanted to stop him. He couldn't explain this away, and it wasn't necessarily something that he should be forced to explain, anyway. He had a right to keep his family to himself.

It would have been useful to know that they were going to visit his blood, however. They might have used that to their advantage. Now, she was walking into a family reunion without knowing a thing about them.

Why did that make her so nervous? She should be excited to meet his family.

She supposed it might have been easier if that same family wasn't deciding if she should live.

Blowing out a breath, she eyed the owl woman, who was already disappearing into the fog. "I'm not going to ask too much about this strange circumstance, but I do need to know if she's going to lead us to certain death."

"There's never any way to know with my family." He sighed heavily. "But I think the only option here is to follow her. I didn't think we'd drag up so much of my history, or I would have told you more before we came in."

"Would you?" Freya somehow doubted that. She thought it more likely he would have approached his family before he'd brought her here and warned them not to tell her a thing because he wasn't ready to be that honest with her.

Maybe he never would.

With a heavy sigh, she placed her feet onto the winding path and started after the owl woman. "We're going to talk about this later," she threw over her shoulder. "I know you don't want to talk about it now, and I don't want to push you. But you will tell me everything."

"I know," he replied. "I know that very well."

Gravel crunched underneath her feet as they made their way into the mist. This time, Freya used no magic to see what surrounded them. Somehow, using magic at a time like this felt as though that would be a grave insult to the Owl Mother. Whatever the god wanted hidden should remain hidden.

She tried hard to follow the owl woman, but the faerie disappeared into the mist faster than Freya could follow. One second she was right in front of them, and then Freya would blink. No one would remain other than a swirl of fog where the creature had once been.

But then she'd walk down the path a little farther and look to her left. The owl would appear off the path, cloak precariously balanced on the back of her head, staring at them as though she were a creature who had stepped out of her nightmare.

Finally, Freya had enough of jumping at every shadow. The next time the owl woman did it, she reached out and grabbed onto the woman's cloak.

Hand fisting the fabric, she drew the owl close to her face and snarled, "Stop doing that. We're not playing a game right now, and my test is not to be completed by you. Any intimidation you think is happening? It's not. You're only annoying me."

The woman grinned, though it looked strange on her owlish face. "I don't care if I'm annoying you. You aren't here to be comfortable, Freya of Woolwich. Mortal women are not meant to be here at all, and yet, you snuck in with magic you shouldn't have."

Mist coiled around Freya's wrist, tugging at her grip on the cloak. As if the creature was using magic to get her off.

Freya released her hold, pressing her tongue against her teeth and smiling back at the little monster, who continued to think that she had the upper hand. "This is my magic now. I know it must be horrible to look at a mortal who you think so weak, having something that you want."

"I don't want it," the owl woman replied.

"Yes, you do, otherwise you wouldn't be trying to annoy me. You'd simply take me to the Owl Mother and then you'd be done with the dirty little human you think shouldn't even be in your realm." Freya tilted her head to the side, watching this faerie's eyes flick back and forth. Anywhere but Freya. "You're looking at everything but me. You know you cannot lie, and now that I've caught you in your own deceit, you cannot lie to yourself any longer. Can you?"

The owl woman snapped her beak, then looked behind Freya. "What are you going to do about this, Brother? You're standing there, with not a care in the world, as if this mortal hasn't stolen something of yours."

"It's not mine," he replied.

Freya wrapped her hand around the owl faerie's jaw and forced her to look back to the mortal she so hated. With no small amount of pride, Freya lifted her hand and let the dark stone on her finger do the talking for her.

The owl woman spluttered out a sound that was a mixture of an owl's call and a woman's choked horror. "What is that?"

"Proof that I'm more than worthy of the magic you think shouldn't be mine." Freya released her with a slight jerk. "Now, no more games. I'm not interested in speaking with anyone other than her. Especially if they're all foolish little girls like you."

Again, that horrible, cawing chuckle erupted from the faerie's mouth. "That's hilarious. Brother, you know you cannot help her while she's in here, don't you? I thought you were here to watch the mortal flounder and then fail. But you're actually here to see her win!"

"I love her with every fiber of my being," he replied. "I will not see her fail. But even without my help, I think she would prove herself more than worthy of this power and this position."

Freya watched the two of them argue. She should have been focusing on their words, but instead, all she could see was the resemblance that she'd never put together before.

The tips of Eldridge's tufted ears she'd always assumed were fur. Now that she could see his sister, it was so obvious those tufts were feathers. They even ruffled in the wind differently than fur, and she felt like a dunce for not noticing sooner. Even his claws were not that of a furred creature. His fingers were talons. After all this time, she hadn't noticed until this moment.

She felt like a fool.

"Eldridge, you are going against everything our family has always struggled for. You used to hate mortals just as much as I," the owl faerie snarled.

"And yet, I was always the one who was willing to grow while the rest of you remain stuck in the pit of your own despair. I will not, and never will, become someone who cannot admit when I am wrong." He pointed at Freya with a jabbing motion. "That woman is better than half the faeries I've met in my life, and you would be lucky to call her the Autumn Thief."

"And your opinions are clouded with lust." With a disgusted sound, the owl faerie waved her hand in front of him. "You need to learn a lesson, Brother, and I am not so weak that I cannot teach it to you. Did you forget that you are no longer in your realm, or that of the fae? Whatever I want to do to you, I can."

The spell she cast spilled over the Goblin King like water. Freya watched as the glamour he'd created around himself shivered, shifted, and melted away. She only caught a single glimpse of what he looked like. A nightmarish visage of a half man, half owl, before he let out a cry of horror.

His own magic shimmered to life, a dark cloud erupting to cover the owl head that had replaced his own and the smattering of feathers that spread down his shoulders and arms. Eldridge turned into a great horned owl, then burst into flight and disappeared into the mist.

It all happened within the span of a heartbeat. So quickly that Freya wasn't certain she had seen what he looked like at all.

"There," the owl woman muttered. "Now, Brother, you won't meddle in things you shouldn't. Men."

Freya held her breath and tried to focus. She was alone now. She had power, even though she didn't know how to use it. Perhaps another day would be dedicated to train and learn and grow. But right now, she stood in front of a very powerful faerie who served a god, and who clearly didn't like her.

Eldridge, she thought, *where did you go?*

The owl woman gestured for Freya to follow her. "Listen to me, darling. He is not on trial. You are. But he has always had a soft spot for women he can save. And there is no saving you, because then he'd be the Autumn Thief again. That's not what Mother wants."

"Mother?" Freya repeated.

Eldridge had claimed his parentage was noble, yes, and that they were a king and queen. Gods weren't that, and besides, he wasn't the child of a god. None of that would make any sense at all unless... Unless...

"Wow," the owl woman muttered. "While it's very interesting to watch the thoughts dance over your face, I would very much like it if you'd hurry up."

"Excuse me?" Freya muttered, still in a daze from the reality of her situation.

"Let me just lay it out for you, little mortal. Yes, Eldridge is the son of the Owl Mother. He was born into a life knowing that his mother was a god and that he would likely become the Goblin King. His power comes directly from her, and if it didn't, then he would not be who he is. After all, a Goblin King must have some sort of godly powers or no one would respect him." She added a sniff for good measure. "But here's the thing. The rest of us know he's nothing more special than the others. He was the lucky one that was older than the rest. Nothing more than that."

The owl woman turned with a flounce and started back down the path. But Freya knew that while there was some truth to what she said, the last bit was wrong.

Eldridge was so much more special than these creatures. He saw the future, and he wasn't afraid of it. He saw differences and loved them, rather than feared them. But more than anything else, Eldridge had seen a mortal woman and knew she would do something good with the powers she'd been given.

At least, Freya hoped.

"I think you're afraid of him!" she called out.

The owl woman froze in the middle of the path, turning back around with a wide-eyed stare. "Afraid of who? The little man I just turned back into an owl? Back into the most basic form he could suffer?"

"Yes." Freya straightened her shoulders and squeezed her hands into fists. "I think you're very afraid of him. I think you see Eldridge as someone who challenges the old ways, and the idea of that frightens you. You can't control him."

"I can control him. Did you not see how he's an owl now? No longer a man?" The owl woman scoffed, then turned around and gave Freya her back. "You can keep arguing until you're blue in the face, little mortal. But you aren't in your realm any longer and you certainly aren't in the Autumn Court, either. This is a place of old gods and legends. You don't belong here."

But Freya did. Because she was the Queen Killer, the one person who had brought every single court ruler to their knees and then decided to marry the Goblin King. Freya was no ordinary woman, and not even an owl faerie could convince her otherwise.

She continued down the path in silence, but this time with a courage that brewed deep in her belly. This was no one else's confidence but her own. She didn't need Eldridge here to whisper in her ear that everything would be okay. Freya knew it would be.

Let the trials begin. She'd been ready to be Queen long before stealing the Autumn Court's magic.

CHAPTER 12

She noticed the first faerie not long after their argument. It appeared out of the mist as though it were nothing more than a stone standing at the edge of the path. But when she walked past, the owl creature opened its golden eyes and watched her. It moved nothing other than its eyes, and somehow that was all the more terrifying.

Then another, although this was a goblin she'd never seen before. Its face wasn't the only thing that was animalistic. Instead, it leaned on long arms that were a mockery of wings. The feathers indented into the ground. She couldn't tell if it weighed so much that it had moved the earth, or if it had been kneeling there for so long that it had sunk into the dirt.

Yet another creature, one that looked like the owl who was leading her, appeared on her right. Then another. Then hundreds. Each owl lining the path and watching her with disappointed eyes.

None of them wanted her here. None of them thought she was worthy of the magic that burned in her chest.

Let them hate her, she decided. They wouldn't be her subjects and they could think what they wanted. She had stolen the magic as an

Autumn Thief should, and that would be the end of their ridiculous judgement. She had done nothing wrong.

Freya lifted her chin and focused on the small path ahead. The dirt trail grew more narrow with each step until she was walking through the line of owls so close that her shoulders brushed their chests.

In her experience, most faeries flinched when a mortal touched them. But these creatures? They didn't move at all. Just watched her with those haunting, disappointed eyes.

The faerie she followed disappeared again. Freya raced forward to catch her, nearly at a run in the fear that she'd be left alone in this crowd and swallowed up by a mountain of feathers and disapproval.

Racing forward, she almost didn't see the cliff until it was too late. A sheer drop plunged into the mist and shadows far below her feet. Freya skidded to a halt, her toes hanging over the edge and her arms pinwheeling to catch her balance. If she had noticed the cliff even a heartbeat later, she would have tumbled into the darkness below.

Somehow, she didn't think these faerie creatures would have cared one bit. Her death would have been one less situation they had to take care of, and a far easier end to this trial.

Breath ragged in her lungs, Freya looked over at the owl faerie, who stood a few steps to her right. Eldridge's sister had crossed her arms over her chest and watched her with clear disapproval. "Well, I suppose you're smarter than I gave you credit for," she grumbled.

Freya fought every ounce of her desire to shove the other woman over the edge. It would be so easy. The faerie would never expect that Freya would be so bloodthirsty, and all she'd have to do was push.

"My daughter may make you angry, but touching her would be the last thing you ever did. You have greater things to worry about than the existence of a faerie who inconveniences you."

The voice was deep, like the burble of water. Raspy as though the woman smoked the cheroot cigars Freya had seen so many of the sailors hang from their lips. And power echoed through the very tones of the woman's voice, though Freya was unsure how she knew that.

Slowly, she turned her attention across the great chasm. Mist surrounded her. Freya couldn't see the other side of the gap in the earth, nor could she see the sides where a long rope must have been connected. And yet, there was a thick rope hanging mid air in the fog and a woman seated on top of it.

She wore a long cloak like her daughter, though she hadn't brought the hood up over her head. Her gray cloak pooled around her small figure, dangling into the mist and disappearing into the shadows below. Her barn owl face was like looking at the moon. And her eyes were crystal blue.

This was the Owl Mother. No one else could be.

Freya dipped into a low bow and tried not to stare down too long in fear that she'd lose her balance. Her heart thudded in her chest. This was the moment. She'd been waiting for what felt like forever for these trials to start and now, here she was.

Freya didn't have the faintest idea what the Owl Mother would ask of her. She didn't even know how long such a trial would take. The fae had thousands of years to waste their time. Would they let a court be leaderless for that long? Freya didn't know.

She feared what would happen if the court was on its own, however. The goblins were good, dutiful people. But they were also wild and untamed. They needed someone to lead them so they didn't get into too much trouble.

Wings beat by her ear, though she almost didn't hear them at all. With her heart in her chest, Freya watched a great horned owl fly past her and land on the rope beside the Owl Mother.

The faerie woman shifted underneath her cloak. A clawed hand emerged from the folds of fabric and gently patted the top of Eldridge's head. "Welcome home, my son. You know better than to meddle. Your sister has to have her show, after all."

Eldridge ruffled his feathers and clacked his beak at the Owl Mother's hands. He barely missed one of her talons, and Freya wondered how powerful his jaw was. Could he have cut through the Owl Mother's taloned finger? Most likely.

His mother tsked. "Come now. You're being dramatic, as always."

"In my experience he's rarely dramatic until necessary." Freya watched as the feathers on top of Eldridge's head flattened. "But perhaps that's simply being here. I'm sure being dramatic in your eyes is far different from my reality."

The Owl Mother's ears twitched. She reached into her pocket and drew out a strand of hag stones, each one bone white. Lifting one to her eye, she peered at Freya through the small hole in the center, as though she expected to see something other than a mortal in front of her.

Freya had gotten that from the fae before. They rarely thought she was what she said, and they all needed to realize that she was very much a mortal. But she wasn't afraid of them.

"How curious," the Owl Mother muttered. "You are what you say you are, and yet, you don't act like it."

"Perhaps your experience with mortals is lacking."

"Careful. You still stand before a god and I have no problem wiping you off the face of this earth."

Freya shifted her stance, taking a single step away from the cliff edge, just in case. "I think if you planned on doing that, I would have fallen off this cliff before I even noticed it was here. You're bound to the old ways like the rest of us. I think the only way to get rid of me is to have me fail a trial. Or is that incorrect?"

"Clever and pretty." The Owl Mother pocketed her hag stone and gracefully clasped her hands in her lap. "I suppose you are correct, then. My trial is simple. The Autumn Thief cannot be someone who is dim-witted or dull. Your intelligence is what I'm most interested in, Freya of Woolwich."

She was so tired of the faeries calling her that. She was no longer of Woolwich, or even the mortal realm. Without thinking, she blurted, "You will call me Freya of the Goblin Court."

All the faeries around her stilled.

Silence filled the fog with bated breath as if every living creature and magical mist were waiting for what Freya would say next.

"Explain yourself," the Owl Mother snarled.

"I do not yet call a court my home, at least not one of seasons. But the Goblin Kingdom, the one that the Goblin King calls his own, that is my home." She gulped, then continued. "I cannot say I am a member of any court or kingdom other than that one. And I understand that the Goblin King has no subjects. But he has me."

The harsh set of the Owl Mother's shoulders softened. She glanced over at her son, who stared at Freya with wide eyes filled to the brim with love.

"As you wish," the Owl Mother murmured. "Freya of the Goblin Court, are you ready for your trial?"

She wasn't. But would she ever be? If this was a test of her wit, then Freya knew she could survive this one. Though she worried what the other tests might be.

Clearing her throat, she nodded. "A test of wit it is. Do your worst."

The Owl Mother shook her head and rolled her eyes. "Three riddles, mortal. And I won't do my worst, considering you are not of this realm. There are many things here you may not yet have seen or experienced. But I do keep an eye on the mortal realm. I know your world, although you were quick to judge that I did not. In this case, I will provide you with the most difficult riddles from your own kind. If you know the answers to them, then I will be satisfied with your... intelligence."

That was easier. Why was the Owl Mother not taking this opportunity for difficulty?

Freya narrowed her gaze and widened her stance. In some way, it felt as though aggressive body language might make her more focused. She didn't really know, but she still held her hands clasped behind her back in preparation.

The Owl Mother leaned too far forward on the rope until she looked like she would topple over the edge. "In a land far from yours, there is a god named Odin. He asked a man worthy of being king this riddle. Four hang. Four sprang. Two point the way. Two to ward off dogs. One dangles after, always rather dirty. What am I?"

Ah. So the Owl Mother wasn't playing fair after all. She said that she was using riddles from Freya's world, but she wasn't going to use riddles that Freya might ever have heard of. Odin was the name of a god who didn't exist for Freya or her people.

She took her time thinking about the riddle. Warding off dogs, always rather dirty, the words all jumbled in her head. They didn't make sense. She had no idea what the answer to this riddle was, and it was only the first one.

A farmer? Perhaps? Or maybe a scarecrow, although that wouldn't explain the numbers of four.

The magic in her chest rose and pressed against her throat, trying desperately to be released. Freya didn't know what it was trying to do. She felt like someone else was reaching out of her throat and if she opened her mouth, then a hand might pop out. It hurt. It ached.

Finally she opened her mouth and heard herself say, "A cow."

A what? That wasn't at all what she wanted to say and already she had lost!

The Owl Mother clapped her hands a few times. "Bravo. I see you are quicker than I thought."

Wait a minute. That was right?

The magic inside her head seemed to chuckle, as though someone were quietly laughing in her ear. Of course it was right. The magic might have been locked in the faerie realms for all its time, but it was thousands of years old and had lived in countless heads. Riddles were nothing to a power like this.

"I suppose so," she replied, although it felt wrong to say. She hadn't solved the riddle at all. The magic had.

And yet, the Owl Mother still continued. "There is a house. One enters it blind and comes out seeing. What is it?"

The magic again pressed in her throat, but Freya suppressed it. She had heard this one before. She'd gone into the village with her parents, and a wandering band of minstrels had paused for water at the same time as Freya. The leader of the troupe had said the exact same riddle to one of the others, stumping his entire team before he dramatically revealed the message.

Freya only remembered because she had been so shocked. A wandering band full of ragtag people from all walks of life in her little town? The colors of their clothing had been a feast for her eyes. She'd heard his answer, and it had stayed with her for as long as she could remember.

"A school," she said. "You walk in blind, but you leave with the entire world at your feet. Knowledge is powerful like that."

"Hmm..." the Owl Mother muttered. "I'm glad we agree. How

curious it is to know that you didn't even stop to think about that one."

Freya opened her hands at her sides and drew them out wide. "You never said the riddles had to be ones I had never heard. You chose unwisely with that one, Owl Mother. I have heard it and it was a lesson that remained with me for much of my life. Even as a farmer myself, I always knew to continue pouring knowledge into my head. I refuse to be blinded."

A few owl faeries next to her muttered. They leaned close together, whispering in each other's ears and Freya knew she had impressed them. They thought her nothing more than a wild heathen of a mortal. Likely they had thought she would arrive with her face painted, weapons in hand.

They had forgotten that time passed quickly in the mortal realm. Her people had many centuries of learning since the last time any of these old gods had walked that earth.

"And the last?" Freya asked. She wanted to get this over with sooner rather than later. Yes, she understood that she should savor this moment. Or perhaps even feel a little apprehension that this last riddle would be impossible to answer.

Yet all she wanted was to leave this place. She wanted Eldridge back in the form he drew comfort from and for him to be away from the family that thought him dramatic. Useless. Unworthy.

The Owl Mother narrowed her eyes, and all her owl children fell silent. Freya had the sudden sick feeling that this last riddle was going to be more difficult than any of the others.

"You should know this one as well, if you're as well read as you claim. It's from a rather holy book for your people." Her eyes narrowed with glee. "Out of the eater came something to eat, and out of the strong came something sweet. What is it?"

Oh, that was a difficult one. Freya swallowed hard and waited for the feeling in her throat again. The feeling that the magic would take over because she had no idea. She really didn't.

But the magic didn't know either. She could feel it tossing up its hands in shock because that was a riddle neither of them knew.

Freya met Eldridge's terrified gaze and wracked her brain for something. Anything. There had to be a logical explanation for this, though it was unlike any riddle she'd ever heard before. What could this mean?

A holy book. That was a clue.

The Owl Mother tilted her head to the side, then tapped her claws on the rope. The twanging sound was distracting. "Come on, now. You said you were witty and intelligent. You said I underestimated mortals."

"Stop rushing me," she grumbled.

The Holy Book. There was only one that mortals worshipped more than others, but Freya and her family were unlikely to go to church. Fables were more her mother's interests.

Freya touched a hand to her head, running her fingers through her hair as if that might help pull information from her mind. Her fingers tangled in knots at the bottom of her long strands, and that was what made her remember.

Hair.

Samson.

This was a riddle from the Holy Book. A good, dutiful mortal should know the answer to this. They lived their lives based on the truth written on those ancient pages. But perhaps to the fae, the idea of faith in a god no one had ever seen meant that the stories were only that. Stories.

Freya met the Owl Mother's gaze with triumph burning in her own. "You shouldn't have told me it was from the Holy Book, or you would have stumped me, Owl Mother. Samson killed a lion, and bees made honeycomb in the great beast's carcass. I believe that's what you are referring to."

All movement stopped. Even the mist hesitated in its swirls as it waited for the Owl Mother to confirm or deny what Freya had said.

The Owl Mother sniffed, then nodded her head. "You have passed the first test, Freya of the Goblin Court. Now, I believe I would like to speak privately with the woman my son wants to marry."

The mist swirled. It rose in a great wave that crashed down on Freya's head. She ducked, curling her body tight to her knees and waited until the wind died down yet again. This time, when she opened her eyes, she stood in a meadow on the edge of the cliff. No mist. No ropes.

No owlish faeries staring at her in an army of feathers and disdain.

Instead, Freya was alone in this clearing. And so, she waited until the Owl Mother returned to speak with the woman who would be the Autumn Thief.

CHAPTER 13

Eventually, Freya turned away from the cliff and meandered down the path. Neither Eldridge nor his mother appeared, so she had to assume she should wander. Or find her own way back. At the very least, it gave her time to think. Time to wonder at the magic that had risen to the occasion when she needed saving.

"Are you aware of being inside me?" she asked, her voice whispered low and quiet.

She heard in her ear an answering hum. A breathy sound of someone agreeing with her. As if the magic was answering, yes. It was very much aware of being within her. It had a mind and personality of its own, but for now, it was content to live within the heart of a mortal.

Freya touched a hand to her ribs, wondering if she could feel it. That strange pulse of magic must move through her skin. But she couldn't feel anything. Just her own chest rising and falling with each breath.

"Thank you for helping me," she whispered. "I don't know how long you'll be with me, but I am very grateful for your help."

Another faint chuckle echoed through her mind. Almost as though the magic jested that it knew she had needed it, and that she was lucky it had helped. She'd needed its assistance right out of the gate, but after that, she'd managed on her own quite well.

Freya was proud of that. She'd only needed the magic for one out of the three riddles.

A tree appeared on the horizon. The same tree she'd seen upon first entering this realm. The hag stones danced in the wind and clinked together as they moved. It was a beautiful dance Freya enjoyed watching, and one she might have relaxed with if two feathered figures hadn't soared over her head.

The great horned owl and barn owl moved as though they had flown together a thousand times. As if flying through the air in unison came to them naturally, and Freya supposed it must. How many times had mother and son done this?

They landed on the ground next to the tree, then allowed their magic to fall from their forms. The Owl Mother stood with a stooped back and her white cloak draped over her form. And Eldridge, her sweet, handsome Eldridge, appeared to her as he should have all those months ago.

He didn't hide himself, proving that her first vision of him had been true. The owlish face was warped on him. Half of his features were that of an owl, and the other half only had a sprinkling of feathers. But his eyes were the same. They were always the same.

Clawed, curled hands remained limp at his sides. He let her look over his features with only the slightest of winces. "Hello, Freya."

What did she say to him? That she loved him? The words felt a little too dull, even though her heart still thundered in her chest for him. Only him.

What words could soothe the fear in his chest? She would love him like this, no matter what. Of course she would. No form or figure would ever change the man he was, and how deeply she loved his soul.

Freya stepped closer to the tree, pausing when he looked away from her. "Goblin King. I'm afraid I must ask you to make another deal with me. One last time."

His gaze flicked to hers. "And what would that be, Hero of the Faerie Courts?"

"Let me love you in every shape you come in," she replied. "And I will give you my heart."

The feathers on his face lifted, ruffling in the wind. "That's a horrible deal, Freya."

"It's the only deal I want. For the rest of my life and a thousand times over." She couldn't help herself. She had to walk forward until she was right in front of him, begging with her eyes for him to reach out and take her in his arms. "I don't care what you look like, Eldridge. If you suddenly turned into an owl for the rest of our lives, we'd make it work. I want to marry you. I want to spend the rest of my days waking up and seeing your perfect face in the sunrise. Man or beast. Make this deal with me, and I promise to never break it."

A deep groan echoed in his throat. He reached out with a clawed, curled hand, and cupped the back of her neck. He drew her close until their foreheads touched. "You stubborn, foolish woman. I love you with all my bitter soul."

"It's not all that bitter," she replied with a soft chuckle. "You think so much less of yourself in this form, but you are even more other-worldly to me like this. You are my fairytale prince, Eldridge. Nothing would ever make me give you up."

His breath fanned across her lips before he kissed her. Gently, softly, even as his feathers tickled her cheeks and then slowly disappeared. When they drew back, he had returned to the Eldridge she knew.

Freya reached up and touched her fingers to the tufts on his ears. "I always thought these were fur."

"You were wrong." He smiled down at her. But she knew this wouldn't be the only time she'd see his true form. Something in his gaze had warmed even further. "Now, let me properly introduce you to my mother."

Eldridge lifted his arm in a grand flourish and turned them both to meet the Owl Mother's waiting gaze. The old god really was intimidating to look at, but goodness, she was beautiful too.

The moon shaped white face stared back at her with all the wisdom of the world hidden in her eyes. Freya knew that this goddess wasn't afraid of anyone or anything. She had seen so much in her life that she knew what a waste it was to let fear grow too strong within her being.

A breeze swept at the edge of the Owl Mother's cloak, revealing a strong but wiry body underneath it. The Owl Mother had aged, and time already showed in her limbs. Unlike any faerie Freya had met thus far.

"So, you are the one my son has chosen for himself," the Owl Mother said. She folded her hands at her waist and looked Freya up and down. "There are many who will be disappointed in this."

"And they won't be the first or the last." Freya rolled her eyes. "I don't fear the opinions of others. If they don't want me to be with the Goblin King, then they can take up their concerns with him."

Eldridge bared his teeth in a mockery of a grin. "And I will have very few chosen words to say in return."

Apparently, the Owl Mother was very aware of what her son planned to do. She sighed heavily and shook her head. "I see now why you chose this path. Loving a mortal is a short pastime. But make her immortal? One of us? Then you will have a millennium to learn and grow with each other. It was the only path."

Some tension drained out of Freya's shoulders. At least the Owl Mother understood her decision. Even Eldridge still thought Freya was mad for trying to do this on her own. But the Owl Mother had understood. That had to count for something.

"I love him," Freya replied. "I would do anything to be with him for as long as possible."

"It was a selfish choice." The Owl Mother lifted her hands. Mist swirled around her, then solidified into a table and chairs. The old woman sat down as though standing that long had made her bones ache. "And now you need to learn what happens when you make a choice like that on your own. The Autumn Court cannot and will not be ruled by someone who took the power only to be with another."

"That wasn't the only reason why I took it." It wasn't. Freya knew the main reason was that she had wanted to be immortal, like Eldridge. But there had been another, buried deeper in her mind. "The Autumn Thief was dying. I had to help."

The Owl Mother gestured for her to take a seat. They didn't have a choice to say no. Both Eldridge and Freya sat across from the mist born table and watched as the Owl Mother steepled her fingers and pressed them against her pronounced beak. "Yes, Lark. What did she say when you first found her with that wound upon her neck?"

"An assassin has come to the Autumn Court," Freya replied. "We assumed she meant someone tried to kill her."

Now that she said the words, she realized how wrong they were. And how clear the answer was if Eldridge had only remembered these trials sooner.

"An assassin," Freya repeated in horror. "One of you tried attacking her, so she tried to take her own life before you could."

The Owl Mother inclined her head. "Not just one of us, Freya. Death is one of the greatest old gods to ever live. The three of us are ancient, but he is the oldest. He was the first and will be the last, no matter how much the Horned God and I fight for our lives. Death is inevitable."

"So you are not fae," Freya replied.

She'd assumed as much. Just seeing all the children of the Owl Mother had changed her mind on what they were. Eldridge was obviously one of the fae, and his goblin sisters couldn't be denied that lineage either. Though they were powerful creatures, they were still the same as the other faeries. But the Owl Mother? She was something else.

"No," the Owl Mother confirmed. "Old gods are not what the fae are, but we created them. Back then, there were four of us. I was the mother of the Autumn Court. The Horned God created Summer. Our dear, departed sister created Spring. And Death created Winter. All the courts were meant to live together in harmony. We were seasons of the world that shifted around each other and created a more powerful unity. We were wrong."

"Everyone wanted their own power, I assume?"

Eldridge took her hand and lifted it to his mouth. He pressed a kiss to her knuckles. "Power desires more power. It is how the world turns, no matter whether one is in the faerie courts or the mortal realm."

What a horribly sad history for these people. She couldn't imagine having come from such strife and hardship, although she supposed mortal history was likely as horrific.

Freya took a deep breath and nodded. "Then I understand this position is more important than I realized. The Autumn Court needs a strong leader to help heal those old wounds from years ago."

They were the right words to say. The Owl Mother heaved a relieved sigh and leaned back into her misty chair. "Yes, finally. So many people have come through my trials, passed them, but never understood what I really wanted from them. I hope your words remain true no matter what is thrown your way, my dear."

"Time will tell." Freya hoped she could maintain that trust and hope that the Owl Mother had placed on her shoulders. She wanted to be that person for the Autumn Court.

If there was one thing Freya knew how to do, it was how to love people she thought she should hate. Old prejudices died hard. But sometimes they had to be given up.

"It's not going to always be so easy, you know." The Owl Mother looked pointedly at her son, then back to Freya. "I have a soft spot for my boy, and that clouded my judgement. I could have been much harder on you."

"I know." And she was forever grateful that this first test of wits had been one she could overcome and survive. This was the first step toward making everything right.

A familial urge tried to propel her hand over the table and reach for the Owl Mother's hand. Freya wanted to touch this woman who would be her mother-in-law. She wanted to hold on to her hand and promise that she would take care of this woman's son, no matter what happened to them. Their relationship was stronger than any of these faeries could imagine.

But when she reached across the table, the Owl Mother moved her hand away. "Please don't try to be my friend, Freya. A god has no friends, and there is even less family between the two of us. What you need to do now is the sacrifice portion of your trial."

Sacrifice?

She looked at Eldridge and his expression of horror, then back to the Owl Mother. "No one mentioned a sacrifice. I didn't bring anything with me."

"It's not a sacrifice of an important object." The Owl Mother waved her hand, and the mist on top of the table parted to reveal a small platter. Twin gold knives sat atop it and a chalice decorated with falling leaves. "The Autumn Thief is someone who can withstand not only a battle of wits, but a battle of pain as well. No Thief is a weakling."

CHAPTER 14

The knives glinted in the dim light. They taunted Freya with thoughts of pain and the slicing ache of someone cutting into her flesh because she had dared to want something more out of this life.

Taking a deep breath, she let it slip out of her lips as she stared at the gold.

"What do I have to do?" she asked.

The Owl Mother blinked at her with eyes that were too large for her face. "Becoming the Autumn Thief requires a price. You need to show that you are willing to do whatever it takes. Pain is what I request. Use the knives wherever you wish, my dear. All I need is a true response to pain, and a little blood."

Eldridge slid the knives away from Freya. When she started to argue, however, he wasn't even looking at her. He was glaring at his mother as though the anger and hatred in his eyes could burn her alive. "She's not doing this."

"You know it's part of becoming the Autumn Thief," the Owl Mother replied. "You can't stop this part, neither could I for you. This is what it takes for this court to be handed over."

"I refuse it," he snarled. "She will be giving no one pain simply because of an old, forgotten tradition that no one should follow, anyway."

The Owl Mother shook her head in disappointment, a war battling in her expression. "Eldridge, this is the old ways. You cannot change something like this because you want to protect your pretty little plaything. She has to have some form of sacrifice."

Eldridge stood. His chair fell over behind him, slamming against the ground with a sound like it had struck glass. "It was always the same with you! The old ways are better. That we can't change the tides of history and we should never try to re-correct the boat. But no other court requires such barbaric practices."

"I cannot change this, and neither can you!" she shouted in response. "The other gods will require the same and do you know what will happen if I don't request my dues? They will challenge her right to being the Autumn Thief. If this mortal somehow makes it through all the trials, then she will still not get the throne."

Obviously, that answer didn't settle well with Eldridge. He threw his hands into the air and scoffed. "Of course. You want to change it, but you don't see how you can. Isn't that just like you? Every time I need you to do something for me, you have to refer to the other gods. Do you refuse to take any responsibility for your own actions? You can't always blame them, Mother!"

Freya watched the feathers on the Owl Mother's face ruffle. Then the old god stood as well. She clearly didn't like her son taking such a tone with her. Perhaps there was some truth to his words, and that stung more than she was willing to admit. Even to herself.

Whatever the reasoning, Freya could see neither of them planned to budge on their opinions. As with most of the faerie arguments she'd witnessed, they were not interested in listening to each other.

But she was mortal, and she could easily read between the lines of their arguments.

The Owl Mother still saw value in the old ways, but she was also trapped by the other gods. They were going to challenge the legitimacy of Freya's claim if she didn't do this, and that was something she wanted to avoid. Otherwise, they would all start this whole process all over again and Freya had already proven herself to the Owl Mother.

Eldridge, on the other hand, didn't want the woman he loved to be in pain. He would stop at nothing to protect her, even when he knew that was a foolish thing to do. He knew the risks. He just wasn't willing to give up her well being for the risk of losing a throne.

What they both failed to realize was that this wasn't their decision. They could argue until they were blue in the face, but they weren't the ones that had to sacrifice pain to satisfy anyone else. This was all up to Freya.

With that thought in her head, she reached forward and grabbed one of the knives. It took a second for either of the fae to notice that she'd moved, and Freya could only imagine the picture she made.

A little dark haired mortal sitting in a chair made of mist and fog. She spun the golden knife in her hand, looking down at it as though there was some magic in it she hadn't noticed yet. Of course, it did have some form of magic, but maybe it was only a knife. A knife meant for cutting and slicing.

"Freya," Eldridge said quietly. "Let me handle this for you."

She looked up and met his sad eyes. "You know that's not how any of this works, and that's all right. I'm going to do this for you, for me, and for the Autumn Court that I stole from someone much more qualified than me. And I'm not going to flinch."

Freya held her arm over the goblet and didn't let herself think or hesitate. She drew the knife across her wrist with a sharp slice, hissing out a long breath at the sudden heat that spread up from her arm.

It took a while for the real pain to sink it. About the same amount of time it took for the blood to pour from her skin into the goblet. She hadn't made that deep of a cut, but enough for her to bleed a startling amount.

"Oh," she whispered. "I didn't think it would feel like this."

Like she could feel her flesh actually parting. Hot and cold at the same time as blood warmed her skin, but gooseflesh ran up her arms.

The Owl Mother sat back down across from her, and the sadness on her expression was a warning. "The pain you feel will not remain only physical, my dear. I'm sorry for what you're about to go through, but know it is temporary. And that any pain you find along the path will only become something that makes you stronger in the end."

"What?" Another slicing ache of heat, followed by ice, rolled up her arm into her shoulder joint. Freya twisted hard, losing her grip on the knife that clattered onto the table. "What is happening?"

"The last part of my trial," the Owl Mother whispered.

Eldridge caught her as she fell back from her chair. He cupped both his hands under her elbows and held her tight against his chest. "I will be here with you every step of the way," he said, pressing a kiss to her hair. "You are not alone, my Freya. No matter what they tell you."

She didn't have time to ask who *they* were. Her fingers flexed through the pain and then, suddenly, she was somewhere else. Sure, she was still sitting at a table made of mist. But Eldridge and the Owl Mother were gone. As was the tree full of hag stones that clattered in the wind.

She was completely and utterly alone.

The wound on her arm pulsed. Her heartbeat threaded through the slice at her wrist until she didn't know if the wound had opened up farther. A living wound with a heart that thudded every time she took a deep breath.

Freya wrapped her hand around her forearm and squeezed, slowing the blood to the open slice in her arm. The pounding in her arm and in her head slowed. She blinked, and the mist moved. It revealed a clearing with a hundred figures all standing at attention within it.

"Hello?" she called out. "Who's there?"

One by one, the figures turned their head to stare back at her. There were a hundred goblins, each one strange and unusual. Some wore the heads of owls, others were crowned with horns. Feathers, claws, fangs, and scales all decorated the bodies of every creature waiting for her in that clearing.

"We are the many," they replied at the same time. "You are the one."

Slowly, Freya stood. The ground rolled under her feet and she staggered, losing her grip on her arm. A waterfall of blood spilled from her body and soaked the ground. As she stared, the spots where her blood had fallen turned black and shriveled. The grass died wherever she looked.

"That's not possible," she whispered.

Freya clasped her hand around her arm again and blinked. The grass returned to its emerald green state, if not slightly grayer than it had been before.

Swallowing hard, she walked forward into the clearing and stopped beside the very first goblin. This woman had the head of a vulture and claws for hands. Though her body was still mortal, the rest of her was so unusual that it was difficult for Freya to even look at her.

But there was a message here. A message Freya had to hear.

"Who are you?" she asked.

"I was the first," the vulture replied.

"What message do you have for me?"

The vulture inclined her head, her pale pink neck stretching with the movement. "The Autumn Thief was never meant to be a ruler. We were the ones who stepped outside of the laws. The ones who questioned the royals and wanted to make a safe place for those of us who had fallen out of their graces. You will never win their approval if you cannot see the strange and rejoice in it."

This was the first Autumn Thief? Freya blinked and narrowed her eyes, squeezing her arm even harder until the rest of the vulture came into crystal clear view. The vulture woman wore leather pants and a leather corset that were decorated with inlaid gemstones and jewelry. She dripped with wealth, none of it matching. She must have stolen everything she wore, and yet she had become one of the people she had stolen from.

"Thank you for the advice," Freya said. Then, she stepped to the next person and asked the same questions.

"I was the second," the man with the lizard eyes replied. "Prettier than the first by far."

Freya grinned. "Perhaps a little more human, but I don't know if the other goblins would consider you prettier than her, my friend."

He sniffed and lifted an azure scaled hand. "Prettier by far," he repeated.

She bit her lips, but nodded her head. "Then what advice do you have for me, most beautiful of the Autumn Thieves?"

"Be not afraid of those you cannot control. There will be many who do not wish you to become the Autumn Thief, but you are now part of us. One of us. No one will stop you from ruling the way you should rule." He bared his sharpened teeth in a terrifying grin. "And if they refuse to fall in line, then you must remove them from the face of this realm."

"That seems a little aggressive for someone who doesn't agree with me, or want me to be their ruler." Freya couldn't do that to another person. She was more likely to listen to their opinion. To understand why they disagreed with her.

"You are still thinking of this position like a mortal, as if your subjects will be humans who want the best for their kingdom." The lizard man closed his hand into a fist, miming crushing someone within his grip. "If they do not agree with you, then they will stop at nothing to remove you from the throne. You must be harder than you've ever been before. Destroy all those who are not in your family."

Freya swallowed hard but nodded. She didn't know what it was like to rule any of the fae. And he seemed rather adamant that she needed to learn.

And so it went. She went down the line of all the previous Autumn Thieves who had ruled before her. They each had advice for her, though most only wanted to enforce the fact that she needed to be more than what she currently was. Every time she spoke with one, the pain in her arm would flare, and she'd squeeze it tighter.

Bright purple bruises already marked her skin in fingerprints when she finally reached the end of the line. Only one other Autumn Thief left to speak with, and her mind stretched thin. She was so tired. So tired of pain and anguish and people telling her what to do.

But when she looked up, it was into familiar eyes.

She'd seen this one before. This young owl woman with the bright moon face. She reached forward and gently placed her hand over Freya's. "Let go," the owl woman whispered. "It's time for you to feel it all."

Freya couldn't release her grip on her arm. That was the only thing letting her see all the Thieves. She shook her head, trying her best to bring everything back into clarity. "No. I need to know who you are first."

"You already do," the owl woman replied with a soft squint to her eyes. Like a smile. "Let go of your arm, Freya. You need to let go."

No. Letting go only meant that she wouldn't see all the messages she needed. The woman's fingers turned into claws around her arm, and Freya wrestled to be released. "I don't need to let go. I need to hear your advice first. What message do you have for me?"

The owl woman's outline shimmered, glowed, and then changed. The glamour dropped away and Freya realized it wasn't an owl woman holding her hands. It was the man she wanted to call husband.

Owlish features peeled away until it was only Eldridge looking at her. "Hello, my love."

"What message do you have for me?" she choked out the words again through tears. "I know you have something to tell me."

"Let go."

"No," she said, her bottom lip quivering with the difficulty of holding herself together. "No, I know you aren't here. I need to know what your message is and then I will. I will let go."

He heaved a sigh, then leaned forward and pressed their foreheads together. "You stubborn mortal. Fine. Your message from me is simple. Don't listen to any other Autumn Thief. Take their advice with a grain of salt, because you are the only one who knows how to rule as you wish."

"I don't know how I wish to rule," she replied. This would all be so much easier if she believed this mirage was actually Eldridge. "I never thought I would rule anyone, let alone an entire faerie court. This is all so beyond me that I don't know what to do."

"Then you better find out, Miss Freya." When they leaned away from each other, the owl creature had changed yet again. This time, it was the Owl Mother herself smiling at Freya in that strange, feathered way. "You do not know what precious gift you hold inside you, do you?"

Freya had many things the fae had claimed she hid. Bravery. Power. Even sometimes something as simple as kindness. But she had no idea what she had hid from the Owl Mother. "I don't," she replied.

The Owl Mother lifted a clawed hand and set it against Freya's belly. From deep inside Freya's body, a small golden light bloomed.

"Take care of yourself, and all you hold dear, Miss Freya. There's more to your story than you thought."

Her heart stuttered, stopped, then started up again in shock. A child? Was the Owl Mother suggesting she was with child?

Freya was so surprised, she loosened her hold on her arm. A wave of blood emerged again. But this time, she didn't stop. She let the wash of red obscure her vision and all in the clearing. How was she supposed to focus on anything other than what the Owl Mother had said?

She was with child.

CHAPTER 15

Freya slammed back into her body in the forest. She slowly became aware of her surroundings, but that somehow made everything worse. Eldridge still held onto her elbows. The table and chairs remained in the same place they were in before. And the Owl Mother stared at her with an all knowing gaze that turned Freya's blood cold.

Slowly, the Owl Mother stood and waved her hand at the two of them. "Now get out."

"Get out?" Eldridge repeated. "Did she pass the first trial?"

"She passed." The Owl Mother waved a clawed hand, then walked away from them toward the thick mist. "You're no longer welcome in my kingdom. Until the next time we meet."

Freya tried to swallow, but her throat was so dry. Even her voice sounded hoarse when she spoke. "What does that mean?"

"We need to leave," Eldridge said. He gathered her up into his arms and immediately raced away from the hag stone laden tree.

He never once looked down at her in his arms. But she stared up at him. He pressed his lips together tight until they were little more than a thin line of white. His brows drew down into an angry scowl that meant nothing good would happen if they lingered. And his pulse thundered in his throat.

"Are we in danger?" she asked.

"I don't know," he breathed. "But I know the Owl Mother is no kind woman and if we don't get out when she says to, then we won't be going anywhere ever again. This realm is not one to be toyed with."

So that was that. Freya wouldn't argue, and she wasn't necessarily in the right state of mind to run on her own. How he knew, she couldn't guess.

Eldridge had to put her down when they made it back to the door that left this place. He settled her onto her feet gently, then pressed the right button in the door for her. The metal opened silently, revealing the room beyond.

She didn't want to walk through that door. Freya knew what waited on the other side. Yet another conversation that she wasn't prepared to have. More reality sinking in that her life had changed, not just because of her new responsibilities in the Autumn Court, but for much more personal reasons as well.

The Owl Mother's voice screamed through the mist, "I said get out!"

Then a hand made of magic pressed against Freya's back and shoved her out of the Owl Mother's kingdom. She staggered, falling onto her hands and knees with her forearms cracking against the stone floor a little too hard.

Pain zinged up through her shoulders yet again, and blood from her wound smeared across the polished floor. Gasping, she rolled over and pressed her hands against her stomach. Logically, Freya knew the babe wasn't hurt. After all, she had done more wild things in the early stages of this pregnancy than get thrown across a floor by some magical creature. And yet, the fear still burned in her chest.

Could she even feel the child? Would she know if the baby was alive or not? She hadn't even realized the little golden light was inside her.

Eldridge rolled onto his back a few feet away from her. He put his hands on his chest, blew out a long breath, then said, "Well, that was a horrible experience. One down though, two more to go."

He was right. They had completed one of the trials, and she should be celebrating. By all the faerie realms, she'd done something that no mortal woman should be able to do.

And yet...

And yet.

When she didn't respond, Eldridge flopped his head to the side and stared at her. With the speed of a raging storm, he sat up and reached for her arm. "Let me bandage this for you. I'm sorry, my love. If I had known they were still testing Autumn Thieves in the same way they had with me, then I never would have let you go through the trials."

She watched him tend her wound with a blank expression. "You couldn't have stopped me from doing this, Eldridge. It's what I was meant to do."

"That doesn't mean they had to hurt you," he snarled. His fingers danced over the blood at her wrist, and shadows poured from his fingertips. They knit together around the cut, binding it together and holding it in place. "I cannot heal you, but I can bandage it as no other material can."

And when he finished, Eldridge pressed a kiss above the wound.

Oh, he was breaking her heart, and he didn't even know it. She was sitting on the biggest secret she'd ever had in her life, and Freya knew there were only two paths she could walk.

If she told Eldridge, then he was going to get ten times worse than he already was. He wouldn't let her move, most likely, and anything that he considered dangerous would be the end of this adventure. She wouldn't be surprised if he compromised everything because he worried for her.

But if she didn't tell him, then Freya knew it would have to be a secret she took to the grave with her. That lie would eat her up inside until she couldn't think or eat. But worst of all, this was a secret she already had so much happiness about. Even though it was the worst of timings, she knew this little life inside her would be the best thing that ever happened to her or Eldridge.

She couldn't keep this from him. Freya had already lied enough in their relationship to last a lifetime.

"Eldridge," she said, tugging her arm away from his grip. "The Owl Mother told me something you need to hear."

"If she said anything about who I was as a child, that was a long time ago. I made some foolish mistakes in my life but they do not define who I am."

"No," she interrupted. "She said nothing about you as a child or anything that would put you in an unpleasant light."

"Then if she told you about how I ruled, let it be known that I was not a good Autumn Thief. I wouldn't trust anyone who did what I did." He rubbed the back of his neck. "I listened to her too much when I was the leader of that court, and I regret it."

"It's not that either." Freya held up her hand when Eldridge would have continued on with his speculations. "Stop talking, Eldridge."

He snapped his jaw shut so quickly that she heard the audible snap of his teeth cracking together. Perhaps she had been a little harsh in her tone, but she already didn't know how to tell him this.

It wasn't like they weren't having sex. They both had to have been aware that pregnancy could have happened, but it never crossed Freya's mind. She had assumed that a mortal and a fae couldn't have children together. That a union between two very different species wouldn't allow life to bloom.

She'd been okay with that. Her entire being had wanted a child, but she was willing to give that all up for him. Freya had told herself that everything would be fine, and to enjoy every moment she got with the man she loved. But now, there would be three of them.

She couldn't keep this to herself.

"I'm pregnant," she blurted.

The words felt wrong to say. They weren't ready for a child. They weren't ready for a family or even married at this point. Neither of them knew what the future held. Freya might have to remain in the Autumn Court, and Eldridge would have to remain in his kingdom. They might never see each other and slowly drift apart.

But her entire soul lit up with the words as well. The sheer love that bloomed in her chest pushed aside all that worry and anxiety. This little being inside her was Freya's child. Freya's to love, to hold, to watch grow.

Her heart squeezed so hard she almost couldn't breathe. And in looking at Eldridge, she knew he had lost all the air in his lungs as well.

"What did you say?" He said the words as though they were a prayer.

"I said I'm pregnant. The Owl Mother sensed life in me and when I was in that... that strange place with all the other Autumn Thieves, she showed me that it was the truth." Freya pressed her free hand against her stomach and swallowed hard. "I know the timing couldn't be worse. We have so much else to focus on and I know this will make you so much more terrified of what will happen but..."

Eldridge pressed his finger against her lips, forcing her to stop talking. "A baby?" he asked reverently.

She nodded.

Tears filled those dark eyes that held a thousand galaxies within them. He swallowed hard, his lower lip quivering even as his jaw worked. Eldridge tried to hold himself together, and Freya didn't know if that was a good thing or a bad thing.

He reached for her hand and placed it delicately over hers. Eldridge moved, holding her hands and helping her to stand in front of him. He remained on his knees, staring up at her with those wide eyes full of tears. "You are a goddess," he said, voice thick with emotion. "And I will worship you every day for the rest of our lives. Freya. My Freya."

More gentle than he'd ever been before, Eldridge pressed a kiss to her belly. A single, lingering kiss where he poured all his love and magic into her body. His hands framed her hips, holding her in place as he whispered against her skin, "And you, little one. I will love you until the end of all time."

She let her head fall back and her eyes shutter closed. Her Goblin King was happy, and that was all the blessing she could have hoped for.

What a lucky woman she was, too. So many women had suffered at the hands of partners who didn't want a child. Or worse, thought there was no use for one in their lives. Yet here she was, a mortal woman in a fantasy realm, with a Goblin King who was happy to hold her and their child in his heart.

"I love you," she whispered, dropping her chin down again to look into those beloved, glowing eyes. "And I know our child will love you just as much."

"Oh, all the stars in the sky could combine and their brightness would never rival the love I have for you, dear one." He pressed his lips against her stomach one more time. "A baby. Our baby."

A sudden clatter at the entrance to the hall echoed through the room. Freya froze and glanced over her shoulder, only to find a familiar black and white dog staring at her from the door. "What did he just say?" Arrow whispered, his voice filled with shock, and hopefully not with horror.

She hadn't realized how hard it would be to tell him. He was her dearest friend, and she wanted him to be happy as well. She supposed she wasn't all that ready to tell anyone just yet.

Clearing her throat, she nodded her head. "He said the words right, Arrow. I'm with child."

Arrow padded toward them, his dark eyes wide and glistening. "I never thought I'd see the day when another royal baby was born. A royal!"

She watched him walk toward her with a reverence she didn't think she deserved. Arrow sat down next to them both, and she could see the happiness shining brightly in his gaze.

For the moment, she was not just Freya, but now the mother of someone new. Someone who might be equally as powerful as the Goblin King. Perhaps even more. Whatever this baby ended up being like, it was going to be hers. A part of herself that had stretched away from her body until it snapped off and became its own living, breathing being.

Goodness, she was already so in love with this little bundle of light and she hadn't even met the child.

Freya pressed a hand to her still flat stomach and breathed out a slow sigh. "I'm glad you're both excited. I was so worried neither of you would want anything to do with me now that I'm pregnant."

Eldridge and Arrow shared a look before the Goblin King asked, "Why wouldn't we? Like Arrow said, there hasn't been a new royal born in years. This is cause for great excitement!"

It hadn't hit them yet. Freya could see that, now, they were caught up in the glory of new life and their minds hadn't skipped to the future. She had hoped they would already have thought ahead, but apparently she was going to be the person to burst this bubble of happiness she'd given them.

"Because I still have to go through all the trials," she replied slowly. "I still have to become the Autumn Thief."

Arrow's jaw fell open, and Eldridge's brows drew together.

"You aren't finishing this while pregnant," Eldridge growled.

Freya snorted and crossed her arms over her chest. "I'd like to see you try to stop me."

CHAPTER 16

Freya argued for many hours into the wee evening light. Of course she would continue to become the Autumn Thief. She'd already gotten through one of the trials and no, she would not stop because they suddenly discovered she was endangering more than herself.

Every step of her life in the faerie realm had endangered more than herself. She had wandered through the many realms and courts of the fae knowing that every step could harm many people in the process. Freya knew what she was doing.

Obviously, she had no intention of risking the life she now carried inside her. Not unless it was absolutely necessary for them both.

Eldridge gave up at the same time the moon set on the horizon and the sun blasted beams of light through the shattered stained glass in the ceiling. He disappeared into the winding hallways and Freya knew she wouldn't see him for a while. He wanted time to himself, and he'd earned that right to think without her yelling at him.

But she really wished he had stayed.

Sighing, she ran her fingers through her hair and tried hard not to stare at the bracelet of shadows holding her blood within her body.

Even angry with her, Eldridge would never risk her health or safety and take his magic away.

"What do you think?" she asked Arrow. "Do you think I'm being unreasonable in wanting to continue?"

"No," he replied, though his eyes were large and luminous. "You aren't being unreasonable, my dearest of friends. But I wish we had known you were with child before everything exploded. You're risking so much by attempting these trials with a child inside of you. Everything will be harder now."

"Maybe that will work to my advantage," she whispered. The words fell in the air with so much hope, only to be dashed on the floor when she realized how limp they were.

Of course, the old gods wouldn't care if she was pregnant. The Owl Mother had only been kind because the babe inside her was a grandchild, and even then, she hadn't been careful when throwing Freya out of her realm and onto the hard floor beyond.

Arrow shook his head and reached out a paw for her to take. "We both know that isn't the case, Freya. We're all on our own when it comes to the old gods, and they will stop at nothing to give you the hardest test to prove yourself. It will not be easy, and they won't care about the babe."

"Right." She took his paw and squeezed it in her own. "Then we have to figure out the best way to make sure I get through this unharmed."

"I don't know if there's a best way for that." Arrow glanced back at the three bronze faces, one of them now flattened against the wall as though the owl face had been painted rather than carved. "I think they want this to be difficult for you. More difficult than the others."

Her wrist stung at the words. She had already suffered through the pain of one old god. The Owl Mother had made it very clear that pain would be part of these trials, no matter how much Freya tried to run from that portion. A slice through the wrist was one thing, but what would the others ask for?

They were more terrifying than the Owl Mother. And if she feared them more, did that mean they were going to ask for more pieces of her? More than she could give?

Swallowing hard, she turned away from their dark gazes. "I think I need to talk with Eldridge."

"He's not in any place to be talking with you, I would imagine. You basically told him you were going to risk the woman he loved and his firstborn child on a very dangerous quest that he couldn't partake in." Arrow shrugged. "A man has his limits."

"Anyone has those limits," she corrected. "Does he think I'm not affected by this? Of course I'm terrified. I don't want to be the one who missteps and causes our entire future to dissolve before our eyes. But no one can stop the course this river runs. I have to float, Arrow, or I will drown."

He touched a paw to her hip, staring up at her with an understanding gaze that made tears prick in her eyes. "I know that, Miss Freya. I just wish I could change it."

So did she. But this was beyond all of them now.

With a sharp nod, she strode from that cursed room and out into the halls beyond. Her feet carried her through the Autumn Stronghold as though they knew where to go. And maybe they did.

She could feel Eldridge's power like a thread connected them. A thread that burned bright and golden in her mind's eye. She could trail that thread throughout the entire world if she needed to, because she could sense him with every step she took.

He was in the first room he'd brought them to. The only room in this entire building where he felt it was safe for them to sleep. Though she wasn't entirely certain where he'd hidden himself.

Freya paused in the doorway to the shrine, peering up at the dust motes that swirled in the air. The vines had grown overnight. They hung down from the ceiling and dangled in a soft breeze that toyed with their arrowhead shaped leaves.

"You're still looking for me." Eldridge's voice drifted from the rafters. "You know how I feel about this, Freya. No words or argument will change that. You shouldn't go through these trials."

"I know what I'm risking," she replied. Freya stepped into the room and lifted her hand. She teased the glowing dust motes that looked like little dancing faeries, then blew a breath to make them scatter away. "I wouldn't risk it if I didn't have to. You said yourself, this is a path I cannot walk off. I'm stuck here until I finish the trials."

"There must be another way." His voice shook with sadness and fear.

She wished she could take those emotions away from him. She wished she could change this final adventure into something bright and light for the two of them.

But she couldn't.

No one could. Not even the Goblin King.

"Where are you?" she asked. Her voice floated through the air and met a single white feather that drifted down from wherever the Goblin King hid.

Freya reached for it and caught the downy feather in her hands. It was so lovely. So soft. And she knew what this meant. He wasn't hiding from her anymore. In fact, he was entirely himself for the first time since they had met.

"Up here," he muttered. "There's a ladder to your right. If you think you're so capable of adventures, then you can do it yourself."

The sullen grumpiness with which he said the words was all she needed to guess his current mood. The Goblin King was sulking because he couldn't control this situation. And now he was going to lash out until she regretted telling him that she planned to do things on her own.

Of course, Freya had seen this behavior before, and she would not fall for it.

She could manage a ladder, considering how early into this pregnancy she was. Besides, she had climbed a hundred ladders in her life.

She found it quickly, leaning against one of the pillars that was supposed to keep the ceiling aloft. Few of the stone pillars looked stable, but if Eldridge had climbed up, then so could she. Freya cracked her knuckles, set her hands on the rungs, and climbed.

Careful, of course. The last thing she wanted was for a rung to come off in her hands and cause her to tumble back onto the ground. The fall might not kill her, but it would definitely knock the wind from her lungs.

The ladder held, sure and sturdy, as though it were freshly made.

And it led her all the way into the rafters, at least three stories high. Here, she saw there was a small platform where Eldridge sat, his back to her and legs dangling in the open air.

She made her way precariously across the first beam, with her arms held out at her sides. Freya didn't look down, otherwise her balance would twist and she'd end up on the floor. She made it to the platform with little difficulty, though her lungs heaved with the effort.

"We're very high up," she muttered as she sank down next to him. Freya hadn't realized how uncomfortable heights made her.

Even looking at the floor made her dizzy. She held onto Eldridge's shoulder just to sit, but couldn't take her eyes away from the long fall that awaited her with one wrong move. The room spun. Or maybe that was the floor that shifted in some horrible earthquake that was simply bad timing.

Eldridge grabbed onto her hand and tugged it to his chest. "Look at me, Freya. I promise you, you won't be able to look at anything else."

The air shuddered in her lungs, but she ripped her eyes away from the floor to look at the man she loved. Eldridge had dropped all the glamour he used to keep himself from looking even remotely mortal, and an owl stared back at her.

She was so much closer now than she had been in the Owl Mother's sanctuary. Now she could see the fine lines of dark feathers around his golden eyes. The way one side of his mouth sank into the depths of those soft feathers and how the faint hint of a beak hadn't quite grown over his nose. But mostly she saw the man she loved in his eyes, even though they weren't exactly the same as the silver ones she was used to.

Freya cupped his feathered cheek and stroked her thumb through the soft downy feathers there. "You're still handsome like this, you know. I find you no less attractive."

"I'm monstrous in this form. Just as all goblins are to mortals." He looked away from her, but his cheek leaned into her touch as though he craved the contact. "I know this isn't the visage you fell in love with."

"It's another addition to your strange beauty, my love." She smoothed her fingers over his cheekbones and turned his attention back to her face. "I know you're a goblin. I always wondered why you were so different from the others, and now I know. The glamour was all a way for you to hide."

"Not hide." He shook his head in denial of the words. "I never hid from anyone. But it was a way to make me look more human. More like a ruler rather than some goblin boy who had won himself a throne."

"Oh, my Goblin King." Freya drew him close to her, pressing her forehead into his feathers. "Is that why you're so afraid? Do you think you're going to lose me and be that lost boy all on your own again?"

"I fear it every day." Finally, he lifted his hands and tunneled them into her hair. He touched her as though she had already died. As though all that remained of the woman he loved was a pretty ghost with the promise of love in the afterlife.

"I won't die, you know. I thought you'd have a little more faith in me than that," Freya said. She giggled a little and leaned into his touch with a soft sigh. "I know this hasn't been easy for you, and the addition of a child to the mix only made it more difficult."

"The child made it more *real*."

She supposed she could understand that. But that didn't mean they could stop. Though the inevitability of risking her life also didn't mean Eldridge's fear was invalid.

Sighing, she scooted closer to him and set her head on his shoulder. Touching him like this made the heights not so bad. Just like being with him made everything else not quite so frightening. "I know," she whispered. "I thought the same thing. All of a sudden I was more afraid than when I started."

He snorted. "Of course this is what makes you afraid. Not the fact that you're going to be meeting actual gods who are judging if you are worthy of the magic you stole from the Autumn Thief."

"Hey." She nudged him with her shoulder. "Lark wanted me to take it. Is that really stealing?"

"Yes. It's still stealing."

She shrugged. "Well, then I guess I stole it. But I don't feel bad about what I did. Lark was right, and I trust her."

A long silence stretched between them. The wind ruffled his feathers, and she heard the soft sound like a lullaby in her ear.

"A baby," he muttered. "What are we going to do with a baby?"

"Love it," she replied without hesitation. "We will love our child within an inch of its life. An embarrassing amount of love that will probably make her or him feel smothered until they're old enough to realize what a blessing it is to have us as parents."

Eldridge chuckled and wrapped his arm around her shoulder, holding her tight against his side. "I'm afraid I have little experience with that kind of love."

"Sure you do." Freya took his hand in hers, holding it against her shoulder and squeezing tight. "You've kept me around this long. You know exactly how to love like that."

Eldridge was quiet for long heartbeats. Had she been too forward? Was he consumed by fear that he wouldn't be a good father to their child?

But then he kissed the top of her head and breathed, "I suppose I do. But now what do we do, Freya?"

"Unfortunately there's only one thing to do." She took a deep breath and tried to feel brave. To feel strong. "We keep going with the trials. We keep proving that I'm worthy of this so we can get out of here and love our child the best we can."

CHAPTER 17

Freya stood before the two remaining bronze figures and stared them down. The obvious next choice was the Horned God, the one who looked vaguely familiar. As though she'd seen him in the mortal realm before, but couldn't quite remember from where.

She couldn't make herself press his face. Not yet.

"Why don't you tell me about him before we walk in this time?" she said, without looking over her shoulder.

Both Eldridge and Arrow were staring at her as though something was about to fly out of the sky and strike her. Their muscles were bunched, ready to leap in front of her in case anything went wrong. She didn't think anything was going to go so horribly wrong, but one could never be sure.

Arrow cleared his throat, snuffled as though his nose were stuffy, and then replied. "We know the Horned God to be a trickster. You should be on your guard because nothing is as it seems in that place."

"Right." She could have guessed that. All fae were tricksters. "What else? Anything useful or only that he's not trustworthy?"

Eldridge stepped closer and reached out his hand for her to take. "The Horned God has a soft spot for humans, but he doesn't want to talk with them. A long time ago he was known for keeping... well. Pets."

Right, that was disgusting. She didn't fancy meeting a god who thought of people like her as nothing more than mongrels or animals that could be kept as a plaything for when he wanted entertainment.

"All right. Ominous. I'm not looking forward to that in the slightest." Freya shivered, but then drew herself up.

She was a mother now, or would be a mother soon enough. She didn't have time to fear the old gods because she was becoming godly herself. Mothers were the few creatures who could bring life into this realm. Even this Horned God would have to understand that.

"So I just..." She gestured toward the bronze face and mimed pushing it.

"Yes," Eldridge replied. "The same as last time. There will be a door and we will go through it together."

"Do you have any idea what waits for us beyond it?" She knew the answer, but Freya was hoping that maybe she was wrong.

"Not even the faintest idea. That's the whole point of the trials. Each one is different. Individual to the trait the old god thinks the new Autumn Thief is lacking, but also to what they want to see in growth from the new Autumn Thief." Eldridge touched her chest, palm pressed against her heart. "They can see inside you the moment you take the power into yourself. They know everything about you, my Freya. And that is what they are testing."

"Oh, of course it couldn't be something less sinister." She placed a hand on her belly without thinking. Almost as though she already knew that she needed to take care of this baby more this time. As though the child could give her strength.

Freya sighed and put her hand on the horns of the figurehead in front of her. The metal vibrated beneath her touch. A warning? Or excitement from the Horned God himself who was ready to meet her?

She didn't want to find out, but Freya didn't have a choice. This was her path. And she would walk it with strength and virtue.

Shoving hard, she pushed the head into the wall and continued shoving until the door opened beyond. Nothing but shadows were revealed. The Horned God didn't want her to see what was through the door until she stepped foot into his domain.

So be it.

She swallowed hard and looked over her shoulder at Arrow standing behind them, wringing his paws but ready to remain behind in case something bad happened. "Be careful with this one, Miss Freya. He's not one to be trifled with."

No fae were. They all knew how to bend the world to their will, and how to be dangerous.

She touched a finger to her temple and then nodded. "I'll keep my wits about me, goblin dog. You have my promise."

"I hope that'll be enough."

She did as well, but the words rang in her mind. What if it wasn't enough for her to be aware of the dangers? She'd beaten so many fae at their own games. But these old gods were a new beast. Wise, ancient beings who were so much more powerful because of their years walking this realm.

No, she couldn't let her mind wander like that. Such thoughts could only lead to danger.

"Hold my hand?" she asked, reaching out her hand for Eldridge to take.

He slipped his warm fingers between hers and squeezed. "Until the very end, my love."

Goodness, she hoped this wasn't their end. She had a lot more planned for the two of them.

They walked through the door together and Freya realized that the shadows weren't exactly shadows. They were magic. Dark magic that swirled in eddies around them. Tendrils of the blackened stuff wrapped around her arms like thin, spindly fingers. They threaded through her hair, lifting the strands up as though the darkness were admiring the texture and color of her locks. Perhaps it was. Her hair was the same color as the magic.

Ink slid away from her skin like she stepped through a waterfall, and then the shadows revealed a room beyond. It took Freya a few moments of blinking to dispel her surprise. After all, she'd expected something similar to where the Owl Mother lived. A kingdom or a realm of its own with subjects and people. Instead, they walked into a room as though they were still moving through the Stronghold.

It was a lovely room. Warm mahogany paneling covered the walls, though the large arched windows revealed nothing beyond them. Just pitch black. Candles hung from the shadowy ceiling, and when she peered closer, she wasn't at all certain that there was a ceiling. The shadowy tendrils had receded to the roof, where they tangled around each other.

Waiting for their master to call upon them, perhaps?

"Those shadows," she whispered, feeling as though she shouldn't speak too loud in such a reverent room. "They look like your magic."

"That's because they are," Eldridge replied. His fingers turned cold in her grip. "Or some form of it. The Horned God was the one to give me the gift of my powers, long ago. He said a powerful being like me should be able to control more than the elements."

"Isn't light an element? Therefore shadow must be as well." Freya said the words with confidence that she didn't feel. Nothing made sense in the faerie realm, so she could be wrong.

Eldridge shook his head. "They aren't shadows, not really. They have a mind. Thoughts. Dreams, even, if you ask them in the dead of night. They are more than magic. They are living beings with a heart inside them."

Why did that disturb her? Freya gulped and released her grip on the Goblin King.

She stepped into the room, and the shadows shifted away from her feet. She hadn't even noticed them spread across the floor. The carpet of them parted, revealing a lovely white and black checkered floor. This was a room for nobility to dance in, and yet it remained empty and cold.

"Hello?" she called out. "Horned God, I am here to speak with you!"

For a moment, she thought she heard someone calling back to her. But then she realized it was only her own voice bouncing through the shadows. Repeating through these living, dark beings until the sound wasn't her voice anymore. Not really.

Eldridge sighed, and the sound was one of ancient disappointment. "The Horned God will come when he is ready, and no sooner."

"Then why summon me now?" Freya turned on her heel. "Why would he call upon me and then not show his face?"

A fire burst into life before her eyes. Freya tossed up an arm to cover her eyes, certain the roaring fireplace hadn't been there moments before. Heat blasted over her arms and covered her from head to toe in a welcome wave of comfort.

"Eldridge?" she asked again. "Why wouldn't he be here waiting for us?"

No one responded.

Frowning, she turned around, only to see that no one stood behind her. Eldridge had been right there only moments ago. She knew that he was in the same place where she had left him.

Wasn't he? Why would he have left when he knew how dangerous this place was? He wouldn't. Which could only mean the Horned God was already here.

"That's quite a trick," she said. "But it lacks a certain luster when the magician is not in the room."

Long fingernails raked through her hair, gently detangling an area at the base of her skull. "Who says I'm not in the room?"

"Well, visibly in the room, that is." Freya didn't mind correcting herself, although she was certain this god would have liked her to admit more. "I don't think you're standing behind me either."

The claws curved and pressed sharp tips to her neck. "You sound uncertain, Freya. Of all the things I've heard, all the things I've seen in that pretty head of yours, I didn't expect you to be so uncertain."

Was she supposed to know what was going on here? "I could turn around and see for myself."

"You could," the voice said with a chuckle. "But I don't think you'd like what you find."

There was a challenge in his voice. A challenge that she knew she couldn't deny. He wanted to see how brave she was. How easily she could turn around when she feared the monster standing behind her. Maybe... Maybe there was nothing behind her, and this was all in her head.

She squared her shoulders and balled her hands into fists. Freya had seen more terrifying things than shadows. So she turned.

The long tendrils of darkness had coalesced behind her into a familiar stretched figure. A leering grin stared down at her where light split through the warped shadows and through the slitted gaze of a monster made of shadows.

A scream pressed against her throat. But she refused to show these villains that she was afraid of them. "A Midnight Monster," she whispered. "So these are yours, then?"

The voice laughed again, still behind her, even though she had already turned. "I knew you had met them, but I didn't realize you would hate them so. Many find them to be beautiful, or at the very least, familiar."

She supposed they looked like a person's stretched out shadow when the sun set behind them. That didn't make them familiar. It only made them slightly human, and slightly something worse.

"Go away," she growled. "My business is not with you."

The Midnight Monster reached out a clawed hand and scraped it down her cheek. "Everything that is the Horned God's business, is my business."

"I don't think so," she replied without missing a beat. "You are not the person I came here to see. I came here to speak with a god. Not a mouthpiece."

The Midnight Monster's gaze narrowed until its eyes were little more than slits in the shadows. She glared back with what she hoped was equal intensity. He had no right to take this moment from her. And the Horned God would speak with her himself.

When no one else emerged from the shadows, and the Midnight Monster didn't budge, she widened her stance and ground her teeth together. "You will step aside and let me speak with your master."

"Oh I will?" The Midnight Monster pressed a too long hand to its mouth as if it were surprised. "I think not, little human. If he wanted to speak with you directly, then he would. But he doesn't. So he won't."

"I think he will. I doubt he would want to be the only god who didn't give me an audience. When he speaks with the others, it would only make him look like the weakest of them." Freya crossed her arms over her chest, pursing her lips and looking the Midnight Monster up and down. "I don't think you understand how that works. If you're the only person who didn't take the risk to see someone who should be vastly weaker than oneself? And yet, the Horned God would be the only one who was terrified of a mortal girl who had stolen magic she shouldn't have."

The words were a gamble. She could make the Horned God angrier and more likely to attack her.

And she'd promised herself she wouldn't take risks like this with a little light growing in her belly. But there was no other way. Not that she could see.

Freya had to draw him out into the light. She needed to see the Horned God for herself, even if she didn't understand the gut wrenching desire. The magic inside her rolled, forcing her tongue to move even when she didn't want to say more.

"If he's afraid, I understand," she heard herself say. "Fear is hard to overcome. Even for a god."

The magic rumbled in her chest, and she almost heard a voice whisper in her ear, "Yes, that. That's what you should say to a god like this."

Apparently, the magic appreciated her being a little more forward and more confident.

"Afraid?" the Midnight Monster screamed. "He would show you what fear truly meant."

"Then let him prove it." She leaned forward so close their faces almost touched. "You are his shield. I see that now. However, you are a flimsy and weak barrier made of nothing but shadow. True protection requires substance. Stand aside and let me see this little man."

"Too far," the magic whispered. "Much too far."

Well, it had said to challenge him! She would never understand this place.

She heard the Horned God's growl before a clawed hand slashed through the Midnight Monster. The creature screamed in pain and then split in two. The shadows parted like a wave to reveal the substantial monster who stood behind.

The Horned God was a creature from nightmares. His skin was

leathery and wrinkled, like a loose-fitting jacket hung from his frame. Dark eyes glared at her, but they were hard to look at when twin ram horns rose from his forehead. The skin around their base had split open, and twin drops of black liquid dripped down his temples. He stood ten feet high, easily towering over her head. Chest bare, claws darkened with soot and age, he was a formidable monster that she never should have challenged.

Freya gulped, but tried her best to remain confident and strong. "There you are," she muttered. "I thought I was here to talk with you, not your creations."

"You are a very intelligent woman, but not intelligent enough to escape me." His eyes flashed with a fire in the depths of that darkness, crackling with energy and power.

"I wasn't trying to escape you. I was trying to find you because I need you to acknowledge that I am more than worthy of this title and this power."

"Perhaps someday I will admit that," he snarled, lips wrinkling at the edges and black ooze dripping from his bottom lip. "Your games are only beginning, Freya of Woolwich. I need to see more from you than cleverness and mortal instinct."

He lifted his hands in the air and clapped. The sound hit her ears with all the force of an avalanche, and then everything went dark.

CHAPTER 18

Her cheek was cold. Why was it cold? Freya remembered falling asleep on a comfortable bed, not a floor.

Groaning, she lifted her head only to feel a splitting pain trail down the base of her skull and into her spine. Though it hurt, the pain gave her a small sense of awareness. Awareness she desperately needed, considering she had no idea where she was. Who she was. What she was?

Freya pressed her hands onto the smooth stone floor and hauled herself onto her hands and knees. Once stable, she blinked through the grit in her eyes.

White and black checkers danced in her hazy vision. She didn't remember a floor like this, and she didn't think she'd been here for very long. After all, this place was... It was...

Her thoughts paused. She couldn't remember what this place was at all, could she? Her memory had been wiped clean, like someone had washed her mind with the floor.

She trailed her fingers in between the two colors but couldn't find a seam. Stranger and stranger.

No matter where she was, she had to stand up. Freya knew sitting on the floor would not help her find out what had happened or where she had fallen.

And she must have fallen. Why else would she be on the floor?

She staggered to her feet and held her arms out at her sides. Strange, she felt odd. Like there was supposed to be something in her head, only she couldn't quite find it. Unusual, but she didn't think she should worry about it. Or at least, a voice whispered in her head not to worry. Was it even in her head?

She smoothed her hands down her stomach, only to find that her body was covered with a beautiful gown. White as snow, the crystalized bodice hid many iridescent colors that shimmered as she moved. A large skirt puffed out from her waist like a cloud of mist that moved with her. Was she a princess?

That was a silly thought. She giggled and shook her head. She was no princess, even without her memories, she knew that.

A faint nervous energy moved through her body, only to disappear as quickly as it had happened. Her gut said she should worry, that she couldn't remember anything, but her head said not to worry at all.

It was easier not to worry.

She drifted across the checkered floor toward a window that opened out into a balcony. Maybe a little fresh air would clear her head and she'd remember where she was. Her home, she could only assume. Or perhaps she was visiting a friend.

Maybe she really was a princess. How funny would that be?

Giggling to herself, she opened the balcony doors and stepped outside into the fresh, cool air. It touched her face and she let her eyes drift shut to enjoy the soft massage of her features.

That ugly thing inside her, the one that said to worry, breathed in the air as well. But the air was blistering to that part of her. Hot and stifling, and it made her lungs hurt.

Freya coughed and pressed her hand to her mouth. The air didn't hurt when she breathed. The starry sky was no lie, as she stared at such beauty. Her vision went blurry and when she focused again, there was nothing in front of her but darkness. Just a blank, shadowy darkness with something slithering inside it. Not a snake or a monster, but like the shadows themselves had shape and form.

She hissed out a long breath, blinked, and then everything returned to normal. Twinkling stars in a sky that never ended.

"Strange," she whispered. "I could have sworn there was something wrong with this place."

There wasn't anything wrong at all, though. She was safe and home, and everything was absolutely fine.

Breath rattling in her lungs, she turned around and gasped. The dance floor hadn't been so lonely after all. Hundreds of magical creatures filled the space, each in a gown more stunning than the last. A couple whirled by her, their arms outstretched and their feet flying through a convoluted waltz.

The woman had the face of an emerald parrot, her eyes so yellow they glowed in her head. The man had whiskers instead of a mustache, and his pupils were slitted when he met her gaze. His smile flashed in the candlelight, fangs gleaming.

She pressed a hand to her chest in surprise. They shouldn't exist, these creatures. They looked like something out of a storybook, but then she remembered that maybe they were her people. She had only forgotten. They were hers and she was theirs, and if they were dancing...

Well. Then she should dance.

Freya stepped off the balcony and back into the room that was filled with so much vibrancy and life. A woman with giant dragonfly wings stepped to the side, gesturing with her arms for Freya to walk through the wall of people that parted in waves.

Why? Why did they want her to walk through their ranks when she was just looking for a partner? They all danced with each other, and Freya knew how to waltz. She should find someone to dance with and whirl across the floor like the rest of them. Shouldn't she?

But none of the creatures reached out their hands for her to take. They all stopped dancing, raised their arms, and gestured for her to continue walking through them. All the way to the very center of the dance floor. Was someone waiting for her?

Except... No one was. She was the only person in the center when she finally stood there and no other creatures pointed for her to walk in a certain direction.

Freya paused in the middle of the room and tilted her head back to stare up at the ceiling made of stars and floating candles. She watched the bright lights whirl above her head and marveled at their beauty. Every sparkle, every speck above her, appeared to be magic. The stars winked in and out of existence. And more than that, the firelight that glowed just out of reach gave her entire life meaning.

Again, that ugly thing in her chest lifted its head. But this time, it didn't try to speak with her. Apparently that power had grown tired of convincing her that something wasn't right, especially if she would not listen.

It flowed through her body, pulsing down into her fingertips and filling her head with elation and strength. She wasn't herself at all. She was a glowing woman made of galaxies and a thousand sunsets all wrapped up in flesh that was too tight. And not quite her own.

Looking down, Freya turned her hands and was startled to see the stars sparkling in her own skin now. Glowing underneath the surface like her veins had become filled with an essence of the sky itself.

"Dance," the surrounding creatures chanted. "Dance for us."

She didn't feel like dancing. There wasn't even music. She knew there had to be something in the air for her to dance, and there wasn't even the faintest chord of...

There it was.

She heard the music now. The thready reed of a flute, joined by a violin that filled the air with lovely music. And suddenly, she wanted to dance. She wanted to do more than that with the power that filled her to the very brim.

Lifting her hands over her head, Freya spun in a slow circle that lifted her skirts into a wide arc around her. She stared up at her hands, fingers falling into a graceful, relaxed pose. All those stars in her skin erupted. They poured down upon her like a shower of glittering light that illuminated the entire room in one burst of bright magic.

She spun faster. The power whirled, glowing brighter and brighter until she didn't know what was her and what wasn't anymore. The candles weren't bright enough to compete with her. The stars in the ceiling couldn't glow like she did.

Her feet moved in an intricate pattern that she hadn't known only moments ago. Or if she had, her mind hadn't remembered the steps that led her dancing in circles while a hundred faerie creatures watched her move.

Their lips twisted into smiles when she caught glimpses of them in her wild spinning. Some of them wore smiles that appeared kind, and then in the next moment, they leered at her as though they were ready to leap. To pounce. To feed.

Those were the thoughts that stilled her feet and slowed her dance. She nearly stumbled to a halt in front of a man who looked like he wore the face of a beetle, with eyes too large that were covered in a honeycomb pattern.

His too human lips curved into a smile, but she saw another expression under that veneer of happiness. His mouth opened wide into a cavernous maw that threatened to devour her whole. This creature of the night wanted to take a bite out of her flesh and chew on it for hours, just to savor the taste of someone with so much power.

Freya flinched away from him, far across the circle of her own creation. In doing so, she almost bumped into another creature whose face was bright red, with glittering scales cascading down her shoulders. This faerie woman didn't hide her hunger or how much she wanted to hurt Freya.

Instead of concealing that horrible need for pain, the faerie woman reached for Freya with claws sharpened into wicked points. The faerie scraped her nails down either side of Freya's face. And then the whispered words came with the pain. "Keep dancing, little Freya. We want to watch you dance."

Why were her feet moving again? She didn't want to dance. Nor did she desire to put on a show for these foul, loathsome creatures who were laughing at her pain. How dare they?

The power inside her bubbled, boiled, then spilled over. The light that poured out of her was thick this time. Like a wave of yellow sunshine that splashed onto the floor and made the faerie creatures hiss as they backed away lest they be burned.

"Go away," she whispered. "I won't be your entertainment for the night."

Some unknown presence pressed down on her mind. She could feel it reaching into her head and twisting her thoughts around again. It wasn't that she had forgotten, but that a very particular thing or person wanted her to be lost in this impossible sense of the unknown. It wanted her to be afraid in small snippets of a heartbeat before she fell under its spell yet again.

Her own magic swelled in her chest and she saw the room as it really was. Full of creatures made of stretched shadows with leering grins that towered over her. No candles, only darkness and grim light that faded at the edges into madness.

But then she blinked and everything returned to normal. To brilliancy and vibrant colors that swirled with the creatures as they moved again.

She should give in to the magic. Living in this place was so much better than that nightmarish realm of darkness. But she didn't want to. Freya wanted to be free. She had something to do, although she couldn't remember exactly what.

She spun on her heel, ready to sprint through the crowds of faerie creatures and back to the balcony. She'd hurl herself over the edge if that was what it took to free herself from this realm.

Only she didn't get far. Freya collided with a body that wasn't cold or shadowy at all. She looked up, and all the tension in her body eased.

His face was that of a great horned owl. His eyes held a thousand galaxies within them, and he smiled when he looked down at her. Her soul eased at the sight of this creature, and she didn't know why.

No wait.

She did.

"Goblin King," she whispered, although she didn't remember what the title meant.

CHAPTER 19

"Hello Freya," the owl man said.

He knew her name. And of course he did. She knew him as well, although her mind insisted they had never spoken before in her life. Those weren't her memories, though. She had met him a thousand times over because her very soul stretched with happiness when she saw him. It was like some piece of her heart started beating again at the sight of him.

"Goblin King," she repeated. "Why do I know that name?"

He tilted his head to the side, and a slight breeze ruffled the feathers of his cheek. "I don't know. It's familiar to me as well."

So he had no memories either. Or if he did, he was keeping them close to his chest while she struggled to find her own. The weight of that unknown magic pressed down on her shoulders, and the Goblin King reached out to steady her again.

"Are you well?" he asked. There was a sincerity in his words that she doubted any of the other creatures here were able to voice. As though he did fear for her wellbeing, and that if she hadn't been well, then neither would he.

"I'm fine," she muttered. Freya pressed a hand to her forehead and shook her head. "It all feels so muddled up here right now. Like I'm supposed to be somewhere else or know something about what's happening."

The fog in her mind remained strong and true. No matter how hard she fought against it.

He blinked a few times, brows furrowed as though he knew there were memories to remember in his own head, but he couldn't quite do it either. The Goblin King looked down at his clawed hands and raised them between their bodies.

She stared down at those fingers, and the faintest hint of a memory grazed the back of her mind. She swore those hands had touched her before. Freya could feel the whispered sensation of them stroking down her back. Candlelight flickered along silver skin poured over strong muscles that flexed underneath her fingertips. Claws scraped down her spine, not with the intent to hurt, but because he couldn't seem to touch enough of her.

She remembered that. It wasn't some strange thought put in her head by a magical presence, not her own. That memory was all hers.

Holding tight to that knowledge, she looked up into his eyes filled with galaxies and tried harder. But all that brought was more pain thundering through her skull. Someone was trying to stop her from remembering.

"Perhaps," he started, clearing his throat before continuing. "Perhaps if we dance?"

"I've been dancing already," she replied. "It didn't help."

"But you weren't dancing with me. And I think... I know we should dance together." His fingers flexed, then flattened between them. Waiting for her to put her hands in his. "I don't know why, but I think we were meant to do more than just dance."

Goodness, he was right.

She could see an entire lifetime together, happiness in abundance and their future laid out as though it had been paved with gilded stones.

No, that wasn't right. Those were fanciful thoughts from a little girl who thought she could step into a fairytale. Stories like that didn't happen in real life. Only in books. And she knew better than to imagine a life like that, especially when she lived in a place like this.

Freya lived here. Of course she did.

But even with those scolding thoughts in her mind, she still reached for his hands and took them in her own. "A single dance couldn't hurt," she whispered through the screaming in her head.

She knew it could do more damage than a knife to her chest. He lifted her right hand in his own, cradling it out to their sides as those strange eyes stared into hers. Her other hand he lifted to his shoulder and laid it there with utmost delicacy. She flexed her fingers and the round muscles of his shoulder were familiar. Like she'd touched him a thousand times before and knew the warmth underneath her palm.

The Goblin King set his hand against the indent of her waist and pulled her closer. She let out a tiny gasp at the sudden jerking movement, air catching in her throat.

Lips parted, eyes wide, she couldn't pull herself from the abyss of his eyes. Freya didn't want to. She wanted to remain ensnared in his eyes like a rabbit before a coyote, waiting until she was devoured whole.

His eyes crinkled at the edges and the feathers shook with the slightest hint of a smirk. "Do you even know how to dance?"

Had he said those words to her before? Or was she imagining that?

Freya swallowed those thoughts and let her own lips fall into a smirk as well. "I know how to dance light as a feather, Goblin King. But do you know how to handle a partner who can dance better than yourself?"

He threw his head back and laughed, bright and loud. "You are dangerously interesting, little mortal."

"I don't think that's what you call me," she replied. Brows furrowing, she wondered how she knew.

The Goblin King seemed to pause, then nodded. "You're right. I don't call you that."

"It was something like a storybook." Where were these words coming from? She didn't know these things, and yet... she did.

"My hero," he muttered.

"Yes, that sounds right." The words filled her with a courage and a bravery she hadn't felt since she'd woken up on the floor.

Shouldn't she be worried about that? Any other person might have been a little more fixated on why she had woken up and not remembered lying down, but the thought was pushed from her mind before she could latch onto it.

"Shall we?" the Goblin King asked. His voice eased all the anxiety in her chest.

"Yes," she replied. "I think I'd like to dance again."

The music swelled in the air once again. Violins and flutes that she couldn't see, but assumed were hidden somewhere in the crowd of people who watched them with their hands pressed to their chests.

But, as she whirled past another couple, their smiles didn't sit right on their faces. Almost as though the smiles weren't actually there. Her vision flickered and the sea of grinning faces turned into sneers worn by creatures who were hungry.

No, that wasn't right. She was in a ballroom surrounded by her own people who loved her. Wasn't she?

The Goblin King leaned down and whispered in her ear, "Does something not feel right here?"

"I thought I was the only one." Freya wrenched her gaze from the crowd of creatures and turned her attention back to the Goblin King. "I can't remember who I am. Or why I'm here. Or why neither of those things bother me, when I should be worried about it."

"I only know that I want to dance with you," he replied. "But I also know that I've seen you before. A thousand times over. You make me feel like I was a person before all this, and that I should pay attention to what is happening. But I can't seem to think of one thing long enough to really pay attention."

"I'm glad it's not just me." Only, she wasn't. The pain in his voice was difficult to hear, and she wanted to understand why this was happening to the two of them.

Had they done something wrong in a previous life? Were they terrible people who had been sent here to serve out time for a punishment?

No. Why would they be in a castle like this if they were being punished? But if they weren't being punished, then why couldn't they remember anything?

The only logical jump was that they shouldn't be here at all. That the two of them had been thrust into this room, their memories ripped away from them, and that they were supposed to be good little entertainment. Two people whirling about a dance floor, hoping their captor would clap his or her hands and send them on their way.

"Perhaps we can help each other," the Goblin King said. "What do you remember?"

"Nothing." The lie slipped off her tongue so easily, but it burned the back of her throat and made her cough.

He raised his eyebrows and gave her a pointed stare. "That didn't sound like nothing."

Why couldn't she lie? Freya found herself so caught up on that thought that she almost forgot to answer him. "Um." She shook her head to clear the fog as he led her into a complicated waltz. "When you put your hand on my waist, I remembered something. It was like you had done that before, except, somewhere else."

Her cheeks burned in embarrassment. How did she tell a man like this that she thought they had shared a passionate night? That neither of them remembered?

His hand flexed in hers, his fingers curling around her own and clamping down tightly. "When you put your hand in mine, I remembered a starry night where we held hands like this. We were walking down a beach and a million stars twinkled above our head. The only thing I could think about was how delicate your hands felt in mine. And how much I wanted to kiss you."

Oh, those words were distracting. She wanted to languish in them, bask in the glory that a man like this had been so flustered by her touch.

"So," she whispered on a ragged breath. "It seems we remember things when we touch each other. I'm not sure what that means."

"That we know each other from before this moment. Or from another life."

She supposed that was right, but... What if she touched him again? Freya released his hand that he'd held aloft and brought her fingers to his chest. She laid her palm flat over his heart, and another memory bubbled to life.

A vision of him appeared in her mind. He stood between her legs, smiling down at her with a grin that should have split his face in two. He had his hands braced on the table beneath her, on either side of her hips, and he was scolding her for teasing him when he had to work. She knew that he was a busy man, but he hadn't seen her in so many days, and she wanted his attention. She wanted *him*.

Was it hot in this room?

"I know you," she said. "As if you were part of my very soul. Why do I know you?"

Freya tried to hold herself together as they slowed in their dance. The Goblin King brought them to a halt in the center of the dance floor. He took the hand she'd freed and placed it on her cheek.

"I remember a cave," he whispered, the words echoing through the room like a prophecy. "I was so scared I lost you. I thought you had died in front of me, but then you were there again. Like magic, walking through the fog of a spell and proving that you were alive and well. That you would never leave me like that. Not you."

Tears gathered in her eyes. Why did she feel like crying when he said that? She didn't know this man, and yet... she did.

"I don't know who you are." She wished she did, though.

"You do," he muttered. "And I know who you are."

His hand flexed on her jaw, and then he drew her in for a kiss that blistered her soul. His velvet soft lips shouldn't feel like a bad omen, but all she could sense was magic uncontrollably screaming within her.

The spell shattered as if she were made of glass and the Goblin King's kiss was a hammer to her skull. All the memories that had been suppressed came rushing back through her mind.

Saving her sister.

Defeating all those court leaders.

Traveling throughout every faerie court and falling more and more in love with this place. These people.

This man.

"I love you," she whispered against his lips. "I love you more than life itself. My king. My heart. My soul."

His lips curved into a smile against her own. "I know, my hero. I know you do. Now end this spell once and for all, would you?"

The magic coiled inside her like a snake twisting around itself, ready to strike. All it wanted was for her to let it loose so it could attack every person that might try to hold them back.

So she did.

Freya loosed all the magic inside her and reveled in the feeling of utmost power and control. Her power spread like wildfire. It spread through the room and burned every candle to the base of its wick. All the creatures who wore sneers disappeared in the wake of her light.

The only thing that remained was an empty ballroom and a cluster of shadows at the very back of the room. The teeming mass of darkness pulled in on itself until she could see the vague shape of a man.

"There you are," she growled. "End the spell, or I will burn you with the rest of it."

The Horned God shook himself and pushed back on her magic. The darkness spread around him like a dress spilling from his hips, pooling on the floor in an ink stain she knew would never come out of the floor. "You've proven yourself enough, would be Autumn Thief. Let go of your magic and I will end the spell."

"I don't trust you." He'd taken from her everything that mattered. All her magic. All her memories. Everything that made her Freya had disappeared because he wanted to play in her mind.

"One of us will have to trust the other first," he replied. "And I am happy to put you both under the spell again. It will be harder to break the second time. I see my folly was putting you two together. If you were alone, you might never have noticed."

Freya met Eldridge's gaze. He nodded, and she let the power slowly recede from the Horned God. "Fine, then. You've been bested. Now what?"

He grinned, and the light spilled out of his mouth in a mockery of a smile. "Now, the real test begins."

How dare this horrible creature try to take away what was rightfully hers? Freya had little in this world that was her own. But her memories? She had spent her entire life gathering each individual thing she remembered, and this horrible creature had taken them away from her.

Even for a small amount of time. Such a thing was not something she could forgive.

"You are a monster," she snarled. "Not a god."

"Many have said so." The shadows fell away from the Horned God once again, revealing the leathery skin and the horns that wept black blood. "But your opinions do not change my power. I can destroy worlds if I wanted to."

"I think you're too weak for that. You feed off the suffering of others, and so few would dare step foot into this place where they know a monster waits." She swallowed hard. Her words could end in her death, but someone had to take this being to task for what he had created.

This was a room too similar to the Spring Maiden's horrible home. He didn't care about anyone who came to him for help. And that's what gods were for, weren't they? To help the people who worshiped them. The people who gave them their powers.

This one didn't care. The Horned God thought all people who reached out to him were insignificant. That was his greatest weakness. Underestimating others.

She opened her mouth to scold him even farther, but stopped when she felt clawed hands on her shoulders. Ice cold hands with claws that dug into her skin until tiny beads of blood welled in tiny wounds.

"I am a god," the Horned God repeated. "I know what you're thinking, Freya of Woolwich. I know what you want to say to me. And I know that you think this is all because I'm underestimating you. I am not one of the fae, remember? You forget that you are not dealing with anyone that you've dealt with before. Scold away, little mortal woman. You will learn that I am not someone to fight."

She had no doubt, but someone had to fight him. If he wanted to hurt people, then she had to stop him. That was how Freya had lived her life in the faerie realm. And she would not stop now.

"Good," the Horned God replied. He took another step closer while the hands on her shoulders forced her to stay in place. "You think to fight and that is a good trait. Fight against anyone who denies you the right to what you want. That is the first step to becoming the Autumn Thief."

Eldridge stiffened at her side. He obviously wanted to move away from the approaching god, who had taken his memories as well, but he didn't. He stayed right at her side until the Horned God could have touched her.

And then, shockingly, Eldridge reached out and put a hand on the Horned God's chest. "No closer."

Even the Horned God looked surprised. His eyes widened and those spears of light brightened until they were painful to look at. "Just what do you think you're doing, Goblin King?"

"You know the rules. You cannot touch her," he growled. "Or you will answer to me."

Answer to Eldridge?

Freya looked between the two of them, her brows furrowed and body locked in place. Why would the Horned God answer to Eldridge?

"Careful," the Horned God replied with a chortle. "You awakened more questions than you want to answer, Eldridge."

She wished the god would get out of her head. Of course Eldridge had given her more questions, but she'd ask them when this was all over with. The Horned God could go pound sand and then some if he thought he knew what she was thinking.

The hands rose and grasped her skull, squeezing until she let out a small whimper. "I can't touch you," the Horned God whispered, "but my magic can. And don't think for a second I'm not aware of everything that's going on in this head of yours."

The power inside her rose to the battle. It lifted, growing stronger until it pressed against her throat with words she released. "Get out of my head." Even her voice didn't sound like hers.

"Don't be monumentally stupid, little girl. Even the magic of the Autumn Thief doesn't scare me. I helped make it." But the Horned God released her head with a sharp shake of her skull and then took a few steps back. "The trial I gave you was one of endurance. The Owl Mother is so obsessed with intelligence, but I want to see that the Autumn Thief will be someone who can see through magic. A person of more than just intelligence, but instinct."

Freya was quite certain she had passed that test then. She'd seen through his illusions, even though she had not a single memory to help her through that journey.

"Yes, yes," he muttered. "You saw through it, although I don't know if that was really you, or if it was the help of seeing the man you love. I may have underestimated your relationship with our Goblin King. It's an unusual thing to see a faerie and a mortal whose souls are so entangled."

She should take that as a compliment. Eldridge and she were one functioning unit. They saw a problem, they tackled it together, and that worked better for them. They always overcame whatever was thrown at them. That was the beauty of their relationship.

Instead, she took the words as a veiled threat. Like the Horned God thought he could have beaten her if the Goblin King wasn't involved. Yet again, another person thought she wasn't anything without the help of a king.

"There it is," the Horned God said. "The right train of thought. The reason you're having to undergo so many more trials than anyone who came before you. We don't think you're ready for this."

Anger flared in her chest so brightly she swore it spilled out of her hands in a shower of sparks. "Then I will continue proving you wrong. All three of your kind will give me what I want, which is the understanding that this magic is mine. I stole it, as the thieves of old would have done. I will take what is mine and I will keep it."

"And be impressively aggressive while you are fighting for it, yes yes, I know." The Horned God waved a hand in the air, dismissing her words. "You aren't the first to come up with that idea, and you won't be the last when you lose the magic, eventually. Like I said, there is only one more step for you to complete before I never have to see you again."

Good. She would take whatever he had to throw at her. If it meant she left this cursed ballroom, then she would do anything. "What is it?"

The Horned God reared back, and the candlelight played on the horns atop his head. The light ringed them in a red, demonic glow that had her swallowing in fear. He had created the Midnight Monsters, so surely there was more to this story. More to him than only a god who wanted to see what she would do if he pushed her hard enough.

"Of course there's more," he replied to her thoughts with a booming laugh.

He reached behind him with a flourish, and drew out a single, wicked dagger. This one was warped metal, the blade weaving like a river on a map. The wicked tip gleamed.

"Every step requires sacrifice," the Horned God said. "Owl Mother wanted your blood. She likes to taste the memories there, feeding off your essence. But I want more than that. I want more than your blood or your pain."

Of course he did. Look at him! Freya's gaze swept from the top of his head to the bottom of his feet. She had known this creature would require more than physical sacrifice. More than what the others would even want.

When a person fell so deeply into darkness, it was hard to be satisfied by anything less than the depraved.

"What do you want from me, then?" she asked again. "I don't care for the theatrics. Tell me now. Or I will simply walk away from this knowing that I already bested you."

"You can't walk away, Freya. That's why you're still here." He held out a long, clawed hand for her to take. His fingers had an extra digit of length. That was why they looked so odd.

Freya glanced at Eldridge, but the Goblin King said nothing. This was up to her.

Taking a deep breath, she reached out and put her hand in the Horned God's. He closed those terrible fingers around her wrist and then grinned so wide he almost split his face open. "Good, at least you're learning. Not everything has to be a battle, Miss Freya. Or is it Lady Freya now? You'll have to decide if you make your sacrifice for me."

"You keep talking about it as though I'm not going to do it." Freya knew there wasn't anything she wouldn't give up. After all, if she failed this, then she would die anyway.

The power inside her belly swelled and she could feel a shield slam down between her and the Horned God's mind. It was the barest of moments. A brief respite from danger. Then the power of the Autumn Thief whispered, "You'll give up anything but the babe."

It let her linger in that horror before disappearing.

She tried her best not to think about it. Not to dwell that a monster like this could ask for the one thing she couldn't give. But surely he wouldn't ask for that. No one could be so cruel.

"You're hiding something from me," the Horned God said while leading her away from Eldridge. With a wave of his hand, the floor opened up and a small altar rose. "You're getting good at hiding things you don't want others to see. Good. You're learning, and that means that you might survive all this."

"I don't know if you're warning me, threatening me, or trying to teach me a lesson." She schooled her thoughts ever more, trying her very hardest to not think about that light which could not be thought of.

"All of them, actually." The Horned God nodded toward the altar and held out the knife with his other hand. "One last test, and then you're done."

"You said you didn't want blood or pain," she replied.

"I don't. I want something that is important to you. Something that symbolizes a great love. A piece of yourself is owed. A piece that you cannot take back, but that stands for the rest of your life. It's your choice, one who would become the Autumn Thief. But I grow hungry, so you haven't much time left." His eyes glowed brighter, this time with a red hue.

He must know, she realized. He knew she was hiding something so important to her that she might think of it even while she desperately tried to hide it.

But riddles had multiple answers, and she could figure this out. He didn't want that thing she couldn't think of. He wanted something important to her. Something that stood for all that she wanted in this life. For all that she loved.

She looked over her shoulder at Eldridge and saw he also wore an expression of horror. "No," he said, his voice floating through the air like he shouted through water. "You will not harm her!"

The Horned God lifted a hand and threw up a wall of shadows between them. He looked back to Freya and smiled that horrible grin. "You have no help this time, Freya. Your choice must be your own. Make the sacrifice."

Once again, he had given her too much time to think. She had looked at Eldridge and realized her entire life was wrapped around him. He had given her this gift. He had saved her from her boring old life and given her an entire kingdom at her feet if she wanted to take it.

Her life started and began in those starry eyes.

Who was she without her Goblin King? She was just a girl living on the edge of the forest, plagued by fears that were so unfounded. Tears gathered in her eyes until the altar grew blurry.

Freya spun the ring on her finger, hoping the mere action might ease the torment in her mind. It didn't. There wasn't time to second guess herself right now, so she slipped the ring off her finger and put it in her pocket.

She then took the offered knife and steadied herself with a single breath. She couldn't hesitate. If she did, then she'd never go through with this. And it was the only option that she could see in this horrible place where creatures fed off blood and pain.

Freya set her hand on the altar, drew the blade back, and brought it down on the ring finger of her left hand. She'd thought it would be hard. That her body wouldn't let her hurt herself so badly. She'd thought her hand wouldn't go through with it.

But she stared down at her severed ring finger, and belatedly waited for the pain to hit her.

"A finger?" the Horned God chortled. "That's all you have to offer? I do not accept!"

Thunder boomed over her head, and she knew that there wasn't much time for her to argue. If she didn't open her mouth, then she would die. And all of this would be for nothing.

But that was her *finger*.

She'd cut it off.

Freya licked her lips and tried not to scream. Was she breathing? The floor was opening up beneath her, ready to swallow her so the Horned God could play with her for the rest of eternity and she couldn't talk.

Her lungs expanded in a massive gasp. On the exhale, she found her voice again. "In the mortal realm, a man and a woman show their everlasting dedication and loyalty to each other by wearing a ring on that finger. It is the most honorable way to pledge yourself to another. Your life. Your future. All wrapped in a band of metal on your hand. And..." She swallowed down vomit as her entire body shook with the pain and blood loss. "And now I can never make that pledge to the only man I have ever loved in my life."

"Ah, that changes things." The Horned God stepped into her line of vision. He picked up her finger between two of his own, delicately holding it in front of Freya's face. "Now this, Freya of Woolwich, this is a sacrifice."

And as she watched, he lifted her finger above his head and dropped it into his mouth.

The sound of her bones crunching between his teeth made sparks fire in the edges of her vision. His expression twisted into one of pure pleasure before he flicked his own fingers at her. "I change my mind. I accept your sacrifice. Away with you."

The wall of shadows fell behind her with a sound like shattering glass. Freya wasn't sure if she turned first or if Eldridge scooped her into his arms before she had even moved. All she knew was that he had her against his chest as she cradled her bleeding hand.

<h1 style="text-align:center">CHAPTER 21</h1>

Eldridge set her down on her feet in the Stronghold, though he kept his attention on the hand she held close to her heart. Freya couldn't let go of it. Every time she released pressure on her wrist, the wound started spurting blood rather than the slow trickle.

It was a second heartbeat that her body wouldn't shut up about. She could feel it thundering, slamming, pounding repeatedly. No matter how hard she tried to ignore it.

Of course, that all made sense. She had cut off her finger, after all.

The skittering sound of claws crashed through the Stronghold and Arrow veered into the room. "I smell blood!" he shouted, eyes wide with panic. "What happened?"

"The Horned God happened," Eldridge snarled in response. "I don't even know if I can stop the bleeding on this one."

Stop the bleeding? Oh right. She had drifted off into her mind for a bit there, and Freya had forgotten what had happened. Was this what shock felt like? She'd seen a young woman succumb to shock before. The woman had been bitten in the face by a dog. A neighboring crea-ture who had likely been attacked by a slathering beast from the wood.

The dog had always been kind before it bit the strange woman on its land.

"Freya?" Fingers snapped in front of her vision. "I need you to stay with us until we finish bandaging your hand, my love."

Right. She'd cut off her finger.

Why couldn't she stop thinking about those words? She damn well knew what had happened. The throbbing pulse where her finger had once been would never let her forget what had happened.

Arrow nudged Eldridge's thigh with his muzzle, then shoved hard with two paws against his thigh. "Move. I know what to do. I can stop the bleeding."

He could?

Brows furrowed, she sank down onto her knees in front of the goblin dog. "You can? I thought you knew little magic."

"Goblin magic differs from whatever shadowy things you and the king do," he grumbled. Standing on his hind legs, he sort of looked like a person through her blurry vision.

He reached for her with his hands outstretched. No, not hands. Paws. His paws cupped her hands, and the blood soaked through the fine white fur of his paws. "My dear," he muttered. "What did that horrible god make you do?"

"He wanted a sacrifice of something important to me," she whispered. "So I gave him the only thing that humans use to pledge themselves to each other. I... I gave him the finger."

Staring down at it, she belatedly remembered putting the ring in her pocket. As Arrow muttered over her hand, turning it this way and that, she withdrew the gorgeous ring with her free hand.

Tears in her eyes, she looked up at Eldridge and choked out, "I'm so sorry."

"Oh, no. No, my love." Eldridge sank onto his knees as well, taking the ring from her hand and closing his fingers around it in a fist. "I don't need you to wear a ring on your finger for everyone to know you're mine. You are all that matters to me. You know that."

"I do." She thought she did, at least. But what would she do now? A ring was the best way to prove her loyalty to this man, and she didn't know how else to do so. She'd so willingly given it up because she couldn't have given up the child.

The child. She had a baby inside her. She was supposed to be marrying a Goblin King. And all through this entire ordeal she was trying to keep magic inside her that could make her immortal.

What had her life become?

And she was cold. So damned cold.

Shock, she realized. This was definitely a shock and she should be worried about it. Freya should be able to feel her fingers and her toes. The pain should keep her awake but... Well she didn't feel it anymore.

"There," Arrow muttered. "That ought to do."

Freya looked down at her finger and realized the bleeding had stopped. He'd somehow healed her hand so that it looked as though the wound had happened a month ago. Just a nub remained. Even the ragged edges of the wound weren't quite so harsh.

"Ah," she said, her voice shaking. "That was quick."

"I do try to be fast." Arrow put his paw over her hand, hiding the sight from Freya's eyes. "You shouldn't look at it yet, though. Losing a piece of yourself is difficult at the best of times. Let alone with everything else happening."

The shivers shook her entire body. They wobbled through her shoulders and into her spine until she couldn't control them at all. She shouldn't feel like this anymore, right? The wound was done. It had been healed, and it wasn't even visible right now.

Eldridge hissed out a long breath, then drew her into his arms. "Come here, sweetheart. You're all right. You're here with us."

"Am I going to be all right, though?" she asked through chattering teeth. "I didn't think it would be like this. The faerie realm has always been difficult, but it has never taken parts of me. It's never asked for sacrifices like this."

He pressed his lips to her forehead and sighed. "The Autumn Court is different. The faeries here are not kind, nor do they have any desire to follow in the path of others."

"The Autumn Court I know was always kind to me. I remembered this place as a blanket of fiery leaves and tiny goblin children who stole food from each other across a table made from ten different trees."

Her mind wandered through the memories with fondness, though they had dulled since being here. "I remember a hallway full of paintings whose eyes followed me as I walked down their illustrious halls. I thought that was the court I would take over."

Eldridge ran his fingers through her hair. "When will you learn none of the courts are just one thing? The Spring Court looked beautiful when you first saw it, but then you realized half the court was underground and dying. The Winter Court was frozen entirely, its people long past dead. The Summer Court suffered from a poison deep within. Here, it's a different kind of darkness, I agree. But we are the ones who uphold the old ways so the others can make their own mistakes."

"Perhaps the old ways should die," she whispered.

"If only that were possible." He wrapped his arms firmly around her shoulders and squeezed her. "If only I could take this pain from you. I wish I could."

So did she. And that was a horrible thing to think.

Freya snuggled deeper in the warmth of his embrace and tried not to think too hard about what had happened. She was safe, for now, and she could drift into the dreaming realm as an escape. At least for a little while. There was still one more test. One more god to defeat and she could only imagine how horrible and nightmarish the last would be.

Even in her dreams, she saw the skull with red eyes staring back at her. She saw the cavernous mouth opening as Death called for her soul. It wanted to feast upon her, as all the other monsters did in this realm.

Freya woke from the nightmare, frozen in place and holding her breath. Even in her sleep, her body had learned not to let anyone know that she was aware. And in this case, it was the right thing to do.

Murmuring voices whispered near her. She kept her eyes shut for a little while, listening to the sound of familiar people talking in hushed tones. Her hands curled on warm furs, and she realized that Eldridge must have moved her back to the safety of his nest. Far away from those figures that wanted to harm her.

Warm candlelight glowed beyond her closed eyelids. Carefully, so slowly she didn't even exhale, Freya tilted her head to the side and opened her eyes into tiny slits. No one would even know she was watching them. She hoped.

Three figures sat around a fire they had built inside the building. A little dog who wrung his paws and had his tail tucked between his legs. Eldridge, whose skin turned golden in the light of the fire. And a third figure who had once had horns atop her head.

Lark. What was Lark doing here?

"You know this was an impossible quest to send her on," Eldridge snarled, his voice deep with anger. "There were other ways to reach the same end. If she dies, this is on you."

"I know you will believe that until the end of time," Lark replied.

"I still don't understand why you would even consider this path." He shoved a stick into the fire, perhaps a little too aggressively. "Of all the mad quests you could send her on, you had to make her take your place."

"I already explained myself to you, Eldridge. You know there was no other way for her to become immortal, and I wouldn't see you end up alone. Again." She looked down at her empty hands, then back to the Goblin King. "And perhaps it was a little selfish. I couldn't keep catering to them any longer. I couldn't stand them, or the goblins, or the entire realm. I needed a break."

Arrow bristled, the hackles at the back of his neck raising. "You wanted a break, so you sent an innocent girl to her death?"

"She's not going to die." Lark shivered, then rubbed her hands up and down her arms. "She's stronger than either of you give her credit for. And she already had magic. Her father gifted her that from his time here in the realms. Changelings. Who would have thought he could absorb magic like that?"

Absorb magic? What had her father done?

Freya almost feigned waking, but Eldridge spoke, and she stilled her restless limbs.

"He no more stole magic than I asked to become a god." Eldridge wiped his palms on his pant legs as though they were sweaty. "Which I'm quite certain she heard the Horned God say to me."

"You're not a god," Lark replied with a scoff. "They tried to make you one because they liked the number four. But they didn't. There were Goblin Kings before you and there will be after you. All they did was give you enough power to rival them, and then they regretted it when you refused to become their puppet."

"Like the others," he murmured.

"Like the others." Lark sighed again, and her head tilted to the side just slightly. Enough that Freya knew the old Autumn Thief was aware that Freya watched them.

"I can't step in," Eldridge said, his voice cascading through the room. "I have to let her win this on her own, but do you know how hard this has been? I watched him cut off her finger, and I almost killed him. I almost killed a god for her. Our world would run red with blood if I'd done that. I have to trust her, and yet even now I want to watch my magic skin him alive."

Should Freya say something? Should she turn and stretch, or perhaps cough? The old Autumn Thief was obviously aware of what was happening, and yet... Freya didn't want to interrupt. Not when Lark lifted a finger to her lips and indicated for Freya to stay quiet.

What was she up to now?

"Eldridge, I need you to listen to me. Freya has said it many times, and now I will, too. She can do this. You know that. I know that. Not a single fiber of my being worries that she won't survive these trials. She'll impress the old gods the same as I did. As you did."

Eldridge looked up from the flames, and the sorrow in his eyes nearly wrecked Freya. "But will she be the same person in the end?"

So that was what he worried about the most. That Freya wouldn't be the woman he loved.

Honestly, Freya feared the same thing. After so much pain and heartbreak, would she be the same person? She curled her fingers into fists, noting the missing finger that should have moved as well.

Maybe she'd be someone else, but she would still love him. No experience could change how much she loved him with every breath she took.

Lark reached across the fire and took Eldridge's hand. "Of course she's going to be different. She's going to be one of us. A faerie. She will have fought through every court and every god that remains in this realm. She will become a woman made of fire and brimstone and ash, because that is what our court is made of. My King, you will love her all the same. Every love changes. Every person changes. You couldn't expect her to remain stagnant the rest of her life."

He stared into Lark's eyes, and Freya watched the tension ease from his shoulders. "I loved her when she was the mortal woman who crashed into my kingdom, threatening me to find her sister."

"And you love her now. The daughter of a changeling and a woman who had dedicated her life to understanding the fae." Lark released his hands and leaned back, legs crossed and firelight dancing over her face. "She's quite formidable. Even I was frightened of her when I first met her."

"All those years ago?"

"Years? My dear man. That was a few months ago, at best, a year. You've been traveling so much the passage of time has escaped you."

"Perhaps," Eldridge replied with a chuckle. "But every moment of that passage is precious to me. I never thought I'd find someone like her. And a mortal, at that."

Lark looked over her shoulder once again, and Freya saw a sparkle of mischief in her eye. Perhaps the old Autumn Thief wanted the new to see how much her man loved her. Without having to fear that Eldridge knew she was listening.

Either way, she was grateful for this moment of respite.

"How so?" Lark asked, returning her attention to her old friend. "She's a mortal, Eldridge. You'll have to work rather hard to convince me that you're captivated by her mortality."

"I'm fae." He seemed to struggle to find the words, brows drawn down in concentration and hands waving in the air. "I've seen hundreds of years pass by and nothing changes. The world follows itself in cycles. Repeating mistakes and souls over and over again. But her? She stepped out of the circle and started a new path. I've probably seen it before but watching her do that lit a fire in me."

Arrow snorted. "A fire? You never were a poet, Eldridge."

"No, I never claimed to be." He leaned forward and a dark swath of his hair obscured his eyes. "But I don't think I've ever really loved anything before her. I've said the words. I've whispered them in the ears of a hundred lovers, and I went through the actions. But I didn't love them. I didn't even know love could feel like this."

The other two faeries were hanging on his every word now. Even Arrow leaned forward as if the next thing Eldridge said were the words of a prophecy. "What is it like, then?"

He opened his hand and stared down at his spread fingers. "Like the worst day with her would still be the best of my life. And the best day with her would show me what nirvana tastes like."

Freya closed her eyes and let the words settle deep into her soul.

Oh, how she loved him.

CHAPTER 22

Freya stood in front of the wall where the last figurehead remained cast in bronze. The deer skull stared back at her with almost a smile on its face. As though it knew it was the most difficult of gods for her to defeat, and that she was unworthy of this position.

Eldridge stood beside her, Arrow stood on her other side. They wouldn't let her fail, no matter how difficult this became.

She took a deep breath and nodded. "This is it then. The final trial."

"It is." Eldridge took her hand. He drew her attention to him, where he held something out. A twisting cord of shadows suspended the ring he had given her. The dark gemstone glittered even without a single speck of light touching it. "Just because you can't wear it on your finger, doesn't mean you can't wear it at all. I thought you would want this back."

Her eyes burned with tears. This was what she needed. An omen of hope that she could hold on to the moment that deer skull became real and watched her with glowing red eyes.

She took the necklace in her grasp and pulled it over her head, as if the chain might break with the slightest movement. "Thank you," she whispered. "This helps."

Eldridge pressed a kiss to her forehead and then turned her to look at Arrow. The little goblin dog stood wringing his paws, staring at her feet as though he couldn't bear to look her in the eyes. "Miss Freya," he started, then swallowed and stopped talking.

"I'm going to come back, Arrow." She hoped. Oh, how she hoped she would return as the same person they knew.

"No, it's not that." He cleared his throat with a soft growl, then looked up to meet her gaze. "I'm coming with you this time. Everything bad seems to happen when I'm not there, and I think it's important that I... Well. I need to be there with you this time. I won't hear any arguments."

Damn these tears. Arrow couldn't come with them. He was too pure, too precious, too dear to lose to an old god who might use him against her.

But she also couldn't deny him if he wished to be the hero this time. They had done so much without him already, and he wanted to help. Who was she to say that he couldn't?

She loved him as much as she loved Eldridge. They were a family, the three of them. No matter how hard life got, or what life threw at them, they would meet the difficulties together. This situation was no different.

Freya dropped onto her knees in front of him and cupped his dear face in both her hands. "Of course. I wouldn't have it any other way."

His eyes widened and glazed with tears, though she knew the goblin dog would never let them trail down his cheeks. "Good. That's good, Miss Freya."

She squared her shoulders and turned back to the bronze figure waiting for her to take her fate into her own hands. "Eldridge?"

"Yes, love?"

"What did you say this one was called again?"

There was a long pause before he reluctantly replied, "Death."

"Of course." She nodded. "And that's the only name he goes by?"

Eldridge didn't reply, but that was all the answer she needed to know what he meant. He didn't go by another name, and he was a personification of something she should fear.

For what was the most terrifying thing to a mortal if not Death itself?

No time for hesitation. She reached out and put her hand on the face of the skull and gently pushed. It sank into the wall as though the metal face melted, leaking into the warm wood and then depressing into nothing. The door beyond swung open and revealed nothing but darkness beyond.

The pitch blackness sent a shiver down her spine. What waited for her this time? What would this monster desire as a sacrifice?

She held out her hands. Eldridge slipped his fingers into her right, his own long and lean. The warmth of his palm held a strength that she fed from, and let sink through her entire body. He was here. He would never let her go.

Arrow put his paw in her other hand, and each toe pad reminded her that she was loved. The fur on top of his feet was proof she had come so far in her life. After all, she had started this journey hating goblins, and all they stood for. And now? She couldn't live without this goblin dog who was her greatest companion and who supported her in every wild and crazed journey she took them on.

Squeezing both their hands tight, she guided them into the darkness with her.

It was so quiet in this place. She almost thought she couldn't hear a thing until Arrow let out a particularly loud breath.

"It's cold," he muttered. "Too cold for it to be natural."

Gooseflesh rose on her arms, and she had to agree. It was a terrible cold that sank beneath her clothes and ate away at her flesh. The frigid air wiggled all the way down into her bones, turning her entire body so stiff that it was hard to walk.

"Come on," she said. "We have to keep going."

"Where are we going?" Arrow asked. "How do you even know what direction to walk?"

She didn't. But that power inside her seemed to know what direction to take her, and it wanted her to move forward. Ever forward. It didn't matter what direction really, only that she kept their feet moving because there was something coming. Something behind her that could devour them all whole if she didn't keep them safe.

Freya imagined the little light in her belly. The one that meant more than anything else in this entire universe. That light guided her forward, and it tugged her toward a future where she and that little life were safe. Where they could live together in a castle made of starlight and the dust of a thousand universes.

"Forward," she repeated. "We just keep going forward."

And so they did. For what felt like hours but she knew they were fighting against a power that she couldn't see or feel. She could sense it. All around her. That cold sensation wasn't just the place they were in. It was a person who was watching. Waiting. Contemplating whether she was worthy of seeing it.

Or him.

Death waited for her. She knew that without question. And as the last step between her and becoming the Autumn Thief, she was waiting to see him, too.

Finally, the shadows parted before them like curtains on a grand stage. The cold slid from their shoulders as though they had been wearing it like some horrible, hooded cloak. And her eyes cleared.

Floating in the center of all that darkness was a small, red glade. The ground was a circle of sunshine and autumn leaves surrounded by oak trees burning bright red. Another tree stood in the center, though this one was much older than the rest.

The cold air warmed at least a little. Not enough for the gooseflesh to disappear on her arms, but it was a start.

Freya released the hands of her companions and took one step onto the bed of leaves. They crunched beneath her feet, the sound satisfyingly loud after so much silence for what had felt like a lifetime.

"There," she said with a long sigh. "We made it, I suppose."

"Freya..." Arrow's voice was filled with a sense of foreboding. "Look at what the magic did to your clothing."

She stared down at her sensible brown pants and white shirt, only to find that they had disappeared. She wore a blood red dress she didn't recognize. It covered her body like someone had poured liquid over her. From neck, to wrist, to feet, she was swathed in crimson fabric. Like the Autumn Thief had been, long ago. Although, she didn't remember Lark ever having worn something quite so tight.

She hummed under her breath. "Well, I would hazard a guess that Death didn't like what I was wearing for the first time meeting him. Is that a fair enough assumption?"

Eldridge walked in front of her, wearing the same clothing he'd had on before. Travel clothes, certainly. And matching what she had brought with her on this trip. Freya looked to her left and saw Arrow was wearing the same thing as well.

Her stomach twisted into a knot. Why had she been the only one to change her clothing? The other two were here to see this old god with her, were they not?

But she already knew the answer to that. Of course they wouldn't be there with her. They hadn't with any of the other trials either. They had always been kept away from her while she fought on her own.

She met Eldridge's worried gaze and tried her best to smile. She didn't want him to think that she was afraid when he had obviously come to the same conclusion as her. He knew how this worked. He knew they couldn't change the way this had to all play out, even if he was god-like himself.

She hadn't even told him that she knew. Oh, heaven's above. There was so much she hadn't said to him yet, and not enough time for her to say it all.

"I love you," she said, staring into those starry eyes and hoping he saw how much she needed him to be okay. "I'm ready for whatever comes."

Slowly, as if he were moving through water, Eldridge put his hand on her belly. The warmth from his palm seeped through her skin and rattled her to her very core. As if the life that was growing inside her, barely perceptible as it was, recognized the magic of its father.

"Stay safe, my love, my life, mother of my child." His fingers flexed on her belly, but then he withdrew. "I don't want you to do this alone, but I fear I don't have a choice."

"Neither of us do."

Movement shifted through the trees behind Eldridge. But she wasn't ready for that yet. Not when there was so much more left to say.

She looked away from whatever approached them and laid her hand on Arrow's soft head. "Thank you for coming with me, even if it was for such a short amount of time."

"I'm going with you all the way, Miss Freya." Her dear goblin companion drew himself up straight as his namesake. "They can try to stop me."

"I don't know how I got so lucky as to have you in my life, but I am grateful for it every day. You're the best friend I could ever have asked for, Arrow. My sweet, brave, handsome goblin dog who has never once let me down." She tried so hard to keep the tears from falling down her cheeks. "But I don't think you're going to have a choice."

He opened his mouth to argue, and then his eyes glazed over. The expression on his face was similar to the one she had seen in the caves in the Spring Court, when magic had overwhelmed both him and Eldridge. But this time he was half aware of the world around him.

A shiver traveled down Freya's spine. It was long past time for her to see what Death himself had sent.

She turned to see two women peel themselves from the bark of nearby trees. They were entirely nude, or perhaps their skin was the same as the bark. Rough textures decorated their body in tiny pits and raised edges. Their hair was made of long, pale, sticky ribbons. That hair attached them to the trees they had peeled themselves away from. Freya wondered if these women could ever escape from the prison of this place.

They reached for both Eldridge and Arrow, drawing her companions into their arms and holding them tightly against their chests.

Arrow crawled into the tree woman's arms. The strange being drew him to the roots of her tree and then sat cross legged. Arrow curled up into a tiny ball in the space her legs created. He looked like a fox tucked in for a long winter with his tail over his nose like that.

Eldridge slowly sank onto the ground, one leg outstretched before him and the other raised so he could prop his elbow on his knee. His eyes saw her movements. He tracked her as she walked in front of him, but he didn't use anything other than his eyes. The strange creature kept her hand on his shoulder, but it didn't look like she was forcing him to remain in place.

"They are helping for a little while." The deep voice sank through all her anxiety and fears, dispelling them immediately. He had the voice of an actual god. The kind of voice that made her want to fold up in his arms and listen to him talk for hours.

Tears pricked her eyes again, for some strange reason. She didn't know why. Or how.

But she knew who was in the glen with her.

She straightened her back, squared her shoulders, and balled her hands into fists. She would not be afraid. She would not give him that satisfaction.

And then she turned to greet Death.

CHAPTER 23

Death was a terrifying being to look upon. Little more than a black-cloaked figure, the only part of him she could focus on was his skull. The white bones were glaringly bright, even in the glen filled with red. That was the kind of bone one would find wandering in a forest, and a horrible sense of pity would overwhelm the viewer.

Such a thing only died in pain and fear. She knew that deep in her very soul.

He stood beside the largest tree in the center of this barren place. Red leaves swirled at his feet as a tempest burst into life. The movement only made him more terrifying. More ominous.

"Hello, Death," Freya said. Her voice was raspy with fear. "Have you come to give me my last test?"

"Why do you think I'm going to test you?" He lifted his head and for the first time, she saw his eyes.

They weren't red, like she had thought they would be. His eyes were blue as the brightest ocean water at night. And they were sad. They swirled with a deep emotion that burned her soul and made tears prick her eyes. He was sad. So incredibly sad, and she didn't know why.

How could Death feel remorse or sorrow? His job was to collect all the souls who didn't want to see him.

At least, that was the mortal thoughts of who he was. Maybe he wasn't the same in the faerie realm. Or maybe he was the person she had rightfully feared for her entire life.

"All the others have," she finally replied. "That's the entire point of all this, isn't it? I took magic that wasn't mine to take, and now you have to prove that I'm worthy of this magic that grows stronger with every minute inside me."

He tilted his head to the side and his horns caught in the light. Sunlight through the leaves burned behind them, outlining the rippled edges with bright red fire. "A trial always has to be completed for the Autumn Thief. The magic you stole wasn't yours, in a way. But like you said. A thief is what you wanted to become, and so you have already proven yourself ready to take the title of... Thief."

That stopped her anger in its tracks. Was he agreeing with her?

No, that wasn't possible. None of the other old gods had agreed with her, and both of the others had been tricksters. Just like the other fae.

Freya glanced to her side to make sure that Eldridge and Arrow were still where she had left them. Her faithful companions hadn't moved at all. In fact, they didn't seem to even be blinking.

Now, that wasn't normal for either of them to do. She turned back to Death and bit her lip. "What did you do to them?"

"Nothing that they wouldn't have agreed to. They can see. They can hear. I didn't take away their free will or their memories." Death lifted a skeleton hand and swirled the bones of his fingers in the air. A gnarled staff appeared, and he gently closed his fingers around the knotted end. "I am not the Owl Mother who will force your Goblin King into a certain form when he doesn't want to be. And I am not the Horned God who likes to manipulate and control people so that they will eventually worship him."

She followed his words, but Freya didn't understand why he wasn't like the others. A question fell from her lips and danced on the breeze. "Why aren't you like them?"

His bright blue gaze found hers. "Because people already fear me,

Freya. I am the end of all things and the beginning of a new path. I am eternity and the final breath."

Her knees quaked at the words. "So you are the same person who mortals fear, then?"

"In a sense. There are many iterations of Death itself, and we are all connected in some way or manner. But you do not have to be afraid of me, Freya. Someday I will meet you at the river, where you will hand my maidens your clothing and allow them to wash the filth of life from you. But I sense that day will not come for a very long time." He held out his hand for her to take. "But that remains to be seen. As with my brethren, you will need to walk with me."

"I don't want to walk with you," she spat. "I want this all to be over with. I want to go home with the people I love and start the life I was promised."

"You cannot do that, though. You stole magic from the Autumn Thief and therefore, you have more responsibilities than living in happiness." He walked toward her with a significant limp in his gait. "Surely that thought occurred to you long before you took the magic from Lark."

The name stunned her. "You know Lark's name?"

"I know all their names." He lifted his free hand, and a wave of magic shimmered beside him.

A woman with an owl's head stood there, before the image changed into a man with lizard scales. Over and over, countless goblins appeared in the air beside him. Each one turning into another with a quick flick of his wrist. Some of them she recognized from her vision in the Owl Mother's sanctuary, others were entirely new.

Eventually, the mirage turned into two faces she knew very well. Eldridge, though in the owlish form he liked to hide from the world. And Lark, with her antlers that were so much larger than life. Freya missed them, she realized. Those antlers had been part of who Lark was for such a long time, and now... Well, she supposed now Lark was who she wanted to be.

"So you see," Death continued. "I have met with every one of them. I have spoken with them all, and I know their stories. I know how each one of their stories would end though I doubt you're interested in hearing what will happen or what did happen."

"No," she quickly replied. "I have no interest in hearing that."

"Probably for the best." He waved his hand again, and the mirages disappeared. "Some of them were not very pleasant ends, I'm afraid."

"That's what I'd rather avoid, if you don't mind." She cleared her throat and looked back to Eldridge.

Could he see everything that was going on? What would he say to her at this moment?

She already knew the answer. Trust no one, not even Death itself. But so far, this creature wasn't at all like the others. He didn't seem to be playing games with her. He seemed to be rather honest, which was a surprising trait among the fae. Even though they couldn't tell lies, the ones she had met so far were very good at hiding the truth.

"Can I ask you a question?" She put her hand on her belly, gently touching the hollow between her hips as though her touch might sink through to the life within. "It's a short one, and then I promise I'll go with you."

Death inclined his head, slow and methodical as all his movements appeared to be. "By all means, Freya. I will answer any of your questions that I can."

"Am I going to be a different person when this is all done?" There was only one logical response, and it wasn't that she remained as she was right now. There was too much riding on her becoming the Autumn Thief. And all the difficulties of the life that came with.

She'd been a foolish little girl to take the magic from Lark without asking more questions. But she'd wanted to help a friend. She'd wanted to be the hero one more time, and if taking a little magic was the answer to that, then why shouldn't she?

Well. She was living with the consequences now.

Death's eyes blinked in and out of existence, obviously watching all those thoughts play across her face. "I think you already know the answer to your question."

"I do, but I want to hear you say it. I want to know for sure that what I'm thinking is right."

He took a deep breath and sighed. The robes around him swayed in the breeze, and a gust of wind kicked up more leaves that danced at his feet. "No. You won't be the same person. How could you be? You will have defeated every court imaginable, and then you will be walking into a life that isn't the same. A life that has subjects and castles. Kings at your beck and call. You will be very busy and likely have no time for yourself or the life inside you that you hold so dear already."

What a life! It sounded awful.

Death took another step closer, so close that she could see the fine cracks around the mouth of his skull. "But if you succeed, despite all the madness you're welcoming into your life, you will be happy, Freya. I can promise you that much."

And that was all she needed. Happiness. A breath and a break every now and then before she dove back into being busy. Freya liked to work, she enjoyed helping others. All she needed to know was that she would be happy.

She looked one more time at the two men she loved. "Will they be all right while I'm gone?"

"My maidens will take good care of them." One more time, Death stretched out his hand for her to take.

"And your maidens won't drag either of them to a river to wash their clothes?" Her lips quirked in a half smile that she hoped conveyed the joke. She still didn't know what he meant by all that, but maybe he was giving her a glimpse of what real death was like.

He shook the giant skull of his head, and she swore those blue glowing orbs crinkled with a smile. "Your companions are safe. There will be no river, nor clothing washed for either of them. They both have long threads of life left to live."

Good, at least she didn't have to worry about that, then. The only question still lingering in her mind, the one that stopped her from placing her hand in his, was an age-old question that she'd feared since the moment she was born.

"I find I'm not quite ready to face Death on my own," she whispered. Her hands curled into fists at her sides and her throat tightened. "I'm afraid. Of you, of what you're going to ask me to do. Of the future I may or may not see."

Death sighed. The sound mixed with a gust of wind that threw leaves up into the air.

The crimson leaves rained down on her shoulders, gently tangling in her hair and smoothing down her shoulders. As though Death was trying to comfort her.

"You have yet to learn that death is the last thing you have to fear." He chuckled, warm and inviting. "Fear spiders and snakes and shadows. They are what hurts and what lingers. But you do not, under any circumstances, have a reason to fear me. Of all things in your life, I am the kindest creature you will meet. My hope for everyone is that I make the passing a little easier. Not frightening."

"But I'm not..." She couldn't even finish the words.

"Freya. I think the time for questions has passed. I need you to come with me to become the Autumn Thief, or come with me because you denied your future. Either way, your story ends or begins with me." His skeletal fingers twitched, waiting for her to make her choice.

It was ridiculous for her to wait any longer, wasn't it? She already knew what choice she had to make. She already knew there was no other option.

Freya pressed her hand to her belly and whispered, "I'll take care of you. I promise."

Death's eyes crinkled in that strange smile once again. "And I will take care of you, Freya. Come. It is time."

She put her hand in Death's, and let him guide her through the glen.

CHAPTER 24

Freya wasn't sure why she'd thought something else might happen when she took Death's hand. Maybe a large bang as the world rearranged itself because the Autumn Thief had taken the hand of someone so powerful. Or perhaps that the ground would open up beneath her feet and swallow her whole.

None of that happened, however.

Death simply wanted to walk with her through the glen. He strode with her by the large tree that rained red leaves down over their head, and she realized there was a larger path beyond it. Of course, the path also seemed to float in the darkness that spread around them, as though no light could penetrate the strange realm they stood inside.

The path was covered in bright leaves that crunched beneath her feet as they walked. Death seemed quite content with listening to the sound. He didn't say a word until they were far from her companions and the path had become decidedly familiar.

"Is this the same place I was when I first arrived in the faerie realms?" she asked, looking around them. They were moving, but the trees weren't.

The memories struck her hard, and she couldn't stop thinking about that very first moment when she had arrived in faerie, chasing after her sister like a madwoman. This path had frustrated her to no end. Freya had been ready to cut down every tree that she possibly could if it meant getting to her sister in time.

"It is," Death replied. "Entering faerie is sometimes a form of death for some mortals. You were smart and kept your wits about you, or you would have ended up in this purgatory forever."

"Purgatory." She repeated the word with a small snort. "I think I would have stayed here forever if it wasn't for the bravery of a goblin dog."

How strange to end her story at the beginning. Freya scuffed her foot on the ground, disturbing the leaves with the faint impression that she might find her own footprints in the ground here. Just waiting for her to see them once again.

"Perhaps, but I think you would have figured it out all the same. I've been watching you since you stepped foot in this realm, I'll admit. Your journey has fascinated me."

She cleared her throat and removed her hand from his arm. "I don't know how to reconcile the fact that Death himself has been watching me while I've been traveling. It's a little uncomfortable to hear, if I'm being honest."

"I wouldn't expect less from you. Most people are uncomfortable with talking to me, let alone knowing that I've been invested in their lives." He laughed as though what he'd said was funny. "But I suppose that's the way of life in general. There's always going to be some version of Death watching you. Waiting for the moment when you make a mistake and you come to see us for all eternity."

And there he went again. Talking in such a way that made shivers dance down her spine and reminded her that this conversation wasn't normal in the slightest. Nor did she want to continue it for any longer than she absolutely had to.

Freya tucked her hands behind her back and tried very hard not to look at the dress that was poured down her body. "I have no wish to insult you. However, I have to ask why we're standing here of all places. You are supposed to be testing me and deciding if I am worthy of this power and this position. Not taking me down a path of memories."

"But this is where it all started. Not just for you, my dear, but for everyone." Death pointed at the trees with his cane. "I've already made my choice about you, Freya. I've seen you struggle and fight to get everywhere in this realm. And I am most impressed. But there are many things you should know before you take all this on, and there is one more sacrifice to make."

She thought about his words and tried hard to ignore the fear churning in her belly. A thousand questions popped into her mind at the mere thought of what he was implying.

What information could he tell her about being the Autumn Thief that could be worth choosing death over taking this role?

Considering the other gods she had met thus far, she was very afraid of what he was about to say. But again, she realized how little a choice she had in this matter. He had to tell her. She had to take those words and understand that she couldn't change them. And then she had to decide if she wanted to make a sacrifice and continue forward on this path, or branch off down another.

Sighing, she nodded firmly and turned toward him. "Then please, Death. Tell me what it is that I need to know about this place. This magic. What secrets have yet to unfold in front of me?"

Those glowing blue eyes crinkled in the corners again, as though he were pleased with her answer. "I knew you would want to know more. You never have been the heroine who was happy to charge into battle without knowing all the facts." He held his arm out again for her to take. "Would you like to find out what is at the end of this path then, my dear?"

"You mean it's not just an illusion?" She took his arm a little too quickly. "I thought this path went nowhere. That no matter how long I walked on it, that it would always remain the same."

"In a sense, for some, this path will always remain stagnant. But there is a deeper end to it that you should be thankful you never discovered." His cane struck the ground a little harder and suddenly they could walk freely down the path.

How quaint it was to see the trees moving and feel the ground give beneath her feet. Freya had been so certain that wasn't possible in this place.

But, as with everything in the faerie realms, the impossible was never the truth.

She tried her best not to marvel at the change, and instead, listen to what Death was saying. "How unusual. Do you think I ever would have figured out how to make the path continue forward?"

"I would imagine you had about three or four days before your thirst got the better of you. And then, when you thought all was lost, you would have suddenly had more vigor than you've had in years. You'd have gotten up and bounded down this path toward where we are going." He inclined his skull head, pointing in the direction they walked. "Though, by the time you reached the end, you would have understood what had happened to you."

Freya noted how his grip changed while he said the words. Death clutched onto her arm a little harder, a little more forcefully. As if he feared that she would take off the moment she realized they were walking down a path where the dead walked.

But she trusted him. She had realized that truth a little belatedly, as usual, but she didn't think he was trying to kill her. After all, if he'd wanted to do that, then it would have been easier to do it without all this fanfare. That meant he really did have something to show her, and she intended to find out what that truth was.

"Ah," she whispered. "I suppose that should frighten me more than it does."

"Usually. But this is the same path that all the thieves have walked since the beginning of time. You know, it used to be all the court leaders but then..." He sighed. "Then they all wanted to avoid the old gods and the old ways."

She sidestepped a tree that had fallen over the path. The longer they walked, the more untamed the path became. And in the distance, she swore she could see some kind of clearing, or perhaps another grove of trees like the one they had just left.

"Why did they want to divert from the old ways?" she asked. "No one has told me that part, only that they didn't want to worship you anymore, and that the Autumn Thief was one of the few who keeps the old traditions alive."

Death shifted his weight in his shoulders, clearly uncomfortable with her question but ready to answer, nonetheless. "Children want to grow up and leave the home. They want to find their own answers to questions they thought they already understood. It is natural for them to leave, but some of the gods don't share that same opinion with me."

Ah. So they were a rather dysfunctional family, and none of the parents wanted to take responsibility for driving out their own children. In a strange way, that made more sense than anything anyone had told her thus far.

"Right," she replied. "So, the old gods have to be worshipped to stay alive?"

"Something like that. We'd still be here, of course. But the Autumn Thief has always seen the reasoning behind continuing to worship three very powerful beings who could easily become unhinged." Death raised the hand not holding the cane, holding his palm out flat. "I am very different from my siblings. I wish I could say that I wouldn't also feel a little thrown aside, but..."

"When beings that are used to being worshipped feel like they are no longer useful, bad things can happen."

Freya understood the meaning behind his words. Did she want to be that person? Though she was terrified of these beings, she would still have to see them regularly.

Maybe that was why Lark didn't want to do this anymore. These gods seemed to ask for much, but gave nothing in return. And how was that supposed to be easy for the person who became their mouthpiece?

"All right," she muttered. "So if I want to take up this job, then I will have to be aware that you're all going to be meddling in every choice that I make?"

"And in your life." Death's eyes squeezed at the edges again. "I cannot promise that we won't have opinions on your man, your children, or your court."

"Essentially I'll be welcoming three more parents into my life, as well as having found my blood parents." Freya hated the sound of that. She was just coming into her own as an adult, and now she had to listen to so many others?

"Goodness, don't call me a parent. I'm not that old." Death winked one of his glowing orbs. "More like three older siblings who are certain they know how to live better than you do, my dear."

"Right, and that sounds so lovely."

But she was teasing. Of course she would take this punishment, if that's what it required. All she had to do was listen to them complain? She'd gotten quite good at that in the most recent months.

They finally reached a clearing in their meandering walk. She'd been right. It wasn't a home or anything similar, but a clearing. A large space with swirling shadows around it. No trees. No red leaves. Just a blank space where there might have once been something if she looked hard enough for clues.

"Where are we?" she asked.

"The place where you will make your final sacrifice, if you are still certain that you want this position." Death walked ahead of her into the center of the clearing and put both of his hands on the top of his cane. "You have to be sure, Freya. More sure than you have ever been of anything in your life."

"I am." She wasn't. The words were a horrible lie. "But what other choice do I have? Death or becoming the Autumn Thief. I have to do this."

She could only hope he appreciated her honesty, because there were no other options for her. This was it. The light inside her made it difficult to consider anything else.

Death sighed and gestured for her to join him. "Then come look, my dear. Come and see the last part of becoming the Autumn Thief. The last part of becoming someone entirely new."

Freya strode across the fallen leaves and stood beside him. Death had strategically placed himself where he stood so the dark cloak that undulated around him would obscure a horrible sight.

Graves.

A hundred graves, all open, all spread out in the ground as far as the eye could see. Farther, she imagined, and probably more than she'd have ever guessed.

Freya's eyes blurred with tears and she pressed her hands to her mouth. Why was he showing her this? This horribly sad place where so many people had been laid to rest. Was it a battlefield? A reminder that the old gods were infinitely powerful?

"What is this place?" she whispered through her shaking fingers.

Death pointed with his cane to the grave at their feet. "You can guess at that, Freya. You're smarter than you look."

She didn't want to look down. She didn't want to see what the graves contained.

But she looked. Because she had to.

Curled up in the grave with her legs pressed against her heart was an image of Lark. A younger version, perhaps, with tiny nubs of antlers on her head. Her hooved feet were tucked in close to her nude behind, and someone had crossed her arms over her chest. She looked very much like she had fallen asleep in that hole in the ground.

Freya couldn't bear to see her dear friend like that. Her eyes flicked to the right and saw the face of an owl, laid out as though he had fallen asleep on his back.

Her Eldridge. Her sweet, wonderful, handsome Eldridge laid cold and dead at her feet.

A horrible whimper burst from her throat as she stared at the images of her friends. Dead. Cold. Long gone from this life, even though she logically knew they were well and alive. She had just left them. And they hadn't been dead.

"Why?" she asked, her voice ragged and thick. "Why are you showing me this?"

"Every sacrifice you have made has led you to this point, Freya. I know it must seem barbaric to you, but there is always a reason behind what we ask of our leaders." Death's eyes turned cold and icy. Unwavering and unrelenting. "Snap yourself out of this emotional turmoil and think back to the other sacrifices. Why did they want those particular sacrifices from you?"

"Because they are cruel and horrible beings." Tears fell from her eyes and she dashed them away with an angry hand. "Because they want nothing more than to see me on my knees before them, begging for their mercy."

"No," Death replied. "That is not the reason at all. You are leading right now with your emotions, and no Thief can do that. You have to rip through what you have been told, what you have suffered, and understand the meaning behind all this."

"There is no meaning," she snarled.

"That's not fair, nor is it logical. I chose you as my Autumn Thief because you were capable of more than the others. Capable of seeing through the magic and the powers into what is really there." Death grew all the more serious, staring at her as though he could burn her to the ground if he wanted to. "Try again, or I will take back my opinion and make you run the gauntlet as the others had."

Well, she didn't want to do that. But she also hated what he was making her do. This wasn't fair to stare at her friends like this. It wasn't fair to face death long before her time.

And yet, here she was.

The life inside her flipped, shifting and moving in her belly as though the baby was already large enough to feel. The child couldn't be, and yet... She knew better than to expect only the possible.

She couldn't argue with him. There was no winning this argument, no matter how hard she wanted to win.

Freya took a deep breath and stored her anger away for another time. For now, there was no place for anger such as this.

"The Owl Mother wanted to test my wit," she finally said.

"No, that was your trial. Not your sacrifice."

Oh, he wanted to know how all the others had hurt her? How morbid. "The Owl Mother wanted my blood. I cut my wrist over a goblet for her to drink."

Death's eyes narrowed. "I'm not going to hold your hand for much longer, Freya. Your sacrifice to her was not your blood. What was the real sacrifice you made?"

She didn't know. Blood had no meaning. The Owl Mother had cared more for proof of her intellect rather than actually gaining anything from her. But if Death thought that it had meaning, then perhaps it did.

She stilled her mind. The power of the Autumn Thief hummed inside her, apparently thinking as well until they figured it out.

"The Owl Mother is intelligent. She'd want to create some kind of fail safe, so she wanted to be able to use my blood in a spell, didn't she?" Freya shook her head ruefully, not even realizing that she'd given away something so precious until this moment. "She wanted a second way to control me if I didn't bend to her will at first."

"A sacrifice of your own free will, should you fail her expectations." Death nodded. "And then you met the Horned God."

"He wanted a finger. A feast." But there had to be more to it than that. Obviously. "So perhaps he wanted to devour something of mine for... I don't know. To take some of my magic, perhaps?"

Death shrugged. "It's fairly close to what he did. If it makes you feel better, he's probably already used all that magic up. I wouldn't say he's the smartest of us."

"I agree with you on that," she replied with a snort. The Horned God was nothing without his Midnight Monsters, and even then, she didn't fear him nearly as much as the other two. "Which leads me all the way to you. Here. In this horrible place of a thousand graves."

She couldn't begin to guess what he would ask of her. Death at the end of either path didn't make sense. She'd been promised this was the only way to live, and that her child would be fine. But if she died, then so did the baby.

Freya pressed a hand to her belly and tried to still the shaking of her fingers. "I don't know what you're going to ask of me, Death, but I want you to know that I'm pregnant. This child is more important than anything else. If you wish me to die for this, then I will have to insist you allow me to give this life inside of me a chance. Allow me to rule as the Autumn Thief, or appoint your own Autumn Thief until the child comes. But I will do nothing that puts my child in danger."

To her utter shock, Death reached out and put his hand on top of hers. "I would never threaten a life that has yet been born. Your child is not just of a mortal woman who stole the Autumn Thief's magic. Your child is that of the Goblin King, a man I consider my very son. This child is my granddaughter. I will not, ever, risk her life."

She should have focused on all those words, but all she heard in her head was *granddaughter*.

"It's a girl?" she asked, her voice wavering with emotion. "Do you know that for certain or are you simply speculating?"

Death's fingers tightened on hers. "I know when a life is sparked who they are or who they might be. I know their entire thread of life and all the stories that come with it, Freya of the Goblin Court. You are going to have a daughter and she is going to be magnificent."

Tears fell freely down her cheeks at the realization that she was going to soon hold a little girl in her arms. Someday, she hoped.

If anything, that light inside her grew ever brighter. As if the child knew that her mother was excited to meet her.

"She is so loved already," Freya whispered. "By me. Her father. A goblin dog who most certainly will be known as her uncle, although I don't know how I'm going to explain to her that her uncle is a dog. She's going to grow up in a rather unconventional family. Goodness, even her aunt has a tail."

Death tilted the skull head back and laughed. The booming sound filled the clearing with unnatural gaiety considering they stood in an open faced graveyard. "She's going to grow up in the faerie realms, Freya. Nothing here makes sense, and it's all wrong no matter how you look at it. Mortal eyes will fail you here, especially in raising your child."

She supposed that was another thing she would need to give up. Looking at this world through the eyes of mortality would only end in her disappointment, or worse, not knowing who or what she might insult.

Swallowing hard, she met Death's glowing gaze and nodded. "All right. What do you want from me then, Death? My life is the only thing I can assume you might desire, but you keep saying that isn't what you're asking of me."

"No. I don't want your life." He looked back at the graves, and the set of his shoulders changed horribly.

Dread set deep into her belly. "You want my mortality, is that it? What could I trade you that Death would desire but a taste of life itself?"

Again, he shook his head in denial of what she asked. "No, I'm afraid it's much worse than that. I know this isn't what you want to hear, Miss Freya. But the sacrifice I claim from all Autumn Thieves is... themselves."

Well, that didn't make any sense whatsoever.

"You're speaking in riddles," she told him. Daring to do more than just stand at the edge of a grave, she reached forward and put her hand on his shoulder. As though Death needed her to support him as he explained. "I think there's a lot of that going around these days, but I'm afraid I'll need you to speak as plainly as possible."

"I forget you're mortal sometimes," he replied, his voice barely more than a whisper. "And I mean that as the highest of compliments."

"I took it as such."

He waved a hand over the image of a thousand graves before them, gesturing to all the lives he had taken. "The Autumn Thief is a newborn babe, in a sense. When they are fully accepted as the leader of this court, they are no longer themselves. That is not because of the power or the ordeal they have gone through. The sacrifice I require is all of who you were before the magic, Freya. I need you to give me the woman you once were and you will join all the others in their graves."

His words struck her over the head like he wielded a hammer upon her skull.

He wanted her to die. Or a version of herself, at least. That would mean that she pledged everything she had been in her life to this creature who she had no control over.

"Um," she stuttered, unsure of what she should even ask him. "Will that version of myself be aware of what happened?"

The worst thoughts she had were what if she would be splitting herself in two? What if that version of herself knew what had happened? What if she was stuck here, aware but never able to escape? It was a fate worse than she could imagine.

"No, she won't be aware of your choice or anything other than the fact that she is gone. I am not so cruel that I would force my own people to relive their lives or to know what happened to them." Death turned his head to the side, watching her too intently. "You will give me who you once were, so that you can become someone so much more than you are now."

She didn't think she needed to become more than what she already was. Freya was very proud of how far she'd come in this life, and all the things she'd done to get herself here.

"Will I be able to remember everything that happened before I split?" she asked, stammering now at all the possibilities this entailed.

"You'll be yourself, yes. You will still remember everything, although it will be... muted." He waved a hand in the air, gesturing wildly with the staff. "You will know that it happened to you, but the emotions will be duller. Easier to think of all those memories without getting emotional."

"But what about love?" She didn't want to give up all that. She wanted to feel like Eldridge stole her breath away for the rest of her life. Not a dulled version of what they had built.

Death's eyes glowed brighter until they rivaled the very sun above their heads. "Even I can not diminish love. That, my darling, is forever."

Well, she supposed this was the best she would get, then. As long as her love for all the people in her life still burned as brightly, still ruled her decisions as thoroughly, then she would give the rest up so she could continue forward. So she could stay with Eldridge until the end of all days with their child still in her arms.

She pressed her lips together and nodded firmly. "All right, then. I accept your terms, Death. The sacrifice will be made, although I do not know how to do it."

His eyes stared down at the graves just in front of them, and he clucked his tongue. "I thought perhaps you would want your own final resting place when I first realized we would be testing you. All the others had wanted their own place to be honored. But now that I have met you, spoken with you, seen what the inside of your mind is like... Well. I think it's more likely that you'd rather rest with him for all eternity."

She followed the line of his finger as Death pointed his skeletal hand to the grave that held Eldridge's former life. Perhaps this was how her Goblin King wasn't as affected by his childhood as she thought he might be. He rarely spoke about his family or what had happened all those years ago.

Maybe Death had taken away the feelings that went with the memories.

"Can I ask why?" Freya met Death's gaze for the last time with a question burning in her chest. "Why must I give up so much to become the Autumn Thief? And what are you all going to do with the things that you took from me?"

Death shrugged. "I'll watch your memories when I get lonely. I've never been to the mortal realm, so they will be a lovely diversion from the memories that I usually watch from all the others here. The Owl Mother will clutch your blood to her chest in the hopes that it will ease her anxiety. And the Horned God will lick his wounds and tell himself that he was the one to beat you because he devoured a part of you."

"None of that is an answer to my question. Why do I have to give up so much?" She took a step closer to Eldridge's grave, toes hanging over the edge.

"Great power requires great sacrifice," Death replied. "Without it, then power might flow throughout all the realms. Unchecked. Unbalanced. And uncontrolled."

And wasn't that what Eldridge had always said? Power and magic never came without a price, even though she never saw the price that was paid. This was hers, and maybe it wasn't the same as the others. But it was still the price she had to pay.

Taking a deep breath, she dropped down into the grave. She didn't want to step on the perfectly preserved image of the man she loved.

The hairs rose on her arms as she slowly laid down next to him. All of this felt so incredibly wrong. Like she'd never realized what was happening until this moment. She really was going to become the next Autumn Thief. She was going to die here in this grave, or at least, this version of herself would.

She laid her head on Eldridge's chest and wished there was a heartbeat to sooth her fears. But there wasn't. Of course not.

"We will be together again, my love," she whispered against his chest. "I promise you, I wouldn't have made this choice if there was any other way."

One last thing before she was ready to go. Freya reached for Eldridge's hand and lifted it. The limb was surprisingly supple for a man who was supposedly dead. She put his palm on her belly over their child. And hopefully, *hopefully*, they would all come out of this together.

For there was no other choice.

"I'm ready," she said. "Let's get this over with."

"As you wish," Death replied.

And she knew no more.

CHAPTER 26

Freya came back to herself in small spurts of magic. A flicker of memory behind her eyes, and a small touch of emotion that brushed against her mind like an eel in murky waters.

She was alive.

She was Freya of Woolwich.

She was the Autumn Thief.

The magic that burned inside her had lived inside a thousand beings before her, and would live inside a thousand more. It whispered that they would do great things together, and it couldn't wait for her to wake up so they could move forward into the future.

But waking was hard. She wanted to stay in this dazed state between awareness and sleep. Freya enjoyed feeling as though the world had stopped for a little. No people looked to her for answers or placed responsibility on her shoulders. She could float here and relax for a little while.

She hoped, at least.

Someone was talking to her, though. Someone that wasn't in her mind, and it certainly wasn't the creature that had made her.

No, not made her. Death hadn't given her anything other than permission to be a more powerful version of herself. He had given her the gift of letting go of her past. She could see the future so much more clearly now that her history wasn't holding her down.

Strangely, her memory had felt like thick cords tying her down to the ground. She'd cut a few of them herself, but there were hundreds and some were so thick a pair of scissors could do nothing to release her from their grasp.

Death had snipped all those ties. He'd released her from the terrible burden of her own making and as such, she could fly.

Gods, she could fly. All that power in her chest made her want to disappear into realms far beyond the fae. She suddenly knew there were more places to visit. More people to meet and more creatures who had no idea who or what she was. The possibilities were endless when she had become a creature with no limitations.

This was what the fae meant when they said nothing was impossible. Power and magic sparked at her fingertips, and unspoken desires filtered through her thoughts. If she wanted, she should take. If she desired, then she should love.

Patience, that old version of herself whispered.

And though the voice was quiet, it was still there. Death hadn't lied. She still had the memories from her old life, but it was almost as if she were two people now. Two severed halves, one that lived in the realm of the living, and one of the dead.

That voice was right, however. She needed to have some patience or she would lose herself. She'd disappear into the magic and would never come out again, even though the temptation was nearly too great to ignore.

Though the appeal was strong, she fought against it. Freya battled through her own worst desires all the way to the surface of her mind. It was a bit like slogging through thigh high mud. Every step, every movement, pulled at her consciousness. It tried to yank her back to that quiet place where she dreamt of all the terrible things she could do.

But not today.

Today she would quiet those thoughts. And the moment she thought that was the moment she blinked her eyes open as a new person. As the Autumn Thief.

The first thing she noticed was that her dress had changed. She remembered falling asleep in that grave wearing a skin tight dress made of blood and liquid. Now, she wore a ball gown made of every color of autumn leaves. They trailed down the tight corset and into a full skirt that burned with bright crimson and brilliant orange.

Ruby encrusted rings covered her fingers, although there was one that was obviously missing. Said hands rested on the arms of a blackened throne. The seat appeared to have burned a long time ago, but the wood remained. No matter how hard the person had tried to destroy this throne, it had prevailed.

Though she couldn't move her hands from it.

Freya cleared her throat, testing out the sound to see if it was new. Not really, although perhaps the deep tones of her voice had a little more power to them now. They were vaguely more intimidating than she remembered them being.

She peered down at her chest and noted more rubies on her skin there, decorating her neck in a ring of gemstones. Someone had placed her body here and dressed her in finery like she never could have seen before. And how lovely was it? She wore more worth than she'd ever seen in her entire life combined.

Then she shifted again, and she realized those weren't gemstones at all. *They were scales.* Crimson scales that dotted across her body and shimmered in the light.

"Freya?"

Right, there had been a voice. Someone had spoken with her through the veil of her magic, though she hadn't remembered who it was. Her memories were still foggy at best. She should have taken more time in that quiet place in her mind so she could play through all the memories that she'd forgotten. Or... Perhaps it was that the memories were dulled. Not forgotten.

What was the right way to think about it?

"Freya, my love, if you're awake, please look at me."

That voice made all the tension in her body ease. She could relax when that person was talking, though she didn't know why or how.

Why was looking up so difficult? Her eyes wanted to feast on the changes that her body must have undergone. After all, she was one of the fae now. Even Esther had gotten a tail from being here for so long. How far did those crimson scales go? Was she covered?

But that other voice, the old voice of her own, whispered to look up. That the best thing imaginable was waiting for her to look up and see him again. That her heart was going to soar the moment she took the time to look.

So she did.

A man stood in front of her with dark hair and eyes that swirled like silver moonbeams. He stared at her with an expression of loss and hope, though she couldn't imagine why. Did she know him? She must. Her entire being lit up the moment her eyes caught upon his form, but she didn't remember... Yes, she did.

Love bloomed inside her like a rose unfurling its petals. She remembered every wonderful moment that had happened between the two of them. She remembered their adventures, their discoveries, and every tooth pulling moment where she fought against her own feelings. And then the moment she fell in love. The moment when everything changed, and she finally gave in to an impossible future.

"Eldridge," she breathed. His name was the spell that broke the remaining control over her body. She felt a shudder run through her entire spine, shaking her shoulders and entire torso. "Oh my god, Eldridge. What happened?"

"You survived," he replied. "I didn't think it was possible, but you did it, Freya. You survived."

All the rest of the details flooded into her mind. She was sitting on a throne in the center of the Stronghold. No, maybe not the center. But she knew where she was. Her back was to the three heads that had opened into doors where she had been tested. Weighed. Measured.

This throne was the same one that many Autumn Thieves had sat upon before. It meant that the gods had accepted her, and it meant the home itself would now bend to her will.

Eldridge knelt before her, his hands hovering over her knees like he was afraid to touch her. Maybe he was. Arrow stood behind Eldridge on his back feet, wringing his paws with worry and stains on his fine clothing.

"What happened to Arrow?" she asked. Her voice was hoarse, as if she hadn't used it in a very long time. "He doesn't like it when his clothing is dirty."

"Death threw us out of the glen very soon after you left with him. Arrow thought it would be a smart idea to fight against the hand-maidens while they hauled us out of that place." Eldridge's lips quirked at the memory. "You would have been very proud of him. He was quite impressive."

"Terrifying," Arrow corrected. "I was terrifying. And I think when this is all over with, you should make me an honorary guard."

Freya chuckled, though the sound felt strange in her mouth. Like she'd never done it before. And, she supposed, in this new version of herself, she hadn't.

Again, she tried lifting her hands from the throne, but couldn't quite pull them away from the burned wood. And something was on her head. It didn't move when she shifted, but the weight was distracting.

"Eldridge," she asked. "Can you help me?"

"Of course, my love." He moved slowly and with purpose. He reached for whatever was on top of her head and removed it. The weight had made her mind feel foggy. Without it, she could feel the horror when he set a crown of thorns down on the floor.

What a horrible crown. What a horrible title to be put upon her head and yet, she was relieved that this was all over with. Or, perhaps, that she knew for certain the power was now hers.

Eldridge sank down between her legs. Setting his hands on hers, he pried her fingers one by one from the throne.

Her digits were stiff with disuse and ached when she brought them to her chest. But the moment her magic realized she was in pain, all that angry hurt disappeared.

"Ah," she muttered. "That will be useful to not feel pain for very long."

Eldridge reached for her hands again and squeezed them in his own. "Are you back to yourself, yet? Or do you need more time?"

"I'm back to myself. Or at least, as much myself as I'm going to get." She hoped, at least. Freya's gut feared that she would miss the parts of herself who were no longer with her, but perhaps that was an irrational fear. How could she miss something she didn't remember having?

"Good." He lunged forward so fast she barely saw him move.

Eldridge cupped the back of her neck with his hand and dragged her lips to his. He devoured her lips and tongue like a starving man. She wrapped her arms around him and sank into the only arms she'd ever want to be held in.

She trembled in his warm embrace. His arms were a haven she never wanted to leave, because she felt like herself when he was wrapped around her. Even through the fog of power and magic, she knew who she was when Eldridge kissed her.

Freya. His wife. His love.

He kissed all her doubts and fear away until there was nothing left but a Freya she recognized, although one that wasn't entirely the same. And when they drew back for breath, she looked up at him with stars in her eyes.

"I love you," he whispered. "All of you. In this life and all the others. I did not know what I would do if I had to live knowing that you would not wake again."

"You don't have to live with that." Freya pressed her fingers to his lips, gently tracing the bow at the top. "Never, my love. Never."

Arrow cleared his throat, interrupting their reunion. "This is all well and good, but I would very much like to get out of this place without vomiting. So if you two don't mind, perhaps Freya can do that thing the Stronghold does and we might get out of here?"

"Thing?" She furrowed her brows, a question in her eyes as she stared at Eldridge.

"Ah, right." He leaned back a little and slid his hand from her neck to her shoulder. "The Stronghold is yours now, and this house is the lifeblood of the court. If you want to open it to the goblins, then it will do so. If you want a portal to get out of here for good, then the house will remain dormant again. You should be able to feel it. The building is an extension of you, in a way, but also alive on its own."

"So I can ask the house to do things?" she clarified.

"It can do a lot more than that." He grinned, a sharp-toothed grin. "Whatever you want, Freya."

She had no idea what she wanted. A house was just a house.

But as she reached out with her mind, she found another presence waiting for her. The house was ready to help her. In fact, it seemed like it had been waiting for a long time for her to reach out and ask for its assistance. That was all it ever wanted.

Deep beneath that desire to serve, Freya could feel how sad it was. How lonely the house had been with all these empty rooms and halls. It had hoped, maybe, she would stay. But the house could see now that she had a husband and a family. And those were far more important than a silly old building.

"Can we have a portal, Freya?" Arrow asked. "I'd like to get home."

"Um." She blinked a few times before meeting Eldridge's gaze.

He looked like he already knew what she was going to say, and he didn't mind in the slightest. Her Goblin King had always been a transient man to begin with, and he wouldn't mind traveling to his old home more often.

"I will get a portal for you, Arrow. But before you go home, would you mind letting my parents and sister know that I'd like them to join us in the Stronghold?" She grinned up at Eldridge, and it felt like their life was about to start. Even though they'd already been living for such a long time.

"You want to what?" Arrow barked back at her before he controlled himself. Sighing, the goblin dog held his head in his hands and shook his head. "I don't understand why anyone would want to live here."

She let her magic bathe the room. She told the house to clean itself and ready as many rooms as possible for a wedding of the grandest standards. And the house jumped with glee, the rafters shaking with its happiness, before a sudden swell of power cleared the room of debris and leaves. The house was perhaps a little too zealous in its excitement, because the magic did sweep Arrow onto all fours before he stood again and straightened his jacket.

"Fine," he muttered. "I'll go get them and bring them here. It can't be worse than the Goblin King's palace, I suppose."

Laughing, Freya reached for her King again as a portal opened beside Arrow.

The goblin dog huffed, but before he hopped through, he said, "I'm glad you're back, Freya. We both missed you terribly."

"I adore you, Arrow!" she shouted as he left, then looked back to her Goblin King. "We have at least an hour before they all arrive."

Eldridge gathered her up into his arms and lifted her from the throne. "Then hopefully your Stronghold has readied our room, my love."

CHAPTER 27

"Stop touching it, you're going to ruin the fabric with your grubby hands." Esther slapped Freya's fingers away from the edge of the cream-colored bodice.

"My hands aren't dirty." Freya replied with a laugh. "When would I have gotten them dirty?"

"I don't know, but I do know that you're more likely to ruin the dress than wear it the right way, and I refuse to let you ruin this day for me." Esther bustled about the bedroom with all the force of a tempest.

Apparently, her sister was taking the wedding to heart. As if it were her own, in fact.

They stood in front of a mirror in Freya's private bedroom that the Stronghold had put together for this reason only. She still slept in the same room with Eldridge, though they couldn't share that space today. Apparently. Esther had clarified that neither bride nor groom was going to see each other because that was bad luck.

Her sister had insisted the Stronghold clear this tower room surrounded by windows. That way, she could see Freya in natural light and get her makeup perfect. Even though doing her makeup and hair consisted of telling Freya to change something in the mirror while her magic did all the work.

Freya rolled her eyes. She wasn't phased by anything that was happening with the wedding. She would have gone out into a field somewhere with Eldridge alone and been perfectly happy. But of course, everyone wanted to make a big deal out of the affair. And likely she should be very happy and grateful they were all helping.

Instead, they had made it more stressful. Particularly her sister, who seemed to think that if this wedding didn't go well, then her own would surely flounder.

Esther had dressed herself in a pale blue gown that rivaled the sky. Magic decorated the edges, so they sparkled in the sunlight. Her blonde hair cascaded down her shoulders in perfect curls, but she still kept touching it as though the hair was out of place.

It wasn't.

Freya looked over her shoulder at the only person in the room with some sense and mouthed, "Help."

Lark nodded firmly and then clapped her hands to get Esther's attention. "Could you get your mother, please? I want to make sure that her dress is looking satisfactory. I'm also a little concerned that her flowers won't match Freya's, and we can't have that."

Esther's face went white as snow. "What if the flowers don't match? Lark, we don't have time to go get new ones!"

Her sister fled from the room as though hounds nipped at her feet. She'd apparently forgotten that all the flowers were conjured up by the Stronghold to begin with.

Freya heaved a sigh of relief as the door slammed shut. "Thank you. I don't think I will survive another minute of her worries. Everything is going to be fine, and even if it doesn't follow her exact plan, it will still be a beautiful wedding."

"Of course it will be." Lark adjusted her own matching blue gown, then turned Freya toward the full-length mirror. "Now, would you look at how beautiful you are? Eldridge is going to faint dead away when he sees the woman he's about to marry. It's not fair, really."

She'd been avoiding the woman in the mirror for a bit now. Not because she was so afraid to see herself, but because she didn't know what she would find. Her sister had run the entire show thus far.

The woman staring back at her had never been more beautiful.

Freya's hair was coiled atop her head, with dark tendrils hanging around her face. Rubies encrusted every inch of her body, from the tiny circlet on her forehead to the cascading ring of crimson scales at her throat. The cream-colored wedding dress hugged her waist and bell sleeves fell off the edges of her shoulders to touch the ground. The skirt hugged her curves even as the sun caught the fabric in a beam of light that made every fiber glow like the sun. One could just barely see the raised bump of her belly where her daughter was showing.

"I do look beautiful," she replied, touching a hand to the changes on her skin. "I didn't think the magic would give me scales, you know. I thought it would give me feathers or fur like the rest of you. Maybe antlers, if I was lucky."

Lark pressed a kiss to her head. "Oh my darling, we take on the attributes of the creature we are most like. And while I'd like to say you are a rabbit, you are much more terrifying than that."

The doors burst open again, and Esther thrust her mother into the room. "I found her! What about the flowers?"

Their mother was not holding flowers, but she looked demure and kind. In fact, Freya didn't think she'd ever seen her mother look more beautiful than at this moment.

"Oh, Freya." Her mother pressed her hands to her chest and sighed. "You look stunning, my dear. Just like a faerie princess."

"I suppose I am one of those now." Freya reached out her arms and tugged her mother in for a hug. "Even though that used to be your worst nightmare."

The watery laugh was her mother's only response. Apparently, emotions had clogged up her voice.

Esther pulled them apart, her own eyes misty with tears. "Stop that. You're going to cry on her dress and then we're all going to be sorry. That dress was difficult to make, you know."

"I made it, not you." Freya swiped her hand underneath her eyes. "But I will ruin the makeup we spent hours deciding on, so you're right."

It felt so good to have her entire family here. Ready to be with her on this momentous occasion that would only happen once in her life. After all, how many times did a mortal woman marry a Goblin King?

Another knock on the door had all the women in the room turning. Her father stood in the doorway, leaning against the door frame with a soft smile on his face. He'd shaved for the wedding, and his handsome face was all angles and sharp edges.

He wasn't the soft father she remembered. He never would be again with that wolf in his eyes, but at least the beast recognized Freya as its child, as well.

"You're late," he said. His voice was a soft rumble, deeper than she remembered. "People are going to start thinking that the Autumn Thief has gotten cold feet."

Butterflies twisted in her stomach, but she was so ready for this moment. It felt like she'd been waiting a lifetime for it.

Freya looked at the other women and smiled. "I'll see you all down there. I'm walking with Dad."

The Stronghold opened a portal for her family to step through as she walked toward her father. Freya had dreamt of this moment since she was a little girl. That her father would walk her down the aisle and a good man would wait for her hand. That no matter what happened in her life, he would always be there to give her away.

And for a long time, she'd thought she wouldn't get this moment because he was dead. But now he was here, and this moment was everything she had ever wanted.

Freya put her hand on his waiting arm. "I'm glad you're here, Dad. Really glad."

"I know." He patted her hand. "I'm not going to mess up your makeup any more than your mother. Instead, I'm going to say that if he hurts you, I will hunt him down."

"He's the Goblin King," she replied with a snort. "I don't know if you could kill him."

"Perhaps I couldn't. But the wolf definitely could." His eyes flashed bright yellow, like twin gold coins. "My beast has killed faeries before and would be happy to again for our daughter."

Actually, she didn't doubt that the wolf could take care of whatever creature it wanted. She'd even wager on that creature if she let it into a room with the Horned God itself.

Speaking of... "Do you mind if we go the long way?" she asked.

"Second thoughts?"

"No, I just want to make sure a couple of old friends see me. They couldn't come to the wedding, but they'd love to see the dress. I'm sure." Freya led her father down the winding halls that were perfectly polished now.

The Stronghold preferred wood floors these days. The entire building had turned into a rather beautiful lodge. Filled with warm woods, brightly colored tapestries, and windows that let all the sunlight into the rooms. Not a single red leaf could be found on the floor, because the Stronghold much preferred a clean residence.

Or perhaps that was Freya.

They paused for a moment in front of the throne room. Three faces stood above the throne itself, each one carved from stunningly bright bronze. Freya released her father to give the old gods one last spin and a curtsey. And if her eyes didn't deceive her, all three faces curved with smiles. Even the skull.

She put her hand back on her father's arm and let him lead her to the front of the Stronghold. The courtyard beyond was filled with long streamers of flowers that attached to the building and created a canopy to a small platform. There, her new husband waited for her.

Eldridge stood in a fine black suit with gold edges. His hair had been slicked back from his face, though a few strands had already fallen in front of his starry eyes. A hundred people stood at the ready to watch their Autumn Thief get married.

An audience full of creatures that were part mortal, part beast, and who she loved more than anything.

Padding footsteps raced down the hall to her left, then skidded to a screeching halt beside her. Arrow was breathing hard, his sides heaving as he straightened his tuxedo jacket.

Amused, she looked down at him with a smile curving her lips. "Are you ready?"

"I wasn't prepared to walk you down the aisle, Freya. I thought I was going to be in the audience with the rest of your family," he huffed. But she could see how pleased he was.

Freya bent down to press a kiss atop his head. "I wouldn't leave you out of this for the world, my dearest friend."

And with that, she turned her focus to the man waiting for her at the end of the aisle. The three of them walked through the crowd, her father's hand in hers, and Arrow's paw in the other.

Everything else faded away. She had no idea what her father said as he handed her off, only that he squeezed her hand. Arrow patted her arm and then joined the others in the crowd. All she knew was that Eldridge stared at her like she had hung all the stars in the sky.

They'd practiced what they should do next. After all, there was no priest who would wander into the faerie realms. And Freya had wanted to honor the old ways, as the old gods had begged her to do.

"You are the most stunning woman I have ever seen in my very long life," Eldridge whispered. "I cannot wait to spend an eternity with you."

"Careful what you wish for," she replied with a soft laugh.

"I will wish for this a thousand times over. That my life will be filled with hours upon hours looking into your eyes. That your laughter becomes the only music I dance to. And that until the last star falls from the sky, you and I will prove what everlasting love looks like." He lifted her hand and kissed the knuckle where her ring finger had once been.

Eldridge reached into his back pocket and drew out a long rope. He raised their hands so all could see them, and then looped the rope over their bound hands.

Power surged inside her, and when she spoke, Freya's voice rang throughout the courtyard. "This cord is a symbol of our lives intertwining."

"Before this, we were separate in life, action, and thought." He winked, as if the mere idea that they were ever separate amused him.

She took the rope in her free hand and looped it a second time. "As our hands are bound, so are our lives."

He threw the rope over their hands a third time, tugging it so tight she gasped. "So are our spirits. Together now, forever, until immortality drains from our forms and the world wanes into a new age."

"I love you," she said. The words filled her with a light that was so powerful it burst from her form. She glowed like the sun standing next to the moon, who she finally, after all this time, got to kiss.

"Love isn't a strong enough word, Autumn Thief. My queen." Eldridge's eyes glowed with a thousand galaxies hiding in the dark orbs. "I worship the ground you walk on, and every one of my kisses is a promise that I will never leave your side. And I will kiss you a hundred times a day, from now until the end of forever."

Using their hands, he swept her into an earth shattering kiss as the surrounding crowd burst into cheers. A thousand red leaves rained down on their heads as the Stronghold shook with happiness.

The Autumn Thief and the Goblin King were finally wed. After all this time and adventure and hardship, they had a future they could look forward to. No more battles. No more fights. Just the two of them and a thousand years experiencing every magical thing the world could offer.

And when they drew back, Freya stared into those eyes she loved so much and she knew that everything had fallen into place.

"I really do love you," she whispered so only he could hear.

Eldridge pressed their foreheads together and touched their bound hands to her belly. "I know. I've never questioned that for a single moment."

Arrow wiggled his way in between them, his beloved face poking at their legs. "Come on now, you two. There's plenty of time for the mushy gushy stuff later on! Everyone wants to congratulate you and if you don't do it, then I'm going to lose my head. So, shall we?"

She sighed but shrugged. "Into the madness, I suppose?"

Eldridge held out his arm for her to take. "Together. Like always."

EPILOGUE

"Now, remember. The mortal realm isn't all that safe. You might look more mortal than the other goblins, but you are not mortal." Freya patted her daughter on the head, making sure every hair was in place.

"Mama," Fiona said, her bright diamond eyes wide with annoyance. "You said I could go to the goblin market. You promised!"

"I'm not saying you can't go." Freya wanted to say that she couldn't go. Then her nerves might settle and she wouldn't be so worried that her daughter wouldn't return.

It was an irrational worry, of course. The Goblin King always went to the goblin markets with the children, just in case anyone tried to harm the little ones. And that meant that Fiona's father would look over her the entire time.

But Eldridge was more likely to coax his daughter into an inappropriate adventure than he was to whisk her away to safety. After all, he thought Fiona was capable of so much more than a little girl should do.

Speak of the devil, Eldridge walked into their daughter's bedroom with his riding gloves in hand. "Ready, little imp?"

"Ready!" Fiona leapt off her bed, jumping straight into the air, expecting her father would catch her. Arms wide. Legs akimbo. Pale hair flying in every direction.

Freya's heart stopped in her chest every time they did this. Even though Eldridge had never dropped their daughter.

He snagged Fiona mid-air, then spun around wildly. "My love! How did the two of us dark things make a little star to light up our life?"

He always said that about their daughter. And in truth, Freya had no idea. Magic had a way of making children look different from their parents here. And Fiona looked a little like them, but mostly she appeared her own person.

She had Freya's face and heart-shaped lips. But her hair was pale as snow from the day she was born. She'd inherited her father's strange eyes, but hers were like crystalized diamonds. They lacked color entirely, but when one really looked into them, the palest ice blue shards were held in that unearthly gaze. Her pale skin glowed in the moonlight, and sometimes she glimmered with moon magic that neither she nor Eldridge understood.

Their daughter was the first of her kind, and as such, they could both expect many surprises from the little one.

"Just be careful, you two," she said. Freya tried her best not to wring her hands as all that worry flowed through her veins.

The Stronghold provided her with a seat to rest in, and the cushion was more comfortable than any other in the building. She sent a mental thank you to the building and tried to calm her nerves. A teacup appeared next to her elbow.

She lifted it and the small plate beneath it, though her shaking hands made them clack together. "Eldridge," she repeated. "I want you two to be careful. Do you hear me?"

"I hear you, love." He dropped their daughter to the floor and rolled his eyes. "It's like you think we're going to storm a castle."

"I wouldn't put it past the two of you. If she batted her eyelashes, you'd give her an entire mortal kingdom to play with." She sipped loudly from her tea. "Keep our daughter safe, or I will bring the entire Autumn Kingdom to your own castle and storm it."

Eldridge met their daughter's wide-eyed gaze with one of his own. "Mommy is terrifying."

"Down right mad," Fiona replied.

"Do you think we stand a chance if we try to bargain with her?"

"Unlikely." Her daughter crossed her arms firmly over her eight-year-old chest and sighed. "I think we'll have to take matters into our own hands. If we don't, who knows what problems she'll cause."

"I do believe you're right. I taught you well." Eldridge mimicked his daughter's posture and stared Freya down.

Freya sighed and put her teacup down. "Don't you dare. Both of you know better than to pull this on me. You won't win."

As if that was the phrase that released them, her husband and daughter attacked. They leapt across the room with unnatural speed. Eldridge caught her around the shoulders, pinning her to the chair, and Fiona sat on her lap while tickling underneath her arms mercilessly.

They knew her weakness. And apparently that was her daughter's tiny fingers digging into her ribs.

Her laughter mixed with theirs, filling the room with so much happiness that it burst free from her in a wave of magic that sent bright red leaves tumbling through the room. Finally, Freya caught her breath for long enough to cry out, "Stop! I give!"

Like always, that was all it took. They'd trained their daughter early on that the only way to form any sort of trust was to know when a person had to stop. Fiona was good at that. She was good at everything, however.

Her daughter rolled over her lap and flopped onto the floor, still giggling like a mad woman.

"Oh, I'm the crazy one?" Freya said while shaking out her skirts. "You, little girl, are the only child in the room that can't stop laughing."

Fiona pointed behind Freya, still hugging her belly.

Of course, Freya turned to see Eldridge wiping tears from his eyes, and still consumed by mirth. Her husband, the other half of her soul, rarely had a day when he wasn't this happy anymore.

He filled her soul with so much love.

She stepped into his waiting arms and let him tug her into his embrace. Eldridge pressed a kiss to her head. "I'll take good care of her. I'll take care of them all, my love. You needn't worry."

"I do, though."

"I know." He pulled back and smiled down at her. "But that's only because you love us so much."

Freya cupped his face in her hand and knew her world began and ended with him. "I do. I love you so, so much."

AFTERWORD

What can I say about this book series that would do it justice? After months and months of hard labor, Eldridge and Freya have their happily ever after. And I don't really know how to say goodbye to them.

The best I could do is keep up the legacy of the Goblin King and Queen who now have the tiniest of daughter's.

So keep an eye out in 2022. Your faerie royalty will be return with a new series and a lovely little Fiona who has a lot of adventures coming straight for her.

But in the meantime, if you want more fae from me, I highly suggest Heart of the Face (by yours truly). If you want more adventure, I suggest Seas of Crimson Silk. If you want more romance, Tempting Hades. And if you want more beastly men, Gilded Rose.

I have a lot of books. I hope you find more adventures in their pages.

In the meantime, stay in touch.

ABOUT THE AUTHOR

Emma Hamm is a small town girl on a blueberry field in Maine. She writes stories that remind her of home, of fairytales, and of myths and legends that make her mind wander.

She can be found by the fireplace with a cup of tea and her two Maine Coon cats dipping their paws into the water without her knowing.

Subscribe to my Newsletter for updates on new stories!
www.emmahamm.com

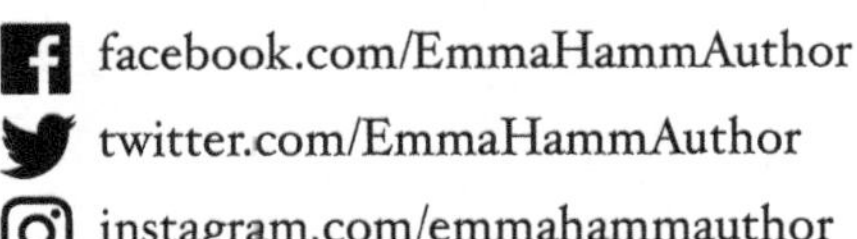
facebook.com/EmmaHammAuthor
twitter.com/EmmaHammAuthor
instagram.com/emmahammauthor